THE ACCIDENTAL ADVENTURES OF YOUNG SHAKESPEARE

From the pen of...

Conn McAuliffe

Cover illustration and design by Luke McAuliffe © 2010

ISBN: 1439268908

EAN-13: 9781439268902

LCCN: 2009913137

THE
ACCIDENTAL
ADVENTURES
OF YOUNG
SHAKESPEARE

Will

Malachi

BY

Conn McAuliffe

DEDICATION

To wife, Martha Belle, who was my most punctilious critic during the writing;

To brother, Frank, who was Malachi in real life and inspired these dialogues;

To sister, Margaret Bedrosian, without whose commitment
this book would never have reached its readers;

To nephew, Luke, whose artistic talent created the illustrations
and cover design;

And to family and friends near and dear.

TABLE OF CONTENTS

Part VII: Drake's Cadiz Raid: April, 1587

Part VIII: A Visit With Montaigne

Part IX: With Raleigh in Ireland: November, 1587

Part X: With Spenser in Ireland: December, 1587

Part XI: Year of the Armada: January To July, 1588

PART I. LEARNING THE ROPES

Chapter 1:
THE APPRENTICE ENTERTAINMENT ASSOCIATION

Wheedle Inn, Southwark, on River Thames outside London, Aug. 1585:

"Indeed, Squire Green, you're absolutely right about that," Malachi nodded.

"He certainly deserves the best beating you can hire done just to civilize him generally, but use caution now. Your planning must be keen to avoid consequences."

"Consequences?" the angry gentleman sputtered. "The only aftermath will be his piteous but satisfying cries for mercy and forgiveness. It does my heart good to teach these young upstarts a lesson in life, for the very foundations of the kingdom begin to crumble when we let apprentices take on such airs. The moral fiber of the nation weakens when people no longer keep to their proper station. "A country can be destroyed from within if people drop their guard and shirk their duty. Rome went that way, you know."

"That's what they say," Malachi nodded.

"Do you know what he shouted at me when I attempted to detail for him—in a constructive way, of course—society's absolute condemnation of his gross behavior?"

"I'm afraid my mannerly mind shudders at attempting to duplicate his mutterings." Malachi shook his head. "I can only imagine it was memorable."

"No question about that," the Squire fumed. "He interrupted me in mid-sentence and characterized my advice by shouting; '*...a tale told by an idiot, full of sound and fury signifying nothing.*' [1] Such arrogant impudence must not go unpunished if we intend to go on living in a civilized society."

"Oh, that's him all right," Malachi affirmed. "He'll start his argument with name-calling right from the beginning and confound the opposition in addition to confusing them. Leaves a sensible man no place to go."

"Confused only at that moment," Squire Green smiled, "but now my course is clear. Since he is a bonded apprentice to you, Malachi, I'd like your legal permission to arrange a vigorous thrashing for him, sound enough to make a real adjustment in his attitude."

"Be my guest," Malachi waved genially. "But the truth is I don't think you need my permission because Wheedle Inn here," he waved about the taproom, "is not in London City proper. Here in Southwark, the laws governing the beating of apprentices—like all laws this side of the Thames—depend heavily on voluntary compliance, and you know how that goes sometimes. No fuss is raised unless the apprentice actually dies in the beating, and then the Master is ridiculed for destroying his best source of cheap labor."

"Splendid!" the Squire said. "I feel very comfortable in a business-like atmosphere."

"I'm a little surprised you don't plan to do the honors yourself, sir. You look as if you're in pretty good shape."

"Oh my, no," said the Squire. "I'm well above that sort of thing now. Actually, I'm under serious consideration for knighthood, and you can see the image problem there. Still, I am able to enjoy the realities of life. One of the real pleasures of wealth is that you can always hire some of the poor to chastise their own brethren when the need arises."

"And your purse decides that need," Malachi observed.

"Exactly," said the Squire. "But don't get me wrong. I'll still be deeply involved when he gets his come-uppance. My heart will race because his impertinence was personal, just as his retribution must be. Once my people have knocked him senseless, I intend to get in a good kick or two to his ribs. I find in this business that broken ribs make a man remember his manners just as well as broken teeth do."

"Oh, I'll have to insist that you stop short of broken bones," Malachi said. "A little bloodshed is acceptable, a broken tooth or two, but only cuts and bruises in this particular case since he must stay fit enough to haul my baggage and do my copy-work. In particular, no broken fingers."

"Well," the Squire gritted, "a disappointing limitation indeed. My people hate those quibbling areas of tenderness which cancel the possibility of a broken-bone beating where the hitters can really show their stuff, but so be it. I have to respect your commercial interest, so I'll instruct my men to lay it on heavy but not deep. They can handle that kind of distinction. I've worked with them before."

"You meet a lot of upstart apprentices?"

"Oh, yes. We even have them at home in Putney. On my business trips to London, however, I nearly always uncover at least one rude, insolent, ill-bred lout, and straightening him out has become a civic duty for me, my personal contribution to the good of the commonwealth."

"Admirable, indeed," Malachi said."If everyone were as civic-minded and as courageous as you, sir, we would soon have things humming around here."

"How do you mean 'courageous'?" The Squire sounded puzzled. "Do you mean it in the sense of my stepping forward and acting out the civic responsibility that falls on every concerned citizen?"

"Not quite," Malachi said. "I mean it in the sense of the pebble-in-the-pond analogy. Courageous in terms of the possible ripples."

"What pebble? What pond? I ain't afraid of no bloody ripples! I've had cheeky apprentices thrashed for years now. There are dozens of uncouth varlets who owe the stiffening of their moral fiber to my instruction, and I've never suffered any kind of consequence, discounting a few baleful glances and muttered imprecations."

"I am certainly glad to hear that, sir. I think that's the way we must all come to feel if we are to hold the lid down on the simmering social unrest which plagues this kingdom. Individual personal responsibility is the key to control of the unruly, sir, and I am happy to see that you are so full of it. Stay on duty, and I'll lead you around to the back of the stable where my apprentice is even now performing, but we must be cautious."

"Performing? Cautious?"

Malachi nodded. "We'll have to approach the stable carefully or he might run off without giving you an opportunity for satisfaction. I'll explain the situation as we go. Just follow me around the back here."

"What's he performing in the stable?"

"Hard to put a name to it," Malachi reflected, "but one might call it 'closet-acting.' It seems innocent enough, and it has certainly speeded his recovery."

"Recovery from what?"

"A head wound he suffered some weeks ago in the line of duty, so to speak. The injury completely erased his memory, and I have been supervising the adjustment of his blank brain back to real life. Since he has recovered enough to limp about the inn, he has managed to wiggle into a very favorable schedule for himself. Whenever his duties permit, he sleeps all morning, and then spends his afternoons with some frolicsome female. On the weekends, he entertains a snickering group of apprentices from the city, deep within the recesses of our livery stable. He refers to this schedule as 'pacing' himself."

"Snickering apprentices?"

"They seem to have an endless appetite for lewd and lascivious matters, so he reads to them from translations of bawdy Italian and French books which travelers leave here at the inn. He also acts out the parts vigorously as he reads. That's what I call 'closet-acting.'"

"Why in the world would he do a thing like that?"

"He is a show-off, plain and simple," Malachi replied. "The stable gives him a theater; the apprentices give him an audience; his lady friends are often maids from the Continent who help him in the translations, so he just hops up on his hay-bale stage and emotes his heart out, which is all he really cares about."

"I'll give him something to emote about," the Squire snarled. "I'll instruct my men to box his ears a little at first to wipe that satisfied smile off his upstart face, and then they can really lay it on him and teach him to play the cripple. At least overnight."

"Well thought out," Malachi observed, "and richly deserved for the impertinence you described so vividly, but you will have to be patient, you know."

"Cautious? Careful? Patient? What the deuce is going on here, anyway?" the Squire demanded. "Just locate him for me, and I'll instruct my people to get started on his instruction immediately. I find that the less time elapses between offense and correction, the more the learning is enhanced."

"We're getting close now, sir, so keep your voice low," Malachi suggested. "I can only wish the country had more like you, your Honor, ready and willing to step forward and do their civic duty in spite of some danger to themselves."

"Danger? What do you mean 'danger'?"

"Here we are," Malachi whispered. "I'll explain later. Let's just slip around the end of these hay bales and hear what he's reading to the group now."

"I don't want to hear him," the Squire whispered fiercely. "I want him punished!"

"Ahh, well now," Malachi sighed, "that's where the patience comes in, you see. No matter how angry you are, no matter how justified your cause, you must not interrupt the proceedings of the Apprentice Entertainment Association—at least, not without giving me due notice."

"What are you talking about?"

"Apprentices find the legitimate theater pretty tame stuff, so they prize this patchwork presentation of erotica so highly that any interruption of their bawdy enjoyment would doubtless enrage them."

"'Enrage' you say? How many are there?"

"His audience varies from twelve to twenty." Malachi bent to peer between the bales. "Ahh, he's standing up there on his hay-bale stage, reading one of those racy Continental stories. My count of the house today puts it at sixteen apprentice caps rapt in attention. Bend down yourself and you can both see and hear him, but be careful."

A clear vibrant voice read with exaggerated expression.

"...The goodwife, knowing the hospitality which the latter did her husband at Barletta, would more than once whenas the priest came thither, have gone to lie with a neighbor of hers...so he might sleep in the bed with her husband, and had many a time proposed it to Dom Gianni, but he would never hear of it; and once amongst other times, he said to her, 'Gossip Gemmata, fret not thyself for me; I fare very well; for that, whenas it pleaseth me, I cause this mare of mine to become a handsome wench and couch with her, and after, when I will, I change her into a mare again; wherefore I care not to part from her.'

"The young woman marvelled, but believed his tale and told her husband saying, 'If he is so much your friend as thou sayest, why dost thou not make him teach thee his charm, so thou may avail to make of me a mare and do thine affairs with the ass and the mare? So should we gain two for one; and when we are back at home, thou couldst make me a woman again, as I am'." [2]

Low whistles of appreciation could be heard from the audience.

Malachi cupped his hand to whisper to the Squire. "I remember this selection. It's a two-hundred-year-old story from Giovanni Boccaccio's _Decameron_. The wife convinces her dull husband to get the priest to work the charm on her, and the priest agrees, but let's listen now as he explains to them that putting on the tail is the trickiest part of the transformation."

"'I know none in the world, except you, for whom I would do this; wherefore since it pleaseth you, I will e'en do it; but needs must you do as I shall bid you, an you would have this thing succeed.' They answered that they would do that which he should say; whereupon, taking the light, he put it into Pietro's hand and said to him, 'Mark how I shall do and keep well in mind that which I shall say. Above all, have a care, an thou wouldst not mar everything, that, whatsoever thou hearest or seest, thou say not a single word, and pray God that the tail may stick fast.'"

"See how he rolls his eyes," Malachi whispered. "He primes his audience for what's coming."

"Pietro took the light, promising to do exactly as he said, whereupon Dom Gianni let strip Gemmata naked as she was born and caused her to stand on all fours, mare-fashion enjoining herself likewise not to utter a word for aught that should betide."

Whistles and catcalls arose from the audience, but the speaker held up a calming hand and smiled, "Behave yourselves. We're just getting to the good part."

"Then passing his hand over her face and her head, he proceeded to say, 'Be this a fine mare's head,' and touching her hair said, 'Be this a fine mare's mane'; after which he touched her arms saying, 'Be these fine mare's legs and feet', and coming presently to her breast and finding it round and firm, such an one awoke that was not called and started up on end."

Amid delighted whoops, while holding the book aloft, the reader, with his free hand, slowly caressed a woman of the mind, a false creation, hovering in the empty air before him.

The Squire bolted upright and muttered grimly, "Good God! He's spreading his lewd manners and licentious ways to the rest of those wretches."

Malachi nodded, "I've seen them scramble here from clear across London when word is out that he is to read. His audience now is almost exclusively the natural leaders among the apprentices since they have quickly come to regard him as a local wonder blossoming in their very midst."

"All the more reason he must be stopped at once!" Squire Green's voice rose with his certainty. "We have quite enough upstart tendencies in this country as is!"

"Careful, sir," Malachi whispered fiercely and grabbed his arm, "your health is at stake here. Let's go back inside and chat over a soothing jar or two."

The Squire made quick note of the sign above the stable as they left. "Nowlan Bros, eh? Good Cornish name too." He shook his head. "Too bad, but that's what happens when you leave public decency in the hands of theatrical show-offs and their untutored audience. In this case, I won't mind taking a little more time to plan his chastisement carefully."

"He often has friends hanging about who might attempt to defend him," Malachi mentioned. "How many men will you get for the job?"

The Squire chuckled. "One thing London doesn't lack is heavy-hitters for hire. I usually have several of my retainers about me, but in a pinch, I could easily round up a tavern full of stout, sturdy fellows with the promise of a drink or two. Most of them are well versed in thrashing wayward apprentices and welcome the opportunity to do a service for their community while working up a new thirst."

"How many do you think you'll need?"

"The beating of your man would call for only two or three stalwart types half-deep in their cups. They would need only one to hold him tight, one to punch him silly, and one to hold the doublets and ward off interference. If there happened to be further need, my resources are such that I could empty several taverns, gather dozens of men. That should solve any problem short of an encounter with the Queen's Guard, I'd imagine."

"That's right, sir, you might well imagine such a solution because you are accustomed to dealing with a few unruly apprentices in Putney, so that dozens does seem like a good bet in conflict with a few, but in London, sir, your dozens could be facing thousands."

"Are you serious? Thousands?"

"The Privy Council has wisely prohibited apprentices from carrying weapons, of course," Malachi nodded, "but they wouldn't need weapons in the usual sense, sir. It wouldn't be that kind of fight, although God knows there's not a single apprentice in London who can't put his hands on a club or a dagger if the need arises."

"What...uh...kind of fight are we speaking of then?"

"Perhaps I better explain a little," Malachi said. "The apprentices of London are a mean, selfish, immature lot taken as a whole, but they are bright enough to join each other in common cause if something they value is threatened."

"Common cause?"

"That is their philosophic base, yes," Malachi affirmed, "but it is their raucous cry of *'Clubs!'* resounding and echoing through the city streets which brings them swarming by the thousands when mention is made of canceling their Sunday afternoon holiday, or forcing them to provide their own apparel, or canceling the bear-baiting, or closing the theater, or subtracting from their entertainment in any form whatsoever."

"And all this has something to do with your apprentice?" the Squire snapped.

"The entertainment part," Malachi nodded. "As you saw, he held that audience completely in thrall with his bawdy presentation, so you can be certain that any mistreatment of their sole source of risqué stories would enrage those leaders, and they would instantly inflame the entire apprentice community against that threat."

"What matter?" the Squire shrugged. "It will be over before they have time to rally. If I once put my mind to it, I can have a sound thrashing carried out in five minutes or less. What can they do then? I'll finish up my business and be home in Putney before they wake up. He is obviously low-born, so he has no connections in high places."

"High enough," Malachi sighed. "Have you ever had a piss-pot dumped on you?"

"What? Of course I have. It eventually happens to everybody who must do business in the streets of London. Less than a year ago it was, just off Fleet Street." He shook his head. "It was the single most degrading and loathsome experience of my life. It gives me shudders even now to think of it. Why?"

"If you do have him beaten, you will immediately become the target of six-thousand apprentices stationed on rooftops and jetties at every intersection in London, intent on subjecting you to an endless repetition of that loathsome experience by dumping well-used chamber-pots on your head every time you appear in public."

"Chamber-pots? Endless?"

"'Endless' may be stretching it a bit," Malachi conceded, "but thousands certainly, by actual count. It would be just as well after the beating if you have no business in London for a while, but if you must be in the city, do remember not to let your loved ones or your business associates walk too close to you for the next few months. But apprentices have a short attention-span, generally, so they will calm down eventually or at least turn their attention to some other object of their rage."

"Thousands of chamber-pots," the Squire mused. "Not quite the same situation we have in Putney, to be sure. You are certain of all this?"

"Positive. The apprentices have done it before when they were deeply offended and, as you saw, the leaders have taken quite a fancy to my man William."

"When I reflect on the matter at greater length, sir," the Squire said thoughtfully, "it occurs to me that while I shall continue in my own small way to make my contribution to the stability of our society, the inescapable fact remains that punishing wayward apprentices is primarily the responsibility of the master. Surely, the Common Cause people can have little objection to that, and, if the harsh truth be spoken aloud, had you performed your legitimate duties correctly in the first place, there would have been no need whatever to involve me in this matter."

"I'm sorry you see it that way, your Honor. God knows I do the best I can, but I could use help from any interested citizen who is willing to share the risk."

"Maybe another time when my own affairs are not so pressing."

"Thank you, sir. I'll look forward to it."

"Although for the life of me, I don't see how you can put up with him as he is. By not correcting him instantly, you appear to approve of his lustful and licentious influence on London's all-too-impressionable apprentices. I think the local bailiff might be quite interested in your responsibility in all this, Mister."

Malachi grinned, "Do as you please, Governor, but you're a young man yet, so for your own future peace of mind, remember that life sometimes pinches down on our choices. This young man suffered his head injury in the act of saving my life by breaking up a robbery where I had already been threatened with death."

"He has courage, you say?"

Malachi chuckled, "We may not know that until he recovers from his injury. It was a complete accident that he saved me. He just stumbled onto the robbery in progress, got hit in the head by the thieves, and distracted them long enough for me to arm myself and run them off."

"He saved you by accident and yet you feel obligated to him?"

"Whether by accident or design," Malachi smiled, "I am still drawing breath today because he suffered an injury, and, in my survival manual, that fact looms larger than logic."

"So you made him an apprentice scribe?"

Malachi nodded. "I had hoped to apprentice him to some craft as soon as his memory returned, but so far there's no sign of that. In the meantime, I noticed that he has an excellent fist for copy work and, because his mind is essentially empty of intrusive thought, he can dash off duplicate fair-copies almost like a printing press. I put him in protective bondage for the next seven years, so he can learn to be a scrivener while he helps me with my copy-work."

"If you hope to be a civic minded master to him, I advise that you institute some heavy-handed, periodic punishment to clear up his faulty focus and teach him some manners."

"Oh, he has much to learn, all right," Malachi laughed. "So far his *tabla rosa* brain has been imprinted with the realization that Elizabeth is our Queen, and the year is 1585. We haven't progressed much past that point yet, but his pace seems to be speeding up, so there's hope for the future. I'll soon be taking him into London now that he has regained his mobility. He tells me it will be his first visit as far as he can remember. He had better learn some manners quickly in the big city, or they'll run him out of town."

"He'll learn nothing," the Squire growled. "The bailiffs will nail him before he sprouts good manners, so I hope your lesson is clear from all this. When masters shirk their duties, the very mortar of the nation's foundation crumbles, and we all know what comes after that."

"Rome?"

"Exactly."

"It has always seemed to me, that particular thesis seriously underrates the efforts of Alaric and his Visogoths."

"Really?" said the Squire. "Your observation is quite telling because it validates something I had already suspected. The fact is now apparent to me that you are the source of your helper's inclination to pointless argumentation, so I'll take my leave and drop a word to the closest bailiffs to watch out for the pair of you. What's the name of your apprentice?"

"William," Malachi said. "No last name. The injury, you know."

"No last name, eh?" the Squire sneered. "In other words, no official record of his obnoxious behavior anyplace, eh? How convenient. I find it interesting that you take his side against the side of a well-ordered society. I'm sure the bailiff will be interested in your choice."

Chapter 2:
LESSONS FROM SIMPLE

That evening at the Wheedle Inn:

"May I ask you a personal question?" William asked his master.

"Anything at all," Malachi replied, "but only after I commend you on your recuperative powers. Your hay-bale exhibition this afternoon indicates you are hale and hardy enough to assume the rest of your duties."

"How do you mean 'rest'?" the apprentice asked. "I thought doing the fair-copies was the extent of my responsibilities, so I have committed all of my energies to excel in that particular endeavor."

"And a splendid job you've done." Malachi shook his head. "It hurts me to say it, but you have the best fist I've ever seen in fair-copy work. No question. You're a natural talent. There's no telling how far you can go in the writing business if you just apply yourself and enlarge your natural ability."

"Enlarge how?"

"Learn to take dictation. Learn that new shorthand that has just appeared on the scholastic horizon. Improve yourself. Make yourself more salable to society and more valuable to me."

"More valuable to you how?"

"I'm glad you asked because your time has come. I have just the spot for you to show your value." Malachi smiled. "But first, let's get your concern out of the way. What were you going to ask me?"

"Oh well, I have grown increasingly curious about several things during my period of recovery. Don't forget, I have no memory but of this time with you, so I have watched your movements pretty closely."

"And found me to be a simple scrivener fleeing hither and thither to record official papers and put bread on the table."

"There was some of that," the young man acknowledged, "but in addition, I noticed that every day there were people sidling up to you with whispers and sometimes small packets to exchange. You are forever off in some isolated corner talking to some shadowy stranger. You are sometimes gone for days at a time. All of these might seem to a casual observer as trifles light as air, but to my fevered brain, they bespeak an unspoken mystery. There is more here than meets the eye. What's going on?"

"Oh well," said Malachi, "I suppose it doesn't hurt to enlarge your horizons, and, indeed, it's gratifying to see that your powers of observation are on the mend. There's no big mystery. In addition to being a scrivener, I am also a governmental handyman. Whenever a pivotal functionary drops out in response to one of life's impositions— death, sickness, prison, desertion, or marriage—they plug me into the gap like a cork until they get a permanent replacement or until the original one returns."

"Why you?"

Malachi grinned. "You'll soon learn that *'Good counselors lack no clients.'* [3] I'm what theatrical people call a quick study. I know the government apparatus inside and out. Perhaps that seems a trifle immodest. Nevertheless, I can keep any station up and running without making costly mistakes."

"In London?"

"Mostly in London, but it could be anyplace in England, with occasional trips to Ireland, Scotland, or the Continent. Anywhere we have information posts."

"Information posts?"

"Survey crews," Malachi nodded. "Checking opinions and gathering information to better direct England's policy of firmness and fairness in all contractual agreements. Mostly we spend our time delivering messages and looking for rascals and rogues both here and abroad in the weights and measurements areas. Usually we just travel about the country and take polls on how people feel about things generally."

"Feel about what, for instance?"

"Anything. Everything. Prices, taxes, immigration, new laws, the Church, the Spanish, the French—everything and everybody."

"Is this a wild curiosity thing?"

Malachi chuckled. "Hardly. The funding comes from high-ranking government officials who are convinced they must keep constant check on the thoughts and feelings of our countrymen in order to govern them wisely and to lead them in the direction they are already leaning."

"You are a government spy!"

"Softly!" warned Malachi, holding up his hand. "But thank you for noticing so quickly. That is exactly what I keep telling them back at Whitehall. "A spy pure and simple, but they always insist I am only a sloppy poll-taker, an over-paid scrivener, and a tardy messenger, but I know exactly why they do it. Government officials don't seem to realize how transparent are their motives to those of us who have had them under observation for several decades."

"May I ask why they do it? Or rather, why they don't do it?"

"Plain and simple. There happens to be a small stipend added to the wages of agents who sometimes do dangerous duty work—a bonus if you will—and the officials don't want to pay it because the less they pay me the more they can keep for themselves. It doesn't seem to concern them in the least that there are months when I earn that bonus twice over."

"Dangerous work, eh? Swords, knives, and poisons?"

Malachi chuckled. "You've been watching too many stage-plays, I'm afraid. The reality is seldom so romantic, thanks be to God. My close calls come mostly from unruly horses, leaky ships, bad directions, and provincial cooking. My sword is seldom called into play, but my patience is often tried. Those of us who travel often must permit expediency to take hostage of our comfort, so we spend many weary hours muttering to ourselves, 'This can't go on much longer'." Malachi paused to laugh. "Hardly the picture the romancers paint of travelers, I would say, but you're fit enough to journey now, so you'll soon find out for yourself."

"So our assignments often involve travel and outdoor work?"

"That pretty well sums it up," Malachi said.

"I think a little travel will suit me in recuperating, but I'm not sure I'm quite strong enough to do any long-distance hauling of luggage."

"Really?" said Malachi. "What happened to your recent wild promises to do anything as long as you were not abandoned?"

"That was earlier. I've stabilized a lot since then."

"We won't worry about that now since baggage-handling will just be your on-stage job anyway."

"And behind-the-scenes?"

"Your role will shift as we go along," Malachi explained. "In doing survey work, we need to fit in unobtrusively wherever we go because some people become self-conscious and clam-up when they know notes are being taken, and others seize the occasion to act up for the reporter, so you can expect your identity to change with various assignments. You'll have to learn to be at home in a variety of settings. Tonight, I've scheduled a little cramming session for your historical perspective. For that purpose I've brought along an old friend of mine who is a wonder at quick-background detail. Open your mind to him. His name is Simple."

Malachi motioned to an adjacent table where a slightly built man stood up, smiled pleasantly, and approached their table, cap in hand. William shook the man's hand and spaced his words carefully. "Hello, Master Simple. That's a beautiful nosegay you are wearing."

"Not that kind of simple," Malachi explained. "Simplification simple. Simple believes he can put all instruction and information into three words. He feels confusion arises when you go beyond three." He turned to Simple, "Show him."

"Nosegays prevent plague," said Simple.

"Any nosegay?" William asked with a sly smile.

"Rosemary is best," Simple replied.

Malachi addressed Simple. "I want him briefed on what he can expect from having become a sudden resident of England."

"'Sudden,' you say?" asked Simple.

Malachi waved a dismissive hand between them, "I'll explain all that later. I owe him a favor, so right now the job is to get him ready to survive in London. Give him a quick rundown on the thinking he will encounter in the city's ale-houses where he will be doing survey work for me during the next few weeks. Get him ready to mix with the vulgar sort and caution him which way to nod his head to keep from getting drawn into pointless brawls and tumults."

"Don't get involved?"

"That's the ticket. Get busy."

"Time allotted here?"

"You can take all evening, but start at the top anyway, so you don't have to rush at the end. Bring him up to date quickly. Let him know what the average Londoner expects from his government in the various areas of policy-making, based on the last twenty-seven years of Elizabeth's rule. Which royal precepts are likely to guide the Queen's hand in any future policy-making."

"The first would be..."

"Postpone all decisions."

"No question about that," Malachi chuckled. "That's number one with her Majesty, all right. Her aim always is to delay difficult decision-making in hopes of enjoying the 'benefits of time'. Number two?"

"Accept no charges."

Malachi nodded. "The Royal purse-strings might just as well be anchor-chains in Elizabeth's hands. Extend no credit without collateral is built into her thinking. Number three?"

"Declare no war."

Malachi winked at William. "The Queen has never trusted the military after the loss of Calais in '58, and she's particularly aware right now how war interferes with commerce. Recent Spanish victories against the rebelling Dutch Provinces in the Low Countries have cut off England's cloth industry by blocking our exports to Antwerp, our main venting port. Thousands of English textile workers have lost their livelihood and have joined the ranks of the discontented homeless, roaming the streets of London." He shook his head. "Bad news piling up there for the government, and no solution in sight. But back to you, Simple, for number four."

"Trust no zealot."

"True. The Queen trusts practical men. They can always be dealt with. Is there a fifth?"

"Advance no idealist."

Malachi laughed. "On the button! The Bacon and Sidney families know all about that policy. The Queen doesn't mind if such families remain a trifle stiff-necked in a world crying out for compromise, but She would never lift Her little finger to help them. As a matter of fact, She seems to exhibit a perverse joy in assigning them duties which She knows are beyond their means unless they bend their necks enough to start imposing fees and taxes on their people, like the rest of their class. I know She was quite aware when She appointed him as Lord Deputy of Ireland three different times, that Sir Henry Sidney would be ruined unless he accepted some kind of compromise with financial reality before his personal fortune was used up by serving Her in that poor country."

"He didn't, so he was," Simple said.

"Ha!" William hooted. "Five words, or even six if you count the contraction as two words."

"Count them all," said Simple. "I sometimes double-up."

"Hyphens are not fair," William insisted. "It seems to me that if you open the door to that kind of fudging, just about anybody——"

"Enough!" Malachi interrupted. "We are at business here, so postpone the nonsense until later. How about Parliament now, Simple? The House of Lords is always predictable. 'Accept no change' does nicely for them, but everybody knows that the House of Commons is beginning to feel its oats lately. What guidelines can William expect to fashion their behavior?"

"Honor the Queen."

"That's right. They still do it today even if it be more with their heads than with their hearts. Another?"

"Raise no taxes."

Malachi chuckled. "Very reluctant to part with any of their newly-gotten riches, and I can't say that I blame them. England has the lowest tax-rate in Europe, and they intend to keep it that way. They are very fearful that even temporary subsidies might be made permanent. Governments, generally, have a bad reputation in that area. There is nothing more permanent than a temporary tax, everybody says. Number three?"

"Promote all trade."

"That's a bit of a scramble these days since our cloth exports have been so recently bottled up. Some merchants in Commons are saying that if war with Spain is inevitable, let's get it over with quickly, so we can get back to business. But there have been no war-preparation subsidies forthcoming from Parliament despite the talk, so it's obvious no central strategy has been formulated as yet. Number four?"

"Watch for Catholics."

"That's right," Malachi nodded. "The alert is on. Since Catholics have been involved in the last three assassination attempts on the Queen's life, even the reasonable men in the Commons have lost patience with the Romans and are in a mood to pass Draconian measures against them."

"For instance?" William asked with a small smirk at Simple.

Malachi filled in the details. "Twenty-pound fines for missing Anglican services and confinement to the estate of some supervising lord."

"I have recently learned that twenty pounds is a great deal of money," William said.

"Just about four year's income for the average Londoner, I'd estimate," Malachi said. "In any case, few could pay such a fine more than a time or two, but its chief purpose is not so much to raise money as to persuade the Catholic nobles to keep quiet and behave themselves or pay through the nose for their spiritual obstinacy."

"What if they don't pay?" William asked.

Malachi shrugged. "Confinement and confiscation of property or banishment from the country if they can't at least pretend to be good Anglicans. Many in Parliament would like to burn them, but Elizabeth won't allow it. It's just as well. We'd be little better than the Spaniards if we burned everybody."

"But we do compel attendance at Anglican services, and we do set a price on being a Catholic, if I have this straight."

"Being a Catholic doesn't bother the government as long as people have enough sense to keep quiet about it. I'd have to guess more than half of England, along with most of the Continent, was still Catholic when Elizabeth became Queen back in fifty-eight. That was only twenty-four years after her father, King Henry VIII, made the big break with Rome, so everybody past that age had been raised a Catholic, and the five years of Catholic Mary's Tudor's reign just before Elizabeth ascended reinforced the Catholic faith in many people. So switching creeds went slowly for many of our countrymen because it involved changing long-held beliefs and overcoming a nagging conscience as well."

"Small wonder!" breathed William. "I once started to read Pope Pius V's 1570 Bull against Elizabeth to the Apprentice Association, but they boo'd me down. It called her a heretic and pretender to the crown."

"Sentenced to excommunication," added Simple.

"*'Elizabeth, the pretended queen of England and the servant of crime...having seized the crown and monstrously usurped the place of supreme head of the Church in all England.... has once again reduced this same kingdom...to a miserable ruin'* [4]," quoted Malachi. "Aye, 'twas a bone-chilling denunciation to keep English Catholics faithful to Rome. Even today there are large areas in our northern counties where the old nobility are still practicing Catholics, but subdued enough to worship without display. As a matter of fact, many northern estates even have small, cleverly concealed rooms called 'priest holes' behind chimneys or back of pantries in order to hide the resident priest if the Royal authorities should call."

"Are there penalties for such hospitality?"

"Elizabeth punished that part of the country when she formed her new government by appointing so few northern nobility to important administrative posts which they had traditionally held in the past. Even at twenty-five, she was wise enough not to invite a daily exchange of pleasantries with nobles who still sided with Rome in judging the union between Ann Bolyn—the Queen's mother—and King Henry VIII as illegitimate since no divorce from his first wife had been sanctioned. Of course that left Elizabeth as a bastard in their eyes, and some of them felt the Stuart bloodlines through Henry II made Mary Stuart the legitimate heir to the English throne since no bastard had previously been allowed to mount the throne of England since William the Conqueror."

"As far as we know," William added.

"There is that slight leavening in the loaf of all Royal assurances," Malachi grinned. "Even today, however, there are many well-behaved Catholics at Court. The heavy fine is kind of an advertising fee. If you want to make a display of your Catholicism by missing Anglican services, it will cost you, and if you really insist on making a nuisance of yourself by publicly blaspheming in front of the Ecclesiastical Court, they will make arrangements to burn you at the stake, as they did earlier this year to a young Cambridge graduate, Francis Kett."

"Was it something he said?"

Malachi nodded. "He insisted on informing them publicly that Jesus Christ was not yet divine as they had mistakenly assumed, but would only become divine upon the occasion of his second resurrection. The Court regarded his two-out-of-three argument as a major departure from orthodoxy and had him burned to a crisp for heresy."

William shook his head sadly. "Good God."

"That's the way to talk," Malachi approved. "Let's get on with your education now, so we can get some sleep later on. I was a schoolmaster earlier in my life, so I know that it is often advantageous to proceed in the learning process from the point of view of the student rather than always from that of the master. Let us pause here and ask which points of interest have already been ignited in your mind by our explanations?"

"There is one thing I am really curious about."

"You have only to mention it," Malachi assured him.

"Is there any action we could take at this moment which would result in speeding up the people in the kitchen? When I extend myself dramatically or scholastically, it etches a hunger in my belly which, for the time being, prohibits thought of anything but food."

Malachi sighed deeply. "Perhaps you're right. It may be time for a break. I've noticed that the absorption rate of your brain slows considerably when you lack food. You know the cook here, Simple, would you mind stepping to the kitchen and speeding the food along?"

"Happy to," Simple grinned and left quickly before William could protest.

Chapter 3:
THE TABLE OF UNIVERSITY WITS

The Black Boar Inn, next night

"You have several times mentioned your desire to become a writer, William, so I want to use your special aptitude for asking questions at the Writers' Table here tonight."

"Writers' Table?"

"Very informal gathering. Mostly Cambridge graduate toss-pots who share a literary bent and a complete lack of modesty since they term themselves the 'University Wits'. I'll sneak you in at one end of the table and pass you off as a student eager to share their creative radiance. Robert Greene holds court nightly to entertain his acolytes and sundry hangers-on by reciting his claim to being the first man in England's history to make his living from his writing."

"How about that Chaucer fellow you mentioned earlier?"

Malachi shook his head. "Geoffrey Chaucer's fame has come two centuries after his death. That certainly puts the author of *The Canterbury Tales* under special consideration as a role-model for writers; however, that same notoriety undoubtedly inflates our view of the commercial success he enjoyed while living. The simple truth is—hold on now! There's Tom Dekker settling down at the table. Nashe will follow in a little while. Then Roydon, Chapman, Peele, Drayton, Marston, or Lodge might drift in during the evening. Greene will make a late appearance. More about Chaucer later, but right now, let's get you into a discussion with Dekker, so you'll be deep in converse when the others join the table."

"Who is Dekker?"

"A friend of Thomas Nashe, recently arrived in London with the intention of becoming a full-time scribbler. He's about your age, but he has already cultivated a great many friends in the writing business. He has some wonderfully entertaining opinions on almost every subject, so it shouldn't be difficult to get him talking."

"And who is Thomas Nashe again?"

"Probably the most talented of the young men attempting to learn from Robert Greene the art of making a living by writing. I think I mentioned that Nashe often joins Greene in the composing and printing of broadside ballads for hire."

"The sheets the ballad mongers sell on the street for a penny?"

"Right. Those poster-like sheets can be used for various purposes ranging from direct commercial advertising to soundly denouncing—in memorable verse—whoever or whatever happens to irritate the person paying the printing costs."

"Denouncing?"

"The subject matter of the ballads often arises from the current tavern talk about politics, wars, executions, prices, murders, religion or any strange happening in the kingdom. The ballads are designed to be sung to the tune of current songs, and they are sometimes illustrated by small but clever woodcuts which help illustrate whatever point of view the customer is paying for."

"So the customer could pay to have something really scurrilous printed to ridicule some other person, like his neighbor?"

Malachi nodded. "Neighbors are the mother's milk of the broadside ballad business."

"And Green makes a living from that kind of writing?"

"Starves to death half the time," Malachi scoffed, "so he is quick to sell his pen to the highest bidder."

"Unprincipled, would you say?"

"'Flexible' would seem more apt a word to me," Malachi said. "Greene is a business-man writer, who is ready to give his patrons whatever they will pay for. I suspect Greene will be a major figure in English literature for years to come if he can manage to stay clear of the Tower. He's a conscientious craftsman, experienced and mature, but we suspect he is renting his talent to some reckless, rabble-rousing people who have come to the attention of our front office. Every time we get an anonymous, inflammatory broadside which is particularly well done, we go out to check on Mr. Greene and his young crony, Thomas Nashe. When they are not involved directly, they usually know who is."

"Inflammatory being worse than scurrilous?"

"Any time there is a deliberate attempt to stir up worker discontent, our government takes it very seriously. Like the recent troublesome broadside criticized England's immigration policies and pointing out that while many of our own people are unemployed, the Flemish among us continue to work because they offer jobs only to their own sort. In short, the ballad writers use hate-mongering and rabble-rousing to incite our working class against the Dutch immigrants."

"So you want me to go over and ask Dekker if he is involved?"

"God bless your simple mind," Malachi chuckled. "I wish our business were that easy and we could get culprits to confess openly as they often do in stage plays, but that is not the way it works for the most part. We don't conduct inquiries in such a direct manner because that would scare everybody into absolute silence. Go over and strike up a casual conversation with Dekker, so we can try to determine in an off-hand manner what his little group has been up to."

"What'll I talk to him about if not his possible guilt?"

"Always start every assignment by doing the most sensible thing. Buy him a drink, tell him you've just arrived in London, and ask him what steps a young writer should take if he aspires to reach the heights Dekker has already reached. That'll get him started, and I'll join you later when I see Nashe come in."

William fetched two tankards to the Writers' Table and offered one to Dekker as an introduction. He soon posed his inquiry and was offered a seat.

"The trick of good writing is in the cultivation of telling details," Dekker instructed him. "How is your ability in that particular area?"

"Telling details?"

"You have recently arrived in London for the first time, so you must have some very strong impressions of the city. How would you render those impressions into words that best convey your feeling of that memorable occasion? In short, what was your reaction when first visiting our city?"

"I admit I was virtually overwhelmed with impressions," William testified. "I thought they would never stop coming, but a few of them stuck out from all the rest."

"For instance," Dekker prodded.

"I found the streets of the city to be dirty, narrow and crowded. Often there is little sunlight because of the second-floor jettys. The city streets are not as open to the sky as streets are in Southwark. Out in the suburbs, there are green fields behind every house and plenty of room to expand."

"Crowded with people?" Dekker inquired politely.

"Oh, yes, people all over the place," William said. "Very disorganized. "A lot of noise and confusion, but some good things too, as you might expect in a city this size."

"Do you remember what I said earlier about the importance of giving details if you wish to be a writer?" Dekker asked.

"That's what I'm doing," William explained, but saw that Dekker was shaking his head. "Do you think you can do better?"

"Glad you asked," Dekker said. "I remember the first time I encountered our fair city. *'In every street, carts and coaches make such a thundering as if the world ran upon wheels: at every corner, men, women, and children meet in such shoals, that posts are set up of purpose to strengthen the houses, lest with jostling one another they should shoulder them down. Besides, Hammers are beating in one place, Tubs hooping in another, Pots clinking in a third, Water-tankards running at tilt in a forth: here are Porters sweating under burdens, there Merchants—men bearing bags of money: Chapmen—as if they were at leap-frog—skip out of one shop into another: Tradesmen—as if they were dancing Galliards—are lusty at legs and never stand still."* [5]

"You are right!" William admitted. "It was very exciting. I'll have to work on details. I was quite impressed by the number of taverns and places of refreshment available to all."

"Human thirst is far from neglected in London," Dekker laughed. "There are 150 licensed taverns in the city and just about the same number of unlicensed. There are signs flapping in the wind at every corner for every taste. What is it that Tom Heywood sings?" Dekker threw back his head and waved his tankard in rhythm to his song.

> *'The Gentry to the King's Head,*
> *The Nobles to the Crown,*
> *The Knights unto the Golden Fleece,*
> *And to the Plough, the Clown.*
>
> *The Churchmen to the Mitre,*
> *The Shepherd to the Star,*
> *The Gardener hies him to the Rose,*
> *To the Drum the man of war'."* [6]

"What are clowns doing at the Plough?" William asked. "Isn't there a Circus Tavern or something like that for them?"

Dekker chuckled. "'Clown' is city slang for all the country people. Anybody with soil under his fingernails is a clown to certain of our city folk. England's prosperous yeomen, however, remain impervious to slander and continue to enjoy themselves at Plough taverns throughout the country."

"And the existence of a Mitre Tavern hints that even the churchmen have a drinking spot of their own," William said. "I must confess that surprises me somewhat. Is there actually a tavern for the clergy?"

"Saving souls must be thirsty work," Dekker said, "for there are three Mitre taverns if you count the one in Cheapside, and, of course, a healthy sprinkling of clergy in all the others too."

21

"I'm surprised church members put up with such behavior," William mused. "What possible excuse could ministers offer for indulging in practices which they often condemn as laxity among the laity?"

"No problem," Dekker laughed. "They are just experiencing life's temptations by nibbling at one of the big ones in order to stay in touch with their sinful flock. Parishioners often feel abandoned if ministers grow too divine. Much salvation gets done over a pint."

"I've heard mention that the Mermaid is an interesting tavern. Great conversations reputed," William said.

"Both of them are," Dekker affirmed.

"Both of them? There's more than one Mermaid Tavern?"

Dekker nodded. "With about 300 ale-houses in London, you can expect some duplication in names. In addition to three Mitres and two Mermaids, we have four King Harry Heads, and three Three Tuns."

"Do the people mix together freely in the taverns," William asked, "or is there always an awareness of who is top dog socially and economically?"

"You are very fortunate because the answer to that question, among others, is even now approaching our table," said Dekker. "Shake hands with Thomas Nashe, who probably knows as much about snobbery and ambition—one way or another—as any man in London. What do you say, Nashe? Does London act as a great stew-pot to permit all classes to flow freely together?"

Nashe smiled in acknowledgment of Dekker's sally. *"In London, the ritch disdayne the poor. The Courtier the Cittizen. The Cittizen the Countriman. One Occupation disdayneth another. The Merchant the Retayler. The Retayler the Craftsman. The better sort of Craftsmen the baser. The Shoemaker the Cobler. The Cobler the Carman. One nyce Dame disdaynes her next neighbor shoulde have that furniture to her house, or dainty dishe or devise, which she wants. She will not goe to Church, because she disdaines to mixe herselfe with base company, and cannot have her close Pue by herselfe. She disdaines to wear what every one weares, or heare that Preacher which every one heares."* [7]

William laughed. "Do they also set their houses apart in that fashion?"

"Surprisingly, London neighborhoods do not always reflect that kind of social exclusiveness," Nashe continued. "Pell-mell was the organizing principal in building London, and catch-as-catch-can was the result. The wealthy merchant may have his five-story, ten-room townhouse, but next door to him is a shopkeeper with his sales window displaying wares, and on the other side is an artificer of one sort or another who share a common wall with him because that arrangement saves the space that an additional wall would have taken up. All the cities, like London, which were walled about in ancient times have the problem of finding room to expand."

"How do they solve such a basic problem?" William asked.

"They end up cramming houses together higgildy-piggildy and extending the upper floors out over the lower floors to attain that jetty effect. Such a structure increases the upstairs floor space while leaving room for tradesmen and carters to function at street level. The search for more room drives the whole thing, because we have an average of eight people per house in London according to our latest survey, and city folk all feel they need more indoor space than do their country brethren."

"The desire for more room may help drive construction," Malachi said taking a seat beside Dekker, "but don't leave out the profit motive for builders. I remember a report somebody did last year for the Queen—of course Elizabeth's solution from on high is that each residence should have at least five acres around it—anyway, the report said: *The desire of Profitte greatly increaseth Buyldings...everie man seeketh out places, highways, lanes, and cover corners to buylde upon, if it be but Sheddes, Cottages, and small tenements.*" [8]

"That's right," said Nashe, "and they don't hesitate to divide up existing structures into tenements to house many families. I know a chandler in Clarkenwell who made fifteen out of one, and I've seen tenements built over stables and in gardens and other odd corners. There seems to be no end to the ambitious avarice of land developers."

"Or anyone else, for the matter," Malachi grinned. "It seems to be a species thing."

Thomas Nashe nodded, "Too true and too sad. In every street in London, we see this tendency acted out. *From the rich to the poore there is ambition, or swelling above theyr states; the rich Cittizen swells against the pryde of the prodigall Courtier: The prodigal Courtier swels against the welth of the Cittizen, One Company swells against another, and seekes to intercept the gaine of each other: nay, not any Company but is divided in it selfe. The Ancients, they oppose themselves against the younger, and suppresse them and keepe them downe all that they may. The young men, they call them dotards, an swel and rage, an with many others sweare on the other side, they will not be kept under by such cullions, but goe good and neere to out-shoulder them...amongdst theyr Wives is lyke warre.*" [9]

"And you can add apprentices to that bunch," Malachi grinned. "Always trying to shoulder aside their masters."

"But at least they can be beaten," said Dekker. "The Bawdy Court always rules that the master may whip an unruly apprentice who attempts to swell above his state."

"Yes, but they dictate no more than six stripes at a time," Malachi pointed out. "Hardly enough for a man to really get his back into the job."

"Well, Malachi, without a lazy back you would hardly be where you are today," Nashe joshed. "You travel extensively. You spend lavishly." He paused to hold up his empty tankard, raising his eyebrows suggestively. "Especially when you are with company that pleases you. And you have an apprentice to thrash whenever the mood strikes you. What more could you ask?"

Malachi grinned and signaled William to fetch another round for the group. "He is my man, true, and a very lively lad. He fancies himself a writer, but at present he is little more than a scribe."

William served them upon return and invited further discussion. "Here you are, sirs, and I confess I gnash my teeth in readiness for more Nashe wisdom."

Nashe smirked. *"Give me the man whose extemporal vein in any humor will excell our greatest art-masters' deliberate thoughts; whose inventions, quicker than his eye, will challenge the proudest rhetorician to the contention of like perfection with like expedition."* [10]

"That's the way I like it too," William said. "Less art and more matter saves us from tear and tatter. Aspiring writers must conserve energy if they are going to make it over the long haul, as we all know. But tell us about your early days as a writer, sir."

All at the table agreed, and Nashe began. *"Having spent many years in studying how to live, and lived a long time without money; having tried my youth with folly, and surfeited my mind with vanity, I began at length to look back to repentance and address my endeavours to prosperity...But all my thoughts consorted to this conclusion: That the world was uncharitable, and I ordained to be miserable."* [11]

William nodded in sympathy. "It feels that way sometimes," he said, "when you look around and see the way things are. But there's no ducking responsibility. What positive steps did you take to insure the success you enjoy today in the writing business?"

"I sat up late and rose early, contended with the cold, and conversed with scarcity; for all my labours turned to loss, my vulgar muse was despised and neglected, my pain not regarded or slightly rewarded, and I myself, in prime of my best wit, laid open to poverty." [12]

"I only regard mine as vulgar when she doesn't put out—so to speak," William confessed with a sly smile.

"Thereby," continued Nashe, *"I came to consider how many base men that wanted those parts which I had, enjoyed content at will and had wealth at command. I called to mind a cobbler that was worth five hundred pounds, an ostler that had built a goodly inn and might dispend forty pound yearly by his land, a car-man in leather pilch that had whipped out a thousand pound out of his horse-tail..."* [13]

"Egad!" cried William softly. "Is this a merry old England or what?"

Nashe turned to the more sympathetic portion of his audience. *"...and have I more wit than all these, thought I to myself—am I better born—am I better brought up—yes, and better favored—and yet am I a begger? What is the cause? How am I crossed, or whence is this curse?"* Nashe rolled his eyes and sighed mightily.

"That's all very true," said William, "but realistically, now, you do pick up some money for those pamphlets you compose with Greene, don't you? And there must be a certain amount of artistic satisfaction in such work, I should imagine."

"Not much," Nashe said. "*Men that should employ such as me are enamoured of their own wits and think whatever they do is excellent...*"

"Perfectly natural," murmured William.

"*...though it be never so scurvy; that learning of the ignorant is rated after the value of the ink and paper, and a scrivener better paid for an obligation than a scholar for the best poem he can make;...How then can we choose but be needy, when there are so many drones amongst us?... or even prove rich, that toil a whole year for fair looks?*" Nashe concluded

"I've heard Marlowe say the same thing," Malachi said. "It's a bad year for writers generally and for highly gifted poets in particular."

"How would he know?" Nashe growled. "He has a patron."

"Nobody knows that for sure," Malachi said, "but it must be admitted that Marlowe seems to have a ready source of pocket money, so he must have formed some sensible alliance somewhere. We all need a little help in this world. How is your collaboration with Robert Greene going? You two have produced some of the most effective broadsides I've ever seen, some funny and some biting, but all entertaining and enlightening. You have a real knack for putting people on the rack." He sent his apprentice a furtive wink. "Have you two produced anything entertaining lately?"

"Interesting that you should ask," Nashe said. "Lately, I have been concentrating on the depiction of the differentiation of national types, how every country produces those who vaunt themselves as superior to others and expend every effort in order to climb to the highest ranks in the eyes of their countrymen. '*Thus do weeds grow up whiles no man regards them. There is no friendship to be had with him that is resolute to do or suffer anything rather than to endure the destiny whereto he was born; for he will not spare his own father or brother to make himself a gentleman.*" [14]

"Hear, hear!" said Dekker.

Nashe continued: "*France, Italy, and Spain are all full of these false-hearted Machiavellians, but properly pride is the disease of the Spaniard, who is born a braggart in his mother's womb; for if he be but seventeen years old and hath come to the place where a field was fought, though half a year before, he then talks like one of the giants that made war against heaven.....and let a man soothe him in this vein of killcow vanity, you may command his heart out of his belly to make you a rasher on the coals, if you will, next your heart.*"

"That's right," Malachi said. "If you want cooperation from a Spaniard, you must chat him up a bit. But the Italians—they are different. They'll chat you up."

Nashe nodded. "*The Italian is a more cunning proud fellow that hides his humor far cleanlier and indeed seems to take a pride in humility, and will proffer a stranger more courtesy than he means to perform. He hateth him deadly that takes him at his word; as (for example) if upon occasion of meeting he request you to dinner or supper at his house, and that at the first or second entreaty you promise to be his guest, he will be the mortallist enemy you have. But if you deny him he will think you have manners and good bringing up and will love you as his brother. Marry, at the third or forth time you must not refuse him. Of all things he counteth it a mighty disgrace to have a man pass jostling by him in haste on a narrow causey and ask him no leave, which he never revengeth with less than a stab."*

"Stay out of Italian alleys," William noted.

"The Frenchman, not altered from his own nature….loves none but himself and his pleasure. Yet though he be the most grand seigneur of them all, he will say 'a votre service et commande-ment, monsieur' to the meanest vassal he meets…"

"I think that's nice—" murmured William.

"He thinks he doth a great favour to that gentleman or follower of his to whom he talks sitting on his close-stool; and with that favour, I have heard, Catherine, the Queen Mother, wanted to grace the noblemen of France…"

"Ah,yes, Catherine." Malachi shook his head. "Not too surprising. The Medici have always been arrogant people."

"A great man of their nation coming in time past over into England and being here very honorably received, he in requital of his admirable entertainment as an evening going to the privy, as it were to honor extraordinarily our English lords appointed to attend him gave one the candle, another his girdle, and another the paper. But they—not acquainted with this new kind of gracing—accompanying him to the privy door, set down the trash and so left him; which he—considering what inestimable kindness he extended to them therein more than usual—took very heinously."

"It is not surprising," offered William, "that different cultures look at things quite differently. No doubt we should keep an open mind—"

"The most gross and senseless proud dolts in a different kind from all these are the Danes, who stand so much upon their unwieldy, burly-boned soldiery that they account of no man that hath not a battle-axe at his girdle to hough dogs with, or wears not a cock's feather in a red thrummed hat like a cavalier. Briefly he is the best fool braggart under heaven; for besides nature hath lent him a flaberkin face like one of the four winds, and cheeks that sag like a woman's dugs over his chinbone….look on his fingers and you shall be sure to find half a dozen silver rings worth threepence apiece. Thus walks he up and down in his majesty, taking a yard of ground at every step, and stamps on the earth as if he meant to knock up a spirit."

"It's probably those wooden shoes," William offered.

"If an Englishman set his little finger to him he falls like a hog's trough that is set on one end."

"I've heard that in the taverns," cried William, "that one Englishman can whip any five—but tell me how do the English rate in the court of world opinion?"

Nashe thought for a moment. *"It is not for nothing that other countries whom we upbraid with drunkenness call us bursten bellied gluttons; for we make our greedy paunches powdering-tubs of beef, and eat more meat at one meal than the Spaniard or Italian in a month... We must have our tables furnished like poulter's stalls, or as though we were to victual Noah's Ark again, wherein there was all sorts of living creatures that ever were..."* [15]

"We've heard," murmured William. "It sounds as if you eat much better than we do."

"And whereto tends all this gourmandise but to give sleep gross humours to feed on, to corrupt the brain and make it unapt and unwieldy for anything?... The Roman censors, if they lighted upon a fat corpulent man, they straight took away his horse and constrained him to go afoot, positively concluding his carcass was so puffed up with glutton or idleness."

"I think that's probably right, Thomas," said Malachi. "I sometimes nap just after I've eaten heavily and suffer bad dreams as a consequence. Would you like another drink?"

"No, thank you," said Thomas Nashe. "I've had quite enough. Well, perhaps, just <u>one</u> more. *'From gluttony in meats, let me descend to superfluity in drink; a sin that ever since we have mixed ourselves with the Low Countries is counted honourable, but before we knew their lingering wars was held in the highest degree of hatred that might be. Then, if we had seen a man go wallowing in the streets or lien sleeping under the board, we would have spet at him as a toad and called him 'foul drunken swine,' and warned all our friends out of his company. Now he is nobody that cannot drink Super Magulum, carouse the hunter's hoop.'*

"What's Super Magulum?" asked William.

"A device of drinking new—come out of France, which is, after a man hath turned up the bottom of the cup, to drop it on his finger nail and make a pearl with that is left; which, if it shed and he cannot make stand on, by reason there's too much, he must drink again for his penance." [16]

"I like games where there are no losers—I'll give it a try." William drained his mug, turned it up and tapped it on his thumbnail. He brought forth a single drop which quivered there. "I did it! There it is. I've won. What reward comes to winners?"

"They get to quit drinking, leave the company and go home."

"Oh my, as you spoke, a giant quiver shook my frame and splashed it to the floor. Condemned again."

"You know," Dekker laughed, "the Dutch themselves, of all people, sometimes clip us drunkards."

"Oh, the Dutch are crafty devils when they drink," said Nashe. "As a matter of fact, they won't bargain with you at all until they're drunk, because that's when their brains work best—submerged in alcohol—with just an occasional dike for footing on which to strike their sharp bargains. I label them as 'foxy' drinkers in the enumeration of drinkers I've listed as part of my next work."

"Enumeration of drinkers?"

"You may think we have only one or two kinds of drunkards but, in truth, I have discerned eight kinds."

"Eight?" echoed all three listeners.

"*Exactly. The first is ape drunk, and he leaps and sings and hollers and danceth for the heavens. The second is lion drunk, and he flings the pots about the house, calls his hostess whore, breaks the glass windows with his dagger, and is apt to quarrel with any man that speaks to him. The third is swine drunk heavy, lumpish, and sleepy, and cries for a little more drink and a few more clothes. The fourth is sheep drunk, wise in his own conceit when he cannot bring forth a right word. The fifth is maudlin drunk, when a fellow will weep for kindness in the midst of his ale and kiss you, saying 'By God, Captain, I love thee; go thy ways, thou dost not think so often of me as I do of thee. I would, if it pleased God, I could not love thee so well as I do', and then he puts his finger in his eye and cries. The sixth is martin drunk, when a man is drunk and drinks himself sober ere he stir. The seventh is goat drunk, when in his drunkenness he had no mind but on lechery. The eighth is fox drunk, when he is crafty drunk as many of the Dutchmen be, that will never bargain but when they are drunk.*" [17]

"You certainly seem to have put a great deal of thought into your work, Nashe. Did you have to travel far to spot all those types?"

"*All these species and more I have seen practiced in one company at one sitting when I have been permitted to remain sober amongst them only to note their several humors.*"

"Must be a wild place with all those crying and leaping and window-stabbing lechers on the loose."

"Well, I'll have to admit I did catch Victor's on a busy Tuesday night."

William turned to Malachi as the others spoke among themselves. "These writers cut people to pieces with their sharp tongues," he murmured.

Malachi grinned. "Indeed they do. And for such butchery, they are deemed wits."

Chapter 4:
WITH MOUTH AGAPE AND EYES AGOG

At dinner a week later in a London Inn:

"You must cultivate good habits, William, if you intend to live comfortably in the city," Malachi advised as he folded his napkin. "Always remember to tip the kitchen people. They will serve you between hours if you are a prized patron. Start today."

"I would be happy to, but I'm afraid my purse has been stolen." William unwrapped a forlorn, leather strip from his belt and gazed at its neatly trimmed ends.

"Again?" Malachi asked quietly.

"It's a real puzzle to me where and how they do it," William said, "because I have never felt any pull or tug. I go out each morning with my purse tied on securely, and I come back each evening with nothing but strings dangling from my belt. Let me ask you if I should properly regard my losses as the normal daily tribute exacted for the privilege of living in this wondrous city?"

Malachi chuckled, "Some claim the local cut-purses are equal to Italian pick-pockets, but I think such people have never visited Rome to observe those consummate villains in motion, or they would not venture such parochial vaunting. Nevertheless, the resident denizens can certainly recognize a prize boob when they see one."

"I suppose that is your introduction to offering me some constructive suggestions about my behavior?"

"You have been in London long enough now to quit walking around *mea culpa* and making yourself an open target for the quick-hand people."

"Walking around how?"

"*Mea culpa*. Literally 'my fault' or 'by my fault' in Latin. But in your case it means 'mouth agape and eyes agog'. You need to master your countenance and try to look like you belong here. If you can cultivate an alert posture, most of the foists and pickers will steer clear of you, but if you continue to wander about in a stupefied daze, you will continue to attract them to your purse. Have you encountered any woman this past week who dropped her groceries in front of you or stumbled against you?"

William started in surprise. "How in the world did you know that? As a matter of fact, I was about to reach the unfortunate conclusion that the women of this city are noticeably clumsy because something very like that has happened to me every day since I arrived in London, although one day it was an older fellow who needed a hand crossing the muddy street."

"And you stopped to help each time, I suppose."

"Naturally," William nodded, "and I don't mind saying that such occasions are a bright spot in my introduction to London and more than make up for the depredations carried out against my purse. I happen to think there is nothing in the world quite as satisfying as helping out your neighbors when they have a bit of difficulty. It makes a man's heart hop happily when he knows that he is being a good neighbor. I think it is the duty of all of us—particularly when we change residence—to expend our effort and energy in such a fashion that people all about us are reassured that a valuable asset has been added to the community."

"Admirable sentiments," Malachi nodded approval, "but costly."

"Costly how?"

"Do a little two-plus-two thinking on the subject. You stop to help each day and you are robbed each day. What does that suggest to you?"

"You mean."

"Exactly. Attention diverted and hands occupied add up to the perfect target. I'm surprised they haven't stolen your doublet as well. But don't worry. All country bumpkins go through some of this when they encounter the rustle and bustle of London's crowded streets," Malachi assured him, "but the wise ones develop an alert posture very quickly, and that's what you must do because I have errands for you to run. That means I'll have to put actual coins instead of buttons in your next purse if you are to eat along the way. Since you seem particularly attuned to your belly's needs, perhaps you'll remember it will cost you your supper if you lose your purse again. Hungry men make good candidates for a little self-discipline, I've noticed, and they can be counted on to remain alert."

"My adjustment to the big city may take longer than I first supposed," William mused.

"While you adjust, let's take a little turn around the square. I find an after-dinner stroll aids digestion."

As they walked, Malachi several times admonished William to be quiet, telling him to practice looking alert. Finally he addressed his apprentice. "I must remind you that our service requires us to remain as unobtrusive as possible at all times, which means that, without fail, we must knuckle under to the rules which society imposes on us, or we risk drawing bothersome attention to ourselves."

"More rules?" William moaned.

"For instance, you need to give way to your betters immediately and always move over to walk outside me."

"But the horses and wagons brush by and splash all that filth on me if I walk out there. Perhaps if we walk single-file, neither of us need get splashed."

"In order to survive at all," Malachi growled, "you must accept the various roles you will be asked to play during our time together. At the moment, you have on the apprentice-cap for all the world to see, and that world fully expects you to surrender the wall to your master and protect him from the splashing of the very filth you mentioned. That's what you're here for. That's your purpose. Nobody wants to see an apprentice leading his master along a wall."

"Could I follow?"

"Courtesy and good manners require that you walk between me and the center of the street. See to it. People are watching."

William crossed to the outside.

"Why don't they build a raised pavement for foot traffic along the side of the street?" he asked. "They could call it a walk-side."

"Good idea," Malachi agreed amiably.

"An uplifted section for walking would profit everybody. We could stay out of that mess in the middle."

"You've been talking too much to young Ben Jonson," Malachi chuckled. "The pair of you are bent on elevating society for its own good, but you have no concept of the economic reality which puts severe limits on such visionary prospects. Do you imagine you are the first person to think of a raised portion along the side of the street?"

"I certainly hope not. I like to think that conscientious people everywhere share a deep-seated desire to—"

"Don't you realize any raised section of the street would not only trip the horses but also rupture the wagon-wheels? Cartmen would never risk it. Delivery of food and drink would come to an immediate halt. London would become a ghost city in a month. Have you any other far-reaching ideas?"

"How often do they rake these streets?" William sniffed.

"London streets are supposed to be raked once a week and most of the filth carted away, but since the Goldfinders only work at night and are poorly paid to begin with, who can say how often they appear?"

"Doesn't anybody check up on them?"

"Some record somewhere will officially show outlay made for street maintenance, so the City Fathers rest easy after spending money on the problem. After that, it's up to either the Justices of the Peace—who are usually abed at night—or to the patrolling Bailiffs, to keep a monitoring eye on this group of cast-off misfits and make sure they perform honorably in their employment."

"Couldn't the JP get up early and take a walking tally of which streets had been manicured during the night and which hadn't?"

"That's the heart of the problem right there," Malachi said. "There is always strong disagreement about which is which. The Goldfinders often leave little sign of their passing."

"I'd say this street hasn't been raked in weeks. Egad, what a stench!"

"Educate your nose to close its passages as all intelligent people learn to do. Assume what we call a 'chemistry nose' and breathe through your mouth as though you had a head cold. Hold on, now. We must move out and give the wall to this gentleman approaching us since he is obviously better dressed than we are and he has several burly attendants in livery accompanying him."

"I will not move one step closer to the center of this street," William declared, "for fear of submerging forever into unimaginable filth."

Malachi grabbed him by the arm and swung with him into a shop doorway. "Your tender sensibility will get us beaten and pitched headlong into the very quagmire you fear if you can't remember your station in life. We have no time for pointless brawls." Malachi bowed his head respectfully as the gentleman swept past with his entourage.

"I really don't see why the streets belong to some of us more than to others."

"It keeps the traffic moving. Everybody knows when to get out of the way and when to steer a straight course. Or nearly everybody."

"Yes, but they know only by rank," William said. "Suppose we had no rank? Suppose everybody counted the same? Suppose everybody was judged on his own individual merits?"

"Unthinkable!" exclaimed Malachi. *"Take but degree away, untune that string, and you would have absolute chaos."* [18]

"Upon reflection, I can see that discord might very well follow such a course," William acknowledged, "but it still might be worth a try. 'Untune that string, hm?" he repeated thoughtfully.

"The point here is you must learn your role and adjust to the way things are. Learn to accommodate. You already caused quite a stir this morning when you ignored your station and shocked the on-lookers."

"You mean at the inn? The chair thing again?"

"Exactly."

"But those benches are so hard to sit on, and nobody was using the chair."

"Everybody sits on benches," Malachi insisted. "The chair was empty because we had a modest company and nobody wanted to assume the role of chairman. Although nothing was said at the time, I felt—and I'm sure the company agreed—that you were the least likely candidate among us to occupy the chair."

"Why didn't somebody say something?"

"I just want you to know that when a real chairman does appear, you may be required to defend your life for your effrontery."

"Defend my life? With weapons?"

"That's the best way."

"You would help me, of course."

"Maybe I would eventually," Malachi said, "but I won't always be around, and the truth is you could use a few hard knocks to sharpen your chances for survival."

"I don't like pain, you know," William confessed.

"That's a good beginning," Malachi chuckled. "While some masters, and some educators, seize upon a future threat of torment as a tool to enhance learning, I prefer to see the pangs of pain crouched in the tall grass just behind you, ready to leap out like a ravenous tiger to disembowel you in a trice and eat out your innards before your very eyes."

"Memorable image, indeed," William grimaced. "I hope there is a moral attached to such indignity?"

"There is indeed. If you concentrate on the art of role-playing in order to fit unobtrusively into any background, you will seldom be called upon to suffer while you are shuffling your way through this mortal coil. In addition, your value to our service will be enhanced by your ability to stay out of sight." Malachi caught William's sleeve. "You are about to pass our inn. Do you not recognize it?"

"Ah yes, the Black Boar! Praise the gods of food and drink. I am about to perish from lack of both!"

"Eat well and sleep well and tomorrow I'll lend you out to Samuel, an old friend of mine who is presently a steward in one of England's leading noble houses. He will review with you the niceties of mannerly behavior for pedestrian travel on the streets of London. He believes in hands-on instruction, so you should pick up the overview very quickly, and come in contact with the public almost immediately."

"Good. I don't have too much patience with theoretical stuff."

❖ ❖ ❖

The following day, breakfast at the Black Boar Inn:

"Oh well," said Samuel the Steward as he finished his toast and tea, "my experience has inclined me to lean t'ward the idea that history is pretty much ruled by strong voices and unexpected consequences."

"Interesting theory," said William, "even if a little general."

"Take the sale of the monastery lands, for example. God knows they needed breaking up. The Roman Catholic Church already owned a third of all estates in England, y' know."

"I've heard."

"And Henry was certainly right in throwing 'em out rather than knuckling under, but, as I say, that's not the end of the matter. There was consequences which was expected, of course. The sale of the church lands got Henry out of debt and made him a rich king, even permitted him to build a brand new English Navy. In consequence, the sale created a large group of landholders that didn't exist before. Up until the dissolution, as they calls it, whatever land was not held by the church was owned by the Crown and the nobles. When Henry threw one third of the nation's land on the open market at bargain prices, the treasure boxes in the homes o' thousands of thrifty men, mostly o' merchants and traders was broken open so that deeds to lands those men had only dreamed of could be duly purchased. It musta been a startling experience for 'em."

"You mentioned unforeseen consequences?"

"Right. You see them all around you, the beggars and homeless. The Church used to handle those problems. There was always a way on monastic lands for a man to work for his supper. The Church took care of the sick and the poor. It kept them people off the street and out of sight, and probably saved their souls in the bargain. So when the Catholic church went, the services went too and dumped all them poor wretches onto the streets of London with their souls in tatters to match their garments. And that's where you come in."

"Me?"

"I hope you realize that ordinarily, a person like you wouldn't have no chance at all of wearing the livery of a noble house."

"Of course."

"But the circumstances ain't ordinary, as I've just explained, and one unexpected thing is that noblemen now have to have more retainers to ease their passage through London streets."

"Malachi mentioned this is a dealing-with-the-public kind of assignment."

"Exactly. Malachi has asked me to acquaint you with the rules of city street traffic, so I am pleased to see that you will be able to impress a kind of rotund presence on the people of London."

"By that I take it you mean that my work will be so all-encompassing as to strike a common note of universality into my audience," ventured William.

"No, I mean you'll be able to push and shove more of that beggarly rabble out of his Lordship's passage. Stout hips helps a lot when you are pushing and shoving, keeping the weight down low for greater leverage."

"Pushing and shoving?"

"Punching too, if needs be. We'll fix you up with a standard on a pole to lead the way. The pole is really a quarter-staff so you'll have plenty of leverage if things get tight. Try not to get the banner bloody. Use the other end for the heavy work. Don't let the beggars impress you when they shout and wave their crutches at you. Remember they are off-balance without their supports, so even a light blow will overset them."

"Let me see if I have this straight now," William said quietly. "You expect me to precede his lordship through the streets, clubbing and punching disheartened home-less people and the pitiful beggars that we encounter along the way?"

"Just shove the homeless aside, but annoy the bold beggars enough so our master may pass unmolested. Nothing serious, just a hard knock or two."

"What you require, of course, is impossible," said William. "I simply couldn't do such a thing."

"Indeed you can. You'll pick it up as you go. Tricks to every trade. You'll learn quick enough the shortcuts."

"Shortcuts?"

"Right. For instance, if you push the beggars sideways instead of straight back, they will often topple several of their brethren as they flail about with their crutches in attempting to regain their balance. Little things like that."

"I don't think you quite understand. When I was offered the job of an advance man to meet the masses of London, I thought we were talking about a kind of public relations thing."

"Yeah, so?"

"When Malachi spoke of meeting the people of London face-to-face each day and influencing the pathways they took in life, he struck a responsive chord in my heart, and I anticipated an opportunity to cultivate a deeper sense of sympathy and concern for the unfortunates of our society, but now it appears to me you want me to serve as nothing more than a common bully, to cudgel and curse the very people who so desperately need our help."

"The cursing is strictly up to you—some do, some don't. But, believe me, it's a waste of time with these people because they've heard it all a'fore. You're not likely to impress them with your genteel vocabulary. I'd say lay on the staff and save your voice. It'll be your responsibility to see that no person below his rank takes the wall from the master."

"Suppose someone comes out a doorway?"

"Plant your staff in their belly and shove 'em back in."

"Women too? What if they should be, you know, increasing?"

The steward of the Great House nodded. "Them in particular. They take up the room o' two. They've got no business showing theirselves in that condition anyway. And most of all, if you see retainers of any new-rich merchant house, the master has ordered we whack them a time or two to remind them there's still a big difference between people who have scrounged wealth by crass commerce and gentlemen who's been born into their riches."

"Whack the retainers, you say? What possible good can it do to brutalize another human being who is only carrying out his orders?"

"Quite right there. Can't have advance men making policy, that's not their function."

"What is?"

"You'll soon see as you act out your part."

"I act best when I am sure of my motivation," William confided. "Tell me clearly then, if you will, what driving force should govern my thoughts and thereby my actions?"

"I suppose a little understanding might help," admitted the steward.

"I'd appreciate it."

"Generally speaking, then, each lord is like a small prince, who has to protect his person and his seat of power. His estates is like the prince's capital city. Capital cities is always situated well inland from the coast, so's not to be taken by surprise, overthrow'd and captured. They're always built by some easy defended river, too, with plenty of real estate betwixt the government and any invaders, but with plenty of room for commerce and supply."

"Yes, that seems well thought out."

"And lords work the same way. They have their boundaries patrolled regular by handy retainers, who keep back any trespassers. Broken-bone beatings usually make the point, but sometimes civil proceedings is necessary. Either way the lesson is clear: Don't approach the seat of power 'thout permission. Also, border guards and game wardens and advance men serve as early trouble indicators."

"Indicators?"

"They are in position to intercept trespassers in the field and then return to their masters, even if bloody and bedraggled, to raise the alarm."

"How often does that happen in this advance man job?"

"Never to any sensible advance man who keeps his wits about 'im and doesn't break any of the accepted rules."

"Accepted rules?"

"There's many that governs your position," the steward affirmed. "For instance, if any fool of an advance man happened to bow first to a retainer from any house lesser than his own, he'd deserve whatever bloody thrashing he'd get as a consequence."

"How can he tell which House is greater?"

"Everybody knows that; we all grow up with it. Closeness to the line of succession makes a House greater. All you have to do is review the bloodlines of John of Gaunt and his seven children for the last hundred years and govern yourself accordingly."

"Hold on!" cried William. "I'm sure you mean the Tudors!"

Samuel snorted. "Any schoolboy knows the Tudors came by their royal blood through their vague descent from John of Gaunt, after Elizabeth's grandfather, King Henry VII, cleared the field of heirs by killing King Richard III at Bosworth Field in 1485. Look it up! Now, another thing that makes a house great is enormous holdings. Just fix in your mind the relative wealth of the leading Houses of the Realm."

William groaned. "Suppose I meet him coming around a corner?"

"Who?"

"The other retainer. How will I know who he is so quickly? How will I know whether to bow first or second? It'll have to be a split-second decision, you realize."

Samuel shrugged. "It's all instinctive. Just glance at the family coat on the livery, and the rest falls into place. Don't think about it, just do it."

"Let me see if I have this straight. I should be able to recognize the coat of arms of each leading family in England so that I may identify them instantaneously as to relative wealth and access to the succession?"

"Good. I'm glad that's clear. It's plain this work is harder here in London than in the rural areas where you only encounter neighboring nobles, but things are generally more complicated in the city; everybody knows that. It's part of the price you pay for the excitement. Just don't forget you represent one of the noblest houses in the realm when you wear our livery, so don't do nothing to disgrace it. Don't worry about the other thing. There are few houses in the land you need bow to."

"But that's just the point, you see: there are some. Suppose I get caught in one of those fifty-fifty things and can't tell whether to bow or wait? Is it all right if I lean a little in the direction of bowing until I get the whole thing straight in my mind?"

"Good God, no! What are you thinking of? You can't bow first to a lesser House! The whole system would fall apart. Get that clear out of your mind!"

"Well, I didn't want to make a mistake the other way—you mentioned they hurt people for that particular failing."

"They'll beat you whichever way you fail. If you bow first to a lower House, your fellow attendants will kick you and trounce you so you won't know your front-side from your backside."

"Perhaps I could be one of the men who follow the advance man until I familiarize myself a little more with the identification procedures?"

"No chance," said the steward. "The employment opening is at the point of our phalanx, as I told your master. All other positions are filled. Here is Malachi now."

William turned to Malachi, "Oh, so you knew all about the position I would get even before you assigned me?"

Malachi grinned. "You'll have a chance to make an imprint on London society for a week or so until I get back. It'll smarten you up about proper behavior on the streets of London."

"What happened to your last point of the phalanx' person, if I may ask?"

"As a matter of fact," the steward said with a smile and a quick wink at Malachi, "he retired to the country on pension, after a long and honorable career."

"Just as they all do," Malachi laughed.

"Could you do me one small favor the first day?" William asked.

"Anything," said the steward. "Just ask. Don't forget now, when you wear the livery of one of England's oldest Houses, you don't have to fear asking for assistance. Any refusal would be an insult to our patron, and few in England would dare to lose his favor."

"You don't know how much that relieves me," said William, "because I must confess to you that I do not have absolute confidence in my ability to perform the duties you've described."

"That's bad."

"Perhaps you could see your way clear to have an advisor accompany me the first day so that I do not make any major mistakes in interpreting rank and riches instantaneously, which is basically what this job seems to be all about."

"A nanny? A monitor? A strong shoulder for our point man to lean on? Do you have any idea what kind of message that would send to the people you are trying to influence?"

"Message?"

"Have you no idea how ridiculous and non-productive your suggestion is?"

"Excuse me, but before you flail me further, tell me first what happened to the cooperation I was supposed to get on any request I made?"

"Forget that! This is in-house stuff! You can't expect us to send along a nursemaid for the very man we expect to take the best blows and insults the untidy have to offer. Half the value of the point man's effectiveness comes from the fact that the general public knows he is expendable. When the real crunch comes, he goes first. They know that and they behave accordingly. What do you imagine they will think when they see a point man coddled and protected from harm by bodyguards?"

"If they have any brains, they'll say that's a very bright point man."

"Forget about such nonsense and concentrate on the job at hand," the steward advised. "Just relax as you approach each street corner and you'll make the right decisions. Let events govern theirselves. Everything will go well, you'll see. By the way, I notice you left this next-of-kin card blank. Is that an oversight or do you have no one?"

"Put Malachi's name there. I'm sure he'll do the right thing in the end."

Chapter 5:
THE YEOMEN SPEAK

One week later, the outskirts of London:

"You handle yourself well on horseback," said Malachi to his apprentice as they rode into the countryside. "You may have been a farmboy in your former life."

"Well, it's good to get away from the pushing and shoving of the street," said William. "A week on that job was enough to give me a very bruised body and a mind filled with endless gibberish about rank and station, so I'm ready for something a little more down to earth, like a ride in the country. Gad, the fresh air smells good!"

"I hadn't noticed." The leather of his saddle squeaked as Malachi shifted his weight.

"Look at that field of wheat! Some farmer is going to do well indeed come harvest time." William filled his lungs with a satisfied inhalation.

"Our English farmers are all anticipating a good year, in spite of the unusually cold winter. The summer's been short but good for certain crops."

"Is that what we're doing out here: checking on the crops?"

"That's part of it. We're also checking on the yeomen themselves, how they feel about the coming year. Things like that."

"You say yeomen. Do you mean farmers, or are all yeomen farmers?"

"Yeoman is a general term for a farmer who freeholds at least one hundred acres—150 on the average. England has very close to 85,000 yeomen, as we can tell from the recorded land deeds."

William whistled. "That makes us an agricultural country indeed! But one hundred and fifty acres seems a lot of land for one farmer to work."

"Many lease out ten-acre plots to cottagers, who often, in turn, hire landless peasants to do the heavy work. Recent prosperous years have given England's yeomen a substantial sense of self-esteem, and they now feel their opinions about agricultural matters should be made known to our policy-makers in Parliament."

"Well, certainly, a farmer knows more about farming than a man in Parliament," agreed William. "I realize that if a yeoman is more prosperous than a lesser farmer, his clothes and farm will, no doubt, reflect his prosperity, but are there any other telltale signs to distinguish one from the other?"

"Yes, certainly," grinned Malachi. "Farmers begin to become yeomen when they can afford to use horses instead of oxen to pull their plows, and to distinguish yeomen from the landed gentry above them, you need only check the local graveyard."

"The graveyard?"

"Right. Successful English yeomen have been moving into the blossoming class of English gentry for several decades now, and the graveyard will always tell you exactly when, and if, they've made the jump. If the farmer is still using flat stones to mark his family graves instead of artistic marble statuary, you know he has not yet moved up." Malachi laughed. "But more seriously now, the yeomen are a good cross-section of the English people and often are well-spoken about their situation. They are growing in importance all the time."

"I suppose they do well financially," ventured William.

"Some high, some low, depending on the quality of the land, the luck of the weather, and the management of their holdings, but an average figure between the rich and poor yeomen would be right at £400 per annum."

"Zounds, that sounds like a sturdy income. Is that when they become squires?"

"Right," said Malachi. "That's why we're seeing so many of them appointed Justices of the Peace, and quite a few chosen for seats in Parliament. Thousands more are propping up their own success by shrewdly sending their sons off for a university education in order to have some home-grown lawyers to look out for family interests. Their growing prosperity has secured them a seat at the table of power in England where they have drawn cards to play alongside the Crown, the nobles, and the Church. They are not yet laying down heavy bets, but who can tell what the future will bring?"

"What about the farmers who don't qualify as yeomen?"

"Our Survey Office figures there are about one million men, men who might be called 'heads of household' but who have little influence on national policy. That group includes the small farmers along with mariners, artificers, small merchants, shop keepers, cottagers, and tenants of all kinds."

"And apprentices?" added William.

Malachi nodded. "Indeed, rogues and vagabonds too."

William grimaced. "I sometimes suspect you pull those figures out of the air, Malachi. If not, you are a walking record book."

"You live in a much better ordered society than you are aware of, young man. There are nearly ten thousand church parishes in England, and for most of this century, they have been required to keep a registry of their membership. The Catholics started the record keeping and the Anglicans carried it on. The central government has access to those records, and has, in fact, made a central file of them. Our survey section has found them very useful because, within certain limits, we can solicit the opinion of any man in England at any given time."

"But who counts the rogues and the homeless and the apprentices, too, for that matter? I don't belong to any parish that I'm aware of. What does that do to your figures?"

Malachi shrugged. "Estimates are estimates. We use them; they don't use us. We assign a certain percentage to those who are not recorded for whatever reason, and a certain percentage to those who are counted twice for whatever reason. Fortunately, those percentages turn out to be much the same, so such factors cancel each other out."

"Very tidy book-keeping."

"Until recently," Malachi continued, "the vast majority of Englishmen were easy to count because they stayed pretty close to home, but now we have the problem of thousands of homeless people wandering about, and that complicates the numbers. But persistent poll-taking along with nimble book-keeping can still get the job done."

"Why do we have so many homeless?" wondered William.

"Many are displaced because of the field-enclosures, others because our cloth trade has lost its venting power now that Parma has closed the Dutch ports. All Continental merchants were affected when the Spanish grabbed Antwerp, but none so hard as our English workers who used to vent three quarters of our production through Antwerp."

"I remember that discussion, but what are field-enclosures?"

"It was a sad day for small growers and animal keepers when Parliament empowered owners of large herds of sheep to enclose pastureland, especially those public plots of land that had always been set aside for landless folk. Perhaps Thomas More identified the growing problem best in his 1516 book, *Utopia* when he wrote: *"Your sheep that were wont to be so meek and tame, and so small eaters, now, as I hear say, be become so great devourers and so wild that they eat up, and swallow down the very men themselves. They consume, destroy, and devour whole fields, houses and cities. For look in what part of the realm doth grow the finest and therefore the dearest wool, there noblemen and gentlemen, yea and certain abbots....leave no ground for tillage, they enclose all into pastures; they throw down houses; they pluck down towns, and leave nothing standing, but only the church to be made a sheephouse."* [19]

"But why would Parliament do such a thing?"

"I'm not an expert on the economy, but I do know that early in this century Parliament had a growing number of landowners who felt they could raise sheep with far fewer workers than tilling the soil required. Fencing in the pastures permitted them to double their return on the land, so the practice has snowballed for this whole century. Unfortunately, the enclosures cast adrift thousands of farm families who have not yet found a resting place in our society." Suddenly, Malachi pointed to a farmhouse that appeared through the trees. "See that grand manor? That belongs to Squire Nowlan, once an ordinary 150-acre yeoman, but he has prospered mightily since then."

"That man in the field there, supervising the workers, could he be the squire?"

"Sharp lad! I believe it is. Squire!" he shouted. "Can you spare us a minute or two?"

The squire waved and grinned and made his way to the fence. He was a burly man, well dressed in corduroy and leathers. His red hair and beard gave him a look of great energy, as did his long stride and warm greeting. "What brings a pale, bent-back like you out into the country, Malachi?"

"I'd hoped to see you, Squire, and maybe some of the other men to get an estimate of this year's crop situation for the Queen's record keepers."

"Well, it's going along, Malachi. Some bumps, some changes needed. I sent the boy for my horse. We'll go down to the village and catch the lads at their noonin'." He stopped to stare at William. "What's that you're munchin' on, boy? It smells like rye."

"Yessir," choked William, swallowing his bite of bread. "I often find that between meals—"

"Rye makes a low-class bread, boy. We yeomen have worked long and hard to grow a better grain, and we expect our fellow Englishmen to dig their teeth into the wholesome all-wheat bread the country now calls 'Yeoman's bread.'"

"Rye bread is low-class?"

"Compared to ours, it is. Rye bread and barley bread too. No person of distinction would choose either of those over wheat bread unless driven to it by necessity. Some sections of the country don't grow wheat, of course, but the gentry have it shipped in from enterprising yeomen to provide good bread for themselves and for influential people in their community. If you accept rye bread or barley bread as a staple, you are confessing that you have not risen above the lower classes."

"Egad, my bit of rye bread marks me as a lowly something or other?"

"Indeed it does. That low class balloons during times of dearth when most of our countrymen must settle for bread made from either oats or beans or peas. And when things really get bad, those breads are seasoned with acorns."

"Ugh, such a prospect makes this bit of rye even more delicious," William said, nibbling.

The squire's horse arrived, and he mounted, saying, "We'll get you a mutton pie at the Plowman. That's something to fill your belly." He put his horse to a brisk walk, and the others followed.

"You have a very prosperous-looking farm here," said William politely. "It makes a man think about getting busy and trying to join you."

"To tell you the truth," said the squire, "a yeoman's survival in England today is a tricky business. I shudder at the prospect of beginning afresh with a heart set on attaining my position."

"Tricky?"

"Aye," Squire Nowlan confirmed. "I recently heard one of the Fuller family describe the entire yeomen group as '*an estate of people almost peculiar to England, living in the temperate zone betwixt greatness and want.*' [20] He chuckled. "Tricky, indeed. Poised betwixt the gentry above and the peasantry below, ours is a balancing act. It only takes one bad year to tumble us down, but it takes a dozen good years in a row to jump us up."

"Jump up to gentry status, you mean."

The squire guffawed. "Sure, not all aspire to that lofty goal. Not by a long stretch. But some with ambition and a willingness to work hard and a policy of systematic underspending can do it."

"Savings, you mean?"

"I do," said the squire. "Enough to make it through a lean year or two, and enough to make a move when them who systematic overspend must sell their lands to pay their bills."

"The lesser gentry?"

"All the gentry. That's the way it works. The better part of them—even of the most well off—lives at arm's reach of their fortunes from year to year, and a certain number of them trip up annually, and their lands fall to the abiding yeoman."

"Who then becomes a gentleman-farmer?"

The squire nodded. "If he's lucky and works hard, good things can happen. Some say that gentility is nothing more than ancient riches, but I've found," he leaned over to poke William playfully in the ribs, "that new-found riches serves just as well."

"As long as one has the money, I guess."

"Not money so much as income. I suppose, in simple form, the real definition of a gentleman today is him who lives comfortable off his income."

"Without lifting a finger," ventured William.

The squire laughed. "Oh, he'd lose his lands soon enough if he didn't manage 'em well. I've seen plenty of men go under."

"Just how much annual income would a man have to enjoy in order to be considered a gentleman?" William asked.

"Plan some social climbing, do you?"

"Just interested."

"Well, let me figger," grinned the squire. "As apprentice to a kind but somewhat stingy master, you probably get the average London monthly wage of four-shillings?"

"Four!" gasped William. "Not nearly——"

Malachi cut in. "He gets the maximum-minimum average, in addition to his found and a quick box on the ear if he complains too much."

The squire smiled at William. "If you have ambitions of gentility, lad, I advise you to cultivate your fairy godmother. You would need an income of between £300 and £400 per annum anyplace in England, outside London, in order to live like a gentleman."

"It is London I have under consideration."

"Well then, you'd need at least £1000 to settle yourself comfortable. Everything costs double in the city. The price of land has doubled in the last decade."

"That ought to put the quietus on such thoughts for the moment," Malachi chuckled.

"But a fellow could work part-time and still be a gentleman, couldn't he?"

The squire nodded. "He could get away with it as long as he didn't have to."

They had arrived at the Plowman, where two other farmers, dressed like Squire Nowlan, stood waiting for them at the entrance.

"Seen you comin', Dennis," said one of the two, who introduced himself as Farmer Francis. "Hope yor all here to join us for a bite of pie and a pint."

They entered the inn boisterously and sat at the table where several other acquaintances were eating. The squire bellowed for food and ale, made sure everyone had all the names straight, and sat back with his fingers laced over his belly.

"The boy here was askin' about what kind of breaks our people got to permit some of us to prosper and become gentlemen. Ted, you got any ideas what to tell him?"

Farmer Francis cleared his throat and scratched his head. "Should I start with the 1215 Magna Carta or is that going back too far?"

"Oh, everybody knows about the Great Charter," Dennis answered. "I think we can skip on down to recent times."

"What is the Magna Carta?" William asked.

"Oops," Malachi said. "I forgot that my apprentice missed a lot of days at school. If you'll permit me, I'll sketch in a quick background for him while you gentlemen wet down your tonsils."

"An honest salute to that central document never hurt any of us, Malachi," Dennis said, "so go to it."

"1215?" William prodded.

"The great charter which guarantees a jury trial and the right to Habeas Corpus even to the least of us," he paused to smile at William, "was reluctantly signed by King John during that year when his barons felt he had grown too arrogant and was abusing what they had come to feel were their traditional baronial privileges."

"What's a Habeas Corpus?"

"That's Latin for 'you have the body' which means that those who detain others must produce them for trial to justify their detention, and that simple legality has become a touchstone for nearly all civilized societies because it meant the King Johns of the world could no longer lock up their troublesome barons and toss away the key. John later repudiated his signing as having been coerced, and the Pope released him from the provisions, but that brought about a civil war which eventually resulted in all of the conditions being accepted as the Great Charter of the English Common Law. Essentially, then, the Charter is rightfully regarded as a symbol of the supremacy of the law over the monarch, and—more to the point here today—as the opening of the door for ordinary English serfs to rise to the exalted position of the sturdy yeomen in whose company we find ourselves today. I salute you, gentlemen." Malachi raised his tankard and the entire group joined him in a hearty celebration of self.

"With that out of the way, I'll jump ahead a couple of hundred years," said Ted, "and point out that the English working man got his first big break after the Charter when the Black Death swept like a bloody scythe through the English population."

"The Black Death!" cried William. "What kind of break is that?"

"Yep. The Great Plague hit England in 1349, I believe, and cut the population in half in a few months. Killed over 300 people a day in London alone. Millions in Europe.

"And that sounds like a break to you?"

"It was a break for the survivors who profited after that deadly dragon's tail lashed about for a full year and wiped out entire communities. Labor shortage severe. Crops was needin' harvestin' and herds was needin' tendin', and there weren't no serfs to do it. Crews was gathered from neighbors to the north and neighbors to the south. In them days, remember, serfs belonged to the estate where they was born. They had to be bribed to jump the fence. That there is where the workers got their first pay in monies. Before that they had to settle for the leavings after the landlord had paid his legitimate expenses."

"That's the break, then?" William inquired. "Actual pay?"

"Yep. But more choice than pay, in actual fact. When the serf left his home estate, he strapped on his walking shoes and sold his services to the highest bidder. Without that power to choose, we wouldn't be yeomen today. We'd still be serfs on some grand lord's estate, using our best efforts for somebody else's profit."

The men sat back thoughtfully, perhaps contemplating their lives as serfs, rather than prosperous farmers. The food arrived, and the men all dug in.

"Where did the Plague come from?" William asked finally, his mouth still full of mutton pie.

Farmer Francis pondered a moment. "No one knows for sure, boy. Even to this day the mystery ain't been solved, and we still get a visitation now and again, cuttin' a furrow through the land, young and old, rich and poor, healthy or sickly, and not a bloody thing we can do about it. It's never been as terrible as that first time, howsomever. Some say the Jews brought it on us by poisoning the town wells. Thousands of Jews were kilt in retaliation over the years. Others said the lepers bathed in the wells to get back at the healthy. "Papal envoy said that Mars and Jupiter and Saturn came together just as the first plague started. These was pretty much ignorant superstition, says I. I agree with them that say it was brought by ship from Chiner."

"Brought by ship from Chiner? Ah, you mean China."

"Yep. That's about all I know of it. The Eyetalian ships come into southern France, to sell cargo they bought from the Asian countries and somethin' sinister came ashore along with the silks and spices."

William shivered. "Something sinister?"

Farmer Francis nodded. "When a ship unloads cargo, it also unloads sick men and skinny rats in every port it comes to. Them's the cargo that brings the Plague, says I."

Squire Dennis Nowlan tapped his pipe on the bricks of the fireplace behind him. "A happenin' as good as the Plague was that civil war we had in 1455. It lasted thirty year and wiped out a big portion of the nobility. As well as the usual number of ordinary soldiers."

"What caused it?" asked William.

The squire looked over at Malachi for help. "I believe you're referring to the War of the Roses," said he, and the squire waved him to continue. "The ground was laid for that war in the previous century when Edward III simply had too many children. Aside from his bedroom prowess, Edward is best remembered as the King who led English bowmen to notable victories over the French at Crecy in 1346 and at Poitiers in 1356."

"How many children were too many?" asked William.

Again the farmers looked to Malachi for the answer. "In conjunction with his Queen," said Malachi dryly, "he produced twelve claimants to the Crown. "few died young, but the rest divided into powerful Houses and produced additional litters of applicants with distant but valid claims to the Crown. Edward III put a lot of courtly ambition on hold with the production of so many sons because, as you might remember from school, William, the Crown goes to the first born son after the king dies, and when that son has a son, he is named the Prince of Wales, next in line to the succession. Every time the king has a child, whole families—brothers in particular—are shoved further away from any realistic expectation of assuming the throne. Over the years those noble families coalesced around several of the claimants and finally split off into two houses: Lancaster with its red rose symbol and York with its white rose."

"That must be why they call it the War of the Roses."

"Very perceptive." Malachi grinned at his companions. "The high-level casualties started at the battle of St. Albans in 1455 and ran to the death of King Richard III at Bosworth Field in 1485, thirty years later. The ordinary soldiers suffered about the number of casualties you might expect over a period of on-again-off-again fighting: 30,000 casualties over thirty years. Not big numbers, perhaps, but big percentages of armies which often numbered no more than ten to twelve thousand men."

"And somehow such slaughter turned out to be a break for farmers?" William prompted.

With a hand gesture, Malachi invited Squire Nowlan to continue his argument. The squire sat forward eagerly. "Well, y'see, lad, the workingman profited because those armies had a lot of highborn Englishmen in 'em. Since most of the nobles had intermarried over the years, the war was pretty much an all-out family free-for-all, where brothers, uncles, and cousins slaughtered each other like sheep for a king's feast. Three kings were kilt—Henry VI, Edward V, and Richard III. One Prince of Wales was lost, and, if I remember right, nine dukes, thirteen earls, twenty-four barons, and hundreds of lesser noblemen were done in. Like many a civil war or family fight, both sides ended up killing all prisoners."

"But," said William, "didn't that policy also mean the death of thousands of ordinary men who happened to be soldiers?"

"Of course," the squire admitted, "but commoners were often slaughtered after battle anyway, so that was no big change. Nobles, however, were usually kept for exchange or ransom, and that's where the policy change favored the ordinary man."

"The nobles got slaughtered too."

"That's right," confirmed the squire, "and since fathers and sons often rode side-by-side into battle under the family banner, their destruction often cast adrift a large number of scattered properties."

"What do you mean by scattered?"

"Well, boy, a king don't award lands all in one spot to loyal nobles for fear separate kingdoms might blossom if any lord gained control of too large an area. That meant the highborn dead from the War of the Roses left behind thousands of properties scattered throughout England, and opened up the opportunity for thrifty cottagers and even well found tenants to scoop up small parcels from broken estates."

Farmer Francis broke in at this point. "My great-great-grandfather was a domestic in the Tudor House, when Henry VII, our Lady Queen Elizabeth's grandfather, seized the throne in 1485. My ancestor was permitted to buy one hundred fifty acres for his loyalty to his lord, so I say Dennis is right: that's where the common man got his biggest break: the self-destruction of half the land-holding nobility."

Farmer Evans belched and set down his mug of ale with a bang. "You lads don't know what a break means," he joshed them. "A break is when you're permitted to better yourself by your own efforts. Plagues and wars is just historical happenin's, but the real break for the workingman came when William Caxton brought the printing press to England from Germany in 1477."

"He created new jobs?" William ventured.

"He took education out of the hands of the Church and gave it to ordinary people, and that's the best break the workingman ever got."

"Oddly enough," interrupted Malachi, "Caxton was just trying to save himself a bit of repetitious bother when he started printing. In his spare time as a merchant, he had translated several French romances for his friends, and his efforts had grown so popular that he spent much of his time making copies. He complained in letters to friends that his hands and eyes were wearing out doing routine labor, so when he saw the printing press with its movable type, operated by Guttenburg in Cologne, he realized such a device would save him a great deal of labor in the production of duplicate copies. It was a natural."

"Was he getting old to be so worn out?" asked William.

"He was fifty-five when he brought the press over, and he lived to be seventy, happily translating and editing and publishing works which he thought the English people would enjoy enough to buy. He published close to one hundred books before he died."

"God bless him," rumbled Squire Nowlan, blowing clouds of pipe smoke. "He gave us our libraries, he did."

"Aye," said Farmer Evans, "thanks largely to Caxton, every man can now build a library of his own with inexpensive editions to educate hisself and his family."

"Very true," said Squire Nowlan. "A man can make hisself an expert in any area. On my own, I learned about our tax system and, 'cause of it, have been selected for the District Tax Board. I keep track of the farms and estates confiscated for back taxes, farms that can be bought up just by paying them late taxes. I've doubled my acreage during the last six years, thanks to William Caxton."

Farmer Evans nodded. "Before Caxton, only a very wealthy man could afford books 'cause they was all handwritten. "personal library of 250 volumes was thought of as a very rare library, indeed. Nowadays, it's hardly worth the mention. My own library contains 283 volumes and is still growing."

"Have ya read 'em all, Phil?" asked Farmer Francis, his eyes twinkling.

"I raised my boys on several of the books Caxton published: *The Noble Histories of King Arthur and of Certain of his Knights,* for instance, although I guess nowadays most people call it *Le Morte d'Arthur.* All my children read the Bible, of course, but they enjoy the lessons of the Holy Book played out in Sir Thomas Mallory's way of writing. The Arthur legends have taught 'em honor, obedience, compassion and valor—all of them things. My sons often quote from the book in their letters home from the Inns of Court. By the by, I can easy locate them quotes since Caxton took the wobble out of the page-numbering business with his printed editions."

"Sir Mallory must have been very honorable and valorous himself to produce such work," William said.

"He had good days and bad, I've heard."

"I mean, did he possess those virtues himself?"

The farmers did not know, so again Malachi came to the rescue. "He was a mix of both. Sir Mallory showed great valor on the battlefields of France during the Hundred Years War which occupied England in the late thirteen hundreds and early Fourteen hundreds. He was regarded as a hero when he returned to England and was sent up to Parliament from Warwick in recognition of his military service."

"A man like that would certainly be writing from experience when he discussed honor then, would he not?"

"True enough," said Malachi, "but there was a certain gap between what he knew and what he practiced. He served two lengthy jail terms, during which, incidentally, he wrote *Le Morte d'Arthur.* It always strikes me as odd how many writers do their best work while locked up. It must be the result of so few distractions. No wine, no women, no compatible friends. I suppose if enough of us wanted to make that kind of sacrifice, we could fill the world with writers in no time."

William frowned, then asked, "In jail for what?"

"His first conviction involved a series of misadventures. He broke into a neighbor's house and raped the neighbor's wife; then he held up another neighbor for one hundred shillings; and finally he broke into the first neighbor's house and raped his wife again."

"All in one night?"

"No, no. Over a period of time—like a spasmodic explosion of adventuring. "lot of returning soldiers have difficulty adjusting to the pace of ordinary life and are subject to periodic outbursts, but other than that, they make excellent neighbors. It's always well to have a stout hand close by in this age of footpads and vagabonds."

"You mentioned a second jail term."

"Found guilty of breaking into and robbing the Cistercian Abbey at Coombe on two different occasions and of stealing two calves, seven cows, and three hundred and thirty-five sheep."

"Um, a pronounced preference for mutton over beef there."

"I suppose you might say," said Malachi, "that he knew honor from the outside in, which probably serves a writer just as well as the real thing if he happens to be clever. It seems to me a writer could be completely bereft of morals or principles or virtues, an empty shell personally, and still glorify beautiful things in his writings."

"I surely hope so," breathed William.

The yeomen sat about the table in silent contentment while more ale was brought to the table. William, whose ale supply had been cut off by Malachi, suddenly spoke again.

"I seem to remember another land break for the yeomen," he exclaimed. "What about the monastic lands King Henry VIII confiscated and sold off in '34?"

"That's right! The Catholic Church owned one-third of all the desirable estates in England when Henry threw them out," said Squire Nowlan.

"Yep," added Farmer Francis. "There were so much land took that even after Henry parceled out the best properties to his favorites to keep them loyal in his move agin the pope, there were still plenty left for the rest of us crafty folk."

"That was a great time," reminisced Farmer Murphy. "My family bought up 150 acres so's now I can send my boys off to the Inns of Court to be educated as proper lawyers."

"And they will all look even more closely at the tax records," William added.

"Exactly," the yeomen replied in unison.

Chapter 6:
JOUSTING WITH THE SPEAR-SHAKER

Enroute to the Oxford manor, October 1585:

"Before we deliver this mail to the Earl of Oxford," Malachi cautioned, "I should mention that Sir Edward de Vere has a house full of servants who sometimes refer to their master as 'Spear-shaker' or 'Shake-spearer'."

"Oh?"

"I mention this only to avoid confusion if the matter comes up in conversation during our visit."

"A curious appellation," William observed. "I wonder where they got a name like that."

"He was born the Duke of Budbeck under the Oxford coat of arms which shows a rampant lion shaking a broken spear in his mouth. Wonderful symbol."

"Why broken?"

"Symbol of a defeated enemy. The Earls of Oxford have been official sword-bearers of English monarchs for five hundred years. They have been at the forefront of every major battle the Royal armies of England have ever fought, and that crest is an indication that they triumphed often."

"That should be worth something," said William, dropping his voice to a whisper, "but this £1,000 per annum pension–" he patted the mailbag on his shoulder— "is an impressive sum of money."

"That is exactly what Burghley thinks," Malachi grinned. "In addition to delivering this warrant to Oxford, our instructions are to uncover, if we can, what service the Queen expects in return, and why she feels the need to conceal her purpose from her trusted advisors."

"I don't suppose Oxford would tell if we just asked?"

Malachi laughed. "You do have a way about you, young man, which argues for a short but exciting future in a service as sensitive as ours. Lord Oxford is one of those gentlemen whom you may not insult with impunity. He is a very moody, combat-trained swordsman with a quick temper and an unfortunate reputation for having any person with whom he quarrels waylaid and beaten thereafter. In short, it is not always possible, even with infinite tact, to avoid his wrath."

"Why should he be insulted?"

"Because such an inquiry would be none of our official business. It would be presumptuous of us. We are but simple messengers of the Queen on this assignment. We have no authority at all to inquire into the import of those messages, and we certainly have no knowledge of their contents. As a matter of fact, it would probably send Oxford into a frothing rage if he discovered we had ferreted out the contents of his mail, so be on your guard to keep your mouth shut about everything."

"Suppose he speaks to me?"

"He will. He asked specifically that I fetch you along after he heard you were interested in theatrical work. I only meant for you to be careful but not uncivil. Talk as much as necessary but do not reveal anything."

"Does he want me for a theatrical part?"

Malachi shrugged. "Who knows? He subsidizes three companies of common players now, so there may be a bit part for you someplace, but the understanding is that whatever he asks of you must not interfere with your duty to me. I have already explained that to him."

"Could the Queen be sending him money to put on more plays?"

"That makes more sense than a lot of reasons I've heard lately. Certainly Elizabeth is not rewarding him as a former favorite because, in the past, the fatal click of her purse snapping shut has always signaled the cooling of Royal passion and served notice that any romance involved thereafter was in the hands of the bookkeepers at the Treasury Office."

"Permit me to inquire about your relationship to Oxford, Malachi. Are you a glorified servant or what?"

Malachi thought a moment. "Well, over the years, in my capacity as Her Majesty's courier, traveling as I have and developing contacts on the Continent and elsewhere, I have been able to perform many small favors for the nobility—mostly making purchases or handling packets of private mail to-and-from the Continent. I've been accommodating the Earl for so long a time, we've become friends of a sort, as much as a commoner like myself, educated or not, can be considered a friend to an Earl. He trusts me, at any rate. And respects me, I think. I must still keep my place, and keep my mouth shut about certain matters." He gave William a warning look. "And so must you. Particularly about the involvement of Lord Derby."

"Lord Derby! Yes, I remember him," William spoke with pride. "He's the one who has been secretly writing plays with some of his friends."

"Silence, you fool!" Malachi growled. "Never utter those words aloud. You simply have no knowledge that those gentlemen indulge in that unspeakable practice. We are dealing with important matters here, and you will not be permitted to deal flippantly with them or you may imperil the realm."

"Imperil? You mean literally?"

"Quite so," Malachi nodded. "There are significant, national considerations afoot which must not be misshapen by a loose tongue. Before I can permit that to happen, I must hold a personal accounting session wherein I grab myself by the scruff of the neck and hold myself at arm's length, and ask myself some searching questions."

"Searching questions?"

"Whether I am indulging myself at great risk to my country by carrying you with me as a source of fun and frolic?"

"I see."

"Whether I can permit the future of this realm to depend upon your wobbly control of a frisky tongue which often seems to leap well beyond the bridle of reason?"

"I have to admit that my good intentions don't always—"

"And finally, I must ask myself whether a single soul in the world—besides me— would miss you if you were to suddenly disappear along with your loose tongue?"

"Ah. Threats now. That settles it. You have my full attention. What is it you wish of me?"

"I want a complete adjustment in your attitude in certain matters. I would like you to cultivate—overnight if need be—the necessary courtesy and common sense it takes to avoid having the powerful people of the realm reach down and squash you like a bug because you have mortally offended them with your constant inquiries into their personal affairs."

"I'll try to adjust, but the truth of the matter is—"

"Above all else, you must come to realize fully that the line of succession to the throne of England must not be governed by your flapping tongue."

"The line of succession? Really?"

"Exactly. There are a great many intelligent men in England who fear the chaos that Elizabeth's eventual death will bring about if she dies without naming a successor other than the Scottish woman. Because Mary Stuart, Queen of Scots, is the obvious, blood-line claimant to the throne, intelligent Englishmen want to plant the possibility of an alternative to the catastrophe she would bring to England if she ever becomes our Queen. She would certainly reconvert us overnight to Catholicism again, and we would end up getting our orders from Rome and Madrid. Nobody wants that."

"But if someone other than the blood-line claimant ascends the throne," William asked, "are we not forced to see him or her as illegal monarchs?"

Malachi shrugged. "Legality is in the eye of the survivor. There are no illegal monarchs after the first week on the throne. That's plenty of time to silence protestors and to restore or create the legal underpinnings of the monarchy. After the first week, any who doubt monarchial validity are denounced as traitors who are then condemned to die the most painful death our society has yet devised after giving the matter long and careful thought. They are hung, drawn and quartered. In the light of that possible fate, any discussion of an alternative to Mary Stuart—quite possibly the future Queen of England—must be in muted tones until the propitious moment arrives."

William nodded, musing. "Spear-shaker, eh? That name stirs something in the dark recesses of my being. I sense an arrow striking very close to the spot where my soul shall someday come to rest. You did say it is only a nick-name with Oxford? He doesn't use it all the time, does he? He wouldn't, for instance, sign legal documents that way?"

"Nothing like that. Nothing formal. It is now just a holdover from the past, a term of somewhat derisive endearment kept alive in a somewhat jocular fashion by Oxford's household servants who know that if they shirk their duties, they might very well be confronted by the specter of Oxford himself, rampant in the kitchen doorway, shaking a mop or broom or whatever is handy in their faces."

"But the name itself isn't his official name? Anyone could use it, right?"

Malachi stared. "I know what you're thinking, lad. You must be mad. Your arrogance knows no bounds! If you did something like that, you would cause the Earl monumental confusion for which he would not, I assure you, be monumentally grateful."

"No, no!" William protested. "It's not likely I would ever be so presumptuous. It's just that I'm something of an orphan without a last name and every once in a while, I hear something that stirs—"

"Forget about it and get your mind on our present business," Malachi growled. "As the Seventeenth Earl of Oxford, our man is a ranking peer of England. Do you have any idea what that means?"

"Not exactly."

"His inherited title confers on him the office of Lord Great Chamberlain, an honor which puts him close to the Queen's person, very close during the decade 1570 to 1580 when he was often her daily companion."

"I thought that was Leicester's period as her favorite."

"Oh yes. Robert has been around from the beginning, but Elizabeth has always played one faction against the other. She does it with France and Spain, Catholics and Puritans, Commons and Lords, and always with two or three favorites as well as with her trusted advisors. The whirlwind of partisan tensions thus created permits Elizabeth to dance coquettishly between possibilities and keeps all concerned on their toes awaiting her choice-of-the-moment. She can be a shrewish scold, however, to any who attempt to hurry her decision-making."

"What happened in 1580 for Oxford to lose the Queen's favor?"

Malachi sighed. "I better explain that Oxford is still an important and powerful man, out of court but not completely out of favor. He has always been a bad man to cross, and he is still extremely impatient with anything he regards as bad manners, so watch yourself about personal inquiries into his life."

William nodded. "I always appreciate learning ways to avoid trouble with testy people. It sounds like the Earl of Oxford may have been subjected to a very privileged childhood."

"Oxford became Earl at age twelve when his father died."

"The Sixteenth Earl?"

"Exactly. Because of his youth, Oxford became a ward of Robert Cecil, who is now Lord Burghley, Treasurer of the Realm, and he was raised in the Burghley household. He was tutored by his uncle, Arthur Golding, the famous scholar, and went on to earn degrees at both Cambridge and Oxford."

"I've heard of Golding, but—"

"Golding translated Ovid for us. You know Ovid, don't you? Roman poet. Very bawdy in a sweet way."

William made a note. "I'll look into him."

"Try his erotic poem collection, *The Art of Love,* sometime when you need a lift. Anyway, the Queen and her Treasurer arranged an early marriage for the young Earl with Robert Cecil's daughter, Anne. The pre-nuptial arrangement showed the Queen's crafty hand because she had to elevate Robert Cecil to the peerage as Lord Burghley, in order to make his daughter noble enough for a union with Lord Oxford."

"So his daughter's marriage turned Robert Cecil into Lord Burghley?"

Malachi nodded. "And that later seemed to rankle Oxford. There were mutterings heard of his having been 'used'. The two men have not been on good terms to this day, so you must never use Burghley's name in Oxford's house because the very mention of his father-in-law infuriates the good Earl and throws him into a passionate temper."

"Did the marriage survive the Earl's feeling put upon?"

"Hardly. Oxford was traveling extensively on the Continent when Anne gave birth to a child here in England."

"How extensively?"

"Some say nine months, some say ten. Oxford himself chose ten and refused to live with her after we fetched him home on the Queen's command. He busied himself thereafter at Court entertaining the Queen with his poetry and staging interludes of his own composition."

"His writings entertained the Queen?" William asked with interest.

"For nearly ten years," Malachi nodded. "And the Queen has presently given him personal license to dabble in plays as long as he keeps his name off the title page."

"That seems unjust." William shook his head. "If a man does good work in any arena, he ought to get full public credit for it."

"That's just the way things are at the moment," Malachi shrugged, "and it may be nature's way of providing a touch of irony by permitting many of the literary pretenders we see hanging about London to make a living by masquerading as authors. They earn a fair amount of small change by taking credit for plays written by those who dare not claim their work in public. I know the Queen is not nearly as offended by theatrical people as are Burghley and some of the other Lords, but she refuses to fight daily battles with her advisors over licensing and regulating stage productions."

"So she farms out the responsibility to some trustworthy advisor?"

"Right. She is quite aware that some responsible party needs to supervise players because their influence on the public can be compelling, and many theatrical people, unfortunately, lack any social conscience when it comes to turning a shilling or two. Elizabeth hopes that permitting Oxford to socialize with theater people will put a monitor in their midst to discourage the use of the English stage for the depiction of social discord or any type of administrative inconvenience."

"But the 'Spear-shaker' thing is not used in print in reference to Oxford, is it?"

"Sometimes it is," Malachi shrugged. "During the ten years Oxford courted the Queen, he frequently participated in royal tournaments of jousting, and often was the hero of the event—a fate which befalls many a favorite of the Queen," Malachi chuckled. "It has something to do with the nature of politics, I imagine. Anyway, the 'spear' connection has often been applied to Oxford. Gabriel Harvey once wrote a description of Oxford as both a poet and a tournament performer, saying in part: *Thine eyes flash fire, thy countenance shakes a spear.*" [21]

"Oh, that's memorable!" William exclaimed. "'Thine eyes flash fire'...what's the other part?"

"I keep forgetting you have no real feel for poetry," Malachi said.

William chuckled, "So how did Oxford lose his position as a favorite of the Court?"

"After Anne died, he married one of the Queen's ladies-in-waiting after getting her with child," Malachi chuckled. "Oxford never could resist a dark-eyed enchantress, and he wooed and won her with sonnets, it was said. The Queen, of course, was furious at such independence among her 'family' members. She likes to arrange such couplings herself, so Oxford and his lady spent their honeymoon in the Tower. After a few months, Elizabeth relented enough to simply banish him from the Court for two years, and he has never drifted back. In addition, his conversion to Catholicism three years ago further alienated her, and it didn't sit well with his in-laws either, so he is now free to pursue his theatrical interests."

"But he makes no public claim to the shaking-spear idea?"

"Juvenile clap-trap as far as he is concerned—unless you get him angry, and then you may see why his household staff still remembers the old nick-name."

"Our delivery of this money should cheer him up considerably. I wonder what a person has to do to score this kind of windfall."

"Recorded history will show," Malachi pointed out, "that Elizabeth has never extended a single shilling to any man without first assuring her profit somewhere in the bargain. She has watched great noble houses flounder and sink for lack of funds. She has seen expeditions planned and manned, only to decay at the docks without victual. She has permitted her cloth industry to wither away to nothing without subsidy. She simply will not open her purse for any cause which does not promise her a profitable return."

"Sounds like a sharp business woman to me," said William. "What kind of shape is Oxford in financially before we bring him this new money?"

"Hurting. He has been selling off his lands since he got the title and often not paying much attention to the price he gets. I remember while he was in Italy, he had me urge his father-in-law to sell certain estates at any price so long as the money came to Oxford forthwith."

"You were with him in Italy?"

"Periodically. Carrying messages and contracts back and forth. Doing scrivener work. Generally keeping an eye on him for his father-in-law."

"Burghley set you to spy on his own son-in-law?"

Malachi frowned. "You love to dramatize things, don't you? 'Spy' is a trifle colorful for a simple liaison functionary. Burghley not only has the right to stay in touch with members of his family, but in the case of Oxford, he also has the duty to do so since he has been the young man's official guardian all these years."

"What did the Queen get out of the arranged marriage between Oxford and Anne?"

"Good question. Elizabeth's motives are sometimes obscure, but in this case, I think it is clear that she got the kind of safe arrangement she enjoys. She tied one of her favorites down domestically in such a fashion as to permit him to come to Court every day to romance her. She decided very early that the Earl of Oxford's pen was merrier than his sword, so she bound him to her court as a writer and actor in courtly dramas that entertained and amused her for the decade of the Seventies."

"Any good?"

Malachi shrugged. "Full of courtly nonsense and in-jokes which ordinary people wouldn't understand, but admirable entertainment for Elizabeth, her Court, and for visiting diplomats who were sometimes made the subject of references in the dialogue of the play. She often had Oxford instruct the players to include lines which would surprise visitors into revealing themselves in ways which they would otherwise conceal. Courtly drama often amounted to an intellectual game which the Queen and Oxford played together for the amusement of the Court."

"Wouldn't it take a lot of plot juggling to rearrange the basic format of a play just for a specific occasion?"

"Don't be silly," Malachi laughed. "Easiest thing in the world. Just insert the play-within-a-play device without touching the basic structure at all. Change the secondary play to suit the occasion."

"Play-within-a-play?"

"I'll explain it all later. Here we are and there, by Jove, is Oxford himself at the front gate. What's that he's shouting?"

Once more unto the breach, dear friends, [22] let's risk another sally!" Oxford was disclaiming in theatrical style.

"Who is Sally?" William wondered.

"Oh, there you are, Malachi," Oxford boomed; "you have caught me at composing. Glad to see you. I hope you have brought me something I can use." Oxford turned to inspect William. "You certainly are prompt with your promises, Malachi. You have provided me with your stand-in amanuenses, who will be put to the test tonight; and at the same time, perhaps, provided a possible front-man for our Group."

"Front-man?" William asked. "What group?"

"Bad word choice," Oxford acknowledged. "Agent, representative, field-man, or straw man. Whatever you prefer as long as the work gets done and you keep quiet."

"About what?" William asked.

"Later," Oxford waved him off. "Let me open my mail first. The Queen has been saying for months that the money is in the mail. Let us see if she finally means it."

"May I ask a question which some might think impertinent?" William asked.

"Impertinent?" Oxford stiffened and his hand dropped to his sword.

"I really wish you wouldn't," Malachi said.

"Who is your tailor?" William asked. "I really like your outfit."

"Do you?" Oxford purred. "You wouldn't believe the number of our countrymen who have no taste at all in clothing. They wear the same old stuff year in and year out. I like to switch about. Most of this particular outfit I picked up in Italy where style is appreciated."

"Yes," said William. "I can readily see the Italianate influence although you have admirably interspersed it with splashes of your own panache."

"Where did you get so knowledgeable a fellow, Malachi? I feel he and I will have much to discuss before we are done."

Malachi bowed. "I had hoped you might."

"Still," Oxford specified. "I would like a sample of his writing skills before I accept him for such an important transcribing task. Let's have him take notes of our gossip during lunch, Malachi, and I can judge his work along with my dessert."

❖ ❖ ❖

After Lunch:

"My word!" exclaimed the Earl, examining the sheet in his hand. "I wish Malachi had stayed long enough to see this. Even from so brief a demonstration, I must say you are one of the best writers in England today."

"Thank you," smiled William. "I like to think that a skill in such small areas bespeaks—"

"You didn't blot a single line! Not only a fair copy but a fine hand! Italianated enough to please the eye but clerical enough to prohibit any misreading."

"Remarkable work, young man, in this day of shabby standards in most areas."

"I know just how you feel," said William.

"My lord," Oxford corrected.

"I beg your pardon?"

"When you address the l7th Earl of Oxford, you say 'My lord.'"

"I'll try to remember that."

"My lord!"

"I beg your pardon?"

Lord Oxford frowned. "When Malachi offered me your services as a dependable amanuensis, he mentioned there were pluses and minuses connected with employing you, and I am beginning to see what he meant. And I don't think I like what I see."

"My Lord?"

"However, I have disciplined myself away from making harsh judgments before noon when my tendency is to be dangerously rash. I have noticed over the years that I level out a bit in the afternoon and generally make more moderate evaluations later in the day."

"Why do you think that is, m'lord?" asked William politely.

"Oh, I know exactly why it is. All my life I've hated to go to sleep at night. I must fling myself into bed, as it were, by will power alone."

"I'm the same way! I know that if left to my own devices—"

"So logically, I should be ecstatic about getting out of bed each morning, right?"

William nodded. "That follows."

"But my mind does a whirl-about every night as I sleep, for although I hate going to bed, you see, I also hate getting up. Astonishing! I'm convinced it weakens a man to be subject to such conflicting inclinations, so each morning I am customarily choleric as I attempt to reconcile such contending propensities into a rational mind-set so that I may comfortably go about my daily business. And woe betide the man, woman, or child who crosses me during that delicate balancing act. It grieves my inner self to witness how subject I am to the ebb and flow of raw emotion over which I have no control."

"Oh well, m'lord, a decent breakfast should get you ready for a world which will certainly confront you with more significant problems."

"More significant, sir?" Oxford questioned in icy tones.

"Oh, thank you, m'lord," said William. "I don't really know if I am entitled—"

"What plague is greater than the grief of mind!" cried Oxford.

"Even though I sense that is a rhetorical question—"

Oxford ignored him, and struck a pose to recite;

> *The grief of mind that eats in every vein,*
> *In every vein that leaves such clots behind,*
> *Such clots behind as breed such bitter pain.*
> *So bitter pain that none shall ever find*
> *What plague is greater than the grief of mind.* [23]

"Why," William exclaimed, "that's first-rate versifying, m'lord, particularly this early in the day. Some few might find fault with your heavy reliance on repetition—which sometimes indicates a lack of Muse power—but I think you extracted yourself adroitly from that particular quibble right there at the end."

"Muse Power!" Oxford shouted. "You say I lack Muse Power?"

"Oh no, m'lord, not in so many words. Your lines were very clever, even if a trifle self-involved. I was simply indicating that your poetic gifts might be better employed in offering us your insights into such universal matters as the moral contract that exists between modern men and women. For my own part, I know—"

"Yes," Oxford said with a sly smile. "Do let me hear what opinion such an immature, rustic simpleton has on the matter of modern women and their moral standards."

"In truth, m'lord, I know only one, and her standards are as high as mine, I'm sure."

"Well, pull out your foolscap then, fellow, and try to record these lines accurately." William wrote swiftly as the Earl disclaimed:

> *If women could be fair and yet not fond,*
> *Or that their love were firm and not fickle, still,*

I would not marvel that they make men bond,
By service long to purchase their good will,
But when I see how frail these creatures are,
I muse that men forget themselves so far."

"A veritable plethora of deep feeling, m'lord," murmured William, still writing. "You certainly are an accomplished man of letters. I particularly enjoyed the muted 'muse' you slipped in at the end."

Oxford frowned. "I don't trust your tone. Do you, perchance, imagine you could make improvement?"

"Improvements on that *'Frailty, thy name is woman'* theme? [24] Not on your life, sir. I think you've locked up that particular point of view for all time. In splendid five-metered lines."

"I'd like to think so. Success in letters is very important in this household. I am often host to my uncle, Arthur Golding, who never for a moment lets me forget, in his heavy-handed way, that he has done a famous translation of Ovid."

"That tendency seems to be a dominant trait of your family, m'lord." William paused for an ominous moment. "Literary excellence, I mean."

"See here, my boy," warned Oxford, "would it be possible for you simply to take notes and provide fair copies without speaking?"

"Indeed so, m'lord. As a matter of fact, I do a better job of note-taking if I receive specific instructions up front and need not interpret the intent of —"

"Just write what I tell you and shut thy gob!"

"Well, it's obvious your overnight whirl-about still has you in its pernicious grip this morning," William observed. "Let me know when you get over it, so we can get down to the business of the day."

"I see," Oxford sighed. "Malachi mentioned the need for patience and God knows I need the practice. The company this evening, then, will include some of the most brilliant minds in England, or anywhere else for that matter, so we will need an accomplished scribe who copies quickly and accurately. <u>And</u> who keeps quiet about it. I'll try you for a single meeting, young man, and I'll expect a transcribed copy first thing in the morning."

✤ ✤ ✤

Lunch the following day at Oxford's Manor:

"Where is your apprentice, Malachi?" the Earl asked cautiously. "I've just looked over his notes from last night and must make arrangements with him for tonight."

"I left him at the inn sleeping, my lord," said Malachi. "He was quite fatigued by last night's duties."

"No doubt," Oxford nodded. "The truth is, your man is simply the best writer I've ever seen. His general notes do a wonderful job of reconciling the contending parties of the meeting. His verbatim notes are perfect. He never misses anything, and his fair copy is a wonder to behold. You are sure he is discreet, Malachi? He had a bit of a loose tongue during our interview."

"Most discreet, my lord, when on the job. "very intelligent lad, though I never would tell him so. He doesn't lack confidence."

"We really must have him for our meeting again tonight, Malachi. Aside from your doing me a personal favor—which you know I shall not soon forget—you will earn yourself a piece of gold for meritorious achievement if you send him to our meeting."

"No need for gratuities, sir," Malachi said. "The problem here is that my apprentice is difficult to deal with when something throws him into his antic disposition."

"I'm sorry to hear it. Can it be remedied?"

"Perhaps," said Malachi. "Shall I be candid, my lord?"

"Yes, indeed," Oxford insisted. "Little is learned otherwise."

"He complained that you were all talking together last night, and that he was exhausted from the necessity of keeping track of four or five ongoing, simultaneous dialogues. He will be quite pleased that you admired his copy, my lord, but he begs to be excused from further opportunities to record your Magic Circle. Unless..."

"Unless?"

"Unless they learn some...ahem...manners, sir."

"Ma-Manners?" Oxford stammered, drawing back in shock.

"The all-talking-at-once thing, for one. And he mentioned that it was difficult to follow the thinking of other members of the group when Lord Derby and Lord Oxford offered so many picky interruptions." Malachi paused, eying the earl carefully. "You asked me to be candid, sir. He had no idea I would be repeating his words to you."

"Go on," Oxford growled between clenched teeth.

"He told me that only the mediation of the saintly Countess of Pembroke between contentious and quarrelsome members of the company prevented the meeting from disintegrating into a shambles."

"What the deuce does he expect? When people get excited in discussion they always talk over each other. Those are our most creative moments. Nobody can change that."

"He doesn't object to the excitement or the talking part at all, my lord. He can handle that nicely. It's the overlap of the exchange that bothers him. He can't handle it, sir. Overload. Exhaustion. He suggested—to me, of course–that you appoint a monitor to keep order. He thought that the 'celestial and radiant' Countess of Pembroke—he seems quite taken with her, my Lord—would serve well in such capacity, especially if she were given enough official clout to maintain an orderly discussion."

"Yes, yes. Pembroke could be our Sergeant-at-Arms as in the House of Lords. Capital!" The Earl rubbed his hands together. "I welcome the establishment of order any place I find it these days. I tell you honestly, Malachi, there are times lately when I swear the world is going to Hades right before my eyes. We have upstarts poised on every stairway and varlets lurking at every threshold. Take your man William. In the old days, he would have hopped and skipped to do a favor for the Earl of Oxford. I really enjoyed those days. Now, every artificer and craftsman dictates conditions for his employment."

"I'm afraid it is coming to that, my Lord, and like much else in this world, it will no doubt get worse before it gets better. However, I am extremely hopeful of a favorable response from my apprentice when I tell him you listened carefully to his ideas and agree on the need for order."

"I might as well tell you, Malachi—and you can tell him—that it is not only his exquisite hand we wish to hire, although God knows, anything written in such splendid script would bedazzle London's tin-eared theatrical crowd as little as they know about either poetry or drama. I myself have trouble communicating with those villains because they misread my intent—and indeed, misread my specific directions!—at every turn. But please, don't let me start on that again. Back now to your man. In addition to his scrivener duties, I would like to hire him as our front man as well."

"You've mentioned this role generally, my Lord, but perhaps now is the time for specifics."

"As you know, our Magic Circle meets to read and patch up play scripts that have been submitted for license to be acted on the public stage. Sir Edmund Tilney, the Master of the Revels, grants final approval, of course, but our little group operates as his 'back office,' so to speak. We also make sure the interests of the Queen are protected on the stage."

"Ah yes," said Malachi. "Public opinion."

"Elizabeth wants a careful eye applied to weed out any content which might encourage social unrest. She knows well the influence that stage productions can have on the public."

"That means weed out all references to both Religion and Succession," said Malachi.

"The big two," Oxford nodded. "So offstage, she is behind us all the way to the tune of £1000 annual subsidy to further our efforts."

Malachi smiled for a moment. "And William's job would be what, my lord?"

"Well, what we need," Oxford confided, "is a kind of part-time Johannas Factorum: a man to pretend authorship for plays composed by our group. None of us can afford to have his good name besmirched by a direct connection with the theater, so we need a straw-man of some sort. We need a modest, unassuming fellow who takes direction well and writes out a beautiful copy. He would take all the credit surrounding the work and even some of the money. Group authorship never plays well to theater audiences, you know. They need someone to glorify. Under the present administrative climate—mostly my cranky father-in-law—it is not wise to be too closely associated with theatrical people other than as a distant patron, and he frowns even on that. He regards all actors as worthless, idle vagabonds who often steal chickens."

"But I know the Queen doesn't feel that way," Malachi said.

"Certainly not! No monarch ever enjoyed the drama more, either at the theater or at her own Court. I can tell you Elizabeth relishes her turn as queen and dresses for the part every day, but alas, she leaves most routine civil matters in the hands of her advisers, and they do little to encourage stage productions. Our little group, therefore, must stay out of sight until the climate clears."

"So, in short, you want a person who gets all the glory without doing any of the work. William might well be interested."

Oxford nodded with benign satisfaction.

"Of course, my lord," said Malachi. "He must be able to dress the part. Theater people are keen observers of wardrobe and would soon detect any discrepancy between his proclaimed attainments and his actual attire. His present shabby wardrobe would be seen as a sure indication of failure. "few rather fashionable outfits—he admires the Italian influence, as you know. Nothing as splendid as your own or Raleigh's, but..."

"Agreed," said the Earl sourly. "Perhaps some cast-offs from last season would do very well."

"And his treatment by your group will undoubtedly serve as a social model for his treatment by others. Theater people are subjected to daily judgment at the ticket office, you know, so they have a well-honed nose for the smell of disrespect. If they saw you treating him like the boorish baggage-carrier he sometimes appears to be, I'm afraid embarrassing questions might be raised which would eventually imperil your grand deception."

"You expect the Group members to treat him as an...an equal?" Oxford was horrified.

"I would say just about the way you treat a gentleman or one of the clergy. At arm's length, perhaps, but still significant. Depends on how much you want a believable front man, my lord."

"Zounds, let me think. The Countess would be amenable. Sir Philip Sidney and Francis Bacon and Sir Walter Raleigh would probably not balk. But the Earl of Darby—oh my, very touchy—oh no, he would find it very difficult."

"I suggest you introduce him tonight as the younger son of a country family, my lord. Barely a gentleman but respectable." Malachi was thoughtful. "He might be, for all we know. Well-educated and quite impossibly arrogant, as he is."

"He does have a certain wit," admitted Oxford.

"He'll also require a certain amount of money for room and board and moving about with the theater crowd, my lord."

"Perhaps we can set him up as a clerk or secretary somewhere in London."

"Excuse me, my lord, but he is already my clerk and secretary. He needs change in his pocket, not in his job."

"Very well then, we'll arrange a small stipend. Does that suit you?"

"Two shillings per week should see him through nicely."

"We'll work something out later."

❖ ❖ ❖

The Earl of Oxford's manor, the afternoon of the same day:

The Earl's butler announced Malachi and William, and they entered the library.

"He has agreed to all the conditions, my lord," said Malachi graciously.

"Excellent!" said Oxford, pouring himself a goblet of brandy and motioning them to seats at the table.

"As I understand it then, m'lord," said William, "I would serve as a channel through which your Magic Circle would present to the theatrical world the plays which they have actually written, but which I am to take public credit for?"

"That's exactly right." Oxford swirled the brandy in his glass. "I hope you don't mind being made the center of an adoring throng when our plays are staged, but remember that your part will always be that of an in-effect-gentleman who deals very modestly with the applause coming to him second hand, so to speak."

"And I have your personal assurance this will all be pretty high class stuff?"

The Earl laughed. "The best that the English stage has ever seen. We are straining at the bit to have this relationship completed because we have future plans for many major works of dramatic art, and we hope to sprinkle a few tasty sonnets along the way just to spice up the breed."

"Of course, as an in-effect-gentleman," William said, "I must be choosy about the proposed subject matter. What is it your group intends to cover?"

"*Everything! Anything!*" the Earl waved expansively. "*Tragedy, comedy, history, pastoral, pastoral-comical, historical-pastoral, tragical-historical, tragical-comical-historical-pastoral, scene individable, or poem unlimited.*" [25]

"Sounds like a very versatile bunch to cover that much ground," William said.

"Indeed," agreed the Earl, "no group could be better prepared for such an endeavor than our own Magic Circle. Every member is highly educated and speaks several languages. Both Darby and I have traveled extensively on the Continent. Each of us saw military duty in the Low Countries, and Sidney is about to get his exposure to that experience. Raleigh, of course, has had more than a decade of military blood and battles in France, Holland, and Ireland. Most of us have experienced shipwreck at sea and all the other travails to which travelers are subject. Francis Bacon is an absolute fountain of knowledge in all arcane and legal matters. Every one of us is a practiced poet in private, so we foresee striking off some toothsome verse and doing our bit to calm social unrest by staging instructive heroics and portraying tragic figures from the past."

"One must certainly admire your group's goal of social betterment," Malachi said, "but at the back of my mind I keep hearing Montaigne complain about the frequency with which '*super-celestial proclamations are coupled with subterranean actions.*'" [26]

William's eyes widened in admiration. "Quite so," he agreed, then turned again to the Earl. "In short, m'lord, what's in it for you? Why does your group go to so much trouble?"

"Oh, our world grows more cynical every day when you presume ulterior motives behind every artistic endeavor," Oxford lamented. "All right then, I'll fit words to the prevailing view. When we do the plays illustrating England's history, we bring forward the contributions of individuals and families who were not fully recognized in the history books written by Hall and Hollingshed. The Derbys and Oxfords, for instance, won battles and placed crowns on English kings. Imagine the Queen's delight if our plays glorify her grandfather, Henry VII, and show Richard III to be a villain and a pretender. Even a murderer! However, I say again, no one must know of our authorship. That's why we need a front man upon whose discretion we can rely completely." The Earl glanced quizzically from William to Malachi.

"Oh, he'll be all right," Malachi assured him, "once the directions are clear and specific. You might go over the particulars of what you would have him do."

William nodded and Oxford cleared his throat. "Number one, you will periodically pick up a completed manuscript from our group, copy it in your distinctive handwriting and sell it to one of the theatrical groups here in London under your own name."

"Check. What verse form will you be using?"

Oxford thought for a moment. "We like blank verse. Iambic pentameter mostly. Kyd handles it well in *The Spanish Tragedy*, and Marlowe showed us that fascinating effects can be rendered by such a flexible meter in some of his early translations."

"You're in luck there," William said. "You know how some musicians are born with perfect pitch? Well, I was born with a hop-hip mind set. My thoughts naturally fall into the iambic meter. It's all kind of instinctive for me, so you can be assured that whatever you produce will be well examined before it leaves my hand."

Oxford turned to Malachi. "Is there some way of gagging him until he learns his proper place?"

"God bless you, my lord, for such a kindly thought, but you'll find he only grates on you at the beginning. Pretty soon, when things calm down a bit, you'll see his illusion of importance as an endless source of amusement. In the end, my lord, I assure you, he is a very entertaining chap."

"I can hardly wait," Oxford growled. "Number two: You will learn to take applause and public adulation in a modest and gracious manner. We certainly do not want some ignorant popinjay strutting an hour upon the stage as he takes our bows."

"I'm sure he can handle that, my lord, with a little prompting. Got it?" he asked William, who nodded.

"Number three, I think he should periodically disappear from the London scene for weeks at a time to explain his creative bouts."

"That dovetails right into our schedule, my Lord," said Malachi. "Couldn't be better, for we still have a duty to our primary employer, whose name, ahem," he smiled, "I fortunately forget at the moment."

"Lord Burghley," William prompted. The Earl stiffened, and Malachi hissed at his apprentice.

"What? Oh, sorry. No offense meant. Is there a fourth requirement for me, m'lord?"

Oxford calmed himself. "And number four, you must never, under any circumstance, reveal the true source of the plays. It will suit us fine if you go down in history as the author. The security must be complete and absolute. I don't know if posterity will appreciate the risk that Lord Derby is taking by joining us in this venture, but whatever chance he has to be chosen Consort to the Queen would vanish if word of his involvement ever leaked out."

"I guess the theater encourages us to take chances," Malachi observed. "As you well know, my lord, several noblemen already write plays for the stage and publish them under pseudonyms."

"But no one risks so much as he," Oxford pointed out. "The others might suffer some public disgrace if their activities were revealed, but Lord Derby would forfeit his possible marriage to the Queen and the actual possibility of inserting Derby blood into the Royal Succession by having a child with Elizabeth, and thereby elbowing aside Mary Stuart's claim to our crown."

"A worthy drama in and of itself," William interrupted. "By the way, might there be a part for me in the presentation of these plays? A young prince perhaps?"

"We'll take care of that later," said Oxford quickly. "How about it then, Master William. Have we a deal?"

"I'll be happy to undertake the assigned role with the proviso that it is understood I am accepting the assignment only as a temporary sideline."

"Certainly, Malachi has made it abundantly clear your first duty——"

"No, no," William said. "I didn't just mean my work for Lord Burghley——"

"Lord Burghley again!" Oxford shouted. "I am warning you for the last time that I don't want that man's name spoken in this house!"

"I didn't mean to offend, m'lord. The thing is, I have my own career to consider. I was not destined to be an errand boy. Our arrangement, I hope, will not forbid my writing plays of my own when leisure permits."

"Of your own?" Oxford said in astonishment and turned to Malachi. "This is an apprentice talking to me in this fashion, Malachi? Do you realize what that indicates about the very social fiber of our beloved nation? I offer him a situation well beyond the wildest dreams of the most roguish of upstarts, and he smothers me in conditions which I must meet." Oxford pounded his fist on the table. "He wants an entertainment budget! He wants respectful treatment! He wants to make improvement on our plays!" He pounded once more and leaned menacingly across the table to glare at William. "And now He wants the most important assignment of his life to be regarded as a sideline. Do I have all of that quite clear?" he asked William directly.

"That is the complete picture," William nodded, "as long as all parties concerned understand I must have final script approval in this transaction."

"You must have what!" hissed the Earl.

"Absolute and complete," said William. "It would be very much to your advantage."

"You would presume to..." sputtered the Earl. "...mangle the verses...and tangle the enlightened thoughts...of the Magic Circle!"

Malachi made soft, soothing sounds beside the Earl.

"You need not worry, m'lord," William assured him. 'If it is done properly in the first place, there will be no occasion for revision. I'm not a man who goes looking for work, as Malachi will readily tell you, but any material which appears above my name—whatever that turns out to be—will have to be first-rate stuff. And, as the author-of-record, I think I am in the best position to make that judgment."

"Yes, author-of-record and in-effect-gentleman and no-name-idiot," Oxford growled, slowly standing and picking up a chair to swing over William's head. "And now, b'God, you'll swear before me that you'll accept your role as nothing more than a messenger-boy taking bows which belong to others, or I will crown you with this chair and crush your skull right now! Swear! Swear!"

"Hesitate one moment, my lord," Malachi interceded gently, "and think the matter through. A literary fool is exactly what your assignment calls for, and you are about to smash the best possible specimen you could ever hope to come by." He waited for the Earl to lower the chair an inch. "And don't forget, my lord, that the manuscript will be returned to your hands after Sir Edmund Tilney approves it for license and after our friend here makes whatever additions and subtractions he feels compelled to make."

"Ah yes, we could get around him altogether," Oxford purred in relief. "You are a true silver-lining, my old friend, and very welcome company, indeed." He put the chair down and poured Malachi a snifter of brandy. "We'll confound him yet."

"Far be if from me to spoil your fun, gentlemen," said William, "but it seems to me that during that final, unescorted journey I must make to sell the MS to Alleyn or Burbage, it would be just as well if my Muse sensed no discourtesy whatever, or she might be tempted to vent her spleen with some creative transpositions of dialogue or incident in the script by renumbering the pages."

The two men stiffened in mid-toast and lowered their goblets.

"Good God, it never ends!" Oxford moaned.

"Or I could interrupt the players during rehearsal and request a change."

The Earl trembled with rage, speechless.

"And if my Muse is really offended, she may decide to abandon this project altogether and find something better to do."

"Sirrah," the Earl snarled. "You do not play your part well. You are, in short, a bad actor. That dooms you to absolute failure in all theatrical endeavors. I have just about decided we are better off without you."

"Did you say 'bad actor'?" William asked quietly.

"Who doesn't even know his own part in life!" Oxford roared. "Yes, that is my critical estimate of your performance so far. A young man so full of himself that he has no feel for the role in which fate has cast him. A young man who cannot profit from the counsel of his betters because his head is full of errant nonsense. Your injury may account for some of your bizarre thoughts and actions, but I have come to feel, through our discussions, that a sound thrashing would set whatever brains you have left onto the proper path."

"And I must tell you, m'lord," William confessed, "it puzzles me somewhat that you are not the first to reach that conclusion. *'Take note, take note, O world, to be direct and honest is not safe'*. [27] Would you advise me, gentlemen, to practice how to twist and twine my tongue like others in order to conceal my real thoughts?"

"Yes!" the seventeenth Earl of Oxford shouted. "Conceal not only your thoughts but your entire persona, your very being, and your absolute self! I would prefer never again to lay eyes on you. I shall ask Malachi to arrange things so as to minimize our future dealings."

"Suits me," William shrugged. "Get somebody who needs the work to stooge for you."

Chapter 7:
TEN DAYS LOST FOREVER

December 11, 1585 O. S.:

"I wasn't too surprised when you didn't show up at Harwich to sail to Holland with the Earl of Leicester's forces as we planned," Malachi said calmly. "I'm not even surprised to find you here at home three days later, well-fed, comfortable, and relaxed with no indication at all that you even attempted to fulfill your duty. I'm only curious about what compelling reason you will offer this time for failing to follow your assignment. You overslept? You were waylaid? You were drugged? You forgot? You didn't forget, you just lost track of time?"

"That's it!" William affirmed. "The time thing. I'll confess to being monumentally mixed up because I keep hearing that it will cost me ten days off my life—ten days that I'll never see because they'll be gone forever—whoosh!—if I simply cross the twenty-one miles of the Narrow Seas to the Continent. Is any of this true? Are people talking nonsense or magic?"

"Oh, my," Malachi said, shaking his head in admiration, "You offer a clever defense. Tried and true. The Gregorian calendar mix-up is to blame, I see. I presume you were waiting until next week to get on board?"

"I was waiting only for the exact moment the directive assigned me to board at Harwich," William said patiently. "I have the note here. As you can readily see, it says I am to take ship on the eighteenth of December in the year 1585. Since this is only the eleventh of December, 1585, I have difficulty following the logic involved in your accusation of my failure at a duty which is still a week away."

"And what does it say after it says the eighteenth?" Malachi asked. "Does it say O.S. or N.S.?"

"What difference can that possibly make? December eighteenth is still December eighteenth, no matter what comes after it. It says N.S., but I have no idea what that means."

"Everybody who visits the Continent needs to know," Malachi insisted. "N.S. means 'new style' and O.S. means 'old style'. Nearly all European merchants and policy makers have replaced the old style Julian calendar with the more accurate new style calendar offered by Pope Gregory three years ago. They still find it necessary during the changeover, however, to label which method they are using because there is a ten-day difference between the two systems. Since Leicester's expedition is to be a mainland operation, someone obviously thought it would be a good idea to make the date adjustment early by issuing instructions with the new dates."

"That's the source of the confusion then."

"Possibly so. Nevertheless, it appears that everybody understood what was meant except for two notable exceptions, so the Earl of Leicester departed the coast of England three days ago with his forces fully equipped and well-manned except for my apprentice and for a royal herald—who was quickly sent for—because his job is to authenticate the legitimacy of candidates for knighthood, many of whom Leicester obviously hopes to find on the Dutch battlefields among the group of six dozen lords and gentlemen supporters who constitute his social company and serve as his ad-hoc advisory committee."

"Are you trying to tell me that my ship sailed three days ago on December eighteenth although I'm still sitting here on December eleventh getting ready to go?"

"You are beginning to get the picture. The major Catholic countries– Spain, Italy, Poland, and Portugal–adopted the new calendar immediately. France and Luxembourg soon followed, and then the Catholic regions of Belgium, Germany, Switzerland, and the Netherlands joined in the change-over. At the Pope's direction, they all agreed to arbitrarily jump their calendar ahead ten days in order to catch up with the creeping change of seasons built into the Julian calendar and to bring the new calendar in closer synchronization with the equinoxes when the sun crosses the Equator twice a year and the days and nights are equal in duration."

"What creeping change?"

"When the Julian calendar was first formulated, the astrologers somehow calculated the year to be eleven minutes and fourteen seconds shorter than it actually is. Such a small surplus of minutes would not be much of a problem in any given year, of course, since it adds up to just about one day every hundred and thirty one years, but the accumulated error after sixteen hundred years tended to distort the seasonal changes people expect to see as they progress through the annual cycles of spring, summer, fall, and winter."

"Distort how?"

"The first snowfall got a little over eighteen hours behind each century and so did the first of the springtime blossoms. It finally became obvious to everybody that traditional planting and harvesting activities were being held a week-and-a-half later than they had been held in the historical past, so there grew an ominous conviction in many minds that the world was somehow slowing down."

"Or speeding up," offered William, frowning in concentration.

"At any rate, the change-over needed doing if only to calm the natives."

"You seem inclined to have England adopt it even if the orders did come from Rome."

"I don't question any source that offers me common sense on any issue," Malachi laughed. "God knows there is little enough intelligent thinking in this world without ignoring the little bit that does appear. The Gregorian calendar solves some big problems, and England will eventually have to adopt it simply because it works better than the Julian in both the long run and the short run, so I say, the sooner the better."

"What did they do with the missing ten days?"

"Whoosh, they were gone, as you so eloquently put it. Millions of Europeans went to bed the evening of Tuesday, October 5, 1582 and were awakened on the morning of Friday, October 15, 1582, by Pope Gregory calling; 'Abra-cadabra, presto!'"

"And nobody ever had the pleasure of living those ten days?" William half-mused. "That's spooky."

"Always a bright side," Malachi chuckled. "Nobody will mourn those dates on tombstones either, because nobody died during the missing ten days."

"So most of Europe is now Gregorian territory as opposed to Julian?"

"There are still out-of-the-way areas—including, as you've just discovered, merry old England—which resist all Roman dictates and refuse to make the change. They figure both calendars utilize a solar year of twelve months divided into 365 days with one extra day every four years, so why get excited over a couple of minutes."

"I think the ancient astronomers deserve a lot of credit for getting the months and days right so long ago."

Malachi nodded, "That's right, but that accumulation of one full day every one hundred and thirty-one years has developed nearly an eleven-day variance between our calendar dates and nature's cycles during the last sixteen centuries."

"Why didn't Gregory's group drop eleven days instead of ten?"

"That was discussed, but the astronomers and mathematicians know well enough there is always a capricious element in nature's movements which thwarts man's effort to pinpoint them, and the surplus of days did not yet amount to eleven, so it was felt prudent to settle for ten. It was argued successfully that the ten-day figure would permit old style calendars to switch to new style simply by writing the Roman numeral 'X' in front of the appropriate old style number."

"What difference can that make? It's all arbitrary anyway. They're just dates on a paper."

"Plenty of difference. In addition to the troublesome displacement of farming holidays, the Church celebrations, which are determined by date, are noticeably being shifted out of season all over England. Our spring ritual of celebrating Easter, for example, is dropping steadily back into the chilling jaws of winter."

"It begins to sound as if the change was needed, but it must take a mountain of arrogance to tackle something as weighty as changing the way we count the days and particularly to rob us of ten days of our lives."

"As always, the really big guys feel perfectly free to decide important matters rather arbitrarily at times. When the Julian calendar was adopted in 46 BC, Julius Caesar expressed a poetic desire to have the new year start with the Spring Equinox, but his Senate outvoted him and declared January first the beginning of the new year simply because that's when they were called into session."

"It's hard to imagine that such important matters were once decided so randomly–" William shook his head—"and pretty spooky to realize that our lives are still dominated by decisions reached sixteen centuries ago. But I must say January 1st makes more sense to me than when? March 21st?"

"It does seem tidier if not as poetic," Malachi acknowledged. "It is also said that Emperor Augustus, the nephew and heir to Julius Caesar, arbitrarily stole a day off the end of the shortest month in the year. He canceled February 29th to make thirty-one days in his birth month of August because he didn't want the thirty-one days of Julius Caesar's month of July to indicate his uncle was the greater man. So poor February ends up short-changed even on leap years."

"You did say the Julian calendar also had leap years?"

"Oh, yes. As long ago as 250 BC, the Egyptian and Babylonian calendars—on which the Julian system of 46 BC was based—saw the need for an extra day every four years to clean up the pieces of days left over by the inexactitude of mortal measurements–and to keep pace with the equinoxes. It is the disposition of those fragments which is the real test of a calendar's validity."

"But I don't see how they're different then. Both calendars have the same number of days and months and the built-in cycle of leap-years."

"In addition to dropping the ten days as a one-time solution to the long-time build-up," Malachi explained, "the Gregorian calendar also changes the regularity of some leap years by slightly revising the old formula which had produced the extra day every 131 years. On the new calendar, every year divisible by four is still a leap year except when it is also divisible by 100, 200, or 300."

"So dropping a single leap-year day every three out of four centuries will wipe out the eleven-minute build-up found in the Julian calendar?"

"For the moment, yes," Malachi said. "None of this, however, excuses you from failing to join the acting group sailing with Leicester. Their odd appearance and unruly behavior would have given you a perfect cover to keep track of how the expedition is going. We particularly wanted you to notice if Leicester is resisting the blandishments with which those wily Dutch burghers in Flushing are undoubtedly plying their newly-landed savior."

"They are treating Leicester like a savior?"

"That's the rumor, and I'm afraid that Leicester's susceptibility to flattery might easily persuade him to take over the United Provinces of the Low Countries as Lieutenant Governor if he is treated royally enough. His acceptance of such a title would infuriate Elizabeth because she has given him strict orders not to saddle England with such a responsibility. In her curious way, however, she has also ordered him to gain enough authority to levy taxes on any available source of wealth in order to help offset the cost of maintaining an English army overseas."

"The actors got off all right, you say. How did you know I wasn't among them, cleverly disguised?"

"We had a master list and checked off everybody who boarded the five major ships. We also kept close watch on the auxiliaries. We counted off six-thousand foot soldiers, one-thousand mounted horsemen, one hundred liveried yeomen and grooms for Leicester's personal service, scores of menials for fetching and carrying, and a group of about one hundred including ministers, choir boys, stable men, and actors. You were not seen among any of those groups including the four-legged bunch."

"Well," William shrugged. "I hope by this time I've explained all that. What's next?"

"Not so fast," Malachi growled. "I'd like you to reflect for a moment on the chance you have just missed to be part of an historical happening. The governor of the Dutch cautionary town of Flushing, our old friend, Sir Philip Sidney, is probably at this moment discussing with his newly-arrived commander and uncle, the Earl of Leicester, how they will conduct the up-coming campaign. Any day now, soldiers in English uniforms and soldiers in Spanish uniforms will shoot at each other on a Dutch battlefield and somebody is going to get killed."

"That sounds like open warfare to me."

"That's the danger,' Malachi nodded, "and it's the first time in twenty-five years that Elizabeth has risked such a fight against another royal kingdom. She has put down rebellious subjects in England and Ireland, of course, but that's not the same thing as taking the field against another duly-appointed monarch and interfering with the governance of his colonies. In the past, she has often condemned such outside interference in royal affairs, especially when remarks were made at Continental courts about England's policies in Ireland."

"What changed her mind?"

"She made that pretty clear in a public Declaration explaining why England has decided to respond openly to the cry for help from our Protestant allies in the Low Countries, who are presently suffering under a cruel regime. She had the statement printed up in five languages and circulated throughout the Continent to let the world know England's limited intentions in the Low Countries. My friend, Esteban Lopez, who will be with us soon, had a part in transcribing the Declaration."

"Who is Esteban Lopez?"

"An old Portuguese acquaintance of mine, who is an expert translator and scrivener. He's fluent in every major European language and a few from Asia as well, so he does a lot of high-price work translating important documents for whichever country will pay his price. We in the business like to think of him as a leader of our profession: the Super-Scrivener!"

"Is that hero-worship or idolatry?" William grinned.

"He's a standout either way," Malachi chuckled. "For many years, Esteban has plied his trade all over the Continent including Spain and England, usually traveling with diplomatic people for whom he does translating and recording. He often stays over in England to help our geographer, Richard Hukluyt, translate some of the foreign language descriptions of sea voyages recorded by other nations. Esteban and I have had some good evenings together. He is a merry companion as well as a valuable one because he is completely candid and non-partisan in appraising the present struggle between Spain and England."

"He doesn't care?"

"He appears amused by it. His native Portugal is off the battlefield at the moment, so he simply enjoys watching the conflict between the country that grabbed Portugal and the country that didn't come to her aid. He doesn't care if England bloodies Spain or Spain bloodies England. A lot of the Portuguese feel like that. Esteban enjoys the spectacle either way and seems completely candid in discussing whatever he notices of interest in either country. He'll be in soon with the latest news on the Dutch situation."

"I've been meaning to ask: you seem to use the words *Dutch* and *Low Countries* and *Holland* and *Netherlands* interchangeably. Are they the same?"

Malachi nodded. "I'll fill you in. Take notes. The term 'Low Countries' is geographical and applies to the sixteen Provinces of the Netherlands combined with Belgium and Luxembourg and, of course, generally describes the relationship of that area to the North Sea. The word 'Holland' is sometimes used to refer to the Netherlands because Holland is the most influential of the sixteen Provinces. For most purposes, the Netherlands applies to the Provinces as a political entity, which is subdivided into the southern Flanders or Flemish Netherlands which is Spanish-occupied, Catholic territory and the Dutch or Holland northern six provinces which are predominantly Protestant."

William looked up from his note-taking. "I think I've got it. But how did Spain end up owning the Netherlands when they aren't even neighbors?"

"The Netherlands was part of the Holy Roman Empire from the Tenth Century up until the middle of this century when Emperor Charles V grew tired of administering so much territory and split the Empire up, turning the Netherlands over to his son, King Philip II of Spain, and giving the German lands to his brother, Ferdinand I."

"Very impressive gift-giving, even for a monarch," William observed, still scribbling.

"Decidedly so since the industrious, innovative Dutch proved such a boon to the Spanish tax-collectors. In 1566, Protestant resentment against the Spanish government flared into rebellion. The Dutch not only resented the heavy taxation but rightly feared the threat of the Inquisition being turned loose on their blossoming Calvinistic beliefs. At first, Philip sent the fierce Duke of Alva to quell the early dissenters by a quick application of terror. He inflicted some impressive killing and burning on the heretics."

"Spain has been warring in Holland for nineteen years? Amazing! The whole place isn't that big to begin with, is it?"

"The sixteen Provinces together measure about 14,000 square miles—about half the size of Ireland. The northern half of the country is mostly import-export, ship-building, and world-trade businesses. The southern half is involved in dairy products and raising produce on some of the richest farmland in Europe, which the industrious Dutch have reclaimed over the centuries from inlets of the North Sea. 40% of all the Netherlands lies below sea-level and takes an intricate system of dykes to offset flooding. Even though the country is relatively small, it is hard for outsiders to control militarily because all the old towns are still fortified from the dark ages and any campaign against them is slow-going in terms of time and money spent in laying siege."

"You hinted that Don Alva's killing and burning policy didn't serve too well in controlling the Dutch?"

"It killed but didn't cure. Alva's men burned and pillaged Antwerp in 1576 and killed 8,000 of its citizens in what is now called 'The Spanish Fury'."

"8000!" cried William. "The thought makes my belly roil!"

Malachi nodded. "If people are angry enough, however, that kind of cruelty is just going to make them madder. When Philip realized Don Alva's approach was drastically reducing the number of his healthy Dutch taxpayers, he replaced him with his own bastard brother, Don Juan. The new Commander was to institute a more moderate policy of reconciling the dissidents with the Catholic faith. Much of this good work was done by bribing city officials and military leaders—some of whom were still secret Catholics—to surrender the communities which they were guarding. When fever took Don Juan eight years ago, Philip picked his cousin, Italian Alexander Farnese, the Duke of Parma, as his new field commander, and Parma has since racked up a steady succession of successful sieges and buy-outs in the ten southern Provinces."

"I don't suppose the Dutch have any kind of army to fight back with."

"You bet they do! They have a group of mercenaries hired periodically by the Provinces and many volunteers from countries which bear a grudge against Spain. England's best field commander, 'Black' Norris, has been over there off and on for ten years as an advisor and has seen to it that many of England's best officers have been bloodied on the Dutch battlefields. Meanwhile, of course, Elizabeth and Philip pretend nothing has been happening."

"If the Dutch have held out for nineteen years, they must be doing something right."

"Sieges take a lot of time, as I mentioned, and forces in the field ebb-and-flow under the influence of sickness and supply. But last year, their natural leader, William of Orange, was assassinated, and the Dutch have had no military success against Spanish control since. The Spanish, on the other hand, have succeeded in pulling the southern provinces back into the Catholic fold, and Parma's veteran Spanish Army has just now captured Antwerp, the major venting port for England's cloth trade. Spanish control over a deep-water port only one hundred and twenty miles from the coast of England represents a real threat to the safety of our country, and that's probably the strongest reason Elizabeth finally decided to act."

"Only one hundred twenty miles?" gasped William, still writing.

"Such a deep-water harbor would provide them with a very handy staging area to make preparations for the coming war. If they could sail against us from such a close base instead of having to sail all the way from Lisbon—"

"The war is really coming?"

Malachi frowned and nodded. "Many think so. In the past, Elizabeth has averted her eyes from the many English volunteers who have joined the Hollanders on the battlefield against the Spanish. "Dutch negotiating team was here in London for months pleading with the Queen for aid before it was too late, but the Queen is always reluctant to commit herself. I think the fall of Antwerp—along with the persistent urgings of Walsingham and Leicester—finally roused her to the decisive action of extending the Dutch a sizable loan and sending them a considerable fighting force under the command of her most enduring favorite."

"Did the Dutch ever offer Elizabeth sovereignty over the Provinces?"

"They did. The Dutch have no concept of how out-of-character it would be for Elizabeth to bankrupt her chested treasure for the privilege of defending them. I suspect the world has never seen a less ambitious-for-conquest monarch than our Queen. Others can have the glory. She wants neither the trouble nor the expense."

"What about Ireland?" asked William.

Malachi smiled as he explained patiently. "She makes an exception in the case of Ireland, which is assumed to be English territory after nearly four hundred years of ownership. As reluctant as Elizabeth is to take on new lands, she nevertheless does not want to become historically noteworthy for giving English property away."

"So we'll always be pestered by the Irish rebels," William grumbled.

"Into the foreseeable future," Malachi agreed. "But sooner or later, somebody is bound to figure out something intelligent to do with that island. Ah, I see Esteban coming. You will enjoy hearing what he has to say."

Malachi embraced his Portuguese friend and took a report from him to read over. He introduced his apprentice and then took his leave.

Chapter 8:
THE SUPER SCRIVENER OF
EUROPE RAMBLES ON

The conversation continues:

"I see you are a note-taker, nino," smiled Esteban. "Bueno. Carry on."

"Malachi has told me you are a great authority on the affairs of Spain and Holland, Senor Lopez. Is it true that the Dutch have offered Leicester governorship of the United Provinces of the Netherlands?"

"Si," Esteban confirmed. "The Dutch will shop that particular honor around until they find somebody who is foolish enough to fight their battles for them while they tend the market place."

"But Elizabeth will not allow him to accept even though it would give England a foothold on the Continent?"

"Not a chance," said Esteban. "Unlike many rulers, your Queen does not value costly ornaments unless she can wear them. In March, the Dutch offered their rule to Henry III in exchange for French protection against the Spanish. The King of France has his off-days in the brain department, you know—days when, it is rumored, he dresses as a woman with his hair in ruffles and exchanges affection with his small dogs and with his mincing minions."

"I guess everybody has to unwind some way," William mused.

"I'm sure Henry experienced some short-sighted joy at the thought of enlarging French territory and acquiring the impressive title of Overseer or Master or Protector of the Netherlands—the Dutch suggested he choose a title to suit himself—but his happiness would have been erased by close-at-hand criticism. His mother, Catherine de Medici, and his other Catholic advisor, the Duke de Guise, counseled strongly against his acceptance and convinced him that assuming the Dutch sovereignty would cost him greatly in both gold and soldiers just to defend the Dutchmen's right to conduct business as usual."

"Still," said William, "even with its problems, I would think territorial expansion would be a tempting bait for some ambitious monarch to bite on."

"Si, but the Dutch have fished out the possibilities in Europe when they didn't land England."

"But if neither the Queen nor Leicester accepts the Dutch Crown, how can we be assured repayment on that big loan we extended them?"

Esteban shrugged. "Elizabeth did just what any sensible monarch would do: she took hostage of the remaining deep-water Dutch ports she wants to deny to Philip. The Spanish will have to think twice about attacking Brill and Flushing now that they are garrisoned with English troops. Those two ports in particular are good ransom to ensure that England gets her money back or, if not that, gains possession of two valuable ports."

"This is very hot stuff!" exclaimed William, still writing. "England on the brink of a proxy-war with Spain, sending troops to Holland and lending money to the Dutch—money that is really rent for vital seaports. And here we are, her agents, scurrying about, negotiating with both Catholic and Protestant forces while the Dutch offer their country to rulers all around them. Is it possible they are drunkards and scoundrels, as Nashe hinted?"

"Oh no, it would be a mistake to think that," smiled Esteban, sitting back comfortably. "The Dutch are the most practical and amiable people God ever put on this Earth. I like them. Some feel they don't maintain enough social distance with their domestics, I know—which probably explains why there is constant strife with the Dutch domestics you English have working here in London, but it all seems to work very well in their society."

"How do you mean social distance?"

"In the Netherlands, domestics are all part of the family. The Dutch spend most evenings drinking and singing together, so they see little sense in denying the group a first class baritone or contralto just because it comes from the kitchen. It's a little taxing for masters to slip back into cold stares and superior tones after such evenings, so the Dutch just leave the social barriers down and everybody is company for everybody else. The Dutch are jovial because they are relaxed, and they are relaxed because they are quick on their feet."

"I'm not sure I understand," said William.

"Decision-wise. They have no cumbersome apparatus by which they form national policy. The Dutch Estates can decide things with the snap of their fingers, and there is no one to say them nay."

"Estates?" asked William.

"Their parliament." Esteban chuckled. "What some people call the 'Bakers and Brewers'. All other countries have monarchs of one sort or another to whom the legislative branch must defer in making policy. The Dutch have no monarch. All other countries have some form of state religion which helps govern decision-making. The Dutch have no state religion. They tolerate everybody as long as they behave themselves—even the Jews are safe in Holland. So Dutch policies may adjust overnight to changing circumstances without the delay of reconciling Church and State views. That makes them very nimble, indeed, in a rapidly changing world."

"Change laws rapidly," wrote William, muttering.

"Their nimbleness is not confined to legislative matters," Esteban said. "They are quick on their feet in commercial enterprises too. Not too surprising, I guess, since the two are pretty much the same thing for them. I doubt if any other nation adopts improvements as quickly as do the Dutch, or, for that matter, improvises solutions when needed. They developed their flat-bottomed, shallow-draft flyboat to haul cargo right across the Zeeland shoals which border their coast while other deep-draft ships must take the time and trouble to sail out around the hazard. They often seem less hampered by tradition than most other countries are."

"Ship building tradition?"

Estaban nodded. "All traditions. I think the daily exertion to keep from drowning in their below-sea-level country keeps their mind in gear, and they are always ready to examine something which works better than what they had before. The Dutch profited quickly, for instance, from the sailing lessons they picked up from the Portuguese, who have been trading with the Spice Islands for many years. The Portuguese are not only the world's best navigators but are also the masters of long distance sailing, making that eight thousand-mile trip around Africa and past India to the East Indies for eighty years now. And they lose fewer men to sickness on such long hauls than we lose in the twelve hundred-mile sail to the Azores."

"How do they do it?"

"That interested the Dutch enough to find out, and they quickly copied the Portuguese technique of rigging their ships so that sails could be handled in sequence by a much smaller crew. Of course they can't crack it on as fast as you English can, but there really are few occasions to do that since sailing is mostly a matter of modifying your sail-set once you're underway."

"What difference does reducing the crew make?"

"A smaller crew creates a big business advantage for merchants and greater comfort for mariners. A major reduction in the number of sailors on board means more room for each man even while increasing cargo space by building fewer crew accommodations. It means the victuals and water last much longer, permitting ships to sail much further. If a ship does not over-burden itself with extra seamen as replacements for the expected die-off from ship fever, it can better control the filth that piles up on crowded ships and that somehow introduces the scourge of scurvy and fever. Yes, indeed," Esteban chuckled, "despite outward appearances, the Dutch are very quick on their feet."

"It sounds as if they are clear-headed when it comes to business," William said, "but I am still puzzled about how they can offer a crown that doesn't exist?"

"That offer shows exactly how their crafty minds work. They would merely create a temporary monarchy and go happily about their business."

"The business of business, eh?"

"While the Dutch Provinces are all a bit testy with each other when it comes to rights and privileges, there are few conflicting interests in Holland when it comes to business. Dutchmen are all going in the same direction when they march to the market place. For hundreds of years the leading merchant families have filled the Estates General with their sons, so there are few hurdles to overcome when mercantile policy is discussed. It all comes down to the one over-riding question: does the policy facilitate business? Aside from its farming, Holland is essentially an import-export country. They bring stuff in from all over the globe, polish it up, re-wrap it, and ship it right back out at a decent mark-up. I like to think of the Dutch as the northern Venetians."

"Who finances them?"

"They finance themselves; furthermore, they keep many of the monarchs of Europe afloat as well. Every guilder and pfennig goes back into the business. That's why you won't see elaborate merchant houses in Holland. They are clean and tidy and cozy but not impressive compared to your English manor houses. The only decorative furnishings the Dutch invest in are the paintings they hang in every room, but even there, their genuflection to business is in strong evidence."

"How do you mean?"

"When they reward the artist with their guilders, they expect a return of something close to their heart, so even though religious scenes are still prominent in their churches, it is the depiction of the market-place and the counting house which decorate their walls at home. The men who buy the paintings have replaced the saints in the depiction. In the same deep-seated market sense, if a rich Dutch merchant tied up capital by building an elaborate house in the country as you English do, he would no longer be taken seriously in business matters. The other merchants would refuse to deal with him on the basis that he had lost all sense of proportion."

"I can see why they would not care to waste a pfennig on war with Spain," observed William. "They would cease to be amiable at that juncture."

Esteban grinned at the bent head of the apprentice. "Sí. And amiability comes off with the cloak when a Dutch burgher sits at the trading table. That burgher is a very serious man, with an insatiable thirst for profit. He will deal hard and honest with you because he counts on return business, and he won't send you away mad, but he doesn't mind seeing a little chagrin in your smile when the final tally is made."

William scribbled on for several minutes, then sat back. "Well," he said, smiling, "I know a great deal more about the Dutch than I did before, but let me take advantage of your vast store of knowledge and ask about the Spanish."

"They're all abuzz about what your Captain Drake has in mind," Esteban chuckled. "They'd give a fortune to find out where his twenty-six fighting ships intend to call next so that they could prepare a nice reception for him."

"Yes, the office mentioned Seville was quick to post their Drake alert," William nodded. "I know Malachi is reluctant to tip his hat to a foe in the field, but I've heard him express frequent admiration for Phillip's ability to gather information. My boss mentioned that several times in his career he has been brought up short when he first learned of English plans from captured Spanish documents. I know that kind of thing can be very disheartening for people in the business."

"He's not alone, believe me, in feeling the impact of Spain's all-seeing eye," Esteban chuckled. "Philip has furrowed many a royal brow on the Continent too."

"How does he manage it?" William asked.

"It's his network of contacts," Esteban explained. "Philip gets reports from all over the world. Hundreds every month. He reads all of them personally. His New World Viceroy warns that the English pirates must be gathering elsewhere since his coast is clear. His Mediterranean merchants tell him that England has increased its saltpeter order from Morocco. His French Catholic friends tell him that commercial enterprise has been restricted in the Plymouth area. His English Catholic friends tell him that the victualers are scouring Plymouth for supplies. His friendly Irish Chieftains tell him that the English pirates are no longer discharging cargo in the Irish ports. And his military people advise him that Drake is gathering forces to inflict some new outrage on Spain's dignity. With all these reports, it is not difficult for Philip to conclude that something is up. He then focuses all of Spain's considerable resources on discovering the 'when' and the 'where' of Drake's purpose."

"Succinctly summated and lyrically rendered," William said in admiration. "He really reads everything himself?"

"Si, every message," said Esteban. "No man could do more, but because he reads everything, the process itself has become too centralized and constricted. In the final analysis, King Philip has made himself into an indispensable bottle-neck in the governance of his territories. They can't operate without him, but they operate ever more slowly as the python of new responsibilities from his expanding empire suffocates his attention and thereby constricts the effectiveness of the only person in the kingdom empowered to make decisions. Timely administration is the key to success in any flourishing enterprise. It takes one week to get Philip's approval back and forth to Lisbon from Madrid; one month for the same process to his armies in the Low Countries, and over two months to go back and forth to Havana."

"Why doesn't he delegate?"

"When Philip was younger and answering his daily mail, he employed several secretaries to keep things moving, but he has changed over the years and the system has slowed accordingly. He has grown distrustful of his helpers and has dismissed most of them. Either they were not efficient enough to please him, or trustworthy enough, or Catholic enough, or Spanish enough, or they were upstarts who presumed to offer him advice. He now attempts to move mountains of minutia every day with little help, and the result is that important letters often work themselves to the bottom of the pile while he attends to mundane matters."

"How mundane?"

"He does the paper work on all public spending down to the payroll for military officers who are stationed thousands of miles away in the New World. He's deeply involved in everything overseas."

"His officials in the New World are permitted no authority of their own?"

"Very little. Philip gives detailed directions to his administrators, and there are no acceptable reasons for failure to follow them. He doesn't want to hear reasons; he wants to see results, and he'll hang any man in a minute if he thinks that man has failed his duty. He doesn't seek compromises; he seeks solutions—often final solutions for any who stand in his way."

"Doesn't he realize how his control of everything slows things down?"

"Slow or not, when Philip does decide something, it is not because he has been misled by any one source, as his ambassadors sometimes are. You know Mendoza, don't you?"

"The Spanish ambassador to France?"

"Si. And former ambassador to England until he was thrown out two years ago because of his involvement in the Throckmorton Plot against your Queen's life."

"Not very diplomatic," said William.

"Mendoza may well be too excitable and fiery for diplomatic life, which calls for a concealing kind of temperament. As ambassador to England, he did not hesitate to take cuts at your countrymen. In one dispute over commerce, he denounced the English people, saying, *"Profit to them is like nutrient to savage beasts."* [28]

"Sounds like the kind of diplomat who better travel often in his work."

"Si. He left England shaking his fist and swearing revenge. He's still very receptive to all sources who offer bad news about you English. Mendoza will pay good money to any agent who brings him any story putting the English in a bad light. The independent agents laugh about it among themselves and regard it as a handy way to pick up an occasional piece of change, but Philip would never fall for such biased reports. When he decides something, it is after consulting his worldwide reporting system."

"And you presume that the greater the sample, the more valid the information?"

"Generally, si, but, of course, one specific piece of information in the 'when' or 'where' department, could prove very valuable to anybody who was willing to sell." Esteban grinned at William.

William shrugged. "All I know is that the Admiralty papers Drake filed said they were headed to Alexandria to do some trading."

"Si." Esteban smiled. "One can certainly do some favorable trading when traveling with twenty-six ships bristling with hundreds of cannon. The simple people in Vigo on the northwest coast of Spain were surprised not long ago when Drake brazenly stopped there for fresh water for his fleet—on the very coast of the Spanish homeland! Imagine that! His display of heavy armament not only got him the supplies he needed but also permitted him to loot the city without opposition and to free some English prisoners held by the Spanish."

"Perhaps it's a form of advanced diplomacy, a simple incident," William pondered, "and don't forget, Vigo is on the way to Alexandria."

Esteban chuckled. "I always wonder about little incidents like that, because I would find it very interesting personally to live long enough to see if history itself has space enough to record the micro-view of human affairs as well as the macro-view."

"How do you mean?' William asked.

"I've done much translating and copy work for diplomats, geographers and mapmakers over the years," Esteban explained, "and my mind is filled with descriptions of recent explorations, discoveries, conquests, and political maneuvering. My professional curiosity leads me to wonder which modern 'incident' future historians will pluck like a blossom from the present colorful array in order to characterize our age. I've read enough history to realize that events and relationships which loom large at the present moment are often found to be fleeting and incidental when subjected to the ponderous mill-wheel of time."

"Do you mean you're using history books to determine the most likely present-day events for mention by future historians?"

"Well said—" Esteban saluted William by tipping his glass— "As a matter of fact, however, the recorded history of Europe is not as helpful as one might initially suppose. The Middle Ages—as we call that thousand year period between the fall of Rome about 450 AD and the early-1400's when the Renaissance movement came into view in Italy—produced very little writing of any kind. The degree of loathsome barbarity that was universally prevalent during that period—quite apart from the lack of literature—is difficult for those of us in modern times to imagine."

"Loathsome barbarity, eh?"

"Can you imagine," Esteban shook his head, "a period in history so hard up for irony that for hundreds of years, it permitted the brutish Irish, of all the people in Europe, to retain an almost exclusive ability to read and write?"

"I have heard that the Irish are die-hard communicators in addition to their other passions," William nodded. "They probably resorted to writing when their diverging views reduced the number of possible listeners."

"It was a period so self-absorbed in protecting its feudal system and repressing all interests outside those of the Church, that without the good graces and scholastic interest of our Arab neighbors, we would today have none of the ancient records of the Greeks and Romans. Imagine, if you can, how stark life would be without Greek entertainment and Roman inspiration!"

"Hard to imagine," William agreed. "Is that macro or whatever that other thing was?"

"Si, macro is the big picture. Micro is the small picture. For instance, there's no question that history books hundreds of years from now will still discuss England's dealings with the Spanish at this time. They will undoubtedly—and rightfully so—cast the relationship as a long-term tension between Queen Elizabeth of England and her brother-in-law, King Philip of Spain, over economic and religious differences which will probably end in open war. That is what's going on. That's the macro aspect of history."

"Got it," William nodded.

"I'm simply wondering whether history will grow so crowded with macro events that some of the more interesting sidelights of our era will be elbowed aside."

"What sidelights would that be?"

"By its very nature, you realize, history is acquisitive and accumulative. If people stay on this planet long enough, history books will eventually take notice only of kings crowned and battles won and ships lost and discoveries made and will no longer tell of any event which was not played out on center stage."

"For instance?"

"What do you know about King Philip of Spain?"

William shrugged. "What everybody knows, I guess. Stay out of his way unless you happen to be a practicing Catholic."

"What do you know about your boss, Walsingham?"

"Not much. Good man. Works hard. A trifle stingy with expense money for my taste, but, of course, he plays on a larger stage than I do at the moment, so he may very well have responsibilities and considerations of which—"

"Have you ever thought to compare Philip and Walsingham?"

"Compare?" exclaimed William softly.

"Si. History will record the conflict between Elizabeth and Philip, but will it record the behind-the-scenes battle that has gone on for many years between two men so alike that it is a shame they are not brothers, so they could hate each other even more intensely."

"So alike? King Philip and Walsingham?"

"Si," grinned Esteban. "Which would you say has an absolute abomination of finery in dress and is never seen in anything other than funereal black?"

"That's easy," William smiled. "Walsingham is a Puritan, and plain clothing is a uniform for that membership."

"Both," said Esteban with satisfaction. "Philip regards finery in dress as decadent and fit only for social outcasts. Spanish grandees do not wear their best wardrobe while in Madrid for fear Philip will hear of their extravagance. Now, which would you say works longer hours each and every day than any other person in his government?"

"Walsingham never rests, stays busy every living second. There is no hour, day or night—" William halted mid-sentence. "And you have just told me no official document enters of leaves Spain without Philip's careful perusal."

"Si, each has exactly the same reputation in his own country. Walsingham's work habits are well known in England, but not everybody knows that the affairs of the Spanish Empire are sometimes brought to a halt while the King of Spain writes out helpful instructions to some lieutenant in the New World on the finer points of Spanish grammar."

"Egad! I support proper usage, but—"

"What would you say about humorless, implacable fanaticism?"

"Give in to it only on your bad days?"

"Each man burns so with the white heat of hatred for the other that there is no hope of compromise between them—ever. Walsingham advises your Queen publicly that the peace negotiations are only a smoke-screen behind which the Spanish are completing their plans for invading England. The Queen, however, does not agree. If Walsingham had his way, he would send Drake and Hawkins and Frobisher and dozens more like them to strike the Spanish coast and immediately disrupt the preparation of their invasion fleet."

"I thought you meant religious fanaticism."

"That too. Each regards the other as the Anti-Christ, and each prays daily to the same God for heavenly guidance in removing the other from the face of the earth." Esteban rolled his eyes upward and sighed. "It makes me wonder how much furrowed-brow time must go on up there in Heaven. Furthermore, Walsingham has often testified publicly to the depth of his religious faith in such a fashion as to amaze listeners. It's not amazing that he says it, of course. But it is amazing that he still holds office. He has been heard to say, *'First I wish God's glory and next the Queen's safety'.*" [29]

"And he's in charge of the Queen's safety?"

"Si, he is. It's clear, however, that the two are much alike in his mind. His gratuitous testimony might irritate the Queen a bit, but she puts up with him because he is the best in England at smelling out plots against her life. He has already saved her several times by exposing Catholic conspiracies which were planned or underway when broken up. The constant vigilance which Walsingham maintains, however, comes at some cost to his personal stability. You can't immerse yourself for years in plots and plans and turncoats and traitors without coming to sense menace lurking in every shadow. As a matter of fact, I have often heard Walsingham mutter; There is less danger in fearing too much than too little."

"It sounds as if Walsingham is suspicious of everyone. I believe he has complete faith in my master, Malachi, however—where is Malachi, by the way?"

Esteban laughed. "He slipped out while you were busy writing. You are not as observant as Secretary Walsingham, who never misses a move with those deceptively somnolent eyes of his. And like Philip, he never gives up once he has picked up the scent of the enemy."

"Gadzooks, I would fear to be around him! Would he consider me an enemy?"

"If you interfered in any way with the smooth workings of his duties, si. But you should never be too trusting, nino. Remember what Burghley told his son Robert: *'Trust not any man with thy life, credit or estate. For it is mere folly for a man to enthral himself to his friend, as though, occasion being offered, he should not dare to become his enemy'.*" [30] Many conspirators and plotters give over their closest friends when faced with the rack, you know."

"I'm not at all surprised," William nodded. "But back to more interesting considerations. I hope in the future we can expand our capacity to store information, so we can keep track of such interesting micro along with the macro. For the moment, however, it seems to me just as well that the current fanatics are evenly divided between Spain and England—though I'll take Walsingham any day over King Philip."

"Por favor, Philip is far from being the evil monster you in England think him," said Esteban, holding up a warning hand.

"Think you not?"

"Si, I know it. I hope to write history books of my own some day, so I attempt to be objective in my appraisal of historical figures. In that sense, I see Philip II as a very successful monarch, who has ruled a huge, expanding empire for thirty prosperous and successful years. The Spanish people still profess to adore him, so he stands very much in their eyes as Elizabeth stands in English eyes. I've heard Walsingham say he has never tapped into any conspiracy which featured Spanish principals bent upon undoing their king. Very impressive at a time when gold will create an opposition party in almost any other European country. Of course, Philip does have the Henrecian Advantage."

"The what?"

"When a monarch assumes the leadership of his national church in addition to being king of his country, as Henry VIII did here in England and as Philip does by his power to appoint Spanish bishops. Such a monarch has pretty well minimized the possibility of meaningful opposition to his policies. Even a poor king can survive a long time with such enormous power, but Philip is far from being a poor king because it's pretty clear that he enjoys his job just as your Elizabeth does. He writes and receives letters to and from all his commanders, both local and abroad."

"He writes letters to all his commanders?"

"Si. Very few have ever talked to him personally. That's the way he likes it. Calm, meticulous, and industrious, he has run his domain on an upward curve since he assumed power in 1555. His father, Emperor Charles V, put the crown on his head. A rare happening, indeed, for such enormous power to be surrendered peacefully."

"Malachi told me some of that. It's here somewhere in my notes how the Emperor abdicated because he grew tired of the job."

Esteban nodded. "Si, after thirty-eight years as King of Spain and Emperor of the Holy Roman Empire, he divided up the empire between his brother, Ferdinand I, and his son, Philip II, and went his merry way. He lived out his years in Germany with a beautiful blonde, who had already borne him a son. The child resembled him mightily, and he enjoyed his last years watching that boy grow up to be a happy nobody."

"Talk about shifting goals!"

"He seemed content and happy to all observers, but quite worn down. He may have been simply exhausted because of his energetic leadership, always campaigning in the field against the rising tide of heresy growing out of Luther's efforts, and trusting his advisors in Madrid to keep the supplies coming. He hated the paper work."

"I imagine one wears down quickly if he enjoys combat that much."

"Si," said Esteban, "but Philip is now just the opposite. Years ago, he used to lead his troops in the field, but now he prefers to run his battles from Madrid or hunkered down in his new hideaway at El Escorial. Your office gets copies of most of his letters because your boss has sense enough to enlist friendly domestics who sweep up military posts at night."

"Is El Escorial a town?"

Esteban chuckled. "Not a town but a combination memorial-monastery-mausoleum . Twenty-two years ago, back in 1563, King Philip set 3,000 craftsmen to work on a bare, windy site in the Guadarrama Mountains about twenty-five miles northwest of his capital, Madrid. They finished the job last year, and the resulting complex covers a 682 by 581-foot area containing chapels, churches and courtyards, enough to utilize twelve thousand windows and doors. The whole is enclosed with a grey granite wall."

"Egad! It sounds like an Egyptian pyramid!"

"Si," said Esteban, "and that is a good comparison. Philip is something of a throwback to the Pharaohs of old in his concern for his final resting place. Early in the construction of El Escorial, he had a seat quarried out of rock in the foothills overlooking the project so he could contemplate the progress of his mausoleum over the years. The main structure itself is not a pyramid in shape, of course. Instead it is built in the form of an upturned gridiron with 180-foot towers sticking up at each corner for legs."

"Gridiron?"

"That takes some explaining," Esteban grinned. "Back in 1557, Spanish troops in the field under Philip's command at St. Quentin in France burned the convent of St. Lawrence the Martyr, killed all the priests and raped the nuns. Philip was so shocked by the spectacle of Catholics killing Catholics that he abandoned a military situation which could have changed the course of history. There was no effective military force between his army and the city of Paris. By taking the capital, he could have made France a part of Spanish territory. But Paris is 95% Catholic, and the conquest of the city would have pitted his veteran Spanish regulars against the Catholic citizens in Paris. There was no doubt about the outcome, but Philip wanted no more of Catholics killing Catholics so he turned away. Since that time, he has conducted his military campaigns by letter."

"That shows compassion. But it doesn't explain the gridiron."

"Philip chose the gridiron form for his massive memorial as penance to St. Lawrence, who, in Biblical times, was burned to death on a gridiron. 'El Escorial' means 'slagheap', by the way, and the whole area is treeless, bare, and rocky with freezing winters and blazing summers, ideal background for a penitent."

"Sounds Puritanical. Ideal for Walsingham, too," murmured William.

Esteban grinned. "Si, it is a bit short of creature comforts, but the stern exterior only emphasizes the beautiful interior. Artists and sculptors worked alongside the masons, decorating walls and ceilings with their paintings and statuary. Europe's most delicate ironwork, most finely colored marble, most exquisite crystal and silk, and even some of the beautiful wood from the New World were all incorporated into the construction of El Escorial. Philip moved into his small room next to the chapel as soon as it was finished and hasn't moved out yet."

"You must have quite a file on Philip's activities."

"Much of my work has been in Spain, and dipping into King Philip's affairs as often as my duties have required, has permitted me to shape a different perspective from that of men who have faced his cannon. I am usually out of range, as it were, and can afford a little Christian charity in my view."

"Charity?"

"Well, understanding at least. It's clear that Philip's life has resembled an ar-rowhead in its development. His early life was the broad back of the arrow-head. He mixed well with everyone. He even got a reputation as a flirtatious gal-lant while he was courting your Queen Mary here in England. She introduced him to the social good-by kiss, and he insisted on kissing all her ladies-in-waiting goodnight."

William smirked. "An excellent custom. Was Philip a 'flirtatious gallant' among his own people in Spain?"

"Oh, si. He courted and won four wives, who, unfortunately, died soon after, through no fault of his own, I might add. For many years, he laughed and danced with all the noble families of Spain. He worked well with a large group of secretaries and advisors. At this time, he commanded military in the field, as I mentioned, and gained several notable victories. After his shock at St. Quentin, however, he gradually narrowed his involvement as the point of an arrowhead narrows. He never took the field again. He now enjoys a quiet private life and never socializes anymore. He only faced active opposition once in his reign."

"An opposition party in Spain?"

"Philip was asking his peasants to make sacrifices to aid his war preparations against you heretic English when he noticed the Spanish ladies of the nobility were competing with each other in public by bedecking themselves with costly jewelry. Philip asked them politely to abstain for the duration, but none wanted to be first to give up her decorations, so the King had to get quite harsh with them. He gained his end by decreeing that only pimps and whores might publicly wear jewelry or hats with one side of the brim hiked up."

"Too bad," William laughed. "I like those jaunty hats. Still, he changed the identity of his opposition with a bit of social alchemy."

"That's right, and when the ladies retaliated by increasing the size of their public entourage—some ladies being accompanied by fifty attendants—Philip decreed that no noble lady may appear in public accompanied by more than two attendants unless she were drunk."

William grinned. "I bet the King of Spain is a pretty good chess player."

"Si, but in recent years Philip has quit listening to the broad base of people with whom he used to mingle. He has isolated himself in the Escorial lately with only a few trusted advisors, and I don't know that he listens to them either. It's hard to see that anyone has any direct influence on him these days."

"Not even the pope?"

Esteban chuckled. "No. Philip often spoke disparagingly of Pope Gregory and now does the same for Sixtus when he speaks of him at all. The King believes his gold and his cannon command a lot more influence than any Papal decree."

"So no one advises him?"

"As far as anybody can tell, he gets his direction only from God himself. It's as if during the early years of his reign, Philip entered the broad mouth of a funnel side-by-side with the Spanish people but now approaches the narrow end of the spout with no room for any to march beside him."

"What happened to your arrowhead figure?"

"Same difference," Esteban shrugged. "But back to our comparison of Philip and Walsingham. Which one would you say still uses the old Roman numeral system to the exclusion of the Arabic numbering system?"

"What? That's incredible. Talk about not keeping up with the times. As slow as Philip is in everything else, I'd bet a pound—if I had one—that only he could be that slow."

"Totally and completely wrong." Esteban smiled in satisfaction. "Anytime I do copy work for Walsingham, I must convert his Roman numbers over to the Arabic-Hindu system which he refuses to use."

"Hard to believe," William shook his head. "But I should have guessed from your tone that it was another trap."

PART II. TUG OF WAR: CATHOLICS VS PROTESTANTS

Chapter 1: MARLOWE HIRES A STAND-IN

Malachi's room at the Black Boar Inn:

"Mercy, my dear, this is William, my new apprentice," Malachi said. "And, William, please to meet Miss Mercy Fairgate, who sometimes assists me on certain survey assignments. You need to listen carefully to what she says because she may well be your supervisor on future jobs."

"Apprentice?" Mercy asked. "I knew we had confederates and accessories and dupes and foils and gulls in this business, but this is the first time I've ever heard of an apprentice."

"Medical necessity," Malachi assured her. "As the years go by, I have more work to do and less energy to do it. Both my luggage-handling and my fair-copy work suffer from my reduced state, so I face a bleak and exhausting conclusion unless I manipulate the variables a bit. My new helper gives me a hand with baggage and a fist with copy. He evens out my equation."

"Hello, then, Apprentice William," Mercy extended her hand, and William, awestruck for the moment, kissed it. He then turned to Malachi and said softly.

"There's language in her eyes, her cheek, her lip,
Nay, her foot speaks,
Her wanton spirits look out at every joint
and motive of her body." [1]

Malachi nodded, "That's more or less what everybody says."

"Very pretty," Mercy smiled, "and admirably perceptive on such short notice. Malachi mentioned you were recovering from a serious head injury, but your fine flair for flattery seems to have survived intact."

"His brain is full of lines and rhymes," Malachi said,. "ever since it was set a-twirl by that bump, but he has improved lately, and he is already useful as long as the task is not too complicated nor arduous. Do you have something for me?"

"Yes. That other poet," Mercy paused to smile at William, "is waiting downstairs to see you."

"That would be Chris Marlowe from Cambridge," Malachi explained. "I left word for him to stop by. Please send him up, Mercy, my dear."

"Aren't you forgetting something?" she asked as she glanced at William. "You're not exactly alone, you know."

"Little matter," Malachi shrugged. "His mind is empty as a sea-shell, so he's safe enough if we steer clear of specifics."

"I'll fetch him then, but you might warn your new associate that Marlowe can be a bit loud and aggressive upon first meeting. He says he likes to make a lasting impression and he always succeeds. He seems oddly indifferent, however, whether that impression be favorable or not."

"Oh, well, I'd say 'loud and aggressive' overstates the case," Malachi observed, "but it must be admitted that he is highly animated and often highly entertaining. I would rate Christopher Marlowe among the top ten tavern-talkers in all of England, and I have seen few men who could move an audience as passionately as he does with his audacious comments about everything. He may well be a trifle loud—as are many men his age—but he backs up his braggadocio by getting things done."

"Like what? William asked.

"He earned his BA degree from Cambridge University last year and is working on his Masters now. In order to educate himself in the art of writing creatively, he took time to translate the Latin language of several ancient poets into very readable English verse. Good approach there: don't wait for somebody else to teach you an art form. What is it young John Donne says: *'Don't ask for whom the bell tolls; It tolls for thee'*."

"Does Chris know you've added an apprentice to your service?"

"Oh, yes," Malachi assured her. "We've already discussed it, and Marlowe is coming tonight partially to look him over and possibly to offer him a bit of work. So send the young man up, Mercy, by all means, but let him finish his drink first. No need to attract unnecessary attention."

"Lesson your new man in such matters," Mercy grinned as she left. "I know my business."

"Miss Mercy appears to be on a first name basis with this other poet, this Marlowe fellow," William observed. "Are they old acquaintances?"

"They have worked together in the past," Malachi nodded, "and they share a close mutual friend, who is one of Marlowe's college classmates: Thomas Walsingham. As it happens, young Walsingham is the cousin of Sir Francis Walsingham, the director of our Survey Service and probably the third most trusted adviser to the Queen after Burghley and Leiscester. Or maybe just about even with Raleigh for third. Anyway, classmates often involve each other in profitable pieces of business, so Marlowe was recruited to work for us several times in the past as a kind of courier. He and Mercy have already shared some exciting moments."

"Interesting," William mused, "I wonder if translating verse from a foreign language can ever be as satisfying as creating the verse yourself."

"Good question, and Marlowe is exactly the proper man to ask. I've heard him read from his rhyming play, *Tamburlaine*, which he is presently in the process of trying to sell, and he did major translating during the whole time he was a Divinity student, so he should have a strong impression of which of the two is more satisfying."

"Marlowe was a Divinity student?"

"You know the old story: the poor go for a career in the Church after college while the well-off buy themselves a lucrative appointment in government. Marlowe's father is only a shoemaker, but he has a rich uncle someplace, who pre-paid his early education. And Marlowe was shrewd enough later to proclaim himself a Divinity student in order to take advantage of Archbishop Parker's special scholarship fund for the education of future clergymen to the tune of six paid-up years at Cambridge University."

"Are you suggesting unprincipled shrewdness?"

"Some might think so," Malachi shrugged. "The expectation was that he would be ordained upon graduation if he accepted the scholarship. He did not, however, choose to take the cloth at that time, preferring instead to gain further training as a writer. And he had good urging for his choice judging from the ability he showed in his translations. While I admire his interpretation of Virgil and Lucan, I particularly enjoy his rendering of Ovid because he maintains the same reverence for the human body entangled in amorous couplings which Ovid always expressed. I'm afraid many poets get carried away with bawdiness and bad taste in that particular area."

"Can you think of an example?" asked William quickly. "My Apprentice Entertainment Association."

"Of the reverence?" Malachi grinned.

"Well, yes. That too."

"I recall a short bit from Marlowe's translation of Ovid's Book 1,"

> *In summer's heat and mid-time of the day*
> *To rest my limbs upon a bed I lay..*
> *Then came Corinna in a long loose gown,*

Her white neck hid with tresses hanging down...
What arms and shoulders did I touch and see,
How apt her breasts were to be press'd by me...
Judge you the rest; being tir'd she bade me kiss;
Jove send me more such afternoons as this! [2]

"Rhymed couplets are not that hard to write," William pointed out. "Did Marlowe do them all that way?"

"No. He used something called blank verse in translating Lucan. Very effective."

"Blank verse?"

"I'll let him explain the technical stuff to you if he has time."

"What employment prospect does he hold for me?"

"It's just a wild fancy on my part at the moment, so let's wait and see what he has to say."

"What's your connection with Marlowe anyway?" William asked.

Malachi chuckled, "You are a nosy sort. Still, I guess it does no harm. As I said, Marlowe has run an errand or two for us in the past. Our messengers are assigned to check with me if at all possible before they set off, and that's why you've noticed people chatting with me at odd hours. But I want you to keep absolutely quiet about that arrangement, do you understand?"

"Perfectly," William assured him. "Why do they check with you?"

"Good Lord," Malachi snapped. "You have no idea of what keeping quiet means, do you?"

"Well, I only thought while we were waiting, I might learn something."

"No matter," Malachi waved away his concern. "For the life of me, I can't figure out if it's a fault in me or a gift in you to get me talking so much. The reputation I have gained as a messenger-scrivener for the last twenty-seven years has been based largely on my ability to be trusted with secrets. In the eyes of all I have served, I am a man who has no need to chatter or gossip nor get chummy with the kitchen help, so I am a safe repository for affairs of state in the areas of pickup and delivery. "trusty messenger, as we like to say in the trade."

"Certainly you are that from all I've seen," William testified.

"I try," Malachi grinned. "But I have come to realize lately that I am something more than a trusty messenger. During all those years, there has been a festering desire seething away inside me to spew forth an explosion of candor too long suppressed. I have a growing need to discuss things in the open without carefully considering the consequences."

"Every kettle will boil if held to the flame long enough."

"Exactly," Malachi nodded, "and since the job necessitates that I seek a safe haven for my candor, Providence has been kind enough to send you along with your impertinent questions, your guileless face, and your unencumbered brain. My mind is the full bottom-half of the used up hourglass while yours is the empty top-half, so it is only proper to reverse the glass and set the sands to flowing once more."

"I invite your timely response," William said with a little bow and a sly smile. "Why are all the messengers instructed to check with you?"

"Since I have a particularly good memory, the front office set me up as something of a clearinghouse for our messenger assignments: a route-master, if you will. Within the scope of my duties, I survey the agendas of the leading personages of the realm, so that when an urgent response is required from Lord so-and-so, I can best advise whether he may sooner be fetched at his manor house in Kent or his hunting estate in Essex or his doxy's flat in Cheapside. By taking a few minutes to check with me, messengers often save themselves a period of riding in circles in pursuit of their duties."

"And you say Marlowe has needed a lot of help in finding his way?"

"Quite the contrary," Malachi corrected him. "Christopher Marlowe is a very competent chap who will not suffer direction gladly from anyone because he is so full of it himself. He is also a close friend and drinking companion of those two Cambridge graduates you met at the Writer's Table: Robert Greene and Thomas Nashe. Those two make their livings by whipping out poems, pamphlets, and plays for any customer who will hire their services. Nobody knows the London theatrical scene better than those three intimates, so if Marlowe offers you any counsel on the subject, you can be sure it will be knowledgeable and informative."

"He's not one of those people who offer advice to complete strangers, is he?"

"He's not far from it," Malachi laughed. "At least you don't have to worry about flat spots in conversation while Marlowe is around because his outrageous outflow will keep you so breathless, you'll hardly have time to muster a response. The big secret of dealing pleasantly with him is not to permit his conversational sallies to throw you off-balance. I'll have a word with him on the stairs and then send him in to talk to you. Show some respect when he gets here."

"I'll show as much as I get," William promised.

Christopher Marlowe entered the room a few minutes later and stood staring at William.

"By Jove," he finally said, "I do believe Malachi is right about this. Grow your sideboards a trifle longer for style and cultivate a small mustache, and I think you may be exactly right for the part."

"Part?" William's ears sprang to attention.

"Malachi says you are interested in theatrical work. How old are you?"

"I really can't say."

"I don't blame you at all," Marlowe said. "If you can get one ounce of satisfaction from such concealment, hug it to your bosom and draw your secret joys from it. I can't imagine a more boring life than one spent completely exposed in a sunlit clearing. It doesn't really matter if you won't reveal your age to me." Marlowe circled William, looking him up and down and finally staring him full in the face.

"It isn't that I won't reveal, you see, so much as—"

"Doesn't matter a bit," Marlowe waved him off. "We are clearly of an age within a few months of each other, so that part will go well."

"Is this a horoscope kind of thing? I've heard that every once in a while they really hit one's type so uncannily that it is difficult to—"

"Indeed, you may be just the man I've been searching for." Marlowe pulled back abruptly from his inspection. "I swear, I've looked all over London for the last month to fill this role. What this town really needs is a central casting office. Nobody seems to realize that London's play attendance has blossomed to the point where we have two separate theaters going full blast at this moment with talk of a third being added soon. Centralizing some functions would certainly make things easier for all of us."

"Role, I think you said."

"That kind of setup would permit us creative men to exert our energy in the establishment of the first commercial theater in the history of mankind."

"Stage plays are something new?"

"Hardly," Marlowe scoffed. "The Greeks originated play production five hundred years before the birth of Christ."

"What nonsense do you speak, then? Is it new or fifteen hundred years old?"

Marlowe stiffened, then took a deep breath. "With most men," he finally said, "I am slow to anger, but you have this extraordinary ability to inflame me every time you open—"

"That isn't what your friends say," William interrupted. "As a matter of fact, I have personally heard Thomas Kyd denounce you as something of a hot-tempered bully, always punching people about. It must be admitted he had some drink taken when he said it, but still—"

Marlowe flushed for a moment and then chuckled grimly. "Former roommates are like ex-wives and must be forgiven accordingly. The fact that you can't hide anything from either of them is hardship enough, God knows, without the chilling realization that they will forever attempt to mend your dark side—whatever they presume it to be—so the scurrilous falsehoods and twisted truths they later choose to utter about you, will not only lack Christian charity, but, unfortunately, will also contain some sprinkling of validity since those dedicated fault-finders have had the private opportunity to pick and choose among your various behaviors for public viewing."

"Back-to-the-wall-time, eh?"

Marlowe nodded. "They leave a sensitive man no choice but to cultivate a divine patience coupled with a sublime indifference to detractors of all sorts and sizes. A patience, I might add, so celestial in scope as to be thought by many to be heaven-sent, and so highly principled that it even includes you at this very moment. Your slate is clean."

"Kyd said he quit hanging out with you socially because you caused a scene wherever you went."

Marlowe chuckled, "I'm not the least bit surprised. Dear Thomas doesn't realize that the creation of scenes from the whole cloth is the very basis for writing significant plays. If he spent his evenings as I do in taverns and Common Rooms driving men to the wall in defense of their deepest religious feelings—even challenging them to name the bargain they would make with the devil to attain their highest desire—Kyd might end up with mature material for use in his plays instead of being forced to paste together a papier-mâché mishmash of foreign literary devices."

"That's what you think of his *Spanish Tragedy*?"

"You know," Marlowe mused, "Kyd's play is the hit of London at the moment, and I am rated as just another Cambridge graduate, but when the London audience gets a glimpse of my *Tamburlaine*, they will be forced to confront a really excellent play, and, I'm afraid, my old room-mate may never get over his confrontation with excellence."

"You think *Tamburlaine* will really be so different?"

"The flow of the blank verse alone puts it a cannon-shot ahead of anything Kyd has ever done—or anybody else, for that matter. You wouldn't believe the kind of effort it takes to control your thoughts in such a fashion that you not only propel the action, but do so in pleasing verse."

"Well," William shrugged, "the label 'pleasing' is really in the ear of the beholder, isn't it?"

Marlowe stared at him for a moment and then shrugged. "Malachi mentioned that your rough edges needed some smoothing out. He said further you would profit handsomely from a grand overview of the London theatrical scene, so let me fill in your over-all picture before some self-appointed know-it-all clutters your brain with inconsequential detail."

"I'd like that. The grand overview has always held a certain fascination for people caught in my particular circum—"

"Few people realize it," Marlowe went on, unconcerned, "but when James Burbage erected London's first playhouse, The Theater, just nine years ago in the suburb of Shoreditch, he really threw the history of drama into a hard left turn."

"How so?"

"The moment he collected the first admission charge was the moment he created the modern commercial theater."

"Where the audience pays money to watch, you mean?"

"Right," Marlowe nodded. "Before his playhouse opened, there had always been an element of subtle arm-twisting involved in promoting attendance at the various dramatic presentations. The Greeks used drama festivals to mark religious holidays, and attendance was mandatory on pain of losing citizenship. The Passion plays and Guild presentations of the last few centuries have all been self-serving presentations of the familiar Biblical themes calculated to keep sinners feeling guilty enough to work hard at redemption. Admirable social order was maintained by such repetition, I imagine, but little enlightenment, and a heavy fine for non-attendance. Mark that well. The truth of the matter is that until this very moment in history there has never existed even the possibility of a voluntary audience."

"That is very interesting, of course, in and of itself, and it obviously moves you, but does it have any real significance? Somebody paid for all those theatricals even if the audience didn't."

Marlowe stared at William. "I hope your eyes see more than your mind does, my good man, because the significance you seek stands directly before your gaze."

"I'm looking at you."

Marlowe nodded. "I hope to play a major part in the flourishing of the commercial theater. I have already roughed out a second *Tamburlaine*, which I call *Tamburlaine Two*."

"Zounds!" William cried. "If it's really that easy once you have the formula, I can hardly wait to get started. Does 'flourishing' mean big money for the writer?"

"I certainly hope so." Marlowe drew a manuscript from his doublet. "But don't be misled about the act of creation being easy. I'm having a lot of trouble getting this second one polished up and finished. Perhaps you will do me the honor of serving as a small audience while I read you this one scene I'm having trouble with."

"You want to know if it holds together?"

"See if it flows, "Marlowe said. "My character, *Tamburlaine the Great*, is here instructing his three sons on military matters:

> But now, my boys, leave off and list to me
> That mean to teach you the rudiments of war.
> I'll have you learn to sleep upon the ground,
> March in your armour through watery fens,
>
> Sustain the scorching heat and freezing cold,
> Hunger and thirst, right adjustments of war;

> *And after this, to scale a castle wall,*
> *Besiege a fort, to undermine a town,*
> *And make whole cities caper in the air,*

"Oh, I like that!" William exclaimed. "'And make whole cities caper in the air'—wonderful stuff."

"If you don't mind," Marlowe said quietly, "I'd prefer that you contain your commentary until I finish the piece." He continued reading:

> *"Then next the way to fortify your men;*
> *In champion grounds what figure serves you best,*
> *Ditches must be deep, the counterscarps*
> *For which the quinque-angle form is meet,*
> *Because the corners there may fall more flat*
> *Whereas the fort may fittest be assail'd,*
> *And sharpest where the assault is desperate:*
> *The Narrow and steep, the walls made high and broad.*
> *The bulwarks and the rampires large and strong,*
> *With cavalieros and thick counterforts,*
> *And room within to lodge six thousand men.*
> *It must have privy ditches, countermines,*
> *And secret issuings to defend the ditch;*
> *It must have high arjins and covered ways*
> *To keep the bulwarks fronts from battery,*
> *And parapets to hide the musketeers,*
> *Casements to place the great artillery."*

William interrupted, "Excuse me. I hope you have included a little stage business here of the sons' rubbing their heads, shifting their feet, and scratching their—"

"This is not a comedy," Marlowe fairly hissed. "Pay heed to the words."

> *And store of ordnance, that from every flank*
> *May scour the outward curtains of the fort,*
> *Dismount the cannon of the adverse part,*
> *Murder the foe, and save the walls from breech.*
> *When this is learn'd for service on the land,*
> *By plain and easy demonstration*
> *I'll teach you how to make the water mount,*
> *That you may dry-foot march through lakes and pools,*

Deep rivers, havens, creeks, and little seas,
And make a fortress of the raging waves,
Fence'd with the concave of a monstrous rock,
Invincible by nature of the place.
When this is done, then are ye soldiers,
and worthy sons of Tamburlaine the Great." [3]

"Finished?"

Marlowe nodded.

"It is certainly pretty good if you like that sort of thing, but are you sure you haven't overloaded it with military jargon? How many people in your audience will know what a quinque-angle fort is or a 'rampire' or 'cavalieros' or 'arjin'?"

Marlowe shrugged, "Nearly everybody, as a matter of fact. All have read or heard about castle defenses before. They all know that the walls of a quinque-angle fort are built like a star to present six arrow-like projecting ramparts to the enemy. But it doesn't really matter if they recognize individual terms so long as the writer puts obscure words in a recognizable context. The audience will draw the obvious conclusion. I was hoping you'd say something about the compression. The poetry."

"The compression is admirable," William said. "You covered a great deal of ground in very few lines, and I always find iambic pentameter a regular toe-tapper. It seems such an easy meter to work with."

"Yes," Marlowe growled. "Why don't you give it a try when you find a few spare moments. I'm sure the result will astonish all."

"Oh, I will, I will. It looks like easy pickings to me. I mean, what can go wrong? As long as the writer puts in his creative time, all the rest should fall into place."

"Your view may be a bit premature," Marlowe chuckled, "because the first thing that should occur to any aspiring writer—if he be a sensible person—is that a voluntary audience might very well volunteer not to buy tickets."

William shrugged, "I suppose a glance at the dark side of any undertaking is just intelligent planning, but such a realization would not discourage you, would it?"

"Discouragement has nothing to do with it," Marlow growled. "We're talking business here."

"Business?"

"Because the dramatist must now lure an audience for the first time in history, he is compelled to abide closely to public taste in order to succeed commercially. The desires of the people have become paramount, and from now on, neither the Church nor the State nor the Guild can direct content before the writer sits down to write. Organizations may still object to the results of a writer's efforts, but that's another matter."

"I wonder if this change is good or bad for the writer?" William mused.

"Depends on the writer," said Marlowe. "With the exception of a few rare individuals, well-disciplined hacks have done most of the work in the past because there were so many restrictions built into the system, but a young writer today has limitless horizons before him if he be apt at all. History, tragedy, or comedy—take your pick."

"Very inviting possibilities," William said. "Must a writer decide beforehand, I wonder, which category he intends to tackle?"

"Never!" Marlowe exclaimed. "The writer must never be concerned with such trivia. Let him write his fool head off, and let the audience put a label on it. That involvement on their part facilitates the promotional aspect, and permits your customers to match their humor to the spirit of your presentation. Keep the customer happy. That's the ticket in every theater."

"Have you figured out what entertains them best?"

"Novelty is what they're after. They always want something they have not seen a hundred times before. Since they are now paying for it, they demand something fresh and stimulating. They want some laughter, some tears, a bit of gore, and a clever verse or two. If a man could string any kind of story line around those ingredients, he would be well on his way to fame and fortune."

"Sounds simple enough if one could ever muster enough time in this busy life to get started."

"Starting is the key, all right," Marlowe chuckled. "Hard to get much done without it. Yes, indeed, you'll do nicely. We'll burn those rags you're presently wearing and dress you up as a gentleman, which will lend a pleasing note of irony to our grand deception."

"Grand deception?"

"Malachi was quite right," Marlowe stared closely at William again. "It's almost like looking into a mirror, the resemblance is so close. The same hooded, dark eyes. The same high forehead—sign of intellect, you know."

"I'm relieved to hear it; I thought I was losing my hair."

"Same long aristocratic nose, but the mouth is wrong. After the eyes, the mouth reveals us to the world, so keep those lips firm, confident, and generous like mine."

"I'll work on it."

"Identical high, arching sweep on the eyebrows over well-spaced, dark brown eyes. Nostrils well matched, tight enough but flared just a bit. Same soft, rounded end of the nose. I've always regarded my nose as my least attractive feature, if driven to name one. You have too much space between nose and mouth, looks naked. The mustache will help you there, but keep it small and trim as a kind of counterpoint to your eyebrows."

"This must be a very intimate theater where they'd notice things like that."

Marlowe laughed. "It's always face-to-face in this business.

That's the only way this kind of work gets done."

"Is it a speaking part per chance?"

"I wish it were because you have a pleasing, well-pitched voice, but not in this role."

William shrugged. "Just getting my face before the public is one way to begin, I guess. At least let them know my name….when I get one."

"Oh, no. Not at this performance. The whole point is that you pretend to be me at this sitting. Nothing else will get the job done."

"Sitting?"

"Didn't Malachi fill you in on all this?"

"Not a word."

Marlowe sighed. "For reasons which need not concern you but they have to do with pleasing someone I much admire—I must get my portrait done by Christmas, so I have scheduled sittings for the first week of next month. Posing even for a short time is a bore to me. I don't like to sit still anytime, but to do so for days or weeks on end while there is excitement afoot on the Continent is simply too great a burden for me to bear."

"A portrait?"

"So I will simply have you sit in my place while I tend to business in France."

"Sit? As Christopher Marlowe? But the painter will be painting my portrait rather than yours."

"Not at all. He'll just sketch in bone structure and broad outlines from you. I'll be back for the eyes and mouth."

"So that's what my role comes to? Sitting for a broad outline?"

Marlowe shrugged. "We must all start somewhere. Let me have a closer look at those ears." He looked and sighed. "Oh well, I think I better come in for the ears as well."

"What's wrong with my ears?"

"Nothing in the world, I assure you. They are definitely…ahh, distinctive—one of a kind, so to speak. They are you, but quite frankly, they simple do not radiate nobility." He smiled and added kindly, "Not yet anyway. Oh, one other consideration worth noting: your cheeks are a trifle hollow. How much weight can you gain in a month or so?"

"Weight?"

"I suppose it will take you that long to grow the sideboards and mustache, so fall to at the table in the meantime, and we can always hope you'll gain a little in the interval. Actually, because the portrait will be done by a student of Nicholas Hillyarde, who is so busy himself supplying the nobility with his exquisite miniatures that he has no time for full-size work, we can expect—"

"Miniatures?"

"Small, expensive, flattering paintings of loved ones, which may be carried about on your person and displayed to others at various social gatherings."

"Expensive because flattering?"

"Just so," Marlowe nodded. "My painter will be working in the Hillyarde School to create that delicate charm which characterizes his portraits."

"And my fee?"

"One of the ways Hillyarde manages to romanticize his subjects is to make the face thinner than it actually is, and I'm afraid if he took any more off your present visage, the face would look emaciated or even cadaverous. I'll certainly alert him to that danger. Now, as to your costume. You must wear this dark, slashed velvet doublet, always one of my best outfits. Let's see how it fits."

William tried it on, taking obvious pleasure in the handsome garment.

"Now button the collar just above the doublet."

"Will I wear a ruff?"

"Egad, no! I hate that damned Spanish invention. In my mind, people wearing ruffs always seem to be contenders in a look-alike contest for the final appearance of John the Baptist. Besides, if you happen to have a slim, graceful neck, why hide it?"

"No reason in the world," William agreed. "What kind of mood will you want me to strike in the posing?"

"Dreamy. 'trifle aloof and yet still connected with the world."

"Detached? Eyes averted?

"No," Marlowe shook his head. "Eyes straight on with a banked fire lurking deep inside them. I'll fan those flames at the final sittings."

"As though the mind wished to return to higher thoughts?"

"Exactly. Mouth firm but not grim. Generous but not flabby."

"A dreamily alert kind of look?"

"That's it. Let's see what you've got."

William struck a pose, and Marlowe studied him for a minute. "Generally, not bad. He can easily get a decent general impression from you, and I'll spend a day or two with him when it's time for the specific features. Any questions?"

"As yet, there's been no mention of my pay, and I like to get these small details out of the way early."

"And it is just there that you are very lucky," Marlowe said, "because we face a very fortunate situation on that issue."

"I certainly hope so," William said as he touched the slack and silent purse hanging from his hip.

"Malachi assured me you are pretty handy in the signature-to-order department, so part of the grand deception will involve your sneaking into the Cambridge kitchen the week I'm gone to sign my name as furtively as you can in the buttery-book, indicating I took my meals on campus that week."

"Why?"

"Because that signature will not only establish my presence on campus for the week and thereby qualify me to collect the shilling-a-week in sustenance money from my scholarship, but it will also help me fulfill the bothersome residency requirement I must complete on campus before I am awarded my Master's degree."

"It might help me to know who I am avoiding with all this furtive sneaking."

"You must avoid my proctor, Gabriel Harvey, at all costs. He would see through your impersonation instantly and then all would be lost because he is already so peeved at my frequent absences that he is intent on denying me my degree by proving I am not meeting the residency requirement. The man is a complete throwback to the Iron Age, and a total sell-out to the rigid educational establishment with their inflexible, impersonal rules which force an adversarial relationship upon the very students they are supposed to be helping. What's the difference if I'm not on campus when I get the work done?"

"I know you'll pardon me for saying so, but it begins to sound as if Mr. Harvey might have a case."

"Completely beside the point and none of your business besides." Marlowe growled. "Here now, give me the doublet."

"Where will you be visiting on the Continent?" asked William, sliding his arms from the garment. "What will you be doing there?"

Marlowe laughed. "Egad, you are new to the Service just as Malachi said. You have not yet learned that assignments are secret matters not spoken of loosely, especially not by such obvious country bumpkins as yourself."

"Obvious?" challenged William, then relented. "Aye, in light of my present infirmity, I suppose—"

"But after saying that, I feel compelled to add that the inner restraint which I share with all gentleman, urges me to exercise my Christian charity by lighting at least one candle when I encounter the weak-minded. May I?"

"Please do."

"I'll be visiting Rheims, which is a Jesuit training school in France that has become a haven for young English Catholics fleeing their homeland because of what they call 'religious persecution' here. They receive a Catholic education and training as Seminarians in France and then return home after ordination to spread their Roman discontent among our happy Anglicans. Our service tries to keep track of the bright, rabid ones who might cause real trouble if they should ever be turned loose in England. I visit Rheims socially every once in a while because I have many friends there, and because it's an easy jump to the Continent as long as Proctor Harvey doesn't hear of it. I can go over and visit and still return in a week if the travel-imps take a day off and the wind is right. It will be during one of those weeks that I will soon require your services."

"I am ready to serve—with Malachi's approval, of course. I'm surprised the Rheims people let you in since you're not Catholic. Or are you?"

Marlowe coughed a bit. "First, let me say that the Jesuits will educate any well-connected young man who will listen to them, and such recruits are always welcome to visit for as long as they like. The Blackrobes obviously hope that any visitor who is not Catholic when he arrives, will be one when he leaves. But it is, nevertheless, entirely possible to be educated at Rheims and not turn Catholic at all. My good friend, Tom Watson, did exactly that a few years ago. But, secondly, let me point out that our front office wants all operational details treated as absolute secrets, with no exceptions at all. Often lives are at stake in this business, so for their own protection, people know only what they need to know to get their job done properly. At the moment I don't see any need for you to know more than I've already disclosed, so why don't you return to your janitorial duties, and I'll iron out the details of your schedule with your master."

"I'm not surprised you feel that way," William said. "I suppose that's the way all spies must come to feel in the end."

"Spies!" Marlowe thundered as he bolted to his feet and dropped his hand to the hilt of his sword. "You have the unmitigated gall, sirrah, to characterize my contribution—" He paused for a moment. "Yes, I recall now. Malachi mentioned I would either have to kill you outright or learn to forgive your endless rudeness if I intended to work with you."

"Make up your mind quickly," William insisted. "Whichever way you go, I don't intend to waste another minute in apprehension over the outcome." He stood in an exaggerated pose of complete indifference. "Well, which is it to be?"

"By good St. George," Marlowe exclaimed. "I see you've got some belly to you." He slammed his half-drawn rapier back in its scabbard. "Learn quickly then that we do not refer to our fellow nationals as 'spies' anymore than Drake refers to himself as a 'pirate.' We use the word 'spy' to refer to people who report to Rome, Madrid, Paris, or any front office other than Whitehall."

"Non-English," William observed.

"Precisely," Marlowe said. "Or almost precisely if you discount those few English knaves who have deserted their country for a few bags of gold and now do duty for other countries."

"What do you call yourselves then?"

Marlowe frowned. "Are you not one of us? Was Malachi mistaken when he told me you were generally safe to talk to?"

"Absolutely safe," William assured him. "Just forgetful at times."

"Our generic cover term is 'agent'. Sometimes we are referred to as 'messengers' and, on strictly formal occasions, we are called 'Couriers of the Queen.' I'm surprised Malachi hasn't filled you in on all this."

"He has tried," William laughed, "but coherence dwindles as the evening progresses just as it does for your fellow Divinity students when they dine with you, according to our reports."

"What?"

"When you are actually in attendance at Cambridge, you often buy wine enough to soak your friends in alcohol while engaging them in spirited debates about their deepest religious convictions. I suppose you do the same thing at Rheims?"

Marlowe smiled. "You have good information, but don't forget, I do the drinking part too, so no unfair advantage is taken. I feel a free-and-loose, thrashing-and-tumbling of ideas is what college is all about. During the evening's wine tasting at Rheims, the Anglican Church comes in for heavy criticism, but here at home, we hear little fault-finding with our home-grown orthodoxy except from the boys from Puritan homes and from a few thinly concealed Catholic sympathizers."

"Those are the ones you report?"

"Gadzooks, no! I've never reported anybody for religious differences in my life and never will. When we are not free to exercise inquiry at the University, we will have fallen into a tyrannical state indeed. I couldn't care a fig about the typical Anglican-Puritan-Catholic debate over holy water or crucifixes or rosary beads or tables or altars, and I'm sure that God feels the same way."

"I wonder how He really feels about Catholics, deep down?"

"I've already taxed my presumptive powers enough for one day," Marlowe grinned. "Let me just explain that I simply keep track of the interests and inclinations of college students' opinions on popular issues of the day. I estimate percentages of prevailing opinions, but I do not implicate individuals. In effect, I am the college correspondent for Walsingham's monthly C.T.R. Report."

"C.T.R.?"

"Current Threat to the Realm Report. Walsingham presents it each month to the Queen, because Walsingham's big job—his only job, actually—is protecting Elizabeth by keeping track of England's present and future enemies."

"I thought Walsingham was the Survey Director?"

Marlowe shrugged, "He is. It's the same thing. In the field we refer to him publicly as Mr. Secretary, our boss, the Survey Director, rather than as our boss, the Head of English Secret Service, for reasons which I hope are obvious to you. Survey

Director is a cover. Are you really slow or is your master keeping you in the dark on purpose?"

William smiled, "Some of each perhaps, but who can tell what Malachi is up to? I'm coming to realize there is no limit to his deception. Tell me how things are going on the collegiate level.

What can I expect when I sneak onto the Cambridge campus?"

"The usual late-night collegiate intellectual turmoil for the most part, but big changes are occurring in registration. Cambridge has become a Puritan stronghold, and they are gaining numbers over the more moderate Anglicans just as they are in The Commons. As a matter of fact, Puritan power at Cambridge has gained so much recent muscle, school administrators must be cautious when making policy changes for fear of offending Puritan principles and touching off student rioting which will start with broken windows and monuments knocked over, but end up God knows where."

"Sounds like they are ready to spread their influence," William chuckled.

"The holier-than-thou Puritans are a very pushy bunch and will someday overwhelm the rest of us if this particular trend goes unabated. Simmering discontent among the Catholic-leaning students, however, remains stable, so every term a few leave for Rheims to combat what they regard as England's descent into heresy."

"I suppose religious thinking encourages deep thoughts on the part of the participants," William mused.

"You would think so," Marlowe agreed, "but like many other impressions in this life, such opinions need close examination. You really can't expect the average mind to dwell long on the mystery of Trans-substantiation, or the wonder of the Holy Trinity, or the God-man aspect of Jesus Christ. Once you realize you confront a mystery, all you can do is shrug your shoulders and move on to something you can chew on. The differences in decorative detail for the worship area which seem to preoccupy many clergymen—pointless though these distinctions may seem—nonetheless are discernible and thereby give the mind an area it can comprehend."

"You mean the setting of the stage during service is the principal point of argument among the Anglicans and Catholics and Puritans?"

"That's the core of the onion all right," Marlowe chuckled. "But radiating out from that center, you find many layers of sects who nurture their own little distinctions from the mainstream and cultivate their own brand of animosity toward the opinions of others. In a recent sermon, Bishop Bancroft said: *'The Apostle Paul did prophesy that there should be many false prophets, and we do see his sayings therein to be fulfilled by the number of such prophets as now remain among us—Arians, Donatists, Papists, Libertines, Anabaptists, the Family of Love, and sundry others.'"* [4]

"The Family of Love?"

"Pretty small numbers compared to the growing mass of Puritans," Marlowe grinned, "but a nice touch on Bancroft's part to throw all the non-conformists into one tidy bundle like that. He stirs up an aggressive them-or-us, back-to-the-wall mood on the part of his beleaguered Anglican flock. His position not only saves time and energy by not bothering to draw distinctions between the competing anti-Anglican sects, but permits greater focus on the solicitation of funds for the one true Church, so that our bishops may sink a little deeper into the cushiony fat of the land and argue endlessly about the most arcane elements of theology which their minds can discover at the bottom of port wine goblets."

"I noticed at the Inn that the clergy are rather given to port," William mused. "I wonder why that is?"

"It dulls the dagger of doubt," Marlowe explained. "It provides the perfect anodyne for men who are secretly aware they are frittering away their lives arguing over trifles and trinkets which obviously do not interest the one true God in the least."

"You sound very certain."

"Can you imagine a real God who cares which vestments are worn during Congregation? Who seriously cares whether a table or altar is used during the performance? Who takes note of whether you are standing or sitting or kneeling during the various stages of adoration?"

"I've always assumed God to be flexible and multifaceted myself."

"Exactly!" Marlowe exclaimed. "The old diamond-in-the-sky concept: sees all, knows all, forgives all. Perfectly willing to give you a break as long as you behave yourself reasonably well." He paused to chuckle. "Not quite the wrathful, fault-finding God the Puritans are trying to sell us."

"Malachi mentioned that the Puritans take themselves and the world around them very seriously indeed."

"Not much humor anyway," Marlowe smiled, "but I find that characteristic very endearing when I am setting up an evening's entertainment at the ale-house."

"How so?"

"One has only to say something a little outrageous to get them to sputtering and stammering in such an amusing fashion it would make your ribs ache with laughter. They simply lose it when you drop a conversational petard in their midst."

"Petard?"

"Explosive device. A bomb. Or in the original Latin, a fart. I tell them that Sir Walter Raleigh's man Harriot knows more than their Biblical Moses ever did. I insist that Harriot can do tricks which match the Biblical miracles of antiquity. They become positively incoherent with indignation."

"I suppose people who take themselves too seriously in discourse leave themselves open to more devious individuals."

"You can count on it," Marlowe agreed, "but make no mistake. If I weren't sticking it to them, they would besiege me non-stop with Biblical citations urging me to mend my ways and save myself before it's too late."

William smiled. "And I imagine you have additional theological insights with which to fend them off?"

Marlowe chuckled, "I don't even let them catch their breath before I tell them I have a suggestion whereby they can make a simple but profound change in their religious worship and once and for all radically distinguish the Anglican service from the Catholic mass whose form they carried with them when Henry broke with Rome back in the Thirties."

"I thought I heard they changed a lot of things to distinguish the two different forms of worship?"

"They did some cosmetic changes; no more altars or holy water or rosary beads or crucifixes or signs of the cross or genuflections or ashes on Ash Wednesday or palms on Palm Sunday, and a minimizing of reference to Mary, but they still desire the kind of big sweeping change that I advise in order to dramatically distinguish once and for all the Anglican ceremony from the Catholic mass."

"I'm all ears."

"I encourage them to enlarge upon their successful Holy Trinity promotion by adding to the Communion ritual the drinking of sanctified tobacco fumes to go along with the wafers and wine. In addition to the symbolic body and blood of Christ then, people could actually see God if they were instructed that the sacred smoke was the image of the Holy Ghost. "lot of visual appeal in such an approach."

"You probably find sputtering and stammering more entertaining than most people would," William concluded. "I suppose you have other suggestions to impart?"

"Endless supply," Marlowe chortled. "Since their minds are so fettered and fixated, mine is free to move about and undermine them from whichever angle will best overset their pietistic posturing."

"Might there not be some personal danger for you in voicing such blasphemous thoughts?"

"Danger?" Marlowe exclaimed. "I salute it! The very elixir of youth! Life would be very pale without its sharp nip. I don't think I'd get any writing done if deprived of its unique, acrid taste."

"You seem to like a lot of things heavily seasoned," William observed, "but, believe me, many of us would be happy to do our work without that particular spice."

"Suit yourself," Marlowe shrugged. "Malachi mentioned you would be tied up with some kind of unfinished business for a few weeks, and that works well because my next scheduled absence from school will be next month. I've arranged for the portrait painter to get started that same week, so remember, I'm counting on you to stay in Cambridge at that time. Don't forget to grow the mustache and sideboards and help yourself to seconds at table in the interim."

"Do I get to spend the shilling a week that I forge your name for?"

Marlowe chuckled, "I like to see a man who knows how to press his bet, but don't plan on getting rich so fast. Newly acquired wealth brings its own problems, believe me. However, I'll be happy to set you a challenge—a performance incentive, if you will. If you can be furtive enough to avoid my nemesis, Proctor Harvey, you have earned the shilling honorably, and it is yours with my blessings."

Chapter 2:
LORD BURGHLEY AND
FRANCIS WALSINGHAM

Black Boar Inn, the Common Room, mid-November:

"Are there ever any time-out periods in this employment?" William asked. "Am I ever free to make future appointments with my friends that I will be sure of keeping?"

Malachi answered with a sardonic chuckle. "You might as well get used to disappointing other people while you are in our service because no matter what arrangements you make, God alone knows if you'll be free to carry them out when the time comes. If we're not running errands for one supervisor, we are for the other, and no prior arrangement is allowed to stand in the way of carrying out those duties."

"We have two bosses?"

"Yes, and this seems a good time for me to explain the difference between a B-order and a W-order and why one must always take precedent over the other."

"Start at the beginning, if you please," groaned William.

"Well," grinned Malachi, "aside from a few Court favorites who profit personally from the Queen's indulgent whims, everybody in England, either directly or indirectly, works for the man the Queen calls her 'Spirit': Robert Cecil or Lord Burghley, the Royal Treasurer. He has regulated England's commercial and economic policies during the twenty-eight years of Elizabeth's reign with a far-seeing view which is said to 'neglect present profits.' English commerce has prospered under his light-handed guidance, and he has been alert enough to encourage new enterprises with subsidies and monopolies to prevent a trade imbalance developing with the Continent. He has warned his luxury-loving countrymen for years that *'Nothing robbeth England more than imports over exports'*. [5] He even has the Privy Council invested in Drake's new trip that nobody knows anything about."

"Egad, he must be a master politician to hang onto office for nearly thirty years. What kind of man is he?"

"I've often shared a glass of the good stuff with his household chaplain, who is obviously partisan but honest enough for a good chat. He cites a great many of Burghley's character traits as the foundation for his success, seeing his master as honest, temperate, sociable, and extremely hard working."

"Pretty predictable," William observed. "No surprises?"

"One. The chaplain said that Burghley is *'delighted to talk and be merry with his friends, only at meals; for he had no more leisure. He never had any favourite (as they are termed) nor any inward companion, as great men commonly have. Neither made any man of his counsel, nor did ever any know his secrets: some noting it for a fault, but most thinking it a praise and an instance of his wisdom. For by trusting none with his secrets, none could reveal them.'"* [6]

"So the B-orders will be from Lord Burghley?"

"Right, and they would be our highest priority apart from an order from the Queen. As I mentioned, one way or another, we all work for Burghley, but we are part of the group that works indirectly for him. Indirectly means the connection must never be mentioned nor acknowledged even under pain of—whatever comes along."

"How do we get our orders then?"

"Under Burghley's direction, we report to Walsingham, Secretary to the Queen and head of our Survey Service. In addition to my courier and scrivener duties, I serve as a ready-reference file for Walsingham. Under his direction, I've read every official government document for the last twenty years, and I must admit as a point of pride, getting to the unofficial ones is also part of my job, and I've read most of them too. I read the official ones in his office."

"Why? Can't he read them himself?"

"Oh, he does. He reads everything. "very conscientious man is Mr. Secretary Walsingham. Completely devoted to his job. Reads it all and makes marginal notes on everything."

"From what you're saying I presume some of this is important stuff, even secret stuff, so why in the world would one of England's leading public officials reveal such material to you?"

"Well, that's my main job, you see. Walsingham calls me his letter-box. The truth is that Walsingham has no memory at all. For a man who has to collate hundreds of little scraps of information each month, such an impediment would be quite a handicap if he didn't employ me as his proxy-memory."

116

"He doesn't remember anything?"

"He has an ordinary memory. He can remember the gist of things a few months hence, but not the exact words."

"But you can?"

"Oh, yes. I remember everything word for word. A picture of the page I've scanned springs to my mind if I close my eyes and concentrate, and I just read right off the picture. People who know about such things tell me I have a pictographic memory."

"That's extraordinary." William's eyes were alight with admiration.

Malachi shrugged. "Unusual enough anyway, but there are others with the same ability. You'll meet some of them before we go far."

"How extensive are Walsingham's files?"

"Absolutely voluminous. Walsingham has a greater craving for information than the combined thirst of all of London's ale-drinkers at closing time. He not only has files on all the leading families in the realm but notes on their personal relations with each other and on their arguments, affairs, and agreements. He is not only familiar with the workings of our major seaports but with every creek bed along our coast. He knows who counts in every county and how to contact the men who can get things done in every part of the country. Walsingham likes to cross-check his files often to find any possible connection between certain people and certain other people and between certain dates and certain actions, but he feels he spends too much time scanning endless documents for individual items when I'm not around to pinpoint them for him. As a consequence, he likes to keep me close at hand. He must always know where we are and how to reach us. That will be part of your job."

"Keeping us in contact with Walsingham's office?

Malachi nodded. "When I am busy elsewhere. Sometimes in foreign lands."

"Does that mean I'll have to go back and forth to the Continent alone?"

"Unknowable at this point," said Malachi. "We often have dependable messengers close at hand, however, who may be sent most of the way without your traveling very far, but this is an important responsibility, so, in the end, you are to do whatever it takes."

"Why does the office send you off on travels to foreign lands then? Isn't that a pretty big risk to take for the kind of valuable repository you purport to be?"

"Can't be helped. It's a trade-off strategy we decided on long ago. If you have valuable people, you either isolate them completely—as Walsingham usually does with his in-house code-breaker and forger, Phillippes—or else you hide them by mixing them with the crowd. Spain has friends and agents at all levels in England. They would love to discover which people Walsingham values most, and then do just as they have done in the past: either pension them or poison them."

"Pension them?"

"Put them on salary. They are called 'bridging-agents' but are turncoats, none-theless. Spain makes sure the underhanded payoff exceeds the regular pay from the home agency."

"So by going on ordinary trips, you appear to be an ordinary courier?"

Malachi nodded. "Ordinary in one sense, yes, but everybody knows an observant courier is just about half-way to being a full-fledged spy, and that's a part I enjoy play-ing. I like to look around."

"It must be quite a rest from all that reading."

Malachi laughed. "I don't read things in the intellectual sense. I mean the con-tents don't wander like troublesome banshees through my mind when I'm off duty. It's more of an optical thing. Once I run my eyes over them, they're imprinted in my mind as though they came right off a printing press."

"Why don't they call such extraordinary ability a printographic mind then?"

Malachi shrugged. "Society never quite catches up with the latest scientific devel-opments. By the time they accepted the term 'printographic mind,' there would be some new concept looming over the horizon."

"Back to precedent, then: Walsingham's orders can be upstaged by Burghley's?"

"Yes, because in the big four of Royal advisors—Burghley, Leicester, Walsingham, and Raleigh, Lord Burghley stands highest in the Queen's estimation. More than anybody else, he speaks directly for her, so his orders carry more authority. All you have to remember is that the B-orders are to supercede the W-orders anytime there is conflict between the two."

William frowned. "There really shouldn't be much disagreement between loyal officials in the same government, should there? Aren't they just there to carry out the orders of the Queen?"

"There is room for disagreement even between well-intentioned men with the same background," Malachi explained, "but when you match the convictions of a younger, confident, and aggressive Puritan like Walsingham with those of an elderly, cautious, and skeptical Anglican like Burghley, you have changed possible disagree-ment into virtual certainty."

"Interesting. What differences?"

"Walsingham, for instance, is dead-set on bringing our difficulties with Spain out in the open and publicly declaring war. Burghley is dead-set on carrying on negotia-tions endlessly as long as they avoid open conflict. Walsingham thinks the war is in-evitable, so an open declaration would free up funds to get the fleet ready and arm the trained bands. He says that new information which is now pending adds substance to the rumor that Philip has decided to cross the Rubicon and has ordered up a huge fleet which will come against England in a year or two whether we like it or not, and that no peace conference will stop Philip when he is ready to strike."

"Umm, it's impressive how often our policy makers hide behind that 'new information pending' gambit. Is it a stall or completely bogus?"

"Neither," Malachi growled. "And try to remember there is a price to pay for pandering to your youthful cynicism because, over time, such self-indulgence will constrict your blood vessels and hamper your breathing. As it occurs, our office has just now acquired hard evidence to validate the rumors we've been hearing since summer about Spain's Grand Enterprise. Walsingham has just received documents showing there has been a tremendous increase in the quantity of maritime stores being shipped from the Baltic and Nordic ports straight to Spain and to the Italian ports which Spain controls. That can only mean that Philip has taken the first step in systematically building an enormous fleet."

"What maritime stores? Ropes and sails?"

"Everything from cordage, tar, and tallow to spars and ship timber—whatever it takes to build a ship. Spain has ordered those materials in such large quantities that it can only mean the Dons are laying the foundation for the largest modern fleet ever assembled, whose purpose will be made quite clear to the English heretics in good time."

"How much time?" asked William fearfully. "How soon could Spain put an invasion fleet together?"

"Anybody's guess. There are many variables. For instance, Santa Cruz, Admiral of the Spanish navy, is a brave man but elderly, and, while he has proved courageous in battle and faithful in duty, he may be the wrong man to direct the endless details and tireless supervision required in building such an armada."

"The difference between a man of action and an administrator, right?

But if Santa Cruz could handle the project and things went reasonably well, how long, would you say?"

"It would make a big difference in construction time if Philip dared to strip his New World colonies of protection by having the ten first-class galleons which now guard his bullion carriers and the nine Portuguese men-of-war which guard his newly acquired Asian trade routes transferred over to the proposed invasion fleet. Such an addition would provide a powerful nucleus for any fleet and it would cut the time of assembling that force considerably, but it would leave the colonies—along with Spain's gold, silver, silk and spice supply—much more at risk from pirates and adventurers."

"Assuming he won't risk reassigning his two guardian fleets, how long would it take him to put an invasion fleet together?"

"It would depend heavily on knowing how big a package he proposed. Invasion plans come in big, small and medium packages, you know."

"How big would big be?"

"I can help you there. We have a copy of the contingency plan for the invasion of England which Santa Cruz prepared for Philip three years ago, and, believe me, in this case, the Admiral was thinking big because he was fresh from a naval victory against irregular continental forces off the Canary Islands. His plan called for some five hundred and fifty-six ships, of which one hundred and eighty had to be first-class galleons. In addition, he wanted two-hundred flat-bottomed boats which would be carried on board the bigger ships to be used as landing craft. The ships would be manned by a crew of thirty-thousand sailors and they would carry an invasion force of sixty-five thousand Spanish regulars, who were to be landed directly in England under cover of one hundred galleons assigned to destroy whatever English naval forces might oppose the landing."

William shuddered. "Pretty impressive numbers."

"Impressive but not quite realistic," said Malachi. "For one thing, I don't know if, even today, you could round up a total of one hundred and fifty galleons fit for battle. I imagine Philip knew that the ambition of his admiral was still pumped up after winning the big naval battle against an odd assortment of contenders for possession of Portugal's former Atlantic colonies in the Azores and Canaries and Madeira—all of which ended up with empty flagpoles when Spain annexed Portugal five years ago. Philip is wise enough to discount the ambitious-warrior element in plans from his military since no one knows better than he who it is that must decant those coarse numbers into the fine wine of attainment."

"And you think Philip will reduce the numbers. To what? Medium?"

"Walsingham thinks Philip may be planning a fleet about one third the size of Santa Cruz's proposal, but still the biggest modern fleet ever assembled: one hundred and fifty ships and thirty thousand troops—enough veteran Spanish regulars to give our trained bands a sound pummeling if they ever make it ashore. In a military sense, Spain's new plan seems achievable as far as Philip's treasury is concerned; therefore, the feeling in the Office is that the earliest they could sail against us, even if the construction phase went well for them, would be about mid-1587. So we have until then to get ready."

"Will we do it? Will we get ready? Will the Queen call for subsidies?"

"Not as long as she agrees with Burghley that war is never inevitable, that all difficulties can be negotiated, that war is incredibly costly and, worst of all, plays havoc with trade, and that your native people consequently grow discontent because they lose their livelihoods."

"And this is the basis of the conflicting instructions from B and W?"

"It is. And sometimes the conflict shows up in the middle of a half-completed job, and we have to whirl-about and undo our apparatus without leaving a trace."

"No wonder your hair is graying if you've been dancing to that tune for long."

120

"Gray or not, I'm happy to have any hair at all. I've seen men no older than yourself lose theirs."

"Ah. Does this mean you have had new thoughts on what my age might be?"

"Well, actually, I was talking to an interesting young man in Italy not long ago—name of Galileo. He struck me as very near your age in terms of skin tone and carriage and such. He mentioned he was born in April of 1564, so, for all practical purposes, you could consider that your birth year and month."

"That would make me twenty-one," William reflected. "Yes. That seems about right. You said young Galileo was interesting?"

At this moment they were approached by a surly-looking workman.

"Curb your tongue with this one," murmured Malachi. "He's a hothead, though one of our network. Good day, Simon. In for your midday victuals, are you?"

"Nay, just checking the inns hereabout for caterpillars. Same as you, I don't doubt."

"Caterpillars?" squeaked William.

Simon gave the apprentice a baleful stare. "Who be this knave?"

"This is my scribe, William. We call the Catholic seminarians from France 'caterpillars,' Will, because they slither around England spreading heresy and discontent. We figure there are above one hundred newly ordained priests loose in the realm at this very moment, and when we have nothing more specific to do, it is part of our assignment to run them to ground."

"And then we burn the bastards!" snarled Simon, rubbing his hands together with relish.

Malachi grunted and glanced at William's shocked face. "An occasional one, as an example," he placated, "or a famous one if we can catch him. In my opinion, we had enough wholesale burning when Elizabeth's sister, Queen Mary, burned over three hundred Protestants during her five year reign."

"Aye, Bloody Mary, damn her Catholic soul! And now it be our turn to put the fear of God into the Papists!"

"Ah well, martyrdom is like a recruiting broadside for those people. For every one burned, three or four young men from the old Catholic families in the North run off to Rheims for their share of Catholic bunkum. I myself think it best to keep the whole thing quiet by deporting them with their sacred promise not to return. Quench their fire without public attention, as it were."

"Bosh!" said Simon. "You know well as me that their 'sacred promise' don't mean dirt when 'tis given to heretics such as we be in their eyes. 'Voiding a compact with the devil'—that's their excuse for betrayin' agreement."

Malachi nodded. "Unfortunately, you are at least partially right about that. Some of the young men will return despite having given their word. Honor comes in different forms for different men, but I like to give it a chance to blossom where it will. If we catch them a second time, however, I am in favor of branding them with an 'S' on both seminarian cheeks and casting them out of England forever."

"Might as well give 'em a medal," Simon scoffed. "They'd be celebrated at Rheims for bearing such brands. It ain't our job to set up heroes for exiled English traitors to rally 'round."

Malachi chuckled. "You probably represent the majority view there, Simon, but I suspect history will show more rallying done around martyrs than around heroes. I just hate to see brave, bright young men mistrusted so seriously as to be put to death rather than taken at their word, even if they are on the wrong side, or—more exactly—the side other than ours."

Simon frowned. "You ain't seemin' too happy about your duty here, Malachi. Maybe you ben't the right man to be huntin' down them you seems to admire so much. Mayhap I should tell to Bishop Bancroft some of what's been said here today."

"Please do," Malachi growled. "I don't mention anything to you that I expect to go unreported. And if I could be relieved of this noisome duty, it would relax me greatly. It seems to me we are little better than Spain itself when we burn a man at the stake because his conscience drives him in a direction other than our own."

"You go too far now!" sputtered Simon. "I've a mind to mark down them words—"

"Go right ahead," said Malachi through clenched teeth, "and be sure to include—"

"Malachi! Sir!" interrupted William in alarm. "Perhaps it were best if you wrote out such important thoughts beforehand and then took the time to edit them. We certainly wouldn't want Simon here reporting off-hand remarks in the same conversation where burning at the stake is mentioned, would we?"

Malachi grunted. "Perhaps you're right, lad, but my thoughts on the matter are already known at headquarters."

Simon eyed Malachi slyly. "One thing I'd like to know. If you grabbed a caterpillar and he refused t' promise to stay out'n the country, would you turn him in, even if it meant the stake, or would you let 'im go loose to join his den of Papist vipers, even now when Spain is building up a fleet agin us?"

"I would not turn him loose," said Malachi wearily. "And if he were fool enough to refuse banishment, I would have to turn him in. But it would do my stomach little good."

Simon stared awhile, then shrugged. "I guess a 'alf-hearted patriot is better'n none at all, so I'll just forget about this 'ere exchange. But I advise you t' mind your tongue, Malachi, because there's them in the Service who ain't as understanding as me."

"Really?" muttered William in mock wonder.

Malachi got up, paid their tab, and led William from the inn.

"Is Simon one of those Puritan fanatics?" William asked.

"Mean ignoramus, more like," answered Malachi. "You should know we have men in the Service that can do their job and still maintain a civilized attitude. I'd like you to meet two such, who live here above the market. I hope you aren't too tired for one more lesson."

"No sir, but I pray you contain your displeasure in the future. I am not accustomed to seeing my guardian slipping the bounds of civility, and I was somewhat unnerved."

Chapter 3:
EX-PRIESTS IN ENGLAND'S SECRET SERVICE

Above the market, same time:

Malachi grinned. "Sullivan and O'Brien are former Catholic priests, now loyal to the Queen. Very tolerant of both Anglican and Catholic and well informed on the history of each. Good men to have on our side."

William followed his master to the back of the market and up the stairs, where he stood nervously while Malachi knocked on a door.

"Sean!" Malachi greeted the man who opened the door. "We've just spent a half hour with Simon, and the lad here got a heavy dose of bile against the Purple Harlot of Rome. Are you and Sullivan free to help us wash the taste out of our mouths?"

"Aye, come in, lads. Shamus and I were just sitting down to a glass of wine and would welcome your joining us." Introductions were made, glasses were filled, and the conversation turned to the Catholic issue.

"It will probably aid your understanding of the Catholic Church, Will," O'Brien explained, "if you imagine it as a large consulting firm rather than as the Harlot reference used by those who hate and fear her."

"A consulting firm in the spiritual sense?" William asked.

"Most assuredly, but the Church is not above offering advice in trade and government matters if called into consultation. Moral guidance surely is needed in a marketplace full of sinners and governments full of the spawn of Beelzebub," grinned O'Brien.

"I've heard that too," admitted William.

"Since all policy-makers need spiritual guidance, the Church does not hesitate to go where the need is greatest. And in order to assure that the interests of God are always protected, the Church retains a staff of experienced Florentine and Venetian merchants to advise her in commercial matters. That way she always knows where her best interests lie."

"I bet the Dutch merchants could advise in business matters too," volunteered William. "But, of course, they are mostly Protestant."

"Perhaps you have heard it said," interrupted Sulliven softly, "that the closer you get to Rome, the less spiritual is the atmosphere. One of our fellow priests told us he could scarce hear the Vatican Mass for all the loud talk going on among the Vatican staff." Sullivan grinned. "But to give credit where credit is due, the Catholic Church has fulfilled its mission of guidance for over a thousand years, right up until this century here in England before Henry VIII took over. Single-handedly, throughout Western Europe, the Churchmen civilized the barbarians and restrained the baser side of human nature....for the most part. Those early founders of the Church deserve their sainthood if only for erecting the structure that has lasted for twelve centuries, so far."

"I like baptism best," mused William. "The idea of cleansing a newborn of its sins——"

"I was thinking more of the business end," corrected Sulliven gently. "The institution of Peter's Pence or tithing, for instance, is a direct steal from the Roman practice of Romescot, which followed ancient practice throughout the Mediterranean part of the world."

"Romescot?"

Sulliven nodded. "Don't forget now, the Catholic Church didn't flourish until the collapse of the Roman Empire in 414 AD when Emperor Constantine turned Christian. Up until that time, the Christians had been a persecuted minority. Constantine, of course, saw to it that the men behind the scenes—the accountants and record keepers—joined him in his conversion, and their first assignment was to put the new church on a sound financial basis. They all knew that the success of the Roman Empire's one-thousand year reign was largely due to a judicious application of the Romescot policy."

"Romescot?" William asked again.

The Irishman smiled. "'We're getting there. The Romans were able to govern for so long because they succeeded in stationing garrisons throughout every country they conquered. They weren't just passing through. They were here in England for five hundred years, you know."

"We've heard," grinned Malachi.

"Those garrisons had to be fed and those soldiers had to be paid by somebody. That's where the Romescot tax came in. Generally, it was a 10% cut of all harvests and profits generated by the surrounding countryside. The system worked very well until the Romans got greedy and upped the tax. Then they ran into spirited resistance—most particularly in Jerusalem."

Malachi laughed. "Home of those other astute businessmen!"

"Aye, you might well say it was heavy taxation that resulted in the decline and fall of the Roman Empire," said O'Brien.

Sulliven waited politely to continue. "So, Constantine's administrators had learned their lesson well. They not only changed the name of the Romescot to Peter's Pence, they changed its very nature. It was no longer demanded as tribute, it was solicited in diplomatic fashion. Instead of having Roman soldiers back up its enforcement, it offered indulgences and holy relics, bestowed or withheld to balance its accounts. Also, the early Church knew enough to return to the 10% entitlement, which had worked so well for the Romans. But, alas, in the last two centuries, the Church has made the same mistake the Romans made and, consequently, is suffering the same decline if not yet the same fall."

"They've become greedy," guessed William.

"Good lad," Sullivan nodded. "Most thriving communities can afford the 10% tithe as long as they have been seasoned in the virtues of charity and piety. But if the bite gets much beyond 10%, the solid rock of religious conviction begins to experience fissures of uncertainty. Over a hundred years ago, the Church fathers decided to augment the Peter's Pence stipend by putting the saving of souls onto the open marketplace by selling costly indulgences and blessings to those who could afford them. The escalating cost of assuring a heavenly after-life caught many souls short and encouraged Martin Luther to nail his objections to such a blatant sale of salvation to the door of the Wittenburg Church."

"That certainly stirred some souls," William observed.

"Luther thereby opened a floodgate of taxpayer resentment which has since engulfed the Church in Hamburg and Geneva and, of course, here in England. Any governing body which permits its unruly citizens to center their discontent on a taxation issue, may soon find its right to tax them at all called into question."

"Death and taxes," murmured William. "Hard to avoid. Incredibly interesting that the taxation issue has been so instrumental in the reformation movement away from the Catholic faith."

"Indeed it is," O'Brien nodded. "I would rate the rejection of taxes right up there with the reaction against church holidays when it came to forcing a whole society to reconsider its allegiance to any one faith."

"Church holidays? Who would object to holidays?"

Sullivan patted William on the shoulder. "Yours is the voice of youth, lad. But consider! A great majority of your fellow Londoners are men of business, and being shut down one or even two days a week to celebrate religious holidays was quite costly, even for the workers. You can see a backlog of resentment lay festering in the breast of many an Englishman."

"The Catholic Church had a stranglehold on the finances of all Western Europe," said Malachi. "Early in this century, the Church owned almost half of the wealth of Germany, three quarters the wealth of France, and perhaps a third of England's finest estates. Of course, the Papal States comprised one third of Italy. Excuse me for interrupting, gentlemen. It seemed a good time to slide that information in."

"No, no. You're quite right," exclaimed the ex-priests. "Young William here needs to know that even when Elizabeth ascended the throne in 1558, two-thirds of our English population were still Catholic, especially in the northern and western counties, which were mostly agricultural. Her father's break with Rome was mostly in matters of control and finances. He promoted a quasi-Catholic faith without accepting the Papacy, and the Anglican Church under Elizabeth is still the same. The queen, in fact, enjoys the Catholic ceremony and the drama of the mass. She keeps the crucifix in her private chapel and retains familiar rituals from the Catholic liturgy—all of which pleases her Catholic subjects."

"We're quite sure, in fact, that she feels the Protestant creed has no more validity than the Catholic creed. Like most leaders, she values religious faith for its promotion of domestic tranquility within her realm. It was her sister Mary—now known as the infamous Bloody Mary for all her burning of Protestants—that put the final period to any chance of England ever becoming a Catholic nation again."

O'Brien smiled at William. "Imagine the stir it caused when Mary and her consort, Philip of Spain, tried to take back the Papal properties that had been distributed to Englishmen by Henry VIII."

"Gadzooks," cried William. "Easier to pry a baby from a mother's arms!"

"Very true, William," said Sullivan, "but all is not property and profit that stirs the continuing English debate over how different the Anglican religion must become from its early Catholic roots before it can be regarded as a pure religion of its own."

"The Puritans!"

"Aye, the Protestants who demand absolute change from everything which resembles Catholicism. The purists, in short. And they are more militant than the Catholics, fighting as they are for a new idea and fearful of a repetition of the sufferings of the Protestants under Bloody Mary."

"Have you ever seen John Foxe's *The Book of Martyrs,* published in 1559?" asked O'Brien. "It chronicles the torture and burning of the Protestants under Bloody

Mary in shocking detail accompanied by gruesome woodcuts. It's enough to start a religious war all by itself. And it may yet."

"Did you know John Foxe is a good friend of Francis Drake?" asked Malachi.

"Ah, yes, another example of Puritan vitality. 'Tis fortunate that Drake has chosen the high seas on which to vent his energies," laughed O'Brien. "It's the preachers and politicians who incite the radicals and thus threaten the tranquility of our fair land."

"Aye, they are great ones for condemnation. In Parliament, the growing number of Puritans rail against the Anglican hierarchy of bishops and archbishops as 'a thing introduced to the church by Satan.' Our Book of Common Prayer, they say, has been 'culled and picked out of that popish dung-hill, the breviary and mass book.' Just last week the students of Cambridge University—the intellectual seed-bed of the Puritan movement—staged a revolt, tore up the campus statues, broke windows and skipped classes–all because of some alleged offense against Puritan beliefs." [7]

"Ah yes," sighed O'Brien. "They set the children to spying, looking for omens and portents among the Puritan community–things like 'blasphemy, whoredom, drunkenness, railing against religion, scolds, ribalds, and such like.' Then at their weekly meetings, these so-called sinners are publicly condemned. Dancing is forbidden, along with drinking and gambling, and dining on dainty foods. Festivals are outlawed and theatrical groups are run out of town–"

"Bloody hell!" gasped William.

"And swearing, of course," added O'Brien quickly. "A great deal of this condemnation is aimed at the Court and at our blessed Queen, who is, as you know, gifted in both dancing and swearing."

"Ah yes, our beloved Elizabeth swears by Christ's wounds, by his death, his head, and several other of his organs. And by all the saints, of course." Sullivan sighed. "One Puritan named Fuller left her a note saying, 'By your majesty's evil example and sufferance, the most part of your subjects and people of every degree, do commonly swear and blaspheme, to God's unspeakable dishonor, without any punishment.'" [8]

"They dare to criticize our queen?" cried William.

"Indeed, they do. More and more blatantly. Reverend Wentworth recently ranted before Parliament, 'Certain it is that none is without fault, no not our noble queen, since her majesty hath committed great faults, yea dangerous faults to herself.'" [9]

"Surely." gasped William.

"Oh, yes," laughed Sullivan, "he was hustled to the Tower before he could say more. But these are grim men, these Puritans, full of self-denial and quick to condemn the ordinary pastimes and any self-indulgence by others. They clearly detest any kind of fancy adornment and beauty. But, most of all, I cringe that their scheme of things has no place for humor or joy, which are, of course, the lifeblood of us Irish—when all else fails."

"Aye, God forbid we dance with '*disordinate gestures, and with monstrous thumping of the feet....[or sing] wanton songs, to dishonest verses*'." O'Brien refilled the wine goblets all around.

"They have their own kind of madness and hysteria, which must be an enjoyment to them. At a service at Elizabeth's chapel in the palace, a wild man ran up to the altar, shouting and cursing, and threw down the candlesticks and the cross—those hated symbols of Catholicism—and stomped them beneath his boots. Later he was questioned, and he held up the Bible, saying the book told him to do it."

"They sound very dangerous," frowned William. "Can no one stop them?"

"Both Elizabeth and King James of Scotland recognize that an attack on their bishops is also an attack on their crowns. King James recently said, '*No bishops eventually means no kings*.' But not everyone seems aware of the danger. The last Archbishop of Canterbury, Edmund Grindal, lost his position when he refused to cool off a Puritan revival meeting in his district as requested by the queen. He said he felt such meetings—called prophesyings—were beneficial to spiritual life even if they included such Puritan diatribes as: '*Satan is roaring like a lion, the world is going mad. Anti-Christ is resorting to every extreme, that he may with wolf-like ferocity devour the sheep of Christ.*" [10]

"I might admire their flamboyant style if I could imagine their welcoming me and my plans for the future into their fold," confessed William. "But if I write historical plays, they certainly would forbid me the use of colorful costumes, and no bawdy jokes to please the apprentices would be allowed. Oh, my."

The ex-priests smiled sympathetically. "In times like these," said Sullivan, "we do best, I suppose, to concentrate on pleasing our reigning monarch. Even such hotheads as the Puritans would not dare override the head of state."

Later, as Malachi and William rose to leave, O'Brien clapped his hand on Malachi's shoulder. "You have a delightful and intelligent lad here, Malachi. Bring him along anytime. We will be delighted to help you train him in whatever you are up to for the Service."

Chapter 4:
TO CATCH A PRIEST

Common Room at the Black Boar Inn the following morning:

"Ah, Mercy, my dear," exclaimed Malachi, standing up from the table where he was breakfasting. "Just in time to join me."

"Where is the madcap apprentice?"

"Still sleeping. But I need to discuss business with you, so please sit down with me and eat."

"I thought you might have sent the young fool on his way by now," said Mercy, as she prepared to fill her mouth with sausage and toast.

"You really must learn, m'dear, that you cannot cast aside the fools of this world so casually or you may end up with no friends at all. I have already explained that I am in his debt."

"Surely your precious men's code does not require you to dance endless attendance on strangers who do you a small service."

"Now, Mercy, I refuse to waste another word justifying the male canon of honorable behavior which has always proved such a mystery to you. All you need to know is that I prospered from the moment I crossed paths with that young man, so I am obliged to see him through his crisis. Besides, he amuses me and I like him. Now to business. There are indications we may have an old friend in the neighborhood."

The girl pulled the mug of ale from her mouth long enough to ask, "Who?"

"We have reports that the elusive Father Cavarocchi is in the area."

Mercy whistled softly. "The Welcome-Man himself."

Malachi nodded. "It would go well with everybody to take him down. I have thought of a plan that involves both you and Will."

"You know I don't have much time," Mercy pointed out. "Lord Herndon will be back in London in a week, and I must respond one way or the other to his invitation."

Malachi's eyes widened in pleasure. "Well, lass, I wouldn't want you to miss out on what may very well be the grandest offer you'll ever get. Not every woman, no matter how beautiful, has been invited into the bed of the Queen's cousin. If you can please him—and I have no doubt you will—there is no telling how high you may go. And such proximity to the Queen's family circle promises limitless information and influence. Still, I worry about how well the nobility may treat a rootless waif like yourself."

"We are already well past the pleasing part," Mercy informed him. "His present offer is to set me up in my own place in London where he can visit periodically. It would be very nice to get off the road for a while and have a place of my own. Besides," Mercy's eyes twinkled, "he amuses me and I like him."

"Such relationships are seldom permanent, you know—quite apart from the morality involved. In addition, from what I have seen, the young woman is almost always taken advantage of and lightly held."

Mercy chuckled in delight. "You are a great one to hide behind morality, Malachi—like the chameleon in the garden! But I treasure your concern for my reputation, even if it does arrive a little late on the scene. The simple truth is that I am attracted to the extravagant life-style enjoyed by wealthy people generally and by the nobles in particular. I am determined to give such a manner of living a good try."

"Sell your beauty, you mean?"

"Too late, Malachi!" laughed Mercy. "I've watched you manipulate people with your loaded questions so often in the past that I really can't take your tricks seriously anymore. Besides, I've been selling both my beauty and my brains to the Service these many years for a much smaller reward, and a girl needs to look ahead to insure some security in her life."

"Ah well," Malachi shrugged, "I'll hate to lose you, but if you have your mind made up, I know there's no stopping you."

"You won't be losing me. I won't be able to leave London for awhile, tis true, but Lord Herndon will put no restrictions on my free time. I may even be in a position to do you some favors if things go well. Other than that, think of this as a bit of time out for me and a chance to put something by for my old age." She leaned over and patted Malachi on the arm. "You've always advised me to do so, my good friend. Now, what is the scheme you devised, involving me and the amusing apprentice? Something short-term, I hope."

Malachi sat back. "I thought it might be a good idea if you and Will got married."

"Married?" cried Mercy.

"I've been thinking our situation over regarding the good Father," explained Malachi. "We have used the Extreme Unction gambit so often that our priest is not likely to bite on it. I would like to put that approach to rest for awhile and shift attention to another sacrament."

"But marriage! I think I'd rather be dying." Mercy gave Malachi a little smirk. "Oh well, I suppose Lord Herndon will not care one way or the other—as long as my new husband does not make a nuisance of himself."

"Right!" Malachi responded, leaning forward to throw a fatherly arm around her shoulder. "I knew I could count on you to put the job before your personal preferences. Well then, let's find ourselves a priest who will join together you two youngsters in the sacred state of matrimony under the auspices of the Catholic Church."

Mercy hung her head. "Poor old Father Cavarocchi. I hope we get him, of course, but still it would be an inglorious way to end his illustrious career." She moved toward the door. "And excuse me, you devious old graybeard, if I go off to weep while you explain his upcoming wedding to the bridegroom."

❖ ❖ ❖

"Married? To Mercy?" William stammered. "Good Lord, the thought itself introduces so many possibilities as to leave a man unbalanced. *My mind is troubled like a fountain stirred, and I myself see not the bottom of it.*" [11]

"Take my advice, William, and don't get too involved in abstract matters," Malachi counseled. "You are not up to it in the first place and, in the second, it is not worth it. If your mind is a complete blank at the moment in the area of theoretical metaphysics, count your blessings and make every effort to keep it that way. Our society has fostered so many contentious factions lately, that a man is better off not giving attention to all their competing arguments."

William dug in to what was left of breakfast on his platter. "Don't listen, you mean?"

"Quite the contrary," Malachi corrected. "Modify your alertness until you identify those speakers who have your best interests at heart, and then listen intently to those people. In short, trust me."

"I do, Malachi, but I'm most uneasy about this."

"You admit she is a beautiful, desirable girl?"

"Oh yes, very beauteous."

"And intelligent and spirited?"

"Very spirited, but—"

"Then there is no problem. You yourself are just a country boy, with no family that you know of to prohibit such an alliance."

"That's true. Yet it's all so sudden and so puzzling. And you say she has already agreed? "

"Trust me, William. It will all turn out for the best. Now, listen carefully. As it occurs, I can take care of all the necessary documentation if you can round up a priest to perform the ceremony here at the inn. In my room above-stairs would be best."

"My injury has left me entirely non-denominational as far as I can recall, so I'm not that particular," said William helpfully. "Any man-of-the-cloth will do me fine."

"Not so fast. Mercy must be married in the Catholic faith or she will lose her inheritance."

"Inheritance, eh?" William smirked. "That's icing on the cake! But, of course, you are correct. I must begin thinking about protecting her best interests. I shall round up a priest if I have to chase my quarry to the ends of the earth."

"That's the spirit," approved Malachi. "You can begin right here at the inn. You have only to mention your need, discreetly, to a likely customer, and the neighborhood will soon be flooded with inquiry."

"And you say you can handle the paper work if I can round up the priest?"

"Absolutely," Malachi assured him. "I have friends who can push through the license and post-date the banns. The big problem is getting a priest to perform a sacrament for people he does not know. If he is caught, you recall, he faces the possibility of a particularly painful death."

"We're proposing something illegal?"

"All Catholic ceremonies are illegal," said Malachi, "even though about 25% of all Englishmen are still Roman at heart. That's why you will have to be careful when you advertise for a priest. You must be discreet, on the one hand, and yet convince your listener that you are involved personally and not pulling a trick of some kind."

"No problem there," William assured him. "I have only to think of Mercy and my personal involvement may be observed by all."

"Good man, but beware the shining bauble of lewd thoughts. Smutty images may easily turn a lover into a lecher."

"I'll do my best to keep that distinction in mind."

"Keep in mind also that the state of marriage calls for the best of whatever is in you, on many levels. You must always compromise your own selfish comforts and desires to assure your mate of her just portion of whatever pleasure is available. If marriage is not approached unselfishly, it had best not be approached at all."

"The weighty tone of your profundities impresses me as much as does the wisdom they impart," William assured him, "and I shall always abide by their helpful direction.

Mercy shall have first choice in all matters not pertaining to the traditional male prerogatives."

"That's a start, I guess," Malachi shrugged. "You two will doubtless have a lot of fun defining those prerogatives in the future, so get busy now and locate a priest."

"Shouldn't I know more about the legal-illegal aspect of this business? Might I get in trouble soliciting actions which 75% of my countrymen regard as extra-legal?"

"No chance," Malachi assured him. "Your ignorance and your lack of social grace will combine to protect you from being taken seriously by intelligent people, who will certainly conclude that you are a lovesick fool whose lustful flame must quickly be quenched in its proper channel for the protection of society at large. Believe me, lad, within moments of meeting you, people will strive to outdo each other in speeding you on your way. That's why I'm giving you a few shillings to spread around. The other drinkers will tolerate you as long as you're buying, which will be just about long enough for you to mention your need for a priest."

"I only hope Simon is not in the Common Room," muttered William as he turned to leave.

❖ ❖ ❖

At a temporary altar set up in his private room at the Black Boar Inn, Malachi kissed the bride and patted the groom's shoulder. "You lovebirds be off now," he beamed, "and make sure the guests below share the food and drink we ordered." He then turned to the priest and pressed a crown into his palm with a handshake. "Well done, Father."

Without looking down, Father Cavarocchi hefted the coin in his hand with such practiced ease that he was genuinely driven to say, "That's very generous of you, my son."

"Not at all, Father. Little enough we can do for those who must live their lives on the run. Very tiresome, I should imagine."

"At times it is," the priest admitted, "especially for those of us whose special vice is a tendency to indulge in creature comforts. But I seldom submerge myself in the pool of self-pity when I confront my accommodations, no matter what the temptation. And since this is one of those joyful occasions which give me a special satisfaction in the performance of my duties, I am determined not to complain. The work must be done and, at times, it is not too bad. It is true that I must scuttle like a rat in certain areas of the country, but there are still sections where the leading families have remained Catholic. I've often spent months with them, quite safe and comfortable as far as noteworthy accommodations are concerned. The Queen, of course, is pleased not to bother those families unless they deliberately provoke civil unrest."

"Which families? Perhaps I know them." Malachi poured two glasses of wine.

Father Cavarocchi chuckled. "That information circulates only on a strict necessity-of-knowing basis. I'm sure you understand."

"Of course," Malachi shrugged. "As a matter of fact, as I understand it, when given her choice, the Queen prefers to have her commands carried out by well-behaved Catholic noblemen. Such loyal subjects treat her with more dignity—lest she turn on them—than do the swarms of Puritans who profess the Anglican faith yet feel free to clog her government with endless reproaches and suggestions on subjects she has forbidden them to discuss."

The priest nodded. "Ah yes, a few of them even address uncivil questions to her from the floor of Parliament. Very bizarre treatment to extend toward the acknowledged head of their church if you ask me. We wouldn't dare try anything like that with the Pope. Well, some of those Puritan gentlemen are not really gentlemen at all, and well the Queen knows it."

"Wentworth and John Stubbs and that bunch," Malachi nodded. "Hard-headed men, indeed, but men of spirit, nonetheless. If the Queen ever ordered my hand placed on the block and then cut clean through at the wrist by a cleaver struck with a mallet, because of something I had printed, I don't know that I could maintain the spirit Stubbs displayed before that crowd two years ago. And I'm quite sure I could never top his *'Now that my calamity is at hand'* remark before he fainted."

The priest chuckled. "Indeed. Impromptu also, as I understand it. Until the last moment, he thought he was to be hanged."

"Well, he had a week or so to work on it, actually," said Malachi. "Most of us knew the Queen would have to cool off sooner or later. She can't stay spiteful forever, and the Privy Council is reluctant to let her start hanging everybody who offends her—or we would all be in trouble on her bad days. The Council will always assign a man a little time in the Tower if the Queen orders it, but they would prefer the death penalty be reserved for something more serious than the publishing of offensive pamphlets like *The Discovery of a Gaping Gulf Whereunto England is like to Be Swallowed by Another French Marriage if the Lord Forbid Not the Bans by Letting Her Majesty See the Sin and Punishment Thereof*." [12]

Malachi paused to pour more wine for the priest and himself. "Stubbs was not alone, after all, in his heated opposition to Elizabeth's proposed marriage to the French heir-apparent, Monsieur Alceon. Most of the major men in the government were also against it. Not many went as far as Stubbs in publicly calling Alceon *'the scum of France'*—and, therefore, *'the scum of Europe'*—but most were with him in spirit." [13]

"Alceon earned the comments even if he was a Catholic," the priest agreed. "The reputation for being riddled with syphilis will gain you strong criticism from a lot of sensible people. That's what finally killed him, you know."

"That's why a lot of folk were very pleased when the Queen was prevailed upon to reduce Stubbs' punishment to the loss of a single hand." Malachi leaned forward. "But tell me, Father, did you ever think that you would like to quit all this running around and stay in one place for a time?"

"The dream of my life!" Cavarocchi's eyes glowed. "I have always felt I would do my best work as a permanent part of some community. I would really enjoy it, believe me, but I'm afraid God is not tempted to assign me that kind of soft duty."

"I am happy to offer you a toast to that end, Father," Malachi said, lifting his glass. "Now, if you would care to don your layman's disguise, we could go below-stairs to join the happy pair."

"To what shall we drink now that my lady wife has been toasted?" asked William in high spirits, looking fondly upon Mercy.

"To the eternal celebration of your nuptials and to the granting of Father Cavarocchi's deepest wish."

"And for you, Malachi?" Mercy inquired.

"For me, the completion of a good day's work is celebration enough. Drink up now."

They did, and Malachi went to the door of the parlor and signaled two soldiers, standing just outside the room.

"What are you doing?" William exclaimed in horror.

Malachi bowed to Father Cavarocchi. "Alas, sir, you have displeased the Establishment." The priest slumped in his chair. To the soldiers, Malachi said, "I want every person in this room placed under immediate arrest. They have all participated in an illegal Catholic sacrament. I want them held separately at close quarters until I can question them."

"Separately?" the groom groaned. "On my wedding night?"

"Immaterial, young man. When traitorous acts are committed against the Crown, there are no other considerations."

"Sir!" Mercy's voice cracked like a whiplash.

Malachi glared at her for a moment but saw that she glared back, so he glanced away. "Very well, then. I suppose it will do no harm, but little good can come of it as far as I'm concerned. The two of you may hold yourselves in readiness in one room until I have time to get to you. He turned to one of the soldiers. "Take them to my room and lock them in. Let no one speak to them until I come up."

Mercy gave him a saucy flip of her head and took William by the arm.

Malachi turned to Father Cavarocchi. "And I further charge you with receiving a gratuity for the performance of that ceremony. Guard, search his person for that gratuity."

The soldier found the priest's purse and handed it to Malachi, who promptly upended it on the table before them. A splendid array of gold pieces spilled out.

"The Church does not go unprepared for its struggle in this world, Father," observed Malachi.

"Blessings of God, my son, to help spread His word."

Malachi quickly sorted through the coins and found one which he held up for the soldiers to examine. "You saw me mark this coin before the ceremony?"

The soldiers nodded.

"Remember it when the time comes," he said and then instructed them to follow the newly-married couple upstairs.

"Sit down, Father," he said, "and relax now that business is over. Have a real drink." He poured each of them a healthy drink of brandy. "I feel I owe you one."

"Why is that?"

"Oddly enough, I am never happy to curtail a good man's freedom, and I've chased you long enough to know you are a good man of your own sort, Father, even if we find ourselves on opposite sides."

"I'm sorry for it, my son."

"I hope you meant what you said about being a permanent part of a small community because you might get stuck in the Tower for the rest of your natural life."

"Need it be that bad?"

"That's the good part," said Malachi. "Not long ago there was a lot of pressure to hang, draw, and quarter men like you as traitors to the country. Things have quieted down lately, however, and sweeter voices prevail at the moment, so you probably only face imprisonment for life. You are not the public figure Parsons and Campion were, so there will be no automatic crying out for your execution. But those of us who have faced you in the field, Father, will certainly sleep easier with you out of the action, if you don't mind my saying so."

Father Cavarocchi chuckled. "Have I really done that well? And, just for the record, I'm Italian born."

"Our assessment credits you with setting up and maintaining the delivery system that has so bedeviled us, and we have no doubt that you have succeeded in smuggling over one hundred young clergymen from France to England. We know you set them up with contacts and safe houses here, and we will be very happy to put you out of business, believe me."

"Oh well," Cavarocchi shrugged, "notoriety is one mark of success, I suppose." His attention wandered to the array of coins on the table before them. "Unfinished business," he said with a gesture in their direction.

"Oh, they're yours, of course. I'm no robber but an honest man pressed to make a decent living, as you are yourself, Father."

"That's generous of you, my son. I know that confiscation of valuables is very common in connection with arrests." The priest scooped all but one of the largest coins into his purse. "At least you have earned your 10%."

Malachi shrugged and took the coin. "Still, it is a shame that a man of your ability should rot away in the Tower. The problem is that you dedicated warriors can never leave the battlefield with the issue undecided. I admire your courage and determination, but it does seem pointless when one might accomplish great things elsewhere."

"Are you suggesting that I still have an option, perchance?"

"Your Italian birth makes it possible for me to offer you an alternative arrangement if certain details can be worked out."

The priest sighed. "I'm glad to get that traitor business cleared up anyway. What details?"

"Two conditions. If I let you go, you'll promise to get out of England and stay out for the rest of your natural life."

Father Cavarocchi bit his lip in thought. "So great was my zeal a few years ago, I would have told you to take your offer and toss it. I would have suffered pain with pleasure if it were for the Cause. But I find, as I get older, my desire for comfort, even when held in check, intrudes somewhat on that zeal, and I am ready to compromise as long as the other condition is not personally repugnant to me."

"Let's not forget, Father, that the arrangement is quid pro quo. I give you something; you give me something."

"I've already agreed as long as you don't press my conscience too hard."

"It really shouldn't bother you at all. "minor administrative matter. Just logistics, actually."

"Sounds ominous. Please don't mistake my willingness to entertain your offer—"

"Let's not pretend, Father. We're doing business here, so the less time we spend on posing, the more time we'll have to come to sensible terms. The simple fact is that I must show some gain for letting you exercise Option B. I certainly don't want a bad progress report at this stage of my career. So let's nail down a deal. Give me something important."

"What do you suggest?"

"I'll start with something vital. Our service is frankly baffled by your ability to slip your seminarians into England even after we have beefed up the port watches along all coasts."

"You have some information about our movements from spies of your own at Rheims, I understand."

"Skimpy, second-hand accounts at best. My immediate problem concerns our budget people who are complaining that we spend a great deal of money without visible results. Because you are a Catholic, I' m sure you are sensitive to the plight of all who must work very hard to please the Front Office. So if you wouldn't mind giving us a bit of a sporting chance to nab you, I would like to know simply whether your successful entry is on our east, west, or south coast."

"So I need only betray a simple logistic to you in order to avoid a martyr's fate?"

"That's what it comes down to," said Malachi. "We don't expect you to give us the exact location, of course, just the general area so that our surveillance duties are reduced in accordance with our budget cuts."

"You are being such a terribly good sort about giving information to a man you have every reason to believe will share his knowledge with those abroad, I will enter into the spirit of the occasion by giving you the exact spot you are seeking in this grim battle we all share to satisfy the Front Offices of the world."

"Well," Malachi grinned, "you are being more reasonable than I ever imagined. Let's have it."

"North. Scotland. The Catholic Scots land the young men and pass them on to the northern English Catholics. By the time they get down here, they have friends and safe-houses all along the way."

Malachi grimaced. "Good luck to us on breaking up that cozy little arrangement. We knew you were doing some of that, of course, but we were sure you had an English landing point as well."

"Nothing permanent, really. Scotland works well in our favor since the Queen is reluctant to oversee her northern lords more closely. Those families defend her northern borders, appoint her local officials, and generally go about their duties as loyal Englishman. We have all learned from the past that Elizabeth is reluctant to rattle sections of her kingdom which are not causing her major grief. All princes must season their policy with a little practicality, as Machiavelli says."

"Old Nick himself," chuckled Malachi. "I thought *The Prince* was a book forbidden by your church, and yet you appear familiar with it."

"I am. It is forbidden by Rome, true enough, but human nature being what it is, that particular prohibition has a great deal of allure for conscientious clerics who desire to stay in touch with their sinful flock by just nibbling at the forbidden fruit without getting too involved. I sometimes think our Codex of Forbidden Books serves as a reader's guide for the priesthood—in a scholarly sense, of course."

"Obviously," Malachi agreed. "What other attraction could forbidden fruit possibly hold?"

"Exactly," Cavarocchi replied, and they enjoyed a quiet chuckle.

"I should warn you, Father. Our figures show 112 seminarians operating in this country at the present time. Ah, shake your hoary locks at me, if you will, I expect that. Nonetheless, that is the number that has been reported to the Privy Council, and they are talking about swarms of caterpillars which will require a swift eradication program. That may well mean our stepping on some prominent Northern toes, so your people need to watch their step."

"They refer to us as 'caterpillars'?" exclaimed the priest.

"Your pest-like aspect dictates the term, I'm afraid."

"Demeaning in the extreme."

"That's what you are to us, actually. There was talk early on of labeling you 'vermin,' but that seemed to add a layer of romantic significance to your work, so we settled for the lowly caterpillar who will quietly harvest your crop for you if you do not smash him underfoot."

"That name-calling stuff is for children."

"Ah now, Father," Malachi placated "we do have some among us who are very emotional and childish, if you will, about the differences between us, but I am not one of them. Don't let my chiding push you back to Option A. Think of yourself as choosing to return to Rheims as a battle-hardened veteran, to offer yourself as mentor for the young and eager aspirants there. Far more productive than ending up with all four quarters of your body hanging at various gates of the city and your head on pike-point above London Bridge."

"Ah yes, slither off like a caterpillar into the night." He held up his hand to stay Malachi's objections. "I don't mean to appear unappreciative, only philosophical. I shall remember you in my prayers for your kindness, Malachi."

"I appreciate the thought," grinned Malachi," but I'd be just as happy not to be mentioned at all in idolatrous worship if you don't mind. It seems a form of bad luck to me, as if I would somehow be gaining recognition on the wrong team."

"I'll pray for your soul, nonetheless, my boy. Well then, I suppose this is good-bye, and thanks again for the options."

"Not so fast, Father. We have already made travel arrangements for you. The guards will be with you every second until you are put aboard a Dutch flyboat in Deptford tomorrow night to be dropped off in Calais."

"Any chance we could make Plymouth my point of departure?"

"Don't push your luck, Father. Our thinking is to scoop and bounce you without giving you time to notify your confederates. It is thought we may gain some surcease from our problems if we manage to introduce at least momentary confusion into the organization which you have kept running so smoothly."

"Modesty forbids me—"

"So you are under a direct gag order from now until you sail. If you attempt to communicate with anyone at all, the guards have orders to actually bind and gag you for the remainder of your journey."

"Understood. I wonder if I might be granted a bottle of wine to protect me from the chill on the trip over."

"Absolutely," Malachi grinned. "No way of stopping you, as a matter of fact. You have gold and you have guards, so the oldest barter system in the world is at your fingertips. In the meantime..." He handed Father Cavarocchi a bottle from the leftover wedding feast as they shook hands in farewell.

In Malachi's room above-stairs, William confronted his bride. "You mean we aren't really married?" he frowned. "I'd become quite reconciled to the idea, Mercy."

"It was all a sham to catch the priest."

"But Father Cavarocchi is a true priest. Surely——"

"The papers were forged. A Catholic ceremony is illegal. The wedding never took place."

William threw his arms around Mercy. "But I want you for my wife, Mercy."

"It's too late, Will," said Mercy, not unkindly, peeling his arms from her. "I love another. Besides, I am too old for you."

"We're the same age! Malachi told me so."

"Perhaps in years, Will, but I've been with the Service a long time. I am old in other ways."

"You're not a virgin, do you mean? I don't care about that!"

Mercy sighed. "I'm not an Innocent in any sense. I grew up on the streets of London, Will. I like the excitement and variety." Her eyes danced. "I love jewels and fine clothes, noisy crowds of jolly people, endless flirting and intrigue. If I had been born a lady, Will, I would have ruled in Society. If a woman were allowed on the stage, I would have all of London at my feet. But I must work with what I am, and I am not for you, my dear. You are witty, yes, but you are a dreamer and a poet and poor as a church mouse. Do you understand?"

"Yes, I'm beginning to," he nodded sadly, then brightened. "Would you be adverse to a little love play to celebrate our almost-marriage?"

"Master William! I am not a trollop!"

"That's all too obvious, my dear, and all to the good, because I have no need of a trollop right now. It's true, Mercy, that at the moment, I am a penniless poet, but I am in perpetual need of a muse who will raise me up above such limitations. "A *Muse of fire, that would ascend The brightest heaven of invention: A kingdom for a stage, princes to act, and monarchs to behold the swelling scene!*" [14]

Mercy tilted her head playfully. "Now that sounds more like my kind of crowd, but I've never before played the part of a muse. Do you think you could instruct me?"

Chapter 5:
CAMBRIDGE CHOICES

Cambridge stable, one week later:

"Is it safe to talk here?" Malachi asked as he glanced about the small rough-planked office.

"Only the horses will hear," William assured him.

"Then I must tell you that once again we've come to a dis-accommodation of purpose between us," said Malachi wearily.

"You don't understand!" William exclaimed. "They all want to take the same horse!"

"Calm down!" Malachi commanded. "We don't have time for theatrics. Let me explain our situation to you patiently before Marlowe gets here because he's going to be pretty upset by your actions. I put you in this obscure job because a horse groom blends easily into the background around a stable. Nobody pays any attention to him, and he carries his credentials with him wherever he goes." Malachi paused to sniff the air and roll his eyes.

"Many of us like the smell," William declared.

"How fortunate," Malachi nodded. "You may recall that you had only three simple duties to perform during your wait for my arrival. You were to sit for Marlowe's general outline on the portrait. You were to slip unobtrusively onto the campus and sign in for Marlowe on the buttery book. And you were to keep track of who accompanied whom and who followed whom when the students hired horses for the trip to London, with particular care paid to any movement by Marlowe's friends. Remember?"

"I made a list of all those riders," William said. "but nothing of interest turned up."

"Fortunately for all of us, the realm has not yet collapsed to the point where it is obliged to come to you for meaningful evaluation. Just give me the names and numbers."

"I have the list somewhere. I'll get it in a minute."

"Get it now ! You may not have another minute. Don't you realize that overnight you have leaped from absolute obscurity to the height of community interest. Everybody is talking about you. Over on the campus they are talking about hanging you."

"Seriously?"

"That's the way it's done, yes."

"Well, hang me if they will because my conscience would go to the gallows anyway if I stood by and let them all take the same horse."

"What are you talking about?" Malachi growled. "I'm on the job here, and you stand about babbling nonsense. The Privy Council wants to know if Christopher Marlowe can possibly be awarded his MA degree without making public his special service to the Queen. He has asked for the Council's intercession to explain his frequent absences. If they decide to muscle in and have him awarded the degree, they don't want to get burned later by revelations that he turns out to be something distasteful like a heretic or a smuggler or a rabble-rouser. This is a complicated inquiry. I must check his attendance records, his attainments, and the attitudes he has expressed to his acquaintances over the years. I need the cooperation of every person in Cambridge to get this job done, and when those people discover I am responsible for your presence among them, God help me. Thanks to you, I may be offered a halter instead of a helping hand."

"I really don't know what's expected of me if I can't live by certain principles."

"I expected you to keep quiet, do your job, stay out of sight, and stand by until I contacted you for a sensible report. Instead, I get this ranting and raving about all the horses being chosen by the same person or some such nonsense—a choice which somehow has inflamed this university like no other dilemma since Henry broke with the Catholic Church. This single stable is the topic at every lunch table in Cambridge, and every conversation is through clenched teeth. You've managed all of this in just three days. Remarkable. You would change the world if I left you alone for a month or so."

"Not all the horses by the same person," William corrected. "The problem here is that they all want to ride the young, handsome animals so that they may cut dashing figures on the fifty-mile trip to London."

"And attract the eyes of various damsels," Malachi nodded. "What's wrong with that?"

"What's wrong is that the older, less attractive animals get no exercise at all and grow fat and discontented with their lot."

Malachi shrugged. "Being rejected can do that."

"And the young ones get overused and consequently exhausted, but I have put a stop to this inequity. I was assigned the task of renting horses while the owner is down in London, and I intend to do the job as conscientiously as possible, come what may."

"Come what may, indeed," Malachi scowled. "But how have you managed to enflame an entire community in so short a time?"

"I have rearranged the stalls so that each newly-ridden horse comes in at one end and stands until his turn comes to be ridden again at the other end. Every horse takes his turn, and no rider gets to choose. He can take the horse offered or none. I'll have a better conditioned set of horses very quickly. The young animals will get more rest and the older ones will get more exercise. No horse is ridden out of turn. The students can like it or leg it!"

"What if they hang you?"

William laughed. "Apprentices might, but I bet college students never would. Basically, they are too high-minded."

"You're right that they'd probably only hang you in effigy if this were an academic disagreement, but you are causing these people personal inconvenience, and that's an entirely different matter. Many of these young men are the sons of nobility, you know."

William nodded. "The ones who wear the forbidden rapiers."

"They're not at all used to the idea of having a horse groom tell them which horse they may ride. Such upstart presumption is grounds for retaliation in the minds of most of them."

"A duel, you mean?"

"A duel!" Malachi laughed. "They wouldn't soil their blades on a horse-swipe! More likely a few trusted retainers would seek you out some night and administer to you a sound thrashing with short-handled truncheons so as not to kill you the first time."

"They sound like considerate fellows indeed," William laughed, "but I'll be all right. I sleep well up in the loft, and we'll be gone in a day or two, as you said."

"Yes, and we'll leave this mess you've created right on the owner's doorstep. He'll probably rearrange his stalls when he sees the discord you have caused among his paying customers. Don't forget, he's a business man who has to make a living."

"Let's hope he's a far-sighted one then. One who knows how to preserve the means by which he makes that living."

Malachi shrugged. "Sometimes long term ideals are whittled down by the sharp edge of daily practicality."

"That will be Mr. Dobson's choice to make then, not mine."

"That's right," Malachi conceded. "Dobson can take it or leave it."

"heavy shout resounded through the stable just outside their door. "Where is that villain? Show him to me!"

"Look sharp, now! That's Marlowe and it sounds like he's been drinking," Malachi warned. "He probably won't draw on an unarmed man, but do your best not to irritate him further."

"Why should Marlowe be irritated with me?"

"Yesterday, you ran off the portrait painter because his nose was offended by your occupational aroma. Today, you have fixed it so there is no chance of your ever signing in for Marlowe because there is no chance of you skulking furtively about in Cambridge. There will be a community watch on your movements hereafter, and dozens will leap to examine anything you sign on campus. Through your own inept actions you are out of the deception business in Cambridge, and, consequently, your value to Master Marlowe has amounted to a fat zero."

The door burst open and Marlowe entered. "There you are!" he cried, shifting his wine bottle from his right hand to his left, drawing his sword, and waving it aloft.

"Hold on now, Master Marlowe." Malachi moved between them and extended his arms in a soothing manner. "God knows you have reason enough to be furious with this poor befuddled soul who certainly means no harm to anybody, but who does, nevertheless, only too frequently, it must be admitted—"

"I salute you, Master Dramatist!" Marlowe shouted at William, holding the hilt of his upraised weapon before his face and half-bowing before returning the rapier to its hanger by his side. "Overnight, you have casually provoked more passion and drama in this community than I have ignited in three years of hard trying, At this very moment, all over the campus, there are heated debates raging over where to celebrate the semester's end by hanging you. I haven't seen such passionate spirit generated around here in a long time! You have succeeded in cutting through their apathy! You have a natural flair for provoking drama, and that flair is worth celebrating—" he offered William a pull on his wine bottle— "because it opens up some interesting possibilities if you survive."

"A celebration at semester's end, you say? When is that?"

"End of the week," Malachi said. "We'll be well away."

"Plenty of time to talk things over," Marlowe pointed out.

"None of it was my fault, you know," William explained. "Your painter was just one of those people who sniff disdainfully while you are presenting yourself, and I had every intention of signing that buttery book this evening, but now, I guess, I need not bother."

"Forget all that stuff," Marlowe insisted. "It doesn't matter now. With your permission, Malachi, I have important matters I want to discuss with William. I intend to offer him a reward well past his fondest hopes."

"Watch yourself, William. Sounds like fish oil to me." Malachi grinned

William stared at Marlowe for a moment. "I guess as a dramatist you are empowered to make dramatic statements. I can only hope you are skilled enough to give structure to that last one."

"How would you like to become a playwright—perhaps the greatest who ever lived?"

"Indeed, I had hoped—"

"It wouldn't be a straight shot, mind you, but if you and I can come to agreement, you will have a 50-50 chance to gain that distinction without lifting a finger."

"Deja vu," murmured William as he remembered his discussion with Oxford. "What agreement?" he asked politely.

"I will explain." Marlowe sat down on the bench across from William. "The men who own the London playhouses are in a conspiracy to keep us writers poor and humble."

"You mean Allyn and—?"

Marlowe held up a hand. "It's good you know something of the situation. That will make it easier for you to understand your role in the scheme."

"What role is that?"

"As long as the theater managers are in collusion, you see, they simply will not pay a playwright more than six pounds for the sale of any play. We have no leverage against their arbitrary judgment of our artistic worth. They are then free to grow rich by garnering twice that amount every week from showing our creation on the stage in their theater. Does that sound fair to you?"

"Certainly not," agreed William. "I can only hope that situation is cleared up forthwith."

"I intend to take an honest stab at clearing it up right now," Marlowe said. "I intend to counter their cartel by setting up a dummy Marlowe, so to speak, so I may pummel them in negotiations from more than one direction. This fake Marlowe will have plays of his own to sell and after an initial success or two, he will thereafter threaten to withhold his services entirely unless he receives at least ten pounds for future plays. One stage manager or the other is bound to give in, especially if we approach him while he is facing dismal reports from his ticket office. The other manager will soon follow out of self-protection. It is imperative that we get the theater people into a bidding war for our services because that's where the real money is."

"Let me see if I have this straight, then," William mused. "The fake Marlowe, once he is successful, will put further pressure on the managers by withholding his creations while you continue to make an admittedly skimpy living under your own name?"

Marlowe nodded. "Except that the creations will be my own work in both cases. I can easily handle that kind of production, and I have already laid out a dozen or so future plays which I want to share with you if we can come to an agreement."

"I wonder, just idly, what kind of recompense is involved for those who serve as shadowy literary substitutes?"

"We'll talk about that later," Marlowe promised. "At the moment, I need to know if you're a good enough actor to create the illusion of being an intelligent writer?"

"It may take a little time," William smiled. *"But with a little practice I may change the stamp of nature."* [15]

"That's good!" Marlowe exclaimed. "Keep talking that way. A writer's puppet should appear to be literate in public to fortify the illusion."

"I'd go easy on the denigration, were I you—at least while we're still negotiating," William advised him. "One thing about such an arrangement really bothers me."

"What is that?"

"I know that your style is so singular, your lyric quality so distinctive, your tone so individualistic, they must all grow out of your essential self. It would seem impossible for you to create a second essential self whose creations would be so unique as to mislead your audience to the point where they wouldn't recognize the distinctive hand of Christopher Marlowe at work in any new play."

"No problem," Marlowe assured him. "I can gently pinch down on my muse enough so that the artistry factor in my writing is shaded in favor of appealing more to the groundlings. After that, a well-chosen pseudonym for you will throw them off the scent entirely. Half the stuff printed in London today appears under fictitious names for one reason or another, so one more will slide in quite nicely."

"But they can track pseudonyms," William said. "As I've recently learned, the person registering the false name must appear in person before members of the Stationer's Registry Board in order to obtain the necessary permit."

Marlowe smiled. "And that's the key to the grand deception. My other self will appear from beginning to end. You'll be there when the license is originally issued in whatever name you pick out. Through you, I'll create a successful mouthpiece who will get full public credit for the work I'll be doing in private."

"Behind the scenes, so to speak," William mused, "while the front man is treading the boards of public approval."

"Exactly! You'll be feted and glorified to your heart's content by those simple-minded theater people, and all the while I can chuckle up my sleeve because only you and I will know how little you've done to deserve such honors. How does that strike you?"

"I am overwhelmed at the prospect, of course, but still, this is not exactly the scenario I had in mind for my writing career."

"It comes as a complete surprise to you, doesn't it?" Marlowe chuckled. "That's good. It gives us a head start on the security thing if just the two of us are involved. If we can maintain that bond, you stand a chance of going down in history as the greatest playwright of the Western World."

"I'm always tickled pink when I hear of such possible honors being extended to me, but I have recently learned this is a practical world. Is there any money in it for me?"

"Money?" Marlowe barked, then smiled. "I like that. I trust a man who looks out for himself. Keep things on a business level, say I. As I mentioned, I usually get six pounds from the manager for each play. I don't suppose they'll offer you any more than four pounds for your first play—although it will obviously be worth a great deal more—but after its success, we'll insist they bump you up to seven pounds. Out of that, I can see my way clear to let you have ten shillings for each play sold."

"Ten shillings!"

"Grates on your conscience, eh? Good sign. Keep your values straight. All right then, I'll present you with five shillings per play, and you can help me put a title on each new one to give you a sense of involvement in the process. What do you say?"

"Instant fame without effort is certainly an alluring proposition for anyone," William conceded, "but life has taught me there are complications in all human arrangements. If you are really going to do the work of two writers, that means future public taste will have to decide which writer was greater. It bothers me a bit that my new name might come to eclipse your old one. Public taste may change and, indeed, the number of groundlings may increase to challenge all others in deciding public taste."

"No problem," Marlowe laughed. "I will still be the same person no matter what they call me. A rose by any other name, you know—"

"But I have to wonder if I will be."

"What?" Marlowe said in surprise. "This has nothing to do with you personally, you realize."

"That's the part that bothers me," Will confessed. "I must give it a good think."

"Upon my word," Marlowe exclaimed. "You are an infamous rogue! I offer you the possibility of eternal fame without exertion on your part, and you must think it over! What is there to think about? You are only going to be a Johannes Fac Totum in the arrangement, don't forget."

"Yes, I know, and such a tumble of my aspirations is something to which I must devote a deep think. But you did say it would only be temporary until we erect a big enough straw man to shake at the managers?"

"That's right. Just for a couple of years. You think the matter through as calmly as you can before the students come to hang you, and let me know what you decide. In the meantime, figure out some classy name for yourself and look over these play summaries which I have already planned out for this joint venture." Marlowe drew a small packet from beneath his cape and handed it over. "They are just general notes about the main characters and the basic conflict and eventual resolution of the future works, but they will give you a good feel for the kind of material we'll be handling if you agree."

William seemed surprised at the packet and the purported contents. "I must say, you obviously want this done."

"I do indeed. We've got to fight fire with fire when we battle those greedy bastards at the top. They have a long-term strategy to keep us low, and I'll develop you as a long-term strategy to bring us high. Are you ready then to sign up?"

"We still haven't reached agreement on my recompense."

"Don't worry, that will all be taken care of in a very satisfying manner."

William grinned. "I relish your assurance. The only remaining step then is for me to look around and settle on a name."

"Right," said Marlowe, "but you really need to shake a leg and get it done, so we can get started on setting up your real identity as my false identity."

"The poor man's Marlowe, eh?" William laughed. "Second between equals."

"Not a bit of it," Marlowe assured him "We'll make your name almost equally famous throughout the world. Get busy and decide."

"Don't worry. I spend much of my time thinking about it, and I'm positive I'll recognize it as soon as it comes to me. Let me see now," he mused. "Legshake? Shakaleg? Ah well, for just a moment there, I thought there was a glimmer."

Chapter 6:
MACHIAVELLI'S INFLUENCE

London bookshop, the following day:

The sign over the bookstall just outside St. Pauls named its proprietor as P. Flanigan. Malachi led his apprentice inside, introduced himself to Mr. Flanigan, and requested a copy of Machiavelli's *The Prince.*

"I was discussing this book recently with, ah...a man-of-the-cloth...and realized it was none too soon for my apprentice here to study its principles. In my opinion, despite its growing reputation for unscrupulous thinking, it's a volume which should be in every man's library."

"I agree," said Flanigan. "It may be going a bit underground these days, but its contents are alive and well, nonetheless. I use Machiavelli as a weather gauge of my own state of mind," he confided to Malachi. "Reading *The Prince* when I am in the melancholic humour inclines me to see a greedy, selfish man drawing a blueprint for absolute tyranny—urging princes to use any means to gain their ends. At that point, I am ready to join those who contend the book is an abomination to mankind." He paused to hand the volume to Malachi, who indicated it was to go to William.

"But you doubtless have other humours," William prompted.

Flanigan nodded, "Indeed I do. Francis Bacon once said: *'Choler is a humor that maketh men active, earnest, full of alacritie and stirring, if it be not stopped.'* [16] I have moments like that when I really get some work done and, in that mood, I am forced to see Machiavelli as a weeping patriot, deprived of his illusions by his years in political life, ousted from his diplomatic career by a shift in local politics, and finally banished for life from the city he loved. Even in his isolation, however, he was ready to serve both Florence and Italy as he stripped bare his heart and soul in *The Prince* in order to foster the unification of the City-States into a single, powerful Italy."

"Was he an insider or was he more of a messenger-type attaché in diplomatic circles?" William asked.

Flanigan smiled, "No one outside royalty could have been better connected than Nicholas Machiavelli. He was appointed Secretary of the Florentine Republic in 1498 when he was only twenty-nine, a remarkable achievement. He went on to serve as the face-to-face negotiator with people like the Emperor Maximillian, Ferdinand of Aragon, Pope Alexander, Pope Julius, Louis XII of France, Pandolfo Petrucci of Siena, and of course, Cesare Borgia himself. In addition, he was a friend of both Leonardo da Vinci and Michelangelo. Essentially, he interacted directly and personally with most of the European policy makers for twenty years at the beginning of this century."

"His observations then would be first hand," William said, thumbing through pages. "Very intriguing."

"And first-class," offered Malachi.

Flanigan nodded. "Machiavelli was a brilliant observer. He grew up amidst the diplomatic and military conflicts which Florence had with the other city-states: Venice, Pisa, Milan, and Naples. The competition for control of the Asian silk and spice trade was fearsome. Cunning, corrupt policies which appeared successful were applauded, while thoughtful, honest policies were often overridden by the stampede for short-term profit."

"Did they all seek to shortchange the Asians?"

Malachi snorted. "Shortchange the masters? Hardly. Most Asian merchant families have been in the business for centuries, and they can calculate profit to a fine degree with their beads-on-a-board counting device called the abacus. They not only know how to get a fair return in business dealings, they also know how to pounce at those special moments when the other fellow blinks. Well, William, I will leave you to an edifying exchange with Mr. Flanigan, while I run some errands. I'll return in an hour."

"Machiavelli must have been highly motivated to write such a powerful book," William observed after Malachi left. "I'm always interested in what drives a writer to actually finish something. Did he ever explain why he wrote it?"

"I think he did when he wrote: *'My intention being to write something of use to those who understand, it appears to me more proper to go to the real truth of the matter than to its imagination; and many have imagined republics and principalities which have never been seen or known to exist in reality; for how we live is so far removed from how we ought to live, that he who abandons what is done for what ought to be done, will rather learn to bring about his own ruin than his preservation'."* [17]

"With emphasis on reality rather than appearances eh? Good approach. I wonder who he used for a muse?"

"The Prince is addressed to Lorenzo the Magnificent, you will notice, but the policies and principles which it promotes to make a prince successful are those of Cesare Borgia, at whose Venetian court Machiavelli served for twenty years. During that period, Venice was generally regarded as the most successful of the city-states, in large part because of Borgia's policies."

"Borgia? It seems to me I've heard that name."

"Yes. His sister Lucretia Borgia is reputed to have dabbled in exotic poisons which she sometimes tested on dinner guests. Anyway, Machiavelli glorified Cesare Borgia as a strong, effective leader. Give me the book, my boy. I'll find the place. Ah, here it is: 'On New Princedoms'. He carefully explains here why a strong prince is necessary. *'...It should be kept in mind that the temper of the multitude is fickle, and that while it is easy to persuade them of a thing, it is hard to fix them in that persuasion.... Wherefore, matters should be so ordered that when men no longer believe of their own accord, they may be compelled to believe by force.'"* [18]

"Compelled by force, eh," William observed. "That's motivation enough for most of us."

Flanigan resumed reading: *"Therefore, he who considers it necessary to secure himself in his new principality, to win friends, to overcome either by force or fraud, to make himself beloved and feared by the people, to be followed and revered by the soldiers, to exterminate those who had reason or power to hurt him, to change the old order of things for new, to be severe and gracious, magnanimous and liberal, to destroy a disloyal soldiery, and to create new, to maintain friendship with kings and princes in such a way that they must help him with zeal and offend with caution, cannot find a more lively example than the actions of this man."*

"That's Machiavelli's idea of a lofty spirit? To exterminate and destroy?"

"A prince's affairs are likely to be more complicated than those of ordinary people," Flanigan explained patiently.

"Even so, I would think that ordinary people would despise such a man."

"According to Machiavelli's observations, *'A Prince is despised when he is seen to be fickle, frivolous, effeminate, pusillanimous, or irresolute.'"* [19]

"Pusillanimous?"

"Lacking courage or strength of purpose."

"I don't think such statements hold up well to close examination," William contended. "Queen Elizabeth is certainly irresolute, and it is said that both King Henry III of France and King James of Scotland are noticeably effeminate."

Flanigan shrugged. "Nobody expects perfection. A prince is allowed one out of five. He keeps the affection of his people in other ways."

"I'm surprised Machiavelli even mentions affection. How is the Prince supposed to pull that one off, basically?"

"He announces all victories himself and distributes all rewards personally."

"Of course," chuckled William. "And the bad news? "

"Let me see here. Ah yes. *'Leave to the magistrates responsibility for inflicting punishment, and, indeed, the general disposal of all things which are likely to arouse disquiet'.*" [20]

"I bet Elizabeth memorized that part."

"All administrators do."

"Do you think that's her nature or did she learn it from Machiavelli?"

"Let's just say she probably has a well-thumbed copy beneath her pillow—if only to encourage her natural Tudor tendencies."

William was thoughtful. "We certainly would not want to accuse our Queen of treachery and cunning, so Machiavelli's advice must have its virtues. What prompted him to write since he was doing so well as a diplomat?"

"He didn't really start writing until the government changed and he was let go by Lorenzo Medici, who in 1512, with a little help from Spain, threw out the Florentine Republic and restored his own family to the throne."

"Did Machiavelli retire, then, or was he thrown out too?"

"He was arrested, imprisoned, tortured, and finally banished for life to a small country estate he owned. During the next ten years, he did his major writing—although some say that *The Prince* might have been written just before the Republic was overthrown. Nevertheless," Flanigan mused, "it always strikes me as strange that so many writers do their best work when they are confined."

"Tortured?" William reacted. "Zounds, that could set up a block in the mind of any writer! I would think, however, that an intelligent person—particularly a trained diplomat—could negotiate his way out of such an experience just by cooperating fully and revealing everything."

"He did that," Flanigan said. "Unfortunately for Machiavelli, however, the Magnificent Lorenzo measured the truthfulness and sincerity of other men by his own. He felt there was always something hidden, something left to squeeze so long as a heart was beating. He knew Machiavelli would freely reveal 95% of the secrets of the previous administration in order to conceal the final 5%—always the sticking point in administrative changeovers."

"Who has the key to the loot, you mean?"

"Exactly. So Machiavelli may have suffered the torment that all practical men suffer occasionally. He may have cooperated too readily and had nothing left to forestall his torture. The truth is, however, that they didn't break him up too badly, so I suspect he held out one last prize to preserve himself from serious suffering." Flanigan grimaced. "Indeed, as *The Prince* clearly shows, the man had two decades' worth of the Republic's darkest secrets concealed within his head, so it would be surprising if he couldn't pull one out when he really needed it."

William nodded. "I suppose his reputation would suffer otherwise."

"His book shows that he spent his twenty-year diplomatic career making political and personal judgments which I would characterize as cold and detached, but also keen and compelling for anybody deeply involved in the power game."

"I'm glad to hear he was able to go on," William said. "I hate to think that any writer's spirit might get crushed by mistreatment."

"As a matter of fact," Flanigan confided, "I feel the prison and torture actually turned him into a writer. Gaining revenge by striking back is an intense motivation. It helps to focus the mind and minimize distractions."

"Yet Machiavelli dedicated his book to the very man who had him tortured: Lorenzo de Medichi. That shows a great deal of Christian charity."

Flanigan shrugged. "What else was he to do? Nothing was printed without approval from the top. Besides, he saw Lorenzo as the man who could unify Italy."

"Malachi told me that Rome now lists *The Prince* on the Catholic Index of Prohibited Books," said William. "Why is that?"

"His atheistic leanings probably. Since the Council of Trent in 1559, all his works have been banned by Rome, but important people still read him. I suspect that every prince in Europe has Machiavelli's book. Henry III keeps a copy in his robe, and Henry Navarre makes his a well-thumbed companion. Whether anybody likes it or not, Nicholas Machiavelli presents some very practical advice about the attainment and preservation of power. He removes ethics entirely from political concerns and replaces them with expediency. According to Machiavelli, whatever action preserves the State is excusable."

"Even murder?"

"At that level, it's called 'assassination.' A drop in the bucket, to Machiavelli's way of thinking."

"I'm amazed that his writing is still so relevant after almost seventy-five years."

"Gaining and holding power are always relevant. Tell me, for instance, which present-day country follows this advice when they seize another country. The conquering Prince '...*should make haste to inflict what injuries he must, at a stroke, that he may not have to renew them daily, but be enabled by their discontinuance to reassure men's minds, and afterwards win them over by benefits....Benefits should be conferred little by little, so that they may be more fully enjoyed.*' [21] Who does that sound like?"

"Sounds like all of them to me."

"You don't really have much of a mind for parallels, do you?" Flanigan observed. "It's the Spanish operation in the New World to the last dot. That's how Spain controls nearly half the world with so few men. Hit them hard at first, kill the troublemakers, set up a big church, a small administrative office, and a token garrison nearby."

"Does that mean that even Philip reads—"

"I wouldn't be surprised," Flanigan nodded. "Probably more copies read in Rome and Madrid than anywhere else. The English are also good students in their dealings with the Irish."

"Oh no, not Ireland again."

"Here in his chapter 'How Provinces Should be Governed,' Machiavelli offers three options for governing a captured state: *'The first is to destroy it; the second, to go and reside there in person; the third, to suffer it to live on under its own laws, subjecting it to tribute, and entrusting its government to a few of the inhabitants who will keep the rest your friends'.*" [22]

"Which do we English apply?"

"All three at different times. We are leaning heavily on the last two at the moment since the Desmond Rebellion four years ago left southwestern Ireland in a state of complete destruction as far as crops, cattle, homes, and people are concerned. London, however, follows the book's advice on handling the remaining inhabitants. They forgive O'Neil and Ormand the personal taxes they owe, hoping that O'Neil will keep the peace with England in the north and Ormand in the south. O'Neil was raised in England, you know, a boyhood companion of Sir Philip Sidney himself on the Sidney estate."

"So he's an Irishman by birth but trained as an Englishman?"

"Right, and that helps to explain O'Neil. He's a crafty one, causing Elizabeth much distress when she watches the mutual agreements England has reached with him not exactly broken but neatly side-stepped by some act of Irish impishness. But I guess a man must be crafty to stay afloat in that beleaguered land."

"Perhaps he reads Machiavelli too," suggested William. "What would the practical Italian say is the worst problem in Ireland?"

"That's easy," said Flanigan. "Ireland has the same problem Italy had in Machiavelli's time and still has for that matter. No central government in place. No central State. No one for England to deal with diplomatically except for surly chieftains in Ireland and cynical city-states in Italy. If either country really gets lucky, it may find a leader who will someday read Machiavelli closely enough to shape the contending factions into a national state powerful enough to defend itself from foreign invasion."

"No offense, Mr. Flanigan, but might you be Irish yourself?"

"My parents were born there, but once in England, they became Anglican, forgot their roots, and set up this business. That's very Machiavellian in itself. Practical and ruthless, as it were. I myself am so caught up in my interests here—being an editor-printer, translator, and interpreter—that I have little concern for old family ties."

"Your life is really bound up in letters, Mr. Flanigan," William chuckled. "Do you know this much about all the authors?"

"To some degree, yes, but Machiavelli interests me very much. I have read *The Prince* in the original and, as I said earlier, it both charms and repels me. But there is no doubt Machiavelli is a genius, and a true genius needs an interpreter."

"I'm afraid I don't follow."

"What's clarity for a genius is often chaos for the ordinary reader. What the genius takes for granted has never even occurred to the common man, even if he is well educated. I like to think I serve as a priest-like functionary who is sensitive enough to catch some glimmerings of the universal truths embodied in the writing of the genius, yet still earthly enough to pass them on in understandable language and sequence to a reader like yourself."

"Sort of an extraordinary-ordinary functionary?"

"That's a nice way to put it," smiled P. Flanigan. "The very heart of Machiavelli, for instance, is buried in an obscure conditional sentence at the end of his work where no ordinary reader would ever find it without the firm guidance of an interpreter. He says, *'If one could change one's nature with time and circumstance, fortune would never change'*." [23]

"Is he saying that the sun would always shine for us if we were able to shift color and blend into the background like the chameleon?"

"Something deeper than that, I'm afraid. He really suggests the myth of Proteus as the road to success in human affairs."

"I'm afraid you've lost me there," admitted William.

"Proteus could assume different shapes and forms to alter not only his actions but his very nature as well, giving him a power equal to the gods themselves. Not possible for any human, of course, but, strangely enough, Queen Elizabeth comes very close to overcoming those mortal limitations."

"Overcome her mortality?" William cried in wonder.

Flanigan nodded. "Our distinguished sovereign is Machiavelli personified. She has run this country for nearly thirty years strictly on a policy of shift and delay. When her counselors grow irritated with that approach, she drops it for a strategy of retard and postpone. She keeps all opposition off balance with her capricious financial rewards and punishments. Unlike her father Henry VIII—who made it a point never to change his mind once he decided something—the Queen will not enter into any agreement from which she cannot gracefully withdraw if time or circumstance should sour on her. Essentially, she behaves exactly as Machiavelli directs an effective prince to behave. In short, she feels no compunction whatever to adhere to a predictable self just to please the onlookers."

"She may feel that way safe in her palace, but I know that if I were a French Huguenot captured by the French Catholics, I would feel very lucky if I got a chance to convert immediately to escape slaughter."

Flanigan smiled. "You are beginning to get the picture albeit a trifle dimly. Here is a quotation that might appeal more to your sporting nature: *'... fortune is the mistress of one half of our actions, and yet leaves control of the other half, or a little less to ourselves'*." [24]

"Roughly 55% for luck and 45% for us, eh?" laughed William. "I usually count on luck for a 10% fillip, no more."

Flanigan shrugged. "Well, for whatever part we do control, Machiavelli advises that it is better to be impetuous rather than cautious. *For fortune is a woman who to be kept under must be beaten and roughly handled; and we see that she suffers herself to be more readily mastered by those who so treat her than by those who are more timid in their approaches. And always, like a woman, she favors the young, because they are less scrupulous and fiercer, and command her with greater audacity'*." [25]

"Ah, now we come to the interesting part!" cried William. "How did he make out with women, by the by?"

"His relationship with his wife, Marietta, seems to have been loving enough. I remember she wrote him in November of 1503 after the birth of one of their sons in a letter that was published along with his private papers. She informed him: *'He* [our child] *looks like you; skin white as snow and a head like black velvet, and hairy all over, the way you are! Since he is so like you, I suppose I must call him handsome.'* [26] I'd say that shows her to be a dutiful and good natured wife, but I don't have any idea how—or if—he made out with other women."

William shrugged. "Still, nothing you've told me so far explains why people use the term 'Machiavellian' to denote treachery and cunning. I mean, so far the man seems moral enough even if a little rough on the ladies."

"The charges which got his work banned were atheism and immorality. The immorality charge stems mostly from his advice in 'How Princes Should Keep Faith.' Shall I read the pertinent part?"

"Please do."

"A *prudent prince neither can nor ought to keep his word when to keep it is hurtful to him and if the causes which led him to pledge it are removed.*" [27]

"That seems a trifle dishonorable." William commented. "And it might result in a lot of chaos if no prince could trust another."

Flanigan smiled. "Let me continue: *'If all men were good, this would not be good advice, but since they are dishonest and do not keep faith with you, you, in return, need not keep faith with them; and no prince was ever at a loss for plausible reasons to cloak a breach of faith...But men remain so simple, and governed so absolutely by their present needs, that he who wishes to deceive them will never fail in finding willing dupes...Thus it is well to seem merciful, faithful,*

157

humane, religious, and upright, and also to be so; but the mind should remain so balanced that were it needful not to be so, you should be able and know how to change to the contrary...Everyone sees what you seem, but few know what you are.'"

"He doesn't think much of the ordinary man, does he?"

"Well, don't forget, this book is really a personal letter to Lorenzo to advise him in the project of uniting Italy. Machiavelli didn't want the fortunes of his Prince to founder on false hopes. He probably tipped the scales a bit against optimism to keep his Prince on his toes."

"But you think he was more hopeful, actually?"

"No. I think he was deeply disillusioned with ordinary people. He must have seen some pretty rough in-fighting during his years as a diplomat. At another point where he is giving advice to the Prince on being loved or feared, he gives ordinary people quite a drubbing. *"But since love and fear can hardly exist together, if we must choose between them, it is far safer to be feared than loved. For of men it may generally be affirmed that they are thankless, fickle, false, studious to avoid danger, greedy of gain, devoted to you while you are able to confer benefits on them, and ready, while danger is distant, to shed their blood, and sacrifice their property, their lives, and their children for you; but in the hour of need they turn against you.'"* [28]

"Egad!" William exclaimed, "he must have grown up in a tough neighborhood."

"He does suggest to his Prince, later on, that intimidation has its limits when he advises: *'Nevertheless, a prince ought to inspire fear in such a way that, if he does not win love, he avoids hatred.'"*

"He really should have been writing stage plays with his emphasis so strongly on the brawny conflicts generated by love, hatred, cunning, trickery, betrayal, and loyalty. He lived during interesting times."

"Exactly," said Flanigan. "During his lifetime, Machiavelli watched armies from France, Spain, Germany, and Switzerland march across Italian soil and bloody it in the passing. Many of those armies were invited in and paid by the squabbling city-states to battle against their neighboring states. It must have occurred to any intelligent man that those visiting armies were from countries much more unified than poor, fragmented Italy."

"How fragmented? You mentioned Venice, Florence, Milan, and Naples."

"There are ten independent Italian states but the big ones are those four plus the Vatican or Church State. Maybe also Pisa. When countries like Spain and France were battling each other over ownership of Naples and the southern half of the Italian boot, it was apparent that Italy suffered from lack of central government."

"They had a central Church. Why didn't that unify them?"

Flanigan laughed. "The last thing an entrenched power structure wants is a competing power structure. For all its promise of celestial brotherhood, the Roman

Church was slow to risk its prosperous position by promoting a coalition of city-states which might easily elbow the Church aside in both influence and revenue throughout Italy. In addition, of course, Machiavelli shared the cynical view of Erasmus and others about the church policies at that time."

"They were disappointed?"

Flanigan nodded. "Disappointed and discouraged about the future of the church. In 1513, Machiavelli wrote out this warning to the church; *"Had the religion of Christianity been preserved according to the ordinances of the Founder, the state and commonwealth of Christendom would have been far more united and happy than they are. Nor can there be a greater proof of its decadence than the fact that the nearer people are to the Roman Church, the head of their religion, the less religious are they. And whoever examines the principles on which religion is founded, and sees how widely different from those principles its present practice and application are, will judge that her ruin or chastisement is near at hand."* [29] Four years later, Luther nailed his 95 complaints to the door of the Wittenburg Schlosskirche, and ignited a fire which is still consuming property and people."

"So with the church out of the picture, he turned to Lorenzo?"

"He did," Flanigan said, "and made a direct appeal to him. *"This opportunity, then, for Italy at last to look on her deliverer, ought not to be allowed to pass away....[Her deliverer] would be received in all those provinces which have suffered from the foreign inundation, with what thirst for vengeance, with what fixed fidelity, with what devotion, and what tears, no words of mine can declare. What gates would be closed against him? What People would refuse him obedience? What Jealousy would stand in his way? What Italians but would yield him homage. This barbarous tyranny stinks in every nostril."* [30]

"Zounds!" William cried. "That's good writing! 'Stinks in every nostril.' I'm surprised it didn't get the job done."

"Well, the Italians are still working on it. I suppose someday they'll agree to unite when the right Prince comes along."

"What about the Irish?"

"Don't ask."

Chapter 7.
SIR PHILIP SIDNEY, RENAISSANCE GALAHAD

Flanigan's Bookshop in St. Paul's:

Malachi entered the shop, mopping his brow with a large kerchief. "Ah," he greeted the proprietor and Will. "Hot out there. You're still discussing the 'Old Nick,' I see. As it happens, I've just set up an appointment with one of the few men in England—or the Western World, for that matter—who does not follow the advice of Machiavelli. In fact, I would say he is the antithesis of the great Italian."

"Who would that be?" asked William.

"Let me guess," said the bookseller. "'T'would be our modern-day Galahad, Sir Philip Sidney. Am I right?"

Malachi chuckled. "Indeed! "modern-day Galahad he is, generally regarded as the most humane of the leading gentlemen of the realm, always ready to fight for a just cause even if it doesn't gain him a shilling."

"That might explain why Sir Philip Sidney rates such special treatment from the alehouse whips, who delight in flogging notables," said William. "Nashe, as I have painfully discovered, is not much given to complimenting anybody but speaks of him as 'gentle Sir Philip Sidney.' I envy the admiration Sidney inspires in everybody."

"Envy away," said Malachi. "You'll never comprehend Sidney's unbending virtue from that direction. As for admiration, Nashe will flip-flop all evening for any who will buy his dinner, just as Greene will. When it comes to jingle-makers, they are the sauciest pair of rogues in the realm."

"And I'll warrant you have never considered the drawbacks of such 'acclaim and admiration' as Sidney enjoys," said Flanigan grimly.

"Drawbacks?"

"If you want to understand Sir Philip Sidney's role in our realm, you must start early," said Malachi.

"It's barely past noon," protested William.

"Early in his <u>life</u>," Malachi specified. "Sir Philip is not only the son of a nobleman but also the nephew of the second most important man in the country: the Queen's old-time favorite, Leicester. He is also the godson of the most powerful ruler on earth, King Philip of Spain, and—"

"Godson of Catholic Philip?" gasped William.

Malachi nodded. "Prince Philip of Spain was in England at the time and personally held his namesake in his arms at the ceremony."

"What in the world was Philip doing in our country?" William asked in some wonder.

"He was escorted here by an honor guard of England's finest nobles in a successful campaign for the hand of our Catholic Queen Mary, Elizabeth's elder half-sister. The senior Sidney, Sir Henry, was part of that guard, and he and soon-to-be King Philip became fast friends just as the need for a godfather arose in the Sidney household with the birth of young Philip."

"Is the family still Catholic?"

"Oh no. Like much of the nobility, they converted to the Anglican Church when Elizabeth ascended the throne. The sons' wives are from Puritan families, so the loyalty of the Sidney family has never been in question. And young Philip has lived up to his role with such grace that, in his thirty-four years, he has earned the respect and affection not only of the English but of all Europe as well. What other young man of twenty-one had his Tour of the Continent enlivened by such offers as the kingship of Poland and the lordship of Holland?"

"A Dutch offer even before our Queen got hers?" William sighed. "Universal acceptance at such a young age. Zounds."

"Not quite universal," Malachi corrected. "Elizabeth takes a different view altogether."

"Perhaps because of the godfather thing?"

"As far as any outside observer can perceive," said Malachi. "There are certain areas of the Queen's brain where she does not think so much as she feels and then lets those feelings serve for thought. What other explanation is there for the rather shabby treatment she has extended to the Sidney family for the last twenty-five years? Even spending part of her youth as a next-door neighbor to them hardly explains her extended animosity."

"Besides the godfather thing," suggested Flanigan, "it's possible they went a bit overboard in their support of Elizabeth's sister, the infamous Protestant burner, 'Bloody Mary.'"

Malachi nodded, "The Queen has a wonderful nose for sniffing out competing power, wherever it rears its head in her domain. She does not necessarily stamp it out, but she never encourages it unless it originates in her court under her direction, and then it's not competing anymore, you see."

"And the Sidneys have always been powerful people," added Flanigan, "in a way Elizabeth cannot duplicate. The Queen's power comes from flexibility of principle, and the Sidneys' comes from firmness of principle. The Sidneys gain the admiration of all they encounter by their honorable behavior. Their word is an absolute bond, and they are considerate and polite to everybody with whom they have contact, including those of the lower orders."

"Not Machiavellian at all," said William.

"Such men have many loyal admirers, and the Queen does not like to share the stage of her countrymen's hearts with anyone."

"Jealousy?" squeaked William.

"That's about what it amounts to, yes. Those of us who love her most must sometimes admit to certain twists and turns in our sweet sovereign. She makes a practice of appointing such highly principled men as the Sidneys to heavy responsibilities, promises them appropriations, and sends them off to do some dirty job without taking another step to supply them."

Malachi took up the narrative. "It is known that the Queen often laughs in chambers at the predicament she has cast them into and states that at last they will have to apply the whip-saw of accommodation to their precious principles. It is only when some costly civic duty is yoked across their shoulders, she declares, that they will begin to appreciate what she has endured since the day she was crowned."

"Such monarchical peevishness doesn't sound quite honorable," said William. "After all, a promise is a promise."

"That's certainly what Sir Henry Sidney thought when she appointed him Lord Deputy of Ireland in '67 and sent him off to quell O'Neil eighteen years ago. I think the man exhausted himself battling against the realization that the Queen's sense of honor did not match his own."

"Machiavelli again," murmured William.

Flanigan nodded. "Most of the experienced military commanders know that the Queen will slow her support once they depart from London. They prepare for every expedition by selling off some of their estates or putting them up as collateral for a personal loan from the Queen. She always grants such loans as long as the estates revert to her if the loan is not repaid. Most of them know that the Queen's initial subsidy must be carefully hoarded against hard times."

Malachi snorted. "Which is why the military has informally adopted the system of always paying the man above a little extra and stealing a bit from the man below. Such a system permits the money to funnel upward where it will be used to influence policy-making in London, but it often leaves the ordinary soldier at the bottom of the arrangement with an empty purse and a matching belly."

"Sir Henry, however," broke in Flanigan, "paid every man fairly, even when it meant digging into his own fortune. He kept thinking the Queen would eventually support him. Such men of honor must be watched carefully, alas, for the people may come to love them overly much."

William sighed. "Aside from losing a great deal of money and gaining the love of his soldiers, how did Sir Henry make out in Ireland?"

"Wrought miracles," Malachi exclaimed vigorously. "He brought to bay the most elusive firebrand in Ireland, Shane O'Neil, and stuck his head on a pike above the gates of Dublin. In his first year there, he assembled thirty-four of the major Irish chieftains and escorted them to London, along with their retinues, all dressed in their finest furs and hides."

William whistled. "Thirty-four chieftains and their men! They must have made quite a spectacle."

"Indeed, they did," said Malachi. "The Queen called them 'A brave cavalcade.' They provided grist for many a courtly jibe about clothing and manners and personal hygiene. But in the final political analysis, Sir Henry Sidney formulated a settlement of the clans' grievances and brought England to the moment when a sensible alliance might have been struck between the two nations. Such an agreement would have assured England a helpful ally over the years, but the chance was missed and since then we have, consequently, spent many more lives and much more money just to gain a stand-off with the Irish rebels."

"What went wrong?" cried William.

"First, the Queen dampened any public enthusiasm for Sidney's victory over O'Neil and his followers by pointing out that the Irishman was *'but an outlaw and not some foreign sovereign.'* [31] On the other hand, whimsically enough, she struck bargains with the Chieftains and sent them home with real prospects for a long peace. As a reward for recognizing her sovereignty, she re-granted them their own estates under royal charters, and made earls of the lot of them, so they would have the authority to set up noble houses in Ireland and help run that country profitably for England."

"And neglected to honor Sir Henry Sidney for the triumph, I bet."

"Well, she honored Sidney in her own fashion," Malachi laughed. "Having stripped him of most of his fortune carrying out her policies in Ireland, she made him a baron.

Lady Sidney begged her not to make the appointment since they had not enough money left to support their responsibilities at their old station. The Queen insisted, however, and extended Henry a large personal loan with his family estates in collateral for repayment to her."

"Why would the Queen treat a successful Lord Deputy in such fashion?"

"Because the people admired and trusted him, even the Irish," said Flanigan. "The Queen saw clearly enough that when the Irish chieftains came to London, they hated each other but held their ancient animosities in check out of the deep respect they felt for Sir Henry. Many times after the settlement, Elizabeth was forced to send him thither again to resolve disputes with chieftains who trusted no other Englishman."

"That presumes a personal power in part of her realm which made Elizabeth very uneasy as a sovereign," pointed out Malachi.

"What happened to the agreement with the Irish? You said it was a chance missed."

"After setting up sensible relationships and formulating an effective administration in Dublin, the Queen simply left the Lord Deputies to keep her promises by raising taxes on the Irish. Tax-collecting in Ireland, however, is not only a tricky business, but a risky one as well. All the arrangements collapsed from want of funds, and every Lord Deputy of Ireland since has spent half his time trying to pry a sensible subsidy out of the Queen."

William sighed. "But Sir Philip, the son? How did he offend the Queen?"

"A number of years ago," said Flanigan, "while Sir Henry was still Lord Deputy of Ireland, he sent a letter of advice to his son Philip, who was twenty-one at that time. It is thought to be the first direct correspondence between them. When the letter was made public, it was much admired and often quoted. I myself helped get it copied and published, so it is now a matter of public record."

"Do you, perchance, have a copy of it here in the shop?" asked Malachi grinning. As the bookseller hurried off to get it, he turned to William. "Try not to take any of Sir Henry's advice too personally or become too self-conscious of your own shortcomings."

"Surely things have changed in the last dozen years, so that such ancient advice holds little value for a youth of today," said William stiffly.

Flanigan returned with the letter held triumphantly in one hand and a glass of water in the other. "Sir Henry offered his son these few precepts eighteen years ago: *'Be humble and obedient to your master, for unless you frame yourself to obey others, yea, and feel in yourself what obedience is, you shall never be able to teach others to obey you.'*" [32]

"I don't particularly need others to obey me," William muttered.

"You do want to be a gentleman, don't you?" Malachi inquired. "It's the same thing." He gestured to Flanigan. "Let the recital continue."

"'Be courteous of gesture, and affable unto all men, with diversity of reverence according to the dignity of the person. There is nothing that winneth so much with so little cost. Use moderate diet, so as after your meal you may find your wit fresher and not more duller, and your body more lively and not more heavy. Seldom drink wine, and yet sometimes do, lest being enforced to drink upon the sudden you should find yourself inflamed."

"He certainly has that part right," Malachi acknowledged softly.

"'Use exercise of body, but such as is without peril of your bones and joints: it will increase your force and enlarge your breath. Delight to be cleanly as well in all parts of your body as in your garments, it shall make you grateful in each company and otherwise loathsome. Give yourself to be merry, for you degenerate from your father if you find not yourself most able in wit and body when you be most merry: but let your mirth be ever void of all scurrility and biting words, for a wound given by a word is oftentimes harder to be cured than that which is given by the sword.'"

"Mark that point well, William, and make thy tongue less sharp," Malachi advised.

William grumbled in response.

"'Be rather a hearer and bearer away of other men's talk than a beginner or procurser of speech: otherwise you shall be accounted to delight to hear yourself speak. Be modest in each assembly and rather be rebuked of light fellows for maidenlike shamefastness than of your sad friends for pert boldness. Think upon every word that you will speak before you utter it, and remember how nature hath ramparted up as it were the tongue with teeth, lips, yea and hair without the lip, and all betokening reins and bridles to the less use of that member. Above all things, tell no untruth, no, not in trifles.'" [32] Flanigan put down the letter.

"Is that it? Is that the sum total of a loving father's advice?" William exclaimed. "Egad, if he needed to exercise his platitudes, the least he could have done was refrain from tedious prolixity."

Flanigan gasped, but Malachi held up a hand to him for patience. "You could do better, young William?"

William nodded. "He should have combined the being 'affable unto all men' and the 'think upon every word' elements into something like *'Give every man thine ear, but few thy voice'*." [33]

"Not bad," admitted Malachi. "Any other suggestions?"

"Well," said William, "he left out a lot of important considerations. Finances, for instance. The lives of young people often go astray over money matters. Sir Henry could have said; *'Neither a borrower nor a lender be: For a loan oft loses both itself and friend; and borrowing dulls the edge of husbandry'*." [34] William looked at his listeners for encouragement and, finding none, continued anyway. "Also, his final statement is weak. Just before the curtain comes down, a strong drum-beat is wanted, not that insipid 'tell no untruth' business. One wants a trumpet call to the very soul!"

"You think 'Tell no lies!' would be better?."

William stayed deep in thought for a moment, then looked up smiling. He struck a pose, one hand on his breast, one uplifted. *'This above all—to thine own self be true; and it must follow, as the night the day, thou canst not then be false to any man'.*" [34]

"Remarkable," said Flanigan, visibly impressed.

"Really remarkable," said Malachi, "the way you can take Sidney's thoughts, on the one hand, and compress them into something you've taken from another source, on the other. There are moments when you appear to have a gift for coordinating and blending the ideas of others."

Flanigan nodded agreement.

"Nothing really." William puffed up a bit. "I just blink my eyes in the rhythm I want my thoughts to flow and before I know it, voila! But come now, sir, you've seen me do this before. Why does it impress you on this particular occasion?"

"The speed of your transfer. You are presented with certain information and you adroitly transform it into passable verse without missing a beat. I must tell you that I find your exhibition of smooth brain-work very encouraging because I've had a feeling lately that the time and effort I've put into trying to educate you was a complete waste and that I was being nine kinds of fool for even attempting to turn your mutilated brain into a functional entity. If you live to be one hundred—"

"Excuse me," broke in William, "but I have a depressing feeling that the long-awaited coach of conversational compliments has just whizzed past me and left me by the wayside, waving forlornly. Could we perhaps back up and review that part where I was doing something you admired before you gallop us down the road of inconsequential complaint?"

"When you have earned a compliment, you need not fish for it," said Malachi, turning to the bookseller. "Tell us, Mr. Flanigan, how would you rate the boy's re-wording?"

The scrivener cleared his throat. "Talk about getting left behind by the conversational coach—hrrrumph!" He turned directly to William. "Nevertheless, young man, you should be aware that you have done little more with Sir Henry's lines than erase the graceful expression and reduce the complexity of his thought into something rather stark and simple—and, if I may say so, slightly unseemly as well. As a matter of fact, if you are gifted in any area, it is as a translator of classic thought into the vulgate of the vulgar."

"Is there money in that sort of thing?" William asked.

"Since you are so attracted to simplicity, perhaps the Puritanical axioms with which Lady Sidney barraged Sir Philip's ears throughout his youth might be more to your taste."

"His mother was a Puritan?" asked William, surprised.

"We're not certain how far to the right she was in the Anglican Church, but Philip did marry the daughter of Walsingham," said Malachi. "And one cannot be more Puritan than Walsingham."

"Well," William grinned, "that is a giveaway connection all right. Perhaps Philip reads Old Nick too. Give us an axiom, then, Mr. Flanigan."

"Early each morning, she admonished him to *'Wish the best and fear the worst; suffer then what happen shall.'*" [35]

"Pessimistic breakfast fare," William observed, "but it might provide comfort for people who are somehow scheduled for a rough day anyway."

Chapter 8:
SIR PHILLIP'S SECRETARY GOSSIPS A BIT

Sidney's Penhurst estate along the Thames River:

William turned at the werryman's call of "Eastward Ho!" as he and Malachi climbed up the lawn from the river Thames to the Sidney home.

"That's my first trip in a werry," said William. "It's interesting that you have to wait until the tide turns to come upriver and very romantic, all that river traffic."

"And a great deal more convenient than coming all the way through London on foot or even on a horse. Coming by carriage is unspeakably slow."

"This is a very fine house," said the apprentice in awe. "I would suppose the Sidneys are still very rich, then."

"Try not to gawk, lad. We couriers of the Queen must maintain our dignity."

"Will I see him, the great Sir Philip?"

"I have a job for you today, William. If possible, I will leave you with Sir Philip's secretary to gather any pertinent information you can. If not the secretary, then I'll send you to the kitchen, which is the heart of a household and the mother lode of gossip."

They entered the house soon after and were ushered into the library, where a very young man introduced himself as Sir Philip's secretary, Mr. William Temple.

"You're very fortunate, young man, to be working under such an illustrious personage," said Malachi. "I trust he is not too lenient with you. It is the duty of the wise foxes of the realm to nip at the heels of you empty-headed kits to make you step lively."

"Yes sir," said Mr. Temple politely. "My master, however, seldom nips at any heels."

"No, he is quite young himself and very idealistic. But English policy-makers all recognize the brilliant diplomatic career that so obviously lies ahead for Sir Philip, if not under Elizabeth, then certainly under her successor. They want to season Philip quickly by giving him more important jobs, but the Queen insists that the process be as slow as possible, and the significance of that strategy is not lost upon the Court."

"You are referring, sir, to the many instances of recent years when my master has been deceived and betrayed by the Walsinghams and Leicesters of the Court?"

"You know your foxes," approved Malachi. "That's two of the big three."

"Who's the third?" asked William. "Lord Burghley?"

"Ah, you're learning," said Malachi. "Those three have been chief councilors of the Queen for many years. Sometimes she listens to one and sometimes to another and oftentimes to no one but her own whimsical urgings."

"Hold!" cried the secretary, in some alarm. "Are you trying to tell me something? Are you trying to soften an impending blow to the Sidney household? Do you know the contents of the dispatch you are delivering?"

"Nothing of the kind," Malachi assured him. "Just rambling along while we wait for Sir Philip to arrive and take possession of this envelope. You said he'd be here about this time?"

"That's the schedule," the secretary nodded, "but one can never anticipate the demands of the Court."

"Amen to that," Malachi agreed. "When he comes, may I leave my secretary here to keep you company? I won't be long with Sir Philip."

"No problem there," the young man assured Malachi. "He'll be welcome here with me until your meeting is over. Let me just ask the butler to bring us some wine and biscuits. The time will fly until my master is in our midst."

The butler entered to announce Sir Philip's readiness to see Malachi.

"Take it easy with that stuff," Malachi warned as he left the library. "I don't want you soused when I get back."

"Never fear," the secretary assured him. He then turned back to William. "Actually, good wine clears the head rather than clouds it, and this is the very best."

"Very reassuring," said William, taking the offered glass.

"Sir Philip is a very generous man," the secretary confided. "He insists that all visitors be well entertained, and the household staff accepts it as part of their Christian duty to offer its best hospitality. My friends call me Temple, by the way." He shook hands with William. "I finished Cambridge just last year and will be studying law when Sir Philip thinks I'm ready. I'm a younger son, you know—not the youngest, thank heavens. I wouldn't want to be a clergyman. But I will have to find a position of some kind. Meanwhile, I like it here very much."

"I like my job with Malachi, too. There's so much to be learned, places to go, and people to see. In the end, however, I would like to write, provided I have something to write about."

Temple sat back and sipped his wine. "Sir Philip was knighted two years ago, you know. We were all very relieved."

"Relieved?" William asked.

"Sir Philip had already earned the knighthood over and over, and if it were not for the mysterious grudge the Queen bears the Sidney family, he would have been vested many years earlier."

"Grudge?" William asked slyly.

"Finally knighted," Temple nodded with satisfaction. "He cooked up a clever little scheme with Casimir of Germany when the two visited in 1581. Casimir was in line to be created Knight of the Garter by Elizabeth for some small favor he had done her on the Continent, so he arranged to miss the ceremony while naming Sidney as his proxy. That boxed the Queen in since the only acceptable proxy for a knight must be another knight. She knighted Sir Philip to meet that requirement as a matter of political convenience rather than in recognition of his merits, but I think the two conspirators enjoyed the process, nevertheless. The Sidneys have learned to make the best of the odd position in which the Queen has placed them."

"The grudge thing again," acknowledged William.

"Oh, I say!" cried Temple. "I can trust you to keep this conversation within these walls, can't I? What kind of a writer did you say you aspired to be?"

"A poet."

"Safe enough," Temple decided. "Fetch another glass, and I'll tell you something very curious about Sir Philip."

William got up to fetch. "Curious, you say?" he prompted, upon sitting again.

"You must promise to keep your tongue behind your teeth about all this, William."

"Absolutely, and let me say you have so far maintained an admirable level of sage objectivity."

"Well, privately, I like to match my thinking against Sir Philip's, as it were, and follow the results of his public decisions. I keep a scorecard on how right or wrong I am in comparison."

"Who's ahead?" asked William.

"It doesn't work quite that way," the secretary explained. "I have observed over my time here that he has special characteristics that weigh strongly in his decisions."

"Like what?"

"Nobility, for one. He's way ahead of me on that, but I usually take him on practicality. Take, for instance, three years ago when a major Court faction—led by Walsingham and Leicester—wanted to advise the Queen strongly against her proposed marriage to the Duke of Anjou, the French heir-apparent, who, thanks-be-to-God, has since died of syphilis. They looked all over for a fall-guy to write the letter that would surely offend her, and Sir Philip was selected to express their opinion. They convinced him that the force of his charm, combined with his forthright honesty, was exactly what was needed to do the job properly. They hinted strongly that it was his duty to the country."

"You think he should have turned them down?"

"Oh, definitely. He knew the letter would certainly alienate the Queen further from the Sidney family because she takes all such advisements as personal insults. The originators of such offenses always find their lives thereafter plagued with arbitrary appointments to positions in which they have no interest and refusal of positions they feel are worthy of their place."

"And did it fall out that way?"

Temple nodded and sipped his wine. "Sir Philip was recently refused the Captaincy of the Isle of Wight and even denied a seat on the Council of Wales."

"I had no idea."

"Part of the pattern. He will be refused what he so deeply desires, but will be granted positions which he and the Court both know are beneath him. Slow suffocation of noble ambition is part of the Queen's retribution policy for offenses real or imagined."

"Terribly unjust," William offered.

"I knew you were a man of keen perception," said Temple as he paused for another thoughtful sip of wine. "That's exactly it, unjust but inevitable, following exactly the fortune that fate has cut out for the Sidneys, or the fate that fortune has cut out for them, depending on how you look at it."

"I thought you said the Queen was responsible?"

"Same thing in this realm," Temple assured him, "as far as public placement goes. Our records indicate that in England we have 1,200 appointive offices which pay enough to make them worthy of a gentleman's attention. That means they return to him above 300 pounds per annum if kept in a sensible manner."

"Sensible manner?" William inquired.

"Make a living out of it," said Temple, patiently. "Either sell the lesser offices under you or arrange a payback of some sort from those you appoint. Set up an accounting system to insure your income from fines levied, licenses issued, and goods bought or sold under your name."

"Ah yes," said William. "I believe I've heard that the system works that way. "bit hard on one's underlings, of course."

"Yes," said young Temple. "And you've heard, of course, how Sir Henry Sidney used up much of his personal fortune in Ireland, going against this system. The Queen had no sympathy at all for the man. She presumes a buccaneering spirit in her governors, and the Sidneys seem to lack it entirely. There's no give-and-take in them. That's their problem: they don't do winks or smirks. Father and son, Henry and Philip, both insisted the English tax be applied equally to all landowners in Ireland because that was the only policy which would curb rebellion and keep the Irish chieftains in line. 'Show no favorites' is the foundation for all their policy-making"

"One can't help but admire—"

"Oh, everyone admires them for it. Any sensible administrator, however, would have shrugged his shoulders and complied with the Queen's wishes to make an exception in the case of the Earl of Ormond's land tax, but the Sidneys continued to insist on an equitable distribution of taxes. Philip left off campaigning with his father to return to England and write up his report: '"Discourse of Irish Affairs.' The report defends his father's actions in Ireland and particularly emphasizes the justice of the equitable tax-policy instituted by Sir Henry."

"I'm sure the Queen was not best pleased with that."

"Not at all," admitted Temple sadly. "She regarded it as an open admission that the Sidneys were not prepared to carry out her policies in Ireland, and she responded by yanking Sir Henry out of his Lord Deputy office shortly thereafter. To get along, you've got to go along, as far as the Queen is concerned."

"Do you remember any of the contents of the 'Discourse'?" William asked.

"Well, young Sidney had learned what every Englishman learns once submerged in the bogs and fens of that dreadful land. You simply can't use gentle means nor be lenient with those people. It doesn't work."

"Lenient?"

"He's absolutely opposed to leniency. I remember in his report he said: '*Truly the general nature of all countries not fully conquered is plainly against it. For until by time they find the sweetness of due subjection, it is impossible that any gentle means should put out the fresh remembrance of their lost liberty, and Irishmen are that way as obstinate as any nation, with whom no other passion can prevail but fear.*'" [36]

"He believes that time will solve the whole problem then?"

"Absolutely," said Temple. "Time and the guiding hand of English law."

"From the tavern-talk I've heard," William observed, "the Irish have so far had trouble appreciating the 'sweetness of due subjection', but I also hear they are a slow lot in other areas as well. How many years has England been administering its law over there now?"

"Roughly three-hundred-fifty."

"One would think," William mused, "that the 'sweetness' part would show up in that length of time."

Temple grimaced. "There's no question the Irish are a stubborn lot. Plenty of testimony along those lines."

"I happen to patronize an Irish boot-maker here in London, and while the man does good work, he is certainly uppity when it comes to casting his accounts. He could use some taking down, in my opinion."

Temple laughed. "You certainly know how to make hash out of a discussion of national significance, Will."

"I like to base my opinions on personal experience," William grinned. "By the way, are there any of those high-paying offices open at the moment?"

"Fat chance! We have over 2,500 qualified applicants from the ranks of young noblemen and rising gentry—a little over two men for each office that comes open. Unlike most Continental monarchs, who personally pick only about one hundred of their main people and then let those selected fill the offices under them with friends and relatives, Elizabeth takes a personal hand in every appointment in her government and uses the system to communicate with the people in all corners of her realm."

"Communicate?"

"By appointing some and disappointing others, the Queen indicates which policies and attitudes please her and which offend. Our Queen enjoys it, or so they tell me, because it fits her picture of herself as the doting matriarch of a large family group. Some young men she picks up, some she casts down, and others she ignores through-out their lives which, consequently, are spent breathlessly awaiting her summons."

"You make her sound mean-spirited."

"I'm sorry for that," said Temple, blushing. "It's just the way she runs things, and I've heard it said there's never been a better Prince, man or woman."

"But many are made to suffer—as in the case of your master."

Temple hung his head. "There are only a dozen or so offices which Sir Philip's dignity would permit him to accept. Everybody at Court knows which those offices are, and everybody knows exactly what it means if the Queen appoints him to a lesser one. That is why the staff here is holding its collective breath to see if our master is going to get happy notification from your master's message or further disappointing news. If Sir Philip is not appointed as his station deserves, we may be in for dark days at Penhurst."

"An ironic situation in light of his brilliant achievements during his Grand Tour."

"You've heard of that!" exclaimed young Temple, proudly. "His tour lasted three years, actually, from '72 to '75, starting when he was twenty-one. He won the hearts of mature statesmen in every country he visited. William of Orange offered his sis-ter's hand in marriage if Sidney would accept the lordship of Holland and Zeeland as a dowry. He was asked to become King of Poland unofficially, but if he had said yes, it would have been made official quickly enough. Even crafty old Languet was enchanted with Sidney and arranged to have the carpet rolled out for him wherever he went."

"Who is Languet?"

"A very prosperous and well-connected French businessman and writer, who had important friends in every court in Europe. He was a broker for international trade deals. He took Sir Philip under his wing, and his letters followed him from country to country, full of sound, practical advice for the idealistic young nobleman who he was sure would ascend to great power in England someday. He is dead now, of course. Died in '81."

"I don't suppose you were privileged to read any of those letters."

"Well, actually, yes I was, during my duties as a sorting clerk." Temple smiled as he rose to refill both their wine glasses. "I remember one piece of advice in particular, wherein Languet cautioned Sir Philip not to be too trusting of his fellowmen. He wrote, *'You imagine that all men have the same obliging character as yourself! I consider that in these days men do a great deal if they do not actually betray their friends.'"* [37]

"Sounds as if some of Languet's business dealings may have made a cynic of him," William observed.

"I wouldn't be surprised," agreed George, "but he knew how to get along. Just before Sir Philip came back to England, Languet wrote him this advice: *'When you reach England see to it that you cultivate the good-will of Cecil, who is friendly to you and who can smooth your path in every way. In no way will you be able to secure his favor more certainly than by your affection for his children, or at least by pretending that you love them. But remember that astute old man who has been made wise by his long experience in affairs of state will easily see through the pretences of youth. It will also be to your advantage to cultivate the friendship of Mr. Walsingham; to sum up, it is necessary that he who wishes to live above contempt in the Courts of powerful Kings should moderate his pretensions, digest many injuries, avoid with the utmost care every occasion for quarreling and cultivate the good will of those in whose hands rests his fortune.'"* [38]

"I would say that Philip's marriage to Walsingham's daughter qualifies as showing love for the children of one of the Queen's advisors," William chuckled.

"Languet also advised Sir Philip not to go to Italy. He told Sir Philip he had seen too many promising young English noblemen corrupted by the Italians and turned into Italianate Englishmen who were not at home in either country. I suppose he meant the Earl of Oxford and some of that crowd. Or perhaps he was being mindful of Lord Burghley's single greatest directive to English noblemen upon sending their sons to the Continent for their Grand Tour: *'Suffer not thy sons to pass the Alps; for they shall learn there nothing but pride, blasphemy, and atheism'.*" [39]

"I can only imagine," said William, "that for a young man of spirit, such cautions would only serve to illuminate the forbidden fruit."

"Exactly. Sidney was off to Rome like a shot with Italian-born Ludovick Bryskett as his guide. After he was there a few months he offered this general opinion of Italy in a letter to his brother David, back in England. *'Except Venice, whose good laws and customs we can hardly proportion to ourselves, because they are quite of a contrary government, there is little there but tyrannous oppression and servile yielding to them that have little or no right over them. And for the men you shall find there, although indeed some be excellently learned, yet are they all given to counterfeit learning, as a man shall learn among them more false grounds of things than in any other place that I know; for from a tapster upwards they are all discoursers. In fine, certain matters and qualities, as horsemanship, weapons, painting and such, are better there than in other countries, but for other matters, as well, if not better, you shall have them in nearer places.'"* [40]

"Horsemanship, weapons, and painting get high marks, but empty-headed chatter rates a decided minus, right?"

"Exactly. Sir Philip is not the least bit naive about what goes on in the world. He has deliberately chosen to assume the best about everyone and ignore the worst, but that doesn't mean he is unaware of the worst."

"White Knight label or not, then, Sir Philip Sidney does not live in an Ivory Tower, oblivious to what goes on around him?"

"Oh my, no! Sir Philip is quite aware of how the world turns. Had you heard that he was in Paris in '72 at the very time of the St. Bartholomew Day Massacre? No?" Temple shuddered. "He saw the whole thing from a window of the English embassy. He saw gangs of Catholic noblemen and their henchmen break the truce and slaughter the visiting Protestant Huguenots. Henry of Navarre, whose wedding his fellow Protestants had come to as guests, barely escaped with his life. There were over 4,000 people killed throughout Paris and thousands more when the slaughter extended to the countryside. Sir Philip was so horrified that he swore to himself never to be involved in religious warfare thereafter. In fact, I believe he has come to dislike both Catholics and their religion."

"Did someone order the Massacre or did it break out like a street fight?"

"It was ordered, all right. Some say it was French King Charles, but few believe it. He was too weak-minded. Most believe it was the queen mother, Catherine de Medici, in alliance with the Duke de Guise and the second son, soon to become king."

The two young men helped themselves to more wine in silence, and by the time they had reseated themselves, Temple's nerves were restored.

"I don't expect people dressed as you are to understand this," he said waving his glass, "but my master is regarded as the glass of fashion throughout the Continent, not only in matters of style and dress, but also in matters of morals and manners, so it goes against my innards to say anything that would in any way diminish that public perception of the man."

"'Glass of fashion' eh? Nice descriptive term," said William. "I like the bare intimation of the mirror."

"But those of us who live behind the scenes, so to speak, see quite a different picture of such great and glorious personages when their doublets are unbraced."

"I can well imagine," William murmured.

"Those of us who best love Sir Philip think the public should be let to see some of his private side, so they will appreciate what it costs him to play out such an admirable national figure. He is actually a human being much like the rest of us."

"Umm yes, a little touch of individuality makes a man more interesting, more worthy of discussion," William observed.

"For instance, it is not generally known that Sir Philip has quite a temper when offended. Not long ago, when he was led to believe through some misunderstanding that his father's secretary, Edward Molyneux, was gossiping about the family's private affairs, he had me send Molyneux a note which chilled my blood as I wrote it."

"I can well believe it."

"He wrote, '*Mr. Molyneux—Few words are best. My letters to my father have come to the eyes of some. Neither can I condemn any but you for it. If it be so, you have played the very knave with me, and so I will make you know if I have good proof of it. But that for so much as is past. For that is to come, I assure you before God that if ever I know you to so much as read any letter I write to my father, without his commandment or my consent, I will thrust my dagger into you. And trust to it, for I speak it in earnest.*'" [41]

"Hard to miss a certain note of sincerity there," said William uneasily. "Perhaps we should all heed his warning." He watched as young Temple got up for more wine and indicated to his host that his own glass was still half full. "What happened to Molyneux?"

"He was innocent," Temple assured him. "And devastated as well, but not entirely without defense. Personal dignity can be an effective shield against many of society's arrows. Molyneux knew that Sir Philip was just a rash young man who had simply made a mistake, so his response was measured and direct."

"And you remember it, I'm sure."

Temple could not but smile as he recited Molyneux' answer: "'*Sir:-I have received a letter from you, which, as it is the first, so the same is the sharpest that ever I received from any. But since it is—I protest to God—without cause or just ground of suspicion you use me thus, I bear the injury more patiently for a time, and mine innocency, I hope in the end, shall try my honesty; and then I trust you will confess you have done me wrong Yours, when it shall please you to conceive of me, humbly to command, Edward Molyneux'.*" [42]

"You're right. Patient, judicious and dignified. Did Sir Philip ever apologize?"

"He did," said Temple. "He found he had been at fault, apologized to Molyneux, and thereafter signed himself 'Your loving friend' whenever he wrote to that faithful retainer."

"Justice and dignity triumph! That's the kind of world I like to envision! Such stories lift up people's hearts and make it possible for them to go forward in the constant battle—"

"And that's not all," interrupted Temple. "Sir Philip challenged the author of the Leicester Commonwealth to a duel for slandering his uncle. He also has a coldly dispassionate view about some things that sends a chill up the spine of those of us who are unable to think objectively about our sovereign."

"Objective about the Queen?"

"Most of us assume that Elizabeth will be with us forever because that is a very comforting thought, and because she has been with us throughout our lives, but Sir Philip indulges no such illusion and his appraisal hits the rest of us like a drenching of icy water. He recently wrote of her, *'The Queen, though somewhat advanced in years, yet hitherto vigorous in health; which as it is God's will that our safety should hang on so frail a tread is with good reason earnestly commended to the care of Almighty God in the prayers of our people. When [she] perishes, farewell to all our quietness.'"* [43]

"Certainly measured and realistic," William conceded.

When Malachi came into the library alone a few minutes later, he found his apprentice quietly thumbing through a volume taken from the shelf and Sir Philip's secretary snoring gently in his chair by the fire.

PART III: THE ENGLISH NAVY

Chapter 1:
ON THE ROAD TO PLYMOUTH TOWN

Inn at Ashburton, three days out from London:

"This is our last stop before we reach Plymouth," said Malachi to William, "so eat hearty."

William slid onto the bench of the pub gingerly. "I'm bloody glad we're almost there," he groaned. "My poor arse is no longer enchanted with this adventure across south England."

Malachi chuckled. "You're full of complaints, lad, but you're right. It is a longish ride. 165 miles, all told. We're fortunate English couriers are afforded nine changes of horses between London and Plymouth. Else it would take us longer than three days."

"Think you we'll see Drake's Navy today?" asked William eagerly.

"Indeed. All snugly berthed in Plymouth harbor."

"And Drake? Drake himself? What does he look like?"

"Every time I see Drake, my impression starts with his eyes."

"His eyes?"

"He has a set of piercing blue eyes whose sharp vision funnels out like the beam from a bull's-eye lantern scanning every aspect of our physical world and all its eccentric inhabitants as well. Any man illuminated by that compelling beam immediately comes to attention and faithfully awaits his orders—and I include myself in that large group of underlings who are very careful to get things done just as Captain Drake prefers. Some say that Drake would dare what no man else would dream, and that's what I see in his eyes. A wild, fierce power of effrontery which will respect no restriction and delights in springing on opponents from unforeseen directions."

"But in addition to the spell-binding eyes, what does he look like? Big? Small? Fat? Lean?"

Malachi chuckled. "That question comes home to fertile ground because I recently bent elbows with two fellow scriveners who spent much of the evening comparing the transcriptions they had taken on this very subject from two history book writers, William Camden and John Stowe. May I quote some key passages?"

"I've come to realize that direct quoting is good for your digestion, so please go to it."

"It helps keep the rust out," Malachi grinned. "John Stow said that Francis Drake is *'more skilful in all points of navigation than any ever was...of perfect memory, great observation, eloquent by nature, skilful in artillery, expert and apt to let blood and give physic unto his people according to the climates.'"* [1]

"But his physical appearance?"

"I'm getting there," Malachi growled. "Stow also said Drake is low of stature, of strong limbs, broad breasted, round headed, brown hair, full bearded, his eyes round, large and clear, well-favoured, fair and of a cheerful countenance. He also mentioned what might be regarded as shortcomings in the captain when he said that Drake is ambitious for honor, inconstant in amity, and greatly affected to popularity."

"I think being ambitious for honor and popularity might be true of many of us," William grinned. "But none of that explains how Drake got where he is today. As I understand it, he was born a poor commoner, and yet somehow he has made himself famous throughout the world. How?"

"Perhaps Camden explains his background best," Malachi explained. "After telling us Drake's father was a poor preacher and bible reader for the naval seamen on the King's ships which lay at anchor in the River Medway in Kent, he writes: *'This Drake to report no more than what I have heard from him was...[placed] with a neighboring pilot, who, by daily exercise, hardened him to the sailor's labour with a little bark, wherewith he sailed up and down the coast, guided ships in and out of harbours, and sometimes transporting merchandise into France and Zeeland. This young man being diligent and pliable, gave such testimony of his care and diligence to the old pilot, that he dying issueless, in his will bequeathed, as a legacy, the bark to him, wherewith Drake, having gathered a pretty sum of money, and receiving intelligence that John Hawkins made preparation of certain ships at Plymouth, for the voyage of America, which was called the New World, he made sale of his bark, and accompanied with certain brave and able mariners, he left Kent, and joined his labours and fortunes with Hawkins'.*" [2]

"How old was he then?"

"That was in 1566 when Drake was about twenty, and his cousin John Hawkins was thirty."

"So Drake is about forty now—pretty young to have England's Royal Navy so often referred to as Drake's Navy. Why not Elizabeth's Navy or even Hawkins' Navy?"

"Sir Francis Drake is a hard man to overlook in any company," Malachi grinned. "In many areas of the world, Drake is better known even than Queen Elizabeth. Stowe says that Drake's name is *'a terror to the French, Spaniard, Portugal and Indians. Many princes of Italy, Germany and others, as well enemies as friends...desire his picture...as famous in Europe and America as Tamburlaine in Asia and Africa.'* [3] Spanish mothers frighten their children to bed at night by threatening them with a visit from 'El Draco,' the dragon."

"That's strange."

"What?"

"It never occurred to me that world-wide recognition might be viewed in a negative light by much of the world. This insight makes the whole business of expending time and energy in pursuit of fame much more complicated than one would first suppose."

"Stay at it anyway," Malachi grinned. "It keeps you out of trouble. The funny thing about the public adulation of Drake is that it's all so recent. When he cleared Plymouth Harbor to start his trip around the world in December of 1577, he was already known as the adventuresome sea-captain who had raided Spanish settlements in the West Indies and captured £40,000 in silver from a Spanish pack-train in Panama back in 1573."

"Someone at the inn yesterday told me Drake is presently doing ordinary plumbing work," William mentioned. "Could such a hero fall so far so fast?"

Malachi chuckled. "Somebody is having a bit of fun with you. At this moment, Drake is deeply involved in the admittedly less adventuresome task of trying to engineer a permanent fresh-water supply for his port-city, Plymouth. The city fathers recently selected him for the job on the wonderful supposition that a Master of the Seven Seas—as some call him—should have little trouble directing a modest flow of water through some pipes and ditches. But, never fear, when England is next threatened by Spanish ships and daily affairs are swept aside, and when the decks are finally cleared for action, the English people expect Sir Francis Drake to lead our Royal Navy into battle against the Spanish. The Queen, of course, may have other ideas."

"But John Hawkins is Treasurer of the Navy."

"He is, indeed," agreed Malachi. "And until very recently the affection of the English people was pretty much reserved in nautical matters for our brave, dependable Treasurer, who gave Drake his first command well before he became Sir Francis. But everything changed on September 26, 1580, when Drake returned from his Around-the-World-Trip and hailed the dock in Plymouth Harbor with his famous inquiry, *'How goes the Queen'?"* The *Golden Hind* promptly unloaded the most valuable commercial cargo ever landed in England, and the stockholders enjoyed a return of 4,700% on their investment."

"Zounds!" cried William. "Does that mean that if I had invested ten pounds, I would have a return of £470?"

"That's it exactly."

Sighing wistfully, William asked, "How did the crew make out?"

"Well taken care of. No captain in the world knows better than Drake the value of good seamen. In Plymouth, I hope we'll have a drink with a company of his crewmen from the trip. You'll hear firsthand accounts of their memorable adventure if you keep the ale flowing. One of the side benefits for Drake's Round-the-World crew is the open spigot they encounter everywhere they go for as long as they can wag their tongues. I have never yet seen any other subject take the stage against tales from that voyage. Members of that crew have been subjected to riotous acclaim and secret envy during the five years since they returned."

"If we oil them with enough ale, mayhap they'll tell us how Drake came to surpass John Hawkins in the public's eye?"

"Oh, that's right," Malachi laughed, "I did rather lose the thread of my thought there. Drake's fame blossomed that day in 1580, as I mentioned, but fate itself had nurtured the bloom for the preceding three years. Little was heard from Drake after he left England in December, 1577. It was known publicly that many of his crew had signed on for a proposed trip to Alexandria, Egypt, and it was soon reported that Drake was seen sailing into the Mediterranean Sea through the Straits of Gibraltar. It was not reported, however, that he ducked back out at night and set sail for South America. It is apparent now that the strategy all along was for Drake to sail his small fleet quietly until he reached the Pacific through the Straits of Magellan. He then could turn north along the coast of that southern continent and sweep up Spanish treasure ships as they carried gold and silver from the Peruvian mines up to Panama for shipment to Spain. That west coast had never been raided and was ripe for the picking."

"How far north did Drake sail up that west coast?"

"In the end, he went from about 58° south—in what is now called Drake's Passage, just below the Straits of Magellan—to about 47° north, just about parallel with Newfoundland. He searched the west coast of the New World in hopes of finding the western outlet to the hypothetical Northwest Passage even though we have yet to find the eastern inlet," Malachi chuckled. "The cold drove him south again, and he wintered on shore at a settlement he called New Albion at about 38° N where the *Hind* was greeted by a golden rainbow stretching between two headlands at the entrance of a long, deep bay."

"Could he get fresh provisions there?"

"There were helpful Indians in the area, and they furnished him with a food supply. There were no riches to be had north of Panama, however, and the Spanish pursuit was gathered in that area, so Drake headed west for the Spice Islands as soon as the weather warmed up, well laden as he was with the Spanish gold he had already grabbed."

"He headed west to avoid the Spanish gathering at Panama?"

"That may have influenced him, but he pretty obviously had the trip around the world in mind from the beginning. Anyway, as soon as Drake captured the giant treasure ship *Cacafuego,* just south of Panama, word was flashed back to Madrid that El Draco was on the prowl again."

"Flashed back?"

"The Spanish have been in the long-distance naval communication business for nearly a century now," explained Malachi, "and they have developed light, built-for-speed mail boats which get the news from Havana to Madrid in just about a month. King Philip is quite aware how long it takes to get messages exchanged in his Empire, and he holds his people to very strict compliance as far as schedules go. As soon as the Spanish government learns anything important, however, somebody in the Venetian Embassy is sure to sniff it out, and that starts the bedrock of Spanish security rolling rapidly downhill because every court in Europe then has the story in two weeks."

"How do the Venetians do it? Even I know how often they beat everybody to the dish."

"God knows, but it must be something in their blood because they've been doing it for centuries. Anyway, thanks to the Spanish messenger-service, Drake's trip around-the-world became one of the great audience-participation events of all time. We would get no word at all sometimes for months, and then would come reports of his victories when he brushed up against the Spanish in the New World or the Portuguese in the East Indies."

"Zounds! He was playing out a worldwide drama to a worldwide audience!"

"Exactly," Malachi nodded. "The Spanish, of course, were quite aware that Drake was making international news at their expense so, periodically, they offered England some sleepless nights by reporting that the notorious English pirate had been captured and killed."

"But then he would show up again in a different part of the world!" William showed his excitement. "Wonderful stuff! The man obviously has an incredible sense for dramatic flair since he shapes his activities into such compelling adventures. I wonder if he would be interested in a collaborative effort to strike off a dramatic stage-play or two when he's finished with his naval adventures."

"He'd be a good one," Malachi chuckled. "The presentation of his trip as a suspenseful drama certainly captured the interest of the ordinary people, and it fascinated the military establishment throughout Europe. He did things that they didn't know could be done. He had obviously mastered the art of obtaining stores as he traveled, living off-the-land at sea, so to speak. He kept his men healthy for three years when most captains can't sail for longer than three months without losing half their crew to ship's fever."

"What kind of provisions would he take for a trip like that? Clear around the world! Egad!"

"I once made a copy of the draft plan for Drake's expedition so I know exactly what he started out with. He loaded stores of *biscuit, meal, beer, beef, pork, fish, butter, cheese, rice, oatmeal, peas, vinegar, honey, sweet oil, salt, and lots of wine.*"[4]

"Why so much wine?"

"Reality of shipboard life. Wine keeps a long time while beer tends to sour quickly, and water stored in casks soon becomes foul. You drink the beer and water first at sea and then break out the wine while you search for fresh water. Like Hawkins, Drake is a demon about locating healthy food and water for his crew."

"He must be a great captain to sail under."

"That he is," nodded Malachi. "And it's my great fortune to see him before and after every voyage. He collects maps from all over the world, and I often carry the charts back and forth between Plymouth and London." He patted the pouch hanging safely from his shoulder. "Drake is absolutely opposed to releasing any of his personal charts publicly for fear the Spanish will obtain copies. His maps are always very individual because he carries an artist in the crew to paint in color the various harbors and headlands he visits. His charts are a pleasure to behold and invaluable to any seaman, but he feels public copies would constitute a threat to England, so that's the end of the matter for anybody who does not seek the very personal displeasure of Captain Drake."

"Why do you carry them back and forth then? Why doesn't Drake keep his maps with him?"

"England's finest map maker, Richard Huklyet, always gets the original by Drake's order so he may reproduce accurate copies. I usually take a peek at the charts, and my mind has often been beguiled and delighted by the places it has visited through such careful rendering of scenes from the other side of the world."

"You've seen Drake's personal charts and maps?"

Malachi nodded. "He is a first-class sketcher himself. He has a fine eye for lining up tricky channels with coastal rock formations, church steeples, nearby valleys or river mouths—anything which will help the sailor find his way safely into harbor."

"But exclusively English sailors," William amended.

"That's the way he'd like to keep it," said Malachi, "but he's not having much success with concealment. He was somewhat alarmed recently when he found that all Spanish ships now have copies of the latest edition of Waggoners, the best of the rutters which treat in great detail the harbors of the Narrow Seas between England and the Continent. Drake considers our coastal shoals and tide-rates part of England's natural defense, and he is not happy to share detailed knowledge of them with our enemies."

"Surely everyone agrees with that. It's common sense!"

"Unfortunately, governments can no longer exercise full control on everything printed. Commercial interests have seized their chance and will print whatever will sell, without showing any concern for national interests. Even international borders are no longer a barrier to the trade. If a writing may not be licensed in one country, the author need only travel abroad to find a country where the licensing requirements are less severe. The Dutch will print anything with or without literary merit, as long as someone foots the bill." Malachi grinned. "Make a note of that, lad. If you are really intent on being published some day, the Dutch press of vanity may be your solution."

William snorted. "I have never yet paid for it and I never will."

Malachi grinned. "By the by, keep your eyes open for Sir Philip Sidney's coach. I'm sure he has Temple with him. You two seemed to get along quite well."

"Sidney's secretary, Will Temple?" William stammered. "We just left him three days ago, and he didn't mention coming down here."

"He didn't know it until Sidney opened the message I brought him and found that Don Antonio is due to land in Plymouth any day now."

"A Spaniard!"

"Close," Malachi nodded. "but a Portuguese, and the man who could once again be King of Portugal someday if he can recruit allies enough on the Continent or here in England to help him recapture his country from Spain. Philip claimed the crown when the Portuguese king died without issue five years ago. He labeled Don Antonio a pretender and closed out all other claims by simply annexing Portugal to Spain on the basis of his own close bloodlines, since his mother was Portuguese."

"Where does that leave Don Antonio?"

"He is the offended party, as they say," Malachi chuckled. "For the past five years he has bounced around European courts trying to solicit friends. He was well received at first because he had jewels enough to cover his costs, but as his treasure dwindled, so did interest in his cause. Our Sir Philip Sidney is one of the few English gentlemen who will now go out of his way to receive him."

"Out of his way, indeed, to travel post haste all the way to Plymouth!"

Malachi nodded. "As soon as Sir Philip got word that Drake was ready to sail on his next voyage, he jumped into his coach and flew down here, as it were. By coming to Plymouth, ostensibly to welcome Don Antonio to Elizabeth's court, Sidney puts himself in a position to do more than cheer Drake on."

"How do you mean? Where is Drake to sail? Why would Sidney cheer?"

"Any answer to that barrage of questions would mix restricted information with unfounded rumor, so I had better leave off. We'll watch the drama of the situation play itself out. Meanwhile," Malachi stood up from the table and lay down his napkin, "if you've finished your victuals, m'boy, we'd best be on our way. Provided our post-horses do not founder, we should be arriving at Plymouth in another six or seven hours."

Chapter 2:
PLYMOUTH, A MARINERS' TOWN

Plymouth Harbor, early evening:

William stood on the quay where Malachi had left him gazing out on the sea of spars and sails bobbing about in the far-flung harbor.

"I will return before time to retire," Malachi had said. "In the meantime, I'll send one of our men to show you the ropes. His name is Salty Tom, and he'll cadge drinks 'til Doomsday if you supply him, but he's a good man. You can depend on him."

A grizzled old sailor lounged nearby, several times catching William's eye, then glancing away.

William smiled. "It sends shivers down my spine to know I am standing on the very dock from which Drake launched some of the greatest sea voyages in English history," he said in a friendly fashion, "and from which he may launch many more if our country is lucky and if fate does not see fit to interpose an interfering hand on Drake's glittering career."

"Don't be a blithering fool," the mariner chuckled. "'Tis no more Cap'n Drake's dock than 'tis mine. In Plymouth Harbor, 'tis always 'Berth 'em where your bottom will fit,' and even the good Cap'n takes his chances on a good berthin', same as the rest of us."

"Sir," William frowned. "I clearly heard you tell that group of people who were just here—"

"What did ye expect me to tell 'em? Them folk come all the way from Canterbury and London to see what there is to see o' Cap'n Drake. Would ye 'ave me force 'em to cough up a vague 'maybe' when the folks back home ask if they saw Drake's dock?"

"But I saw you cut off splinters from this dock and sell them to those visitors as keepsakes. That's no better than the Catholics cutting down whole forests to meet the demand for 'authentic' splinters from the Crucifixion cross."

"Aye, ye be putting me in good company for earnin' a 'onest living. Thar's plenty of profit to be made from our 'eroic figgers. An' if I can tell a yarn or two over a mug o' ale, it gives folks both pleasure and refreshment. Speaking of which..."

He motioned William toward a nearby tavern and, after a moment's hesitation, William followed him. "This 'ere's the Whale's Tale Inn, full of lads who 'ave sailed a gale or two on the high seas. Some 'ave shipped with Cap'n Drake hisself on the 'Round-the-World trip. Next to a full tankard, they fancy tellin' their old tales to new listeners, so set up a round, and you'll be in for a lively evenin' o' turnin' on two taps at once, if ye get my meaning."

"My pleasure," William assured him eagerly. They secured their ale and sat down at a large table in the taproom.

"The truth o' it is, I don't get wages and never did. It's always a lucky night when I meet up with a lad like yorself who don't mind oilin' the pump, as 'twere."

"You get no wages? I took you for a sailor, sir. How could you not be paid?"

"I be a sailor, indeed, and t'sea is all I know. Look 'round the streets and taverns of Plymouth, and what do ye see?"

"Sailors?"

"Schools and scuttles of 'em, all over the place. Too many. We've no bargainin' power with the cap'ns 'cause we all needs the work. It ain't possible to get reg'lar wages, so we signs on for thirds and pillage."

"Thirds of what?"

"Prizes took. The cargo be split in thirds. The cap'n and crew get one third, the ship owners get one third, and the shareholders and victualers get the other third. 'Tis the only chance a sailor's got to 'it it rich. That's the bait. That's why the cap'ns can pack their ships with men and not pay them wages. The crew is adventurin' along with the cap'n."

"How long have you been in the business?" William asked.

"Me whole life has been smugglin' or adventurin'. I were raised here in Plymouth."

"Have you made a living at it?"

The sailor shrugged. "Good pillage years and bad pillage years, like ever'thin' else."

"The pillage is in addition to the thirds, then?"

"Aye. Pillage is any val'able on the captured vessel outside the main cargo 'old. The boarding crew 'as the right to all gold, silver, silk, tar, pitch, or cable outside the 'old and splits it up accordin' to rank."

"The crew's and passengers' private belongings too?"

"In partic'lar! Wealthy merchants be fond of rings and gold chains, and many a sailor 'as a brass-cased Bishop's Bible."

"You'd steal a Bible?"

"Nothin' of the kind. No stealin' involved. We sails under t'authority of Letters o' Reprisal. We be retrieving property to a value equal t' property already stole from us by t'Spaniards."

"Exactly equal?"

"We operates on more of a 'there-abouts' scale. Saves fuss n' bother, ye know."

"But the pillaging stops short of the ship's commercial cargo?"

"Oh, aye. Off base altogether 'til the Admiralty official 'as weighed it up and took the 10% Admiralty fee."

"It's wonderful that you can get complete compliance on such a delicate issue from men who lean a little toward boisterous and avaricious behavior, if I may say so. I guess it shows the kind of cooperation that's possible from a well-disciplined crew."

"Not 'ardly complete, laddie," chuckled the sailor. "Depends on the cargo. "prize cargo o' wine don't often reach English port 'thout the cargo 'old bein' rifled t' some degree."

"Now that goes beyond pillage, as I understand it," said William.

"Aye, that's plunder and strictly agin' the terms the cap'n signed in his Letters o' Reprisal, but in t'case of a wine cargo the men takes only what they can drink so ever'body ignores the rule. Not the rest, howsomever. If the crew takes any precious cargo goods such as gold, silk, or jewelry, the Admiralty Court 'unts down the guilty parties and fines 'em in addition to takin' the 10%."

"I suppose you've been in on any number of gold and silver prize splits yourself."

"You'd be supposin' wrong, laddie. *I be a man what fortune hath cruelly scratched*'. [5] Fate 'as brought me mostly prizes of fish, cheese, 'ides, lumber, and a bit o' wine. Enough return to keep change in me pockets, but not enou' t' found me a fortune."

"But you keep assuming the big one is right around the next corner."

"Aye, riches around the next headland. That's what keeps me goin'. Could we have another?"

"Strictly up to you."

"I'll signal the boy then."

"By the way, could you point me to the man they call Salty Tom? Someone said I might find him—"

The old sailor guffawed. "Wal now, ye be talkin' to him, lad. And I'm thinkin' that ye be Malachi's clerk, for I can tell by your complexion ye ben't no workingman."

The tavern boy filled their tankards, and Salty Tom raised his to William. "I welcome ye, nonetheless, t' the Brotherhood of the Sea. Honorary, as 'twere."

"To the Brotherhood of the Sea!" toasted William. "That extends beyond sailors then?"

"Oh aye, to all who lives by the sea, but 'specially sailors, from cabinboy to cap'n. The cap'ns have their own brotherhood, seein' as how they don't mix much with us common seamen but share wi' each other the burden o' leadership. In ever' port, they seeks out other cap'ns to exchange findin's on winds and currents—tools of the trade, you might say—and also ships friendly and unfriendly they met with or have seen. Pirates and privateers and the like."

"But an English captain would never sit with a Spaniard."

"Oh, aye, politics an' nationalities be mostly ignored atwixt 'em. They be business men, ye know. A Dutch cap'n might find his ship berthed in Lisbon atwixt a Spanish carrack just returned from the New World and a Portug'ee galleon still runnin' th' spice trade in t' Orient for t'Spanish."

"That might be very awkward."

"Times so, 'times not," he nodded. "Chances be all three cap'ns 'ld be asked ashore to sup with a rich import-export merchant, eager t' turn a tidy profit. Cap'ns be very keen on which trade goods fetches t'highest prices."

"I wonder that a merchant is tolerated in such august company."

"He talks local tides and winds too, ye know, as well as profits. And so he be part of the brotherhood. Merchants supply news and gossip, too, along with wine 'n pipes of tobac'—that new import from the Virginia colony."

"Tobac, you say?"

"The Virginia natives 'ave a leaf that when ye kindle it, burns slow in the pipe. They pull the smoke inta their mouths and then blow it out. Just the kind o' thing the cap'ns take to. They likes to stay atop changes betwixt countries too, like what's happening in the Low Countries. Did ye know that the Dutch merchants still trade wi' Spain even after English money an' blood went to defendin' them agin' the Dons' control?"

"I'm afraid I'm exactly the wrong person to have much background in—"

"These things be important t'know in the line o' business. Ye can understand that."

"Yes, certainly. But do the captains go to all this trouble just to increase profits for their investors?"

"Wal, as to that, no doubt many a cap'n invests for hisself in the ventures he dredges up, but survival be the real key to it all. Few surviving cap'ns die poor." Salty Tom leaned forward confidentially. "Our own Cap'n Drake has a capture policy what, to my thinkin', ups respec' for capns ever'whar."

"Capture policy? Like a privateer, you mean?"

"Aye. Ever' mariner knows that the Dutch Sea-beggers will rough them up, rob them, and let them go. The Frenchies rob them and kill any who can't keep their gobs shut. An English pirate kills all who resist, but lets t'others go after taking their goods. But as ever' cap'n knows, if Drake takes him, three things will happen."

"Three?"

"First, Drake robs the cap'n an' ship. Second, he gives that same cap'n a valu' ble piece o' booty from his own hoard o' treasures—a silver cup, as often as not—and, third, after dinin' 'im handsomely, he let's 'im go. To a life o' fame an' fortune, as 'twere."

"How fame?"

"Wal, think on't, lad. For all his life, that cap'n can 'old 'is listeners by tellin' the story of 'is capture by the famous 'El Draco' and prove it by sportin' 'is priceless souvenir. It's as good as a open-spigot pension."

"You are almost saying some captains might welcome a capture by Drake."

"Nay, but it carries no disgrace, and it can well be turned to profit. That's why King Philip finally ordered 'is cap'ns to burn their ships—no matter the cargo—if they be in danger of capture by Cap'n Drake." Salty Tom looked around him for the tavern boy. "Me throat is gettin' near parched..."

William returned shortly with filled tankards. "Is Plymouth always this crowded," he asked, "or is someone putting a fleet together for action in the New World, as I've heard some say?"

Salty Tom swallowed a deep drink and then leaned close to whisper, "Ye 'ad best keep mum about what ye think ye know about such things, lad," he said. "There be men at hand who 'olds that loose talk threatens their lifes. Many be alive today because they strikes first and questions after." He made a cutting motion across his throat with his index finger. "Best to avoid certain subjects alt'gether."

William glanced over his shoulder. "I'll remember that. But how about the New World generally? Will we ever break Spain's hold over there?"

"When I permits meself to look at the sit'ation object-like," confessed Salty Tom, "I can't much blame Philip for his hostil'ty 'cause it occurs to me 'ow easy could be t'shoe on t'other foot."

"What shoe? Which foot?"

"Do ye know aught o' the history of Spain and the south countries?" When William shook his head, Tom continued. "Few countries, ye know, ever seen the kind o' change Spain lived through in 1492. "big year all 'round. King Ferd'nand and Queen Is'bella drove them Moors out o' Grenada and out o' Spain for the first time in six hunert year. Then they drove out t'Jews as well. Then, they appoints the first Spanish pope in Rome—one of them Borgias. So in 1492, the Cath'lic Monarchy—as they was called—was undisputed 'ead of t'country and of t' Cath'lic Church in Spain— meanin' they could appoint and dismiss bishops. Then talk about pillage! They got all t'property and treasures the banished Moors and Jews couldn't take with 'em. They was runnin' strong in a high wind! So the balmy but excitin' notions of that pesky Genoese sea cap'n we know as Christopher Columbus began to make sense to them."

"Sounds like a great year for the Catholic Monarchy," William agreed, "and not bad for Columbus either."

"Well, here's the thing of it. If they 'adn't been so flush with success, if they'd a' sent Columbus packin' one more time, he might well a' tried his luck with our Henry II, who was known to have a love o' daring ventures. 'ad it fell out that way, the New World's gold and silver might now belong to England. England an' Portugal woulda split up the known world instead of Spain an' Portugal. England coulda laid claim to the West Indies just as the Portug'ee claim the East Indies. Pope Alexander II woulda had to back us, and the Treaty of Tordesillas in 1495 woulda give England claim to all the lands west of the 42nd Meridian—called 'the line' ever since. Portugal got claim to everything to the east 'cept for the Philippines, which went to Spain. Portugal got Brazil in t'West to even it out."

"Think of it!" exclaimed William. "What would have happened to Spain if England had split the world with the Portuguese, I wonder."

"Well, lad, seems to me, the only thing that 'as made Spain the greatest power o' Europe be the gold and silver she took from the Americas. Ye know, don't ye, that the Spanish buy everything instead o' makin' it theirselves. They hires everything out to other countries. They got next to no shipbuilding industry and 'ad no foundry for cannon until Philip throw'd one together this year for armin' the new fleet he's fixin' to build. The Eyetalians builds the Spanish ships for 'em. The Germans supplies their ordinance, and the Baltic states gives 'em their lumber an' masts an' tallow an' riggin'."

"If England only had a slice of that gold and silver!" cried William, caught up in the vision. "We'd do our own work and become the English Empire in our own right! Would the Pope really have turned half the world over to England?"

"Why not? We was Cath'lics back in 1495, don't forget, before 'ole 'Enry Eight turned us 'round in 1534. And never worry," Salty Tom chuckled, "the Church woulda been gettin' her share no matter 'oo owned the New World."

"And if England had won the West Indies, do you think we would have been more reasonable about open trade?"

"Yo'r wonderin' if England would a' been as selfish and mean as Spain 'as been?" Tom laughed. "Damn right we woulda! And as rich too! We'd 'a kicked those bloody Spanish Cath'lics out of there just as they're fixin' to do us."

"And I imagine we'd object if they raided our outposts in the New Word just as they complain about the raids Hawkins and Drake and the others carry out against them. We'd probably even have called them 'pirates.'"

"I 'spect we would, but the sit'ation be somewhat different."

"How so?"

"A Cath'lic merchant and a Protestant merchant don't hardly bother to argue theology while profits be handy. Trade makes the world go round, a'ter all, but Philip is turnin' trade into a religious war. He don't permit 'heretics'—as he calls us—into the New World for any reason, even just to buy an' sell as we passes through. He burns a Protestant to death or makes him a galley-slave for life if he catches 'im over the line. He's set on defendin' the new territories for the Cath'lic Church, and that there is why the sit'ation be diff'rent. Since England ben't no longer Cath'lic, she don't abide by Roman decisions. No Englishman accepts the Cath'lic order to shut out merchants from the sea lanes. That's why even though Drake and Hawkins be pirates in the eyes of the Spaniards, they be patriotic merchant-adventurers 'ere to home."

"That's an interesting argument," William observed. "Having severed our relationship with Rome, we need not thereafter recognize any agreement that went before?"

"Exactly."

"Then how about Ireland?"

"Ireland?"

"Sure. Didn't I hear someplace that Ireland was given to England by the only English Pope ever to grace that office—Pope Albion back in 1250?"

"Aye, mayhap that be correct."

"Then why shouldn't the Irish decide that our leaving the Catholic Church also negates England's claim on them?"

"Don't give 'em ideas, lad!. They be trouble enough a'ready."

"But if we want to represent ourselves as an honorable nation, a highly principled one, shouldn't the same legal precedent apply in both cases?"

"'Old up a minute, lad. Ireland be England's west flank just as Holland be our east flank. High principles be one thing, but any country that leaves its flanks exposed will end up in the graveyard right alongside those high principles."

"So principles are really only another commodity to be used by the mighty when convenient?"

"Aye, ye be gettin' the picture. Any leader who 'olds rigid to principles what threatens 'is country 'asn't really given the matter much thought."

"Ah yes, a monarch is allowed to juggle principles," murmured William.

"Aye, our Queen be a good 'un for jugglin' principles. She be pretendin' to carry on peace negot'ations with Madrid, knowin' well that Philip be whippin' up a fleet to attack us one o' these days. But our Lady Queen don't lose her head over principle. She plays the diplomatic game with one hand while she builds 'er navy an' sends 'er sea-cap'ns out to challenge Spain in t' New World with the other. Cap'n Drake, of course, be one o' those. Ever since 'e doubled 'er royal income to over half-a-million pounds in 1580 with his 4700% return—that made a right deep impression on our frugal Lady Queen, you best believe—there's been a special relation ever since betwixt Drake and t' Lady. It might be called a friendship, an' it explains why Drake gets so much freedom t' freeboot, as 'twere. Action and profit! God's blood, that's a pair what stirs an old salt's soul!"

"The prospect of a 4700% return does wonders for unsalted souls, too," William testified.

"Aye, them two has grown thick as thieves," Tom nodded knowingly. "She closets with him for hours afore he sails, an' when he leaves dock, only them two knows where he's headed. That be a big part of explainin' his success agin' t' Spanish."

"I've heard that some of Drake's enemies, while in their cups, attribute his success to a compact with the devil."

"Not by no chance!" Tom scoffed. "What man'd use supernat'ral tricks while he be in good supply of nat'ral ones? Enough t' say the Spanish can't keep track of Cap'n Drake 'cause the English can't keep track of him. Grievous to say, howsomever, there be many a' English—Cath'lics and other discontents—what collects dockside rumors o' sailin' plans and ships' provisionin' and then reports it all to Spain. Curryin' favor with the Dons, I spose. Most ships do end up goin' where the rumors say."

"Even Drake can't stifle rumors."

"'Ell no!" cried Tom. "The Cap'n don't never waste time combatin' natural forces. 'E treats dockside rumors like 'igh seas. I've even knowed 'im to originate a rumor or two. 'Is true destination be so precious, you see, 'e defends it with a stockade o' lies. There's most always three main stories goin', with conflictin' details, while 'e be victualing at Plymouth. Deception be a game Cap'n Drake understands and, like any master, delights in playin.'"

"Wouldn't there be some indication of a destination from the cargo he takes aboard?"

"Oh aye. And 'e's been known to load supplies just t' deceive the spies." Tom chuckled. "Any other English shipmaster woulda been 'anged a dozen times o'er if 'e operated as Drake does. Aye, and there's some others as envy and resent his 'igh-'anded ways."

"For the pirate thing, you mean?"

"Ever'thing! All o' it. The Cap'n's carryin' on a personal war agin' King Philip 'thout a murmur from our Lady Queen. Also, 'e's imprisoned and executed agents representin' very 'igh-placed folk at our English Court. Doughty was Burghley's man, ye know."

"Doughty?"

"Aye. Burghley sent him with Cap'n Drake on the Around-the-World trip, hopin' to keep the Cap'n from strikin' too 'ard at the Spaniards and givin' 'em an excuse to invade England. Like our Lady Queen, Burghley wants to 'old off the war as long as possible, bein' as it's mighty costly and interferes with trade. Ye can figure that their feelin' just the same—Burghley and the Lady Queen—makes for 'im havin' a powerful influence on 'er. She listens to all 'is advice on state matters, so they say."

"What was this Doughty fellow supposed to do? Spike Drake's canon?"

Tom chuckled. "'Is instructions was probably as shaky as Burghley's resolve. Typical, the Royal Treasurer wanted it both ways. 'E wanted the Cap'n t' open New World ports t' English trade but t' stay out o' war with Spain, doin' it."

"Quite a juggling act."

Salty Tom nodded. "So Doughty, ye see, was sent along as a sea anchor to keep Cap'n Drake from firin' on Philip's dignity and scuttlin' the peace negotiations. Burghley was figurin' without the Cap'n, howsomever, for Cap'n Drake'ld brook no interferin' in his plan t' circle the globe. Doughty was forthwith dispatched, as they say."

"Why do we always use 'forthwith' with unfortunate occurrences?" William mused. "Why don't we sometimes speak of eating dessert forthwith, or accepting a rise in pay forthwith, or even—"

Salty Tom swigged back the last of his ale. "Wal, I'll be leavin' it to others to fill in the details o' Doughty's fate, ones that was on the scene, as 'twere. Meanwhile, I'll share with ye what others 'ave said, and that is that Cap'n Drake changed England from a pawn to a bishop on the international political chessboard. I don't play chess meself, but I likes the sound of that. The truth of it be the Cap'n 'as put Spain's military reputation in a bad light. Burghley hisself 'as said our fire power in the world's courts is doubled and tripled 'cause of the Cap'n's doin's."

"I imagine it is pretty unusual for an individual captain to get under a king's royal skin as Drake has done to Philip," William said.

"Aye. Philip would scarce miss the gold an' silver Drake takes since Spain 'as millions comin' in each year, but the assault on Spain's military rep'tation be a different matter. Cap'n Drake opened the world's eyes to 'ow thin the defense of the New World Spanish outposts be. In truth, he taught the French and Dutch pirates that prowl the Spanish Main 'ow best to grab Spain's treasures. During his raids, the Cap'n showed 'ow successful be a flanking amphibious assault under cover of ship's canon agin fixed defenses. A lesson no military man'd miss."

"That sounds like the message Burghley wants Philip to get."

"Aye. And the sooner Philip comes to see 'is monopoly be impossible to defend, the sooner we can be loadin' our ships with trade goods instead o' cannon balls."

"Will Philip ever change, do you think?" William asked.

"When a ruler be convinced 'e's doin' God's work and growin' rich in the process, what kind o' inducement could take the field agin' such comfortable convictions? At the Spanish auto-de-fes—"

"Auto-de-what?"

"Act-of-faith carnivals, 'eld mostly for the burnin' of 'eretics along with the singin' and dancin'. Thataway, Philip shows the world exactly 'ow God wants 'eretics treated. When he quits burnin' people to death, and the air is clean agin' of the stench of burnt flesh, mayhap then...but don't be 'oldin' your breath."

"Might not some Christian charity creep in unbeknownst?"

"Ye ben't a religious person if ye think there be a middle ground in this partic'lar face-off. Both sides ends up shooting at you fence-sitters once the action starts. Now! Ye see them lads as just come in? Them's some of Cap'n Drake's 'Round-the-World gang. They'll soon be fillin' that back table with their endless stories o' the trip. Fetch 'em a round and open yor ears if ye wish real entertainment. I'll leave ye for a spell, but ye be fine company, lad, and I hope to set with ye agin' soon."

Chapter 3:
DRAKE'S ROUND-THE-WORLD CREW

Whale's Tale Inn in Plymouth, evening:

"Is there room for me and my burden, gentlemen?" William asked as he approached the table with an armful of brimming tankards.

"Aye, there is," said the sailor Kevin, who rose quickly to help distribute the load. "Any lad who knows how to make a proper entrance is welcome in this company. Here's to ye!" They all raised their drinks in welcome as William sat.

"In truth," William said, "it's hard for me to believe that I'm sitting here with four eye-witnesses to the historical voyage of the century. My mind is a-whirl and can't focus on where to begin my inquiry."

"Belay that," said Kevin pleasantly. "I can help you there. You told the publican you were buying ale for this table, did you not?"

"I did," William said, surprised. "How did you know?"

"And then what did he do?"

"He went to a cabinet and took out the tankards. Why?"

"He went to the cabinet and took out these here four tankards. You may notice you didn't get one of the four."

"I noticed that, but it's not unusual. Taverns often store special vessels for their regulars, and, of course, that's how you knew," William smiled. "Mine is not special but it holds my ale, so I see little difference one from another. As a matter of fact, now that you call my attention to the matter, I notice that the publican served me a much newer tankard than yours. Have you gentleman been paying your bar-bills?"

They all laughed at the sally. "Truth to tell," Kevin said, "we paid heavily for our special tankards. Do you know where Port St. Julian's is?"

"I've heard it's in the New World."

Kevin nodded. "Aye, near the bottom of South America, about two-hundred-fifty miles north of the Straits of Magellan in th' area called Patagonia. We wintered there for two months after the execution of Doughty, all of us so shook by that bloody spectacle that the cold fog that wrapped us tight suited our brooding period just right. 'Twere many a long an' windy night we set on that barren coastline. The layover, howsomever, gave us plenty of time to refit our three main ships—the *Pelican,* the *Elizabeth*, and the *Marigold*—before attempting the Straits."

"Oh, I hope you're not attempting to pull somebody's leg here," William laughed. "The word is out, you know, that Drake sailed around the world on the *Golden Hind* and no other, but you now would have me believe that particular ship wasn't even there?"

"Nay, she was there all right but in a different form, so t' speak," Kevin said. "But her public appearance rightfully comes later in my story, which I will attend to in due time. In the meantime, we need to a'quaint you with the rules of this here table."

"Rules?"

"A visitor ain't never allowed to interrupt a story mid-stream. If'n he does, the penalty is always the same: a round for the table."

"You can't really mean 'never'?" William exclaimed. "You are thereby canceling out the possibility of spontaneous curiosity and honest interest on the part of your listener. Worse yet, you are empowering, God forbid, the unfettered broadcast of endless gibberish from orators who wander from the main plot, mistakenly assuming their audience is interested in their mumbling of inconsequential anecdotes."

"You've a keen eye for the faults o' others," Kevin smiled thinly, "and, worse yet, it must be admitted that you be partly right. No interruptions at all is the target we aims for, but experience 'as taught us such a goal don't mix well with ale. Bein' practical men, we recognize that curiosity and interest be ignited by our spell-bindin' tales. We therefore grants our visitors three offenses afore they pay forfeit of an additional round. One thing more: the management of this here table reserves the right to raise or lower the penalty-points."

"Hear! Hear!" the four sang out in unison as they clinked.

William shook his head doubtfully. "I'll do my best."

"That's one," Kevin said, but one of his mates objected.

"Ahh, give the man a break now and leave off," Seaman Scotty advised. "We must start out the evening bein' fair, or we miss half the fun later on. See if he has any more questions, and then we can keep score."

"How about it?" Kevin asked.

"Only the mystery of the *Golden Hind*, but I'll wait for that."

"Then the rule starts now as I continue my story," Kevin cleared his throat. "Ahem. Now, personally, I've never got used to the upside down weather on the underside of the globe. For June and July to be the middle of winter in South America fair strains my mind. But back to St. Julian's. When we arrived, the nights was cold and long, and attempting the Straits was ill advised. We careened our three ships, instead, and tarred an' caulked an' painted 'til they was sound and ready for the venture. This way, Drake kept the crew busy, but amongst the ten gen'l'men we carried, there was a deal of simmering discontent. This was our second winter in a row, our summer having sailed past when we plunged from 52° north in England to—what did we decide St. Julian's was?" he asked the group.

"49° south," Scotty said. "Almost from the top of the globe to the bottom."

"Aye," Kevin resumed. "The gen'l'men's boredom took the form of leisurely posturin' while the crew worked around them. I had one gen'l'man offer to pull his sword on me because I required the coil of rope he was reclinin' on. So you can see, the sailors was always busy and the gen'l'men was always bored, and the tension between us was fast hardening to hatred. But at that point Captain Drake stepped forward and done a thing what changed the nature of the English Navy forever."

"Ah, changed the Navy forever. How did he do it?"

"He assembled the entire company ashore at Parson Fletcher's service and preached us a sermon that the Royal Navy will never forget. He told us plain that there was to be no more special privilege for anyone—our ships' officers excepted. That meant that the gen'l'men had to share the work of crewing our ships at sea. He said the crew was too unruly dealing with the gen'l'men, and the gen'l'men was too dainty in face of the labor needed to keep our ships afloat. Then he told us that we had a difficult but profitable voyage ahead and would only succeed if we pulled together and subjected ourselves to the rule of a single commander."

"Let me guess," William smiled.

"You be extravagant with your interruptions, lad," Kevin pointed out, "and I hope that means you are a man of endless wealth. Don't forget, you have two on you, so you get only one more."

"I love the effect of a well-chiseled statement," William said. "An extra round to any man who can recite Drake's exact words for me."

The company burst into applause and cries of approval. "That's round two taken care of," they shouted as they toasted.

"Mates," Scotty addressed them solemnly. "Methinks we've fallen into the company of a real sport, and we don't want to scare him off. As soon as we gets round two, let's raise the penalty-points from three to five—for he can't seem to control hisself. I says if we don't empty his purse too quick, we'll mayhap all get a chance to tell our stories tonight."

They all clinked and shouted "Agreed! Agreed!"

"As a tribute to your generosity, lad," Kevin said, "I will conduct a chorus in response to your request." He raised his arms like a conductor. "Ready, mates? We'll begin on Drake's 'wherefore'. Begin. The men sang out: *'Wherefore we must have these mutinies and discords that are grown amongst us redressed, for by the life of God it doth even take my wits from me to think on it; here is such controversy between the sailors and the gentlemen, and such stomaching between the gentlemen and sailors, that it doth even make me mad to hear it. But, my masters, I must have it left, for I must have the gentlemen to haul and draw with the mariner and the mariner with the gentleman. What! let us show ourselves all to be of a company, and let us not give occasion to the enemy to rejoice at our decay and overthrow. I would know him that would refuse to set his hand to a rope, but I know there is not any such here.'"* [6]

"Whilst the company was still digestin' those words," said Kevin, "Drake rammed home his authority further by dismissing all of the officers, includin' the other two captains. Once he saw that no one was fixin' to dispute him as sole commander of the fleet, Drake reinstated the officers into service under himself, and we was ready to sail out from Port St. Julian's and take our chances with the Straits."

"So that's the big thing Drake did? Got the gentlemen off their duffs?"

Kevin looked at William thoughtfully. "You don't grasp things readily, do you, lad? But no matter. Drake's change went deep under the surface. Up until that time, y'see, the English Navy had only one system of command, and that was by committee. The captain always met with his officers before any decision was made, and the officers had a strong voice in that decision. There was a lot of accountability in the system, plenty of witnesses to every decision. That way the Privy Council could get to the bottom of it if anything went wrong. Military thinking: beef up the number of witnesses who can later report."

"But slow down the process too," William suggested.

"Aye, that's it exact." Kevin nodded. "The system was too slow when it come time for action. Take a five-ship squadron and think o' rowin' back and forth for conferences even after the enemy is sighted. Plain to see you are givin' away a lot. So Cap'n Drake borrowed from the Sea-beggers and freebooters, who make the captain absolute boss of his vessel and fleet commander absolute boss of his fleet. That's how they done it for the last fifty years and with unfailin' success too, especially when it's time to clear for action. Any command not carried out on th' mark ends with a body decoratin' the yardarm—or the chopping block like poor Doughty."

"It only takes one of them exhibits each voyage to guarantee a snappy crew," Scotty reflected.

"That's all I need, for sure," Kevin agreed. "When Drake chopped off Doughty's head at St. Julian's, every man jack of us watched. We was ordered to, y'understand. No captain, and Drake least of all, ever wastes the chance to teach his crew a lesson. When Doughty's disconnected head rolled in the dust afore us, I 'spect every lad there promised hisself to do his level best for the rest of the trip. As a result, the _Hind_ was the best-kept ship I ever crewed aboard. By the time we reached the Spice Islands in the Moluccas, we had been underway for two years, and we still had room on deck to store six tons of cloves."

"Half o' which we tossed overboard when we got caught on that reef." Scotty shook his head sadly. "Do y'know what cloves go for on the open market today?"

"Afore we head off for the East Indies," said Buzz the Carpenter, "let me fill the lad in on the tankards?"

"Oh, aye," said Kevin. "T'is your story. Go to it."

"I hopes you're not particular morbid, laddie," Buzz said, "but the mugs we four drink from has a history what starts in Port St. Julian's some fifty-five years afore our ships anchored in her harbor. We all of us knew this was the place where Magellan had hanged three would-be mutineers and marooned two others. That was afore he found the passage from Atlantic to Pacific. The gibbet had stood there half a century and kinda loomed over our proceedin's."

"Did all that hanging and marooning work out for Magellan? Did those extreme measures assure success for his expedition, or did they further fracture his relationship with his crew?"

"Crews, really," corrected Buzz. "Ferdinand Magellan sailed with five ships and 240 seamen when he left Spain on September 15, 1519, and ended when his one remaining ship, _Victory_, struggled into home waters on September 15, 1522 with eighteen survivors after finally confirming that the Earth is round."

"Exactly three years! A good omen. Did Magellan profit for his accomplishment?"

Buzz shook his head. "He was not one of the lucky eighteen. After spending 98 days crossing the Pacific during which their food ran out, and they were forced to dine for a time on rats, ox hides, and sawdust, Magellan got caught up in a local dispute with Philippine natives and was untimely dispatched."

"Is the Philippine part of the Spice Islands?"

"Close," Buzz nodded. "It's a group of islands which, oddly enough, were named after Philip of Spain shortly after his birth by his father, but let me get back to our dealings with Doughty. There was a real problem there ya see because he had made a pest of hisself the whole voyage, complainin' to all who'd listen that Drake was not consultin' him and that the Queen had appointed him co-commander of the expedition."

"Did he offer any proof?" William asked.

"Only the word of a gen'l'man." Buzz grinned at William. "Twas plain he wanted the lot of us to go agin' Drake and obey him instead, so he could establish his authority. I dunno if'n he knew that Drake would call it mutiny, but it certainly dawned on him before it was over. Anyway, Cap'n Drake called a drumhead on him.

"What's a drumhead?"

"Wal," said the carpenter thoughtfully. "It's a kinda quick, informal trial up on deck. It was clear to all o' us that Doughty was strikin' at the Cap'n's authority, so we didn't much doubt the outcome of the trial."

"Was no one on Doughty's side to speak in his defense?"

"We thought him a bit crazed though he was reputed a noble. Some thought him a Spanish spy, tryin' to keep us from Spain's gold shipments in the Pacific. Some thought him Burghley's agent, sent to keep Cap'n Drake from pesterin' Philip with our raids and endangerin' the peace negotiations. Drake hisself saw him as interference. At the trial, Drake told us he would brook no interference whatsoever in carrying out the Queen's commands and showed us documents. He read what the Queen had wrote: *'We do account that he which striketh at thee, Drake, striketh at us'.*" [7]

"Did anyone else read the documents?" William asked.

The carpenter gasped. "Doubt Drake's word, ye mean? No sensible man would be so foolhardy. Like the Queen herself, the Cap'n is a stickler for respect. He waved the papers in front of us in case any wanted a closer look, but the reading he did hisself. He's a good reader too, loud and clear."

"Comes with practice, I imagine," William observed.

"Anyways, Doughty took his sentence well and made the Gen'l'man's Choice 'thout fuss."

"Which was?"

"When convicted at sea, a nobleman c'n be marooned on the nearest land, c'n be returned to London in irons for trial, or c'n be executed on the spot."

"And Doughty chose—?"

The carpenter shrugged. "'Bout what you'd 'spect. Nobles, y'know, have little stomach for indignity or discomfort, and Doughty chose a quick end."

"On Magellan's gibbet?"

"Nay, that wouldn't hold him." Buzz said. "Most o' the timbers was rotten, though some had life in 'em still." The mariners laughed and cheerfully clinked their tankards in unison. "Doughty chose beheadin', and Drake lifted his bloody head after and shouted, 'So die all traitors'!"

"They was good friends too," Scotty observed. "Fought together in Ireland in the early '70's. Received communion and ate together the night afore Doughty went off. Laughed, they did, at their table and talked about the good ole days. Doughty took it like a man and musta realized at the end that he had just pushed Drake too far."

"And so perishes a slow learner," William shuddered. "And the tankards?"

Buzz held up his drink and smiled, "I made one for each o' the lads out of Magellan's old gibbet. Makes me feel like I'm holdin' a bit of history in my hand, it does, when I drink from it. Not morbid at all, you see. Historical. As for Doughty, wal, I figger he was just one of them pushy noble types trying to carve out a little bigger piece of boss-pie for hisself, but he chose the wrong commoner to elbow aside."

Kevin laughed. "Drake on his quarter-deck is like Elizabeth on her throne. Won't tolerate no reach for her scepter. Likewise, Drake will share command with no man. I think Doughty counted on his long friendship with Drake that no drastic action would be taken ag'in him and that after the foam settled, he'd get to take his place as a noble in charge of a upstart commoner. He paid a heavy penalty for such thinkin'."

"A hard lesson indeed," William said. "What was the reaction of the crew?"

"Some of the gen'l'men shared Doughty's fancy, but no crewmen did. The lads knew well enough who our commander was. Doughty was a courtly mariner, y'see, who could not have fetched us home proper and safe, so few was sad to see him go. You may not remember this, lad, but at this here time there was talk that the Straits of Magellan no longer existed. Many a seaman thought an earthquake or landslide musta closed the gap, since so few ships had made it through. The Spanish always concealed their losses best they could, but we knew many a ship had been lost trying to follow Magellan. We needed the best captain we could find to get us through the Straits, and Drake filled that bill just fine for us."

"Did you have a description of the Straits beforehand?"

"Oh, aye. Drake read to us from the record of Magellan's trip, so we knew that the Straits, if we found 'em, would be a real challenge. It were 330-mile from the Atlantic to the Pacific, through a narrow passage two and a half to fifteen miles wide and twistin' its way between islands with steep shores formin' a rocky canyon. "blustery wind blows through from th' west all the time, and there was violent storms all the way. The crew expected some mighty rough sailing and some brisk tacking before we hit the Pacific. After dispatching Doughty, we made ourselves as ready as we could."

"By making tankards from the gibbet," William grinned.

"Only in m'spare time, when m'duties was done," said Buzz. "During them first two weeks, the forge kept me busy. Drake always has a first rate forge crated up and put below deck before he sails anywhere. Sees to it personal, he does—a great one for keeping his ship in good health. I can do minor smithy work on the cook's fire when seas are calm, but I needs to spread out with plenty of fuel for any major metal work."

"I thought you were a carpenter," exclaimed William.

"Aye, but among m'duties was the makin' o' hoops for fresh water casks. I cut a few barrel staves from the warped steps of the gibbet and used the ends for the tankards. Waste not, want not."

The mariners tested the tankards once again, and all fell into a thoughtful silence.

William spoke at last. "Was there any Royal kickback over Doughty's death?"

"Ha!" exclaimed Scotty. "Our Queen likes her sea captains to sweep their own decks. She can't abide a man who, as she puts it, is 'a prey unto delicacy.' When she wants a job done, she 'spects her men to make their own decisions, not refer 'em to her. Aye, officers what have the authority to carry out her business better get it done."

"Sounds like little sympathy for Doughty in that," William observed.

"Very little. The Queen was well enough pleased when she got word that Drake had executed Doughty at St. Julian's. No clapping him in irons and sending him back for her judgment. No bickering with Council members over who had final authority. No endless paperwork with barristers and such-like. 'Hang the bastard and get on with the job,' she is reported to have said."

"I'm a little surprised that Doughty didn't choose one of the other alternatives," William said. "I would have picked marooning in Patagonia long before I bent my head for the ax-bite."

"And open yourself up to a very nasty fate, mayhap," explained Kevin. "Them huge-footed Patagonian savages might well ha' tortured him to death as soon as our ship's cannon cleared the headlands. They had already killed three of our lads afore we taught 'em respect with our wheel-locks. Or they might ha' set him up as a village clown to amuse the women an' children an' dogs. Hardly the best o' fates for an English gen'l'man."

"It's a wonder then he didn't settle for a return to England for trial."

"Wal," Buzz reflected, "Doughty may ha' been no more than a half-mounted gen'l'man at best, but he played that part to the end. He knew Drake had won the struggle for authority, so it was his part to get out of the way. And I doubt if the thought o' being returned to London in chains pleased him." He chuckled. "They tends to hamper the social graces, y'know."

"Unless they're made of gold," William smiled.

"Oddly enough, if he had chose to return, he'd a'reached England just before the news of our takin' the treasure ship _Cacafuego._ All o' London knew what a success that prize meant. The profits was sky-high if we made it home safe. If the Cap'n decided to jettison a bit o' debris whilst winning a fortune, probably there weren't a single dissenting voice—barring relatives—in all o' England. I 'spect Doughty saved hisself some severe heartbreak, having the job done at St. Julian's."

"Let me take our lad back to the birth o'the *Golden Hind*," Scotty said, "before curiosity consumes him entire." Permission was granted. "Drake changed the name of the *Pelican* at the eastern end of the Straits. He ordered our three ships to strike their topsails as a signal that we were dedicating our attempted passage to the Queen."

"Strike their topsails?"

"Nautical equivalent of tippin' your hat. During that ceremony, Drake changed our ship's name to the *Golden Hind*. That was to honor his patron, Sir Christopher Hatton, who has a hind on his coat of arms. I 'spect the Cap'n figgered Hatton might intercede with the Queen if Doughty's death was taken poorly in London. Drake must ha' decided to change the ship's name right after the execution because now, two months later, a carpenter had already carved a new figurehead to replace our old pelican. The new piece were a golden hind, of course, and showed many weeks o' first rate craftsmanship. Good downstream planning, eh?—the kind o' thing Drake shines at."

"And were the Straits as mean as advertised?" William asked. "Or did they turn out to be another of those seaman's yarns that all too often seem to stretch—"

"Sixteen days o' brisk work, with a small anchorage about halfway through. We got out of the wind for awhile there an' took on 3,000 penguins for vittles. But aside from that short stay, it were heavy sailing all the way. Poor bottom for the anchor and the wind snappin' cables. We spent two weeks and two days tackin' back and forth ever' ten minutes in that narrow wind-tunnel, often gainin' only a few yards and sometimes losing in minutes what it had taken hours to win."

"God's blood!" William exclaimed. "Sixteen days to do 330 miles? That's only about twenty miles a day, not even one mile per hour! Couldn't you sail any faster than that?"

The company guffawed, and Scotty said, "Twas unfortunate our ship could not be set at a desired speed. We had to sail the old-fashioned way, takin' whatever nature served up, fast or slow."

"It must have been very satisfying, though, when you finally sailed into the broad reaches of the Pacific Ocean." William made an expansive gesture with his arms, and the company groaned.

"Wal," Scotty grimaced, "the thing we really achieved was to sail into the worst weather any o' us had ever lived through. Storms hit us soon as we cleared the Straits, afore we could find a safe anchorage on the west coast. So that there satisfaction were delayed a full month by the storms what pitched the <u>Hind</u> about like a rat in a terrier's jaw. We was blew mostly southeast an' finally landed on the tip o' the continent. 'Twas here, Drake pointed out, the Atlantic and Pacific Oceans came together as one body—the only place along the whole length o' the New World that happened."

"Egad," breathed William. "It must have been the bottom of the world!"

"About two hundred an' fifty miles south of Magellan's Strait, at 58⁰ south. When Magellan went through the Straits, he named that land to the south Tierre del Fuego, the land o' the fires, because o' the active volcanoes. Since then, the mapmakers, thinkin' 'twas a new continent, named it Terre Australis on all their maps. What we discovered then was that no such a continent ever existed. But the Cap'n made us promise ne'er to reveal our finding to the Spanish because if the Dons knew there was a safer route so close 't'hand, they'd not need to risk the Straits. We named that new route 'Drake's Passage' and sailed north again."

"Did all three of your ships make it then?" William asked.

Scotty shook his head. "The *Elizabeth* 'ad a curious time of it, but she made it back to England. One o' her crewman c'n tell you that story later. We never saw the *Marigold* after we reached the Pacific. Course we had no time to look for her that first stormy month. Later, we had to figger she was lost with all hands. So our fine fleet was reduced to the new-minted 110-ton *Golden Hind* and to us ninety men who was mighty grateful to be alive at that point."

"The *Hind* sounds like a pretty small vessel for all you accomplished," William observed.

"Aye," Scotty nodded. "She is a small galleon, but sturdy. And her small size come in handy when her 13-foot draught often let us conceal ourselfs close to shore. She was a fleet 'un too. She was built with no fore and aft castles even before Hawkins made that shape popular and she answered quick to the helm. We carried eighteen cannon: seven to a side and four in the bow. Enough to handle most problems as we set sail north for the gold mines of Peru."

"An' near lost Drake first thing, with an arrow through his face just below the left eye," Kevin offered. "Near killed the man."

"Zounds!"

"Aye," said Kevin. "We'd landed on Macha Island just off the coast, and some local Indians jumped us. Lost three men, we did, in addition to Drake's wound. The Indians on the island had fled from the Spanish on the mainland and wanted no dealin's with white men. Gave us no warning. Shot us from ambush."

"Probably learned such tactics from the Spanish," William said.

"Oh, the Indians was never angels, y'know," said Buzz. "They had wars enough amongst theirselfs before the Spanish come. We was impressed the way they handled their weapons, so we bugged out o' there quick."

"Captain Drake retreated?"

"Bad investment," Buzz explained. "No gold. No targets for our cannon, an' arrows all over the place. Three dead an' no return. That's not Drake's game. We headed for the mainland 'cause we knew there was treasure there if we could grab it. Spent the next few weeks raidin' north along the coast of Chile. Captured a few fishing boats and then ventured ashore to surprise some Spanish soldiers and frighten some Indian workers at the Spanish silver mines. We took what ingots they had, but there was piles of ore we couldn't load or burn and had to leave. All along we took some modest prizes, but things really changed when we reached Peru. There we learned that the bullion ship *Cacafuego* had sailed north a week ahead o' us, heavy laden and bound for Panama. But that's Mike's story, so go to it, mate."

"Should we stop here to replenish our drinks and mayhap step out back?" suggested William, getting up. "I, for one, need a minute."

Soon all were seated again and Mike began his tale. "Ever'thing changed fast when Cap'n Drake 'eard o' the treasure ship," he said. "Within the hour we cleared from a harbor full o' small prizes and cracked on every yard o' canvas to chase that bullion carrier up the coast like a greyhound after a rabbit. We knew we had to over'aul her afore she reached Panama, so you can bet the *Hind* had the bone in her teeth for the next two weeks."

"Is 'bone in her teeth' a nautical expression?" William asked.

"Oh aye," Mike nodded. "When a sailing ship be in fine fettle and cleavin' fast through the sea, she produces a bow wave—where porpoises sometimes frisk—as she throws curling sheets of foaming water from each side o' her charging prow, lookin' for all the world like she had a bone in her mouth."

"One more question," said William. "Buzz said the bullion ship was called the *Cacafuego*. Does 'caca' mean the same thing in Spanish as it does in English? I know that 'fuego' means 'fire' or 'shoot' in Spanish, but if 'caca' means what I think it means, it's pretty hard to imagine what they had in mind when they named her the *Cacafuego*."

"Meanings sometimes meander when y'switch languages," Mike laughed. "In Spanish *'Cacafuego'* be closer to 'Spitfire'. Officially she be the *Nuestra Senora de la Concepcion*—Our Lady of the Conception. All Spanish ships have nicknames in addition to their regular religious names. 'Spitfire' is not official, o' course, and we learned from the crew later, the name might be a bit derisive. The Spanish crewmen knew well enough when they named her that sailing the peaceful west coast o' South America in their big, powerful vessel 'ad made their ship smug an' fat."

"How does a ship get smug and fat?"

"I don't always understand Spanish humor," Mike confessed, "but I imagine it had to do with the 800-ton ship havin' more cannon than gun crews, or more cannonballs than gunpowder or some such thing what made her less powerful than she appeared. Anyways, y'may remember I said the *Cacafuego* had a week's start on us when we set out in pursuit?"

"The bone-in-teeth time," William said.

"Aye," Mike nodded. "It took us two hell-bent weeks to overhaul our prey, and then we had to slow abruptly and scheme our way to the treasure. Y'recall that King

Philip had give his captains orders to burn their vessels—no matter what the cargo—if they was in danger o' capture by Drake."

"But if you caught them in two weeks after they had a week's start on you, that must mean you could sail twice as fast as they could," William observed.

"Aye," said Mike, "but as soon as we overhauled 'em with our quick sail, speed became our biggest enemy. They sighted us late in the day just as we spotted them. If they learned who we was and how fast we could overhaul 'em, the Spanish cap'n would have no choice but to fire his ship and send its beautiful cargo to the bottom right before our weepin' eyes."

"Couldn't you drop sail or whatever a ship does to slow down?"

"We could, aye, but that wouldn't fool the Spanish commander. If'n he saw us drop sail, yet still keep him in sight, he'd quick realize we could crack it back on and catch him. What we needed was some trick t' make him think he were safe from us even with all our sails set. So Drake kept all four thousand square feet of our canvas in view but commanded us t' trail everything off the stern that would slow us down. We used canvas an' mattresses, casks, pots an' pans an' everything else that would serve as sea anchors. We cut our sailing speed near t'half, so it must have appeared to the Spanish capt'n we could never catch him, even with all our canvas spread. The first night after we spotted each other, he doubtless went to bed feelin' safe, havin' seen we could never overtake him—whoever we were."

"You offered them the ocular proof, eh?" William mused. "No sleeping on the *Golden Hind*, I'll bet."

"We could smell that treasure! No lover ever waited more eager for night to come. As soon as t'was dark, Drake ordered all trailin' lines cut, and the *Hind* leaped forward. The Spanish didn't see us 'til we was alongside. We sent a volley from forty arquebuses across their deck, and Drake shouted out for them to strike their colors. Cap'n Juan de Anton refused to strike, howsomever, and demanded our identification, so we used chain shot from one of our cannon to blow his mizzen mast into the sea along with its lateen sail. While Captain de Anton was digesting that surprise, forty English archers from our longboat landed on the opposite side of the *Cacafuego* and scrambled up the ratlines behind him. From the rigging heights, they commanded the Spanish deck below with their arrows. The Spanish had to admit they was outfoxed and down came their colors.

"Not afore we sent one more eighteen pounder into their hull to speed them up," Scotty said. "I was on that gun crew, so I want it mentioned."

"That surprise we pulled off and the fortune we gained was a great thing!" said Mike. "The men who risks their lifes in such ventures really likes it when bold planning gets the job done clean and fast like that. The less time we sailors spend midst flashing swords and musket fire the better, and the more chance we have to enjoy the booty we've earned. Nothing grieves a poor man worse than dying with newly-gained riches in his pocket."

"Hear! Hear!" the company clinked in obvious agreement.

"And if you ever wanted t' meet a man who don't know how to enjoy his good fortune," Kevin laughed, "here comes old Blinky now. A single jar will tip him downhill, so prepare to hear about the darker side of Cap'n Drake. We'll stay out of it so you can take his first broadside straight-on, and we can see how tight your timbers bind." He winked at his mates and they chuckled together.

"Damn me," Blinky growled as he took a place at the table, a dark, weathered tankard in hand, "but yon fickle public gets 'arder to understand all the time. John Hawkins is the English Navy, same as Old Harry, the Queen's father." He paused to stare intently with his one good eye at the newcomer to the table. "I see we 'ave a visitor. I dunno what they teaches you in school these days, young 'un, but did they tell you 'twas Henry Eight what invented the navy's best fightin' weapon?"

"The Queen's father, right! What weapon?"

"Th' broadside! He lined up guns on th' ship's deck to attack the enemy at right angles as they sailed by. A fearsome weapon it 'as turned out to be. No defense agin it 'cept a bigger broadside or a fleeter set of sails. Harry put the broadside into our clumsy old ships, and Hawkins rebuilt them ships to carry the new guns and still outsail anything the Spanish put in the water. That be our Navy! Ever' Englishman knows it. A few years ago, all the people knowed Hawkins 'ad made England queen o' the oceans the world over. Other nations'd 'ave to scramble t'build better fighting ships t'beat us." One eye was fixed on William. "Mark m'words on it."

"I will," William assured him.

"T'see Hawkins shouldered aside o'ernight," growled Blinky, "by a Johnny-jump-up like Drake—'tis very disturbing. Drake be worse than a interloper. He be a puritanical pirate!" The old sailor glared at William as though expecting rebuttal.

"Keep it down, Blinky," Scotty advised. "You're playin' to a Drake audience, don't forget."

The one-eyed sailor lowered his voice. "Hapless cities he's sacked! 'An grabbed endless fishing boats! Bah! Y'could grab fishing boats from a dingy or from a blowed-up goat skin!"

"The *Cacafuego* weren't hardly a fishing boat," Mike pointed out.

"He 'ad a bit o' luck there," Blinky insisted. "By gore, ye have to get lucky now and ag'in if'n you grab enough of 'em. The point be that Drake used only what Henry and Hawkins gave 'im. I've sailed with Frobisher and Cavendish and Drake as well as with Cap'n Hawkins, and tis the Cap'n what takes best care of his men."

"Drake fetches more prizes," offered one of the sailors.

"Aye, Drake 'as a golden nose, but you be lucky to survive the voyage the way 'e packs 'is men in."

"He just uses the reg'lar old formula for mannin' his ships: one crewman for each one and two-thirds tons," offered Mike. "'Tis true Hawkins made a good argument to the Council for changing that ratio."

"Aye, 'e did that, and I've heard 'im go through 'is reasoning a dozen times. He uses the 500-ton *Golden Lion* to show how the change could be made. The *Lion* is ordinar'y manned by a crew o' 300 officers an' men, at a charge o' £350 a month for pay an' vittles. Hawkins reduced th' crew to 250—one crewman for each two tons—and used the money 'e saved to raise the sailors' wages. The ordinary swab went from seven t' ten shillin's a month, which pretty well guaranteed that the navy'd get the best crewmen in port."

"But that means more work for each man at no savings for the Queen," observed William.

"Wal, I been on sweet ships and sorry ships,' said Blinky, "an' there be no question a content crew of 250 men can do double the work o' a discontent crew of 300 and do it better. An' asides a third more pay, there's more room below decks for a man to keep 'is gear. I likes to waterproof a little compartment to 'old dry clothes, being as how standin' in wet togs too many days in a row brings on the ague."

"Don't forget the vittles. With fewer men, they'll last longer."

"Aye, Hawkins increased the cruising time from six weeks to two months before he had to stop for supplies."

"Afore long, all the good captains will follow his ways though captains are mighty slow to change, I've noticed. It's still only Hawkins' men who they're callin' Limeys because of the fruit he feeds them to keep away the scurvy." All the sailors chuckled, including Blinky.

"I see by your tankard," William ventured, "that you sailed with Drake on the famous Around-the-World trip."

"Aye, that's right," Blinky confirmed, "and t'was just like I said. After a few years o' training under Captain Hawkins, Drake could outsail and outshoot anything the Spanish sent ag'in us. A simpleton coulda done it."

"Well, God knows," William grinned, "we have enough of those around. But it appears you didn't find your service under Drake pleasant. May I ask why?"

"Many a reason, don't y'worry," Blinky answered darkly.

"You're how old?" William asked.

"About fifty, at a guess," the sailor conceded.

"And healthy enough to rot your guts every night with this bilge." The crew tipped their tankards in salute. "And wealthy enough to afford daily dissipation, and sure of a warm bed, a dry roof, and missing only one eye."

"Oh, aye, and well content with dry socks."

"So you're living off your share of the prize money from the capture of the *Cacafuego,* and yet you denounce Captain Drake?" William shook his head, and the sailors around the table laughed good-naturedly.

"Only when 'e shoves aside the real founder o' the English Navy: Captain John Hawkins. Other'n that, I bears Drake no ill will. I resents the man, 'tis true. He be petty an' petulant an' boastful, but I admits I profited from crewin' for 'im."

"What did you do with your portion of the Around-the-World split?" William asked.

"My son-in-law, he's a money-sharp Fleming, invested m'prize money in importin' forks from Italy, spectacles from Amsterdam, and a new company insurin' ag'in glass breakage in Ireland."

"Well, two out of three isn't bad," said William thoughtfully.

❖ ❖ ❖

More men joined the group at the table, and Kevin introduced them as Navigator O'Keefe and Gunner Starkey. The taproom boy now passed their table regularly, and no one was required to get up for refills.

"I have heard," said William to the navigator, "that Drake's maps and charts from the trip are being published for everybody to see. Shouldn't those hard-won charts be guarded more closely?"

"Well, bless you, lad," O'Keefe said, "for worrying about your country. You're right that we ought to be secretive about our rutters, but it's not the end of the world if they fall into Spanish hands. They already have the Waggoners—the best available—but even there, you're still dealing with child's play navigation."

"Child's play navigation?"

"Every serious captain has his astrolabe instrument he can determine his latitude with. He has the conventional rutters containin' all the significant landmarks on the coast of Europe, all river mouths and deep-water channels to major seaports, along with their latitude and soundings. That's conventional stuff. The captain need only shoot the sun at noon, measure its angle above the horizon, check his calendar chart for the angle, and he gets a very good latitude fix on his position north or south of the equator. But east and west—that's the big guessin' game."

"But they must make some attempt to pinpoint their location."

"Oh, yes. As long as the wind is steady and the sea is fair, a seaman can estimate his speed and progress by droppin' the log line off the bow and timin' the number of knots that play out in time with a half-minute glass. But when the wind is whirlin' and the sea is wild and the currents are mixed for days or weeks on end, the best navigator in the world is really only guessing distances east and west. If he's a good guesser, he's a good navigator."

"Not very reassuring. Can't a navigator do better?"

"Not if those three elements—wind, sea, and currents—let loose at once. The currents are rivers in the ocean. If a ship can jump onto a current and also catch the wind, it can appear and disappear from captains who only understand conventional navigation. That's what Drake does. He knows more about ocean currents than any other captain. Whether pressed from behind or chasin', Drake always knows where to go to get a little help. He's the fastest sailor in the world."

"How did he learn all this?"

"Where you learn everything. He was interested. Drake took constant notes during our trip: the color of water, the health of the fish we took from local fishermen. He even kept a keg of beer below, nailed against the hull, which he sampled often to check the outside water temperature."

"That's what he told you, that his beer measured ocean temperature?"

O'Keefe smiled. "He could tell within a degree or two. And that's the way you find the currents. They're hotter or colder than the surroundin' water, so when you get a rapid change in temperature, you know you have a change in sailing conditions, which may help or hinder, depending on how you manage your sails. That's how we find the Mariner's Current."

"The Mariner's Current?"

"Gets you home fast and safe from the New World. The Spaniards were aware of it long before we were. It's the route their bullion fleet uses to come home. It starts near Havana, Cuba. The gulf to the north of Cuba produces a great mass of warm water which swings eastward around the Florida peninsula, cuts sharply north/northeast and finally loops east in the middle of the Atlantic. An easy run home for English sailors. Or Spanish, for that matter."

"Don't all captains know about ocean currents?"

"It's easy to see currents at work in harbors or along the coast where the landscape in the background shifts as the ship is carried along, but it is an entirely different matter at sea where there is no such perspective. Since they can't measure ocean currents, most captains pay closer attention to wind and sun and compass to guide their vessel."

"But Drake can measure the currents."

"Perhaps not measure exactly, but at least acknowledge. Drake always asked the local fishermen about the prevailing currents we encountered during the Around-the-World trip, even on the other side of the planet. Drake knows every current on the coast of Europe. He sailed his own commercial ship after servin' his apprenticeship in the Antwerp-London cloth trade, so he knows all there is to know about the currents of the Narrow Seas."

"This is twice I have heard reference to the Narrow Seas. What might they be?"

"That's the channel between England and France. It narrows, y'know, bein' a hundred miles wide at the west end between Land's End and Brest and just twenty-two miles at the eastern end between Dover and Calais. That funnel shape compresses the tidal surge of the sea four times a day, which produces mighty treacherous currents at the narrow end. Any ship lackin' a seasoned man at the tiller can be overset in a hurry."

"Returning to England from the New World, a captain would be tempted to sail directly northeast after rounding the Florida Peninsula if he did not know about the Mariner's Current," William said. "What's wrong with that course?"

"Shiftin' winds and much becalmed water. Not dependable at all. Ships disappear over there around Bermuda. If two ships rounded Florida together and one swung northeast for a straight line to England and the other headed north-northeast along the coast before swinging east, the second one would reach England sooner every time."

"That dependable?"

"Aye," said O'Keefe, "and five degrees warmer. That's how you know you're in it. It has eddies and flows inside it, but mostly it's a warm, fifty-mile-wide river which loops across the cooler ocean for three thousand miles until it swings south just as it reaches Europe. It brings such warm weather to the coast of southern Ireland that I've seen a small palm tree growin' on the coast of Cork."

"Steers a ship right to Ireland, eh?" chuckled William. "How deep would such a current be?"

"God only knows. It's a powerful force, the most powerful I've ever seen. Mayhap the ocean floor slants that way or somesuch."

"And that rightfully concerns serious navigators?"

"Wal, I prefer 'intelligent' if you don't mind. Or 'alert'. There's a lot of 'serious' people in this world who are plumb stupid, and I've had the misfortune to work with some of 'em."

William smiled. "I wonder if Drake will ever make his records of currents public."

"Oh, aye, he'll certainly pass his knowledge to every English captain he trusts, but he don't trust too many. Genius though he be, Drake sees plots and conspiracies against England and himself whenever things don't go his way. Even our minister on the Trip wasn't safe if he tried to go ag'in Drake's thinkin'."

"Ah yes," said William, "I understand Drake is extremely religious."

"Aye," spoke up Kevin, "Drake be a God-fearing man, right enough, but like most great men, he likes to deal direct with God. Only principals need apply, as they say. He has no patience atal' with God's go-betweens less'n they happens to see God's will just as Drake sees it."

"But a minister was with you the whole way on the Round-the-World trip?"

"Parson Fletcher," Kevin supplied. "Services ever' day. Drake be real strict 'bout religious observance on board ship. No excuse whatever for non-attendance. What the hell, Drake be a born sea-cap'n, and he knows a ship's crew can turn unruly if not held in check. Any sea cap'n who don't tend his crew close don't need to look overboard for deadly shoals. You can bet that Drake will support any discipline what helps 'im govern his men, especially somethin' as powerful as the wrath of God."

"But his own religious convictions come into this, I'm sure."

"That's the point," said Kevin. "'Tis all the same to him. I doubt there's any difference in Drake's mind twixt his role as cap'n and his role as server o' the Lord, striking at the Purple Whore o' Rome by pillagin' and plunderin' Cath'lic ships and outposts. That there attitude was clear enou' when he declared war on King Philip. 'E sent 'im a letter what was also published, mayhap by his own self. Many a mariner 'as lifted a pint and shouted 'About time!' and 'Good show!' when that declaration be mentioned. Probably the first time in history that a commoner was so bold as t'declare war on a reigning monarch."

"Or had enough wit to handle the promotional aspect himself," William mused. "How did Philip take it?"

Kevin chuckled. "The King o' Spain has good reason not to underrate Drake. He knows that e'en 'The Greatest Thief o' the Unknown World'—as the crew names him when we're celebratin'—can't take enou' gold from Spain to do real damage, but the cap'n sets a fearsome example for them other privateers when 'e rampages 'cross the Spanish Main sackin' and destroyin' the fortified settlements as though they was rabbit hutches."

"I've heard that," said William. "And Philip fears the circling-buzzard effect, of course."

"Aye. And 'tis personal too. I don't doubt Philip longs to get Drake tied down and stretched out where he could apply red-hot pincers to 'im. Aye, it's personal all right, on both sides, and a historical lesson to boot."

"Historical lesson?"

"Drake's taught Philip that Spain 'as all she can handle holdin' onto the colonies she already has and that the Dons'd do better puttin' their time an' money an' men into buildin' up defenses and less into huntin' down and destroyin' New World colonies o' other nations—like they did the Huguenot colony in Florida back in 1562."

"Hue-ga-knot," repeated William. "Sounds like an Indian name."

"The Huguenots was French Protestants, fixin' to separate theirselves from the religious wars o' France."

"So French Protestants had a colony in Florida twenty-three years ago?" said William in surprise.

"Aye," Kevin said. "But the Spaniards captured it in 1565 and hanged all the French they could round up. Pedro Melendez de Avila was careful to explain that the eight hundred he hanged was executed as heretics, not Frenchies. Two years later the French returned and hanged every Spaniard they found at the colony, and Dominique de Gorgues of Gascony explained he was not executin' Spaniards but only riddin' the world of assassins."

"Bravo!" cried William. "Just a little tit for tat."

"Aye, but the colony idea were abandoned for awhile, until Raleigh decided t' try his luck. As it stands now, every new colony has a better chance of succeeding because Drake has caused a pullback of Spanish aggression, so Raleigh's colony in Virginia has more time to take root."

"You see Drake, then, as running interference for Raleigh?"

"It amounts to that, aye."

"But back to Parson Fletcher. Did I sense a story there?"

"Parson Fletcher, aye." Kevin took a swig of ale and wiped his mouth. "Generally, the Parson fit in as a crew member. Fact o' the matter, he been so active in th' grabbin' o' prizes, he soon come to argue that our horde o' golden chalices and goblets captured from Spanish churches, should, by rights, go t' him personal as religious artifacts." Kevin grinned. "'E was voted down handsome by both captain an' crew. God's blood, I'd love to sail ag'in someday on a ship that was so heavy laden with booty that we used gold an' silver ingots as ballast. Did I tell ye that it took us six days on the high seas to transfer the treasure off the *Cacafuego* onto the *Hind*? I never saw our crew step so lively as durin' those days, an' ye can bet we slept very sound on the way home, knowin' what lay 'neath our heads. Ah well, the good old days." All the crewman at the table murmured agreement.

"The greedy parson ventured on dangerous ground then," murmured William. "Did he agree basically with the captain on religious matters?"

"There was occasional flare-ups. But they was resolved quick after the Parson found that Drake kept an iron grip on interpretin' God's will aboard his ship."

"What kind of flare-ups?"

"The most serious was when we were in the Malacca Straits, but then it weren't so much a religious thing as 'twas Drake's suspectin' the parson was plottin' a kind o' faint-hearted mutiny."

"Mutinous as well as greedy, eh?"

"Do you remember the earlier mention of our running up on a reef and being stuck hard in the East Indies just off the Celebes?"

"Where you had to abandon your nutmeg?"

"Cloves," Kevin nodded. "We was held tight in the vise o' that reef for a full twenty-four hours with apprehension mountin' every minute. We couldn't move and we couldn't do nothin' to improve our condition. We tried to put an anchor out to windward astern to pull us off, but we couldn't find no seabed for leverage. To lighten our load, we first threw over half the cloves and then some o' our cannon, but the *Hind* wouldn't budge an inch. We wasn't tempted to dump any o' the gold, howsomever lighter it might make us, but other than that, we was pretty desp'rate. The entire crew attended service an' took the sacrament, we was that close to our doom."

"I'm glad you're here," William said, "or I would fear an unhappy ending to this story."

"We was in real danger, right enough. If the seas had roughed up that day we woulda been dashed t' pieces an' scattered t' the deep with our treasure— a'ter we got home, we all agreed bein' perched on that reef were the closest call we had durin' our three-year trip. Finally, howsomever, we catched a flood tide just as the wind switched directions. The cap'n ordered us t'set sail and we backed out of that there deadly embrace like as though we was leavin' dry-dock."

"What damage to your ship?"

"God be praised, we'd run up on a slantin' stone ledge of some sort, so our double plankin' was not torn when we backed off."

"Double planking?"

"Aye, the *Hind* was built sturdy an' had a double sheathin' o' planks with a thick layer o' tar betwixt."

"Speaking of God reminds me of Parson Fletcher again." William smiled.

"Oh, aye, Fletcher's offense," Kevin said, grinning. "When we was in the clear, someone warned Drake that durin' the trouble, Fletcher were heard to say that our bad luck were God's judgment on th' Cap'n for the sin of executin' Doughty."

William gasped. "Egad! And Drake does not take criticism lightly, I recall!"

"Indeed he don't," Kevin affirmed. "He clapped Fletcher in irons an' called the crew together for a speedy judgment on the matter. He said to the Parson: *'Francis Fletcher, I do here excommunicate thee of the Church of God and from all benefits and graces thereof, and denounce thee to the devil and all his angels.'* [8] Then he forbids Fletcher, under pain o' death, to appear in the crew's quarters or afore the mast or to preach to the men. The cap'n set a placard around Fletcher's neck to identify 'im to the crew: *'Francis Fletcher, the falsest knave that liveth.'*"

"Wait a minute now," William said, "how could a layman like Drake excommunicate an ordained minister of the Anglican Church—or anybody else, for that matter? I know sea-captains have extraordinary powers at sea, but that smacks of ecclesiastical encroachment."

"Ye may be right," Kevin laughed, "but once we reached the Spice Islands, we still had 8,000 miles to go afore we reached England, and the Cap'n didn't want no mutiny even if it were faint-hearted, so 'e used his commission as the Queen's personal agent t'act in her place as the supreme head o' the Anglican Church to defrock poor ol' Fletcher."

"That still sounds like overreach to me."

"Mayhap, but a'ter about a week, Drake cooled off after scarin' the bejesus out o' Parson—and the rest of us as well. He finally sent Fletcher back to his reg'lar duties, and we all turned our attention to the journey home."

"Parson Fletcher came close to a quick visit to our Lord there!" exclaimed William.

"Aye," agreed Kevin, "one would have thought the spectacle of Doughty's death woulda' stifled Fletcher's croakings, but I believe the Parson is a thick-headed sort."

At this point, Gunner Starkey spoke up. "Didn't care much for our music either, the Parson didn't."

"Gunner Starkey here is probably the best musician among us," Kevin confided to William. "Tell about our entertainment aboard ship, Bill."

"Wal, you should know, lad," began Gunner Starkey, "that we seamen are musicians of sorts by necessity. The only entertainment we have for months on end is what singing and dancing we can fashion ourselves—to go along with our gallon-a-day beer ration. Each man in his turn is expected to make his contribution to the entertainment of the crew."

"A gallon-a-day beer ration?"

The gunner grinned. "The men'd mutiny without it. It's ale what holds the British seaman to his task. The ale helps deaden 'im to the hard work of close tackin' up some narrow channel into the wind. If'n a man worries about his comfort at them moments, 'tis like he'll bungle the tack and lose the ground that hard work has gained. Ale wraps a man in a cocoon o' comfort so's he can get on wi' his labors—what for my crew, be the mannin' o' cannon."

"It must take terrific hand-and-eye coordination to be a good gunner," ventured William.

"Hand-and-eye, hell," said Starkey softly. "You aims your cannon with your feet."

William blinked. "With your feet! How are gunners chosen then?"

"Meself I chooses 'em with m'flute."

"You mean you charm them?"

"I gives 'em a tune to dance to. The best dancers makes the best gunners. 'Tis the roll of the ship, y'see, that causes a hit or a miss from cannon-shot. That be why a good artillery man on land may make a poor naval gunner. He ben't used to havin' his gun-mount in constant motion. Might never get the feel o' it less'n he be a good dancer. Iffen his feet don't find the tune his gun-rest be playin', he may shoot down many a fish or bird 'thout annoyin' the enemy even a little. The roll o' the ship be most o' what counts in naval gunnery. A gunner can lay 'is piece a few degrees right or left, but most o' his shots are right down the middle. 'Tis up t' the cap'n to position the ship so t'guns are brought to bear, an' 'tis up to the gunner t'feel the roll so's his shot will catch 'em fair."

"Sounds like an old gunner's song," marveled William.

"Here's the odd thing. French and Spanish gunners we 'ave captured tell me they be instructed t' touch off their pieces on the uproll o' the ship. Plain as t'day, touchin' off on the down-roll be a main part of an English gunner's success."

"The down-roll instead of the up-roll," nodded William.

"That there way we skips many o' our near-miss balls into their hulls at the water line. If we touches off a instant too soon on the down-roll, our shot goes into their rigging. An instant too late, it hits 'em at the water line. Both good."

"And that same possibility does not occur on the up-roll," guessed William.

"Nay, the instant you clears water on the up-roll, your guns be pointed at the sky. No chance for a bounce shot."

Several gulps of ale were required from each listener in order to digest Gunner Starkey's technical data.

"Tell the lad about your part in Drake's Trip around the World, Bill," suggested Kevin.

"Were you on that voyage too?" asked William. "It seems to me every sailor I've met—"

"I were there at t'beginning but not at t'end."

"You were not in on the split then?"

"Unfortunately correct," said Starkey. "I were part of Cap'n Wynter's crew on the *Elizabeth*. We missed our chance at circlin' the globe, tryin' to follow Drake through the Straits of Magellan. Hardest duty a crew ever pulled."

"At the bottom of the New World Continent?"

"Aye. We was well aware of the hardships o' the Straits. Cap'n Wynters read to us from the account of Magellan's hardship with that passage fifty-five years before us. It had taken Magellan thirty-seven days to make the 330-mile trip from the Atlantic to the Pacific back in 1522."

"Thirty-seven days! Not too encouraging!"

"Wal, we wasn't too discouraged at first, but by the end of a month, we was ready to take another look at the prospect. We found later that Drake had his usual luck and made it through in just sixteen days. We reached the Pacific twice. But as soon as we did, we encountered direct westerly winds that blew us right back to the anchorage in the middle of the Straits."

"Where the pigeons were," William offered.

"Penguins," Starkey corrected. "Four weeks of desp'rate tacking had not only worn down the men but had taken a terrible toll of our rigging and sails. We'd lost our anchors and cable too. The *Elizabeth* was finally beaten so bad that Wynters decided to turn back and take the easier route to the East Indies around the Cape of Good Hope to meet with Drake in the Spice Islands."

"The route below Africa is easier?"

"Not really, but at least you start with a good wind. That's a big break for men who have been tacking their vessel every ten minutes for a month."

"Between beers."

"That's what keeps us at it, aye. In the end, I've come to feel it was just as well we missed the fame and glory because we also missed the fate of Captain Thomas and the *Marigold*. They made it through the Straits but were immediately swallowed up with all hands by the stormy Pacific."

"'S'blood," whispered William.

"'Twas a sorry fate," said Scotty. "We on the *Golden Hind* were so glum that Drake himself took a hand at lifting our spirits with music and dancing after the storm abated."

"Drake took a hand? Is he a musician too?"

"Aye, he is," said Scotty. "He doesn't trust to chance that each sailor will carry a musical instrument aboard. He keeps a trunkful in his cabin—drums, trumpets, bones, fifes, tabors, spoons, coronets, and guitars—and everybody is encouraged to learn to play. Some of us lads become real good at an instrument or two before the three years was up."

"It's difficult picturing Captain Drake making music with his crew."

"Drake is a crack commander. His orders is specific, and any disobeyin' is punished, but as long as the crew remembers who's in charge, he can get quite relaxed with 'em. He has a jolly side, in fact, and knows it's important for us lads to have a bit of a good time whenever duties permit. That there was the jolliest, healthiest, best-run ship I ever crewed aboard."

"Aye," agreed the crew. William looked at Blinky, who also nodded agreeably.

"Drake cares for his crew the same way he does his ship," Scotty added. "Every six weeks or so during the three years, we would careen the *Hind* and caulk her in some out-of-the-way spot. That crew knew every skill, so whatever was needed, some lad could do it. Drake maintains things. He knows a well-fed crew can be counted on to work hard between meals, so he pays more attention to fresh vittles than do most captains. We ate better on that three-year voyage than any other I've heard of."

"But where do you get fresh food at sea?"

"Wal, the small coasting ships we captured often carried a bounty of fresh vittles even if they had little treasure. Their pantries were always loaded with good stuff for the officers, an' Drake always shared them with us. There was periods when we ate better than were we at home."

"I've heard there is usually a lot of sickness aboard ship," said William.

"Aye, that's right. Cap'n John Hawkins has said scurvy killed 10,000 English seamen in the last twenty years. Not many a English vessel escapes ship's fever after two or three months at sea, but the *Hind* went without it for three years. Mayhap it was the fresh vittles an' water, but also, we wasn't too crowded, seein' as how Drake insisted the ship be kept tidy. That there give us all a little more room to stretch below decks."

"Tell me more about ship's fever," pressed William. "Is it—"

"Nay," interrupted Kevin. "You've generously subsidized our story-telling for the night, but now it's time to pay the piper," and he handed William the reckoning.

"I am always pleased to pay for such superb entertainment," William declared as he reached for his money. His hand came away with the severed ends of his purse strings. "Bloody hell, I've been robbed!" he cried out.

A heavy silence fell across the table.

Chapter 4:
HAWKINS FACES TREACHERY IN MEXICO

The Whale's Tale Inn, Plymouth, that same evening:

William trailed Malachi up the stairs to the sleeping quarters of the inn. "I was never so glad to see anyone in my life, Malachi. I think they might have slit my throat."

"And a good lesson it would have been for you," Malachi growled. "You can't always count on me to dash from the wings in the last act to settle your reckoning."

"There seems to be a surprisingly strong feeling about this business of who pays the bill around here," William observed. "What happened to the warm sense of good comradeship and mutual jesting that prevailed just before the arrival of the charges?"

"It's not who pays the bill," Malachi pointed out, "but, rather, who pays his bill. And in this case, the 'his' was yours. It was explained to me during the negotiations that by your breech of the table's rules, you had lured those simple seamen into a drunken stupor with your frequent interruptions, which, in effect, guaranteed them all they could drink. At some point in the evening, it dawned on them that the faster they told their stories, the more you would interrupt, and the more benefit would thereby flow their way."

"I noticed they began to invite their friends to join the merriment at our table."

"Indeed, it took me a king's ransom to get you out of there in one piece. How could you let your guard down to a cutpurse after all I've taught you? I'm afraid the answer is that you are so entranced by the sound of your own voice that you become a sacrificial lamb tied to a post by all who recognize how defenseless you are while wrapped in your self absorbed fascination. Keeping a safe grip on your coins is a basic skill of survival. A man of the world cannot be caught out without funds like any country bumpkin—"

"Lesson learned," William broke in. "No need for further chastisement. I will never again let my attention wander, no matter what vital information is being told me that might be useful to the Service. *'You shall be as a father to my youth. My voice shall sound as you do prompt my ear, and I will stoop and humble my intents to your well-practiced direction'.*" [9]

"All right. No need for sarcasm. I think we may move on to what vital information you gleaned."

"Well, a one-eyed sailor named Blinky had a decidedly partisan view in his choice between Drake and Hawkins. Almost dangerously partisan, I'd say."

"Yes, I know about Blinky. A bit rough-tongued but loyal enough. Even after sailing under Drake's command and profiting greatly from the Round-the-World trip, he still maintains a dogged loyalty to our Treasurer of the Navy. Blinky first followed Captain Hawkins over twenty years ago in 1563. That was on the *Jesus of Lubeck*, a cumbrous ship of 700 tons, built in the old style, high-charged with castles fore and aft, potbellied, clumsy, and slow to answer the helm. England added her to our Navy back in 1544 when King Henry bought her second hand from some of the merchants in the Hanseatic League. There's a good story about Captain Hawkins' effective commands when fire once broke out on the *Jesus* as she sailed in the West Indies."

"I'm all ears," William said.

"Off Cuba in '67, a careless gunner let his punk go untended, and it started a fire next to the powder magazine below deck. The men scurried about like rats dipping buckets overboard and hauling up sea water, then spilling more than they delivered as they passed the buckets down the ladder. Meanwhile, the fire ate into the hull, and there was no doubt in the men's minds that they were close to perdition."

"The powder magazine, right?"

"Exactly. The paint on the magazine started to blister from the heat, and the men were divided on whether to slosh more water on the fire or loose the hatch-covers for abandoning ship. Finally, Captain Hawkins arrived on the scene, took one quick look at the situation, and gave three terse commands."

"*'Man the pumps!'* he ordered one group, and they sprang to the two mid-ship pumps."

"*'Block the scuppers!'* he commanded another bunch, and they slammed wooden blocks into those openings below the rail where sea water runs back out."

"Then *'Chop a hole!'* he shouted, indicating a spot above the fire. The men fell to and chopped through two layers of deck planking with their axes. The pumps spouted water on the deck, and the blocked scuppers gave the water no place to go but down the hole above the fire. The men below funneled the continuous stream with scoops and swabs directly onto the fire, and it was out very quickly." [10]

"Shades of Simple!" exclaimed William. "The men must have thought him a wizard."

"Indeed," agreed Malachi. "A captain with wit about him will save a seaman's hide sooner than one with a strong arm. Sailors who have spent their lives at sea, know very well how to run a ship effectively in terms of steering and sail-settings, so every captain is under critical observation as soon as the ship leaves the dock. Most captains handle the routine chores well enough, but the smart ones can best be seen during emergencies at sea."

"But couldn't their running water below deck like that sink a ship?" asked William.

"Indeed it could if they did it for long, but as soon as the fire was out, the pumps were stopped, the scuppers cleared, and the deck made new. The relief was great. All hands received a special ration of beer, and you can bet they toasted Captain Hawkins with a great deal of enthusiasm and affection."

"No wonder Blinky has such loyalty for the Captain."

Malachi nodded thoughtfully. "He was also with Hawkins during the San Juan de Ulua battle. Drake was there too, with his first command, the 50-ton *Judith*. He is Hawkins' younger cousin, you remember."

"So Hawkins is a commoner too. Is he also a Puritan?"

Malachi nodded. "I don't know how full fledged he might be, but I'd say there's not much difference between a lax Puritan—if there is such a thing—and a strict Anglican. Hawkins and Drake both see to it that all their crewmen attend religious services every day while at sea. The Spartan life of a ship captain seems to attract strong-willed men like themselves, who feel the need to ask God's blessing daily because that's how often they see the need. Like at San Juan."

"Seventeen years ago, you said. In 1568."

"Right. The voyage began as a delightful cannon-comedy arranged between Captain Hawkins and the New World Spanish. Hawkins had been instructed to behave himself on the trip both by the Queen and by Burghley, his patron. His task was to prove to King Philip that a mutual trade between our two countries in the New World would profit both kingdoms."

"I know the Spanish had gold and silver to trade. What did we offer?"

"Protection, for one. The use of our cannon against the French freebooters, who had just sacked Cartegena and Margarite for the third time. Also, sad to say, we brought black slaves from Africa to sell to the Spanish merchants and growers. And, as always, we had cloth and other English goods to trade."

"But Philip had forbidden his colonists to trade with English heretics, right?"

"Right," said Malachi. "At every port, Hawkins had to talk the Spanish into ignoring Philip's direct command and open trade with us."

"He must be very persuasive."

"Yes, and charming when the occasion calls for it. At every port, he would invite the local authorities to dinner at their best eating place overlooking the harbor. He would then instruct all his ships to use anchors fore and aft to line our gun-ports up broadside to the selected spot. As a result, those dinner guests were looking down the barrels of more firepower than any had ever seen while they digested their meals and listened carefully to Captain Hawkins' proposals for open trade. All the port authorities knew enough to delay their decision while they sought approval from some higher authority in a distant city or on another island or far off in the jungle. They thereby produced what they had desperately sought: an administrative stalemate whereby action would cease for a time so secret steps might be taken."

"By them or by Hawkins?"

"Both. They beefed up what defenses they had and summoned what reinforcements they could. Captain Hawkins made his move by blandly assuming that the interlude of waiting for a far-off judgment was a period during which open commerce was allowed. He quietly opened a trade booth on the dock and went about displaying our best wares. When the ladies of the island saw the quality of the English cloth we carried, and the growers of the island saw the labor force we offered, the whole community usually shrugged its shoulders and let it happen."

"But what did they tell King Philip?"

"That's why the arrangement has been called a cannon-comedy," Malachi chuckled, "or collusive-combat, if you prefer. The English agreed to provide enough smoke and noise to convince Philip, half a world away, that the Spanish had resisted just short of annihilation. Sometimes the port officials would pick out a dilapidated building for the English to blow apart with their guns. Good morale builder for our gun crews and a chance to display some impressive destruction for the pleasure of the onlookers. After a few well-placed shots, there would be celebration with dancing and drinking. Trade would then go on for a month or more."

"Hawkins' fleet would stay in one harbor for a month?"

Malachi smiled. "Pretty hard to disturb an equilibrium which is mutually beneficial. The Spaniards were surprisingly hospitable once they had their cover story for Madrid. The English could buy victuals at each port, and Hawkins always laid up one ship in turn for careening and caulking and refitting. He's a great man for maintenance, but even Hawkins nearly went crazy trying to hold the old *Jesus of Lubec* together."

"Because she was so old-fashioned?"

224

"Right. A high-charged carrack. The stern castle rose forty feet above deck and the forecastle thirty feet. Both solid fortresses. If boarders ever swarmed us amidship, they would be subjected to a murderous crossfire because even the small, swivel-mounted guns atop the castles could be turned to fire down on the boarders. The *Jesus* was solidly built and in good shape when Henry bought her, but badly neglected by James and Catholic Mary as most of the Navy was."

"You mean the *Jesus* was at least twenty-five years old before Hawkins took her to the West Indies?"

"More like forty or more," Malachi nodded. "She had even been condemned early in Elizabeth's reign by men who knew their business, but Hawkins saved her from the grave and fixed her up. He wanted to rebuild her completely, but there was only enough money to do a quick patch-up on her, so he took her to sea knowing he would need a permanent repair crew in addition to the regular maintenance crew."

"What was the worst problem?"

"The ships of that type are essentially top-heavy. The fore and aft castles sway every time the ship lurches in the waves, so they pull and strain the timber fastenings a thousand times a day. The rougher the sea, the harder they yank. Something snapped on the *Jesus* every day, and Hawkins was heard more than once swearing he would sweep his future ships clean above deck. But they were stuck with her, and since she was the Queen's ship, Hawkins was determined to bring her home even at some cost to himself."

"Cost to himself?"

"The contract they sailed under, read that if the *Jesus* sank, the Queen would bear the loss, but if they brought her home, the charge for making her seaworthy again fell to the trade company in which both Hawkins and the Queen held shares, along with Navy board members, Privy Council members, London merchants, Plymouth merchants (including the Hawkins brothers), and an assortment of courtiers who were well aware Elizabeth had a good nose for profit, and aware also that Captain Hawkins had returned 60% profit on a previous trip."

"So it would have been cheaper for Captain Hawkins to abandon her?"

"That's right. As a matter of fact, that's exactly what his advisors told him as they prepared for the trip home after a profitable tour of the West Indies. If they had moved the trade goods and profits from the *Jesus* to the other ships at that point, they could easily have burned her and steered straight for England with a happy crew of newly prosperous mariners."

"But they obviously didn't."

"Right. They turned their attention instead to pouring sand down a rat-hole by repairing the *Jesus*, which was left unfit by frequent storms and unsafe to sail home.

She had leaks the thickness of a man's arm, and living fish swam about in the ballast. They tried Florida first, but found no harbor deep enough for the big ship. Storms drove them west again, and they finally ended up on the Mexican coast at San Juan de Ulua, the port city for Vera Cruz. They knew that the heavily guarded Spanish bullion fleet was due to visit that harbor a few weeks later, but they decided they had plenty of time for repairs before that happened."

"It begins to sound as if they were wrong."

"Right again." Malachi's voice took on a bitter edge. "We sailed into San Juan de Ulua on September 16, 1568, and before we left, Spanish treachery had started a war which burned hatred into the breast of every English sailor—particularly Hawkins and Drake."

"Excuse me, Malachi," William said, "you say 'we,' and some of the details of this story seem to have grown quite personal for you. Is it possible that you were there?"

Malachi grimaced. "It was the beginning of my 'diplomatic' career. Captain Hawkins used me now and again as a Spanish interpreter, so I can give you an eye-witness account of that infamous battle." Malachi stared into space. "Six hours we fought. Six bloody, desperate hours."

"Zounds! A sea battle!"

"The Spanish had mounted cannon on a shoal at the end of a spit of land which formed the outer lip of the harbor about 500 yards from the mainland. They set up a quay for docking beneath the cannon, but the berthing area was only a bow-shot in length each way, so visiting ships were obliged to nose into the dock side-by-side and then set out a stern anchor to hold them out straight."

"Er, how far is a bow-shot?"

"A sturdy shot is generally accepted as 240 yards. Anyway, we entered the harbor flying only our oldest and most weather-beaten pennants, and there was enough confusion about our identity that we were able to grab their cannon on the quay before they could organize resistance."

"You captured their cannon!" exclaimed William. "That doesn't sound too peaceful."

"Couldn't be helped," Malachi shrugged. "We meant them no harm, but we still couldn't risk pointblank cannon fire raking us from stem to stern with chain-shot before we had a chance to explain that we simply wanted to buy victuals and repair our ship. Hawkins had lunch with the authorities and sensible arrangements were concluded without a casualty on either side."

"Captain Hawkins' diplomacy won the day again."

"Exactly," Malachi said. "The next morning, however, we saw thirteen large Spanish ships riding at anchor just outside the harbor, in addition to the eleven lesser Spanish merchant ships that were in port when we arrived, so now our five English ships were in the constraining company of twenty-four of Philip's vessels. Only two of the twenty-four, however, were men-of-war galleons, but it was clear to our 400 men that we were facing thousands if a battle started. We could keep the bullion fleet from entering the harbor with our cannon and with the guns on the quay, but they effectively blockaded us from leaving, so negotiations were held for two days and honorable agreement reached and sworn to."

"Agreement that you would not attack each other?"

"That's correct. We were to exchange ten English gentlemen for ten Spanish gentlemen as ransom for our honor, and the Spanish showed their disdain early for the oath they had just taken by trying to palm off ten ordinary seamen on us in the exchange. Captain Hawkins detected the ruse by noting their callused hands. One of them was insulted by the disclosure that he was not a gentleman and tried to stab our Captain, but he was quickly restrained, so no harm was done."

"But the agreement was sworn to!"

Malachi nodded. "A truce was agreed upon, a celebratory trumpet was sounded to mark the beginning of the pact, and the bullion fleet entered the harbor unmolested. Spain's newly appointed Viceroy for the West Indies, Don Martin Enriquez, ranking just below the King of Spain, arrived with the fleet. He signed with his hand and sealed with his seal the conditions of the truce, which—we later learned—he had every intention of betraying at the first opportunity. For one thing he agreed to permit us to keep control of the cannon on the quay during our stay, and that relaxed us somewhat. We spent the next two days warping ships around to put all the English ships in one bunch and all the Spanish in another."

"Warping them?"

"Positioning them with our longboats and cables. No room to maneuver under sail. On the third morning after we admitted the fleet of Viceroy Enriquez into the harbor, we began to notice suspicious troop movements among the Spanish ships. We were particularly troubled by the number of Spanish troops who went aboard the big Spanish 900-tonner which was berthed closest to our second largest ship, the 300-ton _Minion_. The two ships, berthed nose-in to the quay as they were, marked the dividing line between our vessels and those of the Spanish. The beefing up of the closest outpost to us rightfully concerned Captain Hawkins, so he dispatched Robert Barrett, Master of the _Jesus_ and fluent in Spanish, to inquire of the Viceroy what was meant by such maneuvers while the truce was in effect. Robert Barrett was a cousin of Drake's and met a fate as sad as any imaginable—but that's for later. The Viceroy realized that our inquiry indicated our growing suspicion, so he seized what surprise he might by clapping Barrett in irons and launching an immediate attack on the rest of us."

"He broke the truce!" cried William.

"The signal to begin the hostilities came from the same instrument which had marked the truce, but this time the trumpet's note was a shrill and urgent call-to-arms for both sides. At the signal, a large section of Spanish troops leaped onto the quay from the big ship next to us and overwhelmed our sailors guarding the island's cannon. Before our very eyes, they killed every English sailor they caught on the quay and then loosed their cannon-fire on our five ships. The gunners on our ships had never been completely lulled by Spanish assurances, so our cannon were loaded and ready to fire, but the docking arrangement meant that few of our guns could be brought to bear on the guns on the quay or on the enemy ships."

"The side-by-side thing."

"Right. All the English ships except the *Jesus* immediately loosed the headfasts which bound them to the quay and hauled away on their sternfasts to back out of that trap and bring their guns to bear against the quay cannon and the two men-of-war."

"Why didn't the *Jesus* pull out?"

"The Spanish guns concentrated their fire on Hawkins' flagship, and the masts and yards were soon shot to splinters by the pointblank fire from the gun emplacements atop the quay. It was impossible for any sailor to live on the deck amidst the murderous crossfire, so for a time it was thought best to use her as a bulwark to protect our other ships. Three-hundred men from the big Spanish ship attempted to board the *Minion* while she was hauling out, and some gained the deck. There was bloody, back-and-forth, cutlass and musket work for a time, but they were finally driven off. We pulled the *Minion* around to be partially shielded by the *Jesus,* but only after she had also taken a beating from the ordnance on the island. With the *Minion* out of the way, some of the Spanish boarders got over the rail onto the *Jesus.*"

"Amid-ship?"

"Right where we wanted them!" growled Malachi. "And the very ship which had brought about our predicament rose to glory in her final hour. The *Jesus* was built for such an invasion, and we poured a torrent of fire on the heads of those Spanish troops clustered between forecastle and sterncastle. We finally drove them off with heavy losses on their side. The shore battery crews, which had slacked their fire while their comrades were aboard us, went back to their deadly work as soon as the boarding party was driven off."

"And the Spanish ships were shooting at you too?"

"From every direction. Never before had I heard so many cannon go off in such a confined space, nor seen destruction and death come from so many different bearings. In addition to the shore batteries, the two galleons added their eighty cannon to our discomfort. Finally, the smoke permitted us to free the *Jesus,* and we got her out where we could use her guns on the two galleons. Only two ship-lengths apart, Spanish and English gunners poured shot and shell into each other for a desperate, bloody hour. Finally, English gunners prevailed. One galleon was sunk and the other set ablaze."

"But I imagine the *Jesus* must have been in bad shape too from such close gunfire."

Malachi nodded. "The *Jesus* was shot to pieces by now, so we knew her sailing days were over, but she was still useful in protecting the *Minion* and the *Judith*. By this time the Spanish had sunk our 33-ton *Angel* and captured our 100-ton *Swallow*. The shore batteries were now our greatest threat—at least that's what we thought until Viceroy Enriquez pulled another surprise on us by sending two great fire-ships down on the tide against the *Jesus*. We knew she would have to be abandoned since she could not be maneuvered."

"Fire-ships are boats on fire?"

"Right. Ships loaded with combustibles and gunpowder, sails set, fires started, rudder lashed to sail the deadly cargo on a collision course into the wooden ship of the anchored enemy. We had little time to act when we saw them bearing down on us. It was, without doubt, the end of the *Jesus*. The treasure and some scant supplies were speedily loaded into the *Minion* and the *Judith,* and the *Jesus* was abandoned. Captain Hawkins insisted on being the last man off his flagship and nearly got left behind when the *Minion* and the *Judith* managed to jury-rig whatever sail they had left and make their way out of range of the shore batteries. Many sea captains since have imitated Captain Hawkins' decision to stay with his ship when faced with the same unpleasant prospect."

"God's blood!" breathed William. "Captain Hawkins almost left behind in the chaos!"

"So, of the five English craft that sailed into San Juan, only two managed to limp out of there." Malachi paused, hard put to continue. "Not only were the ships battered, our sailors were in terrible shape. Few men were without a deep wound of some sort. Drake and Hawkins brought what was left of us together on a small island a mile away from the battle and took a count. Men wounded in the fighting were dying every hour, so it was hard to get exact figures, but the 300-ton *Minion* under Captain Hawkins had close to 232 men and provisions for only a fraction of that number. The 50-ton *Judith,* under Captain Drake, got out of the battle with twenty-eight men and few provisions even for that number. We lost 150 men in the fight, and we got scant provender off the *Jesus* for those who were left."

"A desperate situation," William murmured.

"It was decided to transfer 100 men from the *Minion* to Drake's ship and that was speedily done, but neither ship had provisions to speak of. The two companies somehow lost touch in the night, and Drake headed home with 128 badly battered sailors on the *Judith*. I was one. The next four months were a nightmare. It was an endless struggle to keep our smashed-up ship upright in the water long enough to fetch us home. We tried to ignore the piteous cries of our starving wounded. We buried half our company at sea before we reached England. Sixty-two men succumbed to their hurts and their thirst. In the end, I was surprised any of us made it home."

"And the *Minion*? How did she make out?"

"Drake's *Judith* reached Plymouth on January 20, 1569, four months after that September battle. Captain Hawkins brought the *Minion* home a week later with scarce fourteen men left alive out of the hundred-and-thirty he started home with—not enough to man the ship. He had dropped off a hundred sailors in Mexico at their own request before he left the New World because they preferred to take their chances on land rather than face the prospect of a long sea voyage with such scant victuals."

"What a desperate choice! Did the Spanish find them?"

"Details are sketchy, but we know that exhaustion and starvation killed many. The rest were rounded up by Spanish authorities and turned over to the Inquisition. Two were burned outright, but several others were given two hundred lashes and condemned to eight years' service on the Spanish galleys."

"Two hundred lashes!" cried William. "That would kill a man ten times over! And eight years as a galley slave of the Spanish! God's blood! Is that what happened to Drake's cousin?"

"Robert Barrett was taken to Spain in irons, imprisoned for two years, and then burned at the stake in Seville during an auto-de-fe."

William shook his head. "No wonder English seamen hate the Spanish. And no wonder this conflict with Spain is so personal for Hawkins and Drake."

Malachi nodded. "It started at San Juan de Ulua, but it is far from finished."

Chapter 5:
CAPTAIN JOHN HAWKINS HIMSELF

The Admiralty Office in Plymouth, the following day:

"Ahh, Malachi," said Andrew, the Admiralty man in Plymouth. "Captain Hawkins said you might show up soon. He's been waiting weeks for his copy of the Second Bargain with the Queen, so I hope you have it in your magic pouch."

"He does have Royal mail," Malachi affirmed as he patted the pouch, "but, of course, I have no way of knowing its contents. Is he about?"

"Back in a jiffy," Andrew smiled. "Always on the move. Not content until he sees everything is done just right. While he's been Treasurer of the Navy these seven years, he has rebuilt two dozen ships to be better than new."

"How many actual new ones has he built?" William asked.

Andrew stiffened and turned to Malachi. "Who is this?"

"Just my apprentice," Malachi explained. "He's not quite housebroken socially."

"Can he be trusted?"

"Oh, yes," Malachi grinned at him. "He's slow but not sneaky. He has much to learn and no time to spare, so tell him a little about Captain Hawkins' revolutionary rebuilding of the Navy while we wait."

"Revolutionary is right," Andrew replied enthusiastically. "Ever since his sad experience with the old *Jesus of Lubeck*, Captain Hawkins has done his level best to clear our Royal Navy ships of all extraneous clutter like stern castles and forecastles. He even drops the cargo decks to the water line and mounts a sturdy gun deck above them. Only the captain's quarter-deck rises much above the gun deck on all the rebuilt ships. The result is that English galleons are much more nimble than those which still carry their castles."

"Is a galleon a class of ship?" William asked.

"Right," Andrew nodded. "Any big craft which has a keel three times the length of its beam can be called a galleon. Generally, it has become the accepted class for the ocean-going warships of many nations, in addition to being used for long-range merchant ships. The 500-ton *Revenge*, built in 1575, is a medium size galleon and has become something of a model for the class."

"A model, you say?"

"Right. All of the Treasurer's efforts to reshape the Navy have leaned heavily in the direction of duplicating the features of the *Revenge.* She is three-masted and square rigged with a lateen sail on the mizzen mast. With a 92' keel and a 32' beam, she is sleek enough to outrun anything bigger than a pinnace, and her forty cannon would give good battle to any ship afloat as well as to the forts of most small cities."

"What's a pinnace?" William asked.

"Any small craft larger than a ship's boat is a pinnace," Andrew explained. "They carry sails and oars and can range in size from twenty to sixty tons. The larger ones are usually decked over and serve as fast, independent scouting units of the fleet. The smaller ones are undecked and are sometimes broken down and carried aboard the larger ships to be assembled when needed. Part of Captain Hawkins' rebuilding program has been to make sure our fleet will have pinnaces-a-plenty so that ship-to-ship and ship-to-shore communication will be swift and reliable. He has produced sixteen new pinnaces since he took over."

"How many big ones do we have?" William asked.

"Are you sure he's safe?" Andrew asked Malachi.

Malachi nodded.

"Good," said Andrew, "because I could use a brand new face for a little duty tonight—with your permission, Malachi, of course."

"Certainly," Malachi assured him. "Duty first, last and always, but we might be called away. What did you have in mind?"

"Two strangers have been buying drinks along the docks and quizzing sailors about the tonnage of our ships. We suspect they might be Catholics trying to get our formula for figuring tonnage in order to turn it over to the Spanish. They seem particularly interested in how we rate the *Revenge*."

"Englishmen?" Malachi asked.

"Right. I'd like your man to join them for a drink this evening and see if he can mislead them about the process."

"Let me check my messages above-stairs to see if we will be here," Malachi said. "I'll return shortly."

Andrew turned to address William. "When they start to ask you about the tonnage formula, you must have it absolutely committed to memory, so that you may hint at various aspects of it without giving the whole thing away."

"I'm not too adept at math."

Andrew frowned. "If you don't feed them some good stuff occasionally, they'll quit buying drinks. That's your signal that you must dangle a little more bait before them."

"Mislead them and then try to get information," William repeated.

"That's the old service spirit!" Andrew said. "For whatever reason, the Spanish rate all ships at about one-third greater tonnage than we rate them, so we know there is some basic difference in formula. We rate the *Revenge* at 500-tons, and we know from their reports they rate her at 700-tons. They can't go about measuring our ships themselves without arousing suspicion, so they may try to gain our formula from you."

"And they'll think I know all this stuff?"

"You <u>must</u> know it! Don't worry. I'll drill it into you so you will know exactly what to keep concealed."

"Wouldn't it be a lot simpler—" William began.

"Please," Andrew interrupted. "We know what we're doing. There are several English formulas for determining the tonnage of a ship, but we shall confine ourselves to the most popular one."

"Good. Popular means easy," William said. "Tons of what?"

"Actually the term originated several centuries ago as a measurement of a ship's cargo capacity. The tonnage figure indicated how many tuns of olive oil or good old Bordeaux wine a ship could transport."

"Is 'tuns' different from 'tons'?" William asked.

"Strange that you should notice the difference," Andrew smiled. "Yes, a tun is a large barrel usually called a double-hogshead which has a 252 gallon capacity. It was the largest bulk-container that ship winches could handle easily, so it became a pretty standard measurement throughout Europe."

"So you measure a ship's capacity by stuffing it full of big barrels?" William smiled.

Andrew stiffened for a moment and cleared his throat. "To measure tonnage properly, you must first multiply the length of the keel in feet by the width of the beam."

"...by the width of the beam." William repeated. "Got it."

"Then multiply by the point of greatest beam to the top of the keel."

"...keel. Got it."

"Now multiply that product by one-sixty"

"...One-sixty."

"Now divide that figure by 15, 552."

"You must be kidding," William said. "Why all this bother? Why not figure little ships and big ships and medium-size ships?"

"Just get it into your memory the way I gave it," Andrew insisted.

"Can I presume that this convoluted process will then give us a pretty definitive tonnage figure?"

"No," Andrew explained. "The formula up to that point gives you a two-thirds tonnage measure, and you must add an additional third to get your final result."

"Egad!" William cried, "That's not only complicated, it's arbitrary!"

"Hold your tongue until you can do better," Andrew ordered. "It's what we use at the moment, so keep the details well concealed. If you get a chance, tell them the keel of the *Revenge* is only 90-feet long. That will throw off all their calculations if they are trying to duplicate her class."

"Why their particular interest in the *Revenge*?"

"Drake is more like a ghost than a dragon to the Spanish. No man catches him because no ship can keep up with him. The Dons know that Drake puts a premium on nimbleness in a fighting ship. They know he can pick whichever English ship suits him, so the fact that he chooses to fight from ships in the 500-ton class rather than the bigger vessels is not lost on them. The Spanish know well there is no better judge of fighting ships in the world than Captain Drake. They would like to incorporate some of his judgment into their own shipbuilding efforts, and the exact dimensions of the *Revenge* are important to that project. Mislead them on the *Revenge*, and it will throw everything off for them."

"I honestly don't see what there is to throw off," William confessed.

"From what you've explained, any official listing of ship tonnage could be 200-tons up or down from its actual capacity. Do I have a realistic concept of the situation?"

Andrew shrugged. "You said it yourself. Big ships, medium ships and little ships. We need some authoritative way to distinguish one from the other."

Malachi returned. "I've just learned we must be off as soon as I see Captain Hawkins, Andrew, so I'm afraid you'll have to round up some other new face. Sorry, though I'm certain William learned something of value in your lesson."

Andrew grimaced, but William nodded enthusiastically.

"Well then," smiled Malachi. "We await Captain Hawkins. I will take this occasion, William, to fill you in on a little historical background of our fleet readiness."

"Please do."

"In 1547 when he died, Henry VIII left fifty-three English warships in fine fettle. Eleven years later, however, Elizabeth inherited a reduced fleet of twenty-six badly neglected ships because Henry's other two children, Edward and Mary, cared little about the Navy during their time on the throne. In addition to neglecting all the ships, they sold off several of the major craft for handsome returns. Under Elizabeth, routine dockside maintenance was finally established, mostly at the insistence of Burghley, and new repair facilities were put in place, but there was never funding enough to upgrade the vessels nor to build new ones. All of that changed in 1577 when Captain Hawkins handed Burghley his list entitled *'Abuses in the Admiralty Touching Her Majesty's Navy, exhibited by Mr. Hawkins.'"* [11]

"He blew the whistle on the Admiralty?" grinned William.

"You might say so, and he backed it up with notes taken from Mr. Gonson, the then Treasurer of the Navy, who happened to be John Hawkins' father-in-law and a man who had grown tired of the Admiralty Board's abuse of the Queen's purse. John introduced figures and named names in his talk with Burghley. He indicated, for one thing, that the five-man Admiralty Board, dominated by Sir William Wynter, had charged the Queen £4,000 for building the *Revenge* with its accompanying pinnace, when the cost should more properly have been £2,200."

"My God! Just about half."

"And he gave time and place and figures showing where members of the five-man Admiralty Board had lined their own pockets with the Queen's property. They had used her timber to build their own ships and then sold the ships for personal profit. Sometimes they sold off whatever timber they hadn't used."

"Pretty powerful accusations," William murmured.

"They were that," Malachi chuckled, "but power and powder too are what you need to dislodge deeply entrenched vested interests. Two of the other board members were relatives of Sir William and defended his every action even after Hawkins had openly accused him of 'wilful covetousness'. Burghley listened to both sides and then appointed John Hawkins Treasurer of the Navy on the first day of the year 1578, at which time Hawkins began to clean house and rebuild a modern navy."

"How many new ones has he added?" William asked.

Andrew frowned at him. "Did your brain blink and miss my mention, earlier, of his emphasis on the rebuilding program? He has completely rebuilt the existing twenty-two, added one new galleon, and the sixteen new pinnaces. In addition, each year he has fulfilled his First Bargain with the Crown by saving the Queen's Treasury £4,000 pounds per annum and doing an infinitely better job of refitting the fleet."

"My word," William said. "£4,000 would almost pay for two new *Revenges* if I have it figured correctly."

"Right," Andrew said, "and such a fleet is just over the horizon now that we have brought our present fleet up to date—Hold on now! Here is the man himself."

The brisk, burly form of John Hawkins filled the doorway, and greetings were exchanged. William had trouble drawing his breath when he shook the man's hand.

"Breath deep, son," Hawkins advised good-naturedly, turning to Malachi. "You have something for me, Malachi?"

"Indeed I do, Captain," Malachi said as he handed over a packet from the pouch.

Hawkins opened the sealed message, glanced at it, and beamed. "We are in business, Andrew," he announced happily. "This is the signed copy of the Second Bargain, so open that bottle of Madeira on my desk and let's do justice to the occasion."

"It sounds like Burghley still takes your word over that of Sir Wynters," Malachi observed.

"He's a very perceptive man, who is not easily fooled," Hawkins nodded. "But Burghley doesn't take chances on big outlays like this. He put a committee of captains together two years ago to check up on my repair and rebuilding work just because the Wynters' crowd was filling everybody's ears with their nonsense about how I was mistreating the Queen's ships."

"What kind of mistreatment?" William asked.

"They complained that my elimination of the castles on deck made our warships appear no more formidable than merchant ships. Sir Wynters had done most of his sailing in England's home waters—the Narrow Sea, the North Sea, and the Irish Sea—so he had little idea what ocean travel does to high-charged ships. Fortunately, the other captains were ocean-going mariners who had learned as I had that top-heavy craft were ill suited for long ocean voyages, and that their sailing characteristics improved markedly when their wind-catching superstructure was removed. So the captains approved of my work, and the Second Bargain has been struck."

Andrew set out four glasses and, filling them, raised his. "I propose a toast to the Second Bargain and to the creation of a new fleet which will permit Britannica to rule the waves forever!"

"Hear! Hear!" they all cried and did honor to the occasion.

"If the new arrangement permits you to make the kind of improvement you made under the first pact, Captain," Malachi said, "England will be well served, and we'll be ready for the Dons when they come. It must please you to see the fleet in sailing condition after the mess you inherited when you began the rebuilding."

Hawkins nodded. "It does indeed. Very gratifying. When we first looked at what was left of Henry's once-proud navy, we found it had been allowed to rot away at the wharves."

"How long does it take a ship to rot?" asked William.

"Not long at all if the ship is not maintained. When mold and fungus are allowed to have their way with damp timbers, they can cripple the best of ships in a few years. We replaced a lot of timbers in the old fleet, but to get our navy fit again, there was more than refitting the ships to be done."

"Commercial arrangements?" suggested Malachi, grinning.

"Aye, some asinine fool during the reign of Bloody Mary back in the fifties, sought to save money by cutting off the subsidy we always paid to the Hanse." He paused, looking at William. "The Hanse is the largest commercial organization in northern Europe and has a monopoly on the Baltic market, where we get most of our naval stores—spars, masts, cables, oakum, and such. The subsidy allowed us to deal directly with the Baltic suppliers but when we stopped paying it, the Hanse became the middleman, requiring an even larger fee. In short, the Hanse had us by the nose."

"Which also brought up a security issue," Malachi explained to William, "because the Hanse has many ears and more than a few tongues."

"Aye," Hawkins nodded. "Burghley and Walsingham quickly realized that if we had to order through the Hanse while we rebuilt the Navy, the heavy purchases of naval supplies would inevitably be reported in Rome and Madrid, and they would be able to track our preparations. Burghley solved the problem in 1579 when he renewed the subsidy and set up the Eastland Company which deals directly with the Baltic suppliers of naval stores."

"And I presume that arrangement permits us to keep our dealings confidential," Malachi added, "and lets you work somewhat unobserved by our enemies."

"Somewhat is right," Hawkins nodded. "There are always snoops around. For my part personally, the rebuilding of the Navy really started the first day of 1578 when Burghley himself asked me to remain ashore to carry out my newly-appointed duties as Treasurer of the Navy until we could get the fleet back in fighting shape. That was seven years ago. We were both alarmed at the decay of our great ships. I think the Spaniard would be very surprised, indeed, to see the changes we have wrought in those intervening years. It hasn't been easy, mind you, to do this job without running up charges for the Queen."

"Particularly while fending off the accusations of Sir Wynters and his bunch that the changes are making the ships less powerful," added Andrew.

Hawkins snorted. "When we reorganized the workings of the Navy Board, we had to cut through the monumental inefficiency and overcharging which had characterized naval endeavors ever since Henry's time. We made a supreme effort to assure that every pound spent went to the Queen's service. A host of fat, well-cared-for toes got stepped on in that process, and we have been hearing outcries from their owners ever since. They have slowed us down at times, but despite their shrill efforts, we have got the job well under way."

"Did Sir Wynters pay for his thievery?" William asked. Was he arrested?"

"No, no," John Hawkins chuckled. "That's not the Queen's policy. Elizabeth doesn't mind jailing incompetent lawbreakers, but she is very slow to lock up rascals who know how to get her work done for her. She knows well enough that if she slams the jail door on every thief and cheat in her service, there'll be no one left to turn the key. She didn't jail Wynters as other monarchs might have, but she let him know that his future actions would be under her personal scrutiny."

"Is that an effective remedy for law breaking?" William asked.

Hawkins' eyes widened. "To be under the personal gaze of the most powerful force in this country who also happens to be a champion faultfinder? Effective? It freezes your blood!" He shouted with laughter. "Wynters has behaved like an angel since, and, despite some loose tavern talk, he and I have grown friendly again."

"It almost gives me a headache when I imagine the organizing you had to do to move such a large enterprise along," William said.

"I had a lot of help along the way," Hawkins said. "In addition to setting up the Eastland Company to supply our shipyard directly with unlimited quantities of naval stores at a reasonable cost, Burghley also had the foresight to establish trade relations with Turkey in 1581."

"Trade with Turkey was important?"

"Aye, it meant sailing past the French pirates of La Rochelle and the Barbary pirates of Africa, and the Spanish patrols in the Mediterranean. It meant each English merchant ship had to carry her own protection. It meant more guns per ship and longer ships to mount the new cannon along the decks. It meant every English sailor had to take his turn working the guns. In the end, it meant that every English merchant ship was virtually an English warship, and every English sailor was part of a seasoned gun crew. In short, some of what we've done to improve our Navy in the last decade has been done by accident."

"By accident?"

"Aye, it took us quite a while to realize that while we were lengthening our ships to accommodate more guns for heavier broadsides, we were also improving their sailing qualities. They can sail much closer to the wind than most Spanish vessels can. When Spain annexed Portugal in 1580, they inherited a dozen beautiful Portuguese galleons which they now use to protect the bullion fleet and the Asian spice trade, but many of their other ships still have the two-to-one ratio of length to width which produces cavernous holds to carry cargo and soldiers but impairs the sailing qualities markedly. Those big-bellied ships can't shove enough water aside to point into the wind at all. Apart from their Portuguese galleons, I'm ready to say that the worst of our major warships can sail circles around the best of theirs."

"Our ships are sleek and cut through the water better?"

"That's it exactly," Hawkins nodded. "Our ships slip through the water like dolphins while theirs lumber along like worn-out whales."

All four men sat back in comfortable silence, sipping their Madeira and contemplating the superiority of the English navy.

"I suppose then," ventured William at last, "that the San Juan de Ulua treachery taught us many valuable lessons."

Captain Hawkins stared at him blankly, then jumped to his feet. "Andrew, fetch those damned documents, the letter to Philip as well as the report to Her Majesty. By God," he growled, "I read over the details of those bitter times once a week so as never to forget them. Or to forget my brave men—those who died, and those who lived through starvation and hopelessness, and those who fell into the hands of those blasted, treacherous Spaniards." He turned to Malachi. "Did you know I was able to save about half of those held in Spanish prisons?"

"By God! Never say so!"

"Aye, after three years of brooding over my captured men, I was suddenly given a chance to help them. In 1571, Walsingham uncovered a large conspiracy against the Queen's life because some inept plotter was careless enough to include a handy code book along with the encrypted messages, which our people intercepted. The plan involved an agent of the Pope, Roberto Ridolfi; the Duke of Norfolk; Mary Stuart's ambassador to the English Court, the Bishop of Ross; and the Spanish Ambassador to England, Guerau de Spes. They had proposed to dispose of Elizabeth and install Mary Stuart on the English throne in conjunction with an invasion of England by the Spanish army from the Low Countries under Duke Alva. Once we had the details, I approached the Queen and Burghley with an idea I had to write to Philip, hinting at my disillusionment with English policy and the possibility of aiding the Spanish cause."

"You offered to play at being a traitor?" William whispered.

"I did," Hawkins said. "In negotiations through de Spey, I agreed that I would use the English fleet under my command in Plymouth to cover Spain's invasion barges as they crossed the Narrow Sea, and Spain would release my crewmen from their prisons. The plan fell through when Alva denounced Ridolfi as a windbag and Norfolk as a coward and refused to risk his men in any plan of theirs."

"Zounds!" cried William softly. "A treasonous venture, sir! And dead dangerous to your reputation!"

Hawkins grunted. "I had powerful allies to scotch the rumors, but I admit I've taken some broadsides on the matter. However, 'twas well worth it. Before the plan fell through, Philip released most of the lads held at Seville and sent 'em home." He frowned. "A scraggly lot they were, too, hardly fit for duty. But they recovered. Good men. Stout hearts." Hawkins stomped to the far end of the room and back.

Andrew handed him some papers. Hawkins held up the title page and read: "'A True Declaration of the Troublesome Voyage of Mr. John Hawkins to the parties of Guynea and the West Indies in the Yeares of our Lord 1567 and 1568.' [12] Written in 1569 by myself."

"Read the part about the Spanish attack at San Juan de Ulua," cried William, excited.

"Aye, let's see. Here it begins. *'Then we laboured 2 days, placing the English ships by themselves and the Spanish by themselves, the captains of each part and inferior men of their parts promising great amity of all sides; which even as with all fidelity it was meant on our part, so the Spaniards meant nothing less on their parts; but from the mainland had furnished themselves with a supply of men to the number of 1,000, and meant the next Thursday, being the 23 of September, at dinner-time, to set upon us on all sides.'* Thursday morning," said Hawkins, looking up, "we saw some suspicious goings-on, and I sent Master Robert Barrett of the *Minion* to check it out. Good man, Barrett. They burned him, you know. He wouldn't recant, wouldn't lie to 'em about his religion—though none would have held it against him. Seized him, kept him in chains for two years, then burned him at the stake, by God. An envoy and a captain! Nothing we could do. Well, aye, the attack, then."

"Don Enriquez, the Viceroy, *'now seeing that the treason must be discovered, forthwith stayed our master, blew the trumpet, and of all sides set upon us. Our men which warded ashore, being stricken with sudden fear, gave place, fled, and sought to recover succour of the ships. The Spaniards, being before provided for the purpose, landed in all places in multitudes from the ships, which they might easily do without boats, and slew all our men on shore without mercy. A few of them escaped aboard the Jesus.'"*

As Captain Hawkins continued reading, William glanced at Malachi, at his clenched fists and stiffened posture, then at Andrew, whose less emotional listening seemed to indicate he had not lived through the battle.

Hawkins read of the destruction of the *Jesus*, the attack of the dreaded fireships, and of his own narrow escape to the *Minion*. Then, *"'So with the* Minion *only and the* Judith, *a small bark of 50 tons...'"*

Drake's ship, William remembered.

"'...we escaped; which bark the same night forsook us in our great misery.'"

Not deliberately, surely, thought William. With all the panic and confusion, the ships could easily have lost contact. Then each man for himself, none expecting to live.

"'Saturday we set sail, and having a great number of men and little victuals, our hope of life waxed less and less. Some desired to yield to the Spaniards; some rather desired to obtain a place where they might give themselves to the infidels, and some had rather abide with a little pittance the mercy of God at sea. So thus, with many sorrowful hearts, we wandered in an unknown sea by the space of 14 days, till hunger enforced us to seek the land; for hides were thought very good meat, rats, cats, mice, and dogs, none escaped that might be gotten, parrots and monkeys, that were had in great price, were thought there very profitable if they served the turn one dinner.'"

William listened to the further detailing of miseries and at last cried out, "But you made it home!"

"Aye, God be praised," nodded Hawkins. "On January 20, 1568, we arrived in Mount's Bay in Cornwall, fifteen of us. "crew came from Plymouth to steer us into port there."

"But you'd lost all your treasure," mourned William.

"Not a bit of it," Hawkins countered grimly. "London would never forgive us for losing the treasure. We took them four horses loaded with gold and silver. Mayhap it helped pay for our losses, which the High Court of Admiralty put at £28,000—a gross exaggeration, to my thinking. The loss of my men, the four months of misery and starvation—no price on those." Captain Hawkins looked hard at Malachi. "I read this report once a week to keep the Spanish treachery fresh in my mind. Hatred fuels the blood. On the other hand, a man can't work carefully in its heat, so I read it the night before Divine Services, nursing my hatred overnight but 'forgiving and forgetting', as it were, the rest of the week in order to accomplish my utmost for the English navy."

Malachi nodded solemnly, then spoke in a voice thick with emotion. "Here's to our defeats, Captain, which bring about our victories." And the last of the Madeira was downed.

Chapter 6:
AN UNPLEASANT DUTY

Courtyard at a roadside inn outside Plymouth, twilight:

"This is bad," growled Malachi, pacing restlessly near the gate. "Not at all in order. The galloper was supposed to be here when we arrived. Drake isn't going to like it. He wants this message to go to the Queen as soon as possible." He turned to William, who followed behind. "We'll wait an hour or so, and if he hasn't shown up by then, you'll have to do the first leg as a galloper."

"Is a galloper pretty much what it sounds like?"

"Indeed. He is a man who must sit saddle for a day and a half to get a message from Plymouth to London with all speed."

"And 'first leg' is pretty much what it sounds like?"

"Right again. The 167 miles between the two cities contain nine remount stations. I was often a galloper when I was younger, and in my time we used to do the remount on the fly, just to thrill the spectators." He chuckled. "Then we'd slow down around the first bend. But the significance of this information for you would come only after you divide nine into one hundred sixty seven. What do you get?"

"Not quite twenty, I'd say offhand."

"So you won't have far to go on the first leg, just twenty miles. There'll be a standby galloper at that point."

"How come we don't have a standby galloper here?"

"We do," Malachi said. "I've just put him on notice."

"Oh." William groaned. "In an hour you say? May I eat first?"

"You would do better riding without a bloated belly," Malachi cautioned. "Why don't you wait until you get back?"

"Because it is my time to eat, and my stomach is speaking to me. It says if I have to wait until my return, my galloping horse would soon be outpaced by the speed of the corrosive acids racing through my stomach and etching their way through the lining of my belly just short of paralyzing pain. Even the horse himself could be in danger if there were no other sustenance available." William tried to hide a smirk.

Malachi stared at his apprentice. "I perceive I did not fool you this time. The galloper still has a few minutes to get here."

"You didn't have your whole heart in it."

"Aye, I'll feel better when this letter is on its way to London and out of our hands."

"What's the message?" William asked softly.

"I'm afraid it's bad news for our friend, Philip Sidney, who had hoped to sail off to the New World with Drake even though he does not have the Queen's permission to leave England."

"How bad?"

"Pretty bad. Drake is informing on him. This message informs the Queen of Sidney's real intent."

"There always seem to be wheels within wheels in much of what we do," complained William, "and I end up totally confused. Whose side are we on anyway?"

"Confusion is a natural state at the moment," Malachi confessed. "As a matter of fact, much of what has happened lately has puzzled the hell out of me too. The confusion started a week ago when Drake quietly notified Sidney in London that the fleet was ready to sail even though we could see damn well it wasn't."

"I remember that's when word came that the claimant to the Portuguese throne— what's-his-name—was on his way to England and everybody got very excited."

"That's right." Malachi continued to pace. "Don Antonio is a special case. Sidney needed some time to arrange permission to leave Court, so he used the arrival of Don Antonio as an excuse to travel to Plymouth. The Queen was only too happy to have one of her most esteemed subjects stand ready at dockside to greet such a potentially powerful visitor and offer him a gracious welcome to England."

"Potentially?"

"Right. The Queen knows that the wheel of fate may yet turn enough to validate Don Antonio's claim to the throne of Portugal. From that position, he could easily share lucrative Spice Island contracts with whoever helped him in his struggle. The Queen doesn't like to abandon such possibilities when a little delay, or a polite postponement, or a need for further clarification might easily keep the prospect alive without spending any money on it. I suspect, however, Elizabeth has no idea that Sidney really plans to sail off with Drake to the Americas."

"And now we're supposed to tell her," groaned William.

Malachi nodded. "That's our job."

"Why would Drake tip her off?"

"Only God and Drake know that." Malachi leaned his forearms on the stone wall and William did likewise. "Organizing the voyage has been mostly Sidney's show right from the beginning, you know. He made his plan plain when he said he wished; *'to carry war into the bowels of Spain,…..and surprise some well chosen place for wealth and strength, easy to be taken and possible to be kept by us'.* [13] Sidney even picked most of the officers for the trip—and a stout military bunch they are. Sidney hoped to set up some kind of defensible base right in the middle of the Spanish colonies. Probably try to take Cartagena or Havana or Panama and strike out at the gold shipments from there."

"Wouldn't that be an open declaration of war? Grabbing Spanish territory like that?"

Malachi smiled. "You'll make a diplomat yet, drawing such distinctions. You're right. Both Queen Elizabeth and King Philip would probably have to recognize officially that the ante had been raised. Taking a monarch's territory and holding on is very different from grabbing his gold and sailing off. Drake likes the second method and Sidney the first."

"Maybe that's why Drake is turning Sidney in," suggested William.

"I doubt it. Drake would like nothing better than a declared war with Spain. He's been at it for twenty years, so he wouldn't mind a little more company. No, I suspect it's the leadership thing again. Certainly, Drake was able to assemble this fleet and provision it much more easily using Sidney's credit than he would otherwise have been able to do. The influence of a man of Sidney's stature cuts down the scramble time it takes to get any big enterprise off the ground. But now that the fleet is almost ready, the leadership question arises again."

"Reverberations of the Doughty episode."

"Right. The informal arrangement was that Drake and Sidney would share command once the expedition had sailed and the Queen could no longer recall Sidney. That might have worked, too, since Sidney is a very reasonable man even if Drake is not. At least it might have worked until they got to the New World where their strategies would have clashed. Sidney would be for taking and holding while Drake would favor raiding and running. Come to think of it, Sidney's insistence that they take Don Antonio along with them might be the reason Drake is taking this puzzling step of turning Sidney in to the Queen."

"How is that?" asked William.

"A whole generation of English nobles may have to die off before they understand what Drake is telling them: that the man who drives the ship through the water is the man to make the decisions about the expedition, no matter how many earls or lords or monarchical pretenders are lounging about the deck. Direct control is the chain of command that has been used successfully by the Barbary corsairs and the La Rochelle Huguenots and the Dutch Sea Beggars for many years, and you can bet that Drake would be the first to see the advantages of such a system."

"So Sidney's insistence that Don Antonio accompany them might have been the last straw?"

Malachi nodded. "I'm sure Drake already had severe reservations about sharing command with Sidney. For one thing, Drake rules with an iron fist and Sidney is much too lenient, lacking the 'severity to command,' according to Languet—you remember Sidney's French friend Languet? Second, when Sidney insisted on adding the unseated monarch of Portugal to the expedition, Drake must have decided his council table might get a little crowded, so he sent us on our way with this note. Besides, Drake would be very reluctant to risk offending the Queen by being a party to Sidney's sailing off without her permission."

"But he didn't worry about that during all the time he was using Sidney's credit to get the expedition organized," William pointed out.

"That's right, he didn't. Drake is very selective about principles and when to pay heed to them. I suspect that's the way he gets so much done. Ah, here's our galloper now. Ready for a long night's ride, Jake?" Malachi commented as he handed the letter pouch up to the man on horseback.

"Aye, horse and me is fresh as a virgin's kiss," said Jake, pulling the pouch strap over his head and shoulder, then saluting. "Well, we're off then."

They watched horse and rider gallop off, and Malachi said, "That ends our little part of this confusion. 'Tis time to order supper, then we'll make a night of it here. We'll start our more leisurely trip to London tomorrow."

"I'm feeling so regretful about our part in this business, I've almost lost my appetite," William confessed.

Malachi put an arm across his apprentice's shoulders as they walked toward the inn. "Yes, poor Sidney. Too much a gentleman for the game, I'm afraid."

PART IV: THE ADVENTURERS AND SCHOLARS

Chapter 1:
CURBING THE LONDON DRAYMEN

Crowded street in London, several days later, October 1585

"'Zounds, Malachi," William exclaimed, "I wish you had seen it! If that shop doorway hadn't been handy, I wouldn't be here now. That drayman took direct aim at me! Look at your satchel—all scuffed and muddied!"

"The draymen are the bullies of the street," said Malachi wearily. "If they can't run you down, they settle for spraying muck all over you. Stay out of their way. And carry my satchel on the wall side hereafter."

"But this was more than that. I'm convinced a deliberate attempt was made on my life. The driver looked at me and turned his cart so as to run me down, cursing and shouting all the way."

"You felt it was personal?"

"As the breath of death. He was after me."

"I thought it would take longer, but they are a well-organized bunch."

"What would take longer?"

"Nothing for you to worry about, but from now on, don't wear your regular clothes when you go out without me. And wear a wig too. Put on that Irish one with the forelock down over your face."

"Go disguised? Why?"

"Wear it! That's an order. It will keep you out of trouble until the right time."

"Right time for what?"

"When we have the official witness in place."

"What witness?"

Malachi sighed. "I guess you have a right to know since you'll have a part to play."

"I have a part? A speaking part?"

"The Privy Council is angry over complaints against the reckless draymen. They want a couple of drivers nabbed and fined as an example to the rest. Revoke a couple of profitable licenses and the others will fall into line."

"Excellent idea."

"To nab them, we need witnesses to their recklessness."

"London is full of witnesses."

Malachi waved his hand. "That's general stuff. We need specifics. Where, when, who, extent-of-injuries kind of stuff, in front of reliable witnesses. The Privy Council has no desire to get London's mayor angry with them for being pushy, so they want us to prepare a cool, well-witnessed, airtight case, which will permit them to request the city of London to take steps."

"A case like that might take some arranging."

Malachi nodded. "It has taken awhile. How long ago was it I had you write out that petition to the Council to suggest they incorporate a built-up area along the street to accommodate pedestrians and keep them safe from the carts and wagons?"

"'Walk-sides,' we called them. I remember that. It was three weeks ago."

"We sent it to the Council, and they were drawn to serious consideration of the proposal by your penmanship, as I knew they would be."

"Not by the idea?"

"They liked the idea, but they cut your dimensions in half, envisioning a raised section three feet wide and from four to six inches high. Just wide enough to keep the carts from running over you if you hug the wall and just high enough to keep the muck out of your boots."

"I had suggested a foot high."

"I know—and six feet wide. But all of that was scoffed at as an impediment to commerce. There was enough discussion to indicate something might get done someday but that, in the meantime, we should build a case against today's reckless draymen by giving them a specific target."

"Target?"

"Yes, it was felt that when the draymen learned that a suggestion had been made to curtail their freedom of the road, they would strike back. We could then nail them for reckless endangerment of life and limb."

"That pretty well solves the problem for everyone except the target. How do you get him to hold still for such risk-taking?"

"He is an employee of the government. We will explain things very clearly to him, indicate what his duties are, and know we can count on him to do exactly what is expected of him."

"Ah, a brave and devoted man, indeed. But the government asks a lot. Why not just drug him with drink and shove him out amidst the wild draymen and their murderous carts?"

"We discussed that but decided it was not fair to deprive a man of a chance to be heroic."

"And he has agreed?"

"Virtually. Tell me, were you able to pick up any of the wording of the imprecations shouted at you by the menacing drayman?"

"Funny you should mention that. It was a bit garbled and quite blasphemous, you understand, but he shouted something about getting the hell up on the walk-side where I belonged."

"But there is no walk-side as yet."

"Exactly. I'm sure he meant it ironically, which bespeaks a deep-seated malevolence of sorts."

"Good. That means it is you they're after. The first try was not just a happy co-incidence."

"Me?"

"Who else wrote the petition to curb their freedom?"

"I'm sorry if they look at it that way, but I guess one of the characteristics of a bully is that he is not reasonable. Still, how could the draymen possibly learn that I authored the petition? There is no conceivable way they could possible have—"

"We circulated a quick-sketch of you among them."

"You did what?"

"Come, come, the plan is afoot. You have simply to permit them to brush and tumble you about a bit, and I'll get names and license numbers so that we can nail them in the courts. The Council would like to get at least a mandate requiring all carts and wagons to display their license on the rear of the vehicle where we may record their number after offences have been committed. Drivers are fond of displaying their permits at the bottom of the side corners where it is half concealed by the wheels or beneath the overhang of the seat where they may conceal it with their legs if need be."

"Let me get this straight. You are the expert witness standing off to the side while I am expected to offer myself up under those murderous wheels?" William stared at Malachi.

Malachi snorted. "Now before you submerge yourself into a refuge of self-pity, try to think of it this way: As things now stand, nobody is safe on the streets of

London. Somebody is run down every day, and it's not just the vulgar sort, you understand. Gentry are injured or killed while shopping along the streets, and even the nobility are nicked occasionally."

"It rains on all equally, eh, but it really pours on me."

"You're right. The problem crosses all social and economic boundaries, so the Privy Council has decided something must be done. Each individual driver is licensed by the Draymen's Guild, and the Guild holds its charter from the city of London, so the Council needs rock-solid evidence to cut through all that administrative tangle and get a clear message to the draymen that if they don't slow down, we will bust 'em and ground 'em. We feel that might at least back them off a bit. We all know there is a lot of pressure on the drivers to make quick deliveries in order to boost business profits, but their recklessness is causing us to lose precious social assets. A few well documented prosecutions might save some valuable lives."

"Let me guess," said William dryly. "Lives of much more importance than that of the designated victim."

"That's it. Nobody is asking you to make the supreme sacrifice, m'boy. This will simply call for a little expeditious rough-and-tumble. It's an action role! You'll never reach the pinnacle of the theatrical world without a few bumps and bruises along the way. This is a part where the heroic central figure represents all of mankind's desperate efforts to dodge a hazardous collision with the mechanical forces which have been loosed upon society since the world was set on wheels. It has universal import. If this story could ever be told publicly, you certainly would be regarded as an heroic figure, commanding universal attention and admiration, especially from the ladies who have an eye for acrobatic central figures."

"Sad experience has taught me that you have a way of making things sound safe in explanation which prove hazardous in execution."

"I know," Malachi grinned. "Back at the office, they say I have executive potential. Actually, the draymen themselves are quite skilled as drivers. It's the horses that are unpredictable. Most accidents occur because the draymen bring wild stock into the city, and the poor beasts are panicked by the noise and confusion of the streets. They bolt about in a frenzy seeking escape and then gallop madly along the closest street, sluing their wagon from side to side behind them like a giant scythe, mowing down every stroller and bystander in sight. Remember to stay clear of wild-eyed horses because they are just looking for someone to trample."

"Stay well clear of wild-eyed horses, got it."

"Actually, it's their concern for the livestock that have the draymen so worked up over the proposed walk-sides. They are convinced that any such impediment would trip their horses or possibly tilt their wagons over. That is, of course, aside from their usual complaint about government interference in business."

"They wouldn't trip or tilt if they would drive in the middle of the street where they belong!" William exclaimed.

"Good! I like that. Get a little worked up about it, and channel that energy into successful completion of your assignment. I should think we can grab five or six reckless drivers a day if we move you around fast enough."

"Five or six 'brush and tumbles' a day!"

"You're right, that may be optimistic. We'll just stay busy and see what comes of it. By the way, does your nose bleed easily?"

"My nose?" squeaked William.

"See if you can't knock it a time or two on the wheel as it passes. Blood makes a good witness."

"But any one of those five or six 'brush and tumbles' might become a crack, crush, smash, break or tear. It could kill me, in short!"

"It's entirely up to you to see that it doesn't," Malachi assured him. "If worse did come to worse, remember that you are young and nimble, and your bones will knit quickly, so you have nothing permanent to fear."

"I am not nimble!" cried William. "You are confusing my feet with my wit, Malachi. I will not do it, not for my fellow pedestrians or for the government or even for you! Let me have that ugly Irish wig. I won't come out without it!" He opened Malachi's satchel there on the street, rummaged through it for the wig and put it on.

"Gad, I can't see anything through this hair!" he grumbled. "But I can hear perfectly well, sir, and I hear you snickering. You are the greatest prevaricator in the land, sir. Your joke was cruel and ungentlemanly. I almost left your service until I realized the Council would not accept the same victim over and over. You can't ask me to do this dangerous thing more than once, and I guess I can live with that."

Malachi put an arm across William's shoulders, laughing heartily. "You've picked out the weak spot of my presentation, lad," he half sputtered in mirth. "But never think again of leaving me. You are the greatest entertainment of my experience."

"Will one witnessed assault do the trick?"

"Five or six is what we need. I'll round up the reliable witnesses if you will pick out half a dozen of your apprentice friends who are about your size generally, and dress them up to look enough like you that they'll draw a favorable response from the draymen. You'll have to coordinate this thing so we get all the citations done in a day or two because the draymen will spread the word quickly and warn each other away from our set-up. Tell your people not to worry about injuries because it's easy to just tumble out of the way at the last moment. We don't want anybody hurt on this project. Pick some of the Irish. They're very good at evading things."

"How can one tumble out of the way?"

"You don't know the technique of taking a tumble to prevent injury and fetch you out of harm's way?"

"I don't know anything about technique," William said stiffly, "but when I was faced with the actual necessity——"

"Yes, yes," Malachi said impatiently, "well done undoubtedly, but I'm not talking about a frantic, hysterical plunging about to avoid danger. I'm talking about acting technique, the cold, calculated method which actors on every stage employ in order to enhance their performance while preserving their limbs."

"Method acting?"

"Right. Our stage productions are filled with duels and fights and chases and tumults of every kind, and our actors would all soon appear on crutches if they could not topple about without injuring themselves."

"Is there a manual available where one may learn this valuable technique?"

"No manual needed. We are coming to the establishment of Earl Yarberry, haberdasher to the theatrical world. He has costumes of all sorts and stage craft techniques beyond belief. He'll teach you to tumble." They entered a store under the sign of 'Costumes and Enchantments: Prop. Earl Yarberry.'

"Good day to you, Yarberry. I've brought another student for your magic lessons: my apprentice, William. Do you have that special introductory package ready for me?"

"I do indeed," Yarberry said and fetched a small box from the shelf. Opening it, he presented Malachi with a small pistol. "There you are. First rate work."

"Well burnished," Malachi sounded pleased as he inspected the dagg. "How much?"

"Two pounds," Yarberry said.

"What do you mean two pounds?" cried Malachi. "I only asked you to shine it up, not rebuild it. It's not a two-pound job. I won't pay it."

"Burnishing is expensive these days. You should have checked the price before you ordered the work."

"Nevertheless, it's highway robbery and I refuse to pay it," Malachi fairly shouted.

"Suit yourself, but you'll go without the gun until you pay," Yarberry growled as he reached to retrieve the weapon. A short tussle ensued as the two men grappled for the gun. Malachi finally broke away with the dagg and fired it directly into the chest of Yarberry. William stood transfixed as the stricken man clapped his hand to his bosom to contain a flow of bright red blood which suddenly stained the pale fabric of his shirt. From the pitiful moan that ensued as the victim collapsed, it was apparent the man was dead by the time he hit the floor.

"Egad, sir! You've killed him sure," William gasped.

Malachi blew smoke from the barrel, then quickly reloaded the weapon, tucked it in his boot, and nodded his head. "That should settle our little argument and teach him a very good lesson in the bargain."

"Lesson? Argument? You weren't arguing over anything significant! You killed him for no reason!"

Malachi shrugged. "It's a better world without him. Less interesting, perhaps, but much more orderly. The man was messy and inefficient. Careless even. Who wants to forgive that kind of stuff?"

William glanced quickly at the prone figure and the blood-soaked bosom, and then turned on Malachi. "Malachi, you act as if nothing has happened. There's a dead man at your feet, killed by your own cowardly hand. I hereby sever all relationships with you, sir. I will not learn lessons from a cold-blooded rogue. I'm leaving."

Malachi held up a mollifying hand. "Abide a short time, please. I was perhaps a trifle negligent with my dagg just for a moment there, but it's over now and I'm really sorry it happened. Let's forget about it, shall we? After all, a true friend must learn to bear his friend's infirmities."

"Infirmities? It is only out of past friendship that I do not raise the hue and cry on you before I go. You disappoint me. Your action disgusts me."

"You take all of this life-and-death business very seriously, William."

"Malachi, I don't think you quite comprehend what you've just done. You seem to be in a drunken haze as though this were only a scene you were enacting on a stage."

"Perhaps it is." Malachi shrugged. "And perhaps if I snap my fingers three times, it will all be undone." He snapped his fingers twice.

William groaned "I'm leaving."

Malachi snapped once more, and the bloody body rose from the floor.

"If you'll stay, William, I'll treat to a round," said Yarberry cheerfully.

"You could use a drink," Malachi clapped him playfully on the shoulder, while Yarberry poured drinks all round.

"You tricked me," William squeaked.

"Educated you," Malachi commented. "Let's see what you've learned from our little bit of playacting." He looked carefully into William's eyes. "Your eyes are still jittery, which means your brain is still scrambled. Remember that. The ability to scramble brains is sometimes handy in our work. It monopolizes people's attention for a moment while we switch letters or pilfer pictures or load and unload guns. Is my dagg loaded or unloaded now, would you say?"

"Unloaded. You just shot a man with it. Or appeared to do so anyway."

"Wrong. I primed it again with a blank as soon as I shot. Your senses were suspended for a full minute after the shock of the shooting. In short, a man has a little less than one minute to work behind the scenes if he can get the attention of the audience hooked firmly on the scene he creates."

"The blood," William said in a subdued voice. "Tell me about that."

"Something the company at the Theater worked out," Yarberry explained. "Their business is the creation of illusion, and they keep adding to their bag of tricks. A small pig's bladder filled with chicken blood and hung beneath the white blouse just over the heart. A sharp clap on the bladder sends the blood spurting all over and you have the wonderful illusion of fatal red on white."

"Marvelous. You absolutely fooled me." William's voice was flat.

"And the audience loves the gore. The bloodier the better," Yarberry laughed.

"And you give them what they want," Malachi said.

"Whatever sells tickets," Yarberry shrugged. "Ours is not to wonder why..."

Malachi turned again to William. "You will have gathered by this time that my friend here is also an actor of sorts. Unemployed, however, at the moment."

"Between engagements, I rather think."

"And a foreigner, as well," Malachi grinned. "He is one of a group of immigrants who were identified at customs as having special skills when they entered England. Such people are allowed entry on the condition that those skills may at times be summoned in the service of her Majesty."

"Another spy?"

"Another messenger," Malachi growled.

"I'm more into provisioning than spying," said Yarberry.

"Which brings us to the purpose of this visit, Yarberry. William and several lads he will be choosing to help him, need lessons in tumbling out of the way while faking injury at the hands of our more reckless draymen."

"Has he any experience in acrobatics?"

"I'm afraid not. In addition, he's not especially graceful or quick, but he is highly motivated to avoid pain."

William nodded vigorously. "The chicken blood would be an excellent touch, however, and it would save my nose."

"A few colorful bruises here and there would be handy too, but a skill in tumbling is what we need most. Make acrobats out of his bunch overnight if you can. There is official pressure to get this thing resolved."

Yarberry looked William over thoughtfully. "You may play the optimist all you want, Malachi, but please don't ask me to dabble in the occult for you. We can do it, of course, but I'd say a month's time and two pounds per man."

"Now, now," Malachi chided, "You're not in Ireland anymore, and your new country is calling on you. You must respond with both honor and alacrity. You must avoid even the appearance of malingering or of ingratitude toward the Council by over-charging them for what amounts to another simple job of burnishing. Five shillings per man, and two days in the doing."

Chapter 2:
WHITEHALL, SERVICE HEADQUARTERS

Whitehall, London, several days later:

"Will we see the Queen?" whispered William as he followed Malachi into White-hall's spacious entry room. Benches lined the walls and were filled with gentlemen, some in uniform, some not.

"Oh no, lad, but you might see Lord Burghley. When the Queen moves from her quarters here over to the Council Room or the Throne Room at Westminster, these halls are cleared of us commoners, believe me. Burghley and Walsingham have their main offices here, however, and this is where I always come to consult with them."

"I notice many military men here, both Army and Navy. Is this headquarters for them as well as for us agents?"

"Indeed, and for many others besides. Do you recognize that gentleman who just came in?"

"Why, it's Simple! There, he sees us! Perhaps he was expecting to see us here."

"Hail, well met!" Simple greeted them. "Apprenticeship working out?"

William nodded eagerly, and Malachi answered. "He learns a little more every day, just enough to keep afloat. What news have you for us, Simple?"

"Drake sailed Thursday. Twenty-nine ships. 2300 Plymouth sailors."

"He must have emptied every tavern in the town," chuckled Malachi. "Did Philip Sidney go or stay?"

"Stayed: Queen's orders. Grace or thunder."

"Grace or thunder?" William echoed in puzzlement.

"It's a game the Queen plays with her nobles," Malachi told William. "Whenever one of them gets out of line, she offers him two choices: a little glory and the promise of profit on one hand, or personal disaster totally out of proportion to the quarrel on the other. In short, get back in step with my expectations or else."

"What grace did she offer Sidney?" asked William. Both he and Malachi turned to Simple.

"Governor of Flushing."

"A very important post in Holland," nodded Malachi, "but the profit angle is a bit difficult to see—for Sydney, at any rate." He turned to William. "Flushing is one of the cautionary towns the Dutch turned over as collateral for the loan the Queen made them. It is highly strategic to us because it commands the mouth of the Scheldt River, the outlet to the sea for Antwerp."

"Northern Europe's Venice," supplied Simple.

"Indeed," agreed Malachi. "If one has something to buy or sell, the place to go in northern Europe is the port of Antwerp. In southern Europe, the place to do business is, of course, Venice."

"And Sidney's job at Flushing?"

"Military, not commercial," said Simple.

"Right. Antwerp's extensive harbor facilities are now in Parma's hands, thus posing a real threat to England since they are only one hundred and twenty miles from our coast. Lisbon, on the other hand, is ten times further from London if the Spanish are forced to launch an attack from there, so the capture of Antwerp is a strategic prize Philip has been seeking for years."

"Parma. Am I supposed to recognize that name?"

"Alexander, the Duke of Parma, is Field Commander of the Spanish forces in the Low Countries and a very successful military man. In Flushing, Philip Sidney could blockade any proposed invasion from Antwerp by controlling traffic at the mouth of the Scheldt with cannon from the Flushing fort. There is much glory in such an appointment."

"Do we know the Queen's threat of 'thunder' to Sidney?"

"Cancel Drake's sailing," Simple told them.

Both Malachi and his apprentice were taken aback. "Egad," breathed William. "Cancel the voyage altogether! Sidney would not be popular with Captain Drake or the 2300 seamen!"

"Thus, the Queen reminds her nobles of who is in charge," murmured Malachi. "Her mighty captains too."

"Sovereign's wishes prevail," stated Simple.

A portly and ruddy-faced gentlemen approached them. "Do I have the good fortune of coming upon two of the Queen's most devoted messengers?"

Ah," said Malachi, bowing politely. "The Honorable Malcolm Thomas, MP from the Devonshire District. You know my colleague Simple, of course, and this is my apprentice William. What brings you to Whitehall, Malcolm?"

"With luck, the Queen may need Parliament's approval for a special subsidy and may wish to convene it sometime in the near future."

"Dislikes sharing power," said Simple.

"Very true," agreed the MP. "Does her damn'dest to live within the royal income to keep us out of the picture. She does a good job, too, although I sometimes find myself very pleased that the Commons has some control over her purse strings. Because she has to compromise with us every once in a while, I think it curbs her natural arrogance and keeps her in direct touch with the concerns of the ordinary people."

"You mean, without Parliament, the Queen would over-spend?" interrupted William. "I thought she was frugal."

"Indeed, my boy, she is. Elizabeth knows well that the prospect of government spending holds all ambitious Englishmen at attention while she decides which expenditures to undertake. The Queen dreads being in debt to the Continental money-lenders because she knows that solvency is a monarchical weapon and should not be sacrificed lightly."

"Continental money-lenders?" asked William. "The Dutch, I'll bet."

Malachi grinned. "And the Italians. Mostly Jews because Christians until recently were regarded as usurers if they charged interest on the loans they made, and that took the kick out of the process for many of them."

"But the royal income. Surely that is generous."

"Europe's poorest monarch," said Simple.

"How could that be?" exclaimed William.

The MP shrugged. "Easy to explain. The income of our government remains static no matter how prosperous the country becomes because its tax structure is not tied to the rising tide of commerce. For instance, we have London merchants who are worth £100,000., and the Crown gets only fees and license money from them—small pickings, indeed. Within a few years, such merchants will be lending the crown money and demanding favors in return."

"Favors?"

"Tax-exemptions, write-offs, tariffs on the competition—things like that. The merchants are pushing to join the nobles in getting special concessions from the Crown."

"And the Crown goes along?"

"Crowns always cultivate competing forces which stabilize each other and thereby serve as bulwarks against civil unrest. I expect to see the merchant commoners grow more and more powerful during our lifetimes." A note of smugness crept into the MP's voice.

William sighed. "I take it that all monarchs are not so limited in their funds. How could England have let this happen?"

"Well, for one thing, Spanish silver has flooded the markets of every Continental nation ever since the Dons discovered Potasi, that solid mountain of silver in Peru, fifty years ago. When you get a lot of new money like that, it tends to cheapen the currencies of all countries. We have watched exactly that happen here in England. Everything costs much more now than it did in the time of our fathers. Firewood, for example, costs exactly three times what it did thirty years ago, and that's just when you can find it. I don't know what we're going to burn when all the trees are gone. My guess is that we'll end up burning that filthy, smoky stuff they mine over around Newcastle."

"Higher prices means cheapened currency?"

"Less buying power," explained Simple.

"Some monarchs were alarmed enough to take steps against the prospect of a reduction in royal income—along with everybody else's, of course, but Henry seemed preoccupied with his trouble with the Pope and with his inability to keep a wife in permanent residence."

"Henry misread signs," said Simple.

Malachi nodded. "His purse was soon to be flush with the proceeds of the monastery sales, so he didn't pay much attention to economic matters. He spent a lot of time and energy supervising the building of a strong navy."

"Wooing Ann Bolyn," added Simple.

"That too," agreed Malachi. "Meanwhile, France and Spain instituted taxation revisions which assured their monarchs of a percentage of the new revenues."

"But that was many years ago," protested William. "Couldn't the Queen command Parliament to increase her income somehow?"

The MP chuckled. "It's been tried more than once, but always without success.

Understandably, members of Parliament are reluctant to tax themselves further, but the shameful truth is that if they all paid their fair share now, the national treasury would be perfectly adequate for normal operations."

"Members of Parliament do not pay their taxes?" exclaimed William.

"They all pay some tax, but few Englishmen of the better sort pay more than a token amount."

"Hold on now," William insisted. "That seems like a serious charge to me, and I would be disinclined to put much faith in it without convincing evidence. After all, it would be quite possible for any politician to build a case of wide-spread tax cheating on no more evidence than an obscure tailor in Aldergate skimming money from his cash drawer, for all I know, or some Fleet Street merchant who has miscounted his cloth bales. When you suggest there is widespread and systematic avoidance of tax responsibility in our country, you hinted strongly at corruption in high places, and I, for one, prefer to think that when such instances do occur, they certainly do not involve our best people."

"You want proof in terms of some top government functionary?"

"Exactly. The higher the better. I dare you."

"How high does Lord Treasurer, William Burghley, strike you?"

"The man in charge of the whole system! Surely you do not imply—"

"I won't imply anything, but let me just write this figure down for you." He paused to make a note on a nearby pad. "In 1565, Burghley reported an annual income of £133.6s.8d. And he paid tax on every farthing. However, twenty years have intervened, and Burghley has prospered enormously. In addition to being Lord Treasurer, he also holds the most lucrative appointive office in the land as the Keeper of the Wards. He has also had a chance to invest over the years in any promising voyage or venture and has done so effectively on a pick-and-choose basis because of his insider information. He has had the chance to prosper and he has taken it. So what would you estimate his annual income is today? Malachi?"

Malachi thought a moment. "I imagine there is some fudging going on, but it would seem to me that he would have to report at least £4000. per annum."

"Right on the button. £4000 it is! That is what he makes, but that is not what he reports. Ahem, I can see you gentlemen are slow to take my word for it, so let me give you a glance at a record of taxpayers which Walsingham compiled for Parliament last year. It is a private record, you understand, but if you take an oath not to reveal you have seen it—"

His listeners all swore. "Check this column then and see what our Lord Treasurer reported as his income last year."

"Egad!" William exclaimed. "It's the same figure you said he reported twenty years ago: £133.6s.8d."

"Exactly. He has never changed it in twenty years, and he has never paid on anything more. And he has the monumental gall to grumble annually to the Parliament about the rascals among us who avoid paying their fair share of taxes."

Malachi nodded. "Must be very discouraging to those members who are trying to live up to their responsibilities."

The MP chuckled as he put the report away. "There might be a little discouragement in the back row someplace, but Burghley's harangues usually promote MP guffaws since everybody is in on the joke. Except the Queen."

William shook his head. "With that kind of example, I imagine the other MP's feel perfectly justified in doing the same."

"And nobles too," said the MP. "But it's all part of the survival system. More and more of the cost of government has been transferred to the purses of the nobility and local gentry. Since there is no funding coming from London, Justices of the Peace and deputy lieutenants, sheriffs and assessors of the county, etc. must seek funding on the local level from taxes and fines and fees."

"So the ordinary Englishman pays a willy-nilly mixture of fines and fees and taxes too," William said, "and the well-connected let themselves off lightly by under-reporting their income and appointing reasonable men as their assessors?"

The MP nodded. "That's the basis of the gentleman's agreement which has made English taxation the laughing stock of the world. We didn't fix the system at the proper time, so we have not been able to adjust it since. Indeed, there appears to be a tide in the process of taxation which taken at the flow, leads on to efficient governing, but neglected or delayed—"

"We're not interested in all that philosophical stuff," grumbled William

"Enough that our system is corrupt from top to bottom. A tide taken at the flow, indeed!"

At this time the Honorable Malcolm Thomas was called to his appointment, and the Service trio sat in temporary silence.

At last, Malachi spoke. "Actually, Burghley is an extraordinary executive and has been the Queen's right hand throughout her reign. He started as plain William Cecil, you remember, and earned his title and land through service to her. The Queen trusts him implicitly."

"Highly deserving statesman," agreed Simple. "A bit Machiavellian."

"Right. I respect him very much. His treatment of us in the Service has always been honorable. Not a scandal-monger like some we could name."

William looked from one companion to the other and nodded. "Look at the group of courtiers across the room there. Note the one with the sparkling blue cape!"

"That would be Walter Raleigh. A courtier, indeed, and a man of huge ambition. That cloak is sewn with diamonds and, occasionally, one falls off. Such spasmodic distributions assure him of a large following wherever he goes," Malachi chuckled.

"Zounds! Raleigh has a thing for cloaks, I see! I suppose he is here to further his plans for the New World colony you mentioned."

Malachi nodded. "Roanoke, Virginia. His mapping expedition returned last year, bringing back two New World natives. They lived at Durham House with Raleigh for some time. I chatted with them a time or two. Mateo and Wachese. Handsome, well-built lads. Mateo is so learned and civilized that he could easily pass as a Spaniard."

"If a diamond falls off Raleigh's cloak as we pass, may I pick it up and keep it?"

"I say, what's the latest word from Plymouth?" asked one courtier of Malachi, not quite addressing him directly but clearly seeking a reply. William started to speak, but Malachi stopped him with a touch on the arm. They had caught Raleigh's attention, so Malachi nodded politely and murmured his name.

A very young man, perhaps sixteen or seventeen, sauntered up in the company of an older man, perhaps his father. William took careful note of his rich and beautiful clothing: blue velvet coat with slit sleeves of gold, gold-threaded black hose and slops, and a bonnet of matching blue velvet. Heavy gold chains hung about his shoulders.

"Egad, all this hurry and flurry is a foolish way for our Seat of Government to conduct itself," he said, his voice well-timbered for so young a man but very lofty and proud, to William's thinking.

"No doubt it is an emergency," said William. "Perhaps the Spanish are attacking."

The boy stared. William returned the stare. The boy took a lace-edged kerchief from his sleeve and waved it to clear the air around him of all distasteful fumes. William took up his own well-used kerchief, flourished it elegantly, and waved the offensive odors right back. The boy snorted, and William made an elegant leg. The boy turned away.

At that moment, Burghley filled the doorway, searched for Malachi and, finding him, waved him forward. Malachi touched William's arm to follow. As they passed Sir Walter Raleigh, Malachi gave him a short bow and spoke his name politely.

Recognizing him, Raleigh stayed him with a light touch. "We have not seen you at Durham House since you met our guests from the New World, Malachi. Come out soon, and we can exchange gossip." His voice dropped to a soft murmur. "By the by, what is all the ruckus about this morning?"

"I believe Sir Francis Drake has sent news. It could be anything."

Raleigh laughed softly. "And you will not hazard a guess, I wager. Well, go in and get your orders, Malachi. But plan to visit us soon."

"I would be honored, sir." He nudged William, whose gaze was bent toward the floor beneath Raleigh, and they both followed Burghley into his office.

"I'm calling as many couriers together as I can find, Malachi. I want you to fill them in on the Drake-Sidney thing and the need for speed and complete secrecy to comply with Her Majesty's wishes. Use my anteroom there. And plan on staying the afternoon, until we know what's what."

"I hope he remembers to send in some refreshment," murmured William, watching Burghley retreat. "Of course, you're obviously in charge, Malachi. Perhaps—"

"Be patient. This is no time for pampering oneself. What possessed you to lock horns with young Essex?"

"Who is young Essex?"

"Well, he is far above you, for one thing, even if he is a few years younger. His uncle, Leicester, presented him to the Court earlier this year, and the boy has already attracted the Queen's notice for his charm and wit."

"Neither of which he exhibited today. Rather pomposity and posing, I'd call it."

"No use making enemies for no reason, lad. Who knows but what you might one day need support from those in high places. Ah, here's Andrew and Nathan. Take a seat, gentlemen, while we await Burghley's quick round-up of our corps."

"Can you give us a hint of what's to do, Malachi?" asked one.

As the men talked, William noted how they were all dressed to be inconspicuous in any crowd. Neither shabby nor grand, their gear—like Malachi's and William's own—was of serviceable wool and leather in muted shades of grays and browns. Their half boots were of brownish leather, clean but not highly polished. William was proud of his own moss-green jerkin with its small brass buttons.

"This halfling is my apprentice," explained Malachi, noticing the men's glances. "Quite reliable and learning the business readily. Writes a fine hand, too, and carries my satchel wherever we go. Eats like a horse, however."

The men smiled and nodded. More couriers arrived and were ushered in. Malachi asked the clerk for tea and biscuits.

"Tea?" the men exclaimed softly as the door closed.

"And not much of that if I know our frugal Lord Treasurer," grinned Malachi. "Now let me explain why we're here, lads. Take notes, Master William."

Chapter 3:
A RALEIGH BRIEFING

The Red Rooster Tavern in London, midday:

"While we wait for the Durham House messenger," William said, his mouth full of veal pie, "may I ask you two questions?"

"If you can assemble them in single file," Malachi smiled, "then trot them out. I'll be happy to oblige you, but please try not to overwhelm my wits with metaphysical matters before I've finished my meal. Easy, simple questions only, so I can go right on eating without gastric disturbance."

"Is it my imagination," said William, "or do we really keep cutting Sir Walter Raleigh's trail every way we turn in this job? How could one man be so busy in so many things?"

"He will be busier still when we deliver these two new commissions to him." Malachi patted his mail pouch. "I think you can clearly see Burghley's hand in appointing Raleigh both Lord Lieutenant of Cornwall and Vice-Admiral of the West, in addition to making him Lord Warden of the Stannaries. Essentially, the government has put the whole southwest corner of England under Raleigh's supervision."

"Isn't that increasing the duties of a man who is already pretty busy?"

"Sometimes that's the only way you get anything done. Pile it on the guy who'll do it. Burghley is perceptive enough to see that Raleigh may be the single man who can strap an iron band of unity around the free-booters harboring along our southwest coast. That's Raleigh's home country, and he knows very well that England can't afford to be too tough on the resident buccaneers since they are our first line of defense against any Spanish attack along the soft underbelly of that coast."

"How about the English fleet?"

"They'll do their part and more," Malachi nodded, "because Hawkins has rebuilt them into the best fighting ships in the world, but the English Navy has only twenty-six major warships even when they're all turned out, and the truth is that many of the bigger ones sit dockside for long periods without provision or crew."

"And the resident freebooters?"

Malachi nodded. "There are probably three times that number of what our coastal communities politely call 'armed merchantmen,' who are active and manned everyday. Just as important as their number, however, is the fact that the armed merchantmen not only have the guns, they have the people who know how to use them. Raleigh's appointment to his home ground in the West will assure the residents that London understands the situation and that the Queen expects to work with them as allies in combating the Spanish threat to England."

"But can one man do it all?"

"You've hit upon an odd situation," Malachi said. "Even though Raleigh's meteoric rise in fortune and favor has engendered envy and jealousy in the hearts of many court members, they nevertheless all pay a grudging respect to his work habits. Even men who themselves are regarded as exemplars of industry, make their bows to Raleigh's ability to 'toil mightily', as they all phrase it. He has his thumb in an exceptional number of pies even in this age of burgeoning ideas and projects inspired by Greek and Roman thinking."

"A resurgence of those classical times, eh? A kind of renaissance?"

"Exactly. And Raleigh typifies such broad thinking. He specializes in no one area but cultivates talents in many and gets them to feed each other."

"Some might say that a man who spreads himself thin among many areas might be master of none."

"Not in this case," Malachi said. "He sets up a reciprocal system so that some of his investments feed and support his ventures in other areas. Raleigh's natural interest in navigation and mathematics, for instance, has led to his support of map-making and other navigational aids, which has made his sea-captains very successful merchants and buccaneers, which has pleased the Queen and advanced him in her eyes, which has enormously increased his soundness in the eyes of the business community, which permits him to gather funding for such long-term investments as the Virginia Colony, which, among other things, may turn Raleigh into England's largest landowner—ever."

William grinned his admiration. "Well said, sir."

Malachi chuckled. "As you know, the Queen originally granted the Charter for establishing a New World colony to Raleigh's half-brother Gilbert back in 1578. After

Gilbert drowned two years ago, while exploring the New World coastline, the same charter was renewed last year for another six-year period in favor of Sir Walter."

"And the terms could make him a large landowner?"

"The largest, as far as I can tell. Elizabeth said very clearly, '...we have given and granted to our trusty and well-beloved servant Walter Raleigh Esquire, and to his heirs and assigns for ever, free liberty and license...to discover, search, find out, and view such remote, heathen and barbarous lands, countries and territories, not actually possessed of any Christian Prince, nor inhabited by Christian people...and the same to have hold occupy and enjoy to him his heirs and assigns for ever, with all prerogatives, franchises, and pre-eminencies, thereto or thereabouts both by sea and land.'" [1]

"She didn't mention numbers?"

"Yes, indeed." Malachi laughed softly. "Our Queen has a head for numbers. She made it very clear in the Charter that the Crown would get one-fifth of any gold or silver found in the proposed colony, and then she assured Raleigh's title as England's largest landholder by granting him exclusive rights and powers to a distance of six-hundred miles in any direction from the spot where his company sets up permanent habitation within the six-year period of the Charter."

"Egad!" William exclaimed. "Six hundred miles north and six hundred miles south of Virginia would give him twelve hundred miles of the New World coast and a mighty chunk of the interior as well. That would cover all of England with Ireland thrown in!"

"And a good bit of Europe as well," Malachi nodded. "That's why when we get to Durham House, you'll see a lot of concern and careful preparation to make sure the Virginia colony succeeds within the six-year limitation, because if it doesn't, of course, Raleigh and his shareholders lose possession of that vast holding."

"How is it going so far?"

"We don't know much yet, but I know that the Virginia expedition which sailed in April spent six weeks in the West Indies in order to refit and re-supply before they headed north to set up the settlement in Virginia. Late last month, a courier ship landed in England with reports from that layover. Sidney got mail from Captain Lane at that time, which indicated that San Domingo, among other Spanish New World settlements, was lightly fortified and could easily be taken by a determined force. That kind of information is all Sidney needed to harden his resolve to sail with Drake, but it wasn't meant to be, it seems. We'll know more shortly. Raleigh has so many visitors that Durham House is second only to Whitehall in gathering information."

"I suppose when your interests are as far flung as Raleigh's, you better stay well informed," William mused.

"Right," Malachi said. "And especially if you take chances as Raleigh does. He is one of the very few Englishmen willing to tie up funds in a long-term payoff like the

Virginia Colony, but even when he does plot out something like that for the future, he doesn't lose his head about it."

"Meaning?"

"Would you like to guess which of his sea captains he put in charge of piloting the colonists to the New World? No? The most aggressive of all his free-booting mariners: Simon Fernandez himself. Fernandez is the master of Sir Richard Grenville's flagship, the *Tyger*, and also the pilot for the whole expedition."

"Are you saying Raleigh has put a savage pirate in charge of piloting such an important enterprise?"

"You seriously underrate Fernandez if you refer to him only as a 'savage pirate,'" Malachi chuckled. "He is a great many things in addition to that particular designation. He is one of the best navigators in the world. Since the days of Henry the Navigator, the Portuguese have always produced renowned navigators, who have been grabbed up by every seagoing country in Europe as expert pilots. Fernandez sailed for the Spanish in the New World before he joined us. He has been on several mapping expeditions of the Virginia coast already, and he was there last year as pilot when Roanoke Island was chosen as the spot for the colony attempt."

"What's the difference, by the way, between a captain and a master and a pilot?"

"Good question. Right up until our King Henry's time fifty years ago, our Navy was still referred to as our army-at-sea by most military strategists. Even today, the captain of any English flagship is likely to be an army officer who is in charge of the military decisions for the voyage. He frequently knows little about the details of running a ship, but he establishes the destination and the purpose of the voyage. It is up to the master to set sails, tend the rudder, and command the crew. The master may also be the pilot as is the case with Fernandez, but he need not be. The pilot is in charge of setting the course and telling the master where to steer to get where the captain wants to go."

"But, being Portuguese and a Spanish turn-coat, is Fernandez trustworthy?"

"I suspect he would prefer to be hunting Spanish gold in the Florida Straits to planting English colonies on the Virginia coast, but he knows well enough that Raleigh is counting heavily on the colony's success, so he'll get it done before he guides Granville through the hunting ground of the West Indies in search of fat prizes. If they happen to grab up a bit of Spanish bullion, they could offset the cost of the whole colony attempt."

"Is it permissible for me to make a list of Raleigh's activities and offices, so I don't get these things mixed up?" William asked.

"What do you mean?"

"I judge Sir Walter Raleigh to be the busiest man in the kingdom since I encounter his boot-print wherever I go. I just thought it might help the flow of my thoughts if I had a reference guide of Raleigh's numerous duties, so I could at least begin to guess where his path comes from and whither it goes."

"Don't you realize the business we're in prohibits us from keeping that kind of list?" growled Malachi. "We might be taken and the information used against our masters. Don't write anything down except our regular reports which we send in immediately. We carry no records at all. Memorize everything! That way they'll have to torture us before they can get anything out of us."

"No notes equals torture, eh?" said William thoughtfully. "I'll try to remember that."

"Actually, if it ever came down to torture," said Malachi, "I want you to act like the most knowledgeable of the two of us, so that my torture would be delayed and hopefully prevented. To foster that impression, keep your gentleman's wardrobe handy for instant wear whenever we're on the road, or anytime it looks as if we might get nabbed. The longer you can hold out—"

"Knowledgeable about what?"

"Whatever they want to know. Whatever they're asking about."

"Who are they?"

"Whoever has us in their clutches. It changes with every country. It may all seem a bit hypothetical to you now—and God knows you don't seem to profit at all from abstract discussions—but when the time comes, keep those priorities well in mind."

"Let me see now. You want me to pretend to be more knowledgeable than I really am about some hypothetical subject, so that some unnamed party will continue to torture me while you are given a little more time to make your move. Is that about it?"

"That's the over-all plan," Malachi nodded. "Standard procedure."

"I can only hope we avoid torture altogether then, because the truth of the matter is that I am not particularly heroic in suffering pain, and, as you well know, I don't know much of anything. I can't honestly see myself monopolizing the attention of any conscientious torturer longer than two or three minutes if that will do you any good."

"Mixed news there," Malachi grunted. "Not brave, but honest. Still, many a man half-hearted in barracks has proved heated in battle, so I'll count on you until I learn better. It wouldn't hurt, though, to introduce a red herring to prop you up a bit."

"A second course of lunch?"

"Forget what I said earlier about not taking notes, but keep your notes indecipherable to any but yourself. Henceforth, use your peculiar dot-and-dash system and keep a small packet of such notes in your doublet when we are on assignment."

"They'll find it and torture me further to make me reveal its contents."

"That's where we've got them!" Malachi laughed. "You won't carry notes on anything but your own personal thoughts, you see, so even after they take the time and trouble to squeeze them out of you, they'll still have nothing!"

"You know, Malachi," William concluded quietly, "every once in a while, your enthusiasm seems to bend off at a strange angle."

Malachi smiled, then sobered and asked, "And your second question?"

"Ah yes. Well, I'm doing my best to reasonably follow your directions in writing these reports, Malachi, but I confess there are things about this job that defy logic."

"Well," Malachi reflected, "you certainly are the right chap to remark on reason confronted and logic confounded. What's on your mind?"

"I know you have the right and the duty to correct my notes, and frankly, I find most of your corrections somewhat well-founded, but I must confess this spelling-of-names business completely befuddles me."

"Spelling of names?"

"People's names," William nodded. "Take Sir Walter Raleigh, for instance. Every time I write his name 'Ralegh,' you scribble over it 'Rawlie' or 'Rawley' or some other weird variation. He presently signs his name 'Ralegh', so I've simply been correcting the misspellings. If you want me to pursue some less logical course, instruct me if you will, but please don't subject me to further instances where your corrections contradict each other. God knows, I'm having trouble enough."

"You must not interfere with my subjective shorthand," Malachi broke in sharply. "When you change the original spelling, you are destroying one of our best clues."

"Clues to what? Bad Spellers?"

"Raleigh may be the most talked about Englishmen in the world after Drake. At the very least, he's right up there with Burghley, Leicester, Walsingham, and Sidney. His influence with the Queen in the last few years has been such that he has been mentioned in letters, dispatches, and broadsides not only in England but throughout the Continent. It is part of our job to keep track of all new developments concerning the Queen's favorites. Sometimes our information is used to help those gentlemen in their endeavors, and sometimes it is used to hinder them, but that strategy is not up to us. We are simply collectors of information."

"Excuse me," William said patiently. "You seem to have missed my point. How does that relate to correct spelling?"

"That is the point," Malachi said. "When we collect rumors, slanders, praises and other comments of our prominent men, it is important for us to know the fountain-head of the information so we may make a more precise appraisal of the content. We ask ourselves what self-serving twist might be suspected in the information passed out by that particular vested interest."

"They give themselves away in the spelling?"

"Very often the case," Malachi nodded. "Sir Walter is pretty particular about how his name is pronounced. As a matter of fact, in his youth, he signed himself 'Raw-leyghe' to help people get the 'Raw-lee' idea, but since his rise to prominence, he has always signed himself 'Ralegh', as you say. Others, however, have chosen to ignore his shifting preference and use their own variation of his name. We have recorded seventy-six variations from different sources. Any reference to 'Rawlighe,' for example, probably comes from Lord Admiral Howard. Lord Cobham always refers to him as 'Rawlye.' King James of Scotland spells him 'Raulie.' The Venetians spell him "Ralle.' The French write 'Raleich,' and the Dutch spell it 'Halley.' So you see, it is often possible for us to trace any mention of him to its source."

"What do the Spanish call him?"

"They always refer to him as 'Gualtero,' their form of 'Walter.' The Queen writes him as 'Raleigh' when she is not using one of her nicknames for him. Sometimes it is not a straight shot back to the source, of course, because some men use several spellings. Lord Burghley's son, young Robert Cecil, for instance, intermingles 'Rawley' and 'Raleigh' and thereby follows his father's sage advice on the danger of committing oneself on important matters."

"But it's impossible for one man to have so many spelling variations of his name!" William declared. "It makes a mockery of the whole concept of correct spelling! How in the world can future historians keep track?"

"Historians, eh? Why should they be interested in Raleigh?"

"Well, the cloak thing, not the diamond-studded one but the muddy one, makes a very good story. Even I keep hearing about it."

Malachi nodded, "It's possible, I guess, but only if future history is duller than past history."

"What is the inside story on that cloak episode anyway?"

Malachi chuckled. "To really appreciate the boldness of Raleigh's move in bringing himself so abruptly to the Queen's attention, you must realize he was only a reserve in the Esquires of the Body at the time, vying for the Queen's interest with dozens of other young men."

"Of the body?"

"A group of ambitious young courtiers who are on call to be in attendance wherever the Queen happens to be. They escort her on her trips around the country, host foreign dignitaries, prop up ceremonial occasions, and pass her orders on to lesser folk. Some few sleep in the Presence Chamber each night outside her bedroom quarters."

"Are they government workers on assignment, or is it a position of honor, without recompense?"

Malachi snorted. "They have whatever honor comes from squandering their inheritance to stay afloat long enough in the social wash to capture the Queen's attention and thereby win appointment to an office important enough to command patronage and the disbursement of funds. Many of them have spent years of their lives and thousands of pounds pursuing that office, so you can bet there was a great deal of muttering among them after Raleigh's bold stroke gained him untold riches by the simple expenditure of a muddy cloak."

"Envious muttering, eh?"

"Endless. The topic was a proverbial seven-day wonder. I remember copying some notes for the Fuller family, which described the cloak incident. *'This Captain Raleigh coming out of Ireland to the English Court in good habit (his clothes being then a considerable part of his estate) found the Queen walking, till, meeting with a plashy place she seemed to scruple going thereon. Presently Raleigh cast and spread his new plush cloak on the ground; whereon the Queen trod gently.'"* [2]

"What a showoff!" William cried in open admiration.

"Elizabeth was tickled with his exaggerated courtesy. His inspired gesture not only brought him to her immediate attention, but caused her thereafter to turn him into one of England's wealthiest men."

"All at the expense of one muddy cape," William mused.

"Oh, well," Malachi grinned. "I guess history can use a light touch once in a while."

"Also, if his Virginia thing succeeds, that might be important to historians," William suggested.

"Who can tell?" said Malachi. "History does take some strange bounces, but the truth is that one more minor settlement in foreign lands might mean very little to future generations. Historians will have to take their chances along with the rest of us in making sense out of an imperfect and puzzling world. In the meantime, get busy with memorizing those spelling variations, and don't let your penchant for correct spelling hinder our pinpointing of sources."

"Someone should compile a reference of correct spellings," grumbled William, "not just leave it up to each writer to devise his own."

Malachi shrugged. "Educated men do fairly well, using the spellings most often used in modern books and correspondence. Raleigh, for one, is very conscientious about spelling common words consistently. Sidney is another. The spelling of names is difficult to standardize since individual preference prevails in that area, but, in the end, the printing press will undoubtedly hammer all variations into submission."

"But what about scribes like me? I need a reliable reference right now, preferably one which is cross-referenced to all nick-names, Nom de Plumes, and such."

"Well, then," Malachi reached over to pat him on the back, "get busy and write one, my boy. It would be a worthy life's work for you."

"Um," William reflected. "I see that project more as the work of, say, a fat, pontificating scholar."

"And certainly you are no scholar. Nor are you fat, though if you continue to eat everything in sight."

"But you think I pontificate?" laughed William, undismayed.

"Well, you do have a certain facility with words. A tendency, perhaps, to grow verbose at times."

"The better to fill up government mail pouches with documents so that faithful servants will find employment in delivering them," smirked William.

"This pouch is no laughing matter, you impudent upstart. It contains a confirmation copy of Raleigh's Royal grant to collect taxes on the export of woolen broadcloth from English ports, which the Queen granted him last year. Worth about £3,500. per annum, I would guess, during ordinary years."

William whistled in awe.

"That's in addition to the grant she made him of the import tax on sweet wines brought into England," Malachi continued. "Every wine retailer now must pay Raleigh one pound annually for permission to sell sweet wine in our country. Such handsome presents would make Raleigh a wealthy man if he were not already pretty well fixed from the Queen's past generosity."

"The Queen seems to have an endless supply of such grants."

"Not endless by any means, but she has a dozen or so which she distributes. The favorites of the Queen expect her to augment their incomes at least to the point where they can afford to buy her some very thoughtful presents and to host her handsomely when she goes on progress. Elizabeth delights in giving and getting gifts, and she keeps careful track of what offerings she receives from her extended family of nobles, who are sometimes pampered by the Queen in the exchange and sometimes spanked. In the end, however, no one knows better than she how much of the daily community work gets done by the organizational efforts of the noble houses. Each house forms the command center for thousands of families."

"Thousands?"

"Nobles appoint the judges and the other officers in their communities, including the tax assessors, who thereafter are inclined to show their gratitude in rather obvious ways. Not a perfect system, by any means, but one which helps the Queen run the country, so she has always been reluctant to strike down any noble house for any reason. It would throw a whole section of the country into chaos and would multiply her administrative duties enormously."

"I heard somewhere that she enjoys holding court, hearing petitions, and presiding over her people's affairs."

"She does when things move along briskly, but she dreads the endless details which have to be resolved in the wake of a fallen house. She did strike down the House of Desmond back in 1580. But, of course, Munster was already in such disarray from the rebellion, it could hardly get any worse, and Desmond was a madman in addition to being a traitor. Nobody could work with him. His breakout left the whole southwest quarter of Ireland burned over and without crops or cattle. Famine flourished everywhere. At least thirty thousand Irish starved to death in six months. A real mess. She also struck down the House of Norfolk sixteen years ago, when she hanged that notable traitor. But generally she takes the long view."

"Long view?"

"She knows that if any house breeds a bad bunch one generation, their children might be more reasonable in a few years as long as they are not mistreated. There are many examples of the Queen looking at the individuals rather than at the house itself. She knows well that the greatest of houses can produce blunderers and blowhards, and the least of houses may produce competent, courageous officers in whatever capacity. Elizabeth is very fond of competent people—whatever their background—because, when properly employed, they reduce her workload rather than increase it."

"And are her favorites generally competent people?"

Malachi laughed. "Well, let us say she doesn't choose her favorites for competency although they all have a good deal of it, or she'd have nothing to do with them in the first place. Our Sovereign has no patience whatever with bunglers or braggarts, so she expects her favorites to accomplish great things when she sends them forth with her directives and some small slice of her national treasury."

"How does one qualify as one of her favorites then?"

"Ah well," Malachi shrugged. "Elizabeth is like all the rest of us in her need for a specific companion made up of many parts. The difference is that she may gratify her whims and fancies by selecting many people to satisfy her various needs. She may invite any person in her kingdom to come and live at her court for as long as she desires their company. But Elizabeth has been queen for nearly thirty years now and has heard, many times over, everything which well-mannered voices dare to tell her. In truth, she compels a polite response from her court. On occasion, however, she tires of the stilted courtesy and uses insults and harangues to taunt court members into spirited exchanges."

"That sounds like an impossible dilemma for all."

"Among those court members, she hopes to find the few who are not too servile or obsequious. She especially enjoys the fire in the eyes and in the tongues of the men who become her favorites. It is not surprising, therefore, that Raleigh is from Devon and her new favorite, Essex, is from Wales."

"Devon and Wales?"

"The two wildest corners of the kingdom if you don't count Ireland and Scotland, the areas least disturbed by the Roman occupation and the regions most likely to cultivate exactly those qualities which the Queen finds attractive in a man who is already handsome to begin with. Her favorites are always men who can stand up to her and present her with original and entertaining points of view on old subjects. They are men who are not intimidated by her position as monarch and can thrust and parry verbally with her. Elizabeth spends many cheerful hours with them. By keeping her favorites at court, she crosses swords with them whenever the mood strikes her without caring about winning all bouts."

"It sounds as if she doesn't require the last word, after all."

Malachi nodded, "As a matter of fact, a certain feminine propensity applies itself when she sets out to woo a new favorite, and she seems determined to overwhelm him with her generosity. Once she starts giving him gifts of money, land, or monopolies, she ends up piling it on as if to sweep him off his feet. There's some kind of nameless perversity in the whole process, as though she would flaunt him before the people so that they should grow jealous of his good fortune and not form an admiration society for him."

"Thereby keeping the favorite heavily dependent on her good favor," said William thoughtfully. "Which may help explain Sir Philip Sidney's problems. Not only is he too much of a gentleman to argue with his Queen, he is admired by almost all of England."

"Exactly," Malachi nodded. "Here comes the Durham House messenger now, so I'm off to make delivery. I see two of Raleigh's scribes over at that far table. They can fill you in on more of Raleigh's background. Come, I'll introduce you. Try not to irritate them."

Raleigh's scribes, Jeremiah and Daniel, were well into their cups, as it turned out, and somewhat scornful of William's confessed theatrical ambitions.

"What the devil would you do with fame in the unlikely event you did achieve it?" Jeremiah scoffed.

"I'd wallow in the applause of my audience, first of all," acknowledged William good-naturedly.

"Ha, ha," Daniel laughed. "The vanity of public acclaim! Talk about your gossamer wings!"

"Vanity?"

"Exactly," said Jeremiah. "Remembering that purple is the color of royalty, you will recall what Seneca said: *'None of those whom you behold clad in purple is happy, any more than one of those actors upon whom the play bestoys a sceptre and a cloak while on stage; they strut their hour before a crowded house, with swelling port and buskined foot; but once they make their exit the foot-gear is removed and they return to their proper stature.'* [3]

"Strut their hour," mused William.

"Have you ever noticed how often writers use the stage as a metaphor for real life?" Daniel suddenly asked.

"An obvious parallel," William observed.

"Even the Queen recognizes the validity of the comparison. To a deputation of the Lords and Commoners the other day, she said: *'We princes are set on stages in the sight and view of all the world duly observed'*." [4]

"I understand she has the most complete costume collection in the kingdom," William said.

"Take a guess as to why many people choose to explain real life by relating it to life on the stage?" Daniel persisted.

"Perfectly natural link-up," William said. "The stage cuts through the continuum of everyday life and dramatizes the moment. Conflict is identified, competing voices are heard, resolution arises from the action, closure is experienced in the minds of the audience and everybody is happy when the ticket receipts are counted."

Daniel frowned. "Has anyone ever mentioned your inability to stay on the subject?"

"You mean the obvious then? You mean that real life is just as fleeting and transitory as life on the stage, so we must take care in choosing our audience?"

"You are certainly a man of outstanding limited perception," Jeremiah laughed. "You seem to wallow in the naked glare of the perfectly obvious while the nuances, innuendoes, and the subtleties dance gaily past your indolent eye."

"That may be so," William grinned, "but you have yet to prove it."

"Let me illustrate my central point by comparing real life with life on the stage," Daniel said. "First you need a central figure, half-hero, half-villain, for the sake of human complexity."

William nodded. "I recently attended a cobbler who did excellent work for me, but when it came to the casting of my account—"

"AND, it must be somebody of stature enough to make a real difference in people's lives by the impact of his actions, else the conflict will lack universal import."

"It's easy enough to fill a stage with make-believe kings, princes, and other significant figures," William scoffed, "but just how often do you come across such people at the neighborhood ale-house? Now a cobbler, on the other hand—"

"And that person of stature," Daniel pressed on, "must be dramatically compelled to walk the tight-rope of suspense in order to cultivate tension and apprehension in the audience. Particularly will audience reaction be heightened if the central figure be low born with much to lose if he stumbles. It also helps if he has risen to remarkable heights by virtue of a smooth tongue and a record of military successes."

"Like Sir Francis Drake," William suggested.

"Almost precisely," Daniel noted, "but more to the point, I had in mind my own master, Sir Walter Raleigh, who has come out of the rough West country of Devon to catapult himself into the most vulnerable position in the theater of the court—the 'High Theater,' as Raleigh calls the court."

"Vulnerable how?" William asked. "I've recently learned that Raleigh is generally regarded as the second or third most powerful man in the country."

"Indeed he is at the moment and will remain so as long as he has the Queen's favor; but that's the key to the tension, you see. If the Queen ever turns sour on him, he would tumble all the way to the bottom because there is no safety net in place to catch him."

"Safety net?"

Jeremiah picked up the explanation. "The long-time darlings of Elizabeth—Leicester, Hatton, Oxford—have developed their own factions at court because, over the years, they helped the Queen choose candidates to fill the important jobs in government, and those office holders know how to show allegiance to their patron when conflicts arise. But Raleigh came out of nowhere to capture Elizabeth's eye."

"He came from Ireland to read a report, I heard."

"That's right. Four years ago he was a completely unknown gentleman-soldier serving her majesty in that ugly little business Desmond created in Ireland. He was sent to present a report to the Privy Council. He seized that opportunity to also present to them his plan for cutting in half the cost to the Crown of stationing English troops in Ireland by having the Irish themselves pay half the cost of being supervised. Always alert to save a farthing or two, the Council was impressed enough to arrange his audience with the Queen. The rest is history. The Queen was so taken with his wit and charm that she has spent the last three years making him the most hated man in England."

Hated?" William exclaimed.

Daniel nodded. "I've heard him described as '*The best hated man of the world, in Court, city, and country*'." [5]

"Egad, how does he come to earn such serious unpopularity?"

"For one thing, without a faction at court, he is subjected to an endless barrage of scurrilous broadsides by those who resent his meteoric success. When other favorites are attacked, they simply pass the word to the Archbishop to notify the Master of the Revels to confront the offending printer and offer to lop off his ears if he does not desist. But, of course, lack of media control is not my master's only problem."

"I'm sorry to hear it."

"There is an undeniable arrogance in Raleigh which shines forth with every step he takes, every word he utters. Every man feels it. Not that he can't be witty and charming, mind you. He has so enchanted the Queen with his poetry and sophistry, that she speaks of him as her 'Oracle,' and there is talk that he will soon be appointed Captain of the Queen's guard, a position which requires his presence about the Queen's person at all times, a sure sign that she can't get enough of him."

"From what I've heard, the Queen doesn't mind a little arrogance in her companions," William said.

"She thrives on it!" Jeremiah exclaimed, and Daniel smirked. "God bless our sweet Sovereign, but she does have a wicked bent or two in her makeup. She cultivates arrogance in her favorites and then she flaunts what she has created before the court. The drama of having the man to whom all others must defer, bowing only to her, pleases our Lady so deeply that she keeps fostering exactly that situation. When she starts making large grants to her favorites, she does not scruple for a moment to oust bishops from church estates, by providing historical documents showing that the Crown had prior possession."

William seemed impressed. "She evicts long-term residents?"

Jeremiah nodded. "Before she leased Durham House to Raleigh, it had been the London residence of the Bishops of Durham for many years, and the evicted Bishop did not take kindly to losing his comfortable spot to the Queen's latest heartthrob, but there was nothing he could do about it."

"He couldn't complain?"

"Oh, he could indeed complain. He could complain all the way up the line to the Supreme Head of the Established Anglican Church of England. But you see the problem there?"

"That's Elizabeth," William observed.

"Right, and Elizabeth had already established precedent for her response to complaints from the clergy in a similar case three years earlier. She made it crystal clear at that time that she did not enjoy having her simple request for a little clerical cooperation taken so lightly. She had granted the Holborn residence of the Bishop of Ely to Sir Christopher Hatton, one of her frequent companions in those days. The Bishop of Ely complained so vigorously about his eviction notice that the Queen was driven to rebuke him. *'Proud Prelate,'* she wrote, *'you know what you were before I made you what you are. If you do not immediately comply with my request, I will unfrock you, By God'!"* [6]

"Oh, my." William smiled. "I see a lot of poetic sensibility in such clarity and compression, along with obvious executive impatience."

Daniel smiled. "Some call it the Queen's 'personal diplomacy.' She lets you know up front that she's right on top of things in her kingdom."

"Is Raleigh aware of the ill regard in which others hold him?" William asked.

"None better," said Jeremiah. "In a recent letter I copied for him, he said he had reached such a position *'to be beleved not inferior to any man, to plesure or displesure the greatest; and my oppinion is so receved and beleved as I can anger the best of them'."* [7]

"He's quite candid, isn't he?"

"Why not? He feels little but contempt for the *'rascal multitude,'* as he calls them, and deep satisfaction when the great nobles of the land must bow in deference to his influence. He'll suffer no more perfunctory curtsies, thank you. He doesn't really give a damn what anybody thinks except the Queen."

"It's not surprising that he steps on so many toes, then," William said.

"Everybody labors for a livelihood and nobody appreciates seeing some flash-in-the-pan upstart come from nowhere and be handed large grants of land and money. Working people do not welcome such irrational distortions of the system. It's bad enough when the Queen confers monopolies on her nobly-born favorites, but when she rewards the ill-bred with honor and influence, she is really testing the patience of her people."

"Are you saying that Sir Walter Raleigh is ill-bred?" William asked in surprise.

"No, no," Daniel insisted. "In this particular case I had reference only to Sir Francis Drake and not to my master at all. As a matter of fact, Raleigh grew up in a respectable household at about the low gentry level. His father was charged with piracy a time or two, of course, but he was always acquitted and—ironically perhaps—that involvement makes Raleigh even more acceptable to coastal families."

"Is the Queen aware that she is testing the patience of her people with these extravagances?"

"Oh yes, the Queen knows all the parts very well and enjoys seeing them played out to the very last curtain. Why do you suppose the theatrical world has so prospered during her reign? She enjoys theatrics. She enjoys raising up arrogant fellows to whom sensible men must kneel. She enjoys shaking up the composition of her court and watching that assembly react to the intrusion."

"Knowing that people will come to hate her favorite?"

"Of course. That hatred makes him so much more dependent on her and so much more fearful of losing her favor."

"The tension thing."

"Right. Elizabeth delights in it. She spends many happy hours observing the ebb and flow of her favorite's fortunes as he makes his way through English society under her special protection, against the many malcontents who plot to upset his plans while being careful not to offend her."

"Egad," murmured William. "As flies to careless boys are we to the authorities. They manipulate us for their sport."

Daniel nodded. "She even granted Raleigh the right to use press gangs to take up the men and ships he needed for the launching of his Virginia colony in April."

William shuddered. "I've heard of press gangs in Plymouth. The navy kidnaps men right off the street, away from friends and family, business or farm, to man its ships for two or three years at a time."

"Indeed, a brutal but necessary practice. The Queen sanctioned their use but would not let Raleigh himself go on the voyage."

"Malachi told me that Raleigh's half-brother Gilbert was lost at sea on just such a trip two years ago, so it's not surprising the Queen would wish to protect someone she is fond of. Does she allow her favorites to participate in any dangerous endeavors?"

"Oh, yes," said Jeremiah. "There are no barriers so long as they stay at home. She frequently attends the jousts with them not only to see which knight has the skill to win, but which has the temerity to unhorse his betters. By happy chance, she usually gets to present the winner's ribbon to her very own favorite."

"You're not suggesting collusion?"

"Gad, no," Jeremiah smirked. "What possible motive could there be for rabidly ambitious courtiers to let the influential favorite emerge victorious in a contest which the Queen is inspecting so closely and enjoying so much?"

"Certainly none that I can think of," William agreed and joined the scribes as they clinked their tankards in glee.

Chapter 4:
COVERT OPERATIONS AT DURHAM HOUSE

Raleigh's London residence, early afternoon:

"Come up beside me," Malachi said at the front entrance of the imposing Durham House. "I'll introduce you at Raleigh's, but for the love of God, straighten yourself up! This is a noble house and you must fit the picture. What is this head-askew posture, anyway? It gives you the air of always asking after the nearest privy. Your awkward pose underlines our presence to all. Rather than scheming happily behind the scenes arranging the props, we find ourselves continually revealed to the audience because you keep pulling the curtain on us."

"It's just a symbol I happen to fall into sometimes when I relax. I'll keep your urgings in mind."

"The posture you assume is part and parcel of your wardrobe, and I expect you to select a less bizarre stance in the future. We must blend into the background under all circumstances if we are to get our work done. Symbol of what?"

"My openness to the world. I regard my posture as quizzical, which broadcasts the fact that I am open to enlightenment from all sources. My head injury has left me in a critical condition where I am forever in a need-to-know condition simply to survive. I am also in the process of catching-up on my memory loss. By advertising my need with my posture, a kind of speaking with my body, you see, I find many kindly people who are eager to offer me information and direction."

"You'll mangle your spine that way, you know. You've twisted yourself into a giant question mark, and you'll freeze your bones permanently into that indolent pose if you don't straighten up."

"That's it exactly!" William exclaimed. "A question mark! The symbol for all the information the world holds. I intend to contain the complete works before I'm through."

"Tend to business first. Posture is vital in your disguise. Try to appear the attentive apprentice, without seeming to be an indolent boor, especially in the eyes of the household staff. Until you can remember one cover story from another, our effectiveness may be seriously impeded by your drawing attention to us by your crackpot notions of style. Attention means questions and questions mean delay, so I expect you to work hard on invisibility, as it were."

"I don't see how you do it," marveled William. "You step from one role to the next so completely that you startle me. I don't know that I'll ever succeed in being so many different people so quickly."

"Practice," said Malachi, "and a certain native wit which you have not yet had the opportunity to polish in yourself. Try to think of our various assignments as different stage settings, different props, different costumes—"

"And different roles?"

"Not really," Malachi said, "different appearances, perhaps, but our role is always essentially the same: get the errand run and stay out of the way. Nothing more, nothing less, so I will dock what little pay you have coming if you cannot remember to comport yourself in a pleasing but unexceptional manner while we are in attendance at Durham House."

"I may talk to the girls in the kitchen, may I not?"

"Please do," Malachi invited him. "Slither and slide your way thither, with your empty head askew, and you are sure to mark the height of their social season. But be ready to respond in proper character on the instant when I summon you, and listen carefully to what people have to say." Malachi lifted his hand to the door knocker.

"Psst!" came a clear warning hiss. "Over here behind the shrubs before you knock, Malachi."

"Mercy!" Malachi exclaimed in surprise. He lowered his voice as he approached her, pushing William before him. "Business or pleasure? Visit or visitation?"

"It is you," William stammered.

She smiled. "I'm glad to see your new memory is holding up. Have you had any inkling of the old one?"

He could only shake his head while his eyes enjoyed her face.

She turned to respond to Malachi, speaking softly, "A little of each as usual. I'm happy to track you down, Malachi, and pleased to see you are still fat and funny and that your acolyte has safely negotiated his introduction to the job without disaster."

Malachi grinned. "It's been a close thing at times. He had a slight brush with Drake's Around-the-World crew while we were in Plymouth."

"I heard," Mercy chuckled. "I've just come from Plymouth where every dockside tavern had Drake's sailors, egged on by a boisterous audience, playing out the various parts of the wonderful long evening they spent cadging drinks from your apprentice. Nobody seems to notice that the joke was really on you, Malachi, since you had to settle the tab." She turned to William. "You might be pleased to hear that everybody agreed you are a natural born entertainer."

William nodded dumbly, and Mercy said to Malachi, "The Office said I'd catch you at the Rooster or here as you arrived to see Raleigh. They want you to do a little business during your visit." She slid a dark packet from beneath her cloak and slipped it to Malachi. "They want a very special delivery of these to Hakluyt, the mapmaker, and they think that your new man here would be just the person for a delicate bit of business afterward—business it was felt you were too well known to take part in, Malachi."

"Me?" William exclaimed.

"It's a special job, just as you are, my dear," Mercy smiled and patted his cheek. "How is the poetry going?"

"Well, as a matter of fact."

Malachi broke in. "What's the job?"

"Drake wants these charts of his proposed voyage duplicated immediately, and he wants copies taken to the Queen and Walsingham."

"Sounds like simple messenger service," frowned Malachi.

"Drake's charts for the voyage?" exclaimed William. "Wouldn't Madrid love to get a copy of those!"

"Softly," warned Malachi and then asked Mercy, "What have you heard about Sidney?"

"The Queen has appointed him governor of Flushing to supervise the defense of that most strategic Dutch town."

"The cork in the bottle of Antwerp commerce," supplied William.

Mercy giggled. "I carry day-old news, I see. But we're all glad Sir Philip finally got a posting worthy of his standing as a reward for not sailing off with Drake. I don't know how eager he is for the new job, but he couldn't stand the idea of the Queen issuing a stay order for Drake's fleet. In short, if Sidney would not inconvenience himself a little, she would inconvenience Captain Drake and the 2,300 seamen a lot, by canceling the voyage altogether."

"A trifle high-handed," William observed.

"Indeed so," purred Mercy. "Every once in a while, the Queen likes to show her nobles—no matter how high born they are—who holds the big stick in this country. If the good of the kingdom happens to coincide with the Queen's whims—as it so often does—so much the better. The specter of raw, unapologetic power does wonders to quiet half-hearted discontent."

"And the plan for us meanwhile?"

"After you deliver the charts, William will stay with Hakluyt to provide protection while the charts are being duplicated. Tomorrow, you'll carry the copies to Westminster while I meet with William at the Rooster to celebrate completion of the mission. We'll dine and drink until we're just tipsy enough to become careless and lose track of the originals—as soon as we know that Spanish sympathizers are lurking nearby."

"Lose track?" William gulped.

"False maps," explained Malachi.

"Right," said Mercy. "They will show a proposed trip to the Spice Islands in the East Indies, which was one of the destinations rumored along the dockside before Drake sailed."

"Good strategy. It might slow the Spaniards down a trifle if they have to watch for him on both sides of the world."

"The West Indies are still his real destination, though?" whispered William.

Mercy's eyes twinkled an affirmative.

"We'll hand these over to Hakluyt, then," said Malachi. "Are you away, Mercy, or may we count on your company for a while here at Durham House?"

"Nay, I'll see William at the Red Rooster tomorrow."

"You won't have any trouble getting him drunk, will you?"

"None at all," Mercy smiled sweetly. "He always seems a little woozy around me anyway."

In the library at Durham House:

William stood at the end of a long table where the great geographer, Richard Hakluyt, worked. William's job, as Malachi reminded him, was to seem to be standing guard.

"Does it bother you if I talk while you work?" William asked politely.

"Not in the least," Hakluyt assured him. "I welcome a little distraction. Straight copy work can be tiring without relief. As a matter of fact, the mariners in residence often drop by to chat while I'm working, so I'm used to it."

"Do many sea captains reside here at Durham House?" William asked.

"Most of them stay here while ashore. By serving as a barracks for many busy people, Durham House keeps them handy for instructions."

"And a formidable barracks it is," William chuckled. "I've seldom seen any building built so much like a fortress."

"There's a good reason for that." Hakluyt quit working for a moment. "I suspect no one has shown you Master Raleigh's study, which is right next door. He is not at home this evening, so let me show you the view he enjoys."

"I'm sorry, sir, but I cannot leave these maps untended."

"Of course, of course. What am I thinking? I will just describe the view. Upriver from his study, you can plainly see Whitehall Palace and Westminster just beyond. Downriver is the old, familiar London Tower and the bridge."

"I've noticed that part of this building is built to overhang the water."

"Right. Durham House is situated just at the right-angle turn of the Thames in its progress downriver. This location gives an unobstructed view of river traffic both up and down. The Normans were fully aware of its strategic significance when they constructed it hundreds of years ago and built it like a fortress to protect this stretch of the river from any intruders. Happily enough, it has served as a safe and secure refuge for me for many months. I have enjoyed my residence here very much, even if there are those who feel I may be over-protected in my position."

"I didn't mean to offend you when I said you had an enviable place here in Raleigh's household. Malachi has told me you are the foremost mapmaker in England today."

Somewhat mollified, Hakluyt went back to work after acknowledging, "After Thomas Harriot, perhaps."

"You must admit, however, that being Raleigh's classmate at Oxford did smooth your path to acquiring this position," persisted William.

"I think courtesy and common sense call for clarification here," Richard Hakluyt said stiffly. "It is true that I have been a permanent and honored guest of Sir Walter for some time now. He believes in doing things in a big way, but I earn my keep by supplying up-to-date maps and charts for all of Sir Walter's wide-spread ventures."

"Yes, everybody mentions your value," William assured him. "How wide-spread are those ventures?"

"All the way to the New World," Hakluyt told him. "In addition to my book *Divers Voyages Touching the Discovery of America* printed in 1582, I recently did maps and charts for the group that Raleigh sent out in April to do a reconnaissance for the start-up of his Virginia colony. He has absolutely made up his mind to establish a permanent English settlement in America, and, if he lives, I'm sure he'll get it done."

"The reconnaissance group is not the start-up group?"

"Hardly. It's mostly an informal military expedition of volunteers who are being paid to determine if there is any easy gold or silver to be had, and to locate a usable harbor. They have no women or children or clergymen with them, so it's unlikely they'll stay if they don't strike a bonanza of some sort. But they will be followed by permanent settlers who arrive with seed and stock and a burning ambition to acquire land and make a better life for themselves in the New World."

"I've heard people in the taverns denounce the colony attempt as a hare-brained scheme that's going to get somebody killed before it's over. How can you be so sure Raleigh will accomplish his ambition?"

"Even if the first colony attempt should falter, Sir Walter will eventually succeed. A permanent New World settlement will link his name evermore with Elizabeth's because he plans to set up the chief city in the very heart of the vast land he has named for the Queen. He will name that capitol city of the Virginia colony after himself: Raleighville or Raleighburg or something like that, and it will rest content eternally in the very bosom of his sovereign mistress. He will succeed in this somewhat romantic endeavor because he has gathered together men like myself and given us no duties other than to follow our mortal bent in furtherance of the colony plan."

"And your bent is copying maps?"

"Cartography. Old maps made new by examining accounts of voyages since taken."

William shook his head, "Some people might think mapmaking a rather musty kind of second-hand experience. Why—er, how would a person get into something like that?"

Hakluyt thought for a moment. *"I do remember that being a youth, and one of her Majesties scholars at Westminster, that fruitful nurserie, it was my happs to visit the chamber of Mr. Richard Hakluyt my cousin, a Gentleman of the Middle Temple...at a time when I found open upon his board certaine bookes of Cosmographie, with an universall Mappe: he seeing me somewhat curious in the view thereof, began to instruct my ignorance, by showing me the division of the earth into three parts after the olde account, and then according to the latter and better distribution, into more: he pointed with his wand to all the knowen Seas, Gulfs, Bayes, Straights, Capes, Rivers, Empires, Kingdoms, and Territories of each part, with declaration also of their special commodities, and particular wants, which by the benefit of trafficke and intercourse of merchants, are plentifully supplied. From the Mappe he brought me to the Bible, and turned to the 107 Psalme, directed me to the 23 and 24 verses, where I read, that they which go down to the sea in ships, and occupy by the great waters, they see the works of the Lord, and his wonders in the deepe."* [8]

"I like the idea of the wand," William said. "Permits you to focus attention. Every schoolmaster should have one. A sturdy one."

"Yes," said Hakluyt, "but these *words of the Prophet together with my cousin's discourse, things of high and rare delight to my young nature, tooke in me so deepe an impression, that I constantly resolved, if ever I were preferred to the University where better-time, and more convenient place might be ministered for these studies, I would by God's assistance prosecute that knowledge and kinde of literature, the doores whereof, after a sort, were so happily opened before me.* So here I am."

"Oh, we need a lot more of that kind of vocational guidance to serve the troubled youth of today," William declared. "But did not reading about all those journeys kindle your desire to travel, or does your attachment to documents prohibit travel on your part?"

Hakluyt sighed deeply. "As a matter of fact, I have done some traveling on the job. *What restless nights, what painful days, what heat, what cold I have endured; how many long and chargeful journeys I have travelled; How many famous libraries I have searched into. What variety of ancient and modern writers I have pursued.*" He grinned at William. "God help me, I loved it all. But I have to admit that every job has its drawbacks. I was originally signed on to accompany the Virginia group to the New World when they sailed in April, but it was later thought best that I remain here at the command post for the composing and transmission of up-to-date charts and documents. Dr. White, a splendid scientist and a skilled artist, took my place on the trip. Have you met him?"

"I don't remember where I was in April."

"I was sorry not to go because a visit to America would have been the greatest adventure of my life—for as long as I survived, anyway." He sighed. "But I have few complaints because cartography has been good to me."

"But how do you spend your free time? When you're standing up straight, that is?"

"Over the years, I have *by degree read over whatsoever printed or written discoveries and voyages found extant, either in Greeke, Latine, Italian, Spanish, Portugall, French, or English Languages.*" [9]

"Aha!" William cried. "You are a cunning linguist then. Boccaccio writes—"

"I have my moments," Hakluyt admitted with a grin.

"And do you keep all your new maps secret as the Spanish do?"

"Not in the least," declared Hakluyt. "In my role as a public lecturer at Oxford, I was *the first that produced and shewed the olde imperfectly composed, and the new lately reformed Mappes, Globes, Spheares, and other instruments of this art for demonstration in common schools, to the singular pleasure, and general contentment of nearly everybody concerned.*"

"Nearly everybody?"

"The Drake people resent the fact that my maps indicate there is no continent south of the Straits of Magellan . They don't want the Spanish to find that out."

"You speak of the Drake people as a group, but who would be their counterbalance?"

"The Raleigh people. Drake and Raleigh recognize the basic problem with Spain, but each has a different approach for solving that problem. One short-range and one long-range."

"Drake is the short range?"

Hakluyt grinned. "That's right. He's our smash-and-grab man, and that's just about the only strategy Spain has left open to us since Columbus stumbled onto the New World."

"How do you mean 'stumbled'?" William asked as he watched Hakluyt letter in the place names. "I'm a good hand at lettering, by the way, if you'd care to accept my help."

Hakluyt looked up. "Good idea. Try your hand on this one. Just copy from the original, same size, same place."

William bent to the work. "You say Columbus stumbled?"

"No other way to look at it. Christopher Columbus didn't know where he landed when he got there, and he certainly didn't know where he had been when he got back to Spain. He made four trips across the ocean and was convinced until his dying day that he had reached China and India. Why do you suppose we still call the people in the New World 'Indians'?"

"But aren't you ignoring the high degree of uncertainty involved in any exploration? And you are certainly downplaying the skill and daring of this intrepid navigator. After all, he did get the job done."

Hakluyt scowled. "Oh, the Columbus thing had to happen one way or another because the time was ripe for it historically. The Norsemen and the Vikings have oral records dating back hundreds of years of their voyages across the ocean to a place they called Vinland, and the Irish have always claimed that their Saint Brendan sailed across in some cockamamie cockleshell or something like. So Columbus' feat of navigation is really not too impressive once you realize that you can't miss the New World as long as you keep sailing west from Europe. As a matter of fact, he was outstanding as a navigator only for his good luck. All his mistakes kept rebounding in his favor."

"How is that?" William asked as he finished lettering in 'Aleppo' on the chart before him.

"That's fine," said Hakluyt as he examined the lettering. "Quite legible."

"No, I mean about Columbus' being a lucky navigator."

"In an historical sense," the mapmaker explained, "Columbus' attempt to reach India by sailing west from Europe really got started in 1453 when the Turks broke the walls of Constantinople with 600 pound cannon balls. After that notable victory, the Moslem empire controlled not only the seaports of the Eastern Mediterranean, but also the overland traffic of camel caravans from the Orient with their riches in silks and spices."

"Hold on now," William protested. "I've often heard the ballad-mongers sing, '*In 1492, Columbus sailed the ocean blue*.' What's this 1453 business?"

Hakluyt frowned at him, "If one is so simple as to be concerned only with dates, that is correct," he growled. "Most intelligent men, however, cultivate an interest in the significance of dates. In this particular case, the historical necessity for the Columbus trip began when the Moslem middlemen utilized the capture of Constantinople to intrude themselves into a trading relationship which had flourished for hundreds of years between Italian merchants and Asian spice traders. Ever since that most famous of all Venetian merchants, Marco Polo, returned from the Orient in 1271 with samples of gunpowder, paper, a compass, and an assortment of exotic spices in addition to a pasta dish called spaghetti, a mutually beneficial trade has been carried on between Italy and Asia."

"Profitable?"

"Astronomical! As a matter of fact, the spice-trade profits were so enormous, they permitted the Venetians, Genoese, and Florentines to dabble in the arts to such a degree that the resulting explosion in painting, sculpturing, and knowledge is already being referred to as a Rebirth of Italy by some historians."

"The Renaissance label?"

The mapmaker nodded. "That's it. Before the Turks conquered Constantinople and thereby established control of all import channels from the Orient, Italian merchant families had a golden pipeline coming on camel-back overland and on ships through the Indian Ocean and up the Red Sea. All the Italians had to do was sail to a half-dozen Mediterranean ports and dicker directly with the Asian factors, who were only too happy to dispose of heaping piles of pepper, ginger, cinnamon, cloves, and nutmeg in exchange for a little gold, the great international currency."

"But the Turks, I presume, would not hinder the trade itself, just sit down beside the Italian middle-men?"

"That is correct, yes. The trade continued after the Turks slid into the market place, and their control of the import channels permitted them to apply lessons learned well from the Italians. They were not at all hesitant about applying a ten-fold jump in their fee for trans-shipping the goods to Europe."

"That is impressive!" William exclaimed in sheer admiration. "I've never sought a future in business myself, you understand, but a 1000% markup for repackaging is enough to give a person second thoughts about his vocational choice."

Hakluyt looked at him closely. "Any man who proposes to find profit by elbowing aside Venetians, on the one hand, and Turks, on the other, is a fit candidate for Bedlam House, to my way of thinking."

"Right. I was only speculating," William mumbled.

"You are quite correct, however, in recognizing the profit to be made. The cascading wealth the Italian merchants collected on the trade dwindled to a mere substantial profit after they had to share with the Turks. Enough to maintain the fortunes of

Italy's leading merchant families, but not the pyramiding profits of the previous century. That's why the Turks and Italians still go at each other's throats periodically as they did at Lepanto just fourteen years ago over control of the Mediterranean."

"But Constantinople's fall was well before 1492."

"Just so," said Hakluyt. "With the Asian spice trade in the tight grip of the Turks and Italians, Spain and Portugal needed to get at the East Indian commerce some other way."

"An on-going competition, eh?"

"Exactly," said Hakluyt. "Portugal got a big jump on Spain in the exploring business because their Prince Henry the Navigator had been looking for an alternate route even before the Turks took Constantinople. About 1440, he established a navigational center at Point Segres on the southwestern tip of Portugal which is also the southwestern tip of Europe. Gathering the country's best mapmakers, shipbuilders, astronomers, and mariners together, he helped design vessels and redraw maps which would result after his death in Bartholomew Diaz's rounding the southern tip of Africa in 1488. Diaz originally called the southern point of the African continent 'The Cape of Storms' because that's what he found there, but his king, John II, felt that name might discourage investors, so he renamed it 'The Cape of Good Hope' on Portuguese maps. Every schoolboy knows what happened after that."

"What?" ventured William, red-faced.

"Ten years later, Vasco da Gama reached India by rounding the Cape and opened the riches of the Far East to Portuguese merchantmen."

"So with Portugal headed east to the Indies, Spain decided to go west?"

"More or less," Hakluyt nodded, "but only at the urging of Columbus. It is easy now for us to forget that Spain was not a very wealthy nation back then. They had an economy based mostly on the export of wool from the three million sheep that grazed wherever they pleased across the Spanish landscape, but such trade did not produce enough revenue to support the kind of ambitious military adventures the Dons have undertaken in recent decades."

"Their only industry was three million sheep?"

"No, no. In truth, they also exported their excellent wines to Holland and Ireland and, of course, here to England. A real service to mankind—"

"You mentioned Columbus' luck?" William prompted.

"I'm getting to that part," the mapmaker growled. "Keep your doublet on. I said that Columbus was outrageously lucky as a navigator because everything that happened on the initial voyage—even his mistakes—turned out in his favor."

"Did people really believe the world was flat back then?"

"That's typical schoolbook claptrap," the mapmaker snorted, "to bolster the self-esteem of modern students and permit them to feel superior to somebody; anybody.

The truth is that both Pythagoras and Aristotle declared that the Earth was round five hundred years before Christ was born, and Aristotle also mentioned that there were rumors of lands to the west of Europe."

"Yes," said William, "but did Columbus and the Spaniards read that old stuff?"

"They didn't have to. No man has ever sailed the seas for more than a month without noticing that ships go hull-down at eight miles as they disappear under the horizon, and headlands appear peak-first as they are approached from the sea. No explanation is possible for those everyday occurrences other than the realization that we sail on a curved surface. As a matter of fact any person with half an eye can check the shape of the Earth every time there is a lunar eclipse."

"Of the moon?"

Hakluyt nodded. "Before he sailed on his around the world trip in 1519, Ferdinand Magellan said; *'The Church says that the Earth is flat, but I know that it is round. For I have seen the shadow on the Moon and I have more faith in the shadow than in the Church'.*" [10]

"I'll watch for that. Are we getting to the lucky part yet?"

"Earlier, you were surprised that in light of my background as an historian and author of recently published accounts of famous voyages, extensively documented, I should end up as only a mapmaker. ONLY a mapmaker, you said!"

"Oh, well, I sometimes overleap myself with my verbal sallies and end up falling on the other side. I attribute it to my inexperience at social bantering."

"Do you recognize the name Amerigo Vespucci?"

"There is something vaguely familiar about the first part," William considered, "but the second part sounds like one of those wondrous Italian dishes smothered with cheese and redolent with garlic and oregano and—"

"What do you call the region of the New World when you refer to that area in conversation?" the mapmaker demanded.

"Like everybody else, I call the whole thing the New World. Or the West Indies."

"What else do you call it?"

"I'd probably jerk my thumb in that direction and say something like, over the seas and far away."

"Young man," Hakluyt insisted. "I'm speaking about the designation we now apply to a land mass discovered less than a century ago and nearly equal in size to all known lands up till that time. I am talking here of the name we give to half the world!"

"Oh, you mean all of the Americas," William noted. "I thought our primary focus was—hold on, now! Can that really be the case? Amerigo equals America?"

"Just so," the mapmaker nodded in satisfaction.

"I suppose there is a story behind half the world being named for somebody few of us have ever heard of, instead of for Columbus himself?"

"You bet there is," the mapmaker warmed to the task. "Admiral Columbus returned to Spain after his first voyage with little gold but with maps where he felt future treasure might be found. An independent Spanish captain made a separate voyage to the New World between Columbus' first and second trips and with the aid of a map drawn by the Admiral himself, reaped a harvest of pearls from one of the islands. Columbus later contended in court that part of the pearl profit should be his, but that's another story."

"Yes," William murmured.

"On that trip," said Hakluyt, "Captain Hojeda was accompanied by Amerigo Vespucci, a navigator from Florence, who also sailed along the coast of the Portuguese colony of Brazil and wrote excellent descriptions of that area. In 1507, the year after Columbus died, Rene II, Duke of Lorraine, organized a group of scholars and clerics to construct a brand new map of the world under the guidance of Martin Waldseemueller, a German mapmaker. They did a woodcut print of a new world map that was so detailed it measured eight feet by four-and-a-half."

"Gadzooks!" William exclaimed. "I bet they had a tough time folding that puppy up."

"They did it in twelve sections," Hakluyt explained. "The Waldseemueller map was that big because it included an ocean that many Europeans had never known existed—an ocean first named the South Sea by Vasco de Balboa when he sighted it from a tree in Panama and revealed it to the Western World a mere seventy-odd years ago. Pacific Ocean, we call it now, of course—an ocean whose vastness in breadth was validated when one of Magellan's ships—out of the five that sailed—got back to Spain after circling the globe just sixty-odd years ago."

"Wait!" William protested. "Malachi has had me studying history books without end lately, and I distinctly remember that Balboa discovered the Pacific Ocean in 1513. How could the mapmakers, six years earlier?"

Hakluyt grinned. "Waldseemueller's group incorporated what John Cabot and Giovanni da Verrazzano had mapped of North America, what Columbus charted of Middle America, and what Amerigo Vespucci recorded of South America, and then, like good cartographers, indulged themselves in a leap of faith by depicting a vast ocean between Spain's territories in the New World and the Spice Trade of the East Indies."

"But why Vespucci at the expense of Columbus?"

Hakluyt smiled. "Even on his death bed after four trips to the New World, Columbus was still arguing that he had discovered India, so to avoid confusion, the mapping group looked around for another name. Waldseemueller mentioned in letters that the other two known land masses had been named for women, Europa and Asia, so it was time to honor a man. Vespucci had done pioneer work in describing Brazil and the Spanish Main, so they honored him by affixing his name to that region on the map. Over the years the name 'America' has come to include all of the New World."

"Unbelievable," William acknowledged. "A man gains immortality simply by doing his job and letting luck seek him out. I hope it always works that way."

"Don't forget that societies themselves sometimes get lucky breaks," the mapmaker insisted. "It's not unusual for the director of such important mapmaking projects to apply his own name to nameless areas of the map, so if Herr Waldseemuller had been a seeker of personal glory, the Americas could easily have a different name today."

"Oh. Yes, I see. Egad."

"So, remember now, when you start talking about somebody being only a mapmaker, there are certain advantages that accrue to those of us who have dedicated our lives to providing graphic illustrations of how the world turns."

"And providing information to explain why Columbus was lucky?" William prompted.

Hakluyt sighed. "Columbus sailed from Spain in 1492 on his flagship, *Santa Maria*, a 110-ton nao, which was the biggest of the three ships he took."

"What's a nao?"

"One of the old fashioned, coastal freight carriers which turned out to be too clumsy for oceanic travel. After the *Santa Maria* ran aground and sank in Hispaniola on the first voyage, Columbus wrote *"She was very heavy and not suitable for the business of discovery."* (*Nina* booklet). Thereafter, Columbus relied for several of his voyages on one of his two caravels, the *Nina* which was smaller and much more maneuverable, faster, and had a draught of only seven feet. She had square sails on the main and foremast for sailing downwind and lateen or triangular sails on her mizzen mast for cutting across the wind."

"How big is a caravel?"

"The *Nina* and the *Pinta* were each close to 100 tons, about 88 feet long with a beam of 18 feet, and, as a class, they were used all during the 1400's up until about 1530 when it became apparent that bigger ships were needed to do oceanic service and the galleons began appearing. In their time, however, the caravels served many purposes as cargo carriers, warships, patrol boats, and even as pirate ships because they were sound, dependable ships which could sail five points on the wind and carry close to 2,000 square feet of canvas if the captain was interested in speed."

"An 18 foot beam? Good Lord! I could leap across the deck at mid-ship with three bounding steps. Those sound like very small ships for ocean travel. How big was the crew?"

"The crew size varied a lot but twenty men could easily handle the caravel at sea, and the sleeping space aboard ship expanded enormously when Columbus' people came across the greatest benefit ordinary seaman ever acquired from the discovery of the West Indies: the hammock which the natives were all using for comfortable sleeping. That thoughtful innovation was immediately welcomed aboard and has been used by sailors ever since. The new arrangement created so much more sleeping space that there is an historical record indicating that the *Nina* once transported 121 passengers from the New World to Spain in addition to the crew, but I imagine that was remembered by all involved as a cozy crossing indeed."

"Was the size of the ship part of the luck of Columbus?"

"Not exactly. But by not using the Portuguese Azores Islands—900 miles offshore from Portugal at 40° north—for his jump-off spot to sail west in search of India—as many before him had attempted to do—he proved to be very lucky. Those who tried to leave from that spot wore themselves out battling strongly prevailing westerly winds. For political reasons—Columbus was aware Portugal would regard his voyage as a Spanish attempt to cut in on their East Indies trade—he decided instead to sail an additional 800 miles south and jump-off from the Spanish-owned Canary Islands at 28° north, where he had lived for a time in the past. And from there he was in easy reach of the Tropic of Cancer at 23° degrees north where he picked up the prevailing northeasterly wind we have come to call the Trade Winds because they so readily facilitate travel to the trading area of the West Indies."

"That sounds like a bit of good luck," William said.

"Exactly. He already knew of the prevailing westerly-northwesterly winds north of the Azores because he had noticed trees on the Spanish coast bent in a southeasterly direction, so with the lucky find of northeasterly winds south of the Tropic of Cancer, he soon realized that he had a way to sail west as far as he wanted and a way to return east when the need arose. Because his crew were used to navigating by sailing along the coast with land in sight, however, he had to be careful not to frighten them with big numbers about how far they had sailed from any shoreline. To deceive them, he deliberately understated distances in the ship's official log, but he kept a secret log to show his real estimates. Would you like to guess which log proved the more accurate upon examination?"

"It would kill your story if it were the secret one."

"You are correct. Every navigator uses the sun and the North Star to judge a ship's latitude north or south of the equator, but we have no instruments as yet to determine distance traveled east and west from any given point. Back in the second century, in Egypt, Ptolemy constructed his famous world map with the degrees of longitude marked on it as meridians, using the Canary Islands as the end of the West."

"The meridians are the lines on the map that run north and south, just as the parallels run east and west?"

"Yes, indeed. Meridians run north and south so you can mark how far you have traveled between them, and you thereby know how far you have moved east and west.

Ptolemy calculated the distance between degrees of longitude at the equator to be 60 miles."

"Out of 360?" William mused. "So he was saying the world is about 21,600 miles around?"

"Correct. Big enough to scare possible investors. So Columbus cut it down a little. By creatively using both Arabic and Roman numerals interchangeably in his calculations, he argued that each degree of longitude was only 45 miles. That effectively reduced the earth's circumference to 16,200 miles. It was thought at that time that Asia was 10,000 miles east of the Azores—too far for any ship to carry supplies. Columbus contended, however, that historical projections were wrong, and the distance was only one quarter that far. He claimed that he would fetch Japan by sailing down the 23rd parallel for 2,500 miles, and as luck would have it, that's exactly where he ran into the New World-along the 23rd parallel."

"That was lucky indeed," William conceded, "but there has always been something that bothered me about all this exploring business. All the early explorers we hear about—people like Columbus, Balboa, Vespucci, Cartier, Ribault, Verrazzano, and DeSoto—are all Italian, Spanish, Portuguese, or French. We would never hear of any early English explorer at all if good old John Cabot hadn't sailed from Bristol to discover Newfoundland in 1497. Where were the rest of the English when all of this adventuring was going on?"

"Ahhh," Hakluyt sighed deeply, "I'm afraid things may be worse than you suppose since John Cabot's real name was Giovanni Caboto before he signed on to do some exploring for England. The truth is you have struck a very sore spot in my view of historical development. *'I marvel not a little that since the first discoverie of America — which is nowe full fourscore and tenne yeeres…'* [11]

"That's nearly a hundred years ago," William observed.

Hakluyt nodded and went on. *"After so great conquests and plantings of the Spaniardes and Portingales there, wee of England could never have the grace to set fast footing in such fertill and temperate places, as are left as yet unpossessed of them…..And surely if there were in us that desire to advance the honour of our Countrie which ought to bee in every good man, wee woulde not all this while have foresworn the possessing of these landes, which of equitie and right appertain unto us."*

"Oh well, if we financed Caboto and he showed a distinct national preference when he changed names, I guess we have a claim on at least Newfoundland, but I'll admit such abstract distinctions are beyond me. I'm really interested in what motivates writers to get the work done," William said. "Why did you write your 1582 book?"

"I had heard in speech and had read in bookes other nations miraculously extolled for their discoveries and notable enterprises by sea, but the English of all others for their sluggish security, and continual neglect of the like attempts especially in so long and happy a time of peace."

"You think peacetime is the best time to explore?"

"Oh, yes. I've often heard French captains in their cups say if they could get any kind of stable government established at home, they would fill the Atlantic with French explorers headed for the New World. But under the present circumstances, they do as we do and send only pirates," Hukluyt spat out the last word.

"You don't mean the redoubtable Sir Francis, do you?"

Hakluyt nodded and frowned, "Drake and Hawkins and Cavendish and Frobisher and all the rest. You know, in the eyes of the world community, *we and the French are most infamous for our outrageous common and daily practices.'* [12] You don't see any Spanish or Portuguese pirates, do you?"

"Why not?"

"Because they are the haves and we are the have-nots?" William offered.

Hakluyt nodded. *"They have established colonies in the New World. They have found employment and place for all their discontent people. They have done the thing in a respectable manner and we must learn to do likewise if we want history to respect us."* That's why I think our country is very lucky to have such a far seeing and generous man as Sir Walter Raleigh taking up the challenge on our behalf."

"Lucky indeed," William agreed, yawning. "Are my sleeping quarters close at hand?"

"Mine are," Hakluyt said. "but I have plans for the evening, so I'll lock the charts up and finish them in the morning. I suppose I'll see you then."

"I thought I was to stay with you for the night?"

Hakluyt shook his head. "Not possible. I'm busy. But if you just pop around to the kitchen, I'm sure they'll make some kind of arrangement for your supper and your night's repose."

Chapter 5:
ROMANTIC INTERLUDE

Dawn the next morning, Jeanette's bedroom at Durham House:

"Do you mind if I refer to you hereafter as a clumsy, oafish, insensitive boor?" asked Jeanette, one of Raleigh's maids, as she played affectionately with William's curls.

"I beg your pardon," he responded. "I had rather hoped—"

"Just in public," she hastened on. "We two will always remember the perfection of this occasion. I must confess to you, quite openly, that tonight has been the most enjoyable night of my life. Already."

"Then I don't see why—"

"My sweet love, your endless affirmations of eternal fidelity will ring in my mind forever! I like those lovely, sincere pledges of absolute adoration." She sighed deeply. "They really put me in the right mood for the moment."

"For the moment? I had thought that perhaps—"

"And your youthful enthusiasm! Oh, that is a first-rate titillator of otherwise sedate and reserved maidens such as myself. The glint in your eye, your panting breath, the dewdrops on your forehead, and then, of course, the piece-de-resistance."

"Yes?"

"I must be careful not to stray too far from maidenly behavior so soon again," she said. "Bedroom walls have ears in nighttime hours, but I did not want to leave the discussion without complimenting you on your longevity."

William blushed. "Well, some men are gifted one way and—"

"I don't suppose I slept a full three hours this night, and yet I feel wonderfully refreshed! Glad to be alive!"

"Then, I don't understand about this 'boorish-insensitive' business, Jeanette, my pet."

"To keep those other women away from you while you are here at Durham House."

All very well from your point of view, I suppose," William conceded. "But see here, my dear, are you not entering into possible commission of libel and slander and assassination of my character?"

Jeanette giggled. "Oh, you do take yourself seriously, don't you, pet? I think that's so wonderful! It gives a woman a post to which she may bind you during the shameful act. I've always adored the kind of sincerity men can put on during a coupling. It makes my skin tingle when I recall those intimate verses you whispered to me at the height of your excitement. Aside from the admirable breath control they exhibited, I appreciated the fact that their recitation slowed your natural motion and kept you in the game longer."

William was silent for a moment and then said, "I can see now that sincerity should be made of sterner stuff."

"But don't worry, I'll keep you safe from those preying women. Some of them would hoist their skirts for any beggar who smiles their way."

"Please do not add beggary to my other failings during your public denunciation of my shortcomings," William requested.

"Done," Jeanette assured him, "but apart from all that, it's a regular cat-fight to command any attention at all among the maids when we gather socially. Durham House has fourteen maids out of the forty staff members, so when it comes to holding the floor against spirited and ill-mannered opposition, believe me, the 'clumsy-boor' presentation always holds interest much longer than the 'rapturous-bliss' testimony. There are some details women never tire of sharing. I'll start by proclaiming your insensitivity to the plight of my brother, Geoffrey."

"Your brother! Ye gods, in one night I learned more about Geoff's plight and how he has fretted and vexed you, than I know about any other human being. I know that he has become completely addicted to Raleigh's tobacco, that he will lie, cheat, and steal to get his hands on a stash of it, that it is really Raleigh's fault because he leaves that stuff all over the house and encourages his guests to use it; that you are fearful your brother will lose his present position as footman because of his addiction, and that his care and feeding will then fall upon your skimpy resources if he is to survive. I thought I listened quite attentively and with a commendable level of sensitivity."

"Why are you telling me all that?" Jeanette said, puzzled. "I know you did. I was there. You are missing my point entirely."

"Tell me the point again, sweet lady," sighed William. "The point is that such an approach will give me a legitimate reason to again relate in full detail the troubles Geoff has caused me. By discharging the difficulties with which my life abounds into the public ear, you see, I will experience a deep sense of relief and satisfaction."

"I can see that happening once," said William, "but I don't see."

"The other maids have heard of my trouble with Geoffrey before, of course, but I can use your boorishness first as a pry-bar to gain their full attention and then as a springboard to catapult Geoff's situation into their midst once again. You must admit my special circumstance richly deserves their sympathy."

"Jeanette, my dear, do I understand that you will then justify your recital of your troubles on the pretense that I am so boorish as not to listen?"

"Now you are beginning to get the picture just as I knew you would because you are so alert and so...so..."

William sighed. "Sincere?"

"That's it! I'll take sincerity any day over the arrogant airs so many gentlemen in this house put on."

"You regard Durham House as harboring arrogance?"

"Absolutely! No end to it. Some of the visiting sea captains are down-to-earth and very friendly, but the residents live as though this were a monastery. I've never seen so many grown men with their heads in the clouds: astronomy, navigation, astrology, alchemy, mathematics, and the endless dispute over the nature of the Supreme Being. That's all they talk about, night and day. Other great houses may pretend to hold deep intellectual discussions, but they usually end the evening absorbed in the ribald antics of the resident dwarf. There are no dwarfs at Raleigh's house, however. None in the body and none in the mind."

"I don't see the problem then."

"They're all so busy plotting that there is little hope of my finding a sympathetic ear."

"Plotting?"

She nodded. "Nothing else to call it. Scheming to set up another England in the New World although, for the life of me, I can't imagine what they'd gain by it. I've overheard members of Captain Barlow's party from last year's mapping expedition report their findings to Raleigh, and it is obvious that behind all the promotional talk about opportunities in the New World, there is little over there except savage Indians, starvation, and endless toil. I can't imagine how they talked 108 innocent souls into sailing three thousand miles from home to set up housekeeping in that place. They named it Virginia in honor of the Virgin Queen, you know."

"So I hear."

"But there are no butcher shops or decent lodgings or hat shops or bear-baiting or theater or anything! What in the world is going on in their heads to spend so much effort on such nonsense?"

"It is possible they take a long-range view of things, Jeanette, as opposed to—but hold on now; did you just say that you overheard the report to Raleigh of last year's mapping party?"

The maid giggled "I am curious by nature, so my duties often carry me near the great library when we have company. Usually the doors are left open, but with certain visitors, Raleigh has them closed. That cuts down on the flow of communication somewhat because it is then necessary to put one's ear directly against the pantry wall to follow the discussion, but the problem is that when we have important visitors, the pantry gets crowded, and there is always so much giggling and nudging, your ear gets pulled away just when—"

"Who does he close the doors for?"

"The poetic bunch mostly. The philosophers and doubters–whenever the discussion is likely to 'tempt God out of Heaven' as Christopher Marlowe says. After that, there are arguments and considerations which amount to sheer atheism, if you ask me."

William leaned back comfortably among the pillows. "Really? Like what?" he grinned.

"Well, with my own ears, I've heard Marlowe say things that would enrage Bishop Bancroft or Whitgift or any other official protector of the Anglican Church."

"But you're not offended, Jeanette. Do you discuss what he says with others?"

"Oh, no! I have no wish it get Master Marlowe in trouble with the bishop."

"I like Marlowe too. He's quite clever and only talks to entertain."

"Yes. I heard him say the Anglican Church should use tobacco smoke in their services along with the partaking of bread and wine, so that the worshippers could see the specter of the Holy Ghost in addition to experiencing the body and blood of Christ."

William laughed softly and Jeanette leaned closer. "Can I count on you to keep quiet about all this? I wouldn't want to get anybody from this house in trouble or lose my position just because I gossip a little outside the kitchen, you know."

William put a finger to her lips. "Mum's the word, so tell me more. Provided there will be nothing further about your brother," he added anxiously.

"Oh, no," she giggled. "I'll save him for the maids."

"Tell me who, besides the mapmaker, Hakluyt, has permanent residence here at Durham House?"

Jeanette touched her pursed lips thoughtfully. "Well, there's Sir Walter's West Country cousins. His father married three times, you know, and his mother twice, so there's a parcel of them: the Carews and the Gilberts and the Grenvilles and the Cavendishes. Just when the staff begins to fear they have become permanent residents here," she giggled, "Sir Walter gives them something to do elsewhere."

"But you have some who are permanent?"

"Oh yes, and some big ones too," she nodded, counting off on her fingers.

"There's Henry Percy, 'the Wizard Earl' as many call him. He is often here for long periods. And there's Thomas Harriot, the mathematician and astronomer and developer of many of the new navigational ideas used by Sir Walter's sea captains. We call him our own resident wizard. A third would be Robert Hues, another mathematician and Harriot's assistant. Fourth is Walter Warner, who does medical research here. Fifth is Thomas Cavendish, another of the Master's cousins and a sea captain and explorer. He is often in residence. Raleigh's father-in-law, William Sanderson, is number six. He is a successful London merchant and often stays over while he arranges financing for the Master's ventures. Young Richard Hakluyt is always here in the chart room making maps, and old Dr. John Dee stays with us for long periods. Is that seven or eight?"

"You are a fountain of information, little Jeanette. Do you know why Percy and Harriot are known as wizards?"

"Well, Henry Percy is the ninth Earl of Northumberland, you know. He recently inherited one of England's largest fortunes in an odd way. Two years ago, his father, was on the verge of being condemned to die the torturous death of a traitor: hung, drawn, and quartered, that is. But he took his own life with a smuggled pistol during his third stay in the Tower. His conviction was certain, but it had not been pronounced, so his quick suicide prevented the Crown from grabbing his vast estates, and there are plenty of them! It's policy, you know, for the holdings of all condemned traitors to get taken up."

"So Percy inherited it all. Is he Catholic?"

"I don't know about things like that. I know he has no interest in politics. But he needs to be very careful anyway because there are certain people in our government who are suspicious about where the wizard types get their power. Anyone who knows Sir Percy, though, knows he has little interest outside the fields of astronomy, navigation, mathematics, and exploration. Did you know his family has a frightful history of conspiring against the Queen. His uncle was executed for his part in the Northern Rebellion back in 1569. His father was three times involved with plots to take Elizabeth's crown and place it on Mary Queen of Scot's head. He was arrested the third time just two years ago."

"In '71 and '82, I think those other conspiracies were."

"You know as much as I do!" Jennette cried.

"Oh no, pet. Just what I read in books."

"I try to keep my ears open."

"And hard against the nearest pantry wall," William chuckled, "but tell me more about the wizard."

"Well, in addition to all those other interests that Sir Percy shares with my Master, there is also poetry."

"Sir Walter Raleigh is interested in poetry?"

"Oh, yes! And Sir Percy has the best library in the country on those subjects, and my Master uses it often. Sir Walter loves word play and so does the Queen. She should have been here last night, Will, to hear you go on and on."

William blushed. "The Queen is fond of poets?"

"She is a poet herself! And you know how she loves to be amused. I think my Master woos her with verses and schemes just as her other advisers do with other novelties."

William grinned. "As Burghley does with skillful council, Liecester with long-time companionship, Walsingham with current information, Oxford with topical interludes, Hatton with fashion and gossip, and Essex with youthful tilt-yard bravery. But poetry is difficult and Raleigh is very busy. Where does he find the time?"

"They say he 'toils mightily' with his verses as he does with everything else. Also he has made his cousin, soldier-poet Arthur Gorges, an in-house companion and consultant on all poetic matters. That's nine."

"What kind of poetry do they write?"

"I know one pretty little story. A few years ago while Sir Walter was competing for the Queen's attention, he etched on a palace window pane with his diamond ring the words, *'Fain would I climb, yet I fear to fall'.*" [13]

"Did such a line draw her attention?"

"Oh yes, the Queen took another diamond and scratched out her challenge immediately below: *'If thy heart fail thee, climb not at all'.*"

"Not exactly a sonnet," said William. "I thought he might try something a little more complicated just to take advantage of his professional help."

"Complicated? I'll show you complicated." Jeanette drew forth a sheet of foolscap. "They passed this one around. See what you make of it."

William studied the sheet. "Odd arrangement," he muttered. "How is one supposed to read it?"

"Both ways! Up and down and then across. Try it."

Her face,	*Her tongue,*	*Her wit,*
So fair,	*So sweet,*	*So sharp,*
First bent,	*Then drew,*	*Then hit,*
Mine eye,	*Mine ear,*	*My heart,*

Mine eye,	*Mine ear,*	*My heart,*
To like,	*To learn,*	*To love,*
Her face,	*Her tongue,*	*Her wit,*
Doth lead	*Doth teach,*	*Doth move,*
Oh face,	*Oh tongue,*	*Oh wit,*
With frowns,	*With check,*	*With smart,*
Wrong not,	*Vex not,*	*Wound not,*
Mine eye,	*Mine ear,*	*My heart*
Mine eye,	*Mine ear,*	*My heart,*
To learn,	*To know,*	*To fear,*
Her face,	*Her tongue,*	*Her wit,*
Doth lead,	*Doth teach,*	*Doth swear.* [14]

"Clever," William acknowledged, "But perhaps more of a catalogue than a poem."

"Whatever," Jeanette shrugged. "The Queen liked it, and that's all that matters at Durham House. Everybody in this House is here to pleasure the Queen by service to Sir Walter."

William reached to smooth her ruffled feathers. "Tell me about the resident wizard, pet."

Jeanette pouted a bit, allowing William to coax her into response. "Well, like I said, Thomas Harriot is Sir Walter's own personal wizard. He is not here at the moment. He sailed with the Virginia group in April to lead the scientific inquiry into whatever they find in the New World. John White, who is an artist, and Thomas Cavendish, the adventurer, are in the same group."

"But they don't qualify as wizards. Why is that?"

"Harriot is very young, just three years from the university. He instructs the Master and all of his sea-captains in navigation. That is a rare sight, indeed, seeing one so young hold the attention of such gray and grizzled veterans as they assemble in our library. Men of the world do not always pay attention to scholars, you know, but Thomas Harriot has earned their interest, especially with his Three Marriages."

"He has had three wives? And only three years out of university! Where does he find the time, not to mention the energy?"

"Not that kind of marriage," she giggled. "Harriot put together a series of elements which they say has saved sailors and their ships, both."

"Elements?"

"Let me tell you what was explained to me," said Jeanette. "Seamen figure out where they are, something called latitude—"

"Latitude, yes, using the Polar Star at night and sun in the daytime."

'That's it!" cried Jeanette. "You're as smart as any sailor, Will! Anyway there's always been a little difference between the sun charts and the stars, enough to land a ship on the coast of France instead of England. So Harriot produced new charts for Sir Walter that make the sun and star readings agree 'like sister and brother.' That's what the sailors say, but Geoff and me, we—"

"So the marriages are figurative rather than literal."

She nodded. "Harriot did the same thing with navigational tools that were rough and hard to read. He redesigned them and wrote out rules on how to use them right. Got them to agree 'like husband and wife'—though we all know married folks hardly ever agrees." Jeanette giggled again and rubbed her nose in William's neck.

"Ah then, I conclude wizard means genius."

"One more!" cried Jeanette. "Until recently, all the sea charts ignored the way the earth curves so they didn't agree with what the captains' compasses showed. But Harriot developed a method to make those charts and compasses agree 'like master and mate.'"

"Who would have thought that mariners were such a poetic lot?" William mused. "And who would have thought Geoffrey's little sister was such a learned maid?"

"I have my sea captains to thank for lots of what I know. I think of them as my special tutors, and I don't mind a little slap-and-tickle as tuition. As for you, my pretty Will, you teach me lovely thoughts and a nice way to speak."

William reached for Jeanette's lovely plump self.

"No more, my dear," she sighed. "The housekeeper wants us in the line-up by five sharp. Perhaps tonight—if you are still here at Durham House."

Chapter 6:
GRENVILLE RETURNS FROM VIRGINIA

London, the Red Rooster Inn. October 18, 1585:

Malachi entered the taproom, his apprentice at his heels. They slid onto the bench across the table from two men who looked like country vicars stopping in town for lunch.

"Welcome back from Virginia, gentlemen," said Malachi. "We all await the meeting at Durham House, I see." Introductions were exchanged. "We are honored to keep company with such important members of the Roanoke Expedition. Will you be making reports?"

"Oh no," said one. "We carry papers, in case Sir Richard Grenville has need of them." He patted the bulging packet he wore. "Walter here is in charge of Master White's sketches of the natives and their villages, all to be handed over to Master Hukluyt promptly, as it were." He took a moment to gauge the contents of his glass. "Within the hour, I would say."

His companion nodded agreement.

"Ah," breathed Malachi, "you must have great tales to tell from the New World. You were in Virginia, how many months?"

"Two," said the scribe Matthew. "Not counting the many weeks at sea, going and coming. We sailed with Grenville on his flagship, *Tyger*, with Simon Fernandez as both master and pilot. We departed Plymouth in April, five ships and two pinnaces. There are no deep water ports in Virginia, you know, so the pinnaces were needed for shallow waters."

"*Tyger* is a Royal Navy fighting ship," added Walter, "on loan from Her Majesty as part of her investment in the Expedition. She is a 200-tonner, built along sleek lines to make her fast in the chase and nimble in bringing her guns to bear."

"How many people sailed with you?" asked William.

"Of the 500 people in our Expedition, just about half were sailors to man our ships and crew the prizes we captured. We also carried close to 150 soldiers for protection. When nearly 400 of us sailed back to England after our two-month stay, we left behind 108 brave men well organized for the sake of accountability."

"All men?"

"Correct. No women or children or ministers among them. The lack of clergymen was strange in and of itself because one of the strongest justifications for promoting the Expedition was the goal of spreading the True Faith among the idolatrous heathen of the New World. But I guess there is always some slippage in large undertakings."

"I hope they didn't have to take-up too many men off the street for this expedition," Malachi said, "because I remember that Francis Bacon warned in his essay, 'On Plantation': *'It is a shameful and unblessed thing to take the scum of people, and wicked condemned men, to be the people with whom you plant; and not only so, but it spoileth the plantation; for they will ever live like rogues, and not fall to work, but be lazy, and do mischief, and spend victuals, and be quickly weary, and then certify over to their country to the discredit of the plantation.'*" [15]

"They didn't make that particular mistake," Walter laughed, "but they didn't follow Hakluyt's practical advice on choosing colony members either. He advised they take men skilled in practical areas: carpenters, joiners, and millwrights to take advantage of Virginia's timber resources to construct housing for the Virginia colony; gardeners and farmers to feed the group; soldiers to protect them; and craftsmen in minerals and dyes to develop raw materials for industry. He suggested they recruit colony members from respectable people who had lost their money and from imprisoned debtors and ex-soldiers and the children of wandering beggars, and I remember he specified, *'valiant youths rusting and hurtful by lack of employment.'* [16] He also advised that Puritan clergy be sent along to convert the Indians instead of causing so much trouble at home."

"I remember, however," Matthew chuckled, "that last December when the Privy Council set the terms of the Colony Charter for Raleigh, they specifically excluded the imprisoned debtors group from consideration as possible colonists, and I wondered at the time if some of the debts might be owed to the Council members. They also excluded wards and wives and apprentices because the expedition was set up as a semi-military organization financed mostly by subscription in a joint stock company. The 108 who stayed over there are nearly all friends, relatives, and employees of the stock holders, so they didn't have to take up many additional people, but some they did grab don't seem like good candidates for hardship to me, so I imagine they'll be heard from before long."

"Do they get their own land as reward for going over?" William inquired.

"That's the way Gilbert went about the business of raising funds for his proposed expedition. He sold off pieces of land before the expedition ever left England. Gilbert had done a coasting trip along the American shore in 1580—with Fernandez as pilot, by the way—and then he was lost at sea during another trip in 1583. In the interim, however, he sold huge tracts of land to many people, including sales to a large number of Catholics who hoped to escape what they regarded as a repressive regime here in England."

"So Virginia is really a kind of Catholic colony?" William asked.

"Oh, no," Matthew chuckled. "Even before Gilbert died, word came from Spain that English Catholics would be no more welcome in Spain's New World than English heretics, and the absentee landholders all thought better of the adventure and sold out. The 108 presently in Virginia might best be viewed as adventurers for the stockholders and for themselves to profit from whatever is found during a search of the area. The only recorded landholder in Virginia at the moment is Sir Walter Raleigh."

"Just so they followed Hakluyt's advice about plenty of people to grow food," Malachi offered.

"On the contrary, nearly every one of the 108 has a duty which excuses him from manual labor. I saw very little evidence of organized planting and harvesting."

"Actually," said Walter, "the two main goals of the Expedition have little to do with farming. Governor Lane said it best in a letter to Walsingham: *The discovery of a good mine, or a passage to the South Sea, and nothing else can bring this country, to be inhabited by our nation.*" [17]

"'Passage to the South Sea' is what most people call the Northwest Passage to the Pacific Ocean, high atop the continent," Malachi told William in answer to his questioning look. They again gave their attention to Walter.

"To gain either the gold or a new route to the spice trade, the colony was organized in military fashion with the accent on accountability in the important areas. Sir Richard Grenville was the general and commander of the expedition, of course. In addition to being governor, Ralph Lane is also Colonel Lane for military purposes. He is supported by his Irish deputies and by Sir Thomas Cavendish, another Raleigh cousin and chief judicial officer in charge of settling disputes and enforcing discipline in the colony. There is also Philip Amadas, admiral of the Virginia Fleet, along with several army captains, a twelve-member advisory council, an endless number of assistants and subordinates, and a host of specialists."

"Specialists?"

"Two German miners, a surveyor, and a Jewish mineral expert, in addition to our own Thomas Harriot in charge of the scientific inquiry, ably assisted by Master White, who is doing the art work to record people and things which have never been viewed before."

"Tell us more about Sir Richard Grenville. What kind of leader is he?"

"All who know him say he is a commander who takes great pride in completing assignments successfully no matter what opposition presents itself and no matter what resolute steps he must take to crush that opposition. Along with twenty years of military experience against the Turks in Hungary, the Irish in Ireland and the Spanish in general, Grenville spent some years as a Member of Parliament. In short, he has a lot of experience in getting the job done."

"When Sir Walter Raleigh chose his cousin Grenville to command the Virginia Expedition, he did not pick Sir Richard for his table manners, you may be sure," chuckled Matthew. "Although he hasn't had much experience at sea, Grenville is one of those tough-minded military types who has very strong opinions and is very touchy about absolute obedience when he's in charge. I suppose one might call him harsh, especially in dealing with the enemy."

"The enemy. Would that be the Spanish?" asked William.

"Usually the Spanish," Matthew nodded, "but in this particular case it was the native Virginians or 'Indians', as they are being called. Grenville's diplomatic approach for dealing with the natives involved finding people among them who showed disrespect or lack of cooperation and punishing them severely, even disproportionately, as a lesson to everybody else."

Walter cleared his throat delicately. "His people burned an Indian village to the ground and torched their crops as well when they failed to obey his command to return a silver cup that turned up missing on one of our visits."

"Egad," exclaimed William. "And then left Governor Lane and the "brave 108" to soothe the ruffled feathers, I take it."

"Not as big a problem as you might think," said Matthew. "It's a lot like Ireland over there. Very disorganized. If you offend one village, you may be pleasing another one who regards the first as its mortal enemy. The big difference I saw was that the Indians are organized into tribes instead of into clans like the Irish."

"I seem to recall Ralph Lane building forts in Ireland," said Malachi.

"You're right. While he served in Ireland, Lane updated fortifications along the southwest coast of Munster. It was an important post because that south shore has four deep-water ports which could serve Spain well as staging areas for an invasion of England. He was also sheriff of Kerry for a time, but he ruffled local feathers with his endless grousing about his superiors and his constant scheming to gain personal possession of land confiscated from the rebels, so he was sent packing. He took a handful of his Irish deputies with him when he left, and they now serve him in Virginia to enforce discipline if necessary."

"Now that he has the top job as governor," Malachi chuckled, "he'll have trouble irritating his superiors, who will be safely relaxing from their labors an ocean's width away."

Walter glanced furtively at his companion. "I assume it will soon be public knowledge that there were a few clashes between Lane and Grenville."

Alerted, Malachi spoke softly. "I sense there is a story here."

"I myself made a fair copy of his letter to Walsingham in which Governor Lane complained bitterly about Grenville's '*intolerable pride*,'" said Walter. "And at one point during a dispute over unsolicited advice, Grenville threatened Governor Lane with a military trial where death would have been his sentence upon conviction."

"What did they argue about?"

"Well, you may guess that Lane's main interest was in getting the colony established in Roanoke during fair weather, so he was very critical of Grenville's keeping us five weeks in the Indies on our way over. We all assumed we were there for two reasons: to grab a Spanish gold carrier and to lay in supplies. We did manage to capture four small merchant ships during our stay, and we stocked up heavily on fresh stores by trading English cloth for supplies at outlying settlements well away from organized Spanish defenses, but Lane every day became more outspoken about the delay."

"For such a novel venture, how in the world did you decide what supplies to take?" William asked.

"We heeded the thoughtful advice offered by Bacon. '*In a country of plantation,*'" quoted Walter, "*first look about what kind of victual the country yields of itself to hand; as chestnuts, walnuts, pineapples, olives, dates, plums, cherries, wild honey, and the like; and make use of them. Then consider what victual or excellent things there are, which grow speedily, and within a year; as parsnips, carrots, turnips, onions, radish, artichokes, maize, and the like. For wheat, barley, and oats, they ask too much labor; but with pease and beans you may begin, both because they ask less labor, and because they serve for meat as well as for bread. And rice likewise cometh a great increase, and it is a kind of meat. Above all, there ought to be brought store of biscuit, oat-meal, flour, meal, and the like, in the beginning, till bread may be had.*'" [18]

"No real meat?" squeaked William.

Walter smiled. "As I recall, Bacon also wrote; '*For beasts, or birds, take chiefly such as are least subject to diseases, and multiply fastest; as swine, goats, cocks, hens, turkeys, geese, house-doves, and the like*'. As it turned out, most of the food supply we picked up in the Indies was ruined before we could unload at Roanoke Island, thanks to our pilot, Simon Fernandez."

"He lost the Colony's food supply?" gasped William.

"In a very strange way. As you probably know, Fernandez is regarded as the most experienced pilot of the Virginia coast. Just as we were approaching Fernando Harbor, named for him in '80 and '84 during our first two mapping expeditions, he decided to take a shortcut between two of the long sandy islands which bracelet out from the coast. They contain an inland sea which extends for two hundred miles south of Roanoke, and which is known to be too shallow for ships the size of the *Tyger*. Further, he did not take proper soundings, and the *Tyger* was soon grounded on a reef."

More men had gradually drifted into the taproom and taken their places on the benches alongside the table. Now a concerted sound of disbelief escaped them. Murmurs of "sabotage" and "drunkeness" and "Portuguese arrogance" were heard.

"Indeed," nodded Walter. "Before we could pull the *Tyger* off the reef, her hull was breached enough to let seawater spoil all the wheat, flour, and seed we carried in our hold for the Roanoke colony."

"And you mentioned earlier that Grenville is not the forgiving kind."

"Right," said Walter. "He made no secret of his displeasure and hinted strongly at deliberate sabotage. Strangely enough, Lane defended Fernandez, which further inclined the Commander against the Governor. Mostly, the incident was put out of mind during the business of setting up the colony."

"Governor Lane built a fort right off, I hazard to guess," suggested Malachi.

Matthew took up the narrative. "Indeed, he wanted the main work done before most of the manpower, particularly our ships' carpenters, sailed off. We built a seventy-foot square stockade with two easily defended entrances, some inside rooms, and an upstairs loft for valuable supplies and gunpowder. "nice sturdy little fort, cleverly concealed from the prying eyes of Spanish patrol boats which might come snooping along the coast looking for signs of our colony."

"Not as clever as the palisade fortification he had us build on an island just off Hispaniola during our five weeks in the West Indies," Walter insisted. "He used a river for one flank and a lake for the other with the fort itself opening onto the seashore. We could safely run our boats in and out if under attack from the land, though of course, no attack ever came. It was a clever design, nonetheless, and took only eleven days to build."

Matthew grimaced at this interruption. "Meanwhile, at Roanoke, we put in the plants we had brought from the Indies, but few survived the transplant. Grenville led several expeditions into the interior, looking for easy hoards of gold or silver, but none were found. During our eight-week stay, we consumed most of the livestock. Someone estimated the colony had about twenty days of unspoiled foodstuff left when we departed about six weeks ago, so I can only imagine they are living on whatever bounty the Indians can give them right now."

"Fortunately, the Indians are very generous with their food stores," said Walter. "They supplied us daily with venison, fish, corn porridge, pumpkin, various fruits, nuts and water flavored heavily with sassafras and other herbs. Their king, Wingina, had a maize plot planted for our colony and for a time, he supplied our camp daily with several dressed deer and all the rabbits we needed for our table. But 108 long-time guests will be a heavy burden on any granary, and the colony will need to be re-supplied quickly before they become a real threat to the Indians' winter food supply. That possibility might dampen the hospitality of the Indians, and who knows what might then ensue."

"Are these the same natives who had their village burned?"

"No, that was a neighboring tribe down the coast a way. The Roanoke tribe is not very large, numbering just under one-thousand. They have one village located on Roanoke Island three miles off the coast, and another village close at hand on the mainland. The island, by the way, is about ten miles long and two wide. It is heavily wooded, so there was plenty of raw materials for the fort. But if our colonists begin hunting for themselves, one wonders if the game supply will last."

"Do the Indians have guns?"

"No, not guns, but they have bows about half the size of English long bows, and though reduced in capability, they are deadly up to about fifty feet. That's all they need if they're shooting from cover, and they usually are because they're great stalkers of woodland creatures. They are all expert at imitating the sounds of the animals and thereby attracting game to come within reach of their bows. As a matter of fact, I found it quite disconcerting and slightly threatening that they could use animal sounds to communicate with each other over great distances while we were occasionally in the woods together."

"We only contacted a few small coastal tribes during our short stay, and they seemed harmless enough," Matthew said. "They were fascinated and nearly stupefied by our big canoes, our thunder-sticks, and particularly by our sharp-edged metal axes and knives. Up until our visit, they used only stone or bone cutting-edges because the copper they have for ornamentation is too soft to hold a cutting-edge. They saw the superiority of iron immediately. Their chief bought a metal pot cover, attached a cord and hung it over his chest to ward off enemy arrows. He paid twenty deer and buffalo pelts for the cover and then another fifty skins for a copper kettle."

"My word," William chuckled, "I bet he would give a herd of hides for a full suit of armor. His concern for protection makes it sound as if the tribes do some fighting among themselves."

"All the time. Tribes battle over boundary disputes, fishing rights, hunting rights. Some of the villages are surrounded by a wall of sharp stakes with a small entrance, but others are quite open for anybody to walk right through. I suppose it all depends on the neighborhood."

"One upcountry chief named Powhatten is said to command several thousand fighting men. It will be interesting to see how he reacts to the strangers from across the sea. The Spanish set up a Jesuit mission in his territory back in the '70's, and Powhatten is suspected of causing it to disappear without a trace along with eight of the Blackrobes. Should he decide that we are trying to swindle his lands away from him, I suspect he'll be just as reasonable as Tyrone and Desmond have been in Ireland, and we'll end up with savages chucking spears and shooting arrows at us from behind every boulder and tree in Virginia. It will be Ireland all over again."

"Do they have bogs over there?"

"They have swamps which serve them just as well," offered one of the newcomers in military uniform, "and their forests are thick and wild like Kilkenny Woods. The Indians move through the trees like the Kerne and Gallowglass move through the bogs. It's not the proper work of soldiers to hunt for them in tangles and quagmires like that. That's a job for upland huntsmen!" he exclaimed, prompting his listeners to chuckle.

"That's right," said another soldier, "I'd rather fight an honest day's battle against Parma's troops in the Low Countries anytime than trudge endlessly through terrain ideal for ambush in pursuit of a foe who delights in that particular tactic. The Spanish Tercios stand up to you in battle, and at the end of each engagement, you either toast victory or drown defeat after you take muster and count pennants. You can bring your day to a natural conclusion when the campfires are lit and the sentries are set. No real soldier likes all this behind-the-trees stuff, you know."

"They're savages. What more can you say?" said another.

"Even so," said the first soldier, "they better learn to stand up and march properly or somebody will take their lands away from them, and that'll teach them to go skulking around in the woods."

"I keep wondering how the Indian people themselves are reacting to our presence over there," William mused. "It must appear to them that we have come from another planet entirely."

"Too bad you didn't get a chance to talk to the two Roanoke Indians, Manteo and Wanchese, before they went back to Virginia with us in April," said Matthew. "They spent seven months here in England after we brought them home with us last year from our mapping trip with Barlowe and Amadus. The two Indians were exposed to the same experiences in our society as far as I could tell, and since I often do scribe work for Captain Barlowe and Master Hukluyt as well, I was many times in earshot of their different reactions to our culture."

"It doesn't sound as if they agreed," William smiled.

"Diametrically opposed, as a matter of fact. Manteo learned our language very quickly and is fully optimistic about merging our two cultures in such a way that both will benefit. He serves now as the liaison man between the Colonists and the Roanoke Indians, so the colony's success will count heavily on his ability to blend the two. He is such a key figure, the Queen made him an earl to add to his stature, but our titles have little meaning to the Indians—although they probably celebrated his appointment just as they celebrate everything else."

"Celebrate?"

"There seems to be a community conspiracy to seek out things to celebrate: corn harvested, fish caught, battles won, victors returning, visitors arriving from afar, sun shining, rain falling, a full moon—anything. Even their week-long mourning period for the dead ends in dancing and drinking. Indians are always very respectful of death, and they afford it due recognition in their ceremonies. From what I saw, village life suits the Indians very well. Everyone has chores to do. Everyone has a place in civic life, and there is much activity."

"You say Manteo learned our language quickly," William prompted.

"In just a few months. He's a bright young man. During much of his stay here, he was quartered at Durham House under the care of Thomas Harriot, who fascinated entire Indian villages during the '84 trip when he created fire by shining sunlight through a piece of glass, and by producing funny, inverted images from afar through a linked pair of lenses. Manteo worked with Harriot and White on preparing a dictionary of the Roanoke language. They all admitted it was rough going because the Indian language includes a complicated system of grunts which are not mentioned in our grammar. Those three continued that work when we left them in Virginia."

"But Wanchese did not learn the language?" William asked.

"He learned what I would call 'half-English," volunteered another military newcomer. "The half which allowed him to voice complaints, but not the half which allowed him to heed advice."

"But it must be admitted," Matthew added, "that he was the sensation of the social season. Hostesses forgave him everything just to feature a savage from the New World at their table. Me and Steven here escorted him to dinners all over London and watched him steal place settings from every table he attended. He later melted them down for musket balls in a mold he carried with him in expectation of someday getting himself a gun."

"What did he do after stealing them? Eat with his hands?"

"Oh, he never stole his own. Much too clever for that. He always swiped his neighbor's tableware, anything metal, and hostesses learned to ignore the theft and replace the neighbor's utensils with ordinary wooden spoons of the type common in Indian villages, so the neighbor could go on eating as though nothing had happened.

If a fuss was raised over the missing items, Wanchese happily held his own table setting aloft for all to see the evidence of his honesty."

"And this went on for half a year? Didn't anyone discuss the matter with him?"

"That's where the other half of the language comes in or, rather, doesn't come in. The half which would permit us to transmit our complaints and correctives to him just didn't work as well as the half he used. Even after he appeared to pay careful attention to what we said, he more often than not confronted us with an uncomprehending shrug and went about his business. During his stay, he showed a very selective understanding of our language and grew more and more embittered about the co-mingling of our cultures while Manteo became more and more enthusiastic about the process."

"For some reason," Steven offered, "Wanchese was permitted to visit Bill Riley just before we hanged that notable Irish rebel, and I'm afraid he came away with a jaundiced view of the English from that visit."

"Do your Wanchese imitation," Brian urged Steven. "You've got a brand new audience here. Don't deprive them of the inter-cultural experience."

Steven grinned, removed his hat and tousled his hair into disarray. He opened his doublet to his chest and growled, "Irish good fun. Kill English."

"See here now," said Brian, jumping into his role. "I don't know if that's the proper attitude to hold toward your host nation. You are, after all, a guest of the English government."

Steven-as-Wanchese nodded "English march, shoot, steal corn. No damn good."

"If any corn was taken, it was paid for. I can assure you of that."

Wanchese made a circle with his left thumb and forefinger and plunged his right index finger in and out. "English don't bring women, don't take women. Bad medicine. Leave women out of welcome."

"You're right about that, you devil you," Brian laughed. "But Grenville made it clear to all of us that the punishment would be swift and severe for anybody who messed with the Indian women. We believed him."

"English call Wanchese's people 'savages'."

"Just a figure of speech, I assure you. No pejorative intent. I would characterize our efforts, really, as more of a clumsy attempt to define things in terms we can comprehend. Not personal at all."

"Uncivilized savages."

"Perhaps at times some of the men did go too far, but I'm sure they only meant it as a hearty, manly camaraderie rather than as an overt insult."

A ripple of laughter ran through the audience.

"Irish smart. Hide in bogs. Shoot English."

"That hasn't worked any too well for the Irish, or did your mentor, Mr. Riley, fail to mention that before we hanged him? Apart from all other considerations, of course, you have no bogs in Virginia that we were able to locate."

"Have swamps and woods. Same thing. Hide good."

"But your skimpy bows and arrows don't stand a chance against our musket fire. Each of our guns could kill two or three of you as you advanced into bow-and-arrow range, so you better do your best to stay on our good side."

Wanchese smiled broadly. "Not advance. Irish say spring on English at fords and crossings and passes and hillsides. Kill many. Don't let English get in squares. Very tough in squares, Irish say."

"I'll tell you this," Brian gritted. "We didn't hang that damn Riley one minute too soon. I lost friends in Ireland to just such tactics, so I'll never understand why they let you talk to that murderous bastard to begin with. Don't forget, however, no matter what he told you, our muskets balls will cut you down wherever they strike you, and your stone arrowheads will not pierce our armor, so you have lost as soon as you begin."

"English guns even shoot friendly Indians."

"Hold on now," Brian demanded. "That was an accident as you well know."

William was startled. "Did they really shoot friendly Indians?"

"Only by accident. We did attempt to punish an unfriendly village only to find later that the inhabitants had fled upon our approach."

"What about the friendlies?"

"When our enemies fled, some of the Roanokes had gone in to plunder the empty village. We didn't know at the time they were the friendlies."

"But they didn't threaten you?"

"You might be surprised to learn how little that matters when a concerted military operation is under way. We were there to punish, so we did punish."

"The wrong people."

"As it turned out, yes, the wrong people, but they shouldn't have been there in the first place."

"If English kill friends," Wanchese persisted, "they soon have no friends."

"Lane went to the trouble of apologizing, and I thought it a very sincere apology, well-stated. After all, that deep bronze skin color seems to be shared by all the Virginia natives we encountered. Very hard to tell one from the other."

"You killed only fishermen," Wanchese explained. "You'll see difference when you shoot Powhatten's braves."

"I know you have a right to be angry, Wanchese, because some of your people were killed accidentally, but don't let that anger cloud your judgment. On one of our inland trips, we were treated to a display that Menatonon's braves put on for us, and as a military man I must confess I was mighty impressed. Good God! Eight hundred naked Indian savages dancing and stamping the ground in unison while shaking their spears and quivers and everything else at us was enough to make even military men have trouble swallowing the dinner they had served us, but make no mistake about it. Their weapons would be no match at all against our muskets. Each of our guns would kill three of them before they got close enough to use their bows."

"Take soldier two of your minutes to reload," Wanchese smiled. "Plenty time for spears and arrows to find holes in English armor."

"I know you don't mean to, you red scalawag," Brian laughed, "but you may be making a great argument for sending pike men along with the next colony to protect the musketeers. I suspect Walsingham will be very interested in such insight, so you may have done England a valuable service despite yourself."

"Indian always end up used," Wanchese grumped.

"Don't despair," Brian advised. "There is still plenty of joy in the world to enjoy. Tell me, what is that wonderfully pungent aroma you carry with you, Master Wanchese?"

"Bear grease. Good medicine. Good man smell. Rancid best. Enemy know Wanchese is here."

"But at dinner parties?"

"Use fresh bear grease for dinner parties and for bed-fun with women."

"Are you boasting, my good fellow?"

"Not boast. English women very friendly. Make good bed-fun. Line up for turn with Wanchese. Nobel ladies too. Women say bear grease keep away fleas." He smiled and clasped his hands together in warm memory.

"It becomes abundantly clear that you have learned to take full advantage of our hospitality," Brian said stiffly. "It is a bit of a shame that our generosity has not generated a morsel of gratitude in your savage soul, Mr. Wanchese, and you continue to speak of us as your enemy even as we continue to shelter and feed you."

Wanchese was silent for a moment, then spoke. "I like white man," he explained without preface. "White man think quick and shoot guns. When mirror missing, he come quick and shoot guns. When cup missing, he come quick and burn village. Red man not think so quick. Red man dance and drum and chant, but guns not chant or dance. Wanchese make friends with quick thinkers. He likes white man. I teach him to drink smoke deep. Keep him plenty healthy. Who has tobacco for Wanchese?"

"Come now, Wanchese, you've got to stop caging and bumming your way through society," Brian admonished. "It's time you started worrying about your future. What happens to you when you wear out your welcome by your curious behavior?"

No worry. Queen good friend," Wanchese assured him. "Make Wanchese into Earl. Earls eat good."

The audience laughed.

"You're probably right about that," Brian admitted. "Political reality rears its urgent head once more. Whether anybody likes it or not, when you return to Virginia, you will become a translator of our culture to your tribesmen and to any of your neighbors with whom you are not warring at that moment. Thousands may end up hearing your impressions of us, and Elizabeth would just as soon your report be favorable, so it is possible she may appoint you as an emissary of some sort with an impressive title and a pleasant pension in order to bend your opinion a bit in our favor."

"Pension good," Wanchese grunted. "Wanchese get old some day."

"Pensions do work well sometimes in these arrangements," Brian said.

"Raleigh insists that's the strategy which England has used most successfully in governing the Irish. Pull all the clan chiefs over to England, cut them a piece of the pie by granting them a bit of land and a title carrying a small pension to give them clout, and send them home again to protect the Queen's best interests."

"Good policy," Wanchese nodded with a grin. "Fixed Irish problem, you bet."

"Not quite," Brian admitted slowly and reluctantly. "Its success has been somewhat spasmodic, I'm afraid, because many Irish clan chiefs have the same half-English handicap that afflicts you, Wanchese."

"And even the same uncomprehending shrug," added one of the soldiers.

"Like peas in a pod."

"What you expect from primitive savages?" Wanchese grinned and ended his performance by bowing to the audience who clapped their approval.

"First rate entertainment," Malachi commented and turned to William, "You must remember that exchange to perform for your Apprentice Association. You'll make a great Indian."

"Can I tell them everything?"

"Leave out the bitterness between the leaders. Let's not disillusion the youngsters too soon."

"voice of inquiry came from another table. "You who crewed with Grenville to Virginia, have you got your split yet?"

"Soon," Matthew assured him. "Grenville and Raleigh just got back to London after a personal appraisal of the big prize, the *Santa Maria*. The Admiralty Office has set the value of her cargo at £50,000. Mostly sugar, but also some ginger, cochineal, and calf-hides. Enough, anyway, to assure all crewmen a fat purse for a short time."

"And well deserved it is too," Walter testified, "Not only for the danger we faced but also for the worry we suffered when it looked for a while that Grenville wouldn't get the Spanish prize home at all. We brought *Tyger* back to England twelve days before Grenville showed up with the *Santa Maria*. Long enough for a man to have dark thoughts about the reward he has coming for his dangerous service."

"Why such a lag?" William asked. "They're both sailboats."

"There are significant differences which clarify why it took him so much longer," Walter explained. "Very little comparison in sailing ability between our sleek 200-ton *Tyger* and the captured Spanish prize. "The *Santa Maria* is a big, lumbering, unarmed and heavily-laden 300-tonner, built for cargo and not for speed. She was a straggler from a larger group when we took her, so we knew to begin with that she was not a great sailor."

"Unarmed, you say?"

"Right. Strictly commercial. She very sensibly surrendered as soon as *Tyger* opened her gunports. Grenville decided to sail the captured ship home himself with a prize crew. He kept half the Spanish contingent on board to run the ship, and we took the rest home with us on the *Tyger*. We ran back to England just ahead of some nasty weather, but the *Santa Maria* was still getting organized when storms parted us off Bermuda. Not too surprising that they were so far behind because they had to come through some rough weather to get home at all. What do you imagine our cut will come to, Matthew?"

"Pretty complicated," Matthew said. "The Admiralty will take their ten percent of the £50,000, of course, and the shareholders and ship owners will each take a third of the remaining £45,000, so the 500 expedition members will split up the last £15,000."

"How about the 108 people we left in Virginia? Do they get a full share?"

Matthew nodded. "I would think they get a full share of the profit we picked up on the way over there back in April. You remember we grabbed those four small prizes during our stay in the Indies, so the final reckoning will have to include whatever profit we got from selling off those captive ships and also the bit of ransom we got from our few wealthy prisoners. But the colony people may not have a claim on the *Santa Maria* cargo since they weren't aboard when we captured her."

"I dislike taking money from my own purse," said Walter, "but perhaps it should be mentioned that some of the major stock holders weren't present either at the moment of capture. I don't remember seeing Burghley or Walsingham in the boarding party—or the Queen either, for that matter."

"You may be right," Matthew shrugged. "The 108 are still employees of the Joint Stock Company which financed the expedition, so the Admiralty Court may have to decide what kind of split would be fair."

"You didn't mention any silver or gold or jewels from the prize cargo," Malachi jibbed. "You're not hiding anything, are you, Matthew?"

The mariners all laughed. "I hope we are," Matthew said. "I hope there are even more valuables hidden aboard our prize, but Grenville immediately impounded whatever real treasure there was, and we had no sight of it. I can only imagine he reported it rightly to the Admiralty, and we will get our fair share in the final split."

"What might that come to?"

"Let me see now," Matthew paused to consider. "If you took the worst case and divided 500 people into £15,000., we would all come out with about thirty pounds each. Six year's pay for half a year's work. Not bad at all. So good in fact, that out of respect for the fact that newly acquired wealth is expected to be squandered quickly, I should like to propose that the next round of drinks for such an appreciative audience shall be out of the benevolence of my newly rich shipmate, Walter, the peerless scribe!"

The audience greeted the announcement with enthusiastic applause, while Walter went wide-eyed with shock.

Chapter 7:
A VISIT WITH FRANCIS BACON

At the Inn across from Bacon's apartments, January 10, 1586:

"Malachi said you are soon to visit the Francis Bacon household," said the old scribe, Gary, to William over his tankard. "I spend a great deal of time over there, you know."

"Really?" said William. "In what capacity?"

"I'm only a scribe for Francis Bacon's amanuensis, you understand, but they prefer I do the fair-copies right on the premises, so I'm often there."

"Francis Bacon keeps careful track of his own writings, does he?"

"I'll say he does!" Gary exclaimed. "Very careful indeed. Often sends off fair-copies of his most recent writing to every stationer in London. He is unbelievably prolific. I don't have any idea when the man sleeps. A lot of his science writing is not even published yet, but he's afraid it might get lost in the hustle and bustle of creating new stuff all the time, so he makes sure that copies are spread around for posterity. That's where I come in, but the truth is I'm so busy doing copies, that I have little enough time for my own modest pastimes." He paused to sip from his tankard. "Malachi tells me you do good copy. If you're looking for some part-time work, I wouldn't mind letting out some of this straight copy work for scale, less 20 percent."

"Is that standard?"

"Not really," Gary confessed with a chuckle. "I'd be gouging you about 5% for the uplift value you would receive personally in transcribing such lofty thoughts."

"And cheap at the price, I imagine you'll end up telling me." William smiled. "I don't know yet what Malachi has in mind for me, so I'll have to wait to see if I'm available. What kind of person is Francis Bacon, anyway?"

"A brilliant man, no doubt about it," said Gary, "but he has his odd twists and turns like the rest of us."

"Like what?"

"For one thing, he takes a childish delight from incorporating secret codes, anagrams, and the like into his writings. He chuckles out loud as he does it. He swears that if any future rascal of a writer is rude enough to claim authorship for the works of Francis Bacon, he will be surprised to find there are enough clues embedded in the work itself to indicate the true author despite the faulty credit line."

"He's afraid someone will steal his work?"

"Don't act surprised. There are always ambitious villains lurking about—often non-university types like yourself—just waiting to steal from the few creative people England is blessed with. Master Bacon intends, however, to thwart such persons by filling his writing with cryptology enough to keep scholars contending for centuries about credit for certain works. Such scholastic dispute in itself—as Master Bacon sometimes notes gleefully—is a special kind of immortality."

"He seeks immortality then. I wonder what he would like to be remembered for?" William mused.

The old man thought for a moment. "His mind is divided, I think. He has moments when he is quite envious of the fame and adulation heaped on the likes of Thomas Kyd simply because Kyd is not a gentleman and is therefore free to accept public recognition as the author of a successful stage play. There are sometimes rumors afloat in the Bacon household—often among his retainers, late at night, after drink has been taken—that the author taking the bows is not the writer who dipped the quill. But the truth of the matter is that Francis Bacon's mind is far too lofty to be caught up in mere entertainment for very long. He seeks a grander scale by far."

"Did you say mere entertainment?" William frowned. "Perhaps you'd care to point out a 'grander scale', as you call it."

"I'd say he yearns to be known as the man who turned the world's educational process on its ear and instituted a pragmatic approach to scientific inquiry. I imagine he could desire no finer distinction than being known as the man responsible for convincing society that investigation into the nature of things should not be limited to notes from the reading room nor remarks from the pulpit, but, rather, should be pursued and gathered in fields and laboratories by trained and dedicated observers."

"A pragmatic approach to scientific inquiry, eh?" said William. "But he envies Kyd his public recognition, you say. Not a man to hide his light from this world, I'd imagine, which makes him an energetic and demanding master."

Gary shrugged. "The Bacon family is an excellent example of jumped-up gentry, which might make a man behave like he was dancing on hot coals. You've heard of jumped-up gentry, ain't you?"

"The term sounds familiar. Doesn't it refer to members of the working classes becoming gentlemen through the purchase of confiscated papal lands during the reign of King Henry VIII?

"You've got it. Francis Bacon's old grandfather was a prosperous yeoman, who bought land, gained office, and sent his son Nicholas to school. Nicholas was Francis' father, who brokered his own father's simple beginnings into the office of Lord Keeper of the Seal and the owner of York House—a magnificent estate in London—plus a country estate at Goremsbury, where he retained seventy servants and paid tax on forty-seven hearths. I'd say that was jumping-up in anybody's lexicon."

"It's clear that choosing a frugal grandfather to found the family fortune is the real key to wealth and splendor," William chuckled.

"Well," continued Gary, "Francis and his brother Anthony, despite their great intelligence, seem ill-tuned to keep the family in the upper brackets, unlike their father Nicholas who knew well enough how to please the Queen and dicker in the power game. He knew bargains must be struck and deference shown to other power-brokers in the kingdom."

"Things have changed a great deal in Elizabeth's reign, I guess."

"They have, indeed. I was born about the same time as the Queen and have seen those changes up close. Before Henry sold the monastic estates, we had but three significant voices in the realm: the Church, the nobility, and the monarchy—and London Town, too, I guess, if we really want to talk power, but I'll leave them out since their influence was and is mostly local. But now, for the first time in hundreds of years we have a fourth player demanding to be heard."

"The blossoming gentry," William filled in.

"Just so. Before the land sale, we had only a few hundred merchants, lawyers, and tradesmen who had jumped up their families to gentry status. Now they have been joined by yeomen who got in on the come-who-may sale, and the landowner class has opened up like a freshly plowed field. The sheer number of new gentry has forced a change in the old order of things."

"I can see that," nodded William. "The power of the Catholic Church is out, and the protestant Church of England is still shaky."

"Right enough, but it's the noble houses that are being elbowed aside by the new players in the old power game. Even the Queen contributes to that trend by appointing many gentry to high public office with a consequent lessening of appointments for the nobility. Old Nicholas Bacon was the personification of that trend. The Queen obviously prefers practical politicians, whose families remember hard times from the recent past."

"Compliant people who are afraid of losing their jobs, you mean?"

Gary chuckled. "Be careful. It ages a man terribly to get cynical at too young an age. Let's say rather that such people are simply more flexible in government than are the men raised in wealth and splendor, whose opinions have been catered to since birth. She likes her politicians career-minded so they have something to lose if they go against her wishes. For most of her reign, those gentry members elected or appointed to office were so overwhelmed by their own good fortune that they would have presumed it arrogance to ask for anything more, so, generally, they have been very happy in the past to approve whatever the front row suggested."

"Pretty cozy for the Queen's policies, I imagine."

"Right," Gary nodded. "Apart from the upstart Puritans—who, God knows, are impossible to please—most of the Members of Parliament over the years have been thrilled to be in the same room with such notables of the realm as the Sidneys, Leicesters, Hattons, Mildmays, and Knollys. Most of those MP's lived happy lives in service to their beloved Queen, but all of that has changed now. The Commons which Elizabeth inherited with her crown in 1558 were the first of the jump-up group—the men who had actually made the leap—or their sons. The Bacon family again. But the grandsons are appearing today, and they are all merchants or lawyers—men not so star-struck as were their fathers by the nobles among them." The old man scratched his head in thought. "Aye, an odd assortment of gentlemen make up our Commons these days: merchants, lawyers, yeomen, Puritans, men who know a good deal more about merchandise, manors, manure, and morality than they do about running a government."

"Does this mean they might rule in favor of the English people generally rather than favoring the nobility?"

"Some of that undoubtedly occurs incidentally, but the bigger truth is that these new men know very well how to strike bargains and wring profits. Their approval of Elizabeth's subsidies will not come as smoothly in the future as they have in the past. There is a growing awareness, particularly on the part of the merchants that they can trade with the Queen by giving their approval to her subsidy requests in exchange for tax breaks and tariff controls from which they hope to profit. As a matter of fact, I foresee this country's whole financial chain of command getting a severe shaking by future commercial interests."

"Egad, the English are growing to be like the Dutch, a nation of profiteers."

"You're right there!" snickered Gary. "The merchants are mad as hornets over the franchises that Elizabeth has granted to certain of her favorites. They see a lot of national income going into the pockets of a fortunate few, and they have cultivated an appetite for a piece of that profit-pie."

"Let me guess two of those favorites: Raleigh, for one, and for the other, I think, Leicester."

Dennis sighed. "It's no secret. Raleigh has the import taxes due on all sweet wines brought into England, a considerable sum that goes directly into his pocket. Leicester has a long-standing patent on the sale of sweet wines throughout the country, and the revenue from that, so they say, pays for his city and country estates, his civil and military duties, and his own special secret service."

"Zounds, to think we English drink so much sweet wine!"

"There's monopolies on everything we trade: cloth, coal, iron, whale oil and leather, salt-petre, lead, pots and brushes, salt and vinegar, playing-cards and powder, too many to mention, but you can see why the merchants want in on those deals. The Commons is growing from timidity to truculence in dealing with the Crown, and the voice of the nobles continues to recede as they sell off their estates to the hustling gentry. So what presently appears to be a quick change in the makeup of the Commons has been coming for a long time."

"Are there hard feelings on the part of the nobles?" William asked. "How are they taking the come-down?"

"I remember that Master Bacon comes straight to the point on that particular issue just as he does on so many others—and don't forget he is speaking from personal experience—when he says: *'Men of noble birth are noted to be envious towards new men when they rise, for the distance is altered; and it is like a deceit of the eye, that when others come on they think themselves go back.'* [19]

"I suppose he's right about that. It all depends on how you look at it."

"But it's not a deceit of the eye at all," Gary insisted. "The nobles really are being pushed back."

"Outvoted, from what you've said. And the Puritans are mostly from the new gentry, aren't they? That's a lot of change, indeed. And I've been told the Queen dislikes change of any kind."

"Well, in this case, it's small wonder she resists the change. She enjoyed a twenty-year honeymoon with the Commons following her crowning. Now she must put up with carping and grousing mostly from the growing number of self-righteous Puritans, who are not at all hesitant to offer the Queen advice and correction."

"Ah, well," laughed William confidently, "some nobility may be crowded out, but I'll wager Queen Bess will never give way."

Malachi greeted them both and sent Gary off to make the usual kitchen-door arrangement for their visit.

"The way we keep track of Anthony Bacon," Malachi said to William as they waited, "is through his younger brother Francis. Whenever I must contact Tony on the Continent, I start by examining the mail Francis has received from him."

"With permission?"

"Oh yes. This is all aboveboard on our part, so don't muddy it up with any of your customary shenanigans. Francis knows all about our connection with his brother and is pleased to serve as intermediary for us, but, for legal reasons, he must remain completely isolated from our information gathering and not be involved in any way. He must even be supplied with a witness who can attest to his presence elsewhere when the information is gathered just in case such testimony is ever needed at future legal proceedings. The letters, therefore, will be left lying about in the library or other places where I'm likely to 'stumble' across them, so I'll need you to distract our host at times while I do the searching and reading."

"Distract him how?"

"His busy mind sometimes forgets our arrangement, so just keep him interested with your chatter. Ask questions. But be careful. He's very persuasive, so don't agree with him too easily. Just act thick-headed as you sometimes do and keep him preoccupied."

"What questions should I ask?"

"Almost any topic will keep him going. We may be with Bacon for a few days awaiting word from the Continent on the best time and place to meet with his brother. Special pains are necessary for contacting Tony because he does dangerous work on the Continent and could easily be betrayed by clumsy inquiries from suspicious strangers. If it turns out we are to meet him at Rheims, I'll go as the faithful servant of a young, discontented Catholic gentleman, who is visiting Rheims for the first time to consider training as a traitor."

"That's me!" William was clearly overjoyed. "I'll go back to being Master William, and I'll get to wear the gentleman's outfit again!"

"No way out of it," Malachi shook his head, "but never forget there is no room for buffoonery when you are serving one of our top agents in Europe. Tony has spent eight years—and most of his estate—cultivating the young Englishmen at Rheims socially so he will be able to identify any who dare come to England as seminarians in the future."

"Would he do that? Put the finger on his friends?"

"When the time comes, who knows?" Malachi shrugged. "Some do and some don't. Tony doesn't spend all his time at Rheims, however. We might have to meet him at the court of King Henry of Navarre, the Huguenot leader and heir-apparent to the French throne. They have visited together socially since Navarre pulled Tony out of a legal scrape a few years ago, and Navarre is very candid with Tony about Protestant intentions in France. We might even have to contact him at Montaigne's place in Bordeaux, where he sometimes visits. Tony is also on excellent terms with Theodore Beza, who dedicated his book, *Meditations,* to Tony's mother, Lady Bacon."

"Am I supposed to know who Theodore Beza is?"

"He is one of the chief architects of Protestant theology. He was a strong influence on John Calvin himself, who, incidentally, died in Beza's arms back in 1564."

"Sounds like an unhealthy influence to me," William snickered.

"Give over, for God's sake!" Malachi snorted. "We're on business here. Once we get word from the Continent, we'll cross over and try to convince Tony to remove himself from all those seditious foreign influences," Malachi chuckled softly, "and to heed the summons of the Queen to return to England as a stout and forthright Anglican."

"But why shouldn't he stay in place if he is so valuable?"

"Elizabeth has suspended his license to stay abroad," said Malachi. "She must want to talk to him privately. God knows why."

"Does the Queen know how important it is that he remain on-station?"

"That may be the thorny part of this situation. I don't think she'd call him home if she knew he was supplying the excellent intelligence I've personally carried back from him over the years."

"How could she not know?"

"Part of the process," Malachi explained. "After I contact Tony, I give the information to Walsingham, and he organizes it for Burghley, who summarizes it for the Queen. There is a deliberate effort made to hide the identity of our sources all the way down the line—for their own protection, you understand—so he would not, ordinarily, be revealed to her, but God knows it's virtually impossible to keep anything from the queen."

"But still, she may not know at all what Anthony has contributed?"

Malachi shrugged. "I'm afraid that's what it comes down to. In sending for Tony, Elizabeth is probably reacting to the concern which several Council members have expressed that Anthony has been so long among the Catholics at Rheims, that he may have crossed over, and, of course, she is reacting also to the worries of Lady Bacon."

"How does the Queen know how the mother feels?"

"Lady Bacon speaks five languages, often and loudly. There is no possibility of escaping her thoughts. When aroused, she speaks her mind explicitly in the same kind of rough, shocking language the Queen sometimes uses when she is offended enough to broadcast her displeasure to all within earshot. Lady Bacon's letters to her sons are full of Puritanical dictums to live better lives, to cultivate better health habits, to abandon their present friends and attendants, and to rapidly mature to financial responsibility. She is what one might call a 'rabid gospeleer'."

"Or another might call her 'any old mother'," William chuckled. "Is she right about the Bacon's being financially irresponsible, or is that just a parental excess?"

"The office of Lord Keeper of the Seal provided their father with a fortune, so they grew up with a good deal of money. As the eldest son, Anthony inherited extensive estates, which he has gradually sold off over the years to sustain himself on the Continent. As the youngest child of eight offspring, Francis was left with very little in his terms: barely £300 per annum. More than adequate for most of us, but not nearly enough to finance an ambitious nobleman who must maintain the illusion of wealth until a grateful Queen someday solidifies that illusion by appointing him to high office. It's a tight-rope act all the way. I know Anthony has just about run out of lands to sell, and Francis always has impatient creditors at his back door, so they would indeed appear irresponsible in their mother's eyes."

"But surely Francis has good prospects?"

"They appear excellent, but there is a fly in the ointment. His uncle, Lord Burghley, the Royal Treasurer, already has a strong faction at court, so he is slow to appoint anybody who might later prove competition for his son Robert."

"The hunchback?"

"Robert may not rise to full height physically," Malachi reproved, "but many feel his mind reaches the same altitude as his father's in close thinking. At the moment, Burghley is grooming Robert to succeed him as advisor to the Queen and seems reluctant to introduce another promising candidate in the person of his nephew Francis. I don't know that Burghley will advance either of the Bacon boys at the moment, but the Queen is nevertheless quite aware of them. She already has a nickname for Francis—usually a good sign in measuring the Queen's favor—but, in this case, the honor may be doubted."

"What nickname is that?"

"She calls him 'Watch-candle' because his intensity never dims."

"What's wrong with that?"

"She often speaks of the Puritans' burning intensely too, so the association may be a sorry one. Ordinarily, the Queen admires intensity, but only in the desire to serve her as obediently as possible, and I know that Francis, as a member of Commons, has lately petitioned her to use less severity in dealing with the English Catholics even though he himself is an Anglican. I wouldn't be surprised if the Queen regarded his entreaty as offensive because it proposes to weaken policies which she has spent many years setting in place. Elizabeth does not expect to be offended and can be quite unforgiving if she decides that certain brash young members of Parliament have no business telling her how to be Queen. I think Francis really rolled the dice as far as his career is concerned when he sent her that petition, so his prospects hinge entirely on her reaction."

"But he would have backed up his request with an impressive argument, wouldn't he?"

Malachi laughed. "Indeed he would. The young man is adjudged brilliant by all who encounter him. He can formulate the best arguments in the world from any position, but the Queen admires such ability, again, only when it is used to defend her policies rather than to call them into question."

"A monarch's prerogative, I guess."

"Francis sincerely wishes to serve the Queen and the realm with his energies, I think, and also to enhance his financial position within our society."

"But?"

"He is known as an unrelenting seeker of truth, and that avid pursuit sometimes gets in the way of running a government. The art of governing is the art of compromise, and compromise sometimes calls for squinting a little when confronting truth. I'm afraid Francis has very little squint in him and no compromise at all. He must learn to be more practical if he is to serve the Queen."

"A yes-man, in short?"

Malachi shrugged. "There is no rising in the realm without it, or—please take note—in my personal service either. You might be surprised to learn how little gets done in this world without having some of what you call 'yes-men' on board to follow orders without question. But now to business. We'll meet with Francis in a few minutes, and I want you to keep quiet while I repay his hospitality by recounting to him the gossip from the French Court. He delights in the stories I bring him because, as a lad of fourteen, he spent two years in Paris as an aide to our Ambassador and still knows everybody over there"

"May I ask questions if something confuses me?"

"Moderately, yes, especially do so to keep him busy when I leave the room. It's important legally that he not wander around and discover me rummaging through his correspondence. But keep the questions light because he stutters if he gets worked up. He also is most comfortable looking up while he is speaking to you, so if you manage to draw his gaze down to confront you, please remember to back off because that's a sure sign he is about to start stuttering."

"He gazes up to heaven, you mean? Indoors?"

"Right. He has the quickest, most darting eyes I've ever seen. I've heard people liken them to the eyes of a viper. His direct gaze can be very intimidating. Have you ever gazed into the eyes of a viper?"

"Not that I remember."

"He also speaks mostly in aphorisms."

"He does what?"

"Speaks in aphorisms—short, pithy sayings full of wisdom and guidance."

"Guidance?"

"He gets that from his mother. Still, the aphorism is a difficult form of expression, calling as it does for clear thought and careful structuring of sentences, but he is excellent at it. He is '*felicitous therein*,' to use his own words. His brain seems to function best at that very precise, very demanding, very moralizing form. If any of his utterances catch your ear, by all means write them down, and you'll not only augment your wisdom but also add a bit of style to your discourse."

"I look forward to the very possibility of improvement," William said. "When do we eat?"

"Up and away now," Malachi commanded. "The door is open."

Gary beckoned them through the door and led them along a hall into a small library. "Master Bacon will be with you in a moment," he assured them as he left.

"I suspect lunch is still a long way off at this end of the food chain," observed William. "Perhaps I better take a stroll toward the kitchen to check—"

"We'll wait for our host to come down, if you don't mind," Malachi said. "And quit fiddling with the things on that desk."

"No problem," William assured him. "Here's an odd scrap on the floor. *"Reading maketh a full man, conference a ready man and writing 'a' exact man."* [20] William glanced up with a puzzled look.

"Yes," said Francis Bacon as he entered. He was quite young, William noted, perhaps a few years older than himself, and very slender. "Greetings to all. You've just read one of my early, unfinished notations, but I was never quite pleased with it. My ear tells me there is a clinker in there somewhere, and I won't rest until I root it out."

"May I make an obvious suggestion?" William offered.

"No! No!" Bacon thrust his hand, palm vertical, between them as though to ward off intruders. "Please don't. After all, *'I have taken all knowledge to be my province'*. It wouldn't be a pure experience if I needed prompting from the wings. I'll get it eventually, don't worry, *'being gifted by nature with desire to seek, patience to doubt, fondness to meditate, slowness to assert, rediness to consider, carefullness to dispose and set in order'*." [21]

"A veritable Pandora's basket of gifts," William observed.

"I can see," Malachi chuckled, "you don't need any help in setting out your best wares."

"God knows I'll be the first to admit that such a vaunt seems boastful," Bacon acknowledged, "but because of my commitment to knowledge, I accept certain moral obligations from which I must not flinch."

"Ambition should be made of stern stuff," William agreed.

"But the battle is not for me personally, so much as it is for all mankind," Bacon declared. "We must re-think everything."

"How do you mean re-think?"

"Um, let us take as an example the areas of inquiry which, until the middle of this century, had to be approved by the Church. Men of science did not get that approval automatically, by any means, for it was reserved for those studies which furthered the interests of the Roman Church. That rigid screening-process left many fascinating areas of investigation virtually untouched, as you can well imagine."

"It boggles the mind," William nodded.

"Not only were areas unexamined but methods as well. For the last ten centuries, one thousand years—most scientific inquiry has been done by scholars who ramble through ancient books, take copious notes, and then re-juggle the conclusions of the earlier works to establish new findings. Very few scholars ever look at anything first-hand. We must learn to position ourselves so we may watch an ant-hill from a distance of only a few feet rather than from the distant vantage point of dusty rooms filled with dry pages. We must observe how they organize their colony, who works, who guards, who copulates, who nourishes."

"How close did you say?"

"As close as possible."

"Well, of course," William said, "for you to specify such a specific area of study right off the bat like that is impressive, indeed, but any possible follower of your approach would require greater guidance before tackling something other than rustic anthills. What advice, if any, do you have for him?"

Bacon shrugged. "*Inquire into the length and shortness of life in animals, with the proper circumstances which seem to contribute to them...Inquire into the length and shortness of men's lives according to the times, countries, climates and places in which they were born and lived... and according to their parentage and family...their food, diet, manner of living, exercise and the like, with regard to the air in which they live and dwell; Inquire carefully into the differences of the state and faculty of the body in youth and old age; and see whether there be anything that remains unimpaired in old age.*" [22]

"That sounds like a very Pragmatic Approach to Scientific Enquiry," Malachi observed. "Has anyone taken you up on it?"

"A few, but not, I think, on my advice so much as on their own perception. One is my physician, William Harvey, who is studying the human blood system in just such a manner. I understand he uses cadavers—"

"Oh dear," William shuddered and hastily changed the subject. "Malachi has told me, Sir Francis, that you come from a family of very accomplished people. Your late father was Lord Chancellor of the Realm—or something like that—and your mother is a prominent linguist who translates both Latin and Greek books into readable English, while you yourself have already printed a volume of your own personal writings. Am I right?" William asked.

"Yes, apart from slightly misplacing my father in the Royal household, you have summarized correctly, my friend, even if your purpose is somewhat obscure."

"Let's not get caught up in quibbles, sir," William advised, smiling, "or you'll miss the main thrust of my inquiry."

"Which is?" Bacon asked patiently.

"Such a life as yours—being raised among members of the Royal Court as you were—would be a well recorded existence if ever there was one. There are records, letters, and reports which pretty well indicate where you were and what you were up to throughout your life. You are, by the accident of your noble birth, an important personage. Right?"

Francis Bacon could not help smiling. "Granted, I have enjoyed certain advantages in this life, but I like to think that on my own initiative—"

"I mean, there is very little possibility of future scholars ever confusing your dramatic work with the work of somebody else. Am I correct?"

Bacon thought for a moment. "Essentially that is true, but I have also taken certain precautionary measures on my own. I realized early on that the theatrical community itself makes its living from the creation of images and illusions, so its members are quite at home with the concept of fudging things a bit. They wouldn't blink an eye at assigning a false name to a work of art. To add to the confusion, authors who happen to be noblemen deliberately hide their own names and even conspire in assigning artistic credit to lack-luster stooges. This manner of getting their works before the public is necessary if they are to retain favor at Court, where certain influential officers take a dim view, indeed, of any nobleman's associating with the players at any level other than as distant patron and social monitor."

"Why is that?"

"Basically, governments are in business of regulating the people and of insuring domestic tranquility. Stage plays can be fashioned to create disunity and discontent, so they can be a threat to tranquility unless a watch is put over them. Regulating the actors themselves is difficult because the players travel about the country like tinkers or gypsies, so they have no permanent address. They follow no productive craft which would bind them to Guild rules. They sometimes plant cut-purses in their audiences to fleece the enraptured throng; they seldom pay their bills; and they steal chickens everywhere they go. It is not surprising if authorities are sometimes impatient with them."

"Excuse me," William said firmly, "but that hardly seems to be a completely accurate picture of the world's third oldest profession—if you count soldiering second."

"Quite right," Bacon agreed. "Very careless of me to leave out the fact that they also seduce women and girls in every community they visit because nature has made females powerless to resist males who are practiced in the arts of deception and make-believe."

"Really? Powerless?"

"Precisely," Bacon nodded. "But back to my own problem, I realized early that the shifting tides of the theatrical world might easily result in my own dramatic works being credited to some lesser writer in the future since I can't accept direct credit for my creations."

"Ah yes," said William, "I have heard that you use codes, ciphers, anagrams and such to identify your work, but wouldn't such elements tend to further conceal your identity?"

Francis Bacon smiled. "Did you know that some great painters—for political or financial reasons—sometimes paint an ordinary scene over their best works with a paint-blend which can be washed away if one discovers how to mix the cleaner properly? What pleasure it would give the writer—even in heaven—to have his masterpiece finally revealed when some future scholar finally pulls the curtain to present the true color of his work!"

"I concede that all of that is well beyond my experience up to now, but I really think it indefensible that society should erect so many time-consuming hurdles that keep creative people away from their important work. It's clear to me that the acting profession suffers from not getting its side of the story told. If a greater understanding for the theatrical experience could be generated, perhaps you, among others, would be able to step forward and take your bow as the author of so many great works. Alleged."

"Not likely anytime soon," Bacon smiled, "and to be perfectly clear about the matter, I am often not the sole author, but rather the modifier or reviser of existent works submitted for licensing to the Master of the Revels."

"Oh, now I recall," William said with open pride in the simple act. "Someone mentioned that you were part of that group which meets at Winston House—the House of Poetry—with the Pembrokes and Oxford and Raleigh to censor the stage productions after they are submitted to Master Tilney for licensing."

Bacon held up an admonishing hand, "'Censor' is hardly the correct word. We simply advise, and, believe me, the stage managers are only too glad to receive our recommendations since they have no desire to step on the toes of their patrons, but they don't always know where those toes begin nor end. We simply guide them around the sensitive spots."

"'Guide them' really means that stage companies must follow the social, economic, and political dictums of their patrons if they want to stay in business, doesn't it?"

Bacon shrugged, "Ever since Elizabeth realized how much influence dramatic productions could exert on public opinion, it has been a requirement that all theatrical companies be sponsored by a responsible nobleman to keep the troupe from folly or treason. Obviously, such a man would not betray himself or his class by approving values which are alien to the public good."

"I am wondering where consideration of art come into the picture?"

"Art is always a matter of best-foot-forward," Bacon said. "The true artist will always present his case as skillfully as he can under whatever circumstances prevail."

"Much as a barrister does?"

"Exactly," Bacon said.

"Speaking of legalities," William said, "have you found it necessary when writing for the stage to conceal your legal background for fear your expert knowledge would shine through and reveal your true identity to perceptive viewers?"

"Conceal hell! I secretly flaunt it!" Bacon exclaimed. "It is one of the cryptic precautions I spoke of earlier. When future scholars come across a writer of plays who is also able to apply specific legal terms to human affairs, how long do you think it will take them to figure that one out? After all, how many writers do you know who can toss around a line like '*Where be his quiddities now, his quillets, his cases, his tenures, and his tricks?...with his statutes, his recognizances, his fines, his double vouchers, his recoveries'?*" [23]

"You're the only one, up until now," William admitted. "Your situation in life is certainly unique, so there is little chance that history will short-change you, but I was wondering about the fate of other writers who have not had the soft berth which you have always enjoyed."

"Other writers?"

"People from a less exalted social strata, who have no retainers to collect their papers for them, some of whom are, as a matter of fact, instructed daily to destroy all traces of their existence. Yet these writers have already succeeded, against great odds, in outlining—for future completion—a body of work that possibly reflects an incipient genius. Will they get their just due when scholars put the pieces together, or will history simply list their works in a bundle under the names of the leading noblemen of the period?"

"Why should that be a concern of yours?"

"Just idle fancy and a deep-seated sense of justice, I suppose," William said, "but I always worry about the under-dog being cheated out of his rightful claim to fame."

"Hm, I would say that if the work is good, the world will hear of it, and the lack of personal recognition makes no real difference once the writer has departed."

"Excuse me for pointing it out, but that is not the position you take in regard to your own writing. It is well known that you order fair copies of all your signed works distributed to every stationer in London. How can you then say it makes 'no real difference' once the writer dies?"

Bacon shrugged, "You said it yourself. I am unique and privileged, quite unlike whomever it is you have in mind."

"Indeed? That seems eminently unfair," said William coldly.

"Are you questioning the natural order of things, young man?"

"I do question it," said William. "I thought you believed in honest inquiry."

Francis Bacon was thoughtful. "I do believe in it. And believe a man who asks questions shall learn much. *But let his questions not be troublesome, for that is fit for a poser—*" [24]

"Hold on now!" William broke in.

"And," Bacon continued, *"Let him be sure to leave other men their turns to speak."*

"I beg your pardon," William said. "I thought you were finished. I know that excessive enthusiasm is sometimes a weakness of mine, and I plan to work on it when I can set aside a little time for myself."

Bacon smiled politely. *"Speech of a man's self ought to be seldom and well chosen. I knew one was wont to say in scorn, 'He must needs be a wise man, he speaks so much of himself;' and there is but one case wherein a man may commend himself with good grace, and that is in commending virtue. In.another."*

"Well, in that case, I certainly would like to gain your kind of skill in splicing your sentences together in discourse," said William. "You sometimes seem to cover gaps in meaning by juxtaposing discordant elements."

Bacon frowned. *"Petty points of cunning are infinite, [but] nothing doth more hurt in a state than that cunning men pass for wise. [25]* So let us bypass your dubious attempt at coherence and move to more solid matters. *It is good in discourse and speech of conversation to vary and intermingle speech of the present occasion with arguments, tales with reasons, asking of questions with telling of opinions, and jest with earnest; for it is a dull thing to tire, and as we say now, to jade, anything too far."* [26]

"Would you venture to say, then, that the field of humor is wide open?"

"*As for jest, there be certain things which ought to be privileged from it; namely religion, matters of state, great persons, any man's present business of importance, and any case that deserveth pity."*

"Speaking of pity reminds me to ask where you hope to find the bully boys you need to collect those recusancy fines the Queen has finally authorized you to pry loose from Catholic offenders? Some of those old Catholic women have little money between themselves and starvation, and you'll have to round up some really insensitive brutes to snatch those few coins from their malnourished hands."

"If I do have to re-re-resort to b-b-bully-boys," Bacon said grimly, "I'll kn-kn-know where to f-f-find a na-na-natural leader f-f-for them."

"Is it possible to get another drink around here?" William suddenly asked.

Bacon huffed for a moment, calming himself. "*As we see in beasts that those that are weakest in the course are yet nimblest in the turn, as it is betwixt the grey hound and the hare.*

To use too many circumstances, ere one come to the matter, is wearisome; to use none at all, is blunt.' [27] Nevertheless, refreshments are available in the tray on the sideboard. It was thought wise not to place too much stimulant directly on the table because its presence before lunch might encourage boors and buffoons to come out of hiding."

"Good thinking," William approved as he skipped over to the sideboard. "I don't mind working for my pleasure." He sloshed himself a glassful of Malmsey. "That is, unless the host would begrudge me a further sip of joy?"

"Tut, tut," Francis Bacon chided him. "You do make some disturbing inquiries, none-the-less; *'A sudden, bold, and unexpected question doth many times surprise a man and lay him open'.*" [28]

At this moment, Bacon's butler entered the library and announced that Sir Francis had a gentleman caller waiting in the parlor.

"You must excuse me for a moment," said Bacon. "Please go on with your snack. I'll rejoin you shortly."

When Bacon returned, he found the tray completely empty of food.

William attempted to explain, but his host interrupted. "No apologies from a guest, please. Perfectly all right. A host must occasionally bludgeon his sensibilities past the confines of social nicety and realize that a creature of insatiable appetite makes an interesting visitor to a house of limited means."

"Funny how it came about," explained William. "The ham slices were so thin and the cakes so small, that in no time at all—"

"Quite right, young man. Your portion obviously aroused your individual stomach, so it is not too surprising that you were tempted to sample more. I would say, *Beware of sudden change in any great point of diet, for it is hard to distinguish that which is generally held good and wholesome from that which is good particularly and fit for thine own body.*" [29]

William grinned sheepishly. "I could have resisted, actually. It seemed humorous, at the time, and I became interested in seeing if you might forget altogether whether you had eaten. Ah, well."

Bacon smiled benignly. "*There is in man an ambition of the understanding, no less than of the will, especially in high and lofty spirits.*" [30]

"I hope you include me in that august grouping," William chuckled. "Malachi tells me you studied law at Gray's Inn and were admitted to the bar four years ago, but you're having trouble deciding between law and research."

"That's true," said Bacon. "My need to gain worldly success in serving my Queen is somewhat at war with my will to write and pursue scientific study."

"In view of the proposed new legislation governing taxes and tariffs, it seems it might be a good time to be a lawyer."

"I am proposed not to follow the practice of the law. It drinketh too much time, which I have dedicated to better purpose." [31] Eight years of study are required before one may call himself a barrister, and an additional eight years of practice before there is any chance of a judgeship. Pretty small reward for the time involved."

"Perhaps it's just as well," William observed. "England has plenty of shyster lawyers already—I don't mean that pejoratively, you understand, just a general observation about the reputation you lawyers have recently earned."

"Hmm, well, there is that. Civilization would be chaotic, however, without a few of us to mediate, clarify, and organize. But what of yourself, friend? Have you given any thought to what you'll do if you happen to survive your apprentice service?"

"Every day," sighed William. "I can't wait until I get out of my bond period and all this heavy work. Though I am very fond of my master and am learning a lot, I spend half my time hauling and pushing our baggage all over England. It's quite undignified."

"The rising into place is labourious, and by pains men come to greater pains, and it is sometimes base; and by indignities men come to dignities." [32]

"That's all I want, a little dignity," William insisted. "I need somebody to carry my baggage for a change."

"It is a strange desire, to seek power and to lose liberty, or to seek power over others and to lose power over a man's self."

"Just how do you mean that? I'd certainly have greater power if I had someone to order about."

"Tut, tut," said Bacon. *"Men in great place are thrice servants—servants of the sovereign or state, servants of fame, and servants of business; so as they have no freedom, neither in their persons nor in their actions nor in their times."*

"Hmm, there is a great deal in what you say, Sir Francis. You think, then, that I should set a pace for my ambition and hold my ground, not grow too fast?"

"As for remaining stationary, I know that *the standing is slippery and the regress is either a downfall or at least an eclipse, which is a melancholy thing.*"

"That's funny," William laughed. "Malachi used the same word earlier to describe your career under Elizabeth."

"I beg your pardon," said Bacon. "Which word is that?"

"Eclipse."

"Ah, yes. Unfortunately, he is only reflecting my own estimate," muttered Bacon grimly. "It is, indeed, a melancholy thing to have your essential-self blocked from the sun for so many years. Only too accurate." Bacon squared his shoulders. "But make no mistake about it, my friend. My sun shall shine fully in due time."

"I like that! Upbeat! Positive! I'm-the-man kind of thing! If I didn't have such fond hopes for my own future, I wouldn't mind being in your position."

"I appreciate your words, Friend William. *Certainly great persons had need to borrow other men's opinions to think themselves happy, for if they judge by their own feeling, they cannot find it; but if they think with themselves what other men think of them and that other men would fain be as they are, then they are happy, as it were by report.*"

"I wonder why we struggle so much for the good opinion of others," mused William. "What is this incredible impulse we have to get ahead?"

"I think I can answer that in part. With success comes license to do good or evil and a great sense of power. But *power to do good, is the true and lawful end of aspiring.*"

"I'm glad to hear such a positive note amidst all the cynical chatter one hears these days," said William.

Bacon frowned and raised a hand. *"Good thoughts yet towards men are little better than good dreams except they be put in act, and that cannot be without power and place as the vantage and commanding ground. Merit and good works is the end of man's motion, and conscience of the same is the accomplishment of man's rest. For if a man can be partaker of God's theater, he shall likewise be partaker of God's rest."* [33]

"Oh, I like the way you say that. Do good works in God's Theater! It certainly gives a fellow something to shoot for, and," he glanced at Bacon's face, "look up to. It seems ironic, however, that you think about leaving the Law, which is certainly a 'commanding ground' for action. I think you must know that many others aspire to little more than the life you give up so readily."

"You refer to the nobility class again, I perceive, and have little sense of its value to a nation," said Bacon. "Try to understand. *A monarchy where there is no nobility at all, is ever a pure and absolute tyranny as that of the Turks. A great and potent nobility addeth majesty to a monarch but diminisheth power, and putteth life and spirit into the people but presseth their fortune."* [34]

"The tax thing," said William dryly. "We English avoid absolute tyranny but must put up with petty tyranny, is that it?"

Bacon nodded. *"It is well when nobles are not too great for sovereignty nor for justice; and yet maintained in that height, as the insolency of inferiors may be broken upon them, before it comes on too fast upon the majesty of kings."*

"I never thought of that," William confessed. "You're saying the nobles constitute an insolence-barrier for the sovereign. I suppose if that were indeed the case, the nobility would be only too happy to increase the safety of the Queen by opening their ranks to new members? I, for one, am ready to step forward, and—"

"Not so fast," Bacon cautioned *"A numerous nobility causeth poverty and inconvenience in a state; for it is a surcharge of expense; and besides, it being of necessity that many of the nobility fall in time to be weak in fortune, it maketh a kind of disproportion between honor and means."* [35]

"I take it you speak from firsthand experience, Sir Francis."

"Indeed, that is true," admitted Bacon, "but fortunes can be recovered. *Certainly if a man will keep but an even hand, his ordinary expenses ought to be but to the half of his receipts, and, if he think to wax rich, but to the third part."* [36]

"My observation is that most of the nobility do not deign to keep 'an even hand,' as you call it. In fact, most seem to live in exaggerated splendor."

"And therein lies an interesting point, my friend," said Bacon. *"Out of all question, the splendor and magnificence and great retinues and hospitality of noblemen and gentlemen doth much conduce unto martial greatness, whereas, contrariwise, the close and reserved living of noblemen and gentlemen causeth a penury of military forces."*

"Egad," exclaimed William. "You think lavish spending on a personal level equates with military victory?"

"I do. Consider the Romans, who were masters at maintaining military triumphs over a long period. Their policy contained three things: *honor to the general, riches to the treasury out of the spoils, and donatives to the army."*

"And I'm sure the nobility, who lived in splendor, took their share of spoils from the treasury. By 'donatives to the army' do you mean the soldiers were well paid?"

Bacon grimaced. "I doubt it, friend. Soldiers and sailors are never held to be as important as the equipment with which they fight. I'm afraid most policy-makers get used to the idea of thinking of the men as expendable and are always on the lookout for replacements."

Chagrin temporarily twisted William's face. "Well," he said finally, "as long as we have the Irish to fill in the gaps."

"Indeed. And how lucky for us that the Irish men are as adept at sea as on land, for to be master of the sea is the key to England's mastery in commerce as well as in war. It is certain that *he that commands the sea is at great liberty, and may take as much and as little of the war as he will; whereas, those that be strongest by land are many times, nevertheless, in great straits."* [37]

"The tavern talk says pretty much the same thing," William nodded; "yet Parliament and the Queen withhold the funds necessary to allow Captain Hawkins to build a real fleet. Why is that, do you think?"

Bacon was thoughtful. "For one, it costs a great deal to maintain a standing army and navy. And I rather guess our government hopes the merchants will build the ships we need, for the purpose of commerce, you know. The merchants handle business much better than Parliament, for *there be three parts of business: the preparation, the debate or examination, and the perfection* [and one should] *let the middle only be the work of many, and the first and last the work of few."* [38]

"You mean Parliament would take too long on the preparation and perfection. I can see that. But if they put Captain Hawkins in charge—"

"That would never happen, friend. Politicians like to keep their hands on the controls, and getting the job done with the least fuss and expense is not a high priority with them." Bacon sighed. "I wonder if I could ever survive in public service."

❖ ❖ ❖

Malachi joined them for tea, which consisted of bread and cheese added to the thin ham slices and tiny cakes. William helped himself to generous portions of sugar and milk with his tea and contributed little to the conversation during the first part of the meal.

"I'm beginning to think you deceived me entirely, Malachi," Bacon was saying, "when you recommended your man on the basis of his excellent writings. You said he had a flair that had caught the attention even of the Privy Council members. I thought I was going to play host to a budding literary genius and what did I find? An exact antithesis to my own mindset and personality: frivolous when I am most sincere, irreverent of matters I hold most sacred, and prone to switch subjects just when I am getting down to the core point."

"Quite right," admitted Malachi, "but I knew you would never forgive me if I let you miss the chance to meet a unique specimen, which William most certainly is. Perhaps you simply misinterpreted what I said in the note."

"I have your note right here," said Bacon, pulling it from his doublet and snapping it open. "You say very clearly here, 'His writings impress Walsingham mightily and are commented on by Privy Council members.' Did you or did you not write this note?"

"Indeed, I did, Sir Francis, and meant every word, but you have taken a wrong turn on my meaning."

Bacon sighed deeply. "The ball of blame seems to keep bouncing back to my side of the court."

Malachi shrugged. "Written notations often suffer from lack of gesture and intonation, so it's perfectly understandable that—"

"No more of your Irish nonsense, Malachi. Why did you attempt to fool me? And why have you apprenticed such an irregular man to your sensitive business? Finally, what is this nonsense about Walsingham and the Council?"

"It's really quite simple, Sir Francis. You mistook the word 'writings' to mean content whereas I simple meant it graphologically."

"Penmanship?" exclaimed Bacon softly.

"Exactly so. He is the best penman in the realm. I would stack the clarity and beauty of his writing against those of any other scrivener in the country. And I would bet my income on the outcome."

Bacon groaned, and William stuffed another tiny cake into his grinning mouth.

Malachi continued. "Walsingham is a notorious scribbler. Can't read his own writing half the time. But he knows real class when he sees it. William writes up my weekly reports to him, and those records have received nothing but praise for their clarity. The Council generally agrees that William's S's are the most elegant in the land, and his P's and Q's are not bad either."

"So," Bacon said slowly, "you didn't really deceive me, you only mislead me, which, I'll admit, is not quite the same thing. I can see why you like him, Malachi. You are both full of the same nonsense."

"Now, now, Sir Francis. Did he entertain you? Did he follow your thoughts and respond intelligently? Did he keep you on your toes, finding worthy arguments?"

"Indeed, he did all that. But still, Malachi, I had rather not be tricked. Or ridiculed either," he said, turning to William.

"Oh, nay, Sir Francis, there was no ridicule," cried William in alarm. "I enjoyed all your shared thoughts, and, may I say in all sincerity, brilliant insights! Unworthy as I am, I look forward to further conversations with you, if you will allow it."

"I can vouch for him, Sir Francis," chuckled Malachi, reaching over to rub his knuckles in William's hair. "His very faults are virtues in our business. He keeps our enemies off-balance with his garbled accounts of whatever information they manage to pump from him. His thinking is naturally bent in such a way as to trap the unwary. I have come to regard his as a great national treasure," he grinned at William, "even if it must be admitted that he does have his nincompoop moments."

"I admit, Friend William, that in the beginning I thought you a nincompoop, indeed. Now I see it was dissimulation and well done too. Did you also deliberately provoke me to the point where I could almost no longer carry on a coherent conversation?"

"Sorry about that. I work for Malachi, you understand, and he has trouble keeping his moral boundaries lined up after so many years in the business. A casualty of the trade, I guess. Still in all, it is easy enough for strangers to the trade to pass judgment on men who do the fieldwork. There are certain advantages to disguising oneself when one's life is in danger, you know."

"Very true," agreed Bacon. "*The great advantages of simulation and dissimulation are three: first to lay asleep opposition and to surprise, for where a man's intentions are published, it is an alarum to call up all that are against them. The second is to reserve to a man's self a fair retreat, for if a man engage himself by a manifest declaration, he must go through or take a fall. The third is the better to discover the mind of another, for to him who opens himself, men will hardly show themselves adverse, but will let him go on and turn their freedom of speech to freedom of thought. And therefore, it is a good shrewd proverb of the Spaniard, 'Tell a lie and find a truth'.*" [39]

"What a great image!" William exclaimed. *"Your bait of falsehood take this carp of truth!"* [40]

❧ ❧ ❧

That evening, Bacon was absent from the apartment, having previously accepted a dinner invitation. Malachi and William sat alone, sipping their after-dinner wine.

"Did you get any information from the kitchen staff this afternoon?" inquired Malachi.

"There is no kitchen staff to speak of, only Mrs. Paxton, the cook, who hails from Middlesex and is a widow with seven grown sons and ten grandchildren."

"Yes, yes. Sir Francis keeps a very spare staff, I know that. Well, since there are no pretty kitchen maids to divert you this evening, you may accompany me to the library to go over the Bacon correspondence." He rose from the table.

"I can do that," said William, following Malachi from the room. "We are looking for the whereabouts of the eldest brother Anthony, right?"

"And dates. Keep an eye out for recent dates. Here are several of Lady Bacon's latest letters, addressed mostly to Anthony, who then sends them on to his brothers, as instructed, so everyone gets the family news." Malachi smiled.

William read quietly for a few minutes, then suddenly burst out laughing. "Egad, she sounds like Sir Francis himself. Listen to this: *'Procure rest in convenient time. It helpeth much to digestion. I verily think your brother's weak stomach to digest hath been much caused and confirmed by untimely going to bed and then musing—I know not what—when he should sleep, and then in consequent by late rising and long lying in bed, whereby his men are made slothful and himself continueth sickly. The Lord our heavenly father heal and bless you both as his sons in Christ Jesu.'"* [41]

"Hmm," said Malachi absently. "That's a mother's voice, all right."

"Here she says, *'Let not your men drink wine this hot weather. My sons haste not to hearken to their mother's good counsel in time to prevent. Be not speedy of speech nor talk suddenly; but where discretion requireth, and that soberly then. Courtesy is necessary, but too common familarity in talking and words is very unprofitable and not without hurt-taking—the times being as they are. Remember you have no father. Use prayers twice in a day. Your brother is too negligent therein.'* This letter is clearly written to Anthony, who is among the religious folk in France and, no doubt, praying regularly."

"Lady Bacon knows well that Francis will be reading each letter."

"*'Be not over ruled still by subtle and hurtful hangers-on,'* she writes."

"Egad, she really laces into those hurtful hangers-on. *'Filthy wasteful knaves! Welshmen who swarm ill-favouredly, sinful proud villians, cormorant seducers and instruments of Sa-*

tan!'" William chuckled. "Strange, I've never thought of cormorants that way. Give me a modest, clean, dignified swan every time!"

"Hold up, William! Let me hear no mockery. Or literary criticism either. A man who reads other people's mail in Service of the Queen must maintain objectivity and strive to be non-judgmental."

"Yes, certainly. I apologize for letting myself get carried away," said William. But a few minutes later, "Hear this! *'That bloody Percy whom Francis keepeth, yea as a coach companion and bed companion, a proud profane fellow whose being about him I verily fear the Lord doth mislike.'* Convenient that she has such direct access to the Lord's thinking."

"All the Puritans do. Now if you are quite finished amusing yourself at the expense of the Bacon family…"

"She wasn't really implying anything with that 'bed companion' crack, was she?"

"Well, young man, consider that you and I often share the same bed."

"At inns where beds are in short supply, certainly. Or sometimes to keep warm, like everybody else."

"There's your answer. Now move on to that next packet of letters and try not to lose sight of your goal."

"You read Montaigne?" said Bacon in wonder next morning, over his breakfast eggs and toast.

William nodded. "Due for a visit with him very soon, according to rumors at the office."

"You know him socially?" Bacon cried in dismay.

William shrugged, "As usual, I suppose I've already revealed more than I should about our schedule. Please don't mention it to Malachi."

Bacon sighed deeply. "I am a great admirer of Montaigne," he confessed. "Since his book of essays was published six years ago in 1580, it has caused thoughtful Englishmen, actually men everywhere—to turn their eyes inward to see if they dare to deal as honestly with themselves as Montaigne has done with Montaigne. H-h-he is so disarmingly c-c-candid about his th-th-thoughts that the r-r-rest of us are put to sh-sh-shame by the du-d-duplicities and de-de-deceits we p-p-practice on ourselves."

William looked at his host with interest. "You seem very reverent. Do you know him personally?"

Bacon gathered himself together, sipping his coffee calmly. "Only through his writings," he said at last. "I believe my brother Anthony may be acquainted with him." Bacon paused again. "I was about to say further, that even though it is an original work in the field and a splendid collection, Montaigne's *Essays* is not without fault."

"I'm sorry to hear it. I detected none myself although—"

"He meanders and lacks discipline. He starts a discussion of windmills and ends up describing his gallstones—"

"Well, I would think a certain poetic license should be extended in a case where—"

"—and his digestive tract! And the color of his urine! I do not care to read about such things. On the other hand, I enjoyed his splendid inclusion of classical quotations even though at times he grossly overdid the practice. Heavenly Father, he hardly examines one of his toenails without dragging in some Roman emperor or Greek lawmaker for commentary. Such references should be used more sparingly—perhaps no more than one to a page."

"In summary then," William said, "you fault Montaigne for discussing bodily functions too openly and for using too many quotations?"

"Did I mention structure?"

"'Meandering', you said."

"Yes, I fear so," nodded Bacon. "Montaigne would have done well to subject himself to a much more rigorous editing process. His material would profit from being pruned into tighter, crisper paragraphs."

"The kind of thing you do so well?"

"Very kind of you to notice," said Bacon with a slight bow of his head.

"But tell me," said William, "do you really believe all discussions of bodily functions are indiscreet? After all, *One touch of nature makes the whole world kin.* [42] It seems to me that the shining badge of universal humanity is the plumbing we all share, and such a common bond should not go unexamined, especially in these troubled times when diversity seems to rule the social order. I mean, just basically as humans, we all have a great big hole at the top of our bodies through which we ingest our food and drink along with the air, while at the bottom of our bodies—"

"Desist!" cried Bacon. *"Discretion of speech is more than eloquence; and to speak agreeable to him with whom we deal is more than to speak in good words or in good order."* [43]

William shrugged. "Perhaps most readers are not as squeamish as you seem to be."

Bacon tightened his lips. *"To say truth, nakedness is uncomely, as well in mind as body; and it addeth no small reverence to men's manners and actions if they be not altogether open."* [44]

"Oh well," shrugged William. "I guess we all have different experiences when we take off our clothes. As for dressing up our writing, nothing pleases university men more than exchanging Latin quotes and thereby justifying their education. In my view, that may be a fault in Montaigne's book. I hope the book you propose to publish will not be over-burdened with that kind of raiment."

"You m-m-mock the cla-cla-classical references, my friend, b-b-but these eleg-g-gant inclu-clu-clusions will always enhance a p-p-piece of writing."

"Perhaps, perhaps not, Sir Francis. But it's mostly fluff in writing, all mind and no body. All talk and no action. The groundlings won't go for it."

Bacon closed his eyes and took a deep breath. "What ravings are these? G-g-groundlings, indeed."

"Well, according to Christopher Marlowe, you've got to grab the groundlings if you intend to succeed commercially. They want ghosts and murder, plots and witches, duels and war."

"Are you, by chance, talking about stage-plays?" Bacon asked hollowly.

"What else?"

"I was talking about something entirely different," said Bacon. "My essays, like Montaigne's, will be observations about real life. They will be very different from any previously existing literary form. It has taken our species just this long to become civilized enough to communicate at the exalted level of the personal essay. In any event, the essay is radically different from the stage-play in that the reader of essays must involve his mind in his entertainment while the viewer of plays may engage nothing more than his backside."

"Malachi has said you and Monsieur Montaigne will set the precedent for future essays," said William. "What do you intend to call your collection?"

"I will honor Montaigne's pioneer effort by calling my book, simply, *Essays*."

"Wait a minute now," said William. "Isn't that the same title Montaigne used? Aren't you afraid that hundreds, perhaps thousands, of people will purchase your book of essays under the delusion that they are buying the real thing, or buying your book, I should say, instead of Montaigne's?"

"So?" Bacon retorted. "After all, he named the literary format 'essays', so what else would I call them?"

"Oh, well," William shrugged, "I must remember that the groundlings don't buy books."

"Have you had a chance to glance at any of these books in my library?" Bacon asked, after several moments of silence.

"I browsed a bit," said William, "but I don't quiet see the point of heavy reading. I sometimes have trouble choosing such a passive past-time in this active world. Some scholars might think my attitude reprehensible, but my reading habits have little to do with me personally. Perhaps they are a direct result of whatever happened to me—or, possibly, didn't happen to me—during my schooldays. Or even my recent accident."

"The point of reading, as you so curiously call it," Bacon said, "is quite clear: *Studies serve for delight, for ornament, and for ability.*" [45]

"A trident rather than a point, it would seem," William smiled. "All I know is you can burn up a lot of time reading books."

"To spend too much time in studies is sloth; to use them too much for ornament is affectation; to make judgment wholly by their rules is the humor of a scholar."

"That's what I say," William shrugged. "Why bother."

Bacon raised a hand. "Tut, tut," he chided. *"Crafty men contemn studies, simple men admire them, and wise men use them."*

William chuckled. "At least I'm not simple by those standards, but I don't see myself as crafty either. You might call my reading ornamental, however, for while staying at an inn, I'll often memorize some well-written bit up in my room and then lead the loud talkers in the common room to the bait and confound them with my newly acquired knowledge. I happen to be a quick study," William mentioned. "I can grab men's attention initially by some outrageous statement and then lead them gently into my well-charted subject area. Would you call that 'using' studies?"

"I imagine that you are, indeed, a dramatic chap, Friend William, loving the spotlight, but my advice would be *Read not to contradict and confute, nor to believe and take for granted, nor to find talk and discourse, but to weigh and consider."*

"I believe you have left out the entertainment factor or the promotion of fancy," said William. "Take the Italian Bocaccio and his *Decameron*, for instance. That is a great favorite of my Apprentices' Association but is not, I think, a volume one weighs and considers."

"Ah, you are correct. I have read some of Bocaccio's bawdy stories, but not all. Definitely written to entertain, not improve the mind. *Some books are to be tasted, others to be swallowed, and some few to be chewed and digested; that is some books are to be read only in parts; others to be read but not curiously; and some few to be read wholly."*

"That variety is the problem right there!" William exclaimed. "Every book should have a synopsis or summary printed inside the cover so that a reader could avoid wasting too much time discovering its content."

Bacon frowned. *"Some books also may be read by deputy and extracts made of them by others; but that would be only in the less important arguments and the meaner sort of books, else distilling books are like common distilled waters, flashy things."* [46]

William chuckled, "I don't want to offend your sensibilities, Sir Francis, but I confess that I am part of a very big audience for 'flashy-things', and I only spend my time reading when there is no one around to chat with, or when I don't feel like writing anything."

"Yes, Friend William, I have concluded you are a less thoughtful and sober reader than I," said Bacon kindly, "but remember: *Reading maketh a full man; conference a ready man; and writing an exact man."*

"Ah, I remember hearing or reading that somewhere. And I certainly agree about the conferring and the writing, but I don't know if a man must read that much just to learn what he needs to know generally."

"If he read little, he had need have much cunning, to seem to know that he doth not."

"My point exactly!" exclaimed William. "If you don't read much, you must cultivate cunning, and cunning is exactly what I think you need to make your way in this sly world."

"There is more to it than making our way, friend," said Bacon. *"Studies go to form character; nay, there is no stand or impediment in the wit, but may be wrought out by fit studies."*

"You never seem to run out of good advice," William said, "and it's not that I don't appreciate it, but I notice that in the game of life, a man must count primarily on himself for direction."

When Malachi joined them soon after, Bacon seemed to turn to him in relief. "How goes your detective work, Malachi?" he asked politely.

"Well indeed, Sir Francis. I believe I have found the information I came for, thank you kindly. Perhaps you know that both your mother and the Queen would like Anthony to return to England. As head of the Bacon family, he must be under considerable pressure to marry."

"Ah," sighed Bacon. *"He that hath wife and children hath given hostages to fortune, for they are impediments to great enterprises, either of virtue or mischief."* [47]

"Does that include a man who intends to devote his life to creating art for the eternal entertainment of humanity?" inquired William sadly. "No marriage, no children?"

"Certainly the best works and of greatest merit for the public have proceeded from the unmarried or childless man, which both in affection and means, have married and endowed the public. Yet it were great reason that those that have children should have the greatest care of future times, unto which they know they must transmit their dearest pledges."

"Spoken like a true Puritan gentleman," commented Malachi softly.

"Wife and children are a kind of discipline of humanity," Bacon continued. *"And single men, though they be many times more charitable, because their means are less exhaust, yet, on the other side, they are more cruel and hard-hearted, because their tenderness is not so often called upon."*

"Sounds like a bad lot to me," William said.

"Tut, tut," said Bacon. "I myself have found that *unmarried men are best friends, best masters, best servants, but not always best subjects, for they are light to run away."* [48]

Malachi chuckled. "Since we are all unmarried men here, I daresay we would agree."

"Hold on, now!" William commanded with force enough to draw Bacon's gaze from the ceiling. "I am a married man, even though my marriage to Mercy was not legal. Nevertheless, I am hopelessly in love with Mercy and would not give her up, particularly since I plan to dramatize our spiritual relationship in future stage-plays which will forever glorify the ideal union between lovers of all ages."

Bacon smiled benignly. *"The stage is more beholden to love than the life of man, for as to the stage, love is ever a matter of comedies, and now and then of tragedies; but in life it doth much mischief, sometimes like a Siren, sometimes like a Fury. You may observe, that, amongst all the great and worthy persons (whereof the memory remaineth, either ancient or recent), there is not one that hath been transported to the mad degree of love, which shows that great spirits and great business do keep out this weak passion."* [49]

"Weak, hell!" William retorted. "I've never had an experience to equal it! Mercy is the perpetual star that lights up my life even in the glare of the noon-time sun!"

Bacon listened attentively, then commented: *"It is a strange thing to note the excess of this passion and how it [insults] the nature and value of things, by this, that the speaking in a perpetual hyperbole is comely in nothing but in love, neither is it merely in the phrase; for there was never a proud man thought so absurdly well of himself as the lover doth of the person loved; and therefore it is well said 'That it is impossible to love and to be wise'."*

"Is it really a matter of one or the other?" William asked. "I don't remember being complimented on my wisdom before I fell in love—"

Bacon shook his head. *"Men ought to beware of this passion, which loseth not only other things, but itself."*

"What other things?"

"It was Ovid who told us, *'He that preferred Helena, quitted the gifts of Juno and Pallas.'"*

"What does all that mean?" William asked.

Bacon steepled his fingers and explained patiently. *"For whosoever esteemeth too much of amourous affection, quitteth both riches and wisdom."* [50]

"Quits riches?" William asked in some alarm.

"An exhausted man runs poorly in life's race," Bacon said. "Better for a man to accomplish whatever great work he is capable of, then marry coolly and wisely. *Wives are young men's mistresses, companions for middle age, and old men's nurses."* [51]

Malachi chuckled. "I know of many ladies who would object to such a categorization. Our Mercy, for one, would be all three in every age, plus a mystery and a puzzle and a challenge throughout a man's life."

"Sir Francis' placid view of love and marriage does not include such a human delight as Mercy," laughed William.

"There is in man's nature a secret inclination and motion towards love of others, which, if it be not spent upon some one or a few, doth naturally spread itself towards many, and maketh men become humane and charitable, as is seen sometimes in friars." [52]

William shook his head. "That humane love might suit some men, but, personally, I could never give up my wanton moments."

Bacon frowned. *"Nuptial love maketh mankind, friendly love perfected it, but wanton love corrupteth and embaseth it."*

345

William smiled. "Oh, I only meant wanton moments during friendly love. You two still remember those, don't you?"

Bacon coughed a bit and looked piercingly at William. "My good fellow," he said, "why are you pouring the port wine from my glass to your glass?"

"Oh, that," William shrugged. "I could tell by the way your eyes were cast heavenward that you were probably going to say something significant, and I certainly didn't want to distract you just because a heavy thirst descended on me. Furthermore I was reluctant to monopolize the conversation—unless the company convinces me there is interest in my discourse."

"'Reluctant to monopolize', did you say?" Malachi hooted. "Are you feeling all right, lad?"

"I feel fine," William assured him. He looked about the room. "How much would it cost to furnish a room like this, Sir Francis? You seem to have everything you need without making a garish display of it."

"What t-t-tom foolery is th-th-this?" demanded Bacon. "N-n-now that you h-h-have interrupted our d-d-discourse, what c-c-cunning point d-d-do you w-w-wish to make?"

"You have a crafty mind for pin-pointing cunning, Sir Francis." William bowed to his host and drew several sheets from his doublet. "And now that you have broadcast my ulterior motives and things are out in the open, I must confess I happen to have a few sonnet beginnings which I would like to offer up for the judgment of the company."

Bacon's face twisted into a grimace. "Sonnet b-b-beginnings?"

"Right here," William waved his sheets. "I have the octet done on most of them, but I am having trouble finishing off the various sestets. I could be persuaded to read them aloud if the company were of such a mind."

"P-p-persuaded?" Bacon's eyes flicked quickly down like an adder's tongue. "You not only pro-pro-propose to subject us to an un-un-unsolicited recitation of j-j-juvenile clap-clap-clap-trap in the form of trun-trun-truncated sonnets, but you have the add-add-additional effrontery to s-s-seek our encouragement to do so?"

"I would prefer you call them 'incomplete works', if it's all the same to you."

Bacon frowned. "*It is a point of cunning to let fall those words which he would have another man learn and use.*" [53]

"Oh, let the lad read us his scribblings, Sir Francis," said Malachi good-naturedly. "It will do us no harm, and the practice will do him good."

Bacon considered for a moment. "I will listen to one sonnet, friend, if you will return the favor by making me two fair-copies of these few notes by morning. The notes are a listing of files and indexes to various of my writings."

"Indexes?" said William.

"Ahh well," Bacon shrugged, "The more I write, the easier it is to forget where I have put various things."

"Where you have hidden things?"

Bacon frowned and waved off the discussion. "Forget that now. Let's hear your unfinished poem." He laced his fingers over his belly and sat back.

"Apropos to our discussion, this is a sonnet to my love." William allowed a moment to lapse, then began in a rich, clear voice—

> *Shall I compare thee to a summer's day?*
> *Thou are more lovely and more temperate:*
> *Rough winds do shake the darling buds of May,*
> *And summer's lease hath all too short a date:*
> *. . .*
> *But thy eternal summer shall not fade*
> *. . .*
> *When in eternal lines to time thou growest;*
> *So long as men can breathe, or eyes can see,*
> *So long lives this, and this gives life to thee.* [54]

"It isn't finished," grumbled Bacon.

"I need six more lines in the middle sections. Think you 'tis fit for Puritan eyes?"

"'Tis very fine, lad," affirmed Malachi. "It almost brought tears to these old eyes, Puritan or not."

"Yes, it is very fine, Friend William. Now, to get back to my two copies, it is important that you realize the tightest security must be maintained."

"Absolutely," agreed William, folding and pocketing his papers. "I'll get to them just as soon as I return from my dinner."

"I want them done now," Bacon said pleasantly. "One of my retainers will bring you your meals as you work and remain with you until the copies are done. I trust that will be sometime before dawn tomorrow."

"I hope you realize I'll be disappointing a very sensitive young lady who may never forgive me."

"Tut, tut. That can't be helped," Bacon declared. "The tighter I can wrap the security on these notes, the better I'll feel about it. It is unfortunate if it disturbs your plans, but some things are simply more important than others. My man will be glad to deliver any beg-off message to your lady-friend, however, if you'd care to scribble one out and pass it under your door."

"Just two copies, you say?" William asked quietly.

"Just two and no other!" Bacon ordered emphatically. "That's important."

"That shouldn't be too difficult," William estimated, "but, of course, I will have to allot a little more time to the work since indexes and codes don't really flow in the ordinary sense, and—"

"Codes!" Bacon gasped. "I never said 'codes'. Not once ! No codes. Forget codes. I said 'files,' not 'codes'. Remember that!"

"Files it is then," William nodded genially. "No question about that. And only two copies, just as you say. Happy to do it for the hospitality you have shown Malachi and me."

"One more thing, Friend William. You may make me a copy of that sonnet too. Sign your name to it, of course, lest I forget it's yours."

William beamed. "In the final analysis, I am tempted to say that what goes around comes around, and because that cycle is eternal, all's well that ends well."

PART V: THE PLOT TO KILL THE QUEEN

Chapter 1:
MARY STUART, QUEEN OF SCOTS

Ante-room of Walsingham's office, early December, 1585:

"Why do we have to visit the main office so often in the middle of the night?" William asked with a yawn.

"You know a little about Walsingham by this time," Malachi told his apprentice, "so you know his voice will be heard in whatever company he shares, even in the Royal Chambers. Possessing a university degree and being fluent in five languages may give a man a certain entré to any gathering, but if that man happens to be highly opinionated and dauntless in discourse, it's not surprising the Queen periodically decides that Walsingham's outspoken advice trespasses on her Royal prerogatives and She chases him from Her Court."

"They don't always agree?"

"Worse. They don't always resonate. In deciding things, Elizabeth counts heavily on the strategy of delay in order to enjoy the 'benefits of time' which often untie the soul-searching knots involved in making decisions. Some observers call her 'wisely passive'."

"But Walsingham's soul has answers readily at hand?"

"Right. Godliness is a well-lit path for Walsingham so he is frequently at odds with Elizabeth's wandering through the brambles of doubt and uncertainty. In effect, then, all political decisions are religious decisions for Walsingham, so he has only to consult his Puritan inner light for the right answer. For Elizabeth, however, all religious decisions are political, so she must spend some time reflecting on the reaction of the Continental policy-makers to any decision she reaches. Because they think so differently, those two clash often, which is why she has never raised him to any honors other than his appointment as her Principal Secretary where he protects her life fanatically because she is the leader of the Protestant movement for all of Europe in addition to being its principal paymaster."

"So what happens when she runs him off?"

"During his out-of-grace periods, she communicates with him only through Burghley, so Walsingham must do some office work at night. Day or night, however, something fancy is always fermenting in his fertile and furtive brain, so he is never cast far from the Court."

"And the other man we're to see tonight? Have I met this Thomas Phelippes fellow?"

"I don't think so, but you have probably heard me speak of him. Appropriately enough, as the behind-the-scenes linguist and code-breaker extraordinaire for our Principal Secretary, Phelippes is a man who easily fades into any background—a small, yellow-haired, pock-marked chap."

"Some days it seems as if everybody I meet in London is pock-marked."

"They're the lucky survivors," Malachi observed. "Phelippes mentioned they might have an old friend of mine with them as a visitor-prisoner when they meet us here."

"Visitor-prisoner?"

Malachi grinned. "Somebody we have the goods on but have not yet charged because we expect to get something out of him. In this case it's Gilbert Gifford, an Englishman from Staffordbury who rejected the Anglican Church, went to France to train for the priesthood, and has recently been hired by Thomas Morgan, Mary Stuart's agent in Paris, to carry out an unknown mission here in England. Partly on information I supplied, our people nabbed him when he came ashore at Rye, so I have been recruited to be part of his cross-examination."

"Are those interrogations as brutal as I sometimes hear? Torture and everything?"

Malachi snorted. "Torture is never used in English prisons unless the Queen's person is in immediate danger from some active plot, and even then it's officially denied. So, in effect, torture is never used in English prisons. If you need further proof, sometime soon I'll introduce you to Mr. Topcliffe, who is the official Royal torturer. No one needs to torture Gilbert Gifford, however, since he is an eminently reasonable man who seeks only to get along comfortably in this world."

"Are you suggesting he may be amenable to shifting his loyalties, to becoming a sort of double-agent?"

"Double, you say? Don't make the mistake of minimizing this man's outreach as many unfortunates have done in the past. If we can get him to cooperate with us, it will make him a quintuple-agent by my count."

"How is such a thing possible?"

"I have good reason to believe that he collects pay from at least four different agencies, usually by posing as an exclusive agent. He is a clever man, well-spoken, well-dressed, and a crafty actor. He projects a simple innocence which is all sweet on the outside but scheming on the inside. He has a wonderful ability to seem to be confiding in the person he's speaking to at that moment—he's a great listener, and more importantly, he is Jesuit-trained to periodically insert flattering inquiries into his conversation—so he easily keeps people talking for long periods about themselves and about their activities. After first meeting him, some individuals are tempted to turn their purse over to him for safekeeping. His impersonation of unsullied purity is so convincing as to put your own display of actual innocence to shame."

"Isn't such deception a little dangerous?"

Malachi nodded. "Undoubtedly. The fact that he gets away with it is certainly a tribute to his sprightly mind and even more to his nimble conscience. But the larger truth may be that everybody in the survey business has quietly come to accept the diplomatic necessity of maintaining some throwaway professional agents who can be counted on to do certain well-paid specific jobs, but who can be denounced and disclaimed—or even disposed of—if anything much goes wrong. That's Gifford's position."

"No employer will complain now that we've nabbed him?"

"None, but there are other considerations. Thomas Morgan, Mary's agent, is an important functionary for the Scottish Woman, so you can bet that Gifford's mission is an important one. Morgan, incidentally, has for years facilitated the movement of Mary's personal mail by sending it from Paris to the French Embassy in London in the diplomatic bags—a forbidden practice universally abused. For years, Morgan has been in charge of delivering Mary's £1,200 annual pension as the former Queen of France."

"Even after all these years, she still gets paid as the Queen of France?"

"You bet. Governments know how to treat the people they want out of the way. Mary's mother-in-law, Catherine de Medici, pensioned her off twenty-five years ago after the Parisian Court suddenly became overburdened with former and existing queens of France as a result of two French kings' dying within a year and a half—including Mary Stuart's husband, Francis II—and a third King being crowned during the same period. Anyway, Morgan is one of Gifford's employers."

"Morgan," William repeated, ticking off one finger.

"The Duke de Guise and the French Catholic League are also paying Gifford to keep track of Ambassador Mendoza and the Spanish Embassy in Paris. Mendoza, in turn, pays him to keep track of de Guise and the League."

William ticked off a second and third finger.

"And finally, Rome pays him to keep track of all the others. If he hires out to us, that will make five."

William popped up a fourth finger and his thumb.

"He can accept our small offering and cooperate with us, or he can go to the Tower. The choice will be his. I have little doubt which way he'll choose. People like Gifford are not inclined to be heroes when faced with the rack."

"The rack, which we English do not use on prisoners, right?" William grimaced. "But how can we ever trust such a devious man?"

"No need to trust him," Malachi smiled. "We'll just watch him closely and check him often. Ahh, I hear visitors in the outer office now. They'll be here in a minute. You skip off out the side door now like a good fellow and see if you can't talk the kitchen out of a few bottles of something comforting while I have a private word with our company."

When William returned with refreshments, he quickly realized the ante-room atmosphere had changed. Malachi and Thomas Phelippes were alone in the room, involved in trading shop-talk after a busy workday. It was soon obvious they had discovered a source of comfort apart from the one he was delivering.

"You have me there, T.P.," Malachi conceded, turning his wine glass slowly. "In all candor, I must admit to one or two personal vices, but believe me, I keep them well in hand to prevent the very self-indulgence with which you charge me. On that score, I've always been thankful to the Catholics for classifying sin into two separate categories because the division between mortal sin and venial sin provides enough legroom so that any sensible man may regulate his behavior in such a manner as to continue to enjoy life. For my part, when I indulge myself in my major vices, I cut back sharply on my minor ones, and conversely, when I have to do without my major vices, I feel completely justified in running amok among my minor ones. Self-discipline is always the key, of course."

"Do you regard a flagrant disregard for security as a major vice or a minor one?" Phelippes asked sarcastically. "Mortal or venial?"

"Good God, Phelippes, you spend your entire life hunkered down in your back office and see security as the simple act of locking your door. If you'd knock about on the road more often, you'd soon learn that security is a much larger concept than keys and bolts."

"Whatever. I will not, however, share any information with your man, just on your word. He hasn't been checked out, and all our information is classified." Phelippes glared at William, who endeavored to look blankly innocent.

"Balderdash, T.P. It is all public knowledge at this point—or nearly so."

"Not the bamboo letter opener! That's our latest device, and now someone outside the Service knows of it," groaned Phelippes. "I suppose you were drinking when you broke this idea?"

"A drop may very well have been taken," Malachi conceded, "But I had little choice in the matter since he caught me using it when I thought him asleep. When he saw me slip the probe into the top of the envelope and extract the rolled up contents, he came fully awake and started asking questions which would be embarrassing if asked in public, so I had to explain the device to him."

"Yes, and forget completely that Walsingham had sworn us to secrecy about such methods!" Phellippes declared. "You needed to remember your duty to your country and the obligation you owe the Service, Malachi. We have to protect the tools of our trade and the secrets which good men have risked their lives to protect."

"Oh, my," Malachi sighed heavily. "You are missing the full value of his presence by this caviling, and yet you look like a man who enjoys a little entertainment once in a while."

Phelippes took a deep pull on his wine glass, but his bottom lip remained stubbornly extended. Finally he lifted his open palm and invited Malachi to continue.

"As you may know, I've spent twenty-eight years in the service, roughly ten thousand days. At least half those days are spent just sitting around sharing spirits like this, trying to pry something I can use from clever devils like yourself." Phelippes remained unmoved. "It has reached the point where everybody I visit knows all my ploys for coaxing information, so I end up hearing nothing except very obvious news offered in guarded tones. I need a pry-bar to knock people into unguarded moments. You'd be surprised at what people will blurt out when they are pushed off guard."

"Pry-bar?"

"A weapon, so to speak, which a higher power has providentially provided me in William here." He patted William's back. "There really is no telling what will come out of this lad's mouth at any given moment. He can throw the most stable mind in the world completely askew with a single question. Walsingham himself has called him a wise fool, and that seems pretty accurate to me."

"Walsingham knows about him?"

"I explained William's unique value to Walsingham when they first met, and it was agreed I could keep him on probation. The boss got a quick demonstration of my fellow's gift for projecting confusion and misdirection when I introduced them, but he recovered quickly enough to realize that well-managed mystification and perplexity could come in handy if focused like a ray-gun against our enemies. But Walsingham did warn me to keep my nose full-open for the slightest hint of brimstone because he is not yet convinced that William's gift is heaven-sent. So my man is on parole as long as he responds properly to a few minor restrictions and keeps his antic inclination muzzled when in the presence of the Principal Secretary."

"Nothing about keeping his mouth shut altogether?"

"I'm afraid that's impossible. But he is learning to refrain from using verse form in our reports until he better understands how to write pleasing iambic pentameter."

William chose that moment to ask Malachi, "What about the formula for making envelopes transparent? You said we were to pick it up tonight."

"You didn't give him the envelope-wash thing?" Phelippes protested in alarm.

"You never gave it to me," Malachi pointed out.

"Good," Phelippes said, "and I never shall—since age apparently has curdled your brain."

Malachi chuckled. "While we wait for the others, T.P., I need to run an errand down the hall. It will give you two a chance to get to know each other, and after a little time together, you not only will find him an amusing companion, but you'll be looking for a pry-bar of your own, I'm sure."

Phelippes rolled his eyes. "I'm looking forward to it with all due caution."

"You would be much mistaken," the code-master told William a quarter of an hour later, "to go on thinking that the gift of poetic sensibility is reserved for some few jingle-masters who wander homeless and malnourished through the streets of London. As a matter of fact, poetic inclination shows itself often in our ordinary duties."

"In what way?"

"It shows up everyday right here at the office." Phelippes waved around the small ante-room. "Let me explain by first asking you a question. What single subject would you say has dominated discussion at all political levels in England for the past seventeen years?"

William chuckled, "I may be the worst authority you can find for remembering past events, but from what I gather at the moment—"

"Right!" Philippes declared. "No matter where it begins, every avenue of discussion eventually leads to the monolith at the center of English thought: the succession to the throne of England."

"I heard that Elizabeth has prohibited Parliament from discussing her possible successor."

"She has, but the matter still gets plenty of play in the pubs, and there is no secret made of the distaste which is universally expressed for the logical successor: Mary Stuart. Among the English people, the Queen of Scots has earned a reputation for being much more of an ingrate than one might reasonably expect from a murderous, adulterous, Catholic bitch-whore who plots daily against the life of her only friend in the world, our all-too-gracious Gloriana."

"Is that why she is in prison at Tutbury? She lacks gratitude?"

"She's more of a supervised guest than a prisoner. Her cousin Elizabeth doles out fifty-two pounds per week for her meals and lodgings as well as that of her entourage of forty. Tutbury is a comfortable country estate where she may ride her horses and always be protected by men assigned to keep her from harm. Of course, to keep her free from further plots, we have cut off her mail delivery, and most of her letters are piling up at the French Embassy in London. Her visitors are closely monitored to keep her from further conspiracies against Elizabeth, but that's a small price to pay for the comfort she enjoys." Phelippes sighed deeply. "Good God, imagine fifty-two pounds a week for seventeen years! Does Mary have any idea what fifty-two pounds a week would mean to the rest of us? Even for one year? Even for a month?"

"But she has been a prisoner for seventeen years, not a pleasant prospect."

"Quite right," Phelippes conceded as he refreshed himself. "So, all English policy-makers have had that long to shape an opinion of Mary Stuart, long enough to select the lyrical name they habitually use in reference to her. Lord Burghley, for instance, never refers to Mary Stuart as anything other than 'that Scottish woman,' clearly showing his disdain."

"But a little bland for imagery, wouldn't you say?"

"Perhaps," Phelippes nodded. "Elizabeth usually refers to her as 'that Handmaid of Iniquity'. The Privy Council calls her the 'Daughter of Sedition'. The outspoken Puritan, Peter Wentworth, takes the broad view when he refers to her as 'The most notorious whore in all the world,' and Elizabeth's Court warms to the task by calling her the 'Dragon of Discord'."

"Much better imagery," William approved.

"The Continental Courts recognize the threat she poses to the English throne and refer to her as the 'Mother of Rebellion'."

"A trifle utilitarian," William observed.

"Archbishop Parker once wrote: 'Our good Queen has the wolf by the ears', Mary being the wolf."

"Ready to devour our good Queen's vitals."

"And Mr. Secretary always calls her 'The Bosom Viper' to suggest the close personal danger which the imprisoned Mary has represented to Elizabeth and will continue to represent so long as one flashing fang could seat her on Elizabeth's throne and turn the lives of five million Englishmen topsy-turvy overnight. This sword of Damocles has hung over the head of the English people for a very long time. Twenty-five years ago, when Mary Stuart became Queen of France, she made her desire for the English throne quite clear by having the English leopards quartered on her escutcheon along with the lilies of France."

"I understand there was a group formed for the specific purpose of offsetting that possibility."

"The Bond of Association. Correct. It was formed last year and is made up of thousands of Englishmen who have sworn an oath to execute anyone who might profit from the assassination of our Queen, particularly anyone who might thereafter succeed directly to the throne."

"Which narrows it specifically to Mary Stuart."

"Exactly its purpose. The bond was signed by virtually every important personage in the realm—the kind of unified response that should guarantee any undertaking. It's interesting to note, however, that a few gentlemen, good Anglicans too, recognized the essential lawlessness of the Bond and refused to sign."

"Lawlessness?"

"Indeed so. If Elizabeth is ever assassinated—God forbid—all her royally commissioned officers, the council members, judges, and all government workers would, at that fatal moment, lose their authority to function in office. Since the Queen has not yet named a successor, there would be no legitimate authority other than the legal claimant to the throne, Mary Stuart."

"So, in effect, there would be no interested person left with authority enough to exact legal revenge for the slaying of our Queen?"

"That's right. The English people in their great sorrow would be forced to watch a smirking Mary Stuart ascend the throne even though it was strongly suspected she had gained the crown by killing our Queen and breaking our English hearts. That possibility was too much for loyal subjects to bear without taking preemptive action."

"You're really talking illegal action then."

"Damn right! The lawyers could argue legalities for centuries to come, but the deed would be done, and we would not have a Spanish ruler, but we would have a Scottish one instead, since her son James is the next in line of succession to the crown. James, however, has enough sense to cater to his power base. He'd make no attempt to inflict the Peter's Pence tithing on England by handing us back to Rome. He'd rather keep English gold in Scottish pockets."

"That's an advantage?"

"Certainly. Scotland has fewer pockets and they tend to be less deep."

"It does begin to sound like no misadventure in the world will permit Mary Stuart from ever reaching our throne."

"Right. If an assassin ever takes our Queen from us, nearly every gentleman in England is sworn to arm himself on the instant and race hell-bent to plunge his dagger not only into the assassin but into the heart of the Queen of Scots as well. There would be no stopping them. England would constrict with anger before it succumbed to grief, and Mary would be quickly dispatched."

"Egad, that is a strong message, indeed. I imagine that will give the Scottish woman some sleepless nights."

"Don't make the mistake many have made of underestimating Mary Stuart. When she heard of the Bond, she offered to sign it herself."

"Monarchial audacity!"

Phelippes nodded. "The strange part is that Mary certainly knows the only thing that has kept her alive all these years is the princely vow Elizabeth took when Mary first sought her protection back in '68."

"Elizabeth made a vow?"

Phelippes nodded. "A public vow. When Elizabeth opened England's hospitality to her beleaguered cousin, she promised as a queen she would never endanger either the life or the honor of Mary Stuart during her stay as England's guest, and she has kept that promise all these years—often to the complete distraction of her advisors. Our office gets frequent reminders of how dangerous this living Mary Stuart actually is from the number of conspiracies which we must quell. Yet the Scottish Vixen goes on flirting with her own destruction by encouraging plots against her protector. Even Elizabeth, when she occasionally grows exasperated with the situation, regrets the vow she made. She has sometimes been heard to mutter in private that Mary's head should have been struck off years ago."

"Why hasn't it been done?"

"The Queen won't allow it. As a matter of fact, the original charter proposed by the Association was undoubtedly the most illegal statute ever attempted in English common law, since it provided no trial for the suspects, only execution. Elizabeth made them change it. Two months ago, after all the wrangling, the final form of the Bond of Association became law."

"So now the trials and executions would become legal?"

"Not exactly, but as the lawyers are fond of saying, that's a moot point. Thanks to the Bond of Association, everyone on both sides now knows that Mary Stuart will never succeed to the throne of England by force. If we ever lose Elizabeth through misadventure, or if a Spanish invasion force ever lands on our shore, all of England will descend on the Scottish Queen, sword in hand, and that's the message the Bond hopes to circulate. There will be no profit in killing our Queen in hopes of replacing her with Catholic Mary."

"But what if Elizabeth should die naturally," asked William. "Would Mary Stuart then be allowed to take the throne?"

"That would be a very bitter pill for this realm to swallow, and I don't know that it would go down. There are few Englishmen who would relish a re-submission to Papal authority, especially since orders from Rome would certainly involve transferring English land and money to the same people who thereafter plan to burn us at the stake if we don't exchange our relaxed Anglican pew for their rigid Catholic prayer bench. Worshiping the same God does not make us allies. Mr. Secretary—" he nodded toward the inner office— "like all the Puritans, is livid with anger at the thought of some foreign instrumentality dictating the details of his religious worship. The Puritans feel they already have trouble enough from a skeptical Queen and a suspicious Archbishop."

"Everybody says the last time England turned Catholic was a disaster."

"It was hellish. During the five-year reign of Elizabeth's half-sister, Bloody Mary, from '53 to '58, England was quickly returned to Catholicism, and Queen Mary married the very Catholic King of Spain, Philip II. Queen Mary Tudor—whom some called a Spaniard at heart—helped the Pope regain title to some of the lands which Henry had taken from Rome in the '30's, and the transfer left bitter feelings among all English landowners, even Catholics. Most merchants also fear a repeat of such a change because it brought regular business to a standstill. Land deeds and property rights were called into question during a lengthy legal examination and often ended up being transferred by one legal justification or another to the Pope."

"Bitter, indeed," exclaimed William. "Is it certain that Mary Stuart would return England to Catholicism if she ascended the throne?"

"No question," Phelippes nodded. "She has repeatedly stated she will never leave her imprisonment except as Queen of England. She has already designated Philip of Spain her successor to the throne if Elizabeth should happen to precede her in death and she were Queen of England even briefly. She has named him the most trustworthy and resolute Catholic in the world—which, no doubt, he is, but she might have mentioned vengeful too. I imagine Mary Stuart would happily accept martyrdom if she thought her death would deliver England from heresy. I often think the Bond of Association actually formed in the minds of most Englishmen the instant Mary announced that the Spanish king was to be her successor."

"Have all of the assassination attempts been linked to the Catholics?"

"Catholics and crazies," Phelippes nodded. "It was clear some years ago that Catholic gold was financing what appeared to be annual attempts on the lives of the Protestant leaders after Spanish King Philip outlawed them and put a price on their heads. William of Orange, the strongest Protestant leader on the Continent and the linchpin of the Dutch rebellion, was killed last year even while he was recovering from a wound he received the year before in one of four previous attempts. The official report said he was shot to death by a crazed Dutch worker for some obscure religious reason. Catholic to the core and crazy too. The killer claimed he did the deed to show that no person is above retribution for his misdeeds and to show that no person is so low that he may not serve as God's instrument to carry out his justice."

"Operating by himself?"

"That's the way those things often go. Groups which plan assassinations are often uncovered because someone gets careless, or someone acts suspicious, or someone betrays the attempt, but the job is often carried out successfully by some half-crazed individual whose well-earned anonymity hides him from view and facilitates access to his target since he is not a known threat until the moment after he radically changes the order of the world."

"The death of William of Orange, then, must have been another reason the Bond of Association got started?"

"It helped give form to a central conviction growing in the minds of Englishmen. Ever since the Pope promised forgiveness to anyone who killed our Queen, we have seen Catholic plots boiling with increasing frequency."

"I can't believe the Pope did that!" exclaimed William. "Do we have evidence that the Catholics are always involved?"

Phelippes snorted. "Malachi mentioned you might lack a little background in the business. While our work may not be spoken of publicly, every worker in the Service should know the details of our recent successes, so he may learn who and what to look for. Three years ago, back in '82, we intercepted an agent of the Spanish ambassador to Scotland, who had been running secret messages from Spain to Scotland, disguised as a dentist. Unfortunately, this agent managed to escape by bribing our guards, but he left behind a mirror which concealed letters mentioning what the Spanish call 'The Enterprise.' We determined from the notes that 'The Enterprise' is nothing less than a planned invasion of England by the Spaniards and the seating of Mary Stuart on the English throne after the elimination of Elizabeth."

"And I guess it's pretty certain the dentist-agent was a Catholic?"

Phelippes cracked a laugh. "From Spain? I think you can bet on it. And a year later, in 1583, we followed one of Mary's visitors, young Francis Throckmorton—a Catholic gentleman and the nephew of Ambassador Throckmorton—until we found that he was actually an agent for Mary Stuart, running secret mail for her. We seized his papers when we grabbed him, and they revealed further 'Enterprise' details along with a list of English Catholic noblemen who might be interested in the undertaking. The papers also contained a list of English harbors well suited to receive Spanish landing parties."

"Egad," shivered William. "Incriminating stuff."

"Throckmorton stood up surprisingly well to the rack during his first session, but finally, he was forced to reveal that the Spanish Ambassador to England, Mendoza, was deeply involved in financing the plot. Upon being ordered to leave England, Mendoza promised our Queen that if he could not satisfy her as a minister in peace, he would do so in war. Before war comes, however, we expect the plots to continue. King Philip of Spain certainly knows as well as anyone that a quick knife thrust, or a single bullet, or a poisoned dish, could gain him the throne of England faster and cheaper than the armada he seems to be planning. A fat bag of gold or a promised pension might not tip over all English Catholics, but it takes only one to get the killing done."

"Can't Elizabeth insulate herself from such people?"

Phelippes sighed deeply. "She is very difficult to protect because she refuses to tolerate close personal guards, and she exposes herself daily to danger by holding open court amidst a hundred or so of her attendants and courtiers. She insists on being available to her people and has never hidden her deep desire to be the center of all attention at every gathering. That desire, however, may save her life some day because it requires that every court member keep most of his attention centered on the Queen while she is in attendance. Woe betide the courtier who gets so involved in courtly dalliance that he loses track of the Queen's words and fails to reply in context when she questions him. That man might as well sail for the New World for all his career would be worth in England. Further, no one approaches Elizabeth who has not passed through a gauntlet of jealous courtiers who are conditioned to assess every motion extended to the Queen and who stand ready to intercept any threat which presents itself."

"Is everybody around her armed?"

"The gentlemen of her Court all believe they must wear swords or daggers to protect her, but outsiders are expected to approach without weapons. Even when the Queen is on progress about the country, a mobile security area called the 'verge' is set up around her, twelve miles deep. Extra security precautions are taken within that circle: traffic on the roads is observed more closely, crossroads are watched, troublemakers are jailed, and discontents are questioned directly. When major crimes like murder are committed within the verge, they are investigated by her household legal people."

"That begins to sound like a pretty big household."

"It is, but its very size permits us to stick our security people into the Royal presence on a rotating basis. We usually have some gardeners or porters or servants working close to the Queen to keep an eye on things. We can protect the Queen to some degree even without her cooperation, but the coverage is admittedly spotty. We've been lucky so far. A few years ago, we intercepted a packet containing a letter in code from one plotter to another, describing a plan to seize the English throne by doing away with Elizabeth."

"And since you are the code-master, the difficult task of breaking the code was turned over to you?"

"Usually difficult, but in this case a walk-through. Even you could have decoded it in a few minutes."

"The code was so simple?"

"Not simple at all, but the sender had conveniently included the code-key in the packet to permit the receiver to decode the message, and we used that key to uncover a plot we were not even aware of until that moment."

Phelippes snickered, and William grinned broadly. "Big sigh of relief at the office on that one," continued Phelippes. "And lucky again last year when details of 'The Enterprise' were torn up and thrown overboard when our Dutch allies grabbed the Jesuit, Creighten, on his way to England to make trouble. The wind blew the notes back onboard, and the Dutch put the pieces together to reveal the plot."

"Egad, Elizabeth's guardian angels were really on the job that time," laughed William. "Tell me, does Malachi ever get a chance to serve on the Royal household staff?"

"Most assuredly," Phelippes said. "Happens all the time."

"In what capacity?"

"Whatever they need," said Phelippes. "Could be anything. Even menial stuff."

"I would like to see that," murmured William. "Will Madrid and Rome back off if Mary is taken out of circulation?"

"I imagine neither Spain nor the Vatican is counting on Mary's surviving further attempts on Elizabeth's life, or living past the first day of any invasion on England's shores."

"But her son James, you say, is the next in line for our throne?"

"Right. At the moment, he is the nineteen year old king of Scotland. Mary Stuart is the granddaughter of Margaret Tudor, the daughter of our Henry VII and sister of Henry VIII. Margaret married the Scot king, James IV, when she was thirteen, and they had two surviving sons, James and Alexander. James became king of Scotland at age one and a half and married Mary of Guise—also known as Mary of Lorraine."

"What a lot of Jameses the Scots have had as kings."

"That's true, and two others preceded Margaret Tudor's James IV, who reigned twenty-five years and promoted great growth in such areas as music, poetry, surgery, building, jousting, and science. He died, like his son, on the battlefield–fighting England, as a matter of fact–at a very young age. Mary Stuart became Queen of Scotland when she was one week old, and her mother, Mary of Guise, became regent. She grew up in France and became the Queen of France at seventeen when her husband of one year became King Francis II. A year later her husband died from an abscessed ear, and at age eighteen, she went back to being Queen of Scotland."

"Curious to think of royalty being felled by something so commonplace as an abscessed ear," William mused. "It seems as if there ought to be more drama in the death of a king."

"Perfectly natural," said Phelippes. "Francis had a tendency to be somewhat sickly, but if you relish something out of the ordinary in the way of monarchial departures, let me tell you about the unusual death of Francis' father, Henry II, in 1559."

"Just so it's a French Henry and not another English Henry!"

"This King Henry was the victim of one of those freak accidents which make jousting such a great spectator sport. A young earl's lance splintered when he rode against Henry, and two pieces penetrated the king's armor by entering both the eyehole of his helmet and a seam in the chain mail at his throat. Henry survived for nine days in exquisite pain but finally succumbed to his injuries. Oddly enough his death became the subject of a literary debate which nearly got a French poet-prophet burned at the stake because some people felt he had foreseen the King's death too clearly."

"A poet-prophet predicted Henry's death at a jousting match?"

"I don't know if you've ever heard of Michel de Nostradamus, but he was a French astrologer, born in 1503. In 1555 he published 942 quatrains which are said by some to predict coming events in the way of kings falling, wars starting, tyrants appearing, and natural catastrophes happening. Of course, some feel his four-line verses are so general as to apply to many occasions."

"But one of them applied to King Henry's death?"

"Right. Four years before the king was killed, Nostradamus had written:

> 'The young lion shall overcome the old one
> In martial field by a single duel
> In a cage of gold he shall put out his eye
> Two wounds from one, then he shall die a cruel death.'" [1]

"That 'two wounds from one' sounds like the shattering lance."

"The pro-prophesy group mentioned that point and that the king's helmet, with its gilded visor, resembled a cage and that nine painful days certainly is a cruel death, so they raised an outcry for the burning of the astrologer on the charge that he had prophesied so well and so ill for the king. But cooler heads prevailed, and Nostradamus was allowed to live out his years, gazing at his stars."

"That's good," William said. "I don't like it when the public comes after the poet, whose only desire is to entertain and enlighten, not to confuse the masses with posturing like so many ambitious political people do."

"Many political people seem endlessly ambitious, all right. Even though Mary Stuart has already been queen of France and of Scotland, she still hopes to gain one more European crown as queen of England before her collection is completed. During these last seventeen years, Mary has dropped rank from a queen to a blocked pawn on the ninth file. She is extremely vulnerable, but she is yet within a single move of immense power which could distort every English life for years to come."

"Why haven't we shipped her back to Scotland where her son is king?"

"Mary was never a good fit in Scotland. When she returned from France, a teenage Catholic queen, she ran head on into the fiery Calvinist, John Knox, whose spirited preaching had already won over a large contingent of Protestant Scottish noblemen. None of those were at all happy to have a youthful Catholic queen returned to their midst to show them the error of their ways."

"An older, wiser person might have reduced her fervency, as did our Queen Bess."

"Catholics have a difficult time pulling back, it seems."

"When did she remarry?"

"She refused Elizabeth's offer of marriage to the newly minted Earl of Leicester—Elizabeth's old favorite, Robert Dudley, all polished up. She feared such a union would put an English spy in her bed, and, of course, she did not want her cousin's romantic hand-me-downs. Instead, she married Lord Darnley, who was described in the pubs as a 'handsome, beardless, lady-faced' young Englishman who helped her produce the son who is now the reigning monarch of Scotland, King James VI."

"Lady-faced?"

"Soft, ineffectual, not bright, drank too much, easily flattered into serving as a front man by contentious Scottish groups to exert pressure on Mary. Finally, in 1566, he was persuaded by a group of nobles to lead them into Mary's chambers in order to drag from behind her skirts the man they felt exerted too much French-Catholic influence on Mary, the diminutive Italian David Riccio. Some say he was a dwarf. He was not only Mary's private secretary but also her closest confidante. He frequently shared her table, and some said her bed—outright nonsense, that!"

"Some women like a little novelty."

Phelippes gave William a look of scorn before continuing. "Riccio's assassins dragged him just outside her door and killed him with fifty-eight knife stabs. "year later, Mary's people paid Darnley back with a little murder of their own. An assassin's bomb blew him out of bed one night and set his house ablaze. He escaped through an upstairs window, staggered around in a daze and was watching his house burn when some unknown person seized both the opportunity and his neck and throttled him to death in his garden, still dressed in his night clothes."

"Did they ever find the murderer?"

"Court testimony later revealed that Mary's lover, the Earl of Bothwell—who was a Protestant, oddly enough—along with some of his followers, lit the fuse to the explosion, but it was never quite clear who did the strangling. Bothwell was suspected of the murder, and Scotsmen for a time divided themselves along 'guilty' and 'not guilty' lines in addition to their other deep-seated animosities."

"What was decided?" asked William with great interest.

"Nothing, at the time. While the debate raged, Bothwell abducted Mary from her informal confinement and was later reported to have 'raped' her."

"I thought they were lovers!" cried William.

"They were. The report was political hokum. There was a mock trail, then, charging Bothwell with the murder of Darnley, but he was quickly acquitted. But then he and Mary married, which inflamed all Scot patriots since it infused his blood into the Royal Scottish line of succession. Forces gathered again, and battles raged."

"Was Lord Bothwell's blood so much less noble than Darnley's?"

"I believe Darnley had a drop of royal blood in him, but the conflict was mostly a political uproar over who held power in Scotland. Anyway, Mary and her forces were defeated. She was imprisoned and forced to abdicate the throne in favor of her son James. The game was up in Scotland for Mary and Bothwell both. They were separated and forced to flee. Thus, in 1568, Mary arrived on the English border, hotly pursued by the Scottish people she had ruled for many years, who were shouting things like 'Kill that murderous whore!' and 'Murder the adulterous Catholic bitch!'"

"Oh, ye fickle crowds!" William shook his head. "How about The Earl of Bothwell?"

"He fled to the Continent to raise forces to support his wife and encountered there an unfriendly group with whom he had had previous dealings. They settled an old score by tossing him into a dank, Danish dungeon, said to be an oubliette, wherein one is dropped in and forgotten. He lay there for ten years and withered to the point of insanity before perishing."

"What a price to pay for love!" cried William. "Perhaps our Queen Bess learned from all this that royals can't follow their hearts, and so She gave up Robert Dudley's love those many years ago. Imagine Dudley in a dank, Danish dungeon!" William shuddered, tasting the alliteration on his tongue. "But tell me about James; doesn't the son want his mother back?"

"You would think so," Phelippes said, "and Mary thought so too when she announced to Elizabeth last year that she had made an agreement with her son to return to Scotland and share power with him in ruling the land. The prospect of having Mary out from underfoot appeared so promising originally, it caused Elizabeth to break her fourteen-year vow of never again writing in her own hand to the Scottish Woman. She proposed a treaty which returned Mary Stuart to Scotland as long as Mary swore she would encourage no further plots against the life of Elizabeth. The agreement never reached the signing stage, however, because letters intercepted in the meantime showed that Mary was already telling her people to go on with the plotting even if she signed the agreement."

"Why would a king want such a tricky person, relative or not—back in his country?"

"As it turned out, he didn't want her. King James has no intention of jeopardizing his chance to succeed to the English throne by confronting Queen Elizabeth who still may nominate her successor as long as she is alive. He made his position public recently when he declared; *'How fond and inconstant I were if I should prefer my mother to the title, let all men judge'.*" [2]

Well," William cried, "I am ready to let my best judgment fall on King James and here it is!

> *'How sharper than a serpent's tooth it is*
> *To have a thankless child'.*"[3]

"Hold on now," Phelippes cautioned. "Don't forget that James hasn't seen his mother since childhood and appears to feel little filial affection for her. In addition, of course, he wants to protect the alliance he has with Elizabeth because the £4,000 pension it brings him each year is a big part of his budget in a country that doesn't circulate much hard money."

"Oh, Ho! £4,000 ! Oh, yes, The picture becomes clearer now!

> *See, sons, what things you are!*
> *How quickly nature falls into revolt*
> *When gold becomes her object!'*"[4]

Phelippes nodded. "I suppose money will always have a voice even in the highest circles, but the truth is that the nineteen-year-old King shows no inclination to share his crown with anybody. He is definitely disinclined to introduce a zealous, lying, scheming, ambitious partner into his bickering domain—mother or not. As it turned out, however, there was no agreement with her son. Mary made the whole thing up and was infuriated when James did not go along. She unleashed her fury on the Scottish ambassador, who had served as the go-between for the pair of them, denouncing him as *"worthy to be baptized as a lying knave."'* [5]

"I suppose morality comes on a sliding scale for the top people," said William philosophically.

"Pretty hard to stay out of trouble if you have pledged your loyalty to as many earthly entities as Mary has. She has sworn her unwavering fealty to the Pope, to Philip of Spain, to Elizabeth, to the people of Scotland, and to the people of France. Carrying that much loose baggage makes it only a matter of time before you trip yourself up."

"In the end, then, you don't think the certainty of Mary's death might persuade Philip and Pope Leo to stay their hands?"

"Quite the contrary, I think the Bond of Association has forced their hands. They've each played enough chess to know how to sacrifice a helpless piece. A successful attempt on Elizabeth's life would be regarded as an act of war if Mary were not around to take the blame. As a matter of fact, Philip may be thinking of killing two birds with one stone. If he could do away with Elizabeth and have Mary implicated in the murder, he could clear the board of the two queens and checkmate all other claimants by enforcing his distant claim to the English throne in much the same manner as he annexed the crown of Portugal five years ago."

"Why should he want to get rid of Mary since she is a loyal Catholic?"

"Yes, but French-Catholic. Not the same thing at all. Philip certainly doesn't want to waste Spanish gold conquering England, only to find he has strengthened France. My God! Twenty million Frenchmen! If they ever quit chasing each other in circles, they could overrun all of Europe!"

"How many Spaniards are there?"

"Just half that number, about ten million. And the English are roughly a quarter of that number, about five million."

The door to the inner office opened, and Malachi signaled the two young men to enter.

"Phelippes!" Walsingham called from the front office. "Bring your code book in here! We need to get these facts from Gifford down in black and white while Malachi is here to quote them verbatim." His hawk-like gaze took in William, who stood close to Malachi's sheltering bulk.

"Is Gilbert Gifford's cross exam completed, then?" asked Phelippes.

"Gifford has been quite civilized, actually. He confessed readily to being paid by Morgan to set up a secret delivery system, so the Bosom Viper could receive mail not monitored by our office. Thanks be to God, we stopped them in their tracks! We've got our Viper so isolated, there is no room left for her to continue plotting against Elizabeth. Splendid work all around. Splendid!"

"And well directed, sir!" Phelippes took time to praise his boss.

"Remind him of Mary's servants," William murmured to Malachi.

Malachi grinned. "My man begs to remind us of Shrewsbury, sir, of Mary's ring of servants, working as spies."

"Yes, yes, that will all be attended to. No stone unturned. It was only one servant at Shrewsbury, to be precise, who was involved in exchanging secret correspondence with Mr. Curle, one of Mary's personal secretaries. We jailed the servant and issued a stern rebuke to Mr. Curle."

"How often do stern rebukes work?" William wondered.

"And I'm sure," Malachi said quickly, "that you've taken steps to see that kind of arrangement doesn't get started again?"

"Ah yes, God be praised.. The Scottish Viper is now in the hands of Amias Paulet as honest and alert and incorruptible a soul as can be found in all of England. A Puritan, of course. A good man all 'round. Also the former English ambassador to the French Court. His vigilant care at Tutbury Castle will hold the Viper secure once and for all. He will always be present at any conversational exchange between his servants and hers, set a guard to accompany her servants on every errand outside the residence, and permit no strangers into the castle. We have instructed him to pay particular attention to the coachmen and laundresses and the like; it is often the unimportant people who betray security."

"Indeed, yes," echoed Phelippes, "House security is very tight. Very tight."

"And when the Queen of Scots rides out, I'm sure security is even tighter," nodded William sagely. "I understand she frequently seeks a breath of fresh air by way of horse or coach."

"Paulet has specific instructions on that very subject," Walsingham replied. "Phelippes, where is that list? Ah, yes, here it is: *You shall order that she shall not, in taking the air, pass through any towns nor suffer the people to be in the way where she shall pass, appointing some always to go before to make them to withdraw themselves, for that heretofore, under colour of giving alms and other extraordinary courses used by her, she hath won the hearts of the people that habit about those places where she hath heretofore lain.*" [6]

"Very wise," purred Phelippes.

Walsingham nodded. "She is very sly, that one. Because Elizabeth covers her expenses, she is free to spend her own money buying support by her contributions to local organizations as well as to individuals. How ironic! How vile! The salutes of the ignorant crowds that her money gains her! Do not doubt that insidious viper uses every weapon at her disposal!"

"No doubt Mr. Paulet can be counted on to keep the people away," said William.

"Indubitably!" said Walsingham. "Paulet has pledged himself in no uncertain terms: '*I will never ask pardon if she depart out of my hands by any treacherous slight or cunning device, because I must confess that the same cannot come to pass without some gross negligence or rather treacherous carelessness; and if I shall be assaulted with force at home or abroad, as I will not be beholden to traitors for my life, whereof I make little account in respect to my allegiance to the Queen my sovereign, so I will be assured by the grace of God that she shall die before me.*'" [7] In short, he will never let her loose to become queen; he will die first!"

"Sounds like a good Bond of Association man," Malachi observed. "I imagine Gifford would have little chance to outfox such a vigilant keeper."

"Even if Gifford had managed to set up a secure system, they would have had to deliver her mail in batches," Walsingham intoned. "We cut off her delivery when we moved her in January to a more secure residence. Since then the Viper hasn't received any of her mail. It's piling up at the French Embassy here. It's not surprising they are taking special pains to try to get it delivered, and it's not surprising either, Malachi, that you have once again been a key performer in getting our job done properly. Superb job. Superb."

"Nothing to it," Malachi shrugged good naturedly. "Once we heard from Nick Berden in Paris that Morgan was sending Gifford back to England, I figured he would assume his real identity since that would permit him to return to his home county of Staffordshire very near where Mary is being housed. I simply advised our custom people to watch for a Staffordshire passport and they nailed him."

"What did Gifford disclose, sir?" asked Phelippes.

"Quite a bit," Walsingham said. "Very chatty. Gifford trained for one of the minor orders of priesthood, but I think he's not quite the dedicated Catholic as some. He loves to talk. Told us that Morgan had described for him the complete history of the effort to get mail through to the Viper. The pressure really started to build on her people in Paris when we moved her from the doubtful care of the Earl of Shrewsbury at Sheffield Castle, and cut off her mail completely."

"Doubtful care?" William inquired.

"Not necessarily the Earl himself," Malachi explained softly, "although rumor had it that Mary seduced the Earl. In truth, the situation at Sheffield Castle was simply not leakproof. We closed off all the holes we could control, of course, but the Countess of Shrewsbury—Bess of Hardwick—often joined Mary Stuart in ridiculing Elizabeth within hearing of the servants."

"Ridiculing Elizabeth?" William exclaimed.

"The Countess is infamous for her acid tongue, which does not hesitate to accuse the Queen of insatiable lust with Hatton, Leicester, Raleigh, and any number of foreign delegates, and attribute to her such a foolish vanity that she delights in being told it is impossible to look her squarely in the face since her countenance shines like the sun. It was not surprising, therefore, that such household disrespect encouraged actual breeches in security and permitted secret mail to get through."

"But that's not the case at Tutbury," Phelippes gloated.

Walsingham nodded agreement. "Paulet has the place locked up tight as a drum. We can now sit back and let the Bosom Viper expose herself, God aid us. What we need at this point is enough evidence to convince Elizabeth that the threat to her life is very real—very real, indeed—and that it is finally time to end this Catholic conspiracy. I am haunted by the fact that the Viper is nine years younger than Elizabeth, so that if nature takes its course—"

"So we propose to merely wait for Mary to take action?" William murmured.

"God is just and will respond to England's great need to call that Viper to a final accounting, never fear."

"May I make an observation, sir?" William asked.

"I really wish you wouldn't," said Malachi.

Walsingham gave Malachi a sharp glance. "More advice from this puppy? I thought you said you could keep him quiet!"

Malachi shrugged. "You know how help is these days, sir. They will have their say no matter how soundly we thrash them for it. I'm sure it will only take a moment."

Walsingham snorted. "What is it, then, young man?"

"I admit," William said, "I know very little about politics or statecraft or policy-making—"

"Devil take thee, man, get on with it!" Walsingham growled. "We'll be here all night if you detail for us what you don't know. What do you know?"

"I know that whenever we visit this office, I sense the discussions are conducted at cross-purposes."

"Cross-purposes?" Walsingham repeated in a hollow tone.

William nodded. "You gentlemen spend half your time congratulating yourselves for foiling another attempt by Mary's people to set up a secret mail service, and half your time bemoaning the fact that you can't get the goods on her so you can put her away for good."

"Your point being?" Walsingham asked in a tight voice.

"It just doesn't play well," William pointed out.

"Play well?"

"You're tripping over your own plot lines."

"Plot lines?"

"You're shutting down your character's on-going movement at the end of Act two. You have developed stasis and introduced non-drama."

"Malachi," Walsingham growled. "If he doesn't stop doing this, I shall rise from my chair at whatever cost to my gout and plunge my dagger up to the hilt into his."

"I'm sure he is ready to get to the point now, sir." Malachi assured him and glared at William.

"The point is," William explained slowly, "your plot can't thicken if you pull the curtain on Mary Stuart so soon in the action."

"What are you suggesting?" Walsingham asked. "That we let her set up a mail service and then intercept it? I can tell you right now that we have hoped for that very thing. Mary is a very active intriguer, but she has no conception at all of secret correspondence. In letters we have already intercepted, she suggests that her friends reach her secretly by hiding messages in the hollow heels of her visitor's shoes or writing them with lemon juice so they are only readable if held up to a strong light. She knows only the kinds of things we all learned as schoolboys. She could not succeed in setting up a secret post even if we let her."

"If you want to put legs on your plot," William advised, "set it up for her."

Malachi and Walsingham and Phelippes looked blank.

"Use Gifford to gain her trust and let him set it up. From the stories I've heard, he is a very convincing actor. Lead him onstage while controlling him from the wings."

"It's true he carries a letter from Morgan introducing him to the Viper as well as to Monsieur Chateauneuf at the French Embassy here in town," mused Walsingham. "He could meet her without arousing suspicion and soon gain her confidence."

"Socially, he's all smoke and snake oil," Malachi assured him, "so I think she'll warm to him nicely, if we can get him to work for us."

"Don't worry," Walsingham smiled. "I'll offer him no alternative. We'll also keep a constant check on him. I'm wondering now if we might return the Bosom Viper to Sheffield Castle so it would be easier for Gifford to set up the post in those loose surroundings."

Malachi smiled. "I'm sure Bess of Hardwick would be willing to lend a helping hand if she could thereby further aggravate Elizabeth."

"And I have no doubt the Earl will be happy to see her again," Phelippes leered.

"Gentlemen, please," William interposed. "Let's not blow the top off the brew we're mixing. Mary is certainly aware that her secret mail was stopped when you moved her from Sheffield to Tutbury. When you move her back, won't she sense an obvious trap?"

"Probably. We'll just have to take that chance," said Walsingham.

"Not really, if you know enough to heighten the drama," William explained. "Don't make it easier for her to set up a secret mail system, make it harder. Turn all the lions loose for the final act. Don't work on making her suspicious, work on making her confident that she has overcome real obstacles because only then will she feel free to reveal herself and play out the de'nouement you desire. Don't you have some really isolated estate where you could create the illusion of rigid supervision while permitting Gifford to burrow in out of sight?"

"By Jove," said Walsingham "The Earl of Essex has a moated castle at Chartley, just a few miles from Tutbury. We could get her moved over there in two or three days and then work out the delivery system."

"One of the weekly delivery people already on our payroll," suggested William softly.

"The greengrocer or butcher or brewer could easily hide a packet of letters in their delivery," said Walsingham, taking up the suggestion. "And they would have little trouble concealing outgoing mail in baskets or carts or containers when they leave. We would pay them a little extra, just enough to keep them loyal."

"A beer barrel would be ideal," said William, again softly. At his side, Malachi grinned at his sly tactic and said nothing.

"We'll approach the brewer," continued Walsingham, "because we'll need a barrel-sized letter-box for the accumulated correspondence. Once Gifford picks up her mail from the French Ambassador here in London, he'll deliver it to us and we'll read it through and make copies. Then we'll have Gifford turn it over to the brewer."

"Will the barrel be empty or full of beer?" asked Phellips, spell-bound.

"Full, so we'll have to wrap the letters in oil-skin and maybe even put them inside a small casket that will slip in and out of the barrel bunghole. Gifford can arrange for one of her secretaries to receive it. Her mail will come out the same way. Splendid arrangement."

"Splendid indeed!" Phelippes exhaulted. "Very well thought out. sir."

"Glad it entertains your intricate mind, Master Phelippes," Walsingham smiled, "because I want you to travel tomorrow to Chartley and use your devious brain to make all of this happen. If we could only get a little cooperation from our Bosom Viper in making the move, we could get her transferred very quickly, and then we could set our plot up on its legs. I know she feels Tutbury is too chilly, so maybe we could sell her Chartley on the basis of her health."

"Block off the fresh air to the cess-pool area, and she'll leave in two days," Malachi assured him.

"Good," Walsingham agreed, rubbing his hands together. "Every man now has a job. Phelippes, you get out to Chartley and find some enterprising brewer who is not averse to making a few pounds for a little secret cooperation. Malachi, after I convince Gifford to work with us, I'll want you to consult with him in establishing the practical steps needed to monitor the secret mail as it is delivered from London to Chartley. Whatever it takes, make sure the delivery system is secure from tricks and manipulations other than those originating in this office. First thing tomorrow, you direct Gifford to present his letter from Morgan to the French Ambassador here in London and get a second introductory letter from that office to Mary. That should do the trick as far as convincing her to put her trust in Gifford." Walsingham's eyes gleamed as the scheme unfolded.

"Come to think of it," Malachi said, "I recall that the community of Chartley has no brewery of its own. The closest big town is Burton. They do have a brewery there."

"No problem," Phelippes shrugged. "As long as they deliver."

The men shared a chuckle at the sally, and Walsingham turned to William. "And you, young man, get out to Tutbury as quickly as you can and block up that cess-pool system any way you can."

Chapter 2:
THE BURTON BEER-BARREL SCHEME

Whitehall, February 25, 1586:

"I know remembering things is not your specialty, William," Malachi said, "but do you recall that a few months ago we mentioned that Ralph Lane, on his way to set up the Virginia colony last summer, wrote to Sir Phillip Sidney from the West Indies and told him that many of the Spanish colonial settlements they visited for supplies were lightly defended and could easily be taken by a determined force?"

"I do remember that, yes. It was when Sidney and Drake were still working together before Drake sailed in mid-September."

"Right. Sailed and obviously took a determined force with him, as suggested, since we've just received details of Drake's capture of San Domingo, the capitol of Hispaniola and the legal and administrative center of the Spanish West Indies Colonies. That was in November."

"Egad, San Domingo sounds like a place that would have been well defended."

"Right again. It was heavily fortified against any attack that tried to approach through the narrow harbor entrance, which was covered by well-placed shore batteries. As we know, however, Drake is not a captain who does what the other fellow anticipates—at least not *when* he anticipates it. On the second day, Drake did what the Spanish expected by gathering his ships just outside the harbor entrance to exchange canon fire with the shore batteries and by lowering his longboats as though preparing a direct assault on the harbor. The Spanish naturally drew every man they had into a protective ring around the waterfront."

"And I'll guess that's exactly when Drake's first day's work made itself felt."

"Right. I'm glad to see you are getting a rudimentary feel for the creation of illusion. On the evening of the first day, Drake landed half his attack group—about 1,200 men—several miles down the beach out of sight from San Domingo, and that group spent the first night getting into position just outside the city. The next day, as the Spanish defenders trained all their guns on the threatening boats approaching from the ships, they were suddenly attacked from the rear by a well-coordinated assault group which rolled them up with drums rattling and pennants flying. The pincher-attack soon threw the defenders into disarray which quickly dissolved into dismay at the sudden success of Drake's strategy, and the city was captured with little loss on either side."

"Does that mean another big pot of gold for Drake?"

"Hard to tell. The Spanish don't let much gold accumulate anyplace before it is shipped off to Havana for the trip back to Spain. There is some gold, no doubt, but even that will be hidden, and Drake won't get it unless he threatens to burn the place down, which might be a little difficult since most of the buildings in San Domingo are built of stone. He'll have to hold the leaders for ransom and hope the community spirit is such that they will pay handsomely to get them back."

"I certainly wish him success in collecting," said William. "But tell me now, how well is our decoding of Mary's Stuart's mail going? When I stopped by a few days ago to offer my services in copying, as you suggested, it seemed to me there was still a lot of chaos and uncertainty in the air. My question is, have we succeeded in allaying the suspicions of the Scottish Woman?"

Malachi smiled, "Mary Stuart was absolutely quivering with excitement at the prospect of finally receiving some of her secret mail after waiting a year for it."

"Excuse me for commenting on technique," William said, "but if you could see her quivering, weren't you a little close for a simple shadow-job?"

"I got that report through a maid."

"All this while I was riding hither and yon, stirring up cesspools while you were meddling with maids?"

"Speaking of work," Malachi chuckled. "If I live to be a thousand, I'll never forget the shock you gave our work crew when you crumpled up that bunch of Mary's letters in Phelippes' office. Walsingham was livid. He had been hovering like a hawk, making sure we treated each letter with the greatest care so there would be no sign of our tampering when Mary got it at Chartley. The extra care, of course, slowed us considerably. Then you made your slam-bang suggestion." Malachi chuckled. "You realize, Walsingham is quite uneasy about your dramatic flair in a service as secret as ours, so he holds you on probation, but he was very impressed with your suggestion. Very impressed."

"Nothing really," William shrugged. "Some of us simply forgot that Mary would expect her mail to be crushed and battered when it was stuffed into that oilskin wrapping and squeezed through the beer barrel bunghole. The crumpled letters provided her with validating evidence that her people had overcome real difficulties in setting up a secure and secret mail system."

"Well, it was quite a sight to see Walsingham leap up and begin crumpling letters, laughing at himself—as nearly as Walsingham can come to laughing at anything—and you have, once again, escaped with your life."

"Like a good drama," William grinned.

"A very daring performance," Malachi conceded, "and pretty perceptive as well. Walsingham saw the wisdom of your argument just in time to sheath the dagger he had drawn to keep you from further damaging Royal evidence. I commend you for choosing such a cool-headed man for your rough treatment. Your suggestion allowed us to speed up the process by permitting us to break seals with impunity. We have already divided the bulk of her mail into over twenty parcels small enough to fit into the barrel. We also now have a week between deliveries to work on the deciphering."

"Can you decipher fast enough to keep Walsingham busy reading?"

"Not quite," Malachi chuckled. "He's reacting with so much unaccustomed passion, he can't wait for us to finish translating the next page. He's in and out every ten minutes to interrupt our decoding in order to get the latest paragraph or even the latest sentence. He's really in spy's paradise as he reads the inside story on much that has happened both here and abroad during the past year."

"I imagine you encountered some very important names in her correspondence."

"Indeed. Mary's partisans included agents and well-wishers throughout the Continent. Religious and royal men in France, Germany, Italy, Spain, and the Low Countries: the Pope, King Philip, Parma, Guise, Ross, Morgan—all offering advice and support. Juicy enough so that Walsingham has been reveling in the excitement of having puzzles solved, questions answered, plots revealed, strategies exposed, and duplicity disclosed. I don't think I've ever seen the boss go through such a range of emotions as he has during this past week. One hour he is exultant at what has been revealed, and the next he is bemoaning some chance we missed along the way. I wonder sometimes if the human brain can stand that kind of expanding and contracting for long periods."

William chuckled. "It's a barrage of the 'good news-bad news' presentation, I suppose. But Walsingham seems clever enough to make it all operate in England's favor."

"Right. Mary will keep her two secretaries busy for some time since she has been out of touch with her supporters for the last year. I think I can guarantee they will have a full packet ready every time the empty barrel goes out, and you must follow that outgoing packet carefully until it reaches Phellippes' hands because that's where we expect to hit pay dirt."

"Right! The day Mary says too much and sticks her head in a noose."

"No noose," grinned Malachi. "Royal blood always rates the chopping block—or at least the poisoned dish. Meanwhile, you will be part of the team that tracks the mail going and coming, which will furnish you with a nice excuse for riding about in the countryside, enjoying the coming of spring, while I must labor away here at this stuffy copy table."

"It's February, Malachi, cold and wet."

"Don't let little details poison your dish, lad. You should take great pride in the fact that this assignment constitutes official recognition of your youthful vigor and endurance and your body's wonderful ability to recuperate after long deprivation of rest and food. The curtain is just going up on a new role for you, and eyes will be watching to see how well you play it out. To be successful, you will have to subdue your inclination to make a display of yourself and quietly perform your duties in the prescribed manner. What we don't need here is any kind of center-stage spectacle which calls attention to your purpose. Can you handle it?"

"As a matter of fact, it doesn't sound like a 'new' role at all to me. The curtain is going up all right, but once again you direct me to lurk about in the backdrops. If I subdue any further the shadowy substance of the role I play, I may well disappear in a blue cloud of vapor and be entirely erased from the scene."

"There's little danger of that, my boy," laughed Malachi. "Nevertheless, this is not the time for you to be center-stage. You must proceed quietly, checking up on the ever-elusive Gifford as well as the loyalty of the brewer."

"Egad, even the brewer is suspect?"

"Not a likely suspect," Malachi shrugged, "but, don't forget, he took our money."

"He's a business man, I guess. Better he get a little quiet profit rather than any kind of public recognition for his present role as the secret go-between for the Scottish Woman and her partisans. Does the brewer know that Gifford is our man?"

"Not at all," said Malachi. "As far as the brewer is concerned, he is serving as a government agent—and being paid handsomely to do it—while receiving monies from Gifford to slip packets of her mail in and out of the castle. Mary Stuart's secretary also pays the brewer, not only for the beer but also to deliver funding money to Gifford at the other end of the delivery system. We've noticed, however, that the funding money loses heft during the trip back to Burton."

"The brewer is holding out?"

"His fingers are a trifle sticky, and, in addition, he now claims that the weekly trip to Chartley will so greatly increase his cost of doing business that he has no choice but to raise the price of his beer."

"In addition to the payoffs he gets? *'Of All the Bloody Cheek!'* [8] I wonder if he could use a partner."

"First rule of business," Malachi sighed. "Charge what the traffic will bear. The brewer is aware that neither of his clients wants the arrangement published, so he is free to squeeze everybody. In the meantime, Gifford wants to return to France to collect his fee from Morgan, and he has agreed to introduce to the brewer one of our people as his trustworthy cousin who will handle the mail delivery system while he is away. Walsingham thinks it's a good idea for Gifford to return to France to pick up his pay for a job well done because that will make the whole arrangement look more natural to Mary's people."

Chapter 3:
LEICESTER AND THE DUTCH FACTOR

The Ante-room of Walsingham's office, May 1586:

"I'm Martinbee," said the middle-aged, bearded gentleman jovially as he entered the office and shook hands with William. "I'm just back from the Low Countries with news of confusion and chaos for the Boss."

"Yes," said William, "I was instructed to entertain you until they are ready for you."

"What's all the hubbub inside the Sanctuary?" His thumb indicated the inner office.

"They're decoding and copying some intercepted mail, looking for treasonous plots," grinned William. "What's the news from Holland? Who's in charge over there these days? Have our English troops seen action yet?"

"It's the same old push-pull we've watched in this country for the last twenty-eight years."

"Catholic versus Protestant?" ventured William.

"They are part of the drama, certainly," said Martinbee, "but those groups represent too simple a division to explain the complicated performance we see at Court, where the old standbys are subjected to a push-pull that sometimes makes them do flip-flops, causing pull to become push and push to become pull. And sometimes all movement freezes because our blessed Queen defies the heated urgings of her most trusted advisors and simply decides not to decide. Are you right or left handed?"

"What? Did I miss a transition there?" laughed William. "All right! I like to think I can handle most chores with either hand."

"Ambidextrous! Very good. You can double the work done that way or get your work done in half the time, whichever suits you. I've always been a great admirer of such dexterity. As a matter of fact, I'd give my right arm to be ambidextrous."

William looked at him curiously and then observed, "You're Irish."

"I do have a bit of the blood," Martinbee smiled. "Now, as to your original inquiry about the present situation in the Netherlands, consider the two men who have been Elizabeth's right-hand and left-hand confidantes for the last twenty-eight years: Dudley and Cecil—or Leicester and Burghley, if you will. 'Twas the dashing Robert Dudley who rode into her heart on a white charger those many years ago, to announce that her half-sister, Bloody Queen Mary, had just perished and Herself was the new Queen."

"With a certain amount of flash if I understand Dudley's character."

"Oh, yes, and being a handsome, fun-loving fellow, he soon became her confidant and advised her, as well as entertained her, on a near-daily basis. He became her 'Robin', also her 'Eyes', when she solicited his information about rumors and the current opinions of the people. She appointed him Master of the Horse, an office which kept him near her, and later elevated him to Earl of Leicester. He is constantly by her side, except for such times as when he was jailed in the Tower for marrying without her permission or when, as at the present moment, he is leading her troops in Holland."

"Would you say Leicester is her right or her left hand?"

"Left, for William Cecil has always been her right-hand man. For four years during the Calvinistic reign of Elizabeth's brother Edward and for the five years of her sister Mary's Catholic reign, Cecil was Keeper of the Royal Estates. During those confused times, he sometimes went armed against possible assassins and occasionally thought of fleeing to France, but in the end he survived those tumultuous changeovers with honor and dignity and managed to do his job with industry, efficiency, and notable frugality."

"Which would have brought him to the attention of the new Queen, I'll warrant."

"Exactly. It's true he did not enter her heart as the youthful Dudley did, but he better matched her mind with his demonstrated know-how and common sense. His tightrope walk of survival under the two previous monarchs closely paralleled Princess Elizabeth's experience, so she quickly spotted him as a man who could accommodate to difficult conditions and reach wise decisions despite confusing circumstances. Even at the age of twenty-five, Elizabeth had a quick-eye for trustworthy people who performed their duties in a competent but thrifty manner. Within three days of her coronation, she appointed William Cecil her First Secretary to the Queen and formed a pact with him that, to my knowledge, neither has ever broken."

"A pact?"

"When he took his oath of office in '58, she said to him: *'I give you this charge that you shall be of my Privy Council, and content to take pains for me and my realm. This judgment I have of you, that you will not be corrupted with any manner of gift, and that you will be faithful to the State; and that without respect to my private will, you will give me that counsel that you think best; and if you shall know anything necessary to be declared to me of secrecy, you shall show it to myself only, and assure yourself I will not fail to keep taciturnity therein.'"* [9]

"Nice wording!" exclaimed William. "Clear, commanding, and congenial at the same time. 'Keep taciturnity therein', indeed!"

"That bargain has been kept so well that historians may suffer from never learning the inside story of how those two formed policies both here and abroad during the twenty-eight years of Elizabeth's reign. Chroniclers can only hope one of those esteemed personages is keeping a detailed diary of those private conferences."

"Malachi has mentioned Burghley's importance."

"She eventually elevated William Cecil to the nobility as Lord Burghley, nicknamed him her 'spirit', and has consulted with him daily ever since. I'd go so far as to nominate Burghley's personal chats with the Queen as the single greatest influence on English policy for these many years. He is, in effect, England's prime minister, and some feel he is close to being the subterranean king of England since the Queen is quite content to permit Burghley to decide most of the detail work in running her government. As a matter of fact, his influence has not gone unnoticed by foreign observers who are trained in such calculations. In estimating his influence on Elizabeth, the Spanish ambassador once reported that William Cecil *'has more genius than the rest of the Council put together, and is therefore envied and hated on all sides'.*" [10]

"Envied and hated, eh? Does Leicester hate him?"

"Well, being ambidextrous yourself, you must be aware there is frequent striving between right and left for dominance, so you know well enough that the struggle between your two appendages to become the master of arms—so to speak—never ceases, and such constant striving gets quite abrasive at times and may eventually involve sharp elbows."

"So those two have had their conflicts?"

Martinbee nodded. "Normally, they don't argue face-to-face, but each tries to outdo the other in influencing the Queen. At first, it might appear to be a real puzzle how the Queen can remain loyal for so long to two men who differ so greatly, but anyone who watches her closely will realize that she loves to set up extremes and then chose between them when she is driven to decide something. I heard a visitor from France once declare that Elizabeth governs England *'much by factions and parties, which herself both made, upheld and weakened, as her own great judgment advised.'*" [11]

"Do Burghley and Leicester represent factions?"

"They do that right enough, but factions come and go, so the only way those two have retained influence with Elizabeth for so long is by appealing to different parts of the Queen's brain or heart, whichever."

"Are we talking physically or metaphysically?"

"A little of each. When you add up the right arm and ear along with her head, you get Burghley, and when you add up the left arm and ear along with her heart, you get Leicester."

"Do the Queen's judgments always involve a conflict between head and heart?"

"In decision making, the Queen can accept the cautious pull of her common-sense politician or the flattering push of her charming courtier, or she can choose the middle ground between them. But during those rare moments when the right and left hand decide to join on some issue, she can do no better than mount a stand-off. And that's what we have in Holland at this moment."

"Ah, we return to Holland at last. So, what's the big problem?"

"In a word, the Earl of Leicester himself. The Queen has nearly always forgiven Leicester's small displays of arrogance since that's part of what she likes about him, so she only winced a bit when he doubled his own pay and that of his company of gentlemen shortly after landing in Holland. She bit her lip when he set his herald-in-residence to start the research needed to promote twenty or thirty of his gentlemen-followers to future knighthoods even before they visited a battlefield. But she refuses to budge in her command to have Leicester disavow the title of Governor-General of the Netherlands, which he accepted despite her express command not to do so."

"Egad! Does Leicester have that much authority and control?"

"He does, yes, in the sense that he is the recognized spokesman for what might loosely be called the War Party of the Privy Council–just as Burghley is spokesman for the Peace Party. As such, each voices opinions held by large portions of the English population."

"The War Party and the Peace Party. By Jove!"

"The Peace party is made up mostly of Anglicans—the merchants and traders and moderates of all persuasions who tend to be cautious and somewhat skeptical about any kind of proposed change. They tend to share with Burghley the conviction that *"a realm gains more in one year's peace than by ten years of war."* [12] In the Privy Council, Burghley is joined by the partisans of those groups, particularly by Sir John Crofts and often by the Queen herself, who favor the cautious, frugal, and crab-like approach the group usually takes to the country's problems. While Leicester is busy in Holland, Burghley has lately managed to recruit three more peace-lovers to his party; Lord Cobham, Lord Buckhurst, and Whitgift, the Archbishop of Canterbury."

"And that leaves the Puritans to Leicester?"

"Correct. The Puritans and the military on land and sea, most of the young courtiers, and anybody else who is looking for a fight right now. In the Privy Council, the Earl of Leicester can count on the support of the Earls of Warwick and Bedford along with Walsingham, Knollys, and Mildmay. It was their combined influence on the Queen which over-swayed the Peace Party's arguments and prompted her to send Leicester and six thousand English troops to Holland."

"Interesting that Walsingham is in the War Party."

"The boss helps to hold Leicester's impatient faction somewhat in check because he has control over the distribution of so much information. As a matter of fact, he was at the very center of the recent attempt to give newly appointed Governor-General Leicester more time to form sensible agreements with our new allies—the contentious, squabbling Dutch Provinces—by concealing from the Queen the fact that Leicester had already accepted the title in spite of her prohibition. It was hoped something sensible could be accomplished before Elizabeth's anger descended on all of us."

"Did it work?"

"Not by a long shot. Once she was informed, Elizabeth's fury descended on all her advisors for what she regarded as a traitorous conspiracy. The intensity of her anger even impresses those of us who are not directly involved, and its duration for the past three months indicates the Queen has been deeply moved by what she must feel is a betrayal of trust on the part of her councilors. She is still on the boil, so she refuses to listen to anything they now advise. To make matters worse, the Provinces continue to squabble over whether they are better off with Leicester or without him, better off if England withdraws or stays, better off to have a Dutchman in charge, and, of course, better off not contributing to the defense of Holland as a whole, which each Province must now do."

"But the Queen is especially upset with Leicester, right?"

Martinbee nodded. "In the command she sent to him in Holland by royal messenger, she referred to him coldly as 'her creature,' meaning she had made him and she could just as easily unmake him. She wrote, *'How contemptuously we conceive ourself to have been used by you, you shall by this bearer understand. . .We could never have imagined, had we not seen it fall out in experience, that a man raised up by ourself, and extraordinarily favoured by us above any other subject in this land, would have in so contemptible a sort broken our commandment, in a cause that so greatly toucheth us in honour and therefore our express pleasure and commandment is that, all delays and excuses laid apart, you do presently upon the duty of your allegiance, obey and fulfill whatsoever the bearer hereof shall direct you to do in our name; whereof fail you not, as you will answer the contrary at your uttermost peril.'* [13]

"What did the royal messenger direct him to do?"

"Leicester was to renounce immediately his new title as Lord-Governor of the Netherlands in a public display equal to the ceremony in which he accepted the title, monarchs are often great sticklers about the scale of public occasions, you know. They don't want anybody pulling that 'mine-is-bigger-than-yours' business on them."

"Why is the Queen forcing Leicester into such a humiliating action when all her diplomatic advisors are so set against it. Wouldn't we lose influence with the Dutch if we reject their honorary title so publicly?"

"Well, after three months of our wishy-washy indecision on this one issue, I'd imagine most Dutchmen have already curbed their expectation of being saved by the English, so essentially that damage is already done. But if you are truly interested in the reasons for the Queen's obstinacy in the matter, I could mention a few points that probably influence her thinking."

"Please do so."

"As a monarch, Elizabeth is incensed that any subject—especially 'her creature'– would disobey her direct command. She is also deeply offended that Leicester's acceptance of the title makes a mockery of her public declaration last November that England has no territorial ambitions in sending troops to aid the Dutch. She claims that Leicester's acceptance of the title *was sufficient to make her infamous to all princes.*' [14]

"It's clear our Queen takes all of this political maneuvering very personally."

"Very personally indeed, but strictly from a monarch's view. Her problem is that as long as Leicester does not disavow his governance of the Dutch, he is standing directly in the path of the secret plan for peace in the Netherlands which the Queen is attempting to negotiate with Parma, the Spanish commander."

"She is negotiating with the enemy behind the back of our Dutch allies?"

"Behind everybody's back. Just as there are numerous names which attempt to characterize Mary Stuart, Elizabeth's secret maneuvers have been saluted in Continental Courts where many refer to her—not always disrespectfully, you understand—as the Underhanded Queen. Now that Elizabeth has shown Philip that she is capable of what she calls 'letting out' in the Netherlands by sending troops over, she hopes Philip understands that England will fight to keep deep-water Dutch ports out of Spanish hands. The King of Spain will have to think long and hard before committing himself to further destruction of his troops and treasure by assaulting the seaports defended not only by English garrisons but under the close eye of Royal Navy ships anchored in the harbors."

"And I can only imagine that some of the independent Merchant Adventurers like Drake and Frobisher and Cavendish, and even John Hawkins if he can get away from the office, will quickly join those ships if English interests are threatened."

"That's right. Some of the old gunners who have sailed many times with those famous captains, lick their chops at the challenge they see of directing naval guns to fire over the towns and into the encroaching enemy. They feel a good observer placed in some Dutch seaport steeple could pinpoint the massing of troops or the herding of horses or the buildup of supplies, and could then send semaphore signals to the ships, and direct a barrage of cannon-balls to be lobbed over the city and into any attacking force."

"Gad," William grimaced, "they sound like boys with new toys instead of men dealing out death and destruction. In the end, however, it becomes clear that a monarch must take a very large view of such complications in order to govern effectively. I begin to see why the Queen has dug in against the advice of all concerned."

"Don't make up your mind without hearing my speculation of what more than anything else may have determined the Queen's position." Martinbee grinned. "The Countess of Leicester—the former Lettice Knollys, who has been banned from Elizabeth's Court for secretly marrying the Queen's 'Robin'—is preparing to join her husband at the Governor-General's headquarters in the Hague and has announced plans to establish there a court to rival Elizabeth's Court at home. Such ambition on the part of the Queen's cousin and hated social rival, may have been the last straw, as they say."

"Yes, that would be galling. But what will happen? Here we are three months later and isn't Leicester still in charge?"

"He is nominally, but only because the entire English government other than the Queen has united in the conviction that it would be a dangerous mistake to renounce the only unifying element left for the Protestant cause in the Netherlands, so they conspire to hinder every step involved in enforcing the Queen's command, and the delay they create blocks the first step the Queen must take to achieve her separate peace with Spain."

"She can't bargain away the rule of the Netherlands until her subject gives up the role of Governor. Yes, that makes sense."

"That's the case. Elizabeth was furious when her first order was not obeyed, so she sent her Vice-Chamberlain and close personal friend, Sir Thomas Heneage, to the Netherlands with a second royal demand that Leicester renounce the title. I accompanied him on that trip and the Privy Council managed to delay us with one ploy after another for a full week before we cleared London. Once we arrived in the Netherlands, however, every voice argued against the Queen's command and finally convinced Heneage that any lessening of English authority in The Netherlands would amount to a surrender to Spain and would prove to be disastrous to English safety at home."

"But Heneage held firm, of course."

"Not so!" exclaimed Martinbee. "He was finally persuaded to write the Queen to explain that his delay in carrying out her instructions was only to give him the time to advise her that her command went against the opinions of all the wise English thinkers on the scene and that perhaps she should consider further the negative impact her order would have on the Dutch. What a mistake that was!"

"The Queen took his council poorly?"

Martinbee laughed aloud. "He brought forth some of her finest poetry. *"Jesus,"* Elizabeth wrote, *"what availeth wit when it fails the owner at greatest need? Do that you were bidden and leave your considerations for your own affairs. We princes be wary enough of our bargains: think you I will be bound by your speech to make no peace for mine own matters without their consent? It is enough that I injure not their country, nor themselves, in making peace for them without their consent. I am utterly at squares with this childish dealing."* [15]

"That sounds pretty close to a monarchial boil-over."

"Her unrelenting anger has already terrified Leicester into breaking ranks with his fellow conspirators by accusing both his nephew, Sir Philip Sidney, and Elizabeth's personal secretary, William Davison, of unduly influencing him to accept the title. One of Leicester's least admirable characteristics when the Queen is angry at him is a tendency to submerge himself in sickness and self-pity while casting blame on all around him, and then throwing himself directly on the mercy of the Queen. That particular ploy has smoothed his relationship with her for a very long time even if it has cost him the respect of many honorable men along the way."

"So we are at an absolute stand-still, and nothing is getting done."

"Pretty much so. Even Burghley—now that the deed is done—favors hanging onto the title rather than risk the collapse of the Protestant rebellion, which would not only free Parma's veteran army for further adventures but would at the same moment, present Spain with several deep-water Dutch ports from which to launch invasion fleets against England's east flank."

"So the push and pull are together on this one. Is Leicester proving to be a rallying point for the various Dutch groups, then?"

"Leicester?" Martinbee hooted. "A rallying point? Never! His thick-headed arrogance and heavy-handed cronyism has spread dissention and disaster to every corner of the Low Countries. Not only has he alienated our Dutch allies to the point where they seek only to circumvent his orders, but he has managed to set up a dead-end relationship with the most experienced English military commander in Holland: Sir John 'Black' Norris, who has been on the job over there—formally and informally—for ten years. Leicester humiliates Norris at every turn, and Norris shows open contempt for the battle strategy Leicester has adopted of frittering away the striking force of his army by garrisoning towns in the North and not seeking the enemy in the field."

"Perhaps Leicester is just not a good organizer."

Martinbee nodded. "As a matter of fact, he is a champion disorganizer. Lord Burghley's son Thomas recently wrote to his father about the squabbling which Leicester has managed to stir up between all the parties involved in defending the Netherlands. *"Our affairs here be such as that which we conclude overnight is broken by morning. We agree not one with another but we are divided in many factions, so as if the enemy were as strong as we are factious and unresolute I think we should make shipwreck of the cause this summer."* [16]

"Bloody hell, it sounds as if Leicester is gumming up the whole effort and betraying his companions in the bargain."

Martinbee nodded. "Many see it that way. In a very short time, Leicester has managed to shove the big battle with the Spanish into the wings and set up a three-ring circus of pointless partisan disputes not only between the English and the Dutch but also between the English and the English and between the Dutch and the Dutch. The man has a real touch. In all his dealings with others, Leicester puts me in mind of how the draymen's well-fed horses salute the streets of London–but I imagine that's only because I'm poetically inclined."

"That can be a handicap," William smiled. "But I don't understand how the military can hold out for so long against the Queen's wishes, especially if they're not getting the job done against the Spanish."

"And you can bet their defensive strategy irritates the hell out of our Dutch compatriots, who expected a big military effort after Leicester arrived last December." Martinbee grimaced. "They now see that the only orders Leicester is likely to give are those which promote his gentlemen companions to prominent positions which had formally been held by deserving Dutchmen." Martinbee paused. "Still, to be fair, there are several impediments which hinder Leicester's authority."

"Impediments?"

"First of all, the Queen may have given him secret instructions when she dispatched him. She very likely told him to take it easy and to assume a defensive posture in the ransom towns we've occupied. She may also have instructed him to assume enough authority to empower him to collect taxes which would help her defray the expense of sending a military expedition to the continent. Further, Leicester has little idea which of the Dutch or English commanders in charge of the strategic Northern Province cities may be secret Catholics or unprincipled money-grubbers who will betray their charge as soon as Spain makes an offer."

"How much of that goes on?"

"More than any policy-maker cares to admit. We all know the only reason the Antwerp Burgermeister, St Aldegonde, hasn't been charged with treason for surrendering Antwerp's garrison of 16,000 to Parma's besieging force of 8,000 back in August, is because Headquarters is reluctant to advertise the situation and possibly influence other cities to follow suit."

"Egad!" breathed William.

"We have, however, had examples of English military aggressiveness in the field and of victories, but there are inconsistencies enough to defy logical analysis. In April, for instance, the Spanish had the port of Graves under seige, and General "Black" Norris chased them off. He supplied the town with an additional five hundred troops and stocked it with a year's supply of food. Let me tell you, there was elation and toasting a-plenty at English headquarters in the Hague, and a wave of confidence swept over the camp. One of Leicester's scribes was driven to observe, *'If the Spaniard have such a May as he had an April, it will put water in his wine'.*" [17]

William clapped in delight. "Hooray for General Norris! What a triumph! That victory alone could become the rallying cry for all true Englishmen and, once again, demonstrate that there is no substitute for courage!"

"Rubbish," Martinbee scoffed. "Bribery and treachery will run courage out of town three times out of four, and that's exactly what happened at Graves. As soon as Norris pulled his forces away from what he regarded as a very secure city, Parma's troops renewed the siege. Their initial attack, of course, was handily repulsed by the city's reinforced garrison."

"Followed by bribery and treachery," moaned William.

"Right. On the same day that the Dutch defeated the Spanish attack in the morning, Governor Hemart turned around and surrendered the reinforced and well-supplied city to the Spanish in the evening."

"Surrendered?" gasped William. "Why?"

"Nobody knows. English spirits at Leicester's HQ were dashed into stupefied despair. Hemart and several of his captains are being charged with treason and held for trial next month by Leicester's staff in Utrecht. If convicted, they almost certainly will be executed. The English military simply can't let this treachery go unpunished, especially since Graves is not the first Dutch city to surrender."

"How will the Dutch react to an English execution of one of their governors?"

"It will enrage many of them, certainly. Some Dutch voices have spoken out against Leicester and the English 'occupation' right from the beginning, and such an execution would add an octave or two to their protests. Since Leicester's arrival, as a matter of fact, the Dutch have voted extraordinary powers to young Maurice, the son of William of Orange, and installed him in the office of Studemeister of Holland and Zeeland to partially off-set the power granted to Leicester. Fortunately those two gentlemen are getting along well at the moment, or there would be even more trouble than at present."

"I know you said they don't know Hemart's reasons yet, but what are they likely to be? How do the Spaniards manage to get people to betray the very trust it is their duty to protect?"

"Spanish gold. No doubt about it. For most of this century, Spanish gold from the New World has been very influential in giving Spain a big say in European politics. In addition to the gold, however, they have an assortment of attractions to dangle before the fixed gaze of the civil and military dignitaries they wish to influence."

"An assortment?"

"There is no problem if the officials are attracted by money. Their cooperation is gained by granting them a fat purse and a healthy pension for life. If they surrender because they are secret Catholics, they are given positions in the Spanish military along with promotions in both rank and pay. If they desire greater honors and influence, a title might be arranged for them along with attendant estates and dutiful servants. There is something shiny for everybody in the open closet of Spanish come-alongs, while behind the other door lies slow starvation and fatal sickness in the encircled city."

"How are the English soldiers holding up to so much confusion in high places?"

"They don't have the time nor the energy to worry about high places. They battle daily to round up their personal food supply and fight off Dutch resentment."

"Hellfire," said William sadly.

"Yes, like everybody else in England, our soldiers thought they were coming to the aid of honest Protestant trading partners threatened by the ruthless Catholic Spanish. They imagined their heroic actions would be applauded by the Dutch and might even be rewarded with spoils along the way, so they are bewildered to find that many of the Dutch do not see them as liberators but as invaders, occupying and garrisoning their Dutch cities. The resentment against English occupation is so prevalent in some areas, that the military food sources are deliberately delayed and misdirected. Our soldiers are forced to scour the surrounding country for their meals. And you know what that brings about."

"Foraging, theft, violence, resentment, and hatred."

"You've been there, I see," nodded Martinbee. "A reconnaissance report from Philip Sidney's younger brother Robert described the military conditions in the Ostend area: '*This garrison hath so spoiled the country hereabouts that almost for twenty miles riding every way there is never a house standing nor ever a man out of a walled town to be seen here is want of all things, no victuals in store for above twenty days.*'" [18]

"Egad," said William. "A twenty-mile radius of wasteland. But how did everything go so wrong, Mr. Martinbee? Our soldiers marched off with the best of intentions and the highest of hopes, and now end up confused and unappreciated just as the Crusaders did five hundred years ago. Who's at fault, our national leaders or our military commanders?"

"Hard to say. Sir Philip Sidney was surprised by several things when he first took command of the Flushing garrison late in 1585. Not only were the defensive ramparts and bulwarks in terrible repair, but his muster-master reported to him that the garrison was *'weak, bad furnished, ill-armed, and worse-trained'*. [19] Many soldiers were malnourished and had not been paid in several months."

"And ripe for mutiny, I bet."

"Mutinous mutterings from the military were reported, yes, and history has clearly illustrated that the people with the weapons are the last to starve, so those mutterings made some Dutch communities quite uneasy. Sidney quickly distributed amongst the soldiers the £7,000. which the Council had sent with him, and that put some snap back into salutes for a time. But the real danger, even today, comes from the Dutch people themselves."

"The slow-downs and delays?"

"That too," Martinbee nodded, "but the bigger threat was noted by Sidney in a letter to Walsingham, describing the Dutch situation and urging more aggressive action by the English military: *'The people is weary of war and if they do not see such a course taken as may be likely to defend them, they will of a sudden give over the cause."* [20]

"Does that mean they would deliberately choose to be governed by the Spanish Inquisition rather than by tolerant English commanders?'"

Martinbee shrugged, "Oddly enough, long term choices are often decided by short term inconveniences."

"I know we're not supposed to talk openly about such things, Mr. Martinbee," William lowered his voice, "but how much hope do you hold out for the Queen's secret negotiations with Parma? I've heard that you were part of that back-door negotiating attempt to win him over to our side. Did he appear to listen seriously to any of our offers?"

"Buy him over, you mean," Martinbee laughed. "We offered him everything imaginable. In addition to a hefty personal treasure, we proposed that he accept the sovereignty of the Low Countries—Elizabeth certainly doesn't want that costly burden—and England promised to form an alliance with him against Philip's wrath. God knows Spain has bought the loyalty of commanders from every country in Europe, including our own, so it would have been a nice trick on Philip to turn his top man around."

"But could Parma be trusted if he agreed?"

Martinbee shook his head. "I don't think Parma's loyalty is for sale at any price. He has sworn fealty to the King of Spain, and he is too honorable a soldier to betray his allegiance no matter how much we offer nor how poorly Philip treats him. There is a strategic hope, however, of influencing the Spanish Commander sometime in the future."

"In what way?"

"Parma recruits his soldiers liberally from the ranks of German and Swiss mercenaries—many of whom happen to be Protestants—so it is clear that his ambition as a Field Commander overrides his obligation as a Catholic. In short, while he desires military victories, he doesn't share Philip's burning desire to use his army to convert the world to Catholicism. We need to be on the lookout for rifts between those two men and act speedily to insert a small pry-bar between their two ambitions."

Martinbee fell into deep thought, and William's lively look of interest faded as he realized the agent's report had concluded. He took his notebook from his pocket and wrote down a date or two, the names of a few Dutch towns, and the name of General "Black" Norris.

When Phelippes came in to summon Martinbee to Walsingham's office, he glanced at William and the agent where they sat together. "Beware of this man, Martinbee," he warned. "He'll pry every secret he can out of you, and he has no clearance."

Martinbee gasped, winked quickly at William, then assured Phelippes, "Don't worry. My lips are sealed."

Chapter 4:
THE SALTPETER ASSIGNMENT

Shipyards of Deptford, just south of London, late May 1586:

"May I inquire," William asked quietly, "why you are turning me in to the Justice of the Peace?"

"I am not turning you in," Malachi growled, "so much as turning you over to his care while I'm gone. I don't have much time, so listen closely. I've got a delicate task before me and must travel without you, but I don't want to leave you at loose ends while I'm gone, for obvious reasons. I'm placing you in the care of Justice of the Peace, Bruce Wallingford, who is an old acquaintance of mine. He assigns idle and masterless men in his district to tasks that serve the community, like road building, street cleaning, and the like. He'll see that you are kept busy and out of mischief."

"What kind of time frame are we talking about?"

"Hard to say," Malachi said. "There's travel abroad involved, so it will take a few weeks anyway. Here's the Justice now, so I'll be on my way. Take good care of him, Bruce, and I'll see you in a few weeks."

"Happy to have him, Malachi." Wallingford waved. "The district always welcomes hard workers who come our way, so your man will be well cared for in your absence." He turned to William. "You'll be a temp for a time."

"Temp?"

"Temporary worker. We'll plug you in wherever the need arises."

"Plug me in?"

"Like a bunghole. We'll fill the gap with you and stop the leakage."

"What's leaking?"

"One of our civil servants might be missing," the Justice explained, "and when the system loses one of its functionaries, the whole process slows down. We can't afford that. Malachi tells me your specialty is clerical work, and we can always use record keepers."

"Does that mean I might assume duties in some prestigious office?"

"Not too likely," Wallingford laughed. "Malachi and a few others usually do our high-stakes fill-ins. On the other hand, it is within the realm of possibility. Malachi assures me you are a quick study, and I hope that's true because some heavy duties may well be assigned you."

"Set me to the task, supply me with a few explicit instructions, and watch my smoke!" William assured him.

"Glad to hear it," the JP said. "The Plague scare has hit some departments heavily and some hardly at all. It's funny how it does that. It completely empties one estate or village, skips two or three and then pounces on one or two more. People scatter to the wind when the threat shows up in their neighborhood, and all business ceases. The same pattern appears in our government departments."

"Hold on now!" William cried. "Surely you're not going to assign me to a department which is presently in the process of being depleted by fear of the plague?"

"Very little personal danger involved," the Justice assured him. "Our latest figures from the parish burial roles indicate the Plague scare has started to back off somewhat, and we expect to see it gone from London altogether in a few weeks."

"In a few weeks, eh?" William responded. "The obvious weakness in such an encouraging forecast, of course, is that the Black Death needs only three days to snatch you from happy existence to slimy extinction, so, as far as the time factor is concerned, it seems to me that an assignment outside London itself might prove to be—"

"We need you here and now," Wallingford declared. "Don't worry so much about things that might not happen. We have no time for shilly-shallying. Don't forget, you are much safer with us than you are on your own because we never send a man out, especially into the infected zones, without the very latest safeguard against the fatal sickness."

"Really? What odd and mysterious form does this plague-deflector take?"

"You hit the right word there," the JP nodded. "It does not prevent infection entirely, but it does tend to deflect it when used properly. If you happen to contract the plague, however, your options are entirely open as far as treatment is concerned. We offer no advisories on the matter, since all treatments so far seem to be of equal value."

"'Equal value', eh? Is that your way of saying no value at all? Isn't it true that every living soul who gets the plague dies a cruel, painful, loathsome death?"

The JP nodded. "With very rare exceptions, yes, that is the case, but there is no need to dwell on the dark side of the Black Death."

"Are you suggesting there may be a hidden lining to contracting the plague?"

"Only that you go quickly after your armpits turn black. Considering the pain avoided by early departure—not to mention the social embarrassment—that must rank as something of a small blessing, I would think. But let us turn our attention to the active prevention of the sickness rather than concern ourselves with accommodating to it."

"Exactly what I had in mind. How do I avoid it?"

"Easy enough. Don't go anyplace without your orange."

"Orange?"

"This one." Wallingford handed him an orange encased in a cord net. "Tie it around your neck, let it hang down in front, and never take it off. That's the secret. Don't give the infection even a second to slip past the protective mist which your cloves provide for you."

"Are these the cloves which I see sticking out of the orange itself?" William asked.

"Indeed they are. Try not to cause any disarray in their pattern by your movements, because the placement of the cloves generates a protective vapor screen which rises to your face and deflects the noisome fog of infection."

"And surely you must have laboratory findings and voluminous reports testifying to the effectiveness of this particular safeguard?"

"All you could possibly ask for," Wallingford assured him. "Burghley himself has worn one night and day for years and has never once been struck. I understand he even inclines the Queen to wear one during the worst outbreaks. It is not likely our national leaders would accept anything less than the very latest scientific developments to protect their personal lives, is it?"

"Am I supposed to get a new orange every day or what?"

"Oh, no!" the JP cautioned. "The effectiveness increases with usage. One orange per plague season has been found to be the best preventative."

"When you say night and day, I suppose you mean all night too, while I'm sleeping or whatever?"

"Absolutely! There is a growing body of scientific findings which indicate the disease may be passed to us somehow in our sleep when we are most susceptible."

"It is fortunate that the aroma of crushed oranges and cloves smells so nice," William observed.

"That's the ticket! Best to look on the bright side during plague season," Wallingford agreed. "The pleasing aroma of this particular preventative is indeed a big bonus, especially during that time when the dead bodies start piling up around us after we run low on people to cart them away. One shudders to think of the noisome package that nature could have compelled us to hang beneath our noses if she had chosen to be cruel by adulterating the natural antidote with some offensive filth such as—"

"Please," William broke in. "If you don't mind, before you challenge my sensibilities further, let me acquaint myself with my newly-found cloven-orange aroma, so I will in the future be able to better detect any disturbance of the protective veil."

"Good thinking." Wallingford waved airily. "But you know what I mean. For instance, the possibility of mixing together into one stench-filled caldron the putrefied entrails of a toad and a snake along with a bat and a dog to boil and bake. Talk about your offensive odors!"

"Yes, indeed! Offensive odors," William grimaced. "In the final analysis, are you quite positive there is not a single assignment anywhere outside London for which I might be suited? As Malachi must have told you, I am quite good at a lot of things, and I learn fast."

"Prepared to flee the city like so many others, eh?" the JP sneered. "All right, you shall have your wish. There is important work to be done in the countryside, harvesting saltpeter for the defense effort, and you may indeed be just the type to get the work done." He selected a stamp from his desk and stamped William's assignment sheet with a heavy thud. "You'll be working with the Saltpeter Man until Malachi retrieves you."

"The Saltpeter Man?"

"Here he comes now: Sam the Saltpeter Man. He'll explain the job to you as he posts you to your assigned location. I hope you enjoy your holiday in the country."

"Thank you." William undid the cord from around his neck and carefully passed the orange arrangement back to Wallingford.

"Oh, you better hang onto that," said Wallingford. "You never know when you'll need a bit of aroma to enhance your ambiance." He snickered as he turned away.

The saltpeter man greeted William and led him outside to where two horses stood. "'Hopes ye be up to a little ride in t'countryside," he said.

"Oh, I am. I am, indeed," William said, climbing into the saddle. "I confess that I am pleased to be assigned to duty outside London, away from the infected areas. Perhaps you'd like to detail my responsibilities for me since all I've heard so far is that I'll be gathering important ingredients for the war preparation against the Spanish."

"Aye," said Sam as they rode. "Saltpeter' be what we calls it, but 'tis actual' nitre or potass'um nitrate an' it be t' base for the mix what makes gunpowder."

"Gunpowder! Is this dangerous work we're talking about?"

"Nay, not atal," Sam assured him. "Ye ben't involved wi' t'exploding end, just gatherin' t'raw materials like."

"Like a purveyor?"

"Yep, like that. I 'ave assigned ye six pigeon cotes, one stable, two sheep pens, an' one manure heap."

William's eyes grew round. "Egad," he breathed softly. "To do what with?"

"Ye digs out t'earth from 'neath them locations an' puts it in t' trenches, three foot deep."

"Trenches?"

"Aye, get 'em dug right alongside fer easy fillin'. Ye'll thank me fer that 'cause later ye has to fill them trenches wi' t' dirt ye dig out, along wi' straw an' quicklime. A'ter that, ye'll soak t'mix in each trench in piss. Lots o' piss, ever' day fer three weeks. A'ter that, ye digs out t' trenches, boils t' lot in copper vats an' skims off t' saltpeter crystals what results."

"Completely soak ten trenches every day for three weeks? Surely you don't expect me personally—"

"Nay, nay. Ye can add yer little bit, 'course, but ye'll get barrels o' piss sent o'er. Ye'll jus' dip 'er out an' slosh 'er o'er t' nitre bed, even like, 'cause a even layer be t' key to gettin' t' piss crystals t' prosper."

"You'll pardon me for saying so, Sam, but I had been expecting more of a pastoral experience out here in the country. Herding sheep or something. But my impression so far is that this assignment involves matters so disgusting, so degrading, that my mind revolts from picturing them. I'll confess that such an intimate knowledge of the actual barnyard aspect of the broad agricultural experience was not at all what I had in mind."

"Ye got away from t' city, ain'cha, away from t' Plague?" Sam reminded him. "'Sides, it ben't so bad onct ye gets used t'it. By time t' piss soaks yer coat n' britches, ye'll ha' learned to live wi' it. An' don't be forgettin', tis for t' national defense. Us'n'll need lots an' lots o' gunpowder t' fight them Spanishers whenst they come."

"But isn't there some other way? Some more genteel source of saltpeter?"

"Not lately there ain't," said Sam. "This ten year past, us'ns 'ave traded secretly wi' t' Sheriff o' Morocco. They got saltpeter in t' ground there, Malachi says—'uge amounts o' it. But t' English ships can't get in n' out o' there what wi' so many Spanishers an' pirates sailin' those waters, spyin' us out."

"I'm not surprised to hear my master is in on a secret trade. I suppose we offer the usual in exchange: cloth, coal, wood, and the like."

"Aye, us gives 'em tin and iron too. Them Morocs got a mighty hankerin' for iron. Seems t' Bar'bry Pirates runs through cannonballs purty fast, like, takin' t' ships what squeezes through that there twenty mile gap twixt Spain n' Africa."

"The Straits of Gibraltar, you mean? But are you telling me that our country has entered into an international arms agreement trading cannonballs for gunpowder with the infamous Barbary pirates so they can prey on commercial shipping down there?"

"T' trade was iron fer saltpetre," exclaimed Sam innocently. "Us'n caint say what t' Morocs do wi' raw materials. Would us'ns let 'em tell us what t' do wi' stuff we get?"

"But still," William insisted, "the cannonballs that are flying about the ears of honest English merchants and mariners in the Mediterranean are essentially English-born. Isn't there something morally reprehensible about such an arrangement?"

Sam responded with dignity. "I don' know 'bout 'mor'ly 'pre-hensable,' but us'ns got t' do what's necessary to pertect our country."

"Don't you realize that any country at any time could use that reasoning to justify whatever outrageous acts or preemptive attacks they might contemplate?"

"They do fer certain," Sam agreed, losing interest. "Well, here we be at yor first assignm'nt. Start laying out yor trenches, lad, an' iffen t' landowner 'ere gives ye trouble, pay 'im no mind an' just get on wi' t' work."

"Wait just a minute!" William cried. "Do I or do I not have the legal right to dig the unspeakable excrement from beneath the stables, sheep pens and pigeon cotes assigned to me? I mean if it's even slightly illegal, I would very much prefer—"

"Now don' git yer dander up," soothed Sam. "Ye got t' full legal backin' o' t' Crown. I got me a Saltpeter Man's license, an' ye be my duly-appointed man. Tis true t' courts is still workin' on th' legal ins 'n outs if t' landowner makes a fuss, but 'tis bound t' be settled soon now so as us'n can dig an' soak an' boil to our 'eart's content. Us'll be swimmin' in saltpetre afore too long."

"That may be a welcome change when the time comes," said William.

"Iffen all be clear then," said Sam, "I'll be on me way."

"Ah, one thing, Sam. Would you mind arranging for a carter or somebody to stop by to tackle the actual digging which you mentioned?"

"Good luck gettin' a carter t' take shovel in 'and," laughed Sam. "Differ'nt guild entire."

"But, Sam, if there is digging to be done on this assignment, as you said, and no carter is available, who in the world will do the digging?"

"Wal, lad, 'tis entire up to ye t' put th' finishin' touches on t' local details. Ye be t' boss. My job be the assignin' o' duties, an' that be all I kin handle. 'Tis a fierce workload; 'tis, an' awful respons'bility."

"Speaking of workloads, perhaps you had better skim through the outline of my duties once more. I'm still a little hazy on the details."

"'Twill all come to ye onct ye get started." Sam reassured him. "Startin' from th' top, did ye know there be more'n twenty thousand dovecotes in England?"

"Houses for doves?"

"Aye, an' each o' them dovecotes 'olds five-hundred pairs o' well-fed birds. 'Tis their droppin's what is t' greatest source fer saltpeter in England today, an' us'ns needs that saltpeter t' makes our gunpowder. Yer job is t' gather up these 'here riches for t' defense o' yer country."

"From how many of the twenty-thousand?" asked William wearily.

"That's up t' ye. T' sky be t' limit. This 'ere be a new territory, not yet harvested, an' ye be free to get as many permissions as ye can, quick as you can."

"Egad! Does that mean the landowner's permission has not been obtained yet?"

"Now don't go bustin' yer vessels," warned Sam. "Us don't wants t' step on toes, thet's all. Some o' these 'ere landowners tends t' be real touchy 'bout rights, so us asks nice n' polite afore us harvests."

"I can do that, I suppose. Tell them it's their patriotic duty and all that."

"That be t' ticket! Now, also, ye'll be spendin' yer nights wi' our falconer fer a week. Learn wha' ye kin 'bout t 'awks from 'im."

"Don't you mean doves?"

"Lis'en up now, lad, an' don' be arguin' ever' minut. Thar's nuthin' to learn 'bout doves. Ye feeds 'em, leaves 'em together t' lay ther eggs and fill ther cages wi' t' dirt fer England's defense. 'Awks be what ye needs t' know 'bout 'cause t' gentry loves ther 'awks most as well as ther 'orses an' 'ounds. Also, they be t' onliest folks 'lowed t' keep dovecotes legal, so's when ye be seekin' permissions, ye'll be talkin' 'awks cause gentry don' trust nobody who don' talk 'awks."

"H, H, and H! I think I can remember that," William said with a sly smile. "But suppose they refuse me their droppings? God forbid, of course."

The Saltpeter Man nodded. "Some might, odd but true. Folks refuse fer all kinds o' reasons. Some be just stubborn. Some be afeared th' gov'ment might take ther doves outright. Some be too proud to deal with us'ns an' won't give permission t' any but th' Lord Lieutenant hisself. But ye'll do all right. Ye got a nice way wi' ye."

"What should I do if I can't obtain permission? Go on to the next dovecove?"

"Nay, us needs 'em all. Iffen ye can't get 'em t' agree, do th' next bes' thing. Go in at night an' harvest t' national treasure quiet like. Jus' try not t' create a incident."

"Let me see if I have this straight now," William gritted. "You want me to avoid creating an incident by skulking like a thief in the night beneath some unsuspecting gentleman's dovecove and surreptitiously scooping out the unspeakable drippings and droppings of one-thousand well-fed birds, at the risk of being blown to bits as a trespasser? Is that about it?"

"There be a war on," Sam growled. "Or soon will be, and us'ns must all make sacr'fices an' take risks. Iffen ye comes 'cross a illegal dovecote, by t' by, ye needs not t'be quite so polite wi' t' owner. Ye kin lean on 'im since 'e ain't a member o' t gentry."

"Shovel up the illegal droppings as well, eh? Should I also report the illegal owner to the authorities?"

"Jus' cover yer eyes an' do yer job. Us don't care where t' stuff comes from."

"If I cover my eyes with one hand, I'm afraid I won't get much work done since I've already assigned the other hand to holding my nose."

"Wal, as t' that, 'tis part o' yer assignment t' solve problems as they comes up. But us don't wants a single one o' England's ten million doves to go untended. Wal, I best be on me way. Goodbye t' ye an' good luck."

The two shook hands. "And thank you, Sam, for showing me what it takes to be a patriot in England these days."

"Ye got away from t' city, ain'cha, away from t' Plague?" Sam reminded him. "'Sides, it ben't so bad onct ye gets used t'it. By time t' piss soaks yer coat n' britches, ye'll ha' learned to live wi' it."

William could only shake his head and mutter, *"O, how full of briers is this working day world." "YLI.* I:iii

Chapter 5:
THE BALLARD-BABINGTON PLOT

Walsingham's anteroom, June 1586:

"Did you burn your clothes?" Malachi asked William as they waited in Walsingham's anteroom.

"I did," William testified, "I never thought I would enjoy seeing most of my hard-won wardrobe go up in smoke, but I'm glad you got me out of there in time, Malachi, because my skin was beginning to turn yellow. I think this heavy perfume I've doused myself with will conceal the odor until my body somehow casts off the taint, and I am once again able to resume my social life."

"It will," Malachi assured him. "Just give it a few more days."

"Yes," William gritted, "I keep hearing we all have to make sacrifices. As appreciative as I am, however, for my rescue, I am still puzzled by it. What's the big emergency? Why did you pull me off the salt peter assignment so abruptly?"

"Only one thing could do it," Malachi explained. "The boss has called us all together because a new threat on the Queen's life has been reported and Walsingham wants to get us all busy heading it off. All other business is to be put on hold while we look into this report."

A burly, red-faced man burst into the anteroom and stopped abruptly. "Bloody hell! "What is that God-awful odor? Where is Phelippes? And who are you?" This last was addressed to William, seated at Phelippes' desk.

William looked at Malachi, who sat across the room, reading a report. "I'm with him."

"Well, get your ass out of Phelippes' chair," barked the man, his nose crinkling. "God's balls, it smells like somebody's been pissing in the corner and then pouring perfume on it." He reopened the door to the outside hall and ordered, "Bring the vermin on in here."

Two bailiffs escorted a somewhat bedraggled man with a bloody face into the anteroom and shoved him toward a chair. He missed the chair and slumped onto the floor. William leaped to his feet to help.

"Relax, he's no threat to you." growled the red-faced man. "He resisted arrest and I had to teach him a little respect for law and order." He slapped the truncheon he held into the palm of his other hand and spoke to the man at his feet. "Get the hell up off the floor."

"Arrested for what?" asked William.

"For asking questions," said the other as he watched his captive climb laboriously to his feet and sag into the chair.

"Might you be Mr. Topcliffe, the official Royal rack-master?" William inquired. "I'm heard about you and have always wondered—"

"I am not Topcliffe, you fool," he growled, frowning at Malachi's chuckling. "And since Malachi there ain't going to introduce us, I'm Walsingham's secretary, Francis Milles, and sometimes I have to serve warrants after drawing them up."

"Get to, more like," chuckled Malachi. "You know you love the excitement and power involved in arrests, Francis."

"Yes, certainly," said Milles. "I feel a great allegiance for those who risk their lives in the field while you HQ types play musical chairs with the seat of authority."

"Hold on now," exclaimed William. "Didn't you just say you were the boss' secretary? Don't you do most of your own work right here at the office? Aren't you one of the HQ types you are casting aspersions on?"

"Nevertheless," maintained Milles, "my admiration is for the men who do the tough work in the field. They are the very heart of our service."

"Thank you"

"For what?"

"Well, for the past two weeks, I for one have spent time quite literally "in the field," and though I don't expect to be admired for it exactly.'"

The outer door opened again, and the piquant face of Mercy Lovelace showed itself. "Am I late? Has the meeting begun?" Her nose wrinkled in a fetching manner, but she made no rude comment.

William moved forward eagerly, and Malachi stood up, smiling. "Come in, my dear," he said. "Our meeting has not begun and could not until you arrived." He took her hand and pulled her gently inside and to a chair. William pranced about like a colt, grinning and bobbing his head.

"Oh, William! Are we to be assigned to a case together again? What a delightful thought!" She reached out her hand to touch Malachi. "And, you, my dear, dear sir. What have you conjured up for us in that devious and delicious brain of yours? Oh, Francis! What have you done to that poor man. You will turn his head to mush, and then what will the Boss say? Get us a wet cloth, hurry, so we can wipe away some of that nasty old blood!"

Mercy had jumped up and gone to the arrested man while Milles dragged out his kerchief and moved to the water pitcher behind the desk. While she dabbed at the smear of blood on the prisoner's forehead, William and Francis stood by, watching. Malachi remained seated, hiding a grin behind his hand.

When Walsingham entered the room from his office, this was the tableau he saw, and since he too had a soft spot in his heart for Mercy, he didn't doubt that her distress was real.

"Take your prisoner to the interrogation room, Francis, and, in the name of God, do not injure him further."

"Regarding this latest threat on the Queen's life," began Walsingham as soon as Milles and his prisoner had left the room. "we have a shadow job for you and your crew, Malachi, on a young English gentleman, Anthony Babington, who was recently overheard to inquire of a group of drinking friends whether or not it would be legal to kill a heretic queen. Since Babington is a Catholic, we have a pretty good idea which queen he has in mind."

"What a stupid, foolish boy," murmured Mercy.

"He is twenty-five, old enough to know better," said Walsingham coldly. "His family home is in Derbyshire. He has a comfortable fortune and served as a page for the Scottish Viper while she was lodged in the Earl of Shrewsbury's household. He has carried her messages to Thomas Morgan and the Archbishop of Glasgow in Paris and probably moved some of her secret mail for her."

"Where can we find this gentleman, generally?" asked Malachi. "In London? In Derbyshire? At Chartley?"

"He has quarters in London, the last we heard. Our man Poley has managed to work his way into Babington's confidence and has reported that he is the leader of a dozen or so young Catholic gentlemen who often attend the theater and drink together. He overheard Babington's chilling inquiry and has requested our assistance in tracking Babington while he checks up on a priest named Ballard, who sometimes drinks with the group and is probably the instigator of Babington's murderous thoughts. Ballard has been buying drinks and telling impressionable young Catholics that Spain is ready to send 60,000 Spanish soldiers to reestablish the true faith in England as soon as the English Catholics rise against their misbegotten mistress."

"Why don't we just arrest the priest?" William asked.

Walsingham frowned. "That might scotch the snake without killing it. We would still have a dozen young English radicals on the loose, entertaining a very dangerous idea. Our main task now is to identify them. Will you need more men, Malachi?"

"Mercy and William and Poley should be enough for now," said Malachi.

"Is Ballard English?" Mercy asked.

"English-born, but I can't speak for his blood. He is a Cambridge Catholic, who fled England in '79 to escape the 'terrible' religious persecution of Catholics—as he sees it—and studied at Rheims long enough to be ordained a Catholic priest in '81. Since then, he has slipped in and out of England several times. We have occasionally found evidence of his presence here, but he is always one quick step ahead of our nabbing him. He uses several false names and forged passports to move around. He is clever, devious, and well-funded. Our Paris agent, Nick Berden, reported last year that Ballard was one of the major agitators for action among the Catholic exiles in France."

"And Poley says he's in England now?" Malachi asked.

"Yes. Berden was following Ballard when he slipped over to England two weeks ago after spending the last year convincing the exiled Catholics of France and Spain that 60,000 English Catholics are ready and eager to take up arms against their heretic Queen the moment they see the supporting invasion force land on England's shore."

"Ballard seems very fond of that 60,000 figure," said William, causing Mercy to giggle. Malachi held up a restraining hand.

"It is a number that he must now try to authenticate," Walsingham continued. "He procured an interview with Ambassador Mendoza in Paris to tell this little story but could produce no big names or real proof that he represented anybody but himself. Mendoza treated him quite lightly, obviously deciding that Ballard represented a spasm of wishful thinking and self-aggrandizement. Unfortunately, we can't afford to dismiss him so readily."

"We'll get right on it, then," Malachi said. "Mercy, you and Will get down to the theater and see what you can learn about Babington's cronies. I'll check out his living quarters. Remember to get names."

Chapter 6:
THE THEATER AND OTHER ROMAN REMAINS.

At the back entrance of the Theater, June, 1586:

"I will leave you here, Will," said Mercy in her no-nonsense mode, "and go hang out next door at the Green Door Tavern. Perhaps I will catch a glimpse of Babington and his friends there. If not, I'll join you here to keep an eye on the crowd watching the play. Since it's Thomas Kyd's "*Spanish Tragedy* and Edward Alleyn has the leading role, the young fellows are bound to show up for it sooner or later."

"Will you be safe, Mercy, alone in a tavern?" asked William with concern.

Mercy rolled her eyes. "I'm an agent, Will. I can take care of myself. Oh-oh, here comes that old whore Denise, who pretends to be assistant stage-manager while drumming up business. You take care of your own self, Will." Mercy turned to go, laying a hand on William's arm. "I'll see you after the play starts, down in the Pit. Ta-ta!"

A large-haired woman, well-endowed and well-displayed, sidled up to William and took his arm. "Were that thet little bitch Mercy I just seen 'ere with you?" she laughed. "A pretty young gent like you, dearie, could do much better across the river. She be a bit of a viper. I never sleeps this side o' the Thames myself, what with the freedom an' gaiety o' Southwark a stone's throw jest across the way. Let me whistle up a wheery now, an' we can be off for some nice sport, away from this 'ere walled an' gated city."

"But, Miss Denise, ma'am, as I understand it, we promised Malachi I was to be your assistant stage-manager and learn a bit of stage craft from the backstage professionals. If I don't avail myself of this opportunity, he will think—"

"Oh, all right then, dearie. Another time will do fine. Just remember to let the stage-manager hisself handle all the problems, an' you stay out o' the way, 'less you be needed to lend a 'and. Most of all, 'tis yer job to scowl-off strangers."

"Scowl off strangers?"

"Scowl-off any who 'as no business 'anging 'round. Anybody who ain't busy durin' performance 'as no business backstage, so scowl at 'em til they leaves."

"I hope you don't mind if I try a polite request first because that's more in keeping with my nature, and the truth is I may need a little practice in effective scowling. I will get a chance to watch the performance, won't I?"

"Oh, indeedy, most o' your work is done afore th' show starts, so you'll 'ave plenty o' time to enjoy' th' spell-bindin' Ed'ard Alleyn. I've watched 'im act many a time and enjoys 'is energy an' 'is ability to transport 'is audience to foreign lands like. He likes to talk to fellow actors and 'ear the comments of spectators about his performance. He be that grateful to them that offers suggestions which makes his acting better, as 'twere."

"Really? Egad. Grateful, you think? Even though he is the leading figure in the English Theater? You're sure?"

"Deed so," Denise nodded sagely. "By th' by, if anybody was to challenge you bein' backstage tonight, explain to 'em thet you are 'ere under my author'zation. I owes Alleyn a favor an' Malachi owes me one, so Malachi lent you t' me for th' night an' I'm offering you to Alleyn for th' evenin's performance. Don't be explainin' this t' ordinary passers-by, ya understand, only if management asks. Meantime, I'll toddle off t' South'ark, dearie. Don't forget t' keep them back-stage loiterers on th' run."

"I'll see you to your transport, ma'am," William said as he leaped forward and signaled a distant boatman. "It's the gaiety, then, that you like, ma'am?" he asked as they waited.

"I likes t' think o' it as lively commun'ty spirit," Denise said. "Ever'body in South'ark shares it. When we lines up our ale-houses, our bowlin' alleys, our brothels, our beer gardens, our bear-baitin' pits, an' spices 'em up with talk o' buildin' a theater o' our own, we knows we kin milk all kinds o' merriment out o' the visitin' city folk even if we 'ave to empty their purses to light'n' their spirits."

"You'll do that part quite well, I'm sure," William acknowledged. "And it may seem ungrateful of me to point it out, but the authorities should be informed of how lawless Southwark really is. It seems incredible to me that so many stews can operate so openly and not come to the attention of the city fathers. How did brothels get the name 'stews' anyway?"

Denise laughed throatily. "Well, young gent, it's like a lot o' other things in this 'ere country. The name is from Roman times. Them old-time Eyetalians used th' South'ark fields fer baths an' sweat-houses an' stewed theirselves regular. I guess they was use t' bein' warmer–an' cleaner too, fer thet matter. Well, anyways, over time the baths turned inta parlors for massage an' those turned inta our present houses of joy, and th' name stuck."

"My word, it's been over a thousand years since the Romans left!" marveled William. "Why haven't the authorities been notified?"

"Let me put a bee in your Puritan bonnet, young man," purred Denise. "London is th' biggest city in northern Europe, an' th' most successful city, in lots o' ways. An' it continues to grow an' prosper, so it'll be a model fer all great cities t' come."

"A model?"

"You kin lay money on't. Future city builders'll see th' 'vantages of puttin' a sportin' annex just outside the gates o' town. Gen'lmen always needs their pleasure, an' it's smart to have a overflow area close t' hand but out of the way, as 'twere. Not t'kind o' thing them city builders kin afford t' ignore."

"But I'm sure with conscientious effort and some good will, civil authorities could get most of it cleaned up. Perhaps find more suitable employment for the young girls. Cut down the number of ale-houses. Limit the bear-baiting."

"And yank the welcome mat right out from under me and my girls!" protested Denise. "In addition to going against the will of God?"

William sighed deeply. "The will of God again? You're sure about this?"

"I can only offer you St. Augustine an' Thomas Aquinas, young'un, but they must count for something."

"None better," William conceded.

"Saint Augustine said, *'Suppress prostitution and capricious lusts will overthrow society.'*" [21]

"Egad. But couldn't that be taken to mean-"

"And Aquinas wrote, *'Prostitution in the towns is like the cesspool in the palace; take away the cesspool and the palace will become an unclean and evil-smelling place.'*" [22]

"I think I need to point out here, that when remarks are quoted singly, out of their complete text, they often—".

"And you mentioned 'lawless'," Denise pursued sharply.

"Well, yes, I guess I did say something—"

"Well, I'll 'ave you know thet the land where t'South'ark stews is built 'as been part o' the Bishopric o' Winchester fer five-hundred years. T'bishops farm out th' land to us enterprisin' business types, but they knows well enough why our girls is called t' 'Winchester pigeons'.' It don't make no never-mind to 'em jus so long as we follow th' rules."

"Rules?"

"Well, bein' as I'm t'keeper o' a bawdy house, as 'twere, several o' the rules is fer me. I ain't t' hinder any woman what wants t' quit th' life, fer instance. An' I ain't to keep on perm'nent roster any married woman or nun."

"Nun!"

"Well, we all o' us gets a itch now an' agin," admitted Denise coyly. "Another rule is that if m' girls is loungin' around th' entrance t' our 'ouse, they ain't to solicit except by smilin' purty. Neither is they to cuss at the passin' gents if they don' come in or throw stones at them."

"Throw stones?"

Denise shrugged. "'Rejection does that t' a lot o' people. We hires a lad or two to loiter about an' make sure none o' th' gals gets too low in 'er spirits. Thet was th' job I was thinkin' to offer you, but hit's no good 'less you can stay on call in South'ark."

"Happily considered, but out of the question," said William. "Although I suppose I could drop by for cameo appearances when my duties permit."

"Well, ya do thet—" Denise dimpled invitingly—"but, ya know, if you shows up on your own time instead o' your employer's, you come as a ordin'ry customer."

"Only fair, I suppose," William granted, "but regretted, nonetheless."

"Anyways," continued Denise, "we cultivates th' look o' lawlessness on t'other side o' th' Thames t' catch th' eye o' th' London 'venturer, but truth t' tell, South'ark is th' best organized, best pertected, and most profitable part o' London. Lots o' business types you might know, owns businesses there—Henslowe an' Alleyn, fer instance."

"Really? The theatre people?"

"'Xactly. Them two owns the 'stablishment I manage, an' they keeps a tight fist. They shaves th' earnin's o' my gals by tellin' 'em thet our 'ouse is losing money an' they'll soon be on th' street less'n they 'cept less pay. Henslowe tells 'em th' Theater profits is t' only thing what keeps t' stews in bus'ness."

"Gad," said William. "I never realized the extent of the Theater's social significance."

"Don't go bein' such a babe in th' woods," scoffed Denise. "Them theatre gents tell their actors an' writers t' same thing—thet t' stews supports t' theater so thet the drama people mus' 'cept less money. They calls that policy 'spot management' an' goes their merry way."

"I can see I still have much to learn about the wicked ways of the world," William grinned.

"Did thet jade Mercy tell you she 'ad wangled you a meetin' in t' Green Room wi' Master Alleyn a'ter the performance? Play your cards right, young'un, an' you might gain yourself a influential friend in t' theatre. Well, 'ere's me wherry at last, so 'tis off I be. Don't be forgettin' to make some notes before you talk to Alleyn!"

CHAPTER 7:
YOU CAN'T LOLLYGAG YOUR WAY TO BOMBAST

In the Green Room after the performance:

Still dressed in his elaborate costume from the play, Edward Alleyn stood, arms akimbo, and stared down his nose at the assistant manager.

"Rest assured, young man, that your personal contribution to the evening's production will not go unnoticed. Those of us on stage with *her* could, only with the utmost concentration and dedication to our profession, manage to deliver our lines while waiting for the ax to fall on our necks when the authorities rushed in to drag us to gaol and to close the Theatre down for the entire remaining season. What in God's name prompted you do such a thing?"

"Generally speaking," William said, "after the fact, so to speak, theatrical innovation is exactly what our playhouses need. Audiences respond readily to originality, and they mark that response with their patronage and their applause. There are new ways of doing things on the stage today and new voices are being heard. A whole new day is dawning for the playing out of drama, and I am proud to be a part——"

"Will," whispered Mercy, "cease pontificating and explain what happened."

"Yes, well, it was, in short, not my fault. I want to make clear that I had nothing to do with the situation specifically. What was done was not done deliberately, but rather occurred through a series of misunderstandings, coincidences, and misadventures of sundry sorts, all growing out of the lady's amazing ability to pull the wool over all our eyes."

"Nevertheless," said Alleyn, "the record will show that you are the person who employed her, the person who ushered her onto the stage, and the person who thereby cast aside a tradition which has stood as long as records have been kept, of never having a woman appear as a professional player in front of a public audience in this country. You have earned your footnote in the history of English theatre without speaking or writing a single word. Nice going, is all I can think to say."

"I'm very pleased you see it that way," said William. "I was afraid you might think it entirely my fault without giving due recognition to the circumstances involved. When the lady approached me——"

"Her real name is Mary Frith," said Mercy. "but she is known as Moll Cutpurse, and it's true that she makes a very convincing man."

"Well, in all sincerity, I thought I was sending a young gentleman onstage to fill in for our missing player. Since the stage manager turned up missing at exactly the wrong moment and I was placed in a position of authority as assistant director for the night, it was up to me to solve the problem and keep the production going. I made a split-second executive decision, and I would regard it as eminently unfair for anyone to hold my decision against me just because there was no time to conduct a deep background check. I would get a faint whiff of administrative betrayal from such a policy."

Mercy felt obliged to comment. "You must realize, Will, that we were all simply scared silly. The legal punishment for breaking this particular rule is very severe, and in a moment or two, when we recover our equilibrium, we will forgive you when we perceive that the emergency is a thing of the past. Mr. Alleyn is a very noble and forgiving gentleman and only needs time to recover his spirits from such a close call."

The Green Room had gradually been filling with members of the company, some of whom nodded at Mercy's words and some of whom maintained a frowning condemnation of William's mistake.

"If I'm going to be judged, the fact that everybody was fooled along with me doesn't matter?"

"They were not setting policy and you were," Mercy pointed out. "I'm not surprised they were fooled because Moll Cutpurse makes a very convincing man and would certainly deceive anybody up to a certain point."

"The romantic moment?"

"The policy-making moment. It was your responsibility not to be fooled before you went ahead and completely destroyed a revered English acting tradition by dint of your dreadful decision-making."

"Well, now, as to that," answered William defiantly, "I don't see that women on the stage are a threat to morality or to our profession. Just the opposite. If one of the goals of our productions is to hold a mirror up to nature, the logical place to begin is to have women play the feminine parts and men play only the masculine ones."

Mercy giggled. "Oh, gentlemen, think what fun we all would have. And playwrights could invent so many new and delightful parts. The romantic scenes would be so much more believable to us as well as to the audience."

Edward Alleyn snorted. "You young people are full of unrealistic nonsense, and you don't give a damn about tradition."

"I'm sorry you feel so, sir. Both William and I fully support the traditions of the theatre. It is just that we would dearly love to be more a part of it." She glanced about the room at her male audience. "You must admit, Moll played her part well."

"I had never seen her before," added William, "and I still have difficulty believing the manly rake-hell I sent on stage could possible have been a woman."

"She always dresses in men's clothing and is armed and ready to fight," said one of the players behind Alleyn.

"She no longer cuts purses herself, but runs a school where she trains foists and dips to work for her on a percentage basis," offered another.

"She is the best known London fence for big-ticket thefts like jewels and plate and can be counted on to negotiate return of stolen goods for a hefty ransom if the law is left out of it," said a third.

"It must be admitted she knew her lines," said a fourth.

"Enough of this gibberish!" Edward Alleyn shouted. "The deed has been done and there is no way of undoing it. We have escaped unscathed and will know better in the future not to put matters in the hands of a young know-nothing who seems completely oblivious to the concern of others. Egad! He is presently drinking directly from the bottle of wine which other guests might wish to share."

"Sorry about that, but no glass was offered. When you say 'oblivious to the concern of others' do you think I view myself as I view others, as actors on the stage, awaiting a cue for each stage business?"

"You see other people as though they were players in a drama?" Thomas Kyd, the author of the evening's play, stepped forward and viewed William with interest.

"Of course. Doesn't everybody?"

"Oh, Will," cried Mercy, moving in close. "It's Master Kyd, the author of our play. Sir, no wonder your play is so popular. It has everything—a ghost, murder, revenge, treachery, and such heart-breaking grief. And a play within the play. That is so clever!"

William stuck out his hand, grinning enthusiastically. "Indeed, Master Kyd, it is a most lively performance. Quite an improvement over our usual fare. You seem very young to have thought of such an intricate plot and such a variety of characters. How did you come up with such a grand idea?"

Thomas Kyd blushed with pride. "The idea is not mine. As I understand it, the story is very old, originating perhaps with a 13th century Danish chronicler. It is included in the French collection *Histoires Tragiques* by Pierre de Belleforest, which was last printed just a little over a decade ago in 1570. It is the classic story of a father whose son has been murdered, who suspects the identity of the murderers, but who is unable to retaliate because of his need to be absolutely sure."

"Your poetry is passable, too," continued William. "If I might make a suggestion, however—"

"Passable?" exclaimed Alleyn. "You nincompoop! Kyd's lines roll off the tongue! They practically speak themselves!"

"No-no, Edward," Kyd soothed the actor. "Will is right. My poetry is adequate, no more."

Mercy clasped her hands. "It is far more than adequate, sir! The audience feels the father's agony and the mother's grief and Bel-Imperia's despair and confusion over having lost two lovers and knowing her own brother is one of the murderers. It is all so real. '*My heart, sweet friend,*' quoted Mercy with feeling, '*is like a ship at sea….Possession of thy love is th' only port…*'" [23]

"Yes," agreed William. "The audience was quite moved by that scene."

"Oh, the ladies would have broken down and wept if the boy playing Bel's part had known better how to read his lines," Mercy said. "A woman would have done better, of course, knowing naturally how Bel felt."

"Alas, Miss Mercy," said Edward Alleyn, "a woman would never have the power to deliver such lines. Consider Bel-Imperia's admonishment of Hieronimo in Act IV, wherein she berates him for not taking revenge. A woman could never deliver such lines."

"I know those lines," said Mercy, "from viewing the play this day. May I recite four of them?"

> '*Hieronimo, are these thy passions,*
> *Thy protestations and thy deep laments,*
> *That thou wert wont to weary men withal?*
> *O unkind father! O deceitful world!*'" [24]

The Green Room occupants were silent as Mercy's rich voice throbbed and her words echoed about them.

"Gadzooks," breathed William. "You *are* an actor, Mercy!"

"Indeed, Miss Lovelace," said Thomas Kyd. "The theater will be richer by far when women join our guild of performers." He bowed to Mercy. "Did you note, perchance, that Bel-Imperia had a role in Hieronimo's presentation within the play?"

"I did, certainly," answered Mercy, dimpling. "And that she wielded a knife, against both Balthazar and herself. A very strong and active part. We ladies thank you, Thomas Kyd."

A quarter of an hour later, William was still deepy involved in conversation with the great actor Alleyn.

"Your mention of viewing people as though they were actors on a stage means you have the Pure Proscenium Perspective," Edward Alleyn was saying. Very rare and certainly odd in one so young. I had thought it required intelligence and diligent cultivation, but it seems to come naturally to you."

"Thank you."

"Such talent should not go to waste. You must come and work with our theatrical group."

"Really? What part do you see me in? I rather favor the young, idealistic, heroic type—Horatio, for instance. Of course, that might be seen as type-casting of the most blatant sort, but after all—"

"At this particular moment, our cast happens to be pretty well set," Alleyn said, "but while you wait, we can always use help in building sets and holding horses outside during performance. Theatrical work always starts behind the scenes, you know. We must all wait in the wings until destiny beckons."

"I doubt if my duties will permit me to undertake routine work, but I will try to remember to check with my master to see if I have any holes in my schedule should a cameo spot appear."

"Fine," Alleyn said. "We'll let you know at the first opportunity, but in the meantime, I noticed you taking notes during our presentation of Kyd's *Tragedy*. May I ask what you liked best about my performance in the lead role as Marshal Hieronimo?'"

"May I read from my notes?" William inquired politely.

"Please do," Alleyn invited.

"I would advise, Do not saw the air too much with your hand, thus; but use all gently: for in the very torrent, tempest, and as I may say, the whirlwind of passion, you must acquire and beget a temperance that may give it smoothness." [25]

"Smoothness?" Alleyn muttered, taking a step back.

Mercy stepped forward quickly. "You drunken ass!" she hissed in William's ear. "Do you imagine," her voice grew louder, "that the greatest player on the English stage does not know this? Edward Alleyn has performed seventy different parts during the last two years. Seventy! I hope you will excuse my impetuous and misguided friend, sir."

Alleyn, having recovered his aplomb, waved a dismissive hand. "Perfectly all right, Mercy. It's true he is rude and presumptuous, but one of the hard lessons I've learned in this life is to listen carefully to rude people because they are often on to something even as they overstate the case. In this instance, he has stumbled onto something that often flits across my own mind."

William grinned broadly.

"*The Spanish Tragedy* is a bombastic play. Even Thomas admits that. As the central figure, I must react passionately to every incident in a very busy revenge plot, featuring mad scenes, a ghost's appearance, a midnight murder by hanging, an assassination by gunfire, a suicide, a public execution, and in the final scene three quick murders and two additional suicides, including my own. Doing emotional justice to so much bloody execution—even in make-believe—wears a man down over time."

"Such an endless array of bombast leaves one little time for coasting," William acknowledged. "We can only hope for a deeper, quieter, more thoughtful presentation in the future. Have you had a chance to read the new play that Christopher Marlowe is shopping around?"

"*Tamburlaine?* Yes, I was forced to hear part of it one night when Marlowe showed up drunk and insisted on reading it to everybody he could corner. I remember admiring his poetry, but the play itself presents the same challenge to the actor as Kyd's play does. It's full of grand occasions with trumpets and drums and heavy pronouncements and limitless opportunities for sawing the air. I've played such parts happily for many years, but now I find myself worn thin by the exertions demanded by such performances. You can't lollygag your way to bombast, you know."

"Oh, I do know," said William. "You must become the person—that's what acting is all about. It's really a matter of generating enough creative energy to animate your character in the minds of the audience."

"Thank you for sharing that thought," Edward Alleyn muttered. "But the reason for the bombast is apparent. In the past, while the strolling players were performing on the makeshift stages they set up on trestles in open innyards, they had to compete with some noisy attention-grabbers like the arrival of carriages and hostlers changing the horses and passengers disembarking and servants scrambling for luggage. Bombast was necessary to keep the audience focused on the drama, and it became the acting style. All of the players prominent today, including myself, had our early training on such stages."

"But now?" William asked.

"Since James Burbage built this theater nine years ago—London's first—players have had an alternative to the old style of acting. Actors now have a unique setting for their performances, and a different style of acting has been developing slowly ever since. What's called for nowadays is a style which is not so destructive to the actor's energies and permits him a more subtle rendering of character."

"Subtle," said Mercy. "That's it exactly."

"The indoor theater means that the actors have the undivided attention of the audience for the first time. It means they need not work so hard—or at least so loudly—

to gain that attention. I would welcome a subdued Tamburlaine, who only rants and raves in fits and starts. I'm sure I could lengthen my playing career if I were allowed to pace myself better on stage."

"You mean like a prince who is quietly seething inside himself because he has been wronged?" William asked. "He could even seethe away for three or four acts."

"That's it! That's what I need. A subtle part. A lot of interior motivation." Alleyn paused. "I see you are looking at your notes again. Are we to be honored with another suggestion?"

The listeners in the room tittered and leaned forward to be entertained. William paid them no heed.

'This note is to all actors, not to any one in particular. It offends me to the soul, to hear a robustious periwig-pated fellow tear a passion to tatters, to very rags, to split the ears of the groundlings, who, for the most part, are capable of nothing but inexplicable dumb shows and noise: I could have such a fellow whipped for 'o'erdoing...'" [26]

"Let's not forget that groundlings buy a lot of tickets too," Alleyn interrupted, "so it is only good business to broaden the humor of our presentations to be more in keeping with the limited perception of those spectators."

"True enough," admitted William, "so I add, Be not too tame neither, but let your own discretion be your tutor; suit the action to the word, the word to the action: with this special observance, that you o'erstep not the modesty of nature: for anything so overdone is from the purpose of playing, whose end, both at the first and now, was and is, to hold, as 'twere, the mirror up to nature;" [27]

"Anything else?" said Alleyn. "God forfend you should run out of advice for us."

"One more thing," said William, consulting his notes still. "Let those that play your clowns speak no more than is set down for them; for there be of them that will themselves laugh, to set on some quantity of barren spectators to laugh too; though, in the meantime, some necessary question of the play be then to be considered: That's villanous, and shows a most pitiful ambition in the fool that uses it." [28]

"I'll let our favorite fools, Kemp and Tarlton, know how you feel about it when next I see them," said Alleyn. "And now, having been lessoned to the quick, I must be on my way."

"Thank you for your kind attention," said William, bowing to his audience. "One day I hope to stand among you as a member of the acting guild. I hope there will be room for me among your august company?"

Alleyn shrugged. "No concern of mine. Even though I sometimes profit from the observations of rude people, I do not enjoy their company. Good day."

When everyone had left the Green Room, Mercy grabbed William by the doublet. "I hope you are well pleased with yourself, getting that little tirade off your chest. You've just chased away the best lead we had on the trail of Babington's friends.

Alleyn and the others might have told us who attends the theater as part of his group. We could have pin-pointed some of his cronies if not for your idiotic and egotistical interference!"

"Try not to be so bombastic," William advised calmly, "or you'll get left behind by the new dramatic style. Subtlety will get the same job done, and it is far easier on everybody's nerves."

CHAPTER 8:
THE NET CLOSES:

The Red Cock Tavern in London, June, 1586:

"You are a veritable wonder, Mercy," William confessed as he leaned into the pillows of their secluded snug at the Red Cock Inn. "In all of busy, bustling London, you have secured us a spot where we may cast aside all care and be completely alone to share our innermost thoughts and feelings…..among other things," he paused for a playful leer. "You should have been a hostess or tour director or something that pays a little more than our humble profession."

"That's right," Mercy replied absently, "Move those pillows over so you may butt your ear up against the partition between us and the meeting room next door."

"I don't understand," William confessed, "but if listening to other couples in the midst of their dalliance moves your blood in the proper direction, far be it from me—"

"Stop your nonsense and listen carefully. Since we missed our chance to identify Babington's companions at the theater, we must launch into our back-up plan. Poley says the young gentlemen make a habit of meeting here at the Red Cock Tavern after the theater, so I have reserved this snug next to their regular meeting place. We must try to get their names, as the Boss says, so let's put our ears to work up against that wall."

"I can't hear much of anything," William whispered, "but raucous laughter and loud talk. Just a bunch of tipsy young gentlemen having a good time."

"Empty your glass and up-end it against the wall. You'll hear plenty," Mercy instructed him. "Hurry up. We don't want to miss anything. Poley said Babington has been talking wildly of late."

"How wildly?"

"The question of killing our Queen is wild enough for me."

"I heard that Poley has been socializing with Babington. Does our office pay his bar bill?"

"We have to sustain his cover as a young gentleman, of course, but he has been cautioned not to turn into a good-time Percival. Nothing makes gentlemen more suspicious than a free-spender with a concealed purpose. But enough! Be quiet and listen!"

William listened dutifully but shook his head. "Does Poley pretend to be a co-conspirator" he whispered.

"Not quite. Poley let slip that he sometimes runs errands for Walsingham. That makes him good company for Babington, who is trying to obtain a passport from our office for foreign travel."

"Might Poley be judged guilty if anything should come of this plot?"

Mercy laughed, "Don't be silly. We don't waste government agents so casually. Poley will disappear into blessed oblivion when these misguided gentlemen are brought to ground. What are you hearing?"

"Not much. One deep voice. Six or seven younger voices, marinated liberally in wine, methinks."

"Yes, that's what I hear. I bet that mature voice is Ballard's. Yes! He just mentioned 60,000, his favorite figure for Catholics ready to invade England. Babington at twenty-five, is young enough to fall for it."

"Egad, Mercy, you have a gift for distilling their talk from a background of shouting and laughter."

Mercy pulled away from the wall long enough to whisper, "No gift. Women spend much of their lives trying to make sense out of just such sounds. Shhh! Ballard is talking again. He's telling them that the Jesuits' secret poll shows 98% of English Catholics ready to rise and join them once the blow has been struck."

"Zounds! 98%! They are just foxy enough to be polling each other to get figures like that!"

"Quiet! I hear Babington's voice. Oh blast! He mumbles so softly! He says, '....these six gentlemen...no hired assassins.'" Mercy whistled softly. "They really mean to do it! Ah, Ballard is asking about access to the Queen. Babington says, '....Gentlemen of the chamber....outside her bedroom door.' Damn those bastards! Why don't they mention names?"

"You can't expect them to make our work easier," William said. "What's Babington supposed to be doing while the others are risking their lives attacking the Queen?"

"Shh, shh, he's getting to it now. 'Chartley,' he says, 'with one hundred men to free her.'" Mercy glanced quickly at William. "They fear the Bond of Association people if Elizabeth is harmed!"

"Bloody hell! That kind of plotting detail means these boys may act at any moment! We've got to do something. We've got to identify those six right now!"

"Thank you for such spirited conviction," Mercy smiled sweetly. "But what do you suggest?"

"I'm going in there! Maybe I can remember what they all look like well enough to identify them later."

"I'm going with you! Better still, I saw Ottoman down in the taproom, having his supper as we came through. Being a quick-sketch artist, he'll remember better than we what they look like."

"Excellent!" cried William, swooping up Mercy's glass of wine and sloshed the contents across the front of his doublet. "This will establish my credentials with that crowd. I hope Jim has his sketch pad and charcoal. It's time for acting."

"Don't you mean action?"

"That too!" He grabbed Mercy's hand and pulled her from the chamber.

Shortly thereafter at Walsingham's office:

"This is a disgrace," Walsingham snarled, staring down his long nose at the three disheveled "spies." "Especially you, William. Reporting for duty, drunk as a skunk. I detected the alcoholic stench you have added to your other distinctive aromas as soon as I entered this room."

"Strictly ornamental, Mr. Secretary," Mercy interceded. "It's all part of William's disguise. You'll forget all about it when you see what we've brought you." She nodded at the sketch pad Ottoman was opening on the Boss's desk.

"There, sir, is Babington along with the six Catholic gentlemen he has assigned to execute our Queen," William announced triumphantly. "We don't know all their names, but we did catch the name of John Savage here on the end, and I imagine your man Poley can identify some of the others."

"John Savage!" Walsingham exclaimed. "Good God! They are importing killers from the Continent. Gifford told us about this Savage person who took an oath in France to travel to England to kill Elizabeth. And this man next to him, if I am not mistaken, is Charles Tilney, one of the Band of Gentlemen pensioners to the Queen who guard her Presence Chamber. Good Lord, that puts this plot right outside her bedroom door! This is good work, very good! But how did you come by such a portrait?"

"Compliments of Mr. Ottoman, here," purred Mercy, "whose quick hand and eye followed up on Will's wheedling and flattery, which persuaded those foolish boys to allow Mr. Ottoman to paint a portrait from this sketch of their historical and noble gathering. Fortunately, the priest Ballard had left before we arrived or he may have given them wiser counsel."

"Truly, it was Mercy herself who lured them into posing for the portrait," explained William. "Egad, I hate to see what fools we men are in the hands of a pretty and clever woman." He laughed and grabbed Mercy for a kiss.

She did not resist, but she remained focused on her report to Walsingham. "I'm pretty sure the one on the right is Chidlock Tichbourne, one of Hatton's servants, who is often about the Court," she said. "And I suspect several of the Gentlemen of the Queen's Chamber are involved along with Tilney. They should all be watched closely."

"How much of their plan did you hear?"

"As far as we could gather," Mercy explained, "while the six killers are attacking Elizabeth, Babington himself plans to take six other Catholic gentlemen to Chartley Castle along with one hundred attendants to free the Scottish queen and escort her to the throne of England."

Walsingham was sputtering with indignation. "By Gadfrey!," he exclaimed, "You three have done your country a remarkable service. Now get your odd assortment of odors out of my office and round up Malachi for me. Tell him to bring Poley if he can locate him. I'll fetch Phelippes. I want those six identified as soon as possible and placed under surveillance ready for immediate arrest."

"They seemed to us very close to launching their attack," warned William. "Maybe we should pick them up now."

Walsingham shook his head. "Let's not scare anybody off until we've identified the whole lot. We'll take precautions, of course, but we know that Babington was once a page in a household where the Scottish Viper was confined, and Gifford informed us that our young plotter was recently in Paris talking to Morgan. Let's allow our net to run loose for a short time because it's important that we snag the entire catch before we scoop it up."

Mercy grinned. "Maybe even the big fish you've been angling for during these last seventeen years?"

"I fervently pray so." Walsingham came close to grinning himself.

Chapter 9:
THE POST SCRIPT

Walsingham's Office, July 25, 1586

Walsingham and Phelippes were bent over the candlelit table with grim faces, scribbling furiously on individual pieces of paper when Malachi entered Walsingham's office.

"There has to be a way," Walsingham muttered, "of getting Babington to name the six who intend to kill Elizabeth, so we'll have no trouble convicting them. This is a golden opportunity that I would hate to see wasted. Malachi, sit down with us here and give us a hand."

"Perhaps," Phelippes ventured, "if we read through my translation of her response to Babington one more time, we will hit upon a spot to insert the vital inquiry about the six gentlemen."

"I've sent your original deciphering sheet to Burghley to show the Queen," Walsingham said, "but I'm certain I can paraphrase the Viper's note closely enough to suit our needs. I'm sorry you didn't get a chance to see the original, Malachi, or we could get an exact rendering, but I'm sure I can remember the basic part."

"I've been a little out of touch, I'm afraid," Malachi confessed. "I understand Mary Stuart's reply to Babington's proposal to kill the Queen is so damning that you felt free to scribble a gallows on it after you translated it, Phelippes. Is that right?"

"She laid her head right on the chopping block for us," Phelippes smiled, "by accepting the necessity of assassinating Elizabeth to make their plan work. Even the Queen could not miss the murderous intent expressed in her letter."

"That's right," Walsingham grunted. "She can't miss it, but she still might choose to ignore it. It will shrivel my soul if she does not give the appropriate command now that we have the absolute proof in hand. If she does not execute the Bosom Viper now, I will feel that I have wasted seventeen years of good work."

"But she won't hesitate to kill the dozen or so gentlemen involved in the plot if we can get them all identified," Philippes reminded him.

"You're right, and it's heartening that she will at least do that much," Walsingham smiled. "I need a little pick-me-up once in a while when dueling with our flighty mistress. But to bring you up to date, Malachi, you know that Mary Stuart wrote a note to Anthony Babington at Morgan's suggestion on June 25, and received a reply soon after, detailing a plot in which he and a squad of six English gentlemen proposed to eliminate Elizabeth and establish Mary on the English throne. Unfortunately, he failed to name names. Your people helped us identify two of them with that clever portrait they procured, but that still leaves four unknown killers and six other major conspirators."

"All of whom we must identify before we arrest anybody."

"That's right," said Walsingham. "We know some of them have the same kind of access to the Queen's Court that Babington has, so it would be dangerous to leave even one of them free to strike when we start the roundup. I think the best course of action is to deliver Mary's incriminating letter to Babington as usual and have her ask him to identify the six gentlemen so they may be rewarded when Mary Stuart is the new Queen, which our Gracious God forbid!" Walsingham shuddered.

"We should remind ourselves," said Phlippes, "that she instructs him to burn her letter as soon as he reads it, and if he does that, we will have lost our primary piece of evidence."

"Unfortunate, of course," Walsingham muttered, "but the original is in code anyway, so it doesn't mean anything to anybody else. Everybody will have to accept your copy of the translation, but don't worry–" He smiled– "I'll vouch for you. And we really have no choice if we intend to finesse that list out of Babington."

"And that's where we're running into trouble, Malachi," Phelippes added; "trying to work that inquiry into Mary's letter in an inconspicuous fashion, even though we have no trouble duplicating her secret code."

"We were about to review the paraphrase of her letter and I would appreciate any thoughts you might have on how best to insert the inquiry."

"I'll do my best," Malachi assured them. "Let's hear it."

"This is her note to Babington: *'When your preparations both in England and abroad are complete, let the six gentlemen who have undertaken to assassinate Elizabeth proceed to their work and when she is dead then come and set me free...But do not take any steps toward my liberation until you are in such force that you may be able to put me in some place of perfect security lest Queen Elizabeth should take me again and shut me up in some inaccessible dungeon, or lest, if she should fail in recapturing me, she should persecute to extremity those who have helped me." [29]*

"Mind-numbing in its cold-bloodedness against the only friend she has in the world," Malachi shook his head. "Certainly worthy of your gallows imprint, Phelippes."

"But how should we add to it to gain our end?" said Walsingham.

At that moment William tapped on the door and opened it cautiously. He was invited in but somewhat reluctantly.

"Gentlemen, to a casual observer, you look like a covey of conspirators with your furrowed brows and grim countenances. You must lighten up a bit if you wish to conceal whatever deviltry you're up to. *'Only look up clear....To beguile the time, look like the time, bear welcome in your eye, your hand, your tongue....Look like the innocent flower but be the serpent under 't'.*[30]

Walsingham flung his quill upon the table and turned about on the bench. "Can't you see we're busy with important matters, you scalawag?" he growled. "What is it that can't wait?"

"Just reporting in," William said. "What's the problem?"

Malachi spoke without turning. "We're looking for a way to get Babington to name the names of the six conspirators without arousing his suspicion. I am sure we'll light on it straight away."

William glanced at the papers spread across the table with their arrows and insertions and grinned. "This is the letter that rated the deadly gallows drawing, isn't it? You're probably complicating your own plot in trying to alter it, but you would generate a good deal less suspicion by simply added a postscript to Mary's letter. It's all in code anyway, so her handwriting doesn't matter."

Walsingham beamed, "That's it. "post-script." He motioned to Phellipes, "Start writing."

"What shall I say?"

"Have Mary ask for those names in order to do them honor when the time comes," suggested William.

"And rewards," Walsingham added. "Gentlemen are notoriously short of cash."

"Splendid strategy," murmured Phellipes, writing.

"I've been meaning to bring up that shortage problem," said William, approaching Malachi with outstretched palm and a grin.

Walsingham leaned back in his chair. "Give him a coin or two, Malachi. He has served us well–though we do have a security problem to discuss. For instance, how did he come to know so much about this letter?"

Malachi frowned and admitted, "He often knows things he has no business knowing, but he balances that ability out nicely by not knowing things that a well-versed five-year-old has mastered some years before."

"He must make a fascinating traveling companion," Walsingham said.

Malachi held out the palm of his hand and wiggled it. "Highs and lows, but in the main, ah, interesting."

"How are you coming with that post-script, Phelippes?"

"This is just a rough draft, you understand, but I think I have touched all the key points."

"Let's hear it," Walsingham commanded.

Phelippes cleared his throat; *"I would be glad to know the names and qualities of the six gentlemen which are to accomplish the designment, for that it may be I shall be able, upon knowledge of the parties, to give you some further advice necessary to be followed therein; as also, from time to time particularly how you proceed; and as soon as you may, for the same purpose, who be ready, and how far every one privy hereunto."* [31]

"Fine, fine," said Walsingham concluded. "It resounds with the Bosom Viper's assumed authority, so it will do. Cipher that post-script into her code, Phelippes, and add it to her letter. We will deliver her request to Babington and put this plot up on its legs."

PART VI: THE ROANOKE COLONY RETURNS AND TRAITORS DIE

Chapter 1:
THE ROANOKE COLONY RETURNS
Sea Side Inn, Portsmouth, July 28, 1586

Malachi looked up from his breakfast kippers and sausage in surprise. "Lord love us, William. I was sure you'd be long abed this morning after the grueling ride down from London. Are you too saddle-sore to sleep?"

"Nay, there's too much afoot this morning for sleep," William grinned. He paused by the open window to draw a deep breath and suck up a surge of the surrounding sea air. "B'gad, Malachi, there is something pulsating and energizing about marine air. I'm not surprised that so many sailors find they can't go long without filling their lungs with its captivating vitality."

"They call it 'going to work'," Malachi teased him, "or maybe you wouldn't be so impressed if you had a little more salt in your diet."

"Has Drake's ship made it into port yet? Have Drake and the Colony folk disembarked? Have I time for a bit of breakfast, or shall we hie forth to gather our report for the Boss?"

"That's Drake's 600-ton flagship, *Elizabeth Bonaventure*, directly in front of you with his Vice-Admiral, Martin Frobisher, docked right beside him in his 200-ton Aid. The rest of his fleet is spread around the harbor. Those ships look as if they could use a little touching up, but that's not surprising after their ten-month voyage. The ships didn't suffer as much as the crew, however."

"I heard they lost a lot of men, and it wasn't combat that did them in."

Malachi nodded. "It's very depressing to learn that ship-fever killed off just about one-third of the strong, healthy sailors who manned those twenty-nine ships when they left England last September. Their various battles only whittled off a few dozen men, but they still ended up with 750 dead out of 2300. Unfortunately, that's the way of the sea. It surprises me they find enough men to stand up to that risk, but, in the end, we all have to make a living."

"Not a very promising vocational choice," William muttered.

"I talked to a few of Drake's men from the Francis, which got in two days ago because they left Virginia ahead of the others, and they said that the loss of so many men forced Drake to abandon his plan to hold Cartegena as a permanent English base to intercept the Spanish gold shipments in the West Indies."

"That was the plan he cooked up with Philip Sidney, wasn't it?"

"Right, and Drake did capture Cartegena, but he had to abandon it to the original owners after six weeks when he ran out of men to protect it. Anyway, most of the Roanoke people will be with Drake or Frobisher, so we'll see them as soon as the custom officials finish with them."

"Well, as things usually turn out, they'll show up just as I sit down to eat my breakfast, so I'll order one up just to speed things along."

"It appears you made quite a favorable impression on Mr. Hukluyt," Malachi said. "He asked that you specifically be assigned to interview the survivors because you are not so easily turned aside by the opinions of others and because you ask such penetrating questions."

William smiled happily. "I'm glad he regards those as favorable traits."

"They happen to suit his purpose at this historical moment. He'll be busy elsewhere as the bedraggled members of England's first colony in the New World land here in Portsmouth with the taste of abject failure still in their mouths. Hakluyt has served as a trumpet for Raleigh's effort to set up the Virginia colony since the first reconnaissance by Barlow back in '84, and he is somewhat chagrined that every single one of the colony members gave up the attempt and returned to England with Drake."

"I thought this first colony was a semi-military expedition for looking around, and that's why they had no women with them?"

"True enough, but it was hoped that part of the first group would remain over there with the beginning of a settlement so any new assembly would not have to start from scratch. It has been a bit of a shock to the London backers that the colonists have all returned, and Raleigh and Hakluyt would like to find out why. Your probing inquiries might drive to the heart of the matter, who knows?"

"So I should quiz them on why they failed?"

"Well, indirectly. We won't bludgeon them with the fact of their failure but try to get some authentic impressions from these survivors before they insulate themselves in ale."

"Surely they have many adventurous tales to share."

424

"Indeed. The colonists tried to tell their stories to Drake's seamen on the six-week trip back to England, but those crewmen, having lost so many brothers and cousins and friends to fever, were in no mood to listen to other stories of hard times. I expect the Roanoke people will be ready to barrage any sympathetic audience with a volley of impressions and exaggerations in order to enjoy an open spigot at the telling."

"And we must quiz them before they fall prey to a distortion of the spirits?" William nodded wisely. "I understand."

Malachi grinned. "Hakluyt would like as sober an impression as he can get from as many as we can round up. He wants to help Raleigh organize the next expedition by eliminating whatever went wrong with this first one. Lane, Cavendish, Barlow, Harriot and White will be quizzed by Raleigh in London, of course, but we are expected to pick the meager brains of the lesser sort. And here is your first chance to do some quizzing because that is Mr. Hackett, a minor clerk of the expedition, and his friend Mr. Mason coming toward us in response to my invitation to breakfast. Let's see what a seasoned scrivener like yourself can learn from them while I round up some others."

"Gentlemen," William greeted them, signaling the waiter for food and drink. "I understand you have spent the last year at Roanoke in the New World. How did you find it?"

"We just turned right at the West Indies," Mason snickered.

"Biggest mistake I ever made," said Haskell, "taking serious what Barlow wrote in his tip-sheet report to Raleigh on how to get rich without effort while spending a splendid vacation in rare and exotic lands of the New World."

"Barlow deceived you?"

"You tell me. In the report he gave Raleigh after his reconnaissance trip to Roanoke in '84, he states that the land was *so full of grapes as the very beating and surge of the sea overflowed them, of which we found such plenty…..that I think in all the world the like abundance is not to be found. The soile is the most plentiful, sweete, fruitful and wholesome in the world. Peas were planted and shot up 14 inches in ten days.*' [1] He then goes on to testify that *'The earth bringeth foorth all things in aboundance, as in the first creation, without toile or labour.*' [2] Does that not sound like deception to you?"

"It sounds as if no matter what else went wrong, you would always have plenty to eat over there."

"That's right. That's the way he made it appear to all of us who took the bait, but he forgot to mention that while the soil is indeed very fertile along river banks and along the shore of the sound, it rapidly turns into wooded swamps full of snakes as you move inland…just as all his rosy promises did."

"Mmm," William murmured.

"We look for somebody to explain why we had to 'toile and labour' so hard just to get a mouthful of twigs and beetles to eat that last month before Drake rescued us.

And it wasn't just us. Barlow himself lost twenty pounds during the year, although he still insisted that we were dining on roots and shell-fish while I had trouble swallowing my twigs and beetles. That man has a promotional tract for a brain."

"The promoters among us tend to inflate things," William admitted. "What was the big problem with the food supply?"

"The coastal Indians have a simple food system," Mason explained. "Unfortunately, it is very delicately balanced. They are highly dependant on fish and on maize, or 'corn' as we call it. They gorge in the fall after they harvest the summer planting, and then they starve until the early spring planting ripens. During the time of scarcity, they eat mussels, shell fish, berries and roots. They are well off during most of the year, but they hurt when nature takes a sudden twist, because both crops are seasonal in a sense."

"Fish are seasonal?"

"The shoreline of the Roanoke area is part of a very stormy coast, so fishing is frequently interrupted during the winter by gales which sometimes rage for weeks at a time and tear up their flimsy fish-weirs, which are nothing more than long, reed baskets laid out along the shore of the sound. Their corn crop is mostly dependable, but always there are good crop years and bad crop years."

"Can't they use the good crop years to save up for the bad ones?"

"They know how to store grain in the cold ground and they know how to salt the fish and deer meat for later use, but as soon as they build up any future supply, they call in the neighbors for a grand celebration which often lasts until the cupboard is bare again. In the month before we returned to England, the spring corn crop had not yet ripened and the storms had torn up most of the weirs, so the Indians were reduced to their roots and mussels menu while they offered us the last of their winter corn supply."

"Incredibly generous of them, I'd say."

"Not entirely, I'm afraid. Lane made it clear that military measures would again be taken if we didn't get enough food. At the beginning of our stay, they offered us food as a gift, and when the novelty of our visit lessened somewhat, we had to barter for it. Eventually their desire for our iron and beads ran low just as their food supply hit bottom, so we had to hold some of them hostage to squeeze food from the others."

"You held the Indians hostage?"

"It was that or starve. Lane had twenty years of military service before the trip, so he solved our big problems in military fashion: hostage taking, confiscation, appropriation—that sort of thing. We discovered, however, that while the Indians were pleasant enough on the surface, they harbored a deep resentment about giving up the last of their winter seed supply."

"Not surprising," murmured William.

"Their bitterness nearly got us massacred just a week before Drake returned to take us home to England."

"Gadzooks, I didn't realize you were in that much danger," admitted William.

"Oh, yes indeed," said Hackett. "Once again it wasn't quite what Barlow had promised us. His comments on the Indians were also misleading. He wrote: '*We were entertained with all love and kindness. And with as much bounty, after their manner, as they could possibly devise. Wee found the people most gentle, loving and faithful, void of all guile and treason, and such as lived after the manner of the golden age.*' [3] "'Void of all guile and treason', indeed! Let him explain where the hell all those arrows came from."

"Arrows?"

"After they lured half our party 150 miles up the Roanoke River by their reports of 'shiny metal' in that area, they left us without food and loosed a shower of arrows at us from under cover. Those bronze-skins would have done us in if they hadn't been so afraid of our thunder-sticks."

"You call the Indians bronze-skins?"

"Get used to it," Hackett advised. "That's what everybody will soon call them. They are not quite red and not quite brown, so what else would you call them?"

"Drake showed up just in time, then?" William prodded.

"Oh yes, it was a close thing all right," Mason said. "Under the guise of setting up a memorial service for his peaceful brother, who had just died, the Roanoke chief, Wingina, summoned all of his tribe and some neighboring braves in order to ambush us. He assembled seven or eight hundred bowmen to put an end to the hundred white men. He even set a date for the attack, but fortunately we got word of the plan from one of the friendly Indians, and we quickly took preemptive steps to protect ourselves. That's why I'm thinking of taking part in the colony deal Raleigh is now offering in Munster."

"Raleigh is already offering a second colony deal?" William was startled. "Munster is in Ireland, right?"

"Right. In Virginia we didn't have much choice in terms of staying or not. No English ship came by Roanoke for a full year after Grenville left with the ships that brought us over, so we had to stick with Lane no matter what policy he set. We didn't have a percentage investment either. We were in it just for the wages and adventuring. Of course, there was the possibility of finding treasure like the Spanish have found in the New World, but once it became clear that the gold was not readily at hand and the food supply was a problem, our wages began to look skimpier all the time."

"And a colony in Ireland looks better to you?"

"Much better," Hackett said. "Not like Virginia at all. We wouldn't be trapped in Munster. Believe me, it was a bleak day when Grenville took all the ships home after landing us in Roanoke, leaving us with about twenty days' worth of food. At that point, it became clear that if we couldn't work out things with the Indians, we could be in deep trouble."

"But from Ireland, we could practically swim home across the Irish Sea," Mason said.

"Right. If I'm going to risk my skin among blood-thirsty savages, I'd just as soon get some profit out of it. Raleigh is letting us buy into his colony in Ireland. I'd love to grab one of those £300 Gentlemen's Estates he's offering, but I didn't marry quite that well. My modest dowry will permit me only one of the £25 parcels, but such an estate would be worth ten times that amount if it were situated here in England."

"I wouldn't be surprised," William nodded.

"And the neighborhood is all you could ask for. The best part is that the Desmond Rebellion virtually cleared southwest Ireland of the mere Irish, so there are few of them left to dispute with the new owners of the land. The single biggest group attracted to this acquisition scheme is the well-born second sons of the gentry—although a little light in purse, these men are well trained in arms and manners and seeking a little adventure. They make great neighbors with their hawks and their hounds, and they know how to stage a hunt with the best in England."

"I can well imagine," William nodded. "So you are really convinced there is a future in the Munster plantation scheme? You don't think it will go belly-up like Virginia?"

"No chance," said Hackett. "Safest bet in the country because it has everybody behind it. It already has a military presence and a civic government in place for protection, and Raleigh has convinced Burghley and Walsingham and the Queen that the Munster lands represent a nakedly exposed flank of England's defenses. Its southern coast contains several deep-water ports which could provide Spain with a staging area from which to launch their proposed attack on our shore."

"And Raleigh proposes to offset that threat?"

Hackett nodded. "He suggested that he be permitted to solve the problem permanently at little cost to the Queen by colonizing a small portion of the confiscated Desmond Lands with 320 English families of various skills and levels. Kind of a little England in the midst of the treacherous Irish who might well join hands and welcome the Spanish as Catholic allies against us."

'Indeed, the Irish have earned the right to be watched closely," Mason added. "Raleigh persuaded the Council to grant him 47,000 acres to set up the colony. It'll make for a strong Anglican influence in southwestern Ireland to supervise and protect the seaports and maybe begin to pay the Crown back what it cost them to put down the Desmond Rebellion."

"That would be a novelty, all right," William chuckled, "getting money out of Ireland."

"It would indeed," Hackett agreed, "and it's about time we turned that losing proposition around. With the Privy Council on our side, we'll have a pro-business atmosphere which will permit all to prosper who get in on the ground floor."

"I did hear though," Mason cautioned, "that Raleigh's original partners, Stowell and Clifton, went over to look at the property, found the land unsurveyed and disputed, came back to London, and turned over their claims to Raleigh in disgust."

Hackett shrugged. "Some men are discouraged more easily than others. Raleigh has already set surveyors busy and is dividing up the parcels all the way down to £6 pieces. His big problem at the moment, however, is the new Lord Deputy of Ireland, Sir John Perrot, who is attempting to curry favor with the native Irish by deciding some of the land disputes in their favor. A real stab-in-the-back for the whole Munster Plantation scheme as Whitehall envisions it."

"How much land is left of the Desmond estates if Raleigh walks off with 47,000 acres?"

Hackett chuckled. "In this case, 47,000 acres is the proverbial drop in the bucket. As a matter of fact, when the Crown denounced Desmond as a traitor back in '79, they confiscated 800,000 acres of his holdings which included most of Cork, Kerry, Limerick and parts of Tipperary and Waterford. The Earl of Desmond controlled nearly all of Munster in southwest Ireland before he was struck down."

"He sounds like a grand story."

"If you get a chance, ask Raleigh about the details of the Desmond War sometime. I know he compiled a short history of that episode to help sell his plan for the Munster Plantation."

CHAPTER. 2:
MANTEO GIVES INDIAN VIEW

Seaside Inn, Portsmith:July 28,1586:

Malachi joined the party, accompanied by two other men, one quite foreign-looking but both well-dressed and of the gentry.

"I hope you have squeezed these two scallywags dry, William, because I have a real treat for us in the person of Mr. Harriot himself, who has agreed to give us a few minutes before going up to London."

Harriot shook hands with William. "And here is a gentleman you, no doubt, have long wished to meet: the Lord of Roanoke, Manteo."

"Egad, sir," exclaimed William, his eyes twinkling into Manteo's. "I took you for Sir Raleigh himself!"

"Indeed, yes." replied the Indian. "I am handsome Englishman, dress like Englishman, talk like Englishman, made noble lord by Lady Queen herself." He bowed elegantly to the company

Harriot turned to Hackett and Mason, who were finishing the last of their breakfast and getting ready to leave. "Gentlemen, I understand you have already signed up for the Munster Plantation undertaking. I might very well join you if I ever get all the Roanoke paperwork whipped into shape."

They smiled, spoke happily of the Munster project, shook hands, and left. Harriot turned back to Malachi and William. "It is very fortunate that Manteo is here with us," he said. "There were rumors in the Colony that it was Manteo who tipped Lane off about Wingina's plan to attack our settlement. The rumor was false—Manteo had been off visiting his Croatoan family at the time—but it is hard to live down such reports while you are on the scene, so he decided to come back to England with us until things quieted down back there."

"Who did tip off Lane about the proposed attack?" asked William.

"It was a young brave named Skiko, whom we were holding hostage. His father, Menatonon, is an upcountry chief who could put 800 fighting men in the field overnight if we didn't hold a check on him."

"Skiko was a hostage in addition to the Roanoke hostages you took to insure your food supply?" William asked.

"That's right," Harriot said. "That was Lane's way of keeping control of our situation over there, and he wasn't entirely unreasonable about it. He initially took Menatonon himself hostage for several days and then agreed to release him after the chief offered his son in his place. The Roanokes assumed Skiko would be an enemy of our settlement and confided in him, but it turned out he was more of an enemy of the Roanokes, so he warned us of Wingina's plans."

"Wingina really had a plan to ambush you?" William asked.

"He did indeed," Harriot affirmed, "so Lane and twenty-two men armed themselves and approached the mainland Roanoke camp at night where they found the chief seated at a campfire with some of his people. Lane proposed a parley to resolve their differences, but as soon as Wingina agreed, Lane shouted his signal cry, 'Christ, our victory!' and his men all leveled their guns and shot into the Indian group, killing several. Wingina was only wounded and ran into the woods, but Lane's two Irish deputies, Kelly and Nugent, chased him down, shot him, and cut off his head."

"Head now staked on pole in Sound for all to see," added Manteo. "In England, heads of enemies decorate London Bridge in same way."

Malachi grimaced. "Not a good farewell for the Roanoke Indians to remember when Raleigh's second colony lands."

"Exactly so," agreed Harriot. "Fortunately, the new plan calls for the colony to plant itself one hundred miles north of Roanoke in the Bay of Chesepiyc, where our big ships can harbor."

"Is that far enough away that the tribes there will not have heard what happened?" asked William.

"My people already know," said Manteo, "and Chief Powhatten, who has many braves, also knows and he will not think Wingina's death a gift of peace from English. Good fortune I came away from there for awhile."

"And good fortune we English had you at hand to translate all this for us," William observed. "Do many of your people speak our language?"

"English is very difficult for us," admitted Manteo," just as our language is difficult for Englishmen. Skiko talks with hands, and I was not at settlement to help explain his meaning, but Sir Harriot is wise and understood much."

Harriot nodded. "I had worked with Manteo long enough to get some yes and no answers out of Skiko about the proposed attack. Some of the Indians, though not at all fluent, have mastered a few dozen words which serve for basic communication— words like *food* and *more* and *iron* and *beer*. After that basic vocabulary, most of them sloped off. A few, like Manteo here, proved quite facile and learned the language quickly, but he is the only Indian I know who has developed any real fluency, and he loves to show off his new skill, so if you get him started, he'll go on and on." Manteo grinned good-naturedly.

"Dr. White and Mr. Harriot and me myself tried to write Algonkin dictionary but had to give up. Too hard. Too many differences," said Manteo.

"Manteo is right," laughed Harriot. "We have no grammar to cover their intricate system of grunts and hiccups and the like. Perhaps someday a system to describe it will be devised."

Manteo grinned. "Some white men, many years past, learned to speak by listening. Shipwrecked sailors from Spain and from France and from Dutchland joined our tribes long time past, became servants of chiefs, maybe took wives. Englishmen too. Not so many."

"Do you know all these languages, Manteo?" asked William in awe.

"Not all white men were kind to teach Indians. Mostly they taught us enough words to tell them where the shiny metal was. Copper was the only shiny metal we knew, so we pointed upriver where the copper was. But when they found no gold, they thought we lied and deceived."

"And were angry, no doubt, the greedy bastards."

"Things changed," said Manteo. "At first my people welcomed the strangers. We saw there was much to learn from them, especially about their thunder sticks and about their ships and tools. But soon we saw that it was these sailors who lied and deceived and treated us like children. We had to be careful. But we saw no reason to fear them."

"And you continued to learn their languages."

"When I was young boy, some of our people sailed away with Spanishmen to learn more about where they came from."

"That was back in the '60's," interrupted Harriot. "The Spanish took fifty-six Indians back with them."

"I imagine they got the surprise of their lives when the horizon kept going on and on for weeks or months as they sailed," laughed William. "Did any return?"

"After 'many moons,' as my people say, some returned. They brought back strange and wonderful things and told stories of unusual adventures."

"The Spanish ended up choosing just three to train as interpreters, which supports my guess that only one in twenty is handy at language," said Harriot.

"Were all of the remaining fifty-three returned?" asked William.

Harriot looked at Manteo and frowned. "As a matter of fact," he said, "their presence caused quite a furor in the Spanish Catholic Church because it forced them to decide overnight whether or not Indians had souls, and because the Indians were considered to be a conquered foe, there was every justification for making slaves of them. Fortunately, the Spanish hoped to develop commercial interests in the New World, so it was decided that the Indians did have souls and thereby would profit from the sacrament of baptism. Then, of course, as Christians, they were not subjected to slavery, but only to domestic service."

"There's a difference?"

Harriot grinned. "Sleeping indoors or outdoors is the kind of difference that calls itself to your attention on cold, rainy nights."

"But the Spanish let some of the Indians return home. Why?"

"The Spanish added 'slovenly' and 'lazy' to 'lying' and 'deceitful' in describing my people and sent them home," offered Manteo. "Many of us do not understand the white man's ways."

"Is that why you decided to become a translator?"

Manteo smiled. "We have long tradition of translators. Some of our stories are very amusing. A translator does not always tell the truth. In 1539, many years ago, the Spanish sailor, De Soto, found a good translator when he landed in Florida, a Frenchman who lived twenty years among us as a servant after his ship wrecked on our shores. He spoke several Indian languages, so he could have straightened out the copper-gold confusion straight away, but he did not. Perhaps he thought the Spanish might go home if they learned there was no gold and would leave him to return to his domestic chores—which is what they did anyway." Manteo chuckled. "A man is not always in control of his fate. The fox sometimes tricks him."

Malachi laughed. "I imagine the famous something that is said to be lost in translation is often something deliberately concealed in translation."

"How do you remember the details of long-ago stories like this, Manteo? Do the tribes have written records?" asked William.

"We have story-tellers that remember everything that has happened to our people. Also we draw pictures on animal skins you call leather. We have wampam belts that carry a message by beads. Wampam belts are good size for carrying from tribe to tribe. I myself often carried such a message. We also use smoke signals from fires on high hills to send messages of emergency over long distance very fast."

"Signal fires!" William responded. "We have those too!"

"Our people have much in common and much to learn from one another." Manteo grinned slyly. "But the White Man is proud and does not readily learn from 'savages.'"

"Right you are, Manteo," agreed Malachi. "It is very unfortunate. But William here is storing up information as fast as he can, so he will listen to any wisdom you have to impart. Tell him what we have in common with your people, if you will."

William nodded eagerly, ignoring Malachi's teasing tone.

"Our beliefs in the Beginning of mankind are very much alike, I think, although the Spanish burned some of our people for not believing exactly as they did."

"Oh yes, the Spanish policy of 'turn or burn' has given some Christians a spot of trouble too," admitted Harriot, "which is a real shame because there is great comfort to be had in the arms of the True Church—for Indians as well as the rest of us."

"You were saying, Manteo, that our beliefs are very much alike," prompted William.

"Yes," said Manteo. "Indian tribes generally believe *'that there are many Gods, which they call Montoal, but of different sorts and degrees, one only chief and great God, which hath been from all eternity. Who, as they affirm, when he proposed to make the world, made first other gods....and after the Sun, Moon and stars as petty gods....First, they say, were made waters, out of which by the gods was made all diversity of creatures that are visible or invisible'.*" [4]

"Sounds straight out of the Book of Genesis," said William, "or what our Church fathers have told us of it."

Manteo nodded. *"For mankind they say a woman was made first, which by the working of one of the gods conceived and brought forth children."*

"Oh, my!" William said. "That would not go down well with the Church or the priests either! If Eve and God made the human race without Adam's help, that places men very low on the ladder. What do Indian men say about that?"

"They think that all the gods are of human shape and therefore they represent them by images in the form of men...."

"A great idea," said William. "It makes a man feel good to be ruled by a god-head of his own stature. If men are believed to be made in the image of their parent-god, it should cut down the number of things women can find to complain about."

Harriot smiled. "One would certainly hope so, but I think not. The ladies enjoy finding fault with us hapless males."

Manteo waited patiently to continue. "Our view of the after-life is, I think, much like the Christian view. Indians *'believe also in the immortality of the soul, that after this life as soon as the soul is departed from the body, according to the works it hath done, it is either carried to heaven, the habitation of the gods, there to enjoy perpetual bliss and happiness or else to a great pit or hole, which they think to be the furthest parts of their part of the world towards the sunset, there to burn continually; the place they call Popgusso'."*

"*Popgusso.* Sounds like sausage cooked to the split-skin stage, all right," Malachi murmured. "Odd how many religions consign to eternal flames the people who don't behave themselves."

"Yes," Harriot grinned, "and endless, mind-numbing bliss with harp and halo for those who do."

"With all these similarities in religious beliefs,' said William, "it would seem the leap to Christianity would not have been too difficult for the Indians. What went wrong?"

"Our wisemen and storytellers say the trouble started with the sailor de Soto," said Manteo. "You must know my people are much impressed by military prowess and that battles are always a part of our campfire stories."

"Ah," murmured William. "So much for diplomacy and other peaceful means of communication with you folks."

"Yes, alas," agreed Harriot. "A quarter century before de Soto, Ponce de Leon, back in 1513, landed in Florida, looking for what he called the Fountain of Youth, but the Indians saw his quest as a ridiculous excuse to set up a Spanish colony on their territory, so they finished him off with their arrows, and the attempt was abandoned."

"My people do not speak much of Ponce de Leon around the campfires."

"He should be remembered for mapping out the Mariner's Current—or the Florida Current, as the Spanish call it," offered Harriot, "but the Indians don't care about that."

"No," agreed Manteo, "but our campfires have many stories about the devil de Soto and his time among us. We learned much about the White Man from him."

"The Indians quickly saw that Hernando de Soto was not a Ponce de Leon," said Harriot. "He landed on the west coast of Florida in May 1539, with 600 soldiers, 100 servants, 213 horses, and over 300 pigs."

"Egad, he had an army!"

"Yes, he had grown rich following Pizarro in Peru for fifteen years as a military man, and had a strong appetite to uncover more gold in the New World. As soon as his expedition landed in Florida, six local Indians greeted him at the shore. He had three of them dispatched with his magic thundersticks and sent the other three off to spread the word that his people and animals were both hungry and tired and would require some immediate hospitality."

Harriot's audience sat in stunned silence. Finally William asked, "How did the tribes react to that, Manteo?"

"Our wise men advised we wait and see. My people have a myth about great warriors of the past coming back to life when we need them. The Spanishmen with their pale skins and special weapons might well be ghostly gods, they said, whose natural color had been leeched out in the process of returning from the dead."

"What about the shootings?"

"Our medicine men explained that gods often work that way: strange, mysterious, and arbitrary in order to get the job done. Our smoke signals danced up the Florida headland that day, and before nightfall the people well to the north knew that strangers, possibly gods, had arrived with powerful weapons and hard clothing that our arrows could not pierce. Some remembered the ships and horses and firesticks of earlier days. At any rate, all this gave the tribes a good deal to think over."

"And they gave him food and hospitality, just in case. I presume this depleted their stores very quickly."

"Yes," affirmed Manteo. "Few Indian villages could feed 700 people and 500 livestock for long. De Soto soon learned that the big tribal chiefs collected tribute from the lesser chiefs and kept granaries of maize and dried fish as protection against hard times. The Spanish raided those storehouses. They also took the crops from the fields, the corn and peas and pumpkins. The Indians knew the coming winter would be a time of great shortage, but they dared not refuse."

"De Soto's four-year expedition through Florida and inland was really a raid on one such cupboard after another with the threat of near starvation thrown in between times," offered Harriot.

"What about the 300 pigs?" William inquired.

"De Soto loved those pigs and had them served for supper only on special occasions, so that, before he died in the third year of his journey in May of 1542, his herd of pigs had reached 700 in number, even though many wandered off into the woods and live there now—a great benefit to the Indian people." Harriot grinned.

"Ah yes," breathed William. "One can get used to ham and bacon meals in a hurry."

"A small gift," Manteo smiled. "The gods often carry gifts in one hand, even as they bear death and sickness in the other. Besides the pigs that fill our woods, we now have horses grazing in our meadows."

"I'm surprised that the Spanish would let their horses wander off."

Manteo chuckled. "That's not how we got them. Every tribe saw immediately the benefit of those animals, and none rested until they got hold of a mating pair one way or another, even if it meant inviting de Soto's army for a visit. Many horses now live in our mountains, doing nothing but eating and mating. Some have been traded to tribes beyond the mountains, where warriors used to hunt buffalo on foot."

"We brought some buffalo hides back to England with us," said Harriot. "They are huge animals and travel in vast herds, they say."

"So God in his Great Wisdom used de Soto to deliver horses to the Indians?"

"And sharp-edged iron weapons and tools," added Manteo. "Much better than our flint-stone arrows and stone axes. We set young braves to watching from hilltops how the Spanish used the forge and bellows to put sharp edge on iron. We have found many uses for it, particularly the iron-headed hatchet. It is a fine tool for taking scalps."

"You don't take the whole head as the Irish do?"

"Very bulky and awkward if warrior has a good day. I think English also take heads of their enemies. Is this not so?"

"Yes, you're right. More and more, though, we save that ultimate indignity for any of our nobility who have turned traitor. For lesser crimes by lesser people, we just hang most of them or let them rot in prison." William frowned in thought.

"You mentioned sickness," said Malachi. "What kind of sickness did the Spanish bring? The French pox, I suppose."

"Ah yes," said Harriot. "Though syphilis—also called the Italian pox—was slow-working compared to our childhood diseases that the Indians have not built up an immunity to. Measles and whooping cough have wiped out whole villages shortly after a visit from the White Man."

"Ye gods! Did the Indians know we brought it?"

"Oh yes. On many of our own expeditions inland in pursuit of the 'shiny metal'" Harriot smiled, "we expected to get supplies from the Indians, but they had frequently abandoned their villages upon our approach and left us with no food supply. In addition to their fear of catching sickness from us, we found out later that Wingina had sent word ahead warning the inland tribes that we were coming with weapons to make war on them."

"How far did de Soto get in his travels?" asked William.

"He quickly took his expedition inland," said Harriot, "because he knew the Mexican and Peruvian gold was found well away from the coast in Cusco and Mexico City. The group probably covered close to three thousand miles in a twisting, turning, backtracking path from mid-Florida up through the inland area above Florida, and zig zagging over to the giant river the Indians call the Missip, but they found no gold in their travels, and not much copper either. That mineral seems to be found very far north in the land of the Many Lakes, as the Indians call it."

"We use copper to decorate, to make things of splendid beauty for chiefs, sometimes to trade. But White Man does not value copper as he does gold."

"That's true," agreed Harriot, "but we certainly value your *uppowoc,* or 'tobacco' as the Spaniards call it. It has excellent healing properties and, in truth, I could hardly do without it."

William leaned forward eagerly. "How does it work?" he asked. "Do the Indians just yank the plant out of the ground, stuff it in their pipes, and light it up, or is there some special preparation before drinking the uppowoc smoke?"

Harriot explained; *"The leaves thereof being dried and brought into powder: they use to take the fume or smoke thereof by sucking it through pipes made of claie into their stomacke and heade; from whence it purgeth superfluous fleame and other grosse humors, openeth all the pores and passages of the body by which meanes the use thereof, not only preserveth the body from obstructions; but also if any be, so that they have not beene of too long continuance, in short time breaketh them; whereby their bodies are notably preserved in health, & know not many greevous diseases wherewithal wee in England are oftentimes afflicted."* [5]

"Sounds almost too good to be true," William shook his head, "but if the foremost scientific authority from the expedition testifies that the Indians keep good health with its use, its benefit would be hard to refute. And they don't mind sharing its powers, you say?"

Harriot nodded enthusiastically. *"We ourselves during the time we were there used to suck it after their maner, as also since our returne, & have found manie rare & wonderful experiments of the virtues thereof; of which the relation would require a volume by it self: the use of it by so manie of late, men and women of great calling, and some learned Phisitions also, is sufficient witness."*

"Even if our people did not find gold or silver on this expedition, at least they brought back the recipe for a long, healthy life for all of us."

"The Indians also put great store in the healing powers of the sassafras herb. Some say it cures the pox."

"Ah," laughed Malachi. *"There* is a source of great wealth, William. A cure for the pox, indeed. Many would beat a path to your door for such a cure!"

"But does it really work?" asked William. "Has it been proved?"

"Well, it has not been proved *not* to work and for unprincipled souls, that's basis enough to go into business," grinned Malachi.

"And it has an exceedingly pleasant taste, used as a tea," said Harriot. "That makes it a very easy-to-take medicine, if nothing else."

"But de Soto died anyway, despite these two fine medicines," said William. "What happened to his army and 700 pigs after that?"

"The expedition went on to explore west of the Missip for over a year without de Soto. Near the delta of the Missip, they encountered a tribe of Indians who used the atliati device. These spear-throwing sticks double the velocity and range of spears and turn them into a particularly deadly weapon if a man fails to get out of their path. The Spanish military people expressed surprise to see such an advanced weapon in such a primitive area."

"Oh well, I guess all the big boys don't live in the cities." William shrugged. "But how did they get all those horses across such a large river?"

"They simply lashed together canoes to form platforms—"

"Canoes?" interrupted William. "Barges, do you mean?"

"Oh no," said Manteo. "Our canoes are long and narrow and can be propelled swiftly by paddles along streams and rivers, even against the current. We burn out the interior of a single log and call it the dugout canoe. They can be made for two men or for ten. The smaller ones can be carried across the land, bypassing waterfalls or dangerous rapids or for getting from one stream to another."

"Sounds a mite heavy. What keeps it from rolling in the water?"

Manteo grinned. "Our canoe-makers are artisans; they leave more wood on bottom than on sides, so our canoes do not roll over. In north country, Indian people cover light wood frame with bark of birch tree. These canoes very light and swift. But we do not have birch bark."

"You were saying de Soto's army crossed the big river in dugout canoes. Do pigs swim? Or maybe they were left behind for the tribes this side of the river."

"All animals swim if they have to," said Harriot, "but some were undoubtedly left behind because pigs don't march well. When the army returned to Porto Rico in '43, they had only about twenty pigs and twenty horses, and 311 men. No gold at all."

"Godzooks," exclaimed William. "That expedition was a dismal failure! Better if de Soto had never landed. He brought all that misery to the Indians for nothing!"

Manteo patted William's shoulder. "My people used to hard times, young William," he said. "All our villages have sickness every year, famine every other year, twisting storm every five year, shaking of the earth every twenty year, and bone-chilling freezes once in each man's lifetime, so White Man's visit not too great hardship. Also, we learned much from him."

"You are very philosophical, Manteo," said Malachi.

"The merging of our two cultures will take hard work and much understanding," said the Indian. "There will be communication problems just as between family members. Some will lose tempers and some will die, but it can be done. Good men will work it out." There was a moment of silence, and Manteo added. "I think things went better with your Roanoke settlement—at least for a while—because you left priests at home. They cause my people great confusion."

"Your people did not wish to convert to Christianity?" guessed William.

"That was not a problem. Indians are very practical people. It is true, they like to see two lesser gods—sun and moon—every day and night, guiding them on hunt, helping grow crops. When de Soto and Spanish priests said there was only one god, Indians squint eyes to point between sun and moon and call that spot heaven."

"Good adjustment."

"But trouble starts, say campfire stories, when priests say that One True God includes three people in Holy Trinity. Indians turn away in much confusion."

"A lot of English have trouble with that part too. Did the Indian resentment ever boil over?"

"Sometimes, and sometimes they kill straggler or two among the Spanish, but Indians know they stand no chance in battles against soldiers with armor, fire-sticks, and horses. So de Soto and his priests continued to butt into many areas of tribal life."

"Like what?"

"All tribes treat De Soto as guest since they have to, but even guest must show good manners. Tribesmen much shocked when Spanish say they must cut hair European way, before it touches shoulders. Warrior's hair is big part of war decoration and gives him power by patting him on the back as he runs through the woods with it bouncing behind him. It became clear these Spanish men very bad guests, but many warriors let hair be cut just to keep peace."

"A good thing hair grows back," said William.

"Yes. Next thing, de Soto and priests say each chief allowed only one wife. That create big social problem in tribes."

"Social problem?"

"Tribal policy was for braves to marry the widows of slain brothers or cousins and to adopt children. Many have two or three or four wives—no broken families, then, and every woman has man to hunt for her. This no hardship for anyone, for women do much work in camp and work together. Make husband very well off."

"A sensible plan."

"But Spanish say no. Say one wife per man. That create many homeless people for the Indians. Then Spanish soldiers take many women to serve them when they leave, so problem not seem too big."

"You mean the Indians had to turn their womenfolk over to the Spanish? Egad, that was certainly cause for rebellion!"

Manteo smiled. "My people are generous about sharing company with guests. Our women not considered property of husbands, so they were allowed to go with Spanish. Priests encouraged this, so 300 women joined the gold-seekers. Many returned home when de Soto entered territory of new tribe."

"Hmm," mused William. "I don't suppose the priests had a problem with the morality of the arrangement?"

"Our women cook good and gather much food. They bring big comfort to the camps and make no trouble. De Soto's priests talk to women and explain duties, which I think not include what English call 'forn-i-ca-tion'. But not forbid it either. Our women brought home many white babies, which our tribes happy to accept."

"It seems all the Indians are philosophical in certain areas," said Malachi. "But tell us how the Roanoke Expedition was different from the de Soto Expedition, Manteo?"

"By now, our people knew more about White Men. We knew they not sent by gods. We shared food stores but stayed more apart."

"I take it our people were able to hunt and fish for themselves," said William.

"The climate in Virginia is so wholesome," said Harriot, "that after the first three weeks '*We lived onely by drinking water and by the victuall of the country*'." [6] and on that diet only four out of our 108 died and three of them were '*feeble, weak and sickly persons before ever they came thither.*' As a matter of fact, Drake's crew of 2,700 lost one man out of every three while we lost only one out of twenty-six during the same time period."

Both Malachi and William grunted in amazement.

"As for hunting," Harriot continued, "we felt it best to keep what little powder we had for personal protection in case things turned sour with the Indians which did happen eventually because '*some of our companie towarde the ende of the yeare, shewed themselves too fierce, in slaying some of the people*'." [7]

"Yes, Hackett mentioned that your guns were a big help in keeping the Indians under control. Would you advise that the new colony be more heavily armed than yours was?"

"No," said Harriot. "I'd advise we not send military people to deal with peaceful Indians to begin with. That's where most of our trouble came from right from the start. As soon as Grenville demonstrated our guns and burned the Indian village and destroyed their crops over that missing silver cup—which may still be lying in the bushes somewhere—we succeeded in getting their attention and their grudging respect, but we also introduced a deep-seated suspicion of our motives and our methods. That suspicion simmered all year and finally reached the point where Wingina decided that the most sensible way of dealing with the White Man was to kill him off."

"You wouldn't send the new colony unarmed, would you?"

"Of course not, but I would not send people so ready to solve all of life's problems in a military fashion. Taking hostages, confiscating property, and shooting people do not cultivate trust in a culture where the people are very reluctant to disturb their routine activities to suit the white man, which is why the Indians do not make good servants and certainly not good slaves."

"Who would you send if not soldiers?"

"I would send people who intend to live there, grow their own food, and reach some sensible accommodation with their Indian neighbors based on mutual respect—preferably men with families who will work hard without complaint to insure a better future for all. Francis Bacon has written we should send '*gardeners, ploughmen, laborers, smiths, carpenters, joiners, fishermen, fowlers, with some few apothecaries, surgeons, cooks, and bakers....[*not men who] *will ever live like rogues, and not fall to work; but be lazy, and do mischief, and spend victuals, and be quickly weary....*'." [8]

"What say you, Manteo?" asked William. "Would the Indians tolerate such a group or wipe them out as they did Ponce de Leon?"

"All farmers should have guns, I think, but gifts for chiefs and sharing of English food and cloth would be good for friendship. Also straight talk and no sudden betrayals. Perhaps English cannot do these things. What you think?"

William groaned. "Some English have great honor; some do not. I might guess that the men who are too greedy for gold might be less likely to show honor to the Indians—or to anyone else, for that matter."

"That is what I think, too."

All three Englishmen nodded and sipped their ale.

"What other things might ensure the success of the next colony attempt?" William asked.

"Well, above all else," said Harriot, "Our experience indicates that no colony will ever succeed there without a safe harbor. There is no natural deep-water anchorage for one hundred miles north or south of Roanoke Island itself. A colony has to have a safe port because it must rely heavily on supplies from home until it reaches some beneficial arrangement with the natives."

"But why do you need a harbor? Can't you just park the ships in the ocean off the coast? Isn't that what anchors are all about?"

"As it occurs, Roanoke Island itself lies just inside some outer islands which protect it from the surf. The chain of outer islands slant away from the coast for about sixty miles to the south of Roanoke and then slant in again to form a shallow bay over two hundred miles long and many miles wide in spots—sort of an inland sea behind the string of coastal islands. We can send boats into such shallow waters safely enough, but ships over 70 tons cannot enter that inland bay, so they must be anchored in an exposed position two miles off shore in a location which has earned the label of being a 'sudden coast' by seafaring men."

"Sudden coast?"

"Without warning, the wind and rain can suddenly come out of nowhere and whip the surrounding sea into a frothing fury so that a captain could lose his vessel before giving a single command; his sheets being shredded and his cables snapped by the storm's sudden fury. There is very little coastal eddy when the sea is calm, but when the wind and the tidal surge churn the sea into a vicious lather, a ship may quickly become enveloped in a mariner's nightmare. If a ship is caught on a lee shore with the wind and tide against it and the coastal eddy—from the big, shallow bay I've just mentioned—surging in and out of the inlets between the islands like a huge suction pump gone mad as it chops the sea to pieces, it makes a mockery of attempting to steer the ship with the rudder."

"Gad, Harriot, it sounds as if you've been there! What do the captains do if they can't steer their ships?"

"They do a quick review of all the prayers they learned in grammar school," Harriot declared, "and then, if the vessel be lucky and the captain cool and the master smart and the crew sprightly, it is possible to use small sail to make quick tacks during favorable moments in the shifting fury surrounding them and inch their way away from the coast. I've been through that adventure twice on that shoreline, and each time we ended up running down a narrow corridor just as the doors of disaster slammed shut behind us, but praise be to God, we did squeak through each time."

"Where else would the colony go if not to Roanoke?" asked Malachi.

"There is a big bay the Indians call Chesepiyc about one hundred miles to the North, at about 37° N. which is parallel to Lisbon, Athens, and the bottom of the Italian boot in our part of the world."

"Excuse me, Mr. Harriot, I know you are making a point, but something you just cited has always puzzled me. Every time some specific place is mentioned in the New World, mention is made of its parallel latitude in our Old World. Why?"

"Two big reasons. Number one: When investors hear the Old World places I mentioned as New World parallels to the Mediterranean area, they can presume a similar climate which will tell them what kind of plants can be harvested from that region. Number two—if you don't mind a little simplification for the sake of clarity—all navigators have learned to sail along a parallel to get to the New World; They can check the North Star at night and the sun during the day to hold them on course, so if they want to hit the Chesepiyc area in the New World, they just sail to 37° N. off Lisbon in the Old World and then sail directly west while holding that heading, and they should end up close to their goal. Clear?"

"Yes, thank you."

"To resume then, let me say the Chesepiyc Bay area is said to contain many safe anchorages. We had already planned to move there before Drake arrived, but we had no vessel big enough to move our colony out on the ocean. That's why we were tickled when Drake offered us the 70-ton *Francis* along with her crew because she could enter the shallow inner bay to permit us to load and was still big enough to trust on the ocean itself."

"But you never made it. What happened?"

"Drake had offered us food and provisions along with the ship and crew, so the colony decided to stick it out until supplies arrived from England, but a four-day gale with monstrous water spouts assaulted us at that moment, and the *Francis* was blown so far out to sea that she decided to go on back to England. Drake offered us other ships, but none of the others suited our needs and, frankly, by that time, we were so tired and threadbare in both wardrobe and spirit, that we needed a rest from difficulty, so we came home."

"And Drake had plenty of room for you since he had lost so many of his men."

"He did, but he asked us to write out and sign a request for our transport, so he would not run into trouble with Raleigh or Grenville who he knew were scheduled to bring us supplies."

"On the six-week sail home you must have had a lot of time to think about the long-range implications of the first colony attempt."

"I did, and I'm very much afraid the lack of financial success in the first attempt will be far-reaching." Harriot shook his head. "We didn't bring home any gold or silver—while Grenville captured a £50,000 prize on his trip home after dropping us last year. His success has created a general impression that privateering provides much more substantial and quicker profits than does the business of establishing a colony."

"Yes, an unfortunate comparison. Unavoidable, I'm afraid."

"If investors and seamen think too hard about that contrast, both venture capital and ship's crew will be much harder to come by for a second attempt, and, according to the charter, Raleigh has only until March of 1590 to get a settlement started. A second colony might succeed, it seems to me, if we put more authority into the hands of the people who actually make the trip, so they can adjust quickly to developing circumstances without worrying so much about the shareholders three thousand miles away."

"What kind of organization would you suggest?"

"Cultivate a healthy self-interest by offering families 500 acres to own and develop. Appoint one experienced, civilian statesman as governor and let him help them to select their own officials for self-governing."

"500 acres each to a few hundred families might impress the Indians the wrong way. How do you imagine they would feel about it?"

"Oh, there's plenty of room for everybody over there. The Indians will simply have to come to realize they're living in modern times. Hell, this is the Sixteenth Century, and they still don't have recorded deeds on any of their properties. Manteo says the idea of private ownership doesn't even exist in their culture, but he admits that his people will need to be awakened from their pastoral, dreamlike state."

"Can they be awakened gently?"

"I certainly hope so," said Harriot. "Perhaps we should send some lawyers with this next group to transform them into something of a modern culture and prepare them for the oncoming change. The Indians are certainly going to lose some of their old ways as more colonists arrive, and it will be a big gamble to see if they get back anything as valuable as what they lose."

"Is there food and drink at hand?" Manteo grinned. "Ideas fade in distance when belly growls."

"Excellent idea," agreed William, looking toward Malachi. "I've been smelling the aroma of what I believe to be an excellent batch of meat pies. Perhaps Plowman's lunch is about to be served up."

Malachi grinned and ordered lunch for the four of them.

They fell to eating and, between bites, William said, "I'm amazed, Manteo, at how much you know about the white man and the world outside Virginia. Where did all your information come from?"

"I read," grinned Manteo. "Mr. Hakluyt give copy of his *Divers Voyages touching the Discoverie of America* when I first come to England. Talks about all countries that come to my land. I learn much. Read other books later, but this one most good, I think."

"I suppose Hakluyt presents a strictly English point of view?"

"Oh, no. *Divers Voyages* gives accounts of voyages made to America by all nation since 1492 voyage of Columbus. John Cabot claims to discover Newfoundland five years later, and Gilbert Humpfrey tells of coasting trip in 1580. Hakluyt write down what each man say but changes words if account not clear. Many men better adventurers than writers, is not so?"

"I can well imagine it," said William. "Not all are born with a love of words and the music of language."

Harriot laughed softly. "Fortunately, all the captains had the daily writing practice of recording interesting details of their journeys under the 'occurrences' column of their log books. I myself especially remember Giovanni da Verrazzano's 1524 letter to his sponsor, King Francis II of France, detailing his journey along the coast of America from Newfoundland to Florida. His was remarkably direct prose for a man of action."

William turned to Malachi. "I suppose you have read Hakluyt's *Divers Voyages* too, sir, and remember every word of it?"

"Of course," grinned Malachi. "Every man of letters has read the *Divers Voyages* since it was published in 1582. Would you like me to quote a passage?"

"Indeed, I would. Did da Verrazzano meet any of the New World Indians?"

"Interestingly enough, he left an account of natives he encountered at 38^0 N. which is just about the same parallel we just finished talking about."

"Egad, Manteo. He could have been writing about your very people. Did it seem true to you?"

"I think maybe it true of older times. Sixty years long time."

"Well, tell us, Malachi, sir! I am all agog!"

"In this passage, Verrazzano was speaking of the group of natives who greeted his party as they approached the coast *'and came harde to the Sea side, seeming to rejoice very much at the sight of us; and, marveling greatly at our apparel, shape and whiteness, showed us by sundry signs where we might most commodiously come a-land and with our boat, offering us*

445

also of their victuals to eat. These people go altogether naked except only that they cover their privy parts with certain skins of beasts like unto martens, which they fasten onto a narrow girdle made of grass....Some of them wear garlands of bird feathers. The people are of color russet, and not much unlike the Saracens, their hair black, thick, and not very long, which they tie together in a knot behind, and wear it like a tail. They are well featured in their limbs, of average stature, and commonly somewhat bigger than we; broad breasted, strong arms, their legs and other parts of their bodies well fashioned, and they are disfigured in nothing, saving that they have somewhat broad visages'." [9]

"Ah, that's marvelous, Manteo. He writes that your people are handsome! The broad visage probably comes from smiling so much because you don't have to worry about dressing up when you have visitors. A life without worry or scurrying about would put a smile on a lot of faces in our part of the world too. Did Verrazzano not meet any grouchy Indians, Malachi?"

"As a matter of fact, he did. In his notes, Verrazzano called Maine the "Land of Bad People" because when the whites attempted to land there, the Abnaki Indians in that area lined the shore with warriors waving weapons in a threatening manner. Then, having succeeded in turning the landing party away, the Indians hooted in derision at the whites, bent over, bared their backsides and wiggled them at the sailors."

"Very bad people, indeed!" laughed William.

"These same Indians refused to trade face-to-face with Verrazzano's crew, but they did some small bartering by letting baskets down to the boats from the edge of a steep cliff," added Malachi.

"No doubt the Abnaki had prior contact with the White Man," said William, still laughing. "If they knew the Europeans abducted Indians as slaves and presented them for entertainment purposes to old-world onlookers, they might well drive them away."

Manteo nodded. "That a good answer to bad behavior. My people speak of English taking first Indians away in 1502 and Portuguese taking fifty and seven from Newfoundland to king in Lisbon. Even more early, Columbus took away thirty Indians. Maybe Abnaki people not want to go."

"Zounds," breathed William. "It's a great wonder you were willing to come to England, Manteo, knowing all this."

"Manteo a man of thought," said the Indian lord. "He know to speak and dress as Englishman. Not be so different or frighten people. Also he know to seek out other men of thought, who wish to learn customs and wisdom of other tribes. Harriot one good friend. Now you also."

"Egad, Manteo. It is an honor to be your friend," said William warmly, extending his hand.

Manteo took it. "Young William and master Malachi will never betray trust of friend or of his people," he said, bowing. "This I know."

Soon after, Harriot and Manteo took their leave.

"God save us," murmured William to himself. "Who are the savages here if Lane cut off the head of the Indian chief who greeted our people and fed them and even planted crops for them?"

"What's that you say?" asked Malachi.

"Oh, nothing. Just mulling over what I've learned about the Roanoke Colony."

Chapter 3:
MARY'S INCRIMINATING LETTERS

An Inn near Chartley Castle, August 9, 1586:

"Even though I know the circumstances of your handicap," Malachi said, "I am still sometimes struck with astonishment at your political naiveté'."

"It's small comfort, I know, to astonish one's master for the wrong reasons, but I must confess that I feel some joy in getting your attention at all. I have already told you that I don't understand the task at hand. Everything you have said indicates there is always another level to it, and then another level, and then—"

Malachi waved him to silence. "I think I have your drift. Pay attention now. When Mary Stuart leaves Chartley this morning to attend a hunt—which she has requested for some time—she will be met by a royal troop of horse and escorted to the neighboring estate of Tixall, where she will be held incommunicado while her papers and secretaries are seized at Chartley. We already have considerable evidence against her, but Walsingham thinks a little more won't hurt. There may very well be open admissions of treason or worse in her correspondence–a smoking dagg, so to speak." [10]

"Worse than treason?"

"Ah well, Elizabeth understands power politics. She knows well enough that the heir-apparent may be connected to treasonous plots with or without her consent. It happened to her during the reign of her half-sister, Bloody Mary, and she was nearly executed for a supposed connection with Wyatt's Rebellion. Many have thought that Elizabeth's life was saved at that time because Mary was distracted from her suspicion by the joy of her own pregnancy. After all, she was convinced that she was carrying the child who would be born as the greatest monarch the world had ever seen. A son by Queen Mary and her husband, King Philip II of Spain, would have inherited the Spanish and Portuguese far-flung empires and England to boot—most of the civilized world, more than any ruler had ever governed before."

"That would distract anyone."

"Of course, the pregnancy was false, but by the time that was realized, months later, Elizabeth was off Mary's mind and fairly safe. So the Queen knows about such things. The 'worse' would come if Mary Stuart has dared say anything unflattering personally about Elizabeth in her letters to other Continental Courts. If she happened to ridicule our Queen's hair or teeth or general appearance, for example, she will have come very near to signing her own death warrant. Elizabeth's standards for showing respect to herself as sovereign are very strict. Any piercing of her pride will quickly uncover a flashing fang."

"So she would normally shrug off evidence of treachery and treason and invasion plots against her, but she will be murderously offended if mention is made of her hair turning grey under her wig?"

"That's our lady queen, all right," Malachi shrugged. "Half-Prince and half-woman with little sense of proportion in the woman half."

"So how do we seek out the 'smoking dagg'?"

"We are to accompany Milles, Phelippes, and Waad in the collection of her correspondence, both open and closed."

"Open and closed?"

"Her beer-barrel correspondence is already known to us, of course," Malachi nodded, "and has helped us nab her, but there are some few notes we could not cover. As a queen, Mary was allowed visits from a few carefully screened dignitaries during the past year, and nearly every one of them passed her furtive notes from interested parties."

"Ah, they ran our beer-barrel blockade, did they?"

Malachi nodded. "I suspect many highly placed Englishmen have corresponded with her to offer some sympathy but careful not to offer anything more."

"Keeping a door ajar on the off-chance that she may someday rule."

"Right, but hurtful to Elizabeth, nonetheless, since such letters may come from people who are very close to her and perfectly loyal to her under the present circumstances."

"But hedging their bets."

"Exactly."

"When you say 'close to Elizabeth'—bloody hell, Malachi, you can't mean Council members?"

"I would think so. They are all politicians—among other things."

"Even Leicester and Burghley?"

"Neither would surprise me. Probably young Essex too. Maybe even Francis Bacon. Polite notes, anyway. I know that Lord Chancellor Hatton has notified Mary that he would personally come and release her if Elizabeth should die naturally."

"How about Raleigh?" William muttered.

"I doubt if he would take the trouble. He's not political enough."

"So our job is to find those letters and turn them over to the Queen?"

Malachi shook his head. "Elizabeth doesn't go out of her way to encounter bad news, especially if she knows it's there. Our job on the morrow is just to enter Chartley, take possession of all Mary's correspondence, and place her secretaries in custody. Her files will be inventoried by Walsingham, who will review them with four or five other Council members, and the results will be turned over to Burghley who will then decide what the Queen should see and what would hurt her feelings."

"She certainly puts a great deal of trust in her advisors."

"She should. They've served her well for many years."

"But they could remove incriminating letters. Their own, for instance."

"She would expect them to. One of the Queen's favorite observations from Seneca is 'Video et Taceo; I see, but say nothing'. [11] Successful rulers—like successful classroom teachers—must cultivate a very selective sight and hearing filter, or they soon find themselves enmeshed in minutia while their domain goes down the drain."

William shook his head. "My word, the life of a monarch must be a very puzzling existence."

"It's nothing you need ever worry about," Malachi assured him.

Chapter 4:
HUNG, DRAWN, & QUARTERED: A TRAITOR'S DEATH:

Inn near Chartley, end of September 1586:

"Were you there, Poley?" gasped William.

"Aye, a very impressive production," said Robert Poley. "Even those who aspire to appear on stage"—he smirked at William—"would be happy to stand in the audience during a performance of this caliber."

"Do you go to every execution?" William inquired.

"I was assigned to this one as a special witness to be sure it went off as it should, but to answer your question, no, I don't go to every execution. As a matter of fact, my sensitive stomach gets sympathetic pains if I witness more than one disembowelment a year. Surprised you two missed it."

"We were up in Scotland," said Malachi.

"Well, Babington died a prolonged and painful death just as Walsingham promised the Queen he would. His shrieks and screams of agony will serve as a good lesson to anybody who even thinks about endangering our Queen. He stayed alive long enough after being hung to have his cut-off manhood roasted on a brazier before his eyes and finally stuffed into his screeching mouth. The full treatment."

William blanched. Malachi asked, "And that's what our office ordered?"

"That's right," said Poley. "Babington and Ballard and the bunch that were to do the killing got the full treatment the first day, but the executioner was ordered to ease up and show mercy to the remaining seven the second day, so they were hanged until dead before they were cut up."

"The Queen's blood lust was somewhat sated, I take it."

Poley nodded. "At first, the Queen asked Walsingham to devise a more painful punishment for the men who plotted to kill her. She appeared truly alarmed that these plotters had daily access to her during the months they were hatching this plot. Our office had to remind her that being hung, drawn, and quartered was the legal punishment for treason and anything more painful would not only be illegal but very hard to imagine."

"Amen to that," murmured William.

"She had directed Walsingham to scoop up the plotters immediately because, as she explained, *'Lest by not heeding and preventing the Danger while she might, she should seem rather to tempt God, than to trust in God.'* [12] Fortunately, Mary Stewart chose that moment to write to Babington and expose herself by agreeing to the execution of Elizabeth."

"Right," said Malachi. "That was excellent luck, indeed. Before Walsingham could round up the suspects as Elizabeth ordered, we identified John Savage and thereby found out that the plotters were importing killers from the Continent, so we were ordered to delay just long enough to round up all of them."

"Yes," said William, "but it sometimes seems to me the Boss left the Queen exposed to a rather far-reaching plot longer than he might have."

"Perhaps so. Savage and that whole coterie of sympathizers in Paris were part of the scheme," Malachi said. "Once they learned from Ballard that they had a working plot underway, they circulated a letter among Catholics in England cautioning them to move very carefully for a time. Our native Papists were advised to use only tears and prayers, spiritual discourse, fasting, and other civilized weapons against Anglican suppression in order to hold down suspicion while this plot unfolded."

"You must have gotten to know Babington pretty well in the buildup to his arrest," William said to Poley. "Did it seem to you he would really carry through with the killing of the Queen?"

Poley shrugged. "Hard to say. He had moments when he was full bore for the enterprise and moments when he seemed hesitant, but the risk was always there. He was a rich, young gentleman who had allowed Ballard to place him at the head of a small parade of impatient young Catholics on a deadly mission. They were urged on by the spiritual leaders of their faith, so Babington had little time to rest his baton in order to think things over. As a matter of fact, he may have had a change of heart just about the time his arrest loomed because he offered Sir Walter Raleigh £1,000 to intercede with the authorities on his behalf."

"To no avail obviously."

"And, ironically, the Queen has since turned all of the traitor's estates over to Raleigh for services rendered. Don't ask."

"And how about Mary Stwart? Will the Queen finally agree to dispose of her?"

Poley shrugged. "Who knows? I gave up trying to outguess our Queen a long time ago, but I suspect your trip to Scotland may have had something to do with saving Elizabeth the trouble of having to decide. How about it, Malachi? Did you manage to locate some firebrand Scot who still harbors enough hatred against Mary Stewart to do her in if we left the door unlatched for him?"

"No such luck," Malachi chuckled. "We were only smelling the air up there to see how the Scots feel about the possible execution of their former Queen. Checking the pulse, so to speak."

"Yes," Poley smiled, "checking the pulse and helping to safeguard the delivery of King James' subsidy, as I understand it. How much will they holler if we do rid ourselves of Mary Stewart?"

"She's old news to them. They all figure she's our problem now since we've held her for so many years. They'll file a formal protest, of course, but James will secretly relish moving up from number two to number one in the succession line for England's throne and, as a matter of fact, I doubt if he would put his annual subsidy in jeopardy for the sake of a woman he hasn't seen since his first year. Their view of the situation is not surprising, but what does surprise me is that our English Bond of Association people have turned out to be so namby-pamby now that the occasion has arisen for them to back up all their fine talk about protecting Elizabeth's life."

Robert Poley laughed. "Our brave countrymen delivered whole trunk-loads of sworn statements to the Queen testifying to their determination to get rid of Mary Stewart if she caused further trouble, but now that her guilt has been proven, where are they? Not a single man has stepped forward to save Elizabeth from being embarrassed before the whole Continent!"

"That's the value of brave talk, all right," Malachi chuckled. "The Queen has certainly hinted strongly enough that she would accept some less formal way of disposing of the Queen of Scots, but the excuses are flying wild now that the need is here. Some say they can't get past the security at Chartley. Some claim the time isn't ripe. Some worry it would stain their conscience, and some feel such a murder would unite our traditional enemies, France and Spain, and cause them to form a Catholic Crusade to retaliate against us with an invasion. The only meaningful question remaining in the minds of straight-thinking Englishmen today, however, should be how to assure ourselves that Elizabeth lives longer than Mary Stuart, and the clear response to that uncertainty should be obvious to all."

"Ha!" exclaimed Robert Poley. "Some may call it murder if they wish, but in every other European country, I assure you, this problem would be settled in a much more practical manner than the course we're following."

William scratched his head. "Practical?"

"Whenever a Continental Prince is in danger of public embarrassment, his vigilant attendants see to it that the offending party is quickly smothered or poisoned or thrown from a horse or accidentally drowned in the nearest moat—effectively dispatched, in short, so that official involvement is not apparent. 'Plausible deniability' is all Madrid or Rome or Paris or Edinburgh want. Implicate some poor fall guy and hang him afterward for his crime."

"Oh yes," said William sarcastically. "Very practical, indeed."

"That is how the leaders of other countries understand it. They have all done it. What they don't understand is why our Anglican Queen is planning to kill their Catholic Queen openly and thereby make a public statement to which they must respond publicly. Bloody hell, they all know Elizabeth must get rid of Mary, and I'll wager none of them has serious plans for her. Even Philip knows we would never let her leave our custody alive if his invasion were successful."

"Especially then," Malachi emphasized. "So the Queen is stuck. She's forced to appeal to exactly the wrong man to find some other way to resolve her public relations problem."

"What man is that?" asked William.

"Paulet. Too bad he has done such a good job of isolating Mary."

"True," Poley mused. "Nobody can get near her. Nobody knows anything about her routine or her habits."

"I know that all the anger and apprehension of the last six months have really taken a toll on her sleeping habits," William announced. "She must drink a warm glass of milk with a brace of brandy every evening before retiring just to be able to drift off."

"How in the world do you know that, William?" Malachi asked.

"I've seen Mistress Sally prepare it and take it to her."

"What?" Malachi exclaimed. "Can you get in to see the Queen?"

"Well, not exactly, but Mistress Sally has convinced one of the Chartley guards that I am her brother and that we enjoy reminiscing into the night. He is used to seeing me inside the castle. We do resemble each other in a rather superficial way, but I think, really, he's sweet on her too and would do anything to please her."

"By God!" Malachi rose instantly and produced a small phial from behind some books on the shelf. He held this out to William. "Could you have your lady friend add the soothing contents of this phial to her milk this evening? It's a very special sleeping potion which Leicester sent us from Holland."

William took the potion. "Consider it done," he said. "It's time for me to leave now in order to catch the right guard. I'll see you in the morning," he said as he left.

Malachi and Poley looked at each other quietly in wonder and finally poured another drink before Poley said, "You don't really suppose....."

"It has been done in stranger ways," Malachi shrugged, "so who knows?"

"And the logical man to take the blame?"

"Miss Sally is my nominee, if we can arrange it, but if need be, I guess I could make the sacrifice, although I've grown quite fond of him, but in service to the Queen——" Malachi bowed his head and said no more.

Poley stared at Malachi for a moment, then chuckled. "Ye gods, Malachi, you had me there for a moment. I see now you have a scheme to unfold if the need arises. I'll wager your man is safe enough behind some bulwark in your brain."

The next morning, William returned as usual, looking as innocent and unruffled as ever.

"Did the Scottish woman sleep well?" Malachi asked in greeting.

"Mary?" William said. "Fine. She went riding early this morning."

"Riding? Did you give her the potion?"

"Not really. Actually, Mistress Sally and I started frolicking early and somehow managed to knock the phial off the bedside table. Her small dog licked up the contents and went instantly to sleep. Very effective stuff. Unfortunately, he also perished sometime during the night and oddly enough was stiff as a board this morning. I brought him with me to save her the sight of such a loss." He extracted the stiffened remains from a burlap sack he held behind him. "I'll bury him someplace and let her think he wandered off, and gradually she'll get used to the loss."

"Yes," Malachi gritted, "That's a very thoughtful thing to do. Bury him deep. I see you have the phial there too, so bury that with him."

William frowned. "The dog's death after taking the sleeping potion was such a far-fetched coincidence, that I really have to ask you, Malachi: Are you positive that was only a sleeping potion?"

"Quiet, you fool!" Malachi commanded. "We have troubles enough without you spreading rumors. It's true, I may have accidentally given you the wrong phial. My current mountebank is sometimes not as careful as he should be in labeling his products. Nevertheless, get that animal buried and out of sight immediately."

"I don't feel good about this."

"In moments of crisis, keep this thought uppermost in mind: There are always darker days ahead. That single realization permits you to feast on today's skimpy pleasures."

Chapter 5:
ELIZABETH SIGNS THE
WARRANT FOR MARY'S DEATH

Burghley's Office, February 2, 1587:

"Come in Malachi," said Burghley, "and bring your man along with you. We need you to take notes of this auspicious occasion. Mr. Davison, the Queen's secretary, has just delivered to us the solution to a problem which has bedeviled us for nineteen years. Nineteen gut-wrenching years, if I may say so."

"Just doing my duty as I see it," said Davison.

"We've waited a very long time for our Queen to sign this warrant," said Burghley, holding the document reverently to his chest. "You've done a very wise thing showing it to me, Mr. Davison, especially since Walsingham is still feeling poorly and cannot be counted on to advise his usual precipitous action. This will certainly perk him up. No one has waited with as much apprehension as Francis. What do you think finally pushed her into signing it?"

"It would be hard to say it was any one thing," Davison replied, "but I think the gradual drum roll of pressure finally took its toll."

"What drum roll was that?" William asked.

Davison made a tsk-tsk sound. "Just after Babingon and the others were executed, Elizabeth appointed a commission of forty-six peers, privy councilors and judges—the brightest and best in the country—for the trial of Mary Stuart. They arrived at Fotheringay Castle on October 11 to review Babington's letter and Mary Stuart's reply in addition to the confessions of Babington, Ballard, and Savage, along with the depositions of her two secretaries, and before that month was out, they condemned her to death."

"Such a verdict is not surprising after the presentation of such strong evidence," William said.

"Who could possibly disagree with such a finding after hearing Babington's actual words revealing the plot and Mary's actual letter accepting the killing of Elizabeth? It seems to me this will go down in the annuls of jurisprudence as one of the most frequently cited cases in terms of iron-clad evidence against which there can be no sustained disagreement. I think our legal system profits enormously from having such classic cases which can be endlessly cited by future barristers and which serve——"

He was interrupted by a loud cough and clearing of the throat by Davidson. "Much as I admire your sentiment, sir, I think it important to keep legal matters clear of confusion by paying close attention to small details. It would have done little good to present Mary's actual letter to the Commission since it was written in one of the sixty ciphers we found in Mary's possession when we picked up her correspondence. It was, rather, Phelippes' translation of Mary's coded letter that was read to the Court."

"Oh, my. That does leave ajar an unforeseen door in what I had thought was an air-tight case for conviction. Perhaps, then, it's just as well that Babington saw the light and came forward with his confession to tie this whole plot together."

"In point of fact," Davidson muttered, "He didn't exactly 'come forward' as you say. We had to prod him a bit."

"Oh? The rack?"

Davidson nodded.

"And Ballard and Savage?"

Davidson nodded again, twice.

"Good Lord!" William exclaimed. "What did her defense lawyer have to say about such proceedings?"

"Actually, Mary was tried for treason and no defense is provided for such a charge. It is up to the defendant to state their defense after the evidence has been presented. Mary's only defense was her forceful assertion that our Commission had no authority in the first place to pass judgment on an anointed sovereign."

"Oh, my," William shook his head.

"Excuse me, Young Man," said Burghley impatiently, "but if you want further legal instruction perhaps you'd better enroll at the Inns of Court. The truth is that no one is tried for treason in this country unless they are known to be guilty, so there is no need to confuse the issue with lawyers for the defense. Even after we got our conviction," Burghley added with a grimace, "we needed the Queen's signature which was denied us without explanation until the middle of November last when both Houses presented her with a joint petition requesting the speedy execution of the Scottish Woman. Her reply so befuddled our brains that we were all left speechless and we retired to our chambers to gather our wits."

"Do you remember her reply?"

"Oh, dear," Burghley exclaimed. "I thought everybody had heard of her reply before this, but I am ready to revisit that occasion since it was one of the most puzzling moments of my life. After she read our petition, she thanked us for the care we had shown her, and then she said; *'If I should say unto you that I mean not to grant your petition, by my faith I should say unto you more than perhaps I mean. And if I should say unto you that I mean to grant your petition, I should then tell you more than is fit for you to know. And thus I must deliver you an answer, answerless'."* [13]

"An answerless answer!" William exclaimed. "I didn't know such a thing was possible."

Burghley nodded. "It was possible all right and it left our trained negotiators and policy makers with our brains in a tangle until Walsingham finally broke out of our trance in December and once again made a direct and powerful appeal to Elizabeth to act. He must have insisted too strongly, however, since the Queen was so offended at something he said that she vehemently rejected his council and caused him to take sick leave from the Court. He explained his absence to me thus: *'Her Majesty's unkind dealing towards me hath so wounded me as I could take no comfort to stay there....The delay of the intended and necessary execution doth more trouble me, considering the danger her Majesty runneth, than any particular grief.....Seeing the declining state we are running into, and that men of best desert are least esteemed, I hold them happiest in this government that may be rather lookers-on than actors'."* [14]

"Perhaps that's why the Queen advised me to show this signed warrant to him after it received the Great Seal from Lord Chancellor Hatton," Davison smiled. "She joked that I was to take it by Walsingham's house even though he is still sick in bed and give him sight of it. *'The grief thereof,'* she said, *'will go near to kill him outright'.*"

"It's good to see she can still joke in the midst of her grief," Burghley nodded. "She wept when she had to sign away the Duke of Norfolk back in '61 after we broke up the Revolt of the Northern Earls, but she gathered herself and got the job done. This warrant was even more difficult for her, of course, because the Scottish Woman is not only a relative of royal blood, but was once the anointed monarch of her own realm. Elizabeth very wisely sees a dangerous precedent in permitting a trial by Parliament to result in the death of an anointed sovereign–partially, I imagine, because she herself has been at odds with her Parliament, sometimes for long periods. She believes a sovereign's authority is accountable only to God and recognizes no suitable precedent to sanction the execution of fellow monarchs."

"I imagine the country-wide pleadings in favor of this solution finally persuaded her," Malachi said.

"Doubtless it helped," Davison nodded, "but another reason might be the recent reply to the request she had us send to Amais Paulet urging him to find *'some other way to shorten the life of that Queen.'* Paulet's reply just arrived yesterday and may have convinced her finally that she had no alternative but to sign. He said; *'My good livings and life are at her Majesty's disposition and I am ready to so lose them this next morrow, if it shall so please her, acknowledging that I hold them as of her mere and most gracious favour, and do not desire to enjoy them but with her Highness' good liking. But God forbid that I should make so foul a shipwreck of my conscience, or leave so great a blot to my poor posterity to shed blood without law or warrant'.'*"

"Good Lord!" Burghley exploded, "He chooses just such a time to strike a pose for his posterity! *'So foul a shipwreck of my conscience'*, indeed! What in God's name did he think he was signing up for last year when he took a solemn oath to do away with the Scottish Woman if she threatened Elizabeth again? Did he think he was being invited to a tea party?"

"Exactly the way the Queen responded," said Davison. "*'The niceness of these precise fellows who in words would do great things but in deed perform nothing'*, was her comment." [15]

"I, for one, am not surprised that Sir Amais Paulet won't do it," said Malachi. "even after a personal request from the Queen. He would do anything else for her, I'm sure, but in this instance she is being pinched by her own hand. William, how's your memory? Do you remember how Walsingham described Paulet when he chose him early last year to supervise the close confinement of Mary Stuart to keep her from plotting against Elizabeth?"

"It was so impressive, I do remember," William replied. "Give me a moment." He closed his eyes, hummed to himself for a moment and then produced the voice of Walsingham with a bit of bluster: 'A*s honest and alert and incorruptible a soul as can be found in all of England—and a Puritan as well—in addition to being the former English Ambassador to the French Court, and it is into his vigilant care at Tutbury Castle we have placed the security of Mary Stuart'.*" [16]

"Well done," Burghley chuckled. "You may have overdone Walsingham's bluster a bit, young man, but I think it's clear that you have a great future ahead of you as a mimic of some sort or other."

William shrugged. "Not my fault if Walsingham doesn't yet realize the benefit of dramatizing his thoughts. His testimony of Paulet's character was very dramatic and should be presented forcefully enough to emphasize that Paulet is exactly the wrong man to request the favor of a convenient murder."

"One of the few things we can count on here," Burghley said, "is that after the Queen has elbowed her way through the delays and postponements which seem to crowd her mind in the midst of making important decisions, she often comes down on the side of common sense right alongside the English people." Burghley stood abruptly. "But speaking of delays reminds me that we must get this warrant to Fotheringay immediately because it is entirely possible our sweet Sovereign may at this very moment be writing out a cancellation of this order in the privacy of her quarters. Which of the Privy Council members are in town, Malachi?"

"I'm afraid we have all been caught a little off-balance by the Queen's dispatching the warrant tonight," Malachi said. "Some of the Privy Council members have left town for the weekend, and some are on their way to or from Fotheringay." Malachi paused thoughtfully. "Besides Walsingham and Leicester, I'm sure we can locate Howard, Knollys, and Derby. Cobham and Hunsdon were here this afternoon. Hatton, too."

"Find them, find them! They will all sign, I'm sure," Burghley declared. "They will have to do for now. We cannot risk further delay. If we have to postdate some signatures later on, we'll do it. As we all know, when dealing with our effervescent Queen, there does occasionally come a time to cut corners, and this is just such a time, so let's move ahead as quickly as possible. Let's get those signatures tonight and have this warrant delivered to Fotheringay by Council secretary Beale by dawn."

"There is one other consideration besides the signatures," Davidson said very thoughtfully. "The Queen didn't exactly dispatch the warrant yet."

"But I have it here in my hands, all signed," a puzzled Burghley replied.

"Ordinarily, dispatching signed orders is a two-step process with the Queen," Davidson explained. "First she signs the paper and then she tells me either to dispatch it immediately or to hold it for later delivery. Occasionally she signs papers that are never delivered, but not often. Our Queen does not waste words."

"Nor mince them either," Burghley agreed. "Did she tell you to hold the warrant?"

"She didn't say one way or the other. She signed it, told me to get the Great Seal on it and show it to Walsingham, but then she said nothing further."

"And you brought it here without her direct order?"

Davison shrugged. "It has to get done no matter how. England has to rid herself once and for all of the Viper in her Bosom. With Mary Stuart dead, the Catholic plotters who have been so active in the last few years will have no purpose in further attempts on Elizabeth's life. You know as well as I do that our beloved Lady has the capacity to delay what needs to be done for another nineteen years if we leave it up to her, so here it is." He smacked the warrant on the table. "Let's get it done now, whatever the consequences."

"You are a brave man, Mr. Davison," Burghley declared, "and England will never forget you. The Queen has obviously set you up for the fall guy in this affair, and it takes rare courage for you to accept such a role. It's clear to me that at least for today, she wants this deed done, but she is unwilling to accept the responsibility for approving it."

"What will she do to Mr. Davison?" William whispered to Malachi.

"She'll lambast him until his teeth rattle, hoping to convince the world it was not her doing, and no doubt toss him into the Tower for an extended stay."

Davison sighed deeply. "If the Privy Council members will only refuse to sanction my execution—and I hope I may count on you and our associates in that matter, Lord Burghley—a stay in the Tower will be well worth our accomplishment. And I will be honored to deflect criticism from our Queen."

Burghley clapped Davison on the back. "Look me up when you get out, friend. This office can always use men who see things so clearly. But let's get on with it! The warrant will have to go with only nine signatures! I fear the Queen's certain anger may make some of our colleagues hesitant, but we need to disperse the Royal displeasure by having it fall on as many targets as possible. I would prefer the entire Council get banned rather than a special seven or eight. If she runs us all off, she will have to call us back the sooner just to keep the government functioning."

Davison grimaced, "but there will be plenty of anger to go around, I imagine."

"Why not let William make a quick copy of the warrant and circulate it to the other Council members while the original goes to Fotheringay?" said Malachi. "That way they will actually be signing after dispatch but prior to delivery. That should bind them."

"Splendid idea," said Burghley. "Is he a fast worker?"

"Fastest in the business, sir," Malachi assured him as he signaled William to start. "And never blots a single word.""

"Splendid then," Burghley said. "Get the warrant signed and hand it over to Mr. Beale for delivery to Fortheringay without delay, and, Malachi, I'd like one last word with you when the others are gone."

"At your service, sir."

Chapter 6:
PLAN TO BURY SIDNEY'S
BODY AS DISTRACTION

Burghley's Office: February 2, 1587:

They waved the others off and Burghley turned to Malachi. "You are aware, Malachi, that we are on the verge of an earth-shaking development here; one that will evoke an unfavorable response from every other European monarch."

"I know the Catholic countries–Spain, Italy and France–will protest the execution of Mary, but what complaint will the others have?"

"Catholic or not, every king in Europe will recognize this action as a direct assault on the majesty of anointed rulers. In the past, when a monarch did not suit his people, they usually retired to their pubs and waited patiently for life's mortal limitation to solve their problem."

"I see," Malachi nodded. "So when our legislators voted to execute Mary, they introduced an additional limitation where none had existed before."

"True enough, and because all monarchs spend half their time sniffing out threats to their existence, they will all see this action as a precedent that could consume any of them at any time; if it can happen here, it could happen anywhere."

"So they will set up a legal and moral outcry against such a practice. Elizabeth will be subjected to an extensive Continental condemnation for betraying her own kind even though they all know she is only doing what should have been done years ago."

"Impressively insightful," Burghley complimented him. "You'll make a diplomat yet, Malachi, which is just as well since you'll need such skill for the next job I have for you."

Malachi grinned. "I'm ready to try, sir."

"Good. First, we have to recognize that no monarch will defend Elizabeth's action since that would be against their own best interest. That means they will all pile on, displaying their outrage over the execution of Mary Stuart. That's the nature of politics," he grimaced. "Our concern needs to be in defense of Her Majesty's feelings. She can certainly shrug off some criticism just as she has done in the past, but this assault is likely to go on and on until we figure out a way to trump it with a higher card before it wears her down."

"And you have something in mind, sir?"

"That's how I earn my pay," Burghley grinned. "A little review is in order here. As you probably remember, after the 1200 man honor guard returned the body of Sir Philip Sidney to England aboard *The Black Pinnace* back in early November, he was deposited on Tower Hill and there he remains today in the Minories Church, awaiting burial after the proper arrangements are made."

"Oh, I do remember that, sir. We had the devil's own time wrestling his body away from the Zealanders who were determined to honor him by burying him on their own soil where he died after joining them in their battle against Spain. They finally said good-by to him with many a tear, and then England itself spent the month after his death in mourning. When his wife returned after nursing him in Holland, I remember that we all got caught up in her losing their baby just after coming home. I know Walsingham was doubly distressed, losing his son-in-law and then his grandchild so close together."

"Yes, Francis was so disoriented at the loss, I'm sure that's why he subsequently spoke too sharply to the Queen and was sent from her Court. The truth is that Francis should be giving you the assignment I am about to give you, but until he recovers his health, his good friends must fill in as the need arises."

"The arrangements you mentioned, I imagine, have to do with the fact that the English people are puzzled and uneasy by the fact that such a hero has not yet been buried a full three months after his death."

"Exactly," Burghley nodded. "The truth of the matter is that Sidney's estate has not yet been settled, and even if we attempt to bury him in the middle of the night, hugger-mugger, so to speak—which would certainly be a cowardly thing to do for such a man—we could not escape the chorus of creditors who will disturb the ceremony with their contemptuous catcalls and belligerent belittlements of poor Philip. We simply cannot permit them to disgrace his memory in that fashion. The only solution, of course, is to get his estate settled before the funeral."

"Well, if a pound or two from my pocket will do any good—"

Burghley held up an admonishing hand. "That's not what I need from you. What I need is for you to help me pave the way so that we may openly hold the biggest, most heavily attended funeral this country has ever seen for somebody not of the nobility. It must be a funeral which will be reported in every capitol on the Continent, and involve every foreign diplomat now in England. We must clean the slate of Philip's encumbrances quickly and then invite the attention of the entire world to turn away from castigating our Queen!"

"I'm almost afraid to ask. How much does he owe?"

"That has yet to be determined, but it is an impressive sum. The truth is that Philip has always been lavish with his money in helping others because his family has always been well off, but Sir Henry, his father, used up much of the family fortune during his terms as Lord Deputy of Ireland simply because the Queen closed her purse on him after sending him over there. He did wonderful work for the Queen in Ireland, and, like many on the Council, I felt he deserved greater honors at his death."

"That was last May, I remember. Caught a chill from a ride in a wheery. Ironic end after all the serious perils he faced in Ireland."

"Indeed, and it was a shock to many of us when the queen stubbornly refused Philip's request—and that of his two brothers—to return to England to tend to family affairs after Sir Henry's death. She maintained the same adamant refusal a month later when Philip's mother died, so Philip was unaware of how depleted the Sidney fortune had become, and he went on borrowing and spending in Holland in order to keep his six hundred man garrison in Flushing from starving to death."

"Thinking, I imagine, that London would repay the debt."

"Exactly. Either through noble idealism or through what some might regard as naivete', both father and son fell into the same error of thinking the Queen would eventually reimburse the expenditures they made in defense of the Crown, but alas...." Burghley shrugged heavily and threw up his hands. "Nevertheless, the debt is Walsingham's problem now since Philip married into his family, and given time, I'm positive poor Francis will pay off every farthing even if it takes years and ruins him in the bargain."

"And even now the Queen won't help?"

"Elizabeth has always ridiculed the Sidney family policy of remaining aloof from the money-making possibilities of selling offices and charging fees in their various enterprises, so she is simply amused by the present predicament and feels no compunction at all to aid any settlement."

"What was the Queen's reaction to Philip's death?"

"In a letter to Leicester, Elizabeth offered her official condolence, *'for the loss of her dear servant and your lordship's dearest nephew.'* [17] But privately she was heard to refer to Sidney as *'that inconsiderate fellow, Sidney, getting himself killed like any common soldier.'* Presumably, she was offended that he had thrown his life away in her service instead of preserving himself to continue to serve her. As many of us have learned, it is sometimes difficult to foresee her Majesty's reaction to whatever sacrifice we make in her favor."

"How about Uncle Leicester? I remember he pledged to give the shirt off his back to help Philip just after he was wounded."

"That was while Philip was still alive and could be of further use to Lord Leicester, who, incidentally, is responsible for some of Sidney's debt because he diverted funds which were allocated for the Flushing garrison and used them someplace else for his own purpose. Nevertheless, I've already checked with Leicester, and he has obviously concluded that a corpse is not as fruitful an investment as his brilliant, young nephew had been, so he has decided to withdraw completely from what he now labels as a disgraceful scramble to profit from poor Sidney's death."

"Which conveniently misses the point entirely," Malachi muttered.

"One of Leicester's strongest tendencies," Burghley nodded. "God knows that the whole Dutch enterprise would have gone much better if we had put Sidney in charge in the first place instead of Mr. Willy-nilly himself. That's off the record, Malachi. Don't mention to anyone how I characterize Leicester."

"Mention what, sir?"

"Good. As I said, some of the arrangements have already been made here at home. Several Council members and I will consolidate Philip's English debts by paying off his creditors and turning the final tally over to Walsingham. Unfortunately, Francis has spent his time and energy over the years protecting the Queen and not in compiling a personal fortune as some others have, so I'm afraid this resolution of Sir Philip's debts will hit him hard." Burghley shook his head sadly. "Perhaps something can be done. We'll see. In the meantime, I will invite both domestic and foreign dignitaries to the funeral myself, and I will point out that their attendance will be looked on with favor by the old greybeard of the Realm," he paused to grin at himself, "and remind them that he will not forget their cooperation."

"That covers the home front," Malachi said, "so I guess I'll be traveling."

"To Holland," Burghley nodded, "because time is important here, I want to take advantage of your unique ability to spot the man in the crowd who can be counted on to get the work done. The man who can make the process move. We both know that sometimes that's the boss, sometimes the assistant, and sometimes the person quietly hunched over the desk in the corner, and, as we have often seen in the past, it is your special talent to identify such people without being misled by titles or wardrobe or physical appearance. Find those people in Holland who can give you an accurate picture of how much Philip Sidney owes in that country. I want you to use your Irish charm to chat up those creditors and discover how much each is willing to settle for in terms of instant cash in hand."

"Will I have the money with me?"

"A Fugger man will accompany you with a line of credit on his bank. However, since this is to be a delicate operation requiring speed, let me suggest that you leave your apprentice here with us since at times he seems to be at odds with both delicacy and efficiency."

"That's fine, sir. We can use a break from each other. Do you have something in mind to keep him occupied?"

"Yes, the kitchen steward at Whitehall has asked for some help in his accounting department. We'll stick him in there for a time. Be good experience for him."

"Fine. I'll brief him before I go to quiz the Dutch and disperse the funds."

"Once you determine a debt is legitimate after a handshake and a nudge or two with a few gold coins, the Fugger man will supply the payment and we'll thereby consolidate Sidney's Dutch debt for Walsingham's later attention. Dig deep however, because we don't want any guttural Dutch accents crying out against our Sir Philip at his funeral. The Fugger man will meet you tomorrow morning on the Deptford dock, and you'll sail together aboard the pinnace, *Maura Belle*."

"When do you hope to schedule the funeral? How much time do we have?"

"I'm doing some risky down-stream forecasting here, but sometimes that's necessary on this job. I'm hoping we can dispose of Mary Stuart in three or four days, about the sixth or seventh. We'll give the diplomatic outcry a week or so to percolate and then we'll cut it off by burying Sir Philip at St Paul's on the sixteenth with thousands in attendance. I put Fulke Greville—Sidney's best friend—in charge of getting people in England involved in the funeral procession. Greville is both a soldier and a poet so he can alert certain portions of our population to the need of making the funeral a memorable occasion."

"I've met Fulke Greville," Malachi said. "A good man. He'll speak well of his friend."

"He is already circulating a story which will certainly enhance Sidney's nobleness of character. He tells how Sidney entered the hospital after being shot in the thigh and when offered a drink of water, waved it off without drinking because he saw a desperately wounded soldier gazing at the bottle. He offered it to the soldier, saying, *'Thy need is yet greater than mine'.*" [18]

"Admirable, but those couldn't have been his last words since he spent twenty-five days in the hospital before he died."

"Right. Greville tells us that once Sidney became aware that the gangrene was killing him, his last words were *'I would not change my joy for the empire of the world'.*" [19]

"I know he was extremely pleased to finally be serving the queen in such an important post," Malachi reflected, "and for a man of such inherent nobility, I suppose that pleasure included dying on the job. I remember that Herbert Spencer reacted to his death by saying we have lost *'the wonder of our age'.*"

Burghley nodded. "And Spenser doesn't quit that easily when he gets going. He also added that Sidney was, *'the president of Noblesse and of Chivalry'*. Sir Philip Sidney's death impressed everybody at home, of course, but he was also remembered abroad. Even Ambassador Mendoza, of all people, wrote that he *'could not but lament to see Christendom deprived of so rare a light in these dark times.'* [20] We have also learned that King Philip broke off reading a report when he was notified of Sidney's death and wrote in the margin. *'He was my godson'*."

"From the chorus of commentary, it's easy to see that Sidney deeply impressed everybody of importance in Europe. As if to foreshadow this Continental interest in his passing, Sidney himself once said, *'They are never alone that are accompanied with noble thoughts'*."

At this moment, William scratched on the door, and poked his head in. "The warrant has been copied and is making the rounds for signatures," he announced. "May I hope it is teatime?"

"Yes, indeed." Burghley rang a small bell on his desk to summon a servant and order a meal. "In the meantime, a small glass of sherry would not go amiss." He poured three small glasses.

Burghley raised his glass in salute. "Here's to Philip Sidney. I hope we can provide him with a much more pleasant journey than he enjoyed in Holland."

"Well, at least he died a hero's death, I understand," William said.

Burghley gazed into his glass. "You understand? Perhaps you don't yet know the details of that heroic action in Flanders when Norris led an English attack on a Spanish convoy which Parma had sent to reinforce his people in Zutphen. Norris was unaware of how many Spaniards were actually in the convoy. Ground mist concealed their full number up until the moment the English charged them."

"Two hundred English horse and three hundred foot against a Spanish force of fifteen hundred horse and three thousand foot" murmured Malachi.

Burghley continued, "Despite being outnumbered, Norris led several charges that day. Courageous, indeed, but perhaps a trifle too daring. Just daring enough, however, for Sidney and the young English gentlemen who had been placed in Norris's special custody that day. They were exhilarated by their first taste of real combat. I don't know that Norris could have called them off even if he had tried. Sidney had a horse shot out from under him. That might have taught him caution; but instead, he mounted another to continue the fight. A musket ball caught him in the thigh and he made his way back to the hospital, losing blood all the way."

"I thought our cavalry people had armor to cover their thighs," said William. "That puzzles me. Was Sidney under-equipped for combat? Didn't he have a pair of those—what do you call them—cuisses?"

"He did before the attack," nodded Burghley, "but when he noticed that his companion, Sir William Pelham, was riding into battle without leg armour, he threw his own aside in a noble but fatal gesture of sharing the risk."

"I suppose noble gestures should demand a high price or else everybody would be indulging themselves all over the place," said William. "Still, why didn't it occur to Sidney to share the cuisses instead of the risk? You know: one each?"

"That is curious, indeed," agreed Malachi. "He shared his water but not his cuisses."

"Being noble is a lonely business," Burghley murmured. "It does not lend itself to half-measures nor to group action."

"Bloody Hell," protested William. "He should have stuck to politics and diplomacy and left soldiering to the soldiers."

"Yes," said Burghley, "that's just what the Queen said. Well, if you gentlemen will excuse me, we all have much to do. Malachi, if you would, reassign your man before you go, and I'll see you when you get back."

As William and Malachi left Burghley's office, William inquired, "What's all this about reassigning me?"

Malachi explained things as they found their way to the huge kitchen at Whitehall Palace. "Now remember," Malachi said, "you'll only be here for about two weeks, but during that time, you must be more careful than usual because you are inside the official residence of the Queen, and there are many keen-eyed observers about."

"I am to help the Steward?" William asked.

"That's right. You're filling in for the Steward's accountant. You were chosen because they don't like to go outside our office for temporary Palace replacements— you know, security."

"I add and subtract things?"

"Very carefully," Malachi nodded. "It has been suggested that there is large-scale petty pilfering going on in the kitchen. The front office thinks this is a good time to check up on that report, so keep your eyes open. Don't let anything get by you."

"Like what?"

"Well, there are 1,240 oxen coming in."

"Good God! They'll trample everything!"

"Per annum," Malachi added. "Divide by twelve."

"About 103."

"Now by 30."

"Nearly 3 ½."

"And that's exactly how many oxen you must account for every day."

"I can do that. Even half an oxen would be hard to conceal. Don't worry; there won't be any oxen theft while I'm on the job."

"And 13, 260 lambs."

"Per annum, I hope," William said.

Malachi nodded. "And 33,000 chickens, 310 pigs, 4.2 million eggs, 60,000 pounds of butter, and 600,000 gallons of beer per annum."

William whistled. "Keeping track of such quantities is what I call a tall order. It will take me a month to count that many eggs."

"Don't count them individually. Make intelligent estimates. Count cross-sections."

"Cross-sections?"

"Fill one basket with a given number of eggs and thereafter count the baskets, but be careful not to pile the eggs too high."

"Don't put too many eggs in one basket?"

Malachi nodded. "Always a good policy."

"As I go about my detecting duties, I should know what security measures are presently in place. Is there a check-in, check-out system for keeping track of who enters and who leaves the domestic area of the Palace?"

"Not at the moment," Malachi said. "Every few years the Queen becomes alarmed at the rising cost of keeping an open kitchen at Whitehall even though it does feed an enormous number of people who are in residence here. Periodically, she attempts to set up some kind of control system for access to the cooking area in order to minimize the petty pilfering, and many of the loitering family members and neighbors are run off for a time."

"But just for a time."

"Right. After a few weeks of everybody being extra careful, the security tends to snooze somewhat and hoards of unauthorized attendants swarm back into the Royal pantry and even into the unlocked cellar storerooms. Before you know it, strange serving-men are seen carrying meals out of the kitchen; some go to people in residence, of course, but some simply disappear without a trace."

"Oh, I think we can handle that problem rather handily by delivering periodic harangues to the regular household staff, encouraging them to maintain their alert for strangers. I would hope such an effort would keep the security arrangement in place for a longer period. Just to get some perspective on the problem, however, tell me how many of the Queen's regular household personnel are authorized to appear in the kitchen?"

"All of them, as far as I know. With all the cooking and carrying and cleaning, people are coming in and out and back and forth all the time."

"But how many does 'all of them' amount to?"

"That would come to just over one thousand, give or take a score or two," Malachi explained.

"A thousand! Good Lord, I'll need a great hall just to address them and a hundred eyes to watch them!"

"We're not going to pretend it's easy," Malachi consoled him. "Just do the best you can."

"But I'm not sure my final figures will make any sense after dealing with such enormous quantities for a fortnight."

"Get as close as you can," Malachi shrugged, "and if you need a little slippage at the end of the period, go back and divide by 31 days to lower the daily count."

"I can do that? It's acceptable accounting procedure?"

Malachi shrugged again. "Systems and procedures are there to help and not to hinder our work."

"What kind of budget does the Queen have to cover her enormous grocery bill?"

"She runs the household on an outlay of £40,000 annually. Of course, if she runs a little short, she goes on Progress, and it's up to her noble host to make arrangements in return for the pleasure of her company."

"Progress?"

"Periodically—often during the Plague months in London—Elizabeth moves her Court to different parts of England and visits for weeks with noblemen who can afford to lay out three or four thousand pounds for her entertainment."

"Does she take her household staff on Progress with her?"

"Not all of them. Fewer than half usually, and they bring their own dishes, spoons, and blankets."

"Something bothers me about all this," William confessed. "How is large-scale petty-pilfering possible with all those keen-eyed observers you mentioned hanging about?"

"I'm afraid that's part of the problem."

"You mean....?"

"Exactly," Malachi said. "In addition to your other duties, you must be the observer of all observers."

Chapter 7:
MARY QUEEN OF SCOTS IS BEHEADED

Anteroom to Walsingham's Office, February 15, 1587:

"Welcome home, sweet colleague!" William greeted Mercy. "I hope you had a good time at the beach because you missed a lot of excitement here."

"Don't worry," Mercy laughed. "Brighton is civilized enough to have its share of bonfires and churches too. Egad, I thought they'd burn the city down and blunt their clappers before they finally calmed down. I'm convinced there is no corner of England isolated enough to avoid such excitement." Mercy grabbed William's hands and danced him in a circle. "Before the week was out, some of those church bells seemed almost human. Their reaction was so vigorous and hearty, I felt they must have been holding their breath for nineteen years like the rest of us."

"The noise was overwhelming here in the city," William said. "I was sure it would vibrate a belfry or two right off their foundations, but in the end I had to conclude that *I never heard / so musical a discord, such sweet thunder.*" [21]

Mercy nodded, "I don't ever remember such a sense of relief at the news of another person's death. Long overdue, of course, even though I'll miss her as a cornerstone for much debate and speculation. Did you perchance attend the execution, Malachi?"

"Oh, no, I was busy in Holland, but William did take some informal notes from the Earl of Shrewsbury's vivid recounting to Walsingham of the occasion. Ironically enough, our Boss was still too ill to attend the event which he had orchestrated for so many years. He said it would do his heart good to attend, but it might cost him his life to travel so far."

"Who was there?"

"Many of the same men who condemned her, in addition to another hundred or so knights and gentlemen from the neighborhood. That included some Catholics who, undoubtedly, must have felt they were watching the execution of the legitimate Queen of England, done in by her usurper. We still have some of those people around."

"Especially in the North," Mercy nodded. "But as long as they didn't disturb the proceedings, it's a tribute to a certain bedrock stability of England's government."

"That's right, Mercy m'dear. But pray continue, William. You took the notes."

William rubbed his hands together and began to read from his notes. "Mr. Beale delivered the warrant to Fotheringhay on Sunday. By Wednesday—that would be the 8th of February—the great banquet hall was cleared and a small stage, about nine by twelve feet and two feet off the floor, was built at the head of the hall–kind of like the stage which traveling players put up. Chairs and benches were arranged along the length of the interior. The fresh wood of the platform was covered with black velvet. and a high-backed chair was set out. A black cushion was placed on the floor in front of the chopping block. That's how Shrewsbury described it."

"But the troupe numbered only one that day," Mercy said soberly. "What did the Earl say about her composure, William? How did she hold up?"

"Shrewsbury testified that Mary Stuart faced death as courageously as anything she had ever done in life. She entered the hall by a side door accompanied by six of her attendants, following her in pairs as if going to their prayers. She mounted the steps to the stage without aid and sat in the high-backed chair at the rear of the platform just behind the black cushion at her feet."

"And the charges were read, I imagine, to make it official."

"Right. Mr. Beale read the charges from the warrant, and the Dean of Peter-borough attempted to offer her comfort with a Protestant prayer. But, at this point, she stood up and held her crucifix high above her head and, interrupting the prayer, declared for all to hear: *'Mr. Dean, I shall die as I have lived, in the true and holy Catholic faith. All you can say to me on that score is but vain, and all your prayers, I think, can avail me but little'."* [22]

"Scheming to the end," Mercy said in grudging admiration. "Making it appear she was being executed for her Catholic faith in order to egg on revenge from Spain and France."

"And possibly succeeding," Malachi mentioned. "We've already intercepted a message from Mendoza to King Philip after Mary's death wherein he urges the king to line up with God for a little revenge. He wrote, *"I pray that Your Majesty will hasten the*

Enterprise of England to the earliest possible date, for it would seem to be God's obvious design to bestow upon Your Majesty the crowns of these two kingdoms." [23]

Mercy chuckled. "Fascinating how well some men can read the complicated designs of our Savior, while the rest of us struggle daily for his simple approval of our everyday lives."

"Shrewsbury reported that Mary did not go quietly," William said, "but she did go politely. She knelt quickly at the chopping block and continued praying until the black-masked ax-man struck her dead. When he stooped to complete the ritual by exhibiting her head and shouting 'Long live the Queen,' he held aloft only her kerchief with a wig attached while Mary's grizzled grey head left a bloody trail as it rolled across the stage."

"Merciful God," breathed Mercy, quiet for the next few moments.

"Nevertheless, now that she's gone, perhaps our Lady Queen can sleep a little more peacefully, not having to worry about plotters trying to kill her."

"That time may come, but it is not here yet," Malachi said. "Elizabeth must still do some fence-mending before she can relax. Two days after the execution, she summoned her Privy Councilors and gave them stormy hell—especially Burghley and Davison—by shouting that they had wickedly encroached on her power, and made her an object of hatred to the whole world."

"A declaration to be faithfully reported in Madrid and Rome and Paris and Edinburgh, I suppose," Mercy said. "Well, good luck to her on that score because none of those people are easy to fool, and they are always willing to believe the worst of her. Interesting that she has picked out Burghley and Davison to bear the blame. That will help convince some of them."

"Really only Davison," Malachi explained. "She can't do without Burghley, but Davison has already been tried in the Star Chamber for abusing the Queen's confidence and has been deprived of his office, fined 10,000 marks, and condemned to remain in the Tower at the Queen's pleasure."

"Does she think fining and jailing Davison will convince France and Spain that she had nothing to do with killing Mary?"

"Perhaps not, but Elizabeth has apparently convinced herself by constant repetition to the Scots and the Continental courts that Davidson has actually betrayed her, so she has rounded up a pair of judges who assured her that her royal prerogative gives her the power to hang the terrible Mr. Davison without the benefit of a trial. Perhaps that would convince somebody of something."

"How nice," Mercy purred. "Where the hell were those people when the 'some other way' alternative was under discussion?"

Malachi shook his head. "I don't think she'll succeed in hanging Davison because I know that Burghley feels honor bound to defend him and has already expressed open admiration for the fact that at his trial, Davison begged his judges not to question him too closely."

"Ahh, for fear he would be forced to reveal the Queen's part in turning the warrant loose?"

"Exactly right. Burghley sees Davison as the heroic martyr of this whole episode and is determined that the young man will not be permanently damaged by the Queen's political theatrics. As a matter of fact, arrangements have already been made for him to receive his regular salary as Secretary to the Queen even while imprisoned. That, of course, would do him little good if she did succeed in hanging him, but when Burghley learned what the Queen had in mind, he spoke up forcefully; *'I would be loth to live to see a woman of such wisdom as she is, to be wrongly advised….with an opinion gotten from the judges that her prerogative is above her law'."* [24]

"It does appear," Mercy concluded, "that monarchs generally have a difficult time living within the limits of the laws they themselves have established. However, I'll lose little sleep over the fate of Mr. Davison since I know that anybody who has that grey old beard, Lord B, as his patron in this realm is well provided for. I shall, instead, watch with interest as our Queen attempts to sprinkle pixie dust in the eyes of the entire Continent."

"Our balladeers have taken a very philosophical view of Mary's death," William said. "They are already singing in the streets:

> *'The noble famous Queen*
> *Who lost her head of late*
> *Doth show that kings as well as clowns*
> *Are bound to Fortune's fate,*
> *And that no earthly Prince*
> *Can so secure his crown*
> *But Fortune with her whirling wheel*
> *Hath power to pull them down'."* [25]

"Very impressive," Malachi observed, "but that pretty rhyme neglects to mention that the legal successor to the throne of England is now Mary Stuart's son, King James VI of Scotland, and that 'famous queen who lost her head of late' frequently boasted that *'My end is my beginning.'* I wonder how that will play out?" [26]

"We'll just have to buy tickets like the rest of the world and sit back and watch," William concluded.

PART VII: DRAKE'S CADIZ RAID: APRIL, 1587

CHAPTER 1: THE QUEEN'S MESSENGERS CONSPIRE

Leaving the Blue Boar Inn in London, April 10, 1587 (O.S.):

"My horse will be ready in just a minute," Malachi informed William at the door of the Blue Boar Inn, "but before I leave, let's make sure you know exactly what to do."

"Oh, I know what to do all right, but I must confess that I am truly astonished at my assignment," William replied. "In all our time together, this is the strangest order you've ever given me. You actually want me to 'meander-along' behind you on the road to Plymouth? I'm surprised to find you even have a 'meander' strategy in your play-book."

"Don't over-do it," Malachi instructed. "Just keep moving toward Plymouth, but now is the time to profitably employ all of the subterfuges you have utilized in the past to justify your strange behavior."

"I don't know what you mean."

"Time to unleash your arsenal of excuses," Malachi directed. "Trot out your horse-gone-lame gag, or the way-being-lost, or the connection-not-made, or the orders-not-specific. The kind of thing you're so good at. Just keep moving gradually and stop each night at the inns we usually use when we're not in a hurry, so I can get word back to you when the time comes."

"May I have company?"

"I don't have time to argue, but I must confess I am amazed to see that you are prepared to catch me between a rock and a hard spot even when the future of your country is at stake. If I say 'no company', you will wander off to some doxy's crib just when I need to contact you, won't you?"

"Please permit me to assure you," William said with dignity, "that I never had the slightest intention beforehand on any of those occasions—"

"Never mind!" Malachi barked. "Granted. You may have company, but only in your own room where I may reach you, and remember that I don't know anything about that arrangement if official inquiry should ever be made. The word I send to you will come on the gallop, so be prepared at every moment to drop whatever or whoever you're doing and fly like the wind to Plymouth. I don't know how much time we must buy for Drake at the other end, but if you just jounce along at your customary pace of purposeful self-indulgence, that should give him an extra two or three days to clear Plymouth before he gets this bit of bad news." He patted the Queen's message pouch.

"Does she really forbid the voyage? I know I'm not alone in thinking it's a very sensible strategy to attack the Dons on their own coast if they're getting ready to come after us."

"There's no question about the Spanish preparing an attack force. All our Continental sources report a frenzy of activity in new Spanish orders for maritime supplies. That means they're having new ships built all over Europe and reconditioning their old vessels in every seaport in Spain."

"You didn't mention guns."

"Oh, yes, guns too. They are scouring Europe for every piece of artillery they can find, and have finally reached the point where they're willing to pay £22 a ton for first-class cannon, even though some of those full cannon weigh three tons. Unfortunately, such a premium price has attracted some English foundries which prize their purses over their patrimony. They don't mind dealing with the devil himself— English or not—if it will bring them greater returns, and it certainly does that because English brass cannon are prized above all others on the Continent. Only the Dutch—who have enough enterprise to get tin from England to make brass—come close to creating guns like ours."

"I know our merchants need a license to sell in foreign countries, so why don't we cut off such trade by simply refusing to grant them a license? After all, you can't sneak those three ton monsters out of the country under your coat."

"We have prohibited their sale to foreign countries, but some of our merchants are conniving as well as covetous. No license is required to ship guns from one English port to another, so they list another English port on their manifest and as soon as they are on the open sea, they head for places like Naples or Holland or Cork which always have foreign buyers at hand. Raleigh is pressing the Privy Council for investigation and prosecution of this illicit trade, but there is some hesitancy in that group about taking any action they may come to regret."

"Regret? How can they regret putting a stop to arming our enemy?"

"One of the big drawbacks to maintaining a gun-making capability in this country is that the manufacturers must have a market for their goods if they are to stay in business. If our government decides to restrict their market—and thereby curb production—we may find the gun-makers have released many of their expert craftsmen just when we need them most; like right now."

"So in the end, thanks to our self-defeating trade policies, our enemies may end up as well armed as we are," William sighed deeply. "Just another instance of this world being much too complicated for my comprehension. But tell me about Drake. How bad is the news we'll bring him from the Queen? Does she forbid him to go?"

"Not so much 'forbid' him as clip his claws. The original March 15th commission from the Queen specified that he was to *impeach the purpose of the Spanish fleet and stop their meeting at Lisbon.* He was even encouraged to do so by *'...distressing their ships within their heavens.'* [1]

"That sounds as if he has a free hand," William observed.

Malachi nodded. "Much too free as Elizabeth later decided, especially for a captain who is fond of asserting himself at sea no matter what instruction she imposes. As a result of her rethinking the assignment, we carry this April 9th revision of the original orders. In this more restrictive commission, Elizabeth makes clear to Drake that she is not at war with the King of Spain at the moment, and it is her wish that he not spoil that arrangement by inciting further conflict."

"How much does she change the original order?"

"You decide. She commands him to *'forbear to enter forcibly into any of the said King's ports or havens, or to offer violence to any of his towns or shipping within harbouring; or to do any act of hostility upon the land. And yet, notwithstanding this direction, her pleasure is that both you and such of her subjects as serve there under you should do your best endeavour (avoiding as much as may lie in you the effusion of Christian blood) to get into your possession such shipping of the said King or his subjects as you shall find at sea.'* [2]

"Egad," William said. "That sounds to me like an order to 'do it, but don't do it'."

"Yes," Malachi nodded, "I think you have caught the essence of her meaning very well. I hope you now see the necessity of delaying our delivery as efficiently as possible, because no true Englishman wants this albatross hung around Drake's neck just as he is prepared to do some good for all of us—if he be not hindered."

"I'm puzzled about how our delay will fool anyone," William shrugged. "Walsingham certainly knows we can make Plymouth in thirty-six hours on post-horses. Won't we have to answer to him if we take three or four days?"

"The slow-down order comes from Walsingham. He is very strongly in favor of the Drake strategy of meeting the Spaniards on their own coast. He wants the fleet gone from Plymouth before we deliver Elizabeth's castrating order."

"What's holding them up?"

"Drake's fleet is only victualed for two weeks. Just enough time to get to Spain and then start home again if they intend to go on eating. That's the Queen's way of insuring that none of her captains sail off on some wild trip without her specific permission. At the moment, they're waiting for the supply ships to come around from London. An unfavorable wind is holding those ships up, but as soon as they reach Plymouth, the fleet is ready to go. Essentially, we're in a slow-footed race with those supply ships. Enough strategy for the moment, however, let's get to operational details: you are to be the official messenger if there should be an inquiry, so you must carry the pouch. Actually, I will hide the dispatch on my person and gallop ahead so that Drake may see it unofficially and be able to gauge his deadline."

"So, I'm to amble along carrying an empty pouch?"

"And protect its contents at all costs, don't forget—even with your life."

"There are no contents! I should lose my life for an empty pouch?"

"That's the part we must conceal!" Malachi insisted. "That's the kind of thing that would be hard to explain to an investigative board or to an irate Queen who has the power—and occasionally, the inclination—to shorten your stature by a head. Wear it to bed, sleep with it, eat with it, and let no one have a peek—at the risk of your very neck."

"The royal green and white doesn't go well at all with my russet doublet, you know."

"Wear it under your cloak in back, you fool. Don't let anyone see a messenger of the Queen idling about."

"Well, it will certainly play hob with the drop-line of my cape, but I suppose we must all make personal sacrifices to get the job done."

Malachi nodded. "You are beginning to catch on. Low profile then, and move along steadily but slowly until I get in touch with you. Think in terms of a four-day trip unless I advise you otherwise. Got it?"

"All clear," William assured him.

Malachi shook hands and left.

Chapter 2:
ABOARD THE ELIZABETH BONAVENTURE OFF CADIZ

The Spanish Coast nine days later, April 19, 1587:

"My mind is troubled like a fountain stirred and I myself see not the bottom of it," [3] William confessed on the open deck of the Elizabeth Bonaventure.

"Sea-sickness does that to a lot of people," Malachi observed. "You've been pretty much out of touch since that last storm. What's troubling you most?"

"Methinks I've lost all sense of time and place. How long have I been abed, spewing my guts into a bucket? And what land is that yonder?"

"We are approaching the entrance to the Spanish port of Cadiz just fifty miles north of Gibraltar and we are still with Admiral Drake on the *Bonaventure*. Do you remember I told you we had been ordered to join the Admiral and record his progress?"

"I remember you promised me a Great Adventure when you sent those thugs to Basingstoke to yank me from my rest, toss me on a horse, and race me to Plymouth with the warning I might be left behind if I didn't hurry."

"Yes, I'm sorry that those mariners were such heavy-handed chaps, but Drake gave us precious little time to catch him. He was gone from Plymouth when I got there, as I told you, and John Hawkin's son took over from us the job of delivering the Queen's countermanding order prohibiting Drake from entering this very harbor."

"Did he deliver it?"

Malachi chuckled. "As far as I know, he's still north of us, being tossed about in the Bay of Biscay by that very storm that laid you low but which drove us smack up against Drake's fleet. But at least young Hawkins carries the royal mail pouch you brought to Plymouth and also my heart-felt directions on how best to locate Drake."

"You gave him directions?" exclaimed William.

"Along with a few nudges and winks," Malachi smiled. "Let's just say He understood his duty well."

"Did you tell Drake about the second order?"

"Captain Drake knows Elizabeth well enough to know there might be a countermanding order galloping down the road toward Plymouth, so he lit out, leaving this farewell letter for Walsingham: *'The wind commands me away. Our ships are under sail. God grant we may so live in His fear as the enemy may have cause to say that God doth fight for Her Majesty as well abroad as at home. Haste!'* [4] 'Haste', indeed," Malachi laughed.

"So here we are off the coast of Spain," William said, "searching for enemy ships Phillip has gathered for some unnamed enterprise, which undoubtedly will be launched against England. Is Cadiz a strategic port?"

"It is, indeed," Malachi nodded. "Your head is starting to clear if those things are beginning to register on your brain. According to the information we got from the two Dutch merchant ships we stopped outside Lisbon, Cadiz is full of fat prizes, many of which are without crews or sails and some without guns because they are simply transporting food stuffs in support of the Armada warships, which are gathering in Lisbon harbor."

"Zounds, imagine Drake's being forced to forgo striking a costly blow to the enemy because of a vagrant whim of our very own Queen! Life certainly takes some funny turns at times."

"And sometimes it doesn't," said Malachi. "Have you noticed that the sailors in the rigging above us are presently shortening sail?"

"I see them up there, but they do that kind of stuff all the time. Why is it important this time?"

"Because when they lower two topsails at the same time, it is a signal to the other royal ships in this group to send their captains over to us without delay in order to confer with Admiral Drake."

"To share his disappointment at being called off the chase at the last moment?"

"Now, now," Malachi chided, "It always helps to keep the facts straight. The Queen's second order has not yet reached Drake as far as we know because nobody has heard from Hawkins' son since we left him. He was either swallowed up by the storm, or he never determined the proper direction for the trip to Spain."

"But we know! Isn't it our duty to tell Drake what the new orders are?"

"Are you in a hurry to die?"

"Not particularly, no. I'll do my best to make the adjustment when my time comes, of course, but I'm in no rush. Why?"

"Then forget all about the message we formerly carried and remember that our official duty stopped when we turned the pouch over to the Hawkins boy. It is our business to transport letters, not to read them. If you were to reveal that you knew the contents of the Queen's private correspondence before it was delivered, the prevailing authorities would very likely go to the trouble of treating you to a traitor's death. In short, you would be hanged, drawn, and forced to devour your own well-cooked entrails as your last meal before your body was cut into four major pieces."

"Oh. Never mind then," said William emphatically. "So if Drake is still under the illusion that he has Royal permission to enter the harbor, you think he will take us in with guns blazing?"

"I would be monumentally surprised if he didn't," Malachi grinned. "And surprise is the key word here, because there is no way the Spanish can know we're coming since we let no ship pass us in their direction for the last three days. I think the port of Cadiz is in for a bolt from the blue in just a few hours."

"Isn't it risky, however, to go busting into a strange port without knowing about the forts and the channels and the soundings and stuff?"

"Cadiz is not that strange to us. Many English merchant ships have visited it during our more peaceful days with the Spanish, so the port has been well charted, and we know where the forts and the shoals are located."

"But they will have some warships on guard?"

"Undoubtedly," Malachi nodded, "so there may be some heavy resistance initially and we may suffer some hard knocks for a short time, but our records indicate Cadiz hasn't been invaded by a foreign fleet for hundreds of years, so it would seem highly unlikely if their harbor defense were on any kind of high alert."

"But they will shoot their canon at us." William sounded worried.

"Ah, that's right," Malachi chuckled, "you haven't been shot at much, have you? But you are correct; it should always be a matter of deep concern when hostile forces attempt to puncture the balloon of your mortality. In this case, however, your worry may be minimal. Our batteries will probably outnumber theirs fifty to one, and the Spanish will need some very cool gunners to keep their slow-matches lit in the face of those odds."

"Really? Fifty to one?"

Malachi smiled. "Let's add them up. You might as well start recording notes right now to earn your keep. Cast your eyes out over the fleet scattered along behind us and tell me how many you see."

"I count eighteen big and small as far back as I can see, but they are extended all the way to the horizon so there may be more."

"Close enough," Malachi chuckled. "Drake isn't too particular about sailing in formation, but a final count would include twenty-two which sailed with us from Plymouth in addition to the caravel we picked up as a prize to replace the pinnace we lost in the storm. You'll notice that the three closest to us are all galleons from the Queen's royal navy like ours, regular warships newly rebuilt by John Hawkins. All four are stout, sturdy ships rated at four or five hundred tons apiece and each carrying thirty to thirty-five cannon."

"Thirty five? An uneven number?"

"That's us. The *Elizabeth Bonaventure* under Admiral Drake, with two batteries as bow-chasers, one out the stern, and sixteen to a side. In addition, the *Golden Lion* under Captain Borough, the *Dreadnought* under Captain Fenner, and the *Rainbow* under Captain Bellingham each carry at least thirty cannon, so we're talking one hundred twenty-five guns before we even get to the tall ships."

"Tall ships?"

"Those are the four merchant ships you see sailing just astern of our galleons. They are supplied by the city of London and led by Captain Flick on the *Merchant Royal*. Those ships are ordinarily employed in the Levant trade with the Turks in the Mediterranean, so they are well armed to protect themselves against the Barbary pirates and the Spanish galleys which patrol that sea. They are slightly smaller than our galleons but almost as well armed."

"How well armed?"

"They average twelve guns to the side, so that gives us two hundred cannon without even counting the armament of the additional seven volunteer men-of-war of about two hundred ton, or the four ships Drake outfitted at Plymouth for this venture. I think we can safely round out the tally to at least two hundred and fifty guns aboard the fifteen ships we have fit for fighting, and they can reply to anything the Spaniards throw at us. That kind of firepower should permit you to feel a good deal less threatened."

"I am, I am. My word, two hundred fifty cannon on our side, very reassuring, but that means there'll be a lot of noise, doesn't it?"

"I think you can count on it," Malachi laughed. "A lot of noise and a lot of scouting, dispatching, and general running around by the remaining ten or eleven pinnaces and frigates of less than a hundred tons. But you should find it very comforting that it will be our people who will be creating most of that noise."

"Why did Drake outfit four extra ships when he already had so many warships at his disposal?"

"Drake has never been one to miss out on profit after the main task has been attended to. He intends to smash the Spanish first, of course, but the Queen's decision to have this expedition financed as a private venture—so that her peace negotiations with the Spanish would not be jeopardized—means that this fleet is ostensibly cruising for prizes with the intention of dividing the profits. Since ship owners traditionally get one third of any prize money, the more ships Drake supplies, the greater will be his share of whatever profits are forthcoming."

"No national intentions are afloat here then, just business?"

"Right. And I would be surprised if Burghley has not already explained to Stanton, our Ambassador to France, that Elizabeth has strictly prohibited Drake from raiding Spanish harbors, but, alas, that message may not have reached Drake in time."

"And, as I recall, Stanton is the English diplomat who shares all our official correspondence with Senor Mendoza, who maintains a well-used pipeline to the Escorial."

Malachi nodded. "At least two couriers a week depart on the seven hundred mile trip from Mendoza in Paris to Madrid, so Philip will hear very shortly that whatever happens here at Cadiz is without the consent of the English queen."

"Good Lord!" William exclaimed. "It sometimes appears that all the leaders of the world function within a tissue of lies and deceptions. Do any of them believe all that stuff?"

"Some do and some don't, and some do some of the time, and some don't some of the time. They all twist and turn and spin whatever happens to suit their own ends. It's the political way of the world."

"But how do those of us caught in the middle keep from getting very cynical?"

"Get as cynical as you want," Malachi shrugged. "Nobody cares. It's only your own peace of mind that suffers, along with your digestion and the state of your health. Just remember there are always unforeseen eventualities in every enterprise, even those parented by the devious and unscrupulous among us, so the possibility of a bastard benefit is always lurking even in the womb of the worst of scenarios."

"Does all this mean that we were never intended to get that countermanding order to Drake on time, and that somebody higher than Walsingham ordered the delay?"

Malachi smiled. "You are beginning to catch on. Gather up your tools now and we'll scoot to the ante-room of the captain's cabin because I hear the three captains being piped aboard for the war council with Drake. They'll want us standing by, ready to record."

"Do these naval conferences last long? I've already missed lunch."

"A war council in the English Navy could last most of the day. Ever since Henry VIII instituted the procedure back in the thirties, it is obligatory that the admiral of an English fleet call a council of war to confer with his officers before taking any radical steps. Traditionally, the council involves an examination of charts, an exchange of opinions between the Admiral and his senior officers—whose opinions are to be considered very heavily in the final strategy—a formulation of plans, and finally an issuing of orders which bear the approval of the group. I would guess this one will last as long as Captain Borough, who is the senior officer, has meaningful advice to offer to Admiral Drake."

"And Drake will listen?"

Malachi chuckled. "I've heard it said that Admiral Drake is a willing listener to other men's opinions, but he is mostly a follower of his own. I imagine he'll listen unless he's in a hurry."

"Which one is Borough?"

"That's he there in full uniform leading the other two captains. He's older than the others by far. Really old school Navy and reputed to be a real stickler for naval etiquette. He is presently the Vice-Admiral of the Sea under Lord Admiral Howard for the entire English Royal Navy, and, on this expedition, he is Vice Admiral under Admiral Drake."

"With such impressive credentials, how come he's not in charge of this operation?"

Malachi chuckled. "That's a good question which I'm sure Captain Borough has asked himself a dozen times. Drake is not in the regular Navy, you know, but he has some kind of 'separate but equal' arrangement with them since he presently has Elizabeth's ear. As long as he keeps returning enormous profits for her, his opinion is not likely to be elbowed aside by anybody."

"So if Drake represents the Queen's view, Borough must represent the traditional outlook of the English Navy."

"That's right, but in any vote, Captain Fenner has always been Drake's man and Captain Bellingham will be happy to take the Admiral's orders. When the time comes, Captain Flick will speak for the London merchant investors in any decision making."

"And Captain Borough, you say, is senior officer to Admiral Drake?"

"Not in rank on this trip," Malachi explained, "but certainly in seniority he is. Although his time at sea is limited compared to Drake's, Captain Borough was commanding an English fleet in the Baltic Sea back in the sixties while Drake was still nursing the *Judith* home to England from San Juan de Ulua."

"But Drake and the regular Navy and the merchants should all share a common interest on this particular occasion, shouldn't they? Won't they all be in favor of attacking Cadiz now that we've come this far?""

"I imagine so," Malachi nodded, "but this meeting will determine the 'how' and the 'when' of that attack, and there is room for disagreement even among fair-minded men on those details. Look busy now for a minute or two while they march past us into Drake's cabin. My word, Borough has brought hard-head Baxter along to take his notes."

"Who is Baxter?"

"An inflexible old friend. Quiet now," Malachi commanded.

Borough led the other captains along the deck, all chatting as they approached the bench in the ante-room. The seated writers heard Captain Borough explaining, "I'm not surprised you younger captains prefer the new sleeker lines of the race-built vessels because you've never had the opportunity in battle to command a ship with a castle in bow and stern to support your boarding party by pouring canister fire from your swivel guns onto the deck of the enemy craft. By the very soul of St George," he exclaimed, "that's when you really learn to love those majestic castles!"

"The race-built ships appear to sail better, sir," Captain Fenner said.

"That may be true under certain conditions," Captain Borough granted, "but, in all truth, you should be made aware that your preference for the sleek ships sacrifices military effectiveness for fashionable appearances. You don't seem to recognize that it is the stark irregularity of the high-charged ships which makes them so intimidating in appearance and distinguishes them so readily from the docile outline of the commercial craft. I am not against sensible change, mind you, but change which reduces military effectiveness seems to me–ah, here we are. I'm surprised that Captain Drake has not appeared to receive us, but no matter. We'll just go on in."

Baxter dropped off to seat himself with Malachi and William to await their summons. The two older men greeted each other and Malachi introduced William.

"How long do you think this war council will take, Mr. Baxter?" William asked.

"Not too long," Baxter answered. "If they do it right and no real problems arise in the discussion, we can probably expect an attack shortly after dawn tomorrow."

"But we still have four hours of daylight left," William said. "Why wait so long? We are here now, and we outgun them by a large margin, I understand, so why don't we just go get them?"

Baxter chuckled. "It's obvious you are not regular Navy, so I'm not surprised you appear to have no knowledge of the proper steps that must be taken before we can even think about entering their harbor."

"Steps?"

"War councils such as Captain Drake has just convened must be carried out strictly by the rules originally laid done for their conduct. Even after the charts are examined, strategies devised, consensus reached, and orders issued, the formal notification of our intentions will have to be delivered officially to the Spanish before any attack can take place. If the council succeeds in getting those preparatory details out of the way quickly enough, it might be possible to attack at dusk, but, frankly, tomorrow morning seems more likely to me because I know that Vice-Admiral Borough does not like to risk entering strange harbors in the dark."

"Notify the Spanish of the attack!" William sputtered. "Won't we thereby give away the element of surprise?"

"Of course," Baxter nodded. "But it can't be helped. That's the way naval warfare is conducted by officers of the Royal Navy, so I'm positive Vice-Admiral Borough won't agree to anything less. If Drake does not concur, I know Captain Borough is fully prepared to blow him out of the water with this chart he has prepared." Baxter drew a chart out of his notebook and started to unfold it, but Malachi interrupted.

"Let me just say that if Vice-Admiral Borough succeeds in blowing Francis Drake out of the water in any form whatsoever, he will be the first to succeed in what many others have attempted to their utter dismay."

"Oh, well," Baxter shrugged. "I'm not here to argue. After all, the only point under consideration is that we can't have gentlemen sneaking up on each other. If we did that to the Spanish, what's to stop them from doing the same thing to us?"

"Has Captain Borough ever talked to Captain Drake about what happened at San Juan de Ulua?" Malachi asked mildly.

"Oh, I hardly think Captain Drake will bring up that notable occasion from twenty years ago when he ran out on John Hawkins."

"Ran out on him?" William gasped.

"That's what Hawkins said at the time," Baxter nodded. "He said that the *Judith*, under Captain Drake's command, '*forsook us in our great misery*'. [5] Vice-Admiral Borough has made reference to that incident more than once in my hearing."

"I think most fair-minded men realize Hawkins and Drake were involved in mutual misery on that occasion," Malachi spoke crisply, "since both the *Judith* and the *Minion* had barely escaped from a cowardly Spanish attack which had destroyed three of their five vessels. They both ended up with ships shot to pieces and hundreds of crewmen dead or dying and neither craft with enough food to get the survivors back to England. Hawkins regretted his words later when he realized that Drake was in no shape to help anyone, and the two men have been close friends ever since. I can only hope your captain does not bring up that quotation in front of Admiral Drake because I'm sure that——"

Loud shouting and the rattling of Admiral Drake's door interrupted Malachi. The door was flung open and a red-faced Captain Borough, hat in hand, led the other captains hurriedly from the room before the door slammed shut behind them.

"Incredible!" Borough paused to expostulate while glaring back at the cabin door and refitting his hat to his head. He took several hesitant steps then paused to fume further. "Dangerously rash and completely irresponsible," he muttered, "and unforgivably uncivil. No regard whatsoever for the opinion of his senior officer. No discussion. No exchange. That's simply not the way the Queen's Navy conducts business."

The captain's cabin door flew open and Drake stepped out far enough to shout, "I'll have full sail, Mr. Crosse, if you please, and we'll stand in to Cadiz Harbor immediately. Signal the fleet to follow me in." He half turned to reenter his cabin but then took notice of the stationary group in the ante-room. "I'd advise you gentlemen to return to your ships immediately unless you believe they will function better without you."

"Come, Baxter," Borough growled, "and bring your quill. The queen will hear of this." He stomped off muttering, 'Follow me in,' indeed!"

The command group disappeared over the side and Malachi turned to William. "No matter how the Navy feels about it, Drake would never surrender the surprise element when heading into battle. Now start recording as we round the headland into the harbor. What's the first thing you notice?"

"I notice that Mr. Baxter has dropped the chart from his notebook and has gone off without it. Should I call out?"

"Too late. He'll pick it up later. Let's see what it's about."

They spread the chart and Malachi examined it for a moment. "A sketch of Cadiz Harbor," he decided, "with Borough's name at the bottom. He was well prepared for that war council. Look here now and you'll see that the harbor is roughly of an hour-glass shape with an inner bay and an outer bay. It's about three miles wide and seven deep, and the outer bay is deep enough for all ships, but the inner can only be entered by large ships at high tide. The hour-glass is enclosed by a horse-shoe shaped land mass with the mainland serving as one side and the bottom of the shoe and the other side being a spit of land jutting up from the bottom about three miles off the coast and running parallel to it for five. The opening of the horse-shoe, of course, is the entrance to the harbor which we are entering at this moment, and the city of Cadiz, as you can plainly see, is situated on that high ground off our starboard beam at the end of that long spit of land."

"And Borough has labeled that castle overlooking the entrance as a fort. Yes! See all those cannon sticking out and those men in uniform peering down on us from the gun embrasures. They appear interested but uncertain and some are waving tentatively to us. When do they start shooting? Can't they see we're English? All they have to do is look at our flag."

"If you take a quick glance above, you'll see we've replaced our English colors with the Flemish flag just to give the onlookers the impression that one of their regular trading partners has come to call. Their momentary uncertainty will give Drake time for a quick look around for possible threats within the harbor. That fort and the smaller one inside the harbor by the docks will open on us soon enough when they realize who their visitors are. Write all this down. What else do you see?"

"I see about eighty ships docked and anchored throughout the harbor. Very few appear ready to sail, and I don't see any big warships," said William, scribbling. "Ah, see that very large craft off our starboard beam! She doesn't look Spanish. Her crew is lining the rails watching us and unlike all the others, she seems ready to sail. Is she Italian?"

"Her flag signifies she sails for Genoa," Malachi nodded, "but her lines indicate she's a Ragusan Argosy from the Adriatic. She runs about 700 tons and is very heavily armed for her customary trade in the Levant area. I count twenty gun-ports to the side, but fortunately they are all closed at the moment. Other than her armament, she looks strictly commercial, so I'd be surprised if she starts looking for trouble with four English men-of-war."

"If I leave out the little and middle-sized ones, I'd say there are just about sixty major ships loading and unloading here in the outer harbor. Most of the large ones seem to be tubby cargo ships——"

"The Spanish call them urcas, and they are, indeed, used for cargo."

"I see another dozen or so large ships, which do not appear to be Spanish, lined up along the docks. They all have bare masts. Not a shred of canvas on them. Are they getting their sails replaced?"

"Held hostage is more like it," Malachi explained. "Philip is building onto his Armada by hiring ships from other countries and also by commandeering ships from some of his trading partners. There are German, Danish and Italian ships among that denuded group. They won't have their sails returned until the Armada is ready to sail lest they be tempted to escape Philip's embargo in the meantime."

"Bloody hell, that's kidnapping and intimidation on a grand scale!"

"Exactly right, and on that grand scale, you must shift to a monarchial vocabulary. In the unlikely event a king is ever called to account, he would gladly explain that he is simply annexing and influencing those ships for the good of all concerned. The ability to control vocabulary is often the deciding factor in any discussion—especially in legal matters—and all kings presume such control is their birthright. What else do you see?"

"Quite a number of people standing around gawking at us. I'd have to guess there was a great deal of loading and unloading going on just before we hove into view. Now it appears that all activity has been brought to a standstill until some conclusions are drawn about their newly arrived visitors. So far, there's no real threat—although I expect the cannon from the fort to open on us any minute."

"Since you are seeking out threats, you might take a look forward at those ten galleys lined up along the entrance to the inner harbor and presently dispatching two of their number across to inquire of our business."

"Zounds! They move fast when they get all those oars pulling together. How are they armed? Are they a serious threat to us?"

Malachi shook his head. "They're mostly a threat to other galleys because their big weapon is the bronze ramming head mounted in the prow and delivered with all the force a spirited ramming run can generate. That ram can shear off a whole bank of enemy oars if they manage to sideswipe the opposing craft, or it can cut another galley in half if they catch it amidships at the end of their sprint. In addition to that major weapon, most galleys carry five guns. A swivel-mounted man-killer on each side and a 6-pounder as bow chaser. Galleys have been fighting each other for over two thousand years in the Mediterranean, but since the beginning of this century, the Portuguese sailing ships, their Indiamen, have beaten the Turk and Egyptian galleys in combat while carrying on their Asian trade. They are not much threat to us as long as we are underway and able to turn our broadside to them as we are doing right at this moment."

"Will we fire on them?"

"I think you can bet on it. Our gun ports are now open, and I can hear a good deal of shouting down on the gun deck. You better cover your ears, because I think in a very few seconds——"

Malachi's advice was interrupted by a series of ear-splitting explosions just under the rail from where they stood as a drum roll of cannon fire belched smoke and sound out the port side of the *Elizabeth Bonaventure*. The gun deck weapons fired in a string as they came to bear on the far off galleys. The range was extreme so neither craft was hit directly but each stopped rowing to reconsider the threat presented by the cannon fire of the unidentified invaders.

"They didn't fire back!" William exclaimed.

"They're still about a thousand yards off, so their six-pounders can't reach us from there. Our eighteen-pounders can just reach them but with very little accuracy that far off. It must now be apparent to them that our ship alone can fire more and bigger balls in one broadside than their whole squadron can manage together, and we can fire them further too, so it's time for them to back off and reconsider the matter of attacking us."

Further encouragement for Spanish withdrawal was presented to the galleys when the *Elizabeth Bonaventure* loosed an eight-gun broadside from her port-side forward batteries, quickly followed with another eight-gun barrage from the rearward guns. One of the galleys was hit and part of her wood deck sent flying.

"By damn," Malachi exclaimed. "That's speedy work from our gun crews, loading and firing that fast. The Spaniards are duly impressed, too. Look at them pull back all their galleys."

Suddenly a whizzing noise above their heads was followed by a tearing sound in one of their sails and a sharp boom from close at hand on their starboard side. "My God!" William exclaimed. "What was that?"

"I don't believe it," Malachi said, drawing in his breath. "That idiot Argosy fired on us. He must be crazy to shoot at us while surrounded by four warships with loaded cannon."

Sixteen cannon from the *Dreadnought* answered the single shot from the Argosy, and the *Rainbow* added another broadside bare seconds before the *Bonaventure* contributed her starboard sixteen. Shortly thereafter, the *Golden Lion*, after lowering her Flemish flag and hoisting the Cross of St. George, pulled into position and contributed to the onslaught.

"This is crazy," cried William. "Why in the world would they start a fight against such odds?"

Malachi shook his head. "No doubt some junior officer touched off his battery when he saw us fire on the galleys, and now he has committed his whole ship to defending itself unless they decide to strike their colors and run up a white flag. Their forty guns are enough to make a fight of it if they can get them into operation before we blow them to pieces. Unfortunately for them, however, our one hundred twenty-five guns were manned and ready as we entered the harbor, so the outcome of this conflict is highly predictable, especially at such close quarters."

The merciless hammering of the English guns continued for many minutes, and they watched the pieces of railings and cabins fly to pieces as the sixteen pound balls pounded into them.

"They've already lost their mast, most of their guns are knocked out, and I see holes punched in their water line," William said. "At this range, our guns can't really miss, can they?"

"Every shot is inflicting damage, so it's a wonder to me that they don't surrender while they're still afloat. Their few remaining guns are still firing. By God, that captain is a stubborn man. I wonder if he's protecting his cargo or his pride. She's starting to list now, so if they don't quit firing soon we will simply send her to the bottom."

"I notice the canon from the fort have finally opened up on us, but they sound very far off. Are their guns smaller?"

"Hard to tell in the midst of the noise we're making, but I wouldn't be surprised if they are no more than five- or six-pounders. They wouldn't be as loud as our batteries because they don't burn as much powder for each shot. They don't have much range either, so it's unlikely they can reach us."

"How can such things be likely or unlikly? I mean, don't certain guns shoot certain distances? Can't we figure out their range?"

"You're presuming more science in the gunnery business than presently exists," Malachi explained. "There are few expert gunners in the world because gunpowder is expensive and practice is seldom encouraged. Some gunpowder is simply not dependable due to age, dampness, or a bad mix of the vital ingredients. Consequently, some balls might burp out of the barrel instead of being shot out. In addition, no two cannon are cast exactly alike, and cannon balls themselves are of different sizes.

It is difficult, therefore, to predict results for any given shot or even to firm up any pattern for a second shot. In effect, all hits from cannon fire carry a certain amount of luck with them."

"When I have time, I'll try to figure out whether being struck by chance or by design is the more comforting thought. In the meantime, I notice the Argosy is listing heavily at the bow now, and it looks as if she's finished. I see some men leaving her and swimming to shore."

Malachi shook his head. "And there she goes to the bottom, with her few guns still shooting. That is really strange. I hope we get a chance to find out who her captain is and what she was carrying. In my opinion, that man made some puzzling choices. As soon as we fired on the galleys, of course, he realized we would seize his cargo and probably his ship, so it's not surprising he put up a fight. His ship wasn't Spanish, however, so it should have occurred to him that he would have had a better chance of getting restitution from our Admiralty Court if his ship were still afloat— even if in our possession—rather than scattered across the bottom of Cadiz Bay. Yet he went on shooting. Amazing."

"It's very quiet, now that the shooting has stopped," said William softly. "Does that mean the fighting is over so soon?"

Malachi looked toward the quarter deck where Drake stood, surveying the harbor. At last he turned to his officers and said in a loud, carrying voice, "Well, gentlemen, it looks as if the outer harbor of Cadiz is ours."

Chapter 3:
THE BURNING OF THE CARGO SHIPS IN CADIZ HARBOR

Aboard the Elizabeth Bonaventure that afternoon:

Half an hour later, Admiral Drake addressed eleven of his captains in the wardroom of the *Bonaventure*. "I compliment you, gentlemen, on a job well done. Now we must transfer the cargo from those dockside ships without sails to the Indies ships. Load that Biscayan Indiaman first. She goes about 800 tons, so she can haul a big load, and she's ready to sail; we'll take her with us when we go. Captain Flick, you'll be in charge of the project overall and of the Biscayan particularly."

Captain Flick of the *Merchant Royal* nodded. "Sir, we've seen crew members aboard some of those Indies ships. What if they resist, sir?"

"This is a raid," Drake pointed out. "Subdue any who resist. Some will get hurt, no doubt, but the crews of the Indiamen are mostly Portuguese and they resent the Spanish profiting from their hard work; not likely they'll resist much. On the other hand, they might be stout-hearted fools prepared to defend their ships like those on the Argosy, so stand prepared. But go as easy as possible, gentlemen. Let them help with the loading and even offer to take them with us if they want to stick with their ships. Don't waste time with them, however, since time's short. We've learned that Recalde has a small Spanish squadron at sea, and he might stop by to say hello. Let the Portuguese choose and then get on with moving cargo, with or without 'em."

"Admiral, sir, should we simply take the valuables from the ships, or will we have time to unload the entire cargo?" asked another of the captains.

"Hard to say at this point, Beardsley. Just keep moving in a sensible direction. Start with the valuables and then transfer whatever fresh foodstuffs you come across to our ships. It's always good policy to top-off our food supply at sea especially since we were short when we sailed. When that's done, seek out the most valuable cargo for transfer. Since it's too big a job to rig sails in a hurry on those ships at the dock, we'll burn them before we leave, so get what you can out of them as quickly as you can, but don't burn them until I get a chance to check their chart rooms."

"Admiral, sir, those two batteries from that small dockside fort are still firing on us now and again. Should we get rid of them before we land, sir?"

"Aye," said Drake. "They were installed fifty years ago to guard the harbor entrance and discourage Barbary pirates—principally the infamous Barbarossa—from attacking the City of Cadiz, but they are only six-pound sakers so they don't have the range to protect the whole fifteen square miles of the harbor itself. We could easily stay out of their range, but since we're going to land at their docks soon, Captain Flick will anchor where his ships can knock out those shore batteries and provide cover for the long boats. The longboat crews, of course, should be armed to handle any local resistance."

"Good precaution," observed another of the captains, "but it may not be needed from the number of people I see leaving the docks and streaming toward the big fort in the city."

"How long will we be here, sir? The cargo transfer may take a while."

"I imagine we'll be here until they mount some kind of serious threat to us."

"How about the galleys, Admiral?"

"Oh, we'll hear from them again, I suspect, but as long as we have wind and can turn our broadside to them, they're not going to attack. They've already learned that lesson. While your crews are busy with the unloading duty, gentlemen, I'll do a quick inventory of the cargo ship chart rooms for any maps we don't have copies of. After that we'll use our pinnaces and frigates to round up some of the mariners impressed by the Spanish. If we don't scare them off, many of those foreign sailors will be happy to help us locate the best targets from among the smaller ships that managed to get under sail while we were engaged with the galleys and the argosy."

The assembly chuckled. "There was quite a scramble of those ships going for that inner harbor, sir, where several larger ships are already anchored. Will we go in after them, sir?"

"We will unless they figure out a way to stop us. In the meantime, gentlemen, if all your questions have been answered, let's get cracking. Get the music underway."

"Music?" squeaked William.

"Martial music in a battle situation bolsters the morale of the men," said the Admiral. "It also disconcerts the enemy and diverts his attention away from defense. Serenading the Portuguese and other foreign sailors will reduce the tendency to panic from our ship-burning."

"Oh yes, I see now. Like bagpipes and the fife and drum."

"That's right. Nobody associates plundering and burning with music makers. We may be able to coax some of the foreign mariners to join us if we approach them with pleasant sounds. What is it they say about the effect of music?"

"Do you mean, *'Music oft hath such a charm to make bad good'?" [6]*

"No. The one I was thinking about had to do with savage breasts—something like that. But no matter. Malachi, I'll need you with me on my map hunt. And you, young man, might as well grab an instrument and join Murphy's musicians on the longboat. You'll enjoy the action as you circle my nearby ships."

"I don't have any instrument, sir. I am a recorder."

"Oh, I like that," Drake said. "You don't play one. You are one! I look forward to the kind of music such a close association with your instrument can produce. Get going now. Murphy, here's one more!"

"I don't think you quite understand, sir—"

"Hop to it, lad!" Drake barked. "You eat and sleep on this ship so you follow orders. If your recorder isn't handy, jump on that drum there and set up a tempo."

"I don't play the drum, sir," William protested.

"Nothing to it," said Drake. "Just beat on it loud and steady." The Admiral signaled his crew chief, who was supervising the loading of the long boat. "Murphy, find a drum for this young gentleman and put him in the boat if you will."

William dodged away and had one leg over the ship's rail when Murphy caught him by the neck. "There now, lad. No need to be shy. Ya just beat 'til you get the rhythm. Ta rum, ta rum, ta rum pum pum, over and over. On board now." He gave William a friendly shove.

Drum slung over his shoulder, William found himself seated next to a hard-bitten old sailor, who looked at his drum with interest. "That there's a 'andsome one," he said. "Me, I've always hankered t' drum, but the cap'n he keeps a-sticking me wi' these here spoons. Shoot, any sailor can rattle spoons, but it takes natur'l skill t' get music out o' a drum. Practice long hours, did ye?"

"Not in the least. I was a natural at it from the beginning. But it's not as hard as it looks as long as you get good instruction to begin with. That's the key. I'll never forget—" he pointed to his head—*"whiles memory holds a seat in this distracted globe [7]* the simple direction I first received. It paved the way to all my later achievements."

"By gorb, if that were true for you, it moight be true for me. I've always had a bit o' rhythm m'self. The spoons were'nt no challenge atall. You don't s'pose—"

"Hi ho, a trade! You're on. This tuning up period is a good time to try it out." They quickly traded instruments, and William told him. "Just start out with ta rum, ta rum, ta rum pum, pum and pretty soon you'll swing into something a little more catchy."

Murphy ordered the boat lowered and seated himself beside the tiller-man. "Let me check before we cast off. Let me hear a trumpet," and a musical riff greeted him. "A fife," and a lilting air filled the evening sky. He quickly checked the flutes, tabors, coronet, bones, bells, drum, spoons, tongs and took up the mandolin for himself.

"You men at the oars slowly circle the harbor. Try not to get in the way of my musicians. You music makers, warm up for 'God Save the Queen'. The Admiral doesn't want the Dons to think we're not enjoying ourselves out here, so get ready to show them that we're having a grand old time."

Until darkness descended, they drifted through the harbor rowing and playing as their long boat moved through one bank of smoke after another. William no longer winced at the occasional musket fire or far-off cannon shot. He was gratified to find his dexterity in manipulating his dinner spoon stood him in good stead in music making, and he permitted his contribution to grow louder and louder as he gained more confidence. He was slightly dismayed, however, at the lack of progress his drummer friend was making beside him. He turned to the red-eyed man who was coughing slightly behind his hand. "Try an occasional 'ump pa pa'," he suggested.

"It's hard to get me mind on me music since they cut them ships loose and set 'em afire," the old sailor muttered. "By nab, we're surrounded by so many burning ships, they've blotted out th' darkness alt'gether." He shook his head. "It's ver' strange. Up in me head, I know we're hurtin' the Dons by burning the ships they was fixin' to sail against us, but by gum, somewhere deep down I hates to see good vessels turned into ashes 'thout lifting a hand to help 'em."

"I'm sure you'll feel better when you manage to insert a little more rhythm into your playing."

"I've built ships. I know it takes a year o' hard work to build one, and it somehow ain't right all that work should disappear in an hour. I've sailed ships, and, by God, I've lived on ships fer longer than I've lived on land, and I'll tell you the truth: it don't go down well with me atall to have 'em destroyed so deliberate right afore me eyes." He stood up, removed his drum, and carefully placed it on the seat.

"You! Drummer!" Murphy shouted. "What do you think you're doing?"

The old sailor stepped up on the seat, placed one foot on the gunnels, and replied calmly, "I'm going to put out the fire." Then he dove cleanly into the water and struck off for the dock with a surprisingly sprightly stroke.

"Oh, for God's sake," Murphy muttered.

"The smoke musta got to 'im," offered the coronet player.

"Keep playing, the rest of you lot," Murphy ordered. "Come about," he directed the man at the tiller, "and we'll pick him up before he drowns." But the old sailor was swallowed by a pool of smoke before they could turn the boat. "Never mind," Murphy decided. "Our people will get him at the dock if he gets that far. Get back to your serenading", he ordered, but the men were slow to respond, and it quickly became clear that the old sailor had taken more than himself out of the boat.

"When do we eat?" one voice demanded and Murphy frowned.

"Keep rowing and I'll pull us over alongside that Biscayan they've finished loading, and we'll see what we can round up."

They pulled alongside and were greeted by members of the skeleton crew who invited them to eat their fill of the newly acquired foodstuffs. "They got no ale," the host group explained, "but there's plenty of good wine."

"I am prepared to make do with such an inconvenience," William smiled as he made ready to fill his belly with whatever was available.

"You there! Malachi's man!" came a shout from the forecastle.

"Mr. Baxter," William responded in surprise. "Strange seeing you here."

"Where is Malachi?" Baxter asked as he approached across the deck. "Vice-Admiral Borough would like his Cadiz chart returned and he agrees to ask no questions about its theft."

"Theft?"

"What else would you call it when you are in possession of somebody else's property without their permission?"

"There's a very simple explanation," said William with dignity.

"Never mind that now. Where is the chart?"

"I last saw it back aboard the *Elizabeth Bonaventure*."

"Let's fetch it then," Baxter insisted as he took William by the arm and walked him to the rail.

"Just a minute," William objected. "I came aboard to get something to eat and I'm not leaving until—"

"We are under orders, don't forget, and the Vice Admiral of this fleet is not a patient man by any means." Baxter grabbed a loaf of bread from a hatch cover piled high with foodstuffs and shoved it under William's arm. "That will have to do for the moment. Get aboard," he ordered and indicated the craft at the bottom of the ladder.

"That's just a skiff."

Baxter nodded. "Exactly what we need to move about quickly without having to wait for a crew to assemble and sails to be tended. Drake has anchored our fleet of warships just the other side of these merchant ships. Let's pull over there quickly and get that chart before Vice-Admiral Borough has a fit."

"Where is our oarsman?" William asked as he seated himself in the small craft and munched on his loaf of bread.

"He's up there on deck somewhere replenishing the fires in his belly. He's a big, beefy chap, who pulled us over here so fast we created waves with our small craft." Baxter snickered. "I can only hope you'll do half as well."

"Me? I must tell you, I am not an oarsman, and I have no intention whatever—"

"Let's get something straight right from the beginning. I am the authorized representative of the Vice-Admiral of the entire English Navy, and I have been commissioned by him to complete a vital mission. Therefore, every one of the 2,200 souls who make up this fleet—with the possible exception of Captain Drake—must respond to any request I make without delay or argument. In practical terms, I am the senior officer of this craft, so pick up those oars and stroke us over to the *Elizabeth Bonaventure* without delay."

"I must tell you—"

"No, you must not. This is a combat military situation and I am your commanding officer. Need I remind you what happens to people who refuse to obey orders in the wartime military?"

"Well," William considered, "perhaps a little exercise will do me no harm." He picked up the oars and bent his back until he had them alongside the *Elizabeth Bonaventure*, where Baxter called up for Malachi.

"He's not here," a deckhand answered. "He's over among the merchant ships with the Admiral. In the Admiral's launch."

"You heard him," Baxter said to William. "Pull us around to the merchant ships."

"But the tide is coming in. I'll be rowing against that current."

"Can't be helped. The tide comes in every day. Nothing unusual. Get busy now."

William resumed his exertions. "This is twice as hard now that I'm pulling against the current."

"That should teach you not to complain earlier when you had it so easy," Baxter pointed out. "Why are you stopping! Keep rowing, man! You cancel your own effort against that current every time you pause."

"I hear distant cannon fire behind my back. I need to turn to see where it is."

"Keep rowing and I'll tell you where it is. One of our early prisoners informed us the commander of the Spanish galleys is Don Pedro de Acuna, who is now apparently sending his galleys forward against us in an attack while shooting off their bow chasers."

"Is he coming our way? Didn't he already learn his lesson?"

"It's difficult to make out his squadron out there in the dark but the sound of his guns indicates he is still very far off, out of range for both his guns and ours. I think he is just a naval officer earning his stripes by running a delaying action against us to permit more of the Spanish ships time to seek safety in that inner harbor. I'll be very surprised if he persists in the attack after——"

"thunder-crack of sound over their heads caused them to recoil to the bottom of the skiff only to be enveloped instantly in a bank of heavy smoke propelled by the broadside concussion which surged out the side of the *Bonaventure,* and shoved their skiff out across the fan-shaped pattern of chopped up water caused by the blast.

William coughed on the smoke and shook his head in confusion and disbelief. When the gun-smoke cleared, he struggled to his feet and shook his fist at the gundeck of the warship. "Are you crazy?" he shouted. "Are you insane? Don't you see us out here? Those cannon balls whizzed right over our heads! You almost killed us!"

There was no response.

"Well," said Baxter, in a quivering voice, "all my life I've heard reference to 'being under fire' in combat, but I never thought I'd get to experience that expression so literally. We were directly under their fire," he giggled weakly. "Please move our craft as swiftly as you can from alongside the *Bonaventure.* I don't know that my heart can stand another such salutation."

"I thought you said the galleys were out of range?"

"They are. That was just an invitation for them to stay there."

They finally reached the side of the *Merchant Royal,* and Baxter again inquired for Malachi.

"He ain't here," First Mate Haines leaned over the side to inform them. "He was, but he went off with Admiral Drake—I think to check more chart rooms."

Baxter called up, "By the way, have you seen Vice-Admiral Borough?"

"He was here earlier looking for Admiral Drake to urge him to get the fleet out of Cadiz Harbor before our wind dies. He thinks our Admiral is inviting disaster if he stays until our fleet is embayed deep in enemy territory. When he couldn't find him, he seemed quite upset and went off again to search some more. From up here, it seemed to me he was mumbling to himself when he left."

"I wouldn't be surprised," Baxter growled. "Our Admiral hides from his own officers as well as he hides from the Spanish, and thereby keeps himself well clear of good advice."

"Mister Haines, sir," William called up. "It's getting late and cold and maybe even a little crabby down here. Could the *Merchant Royal* feed and bed two weary travelers for the night?"

"We'd be proud to. Come aboard."

William glanced at Baxter, who only shrugged and reached for the ladder.

CHAPTER 4:
THE INNER HARBOR OF CADIZ

The next afternoon, April 20:

"Wake up, William," Malachi exclaimed, nudging him gently. "I'm lucky to have found you. I've never seen a man who could sleep through as much excitement as you do. I suspect you were the only one in our whole fleet who slept through all the ship burning last night. Hear how quiet it is? A good time to get back to our own ship."

"My lungs are full of the smoke from those fires, sir. Seems to me I was out all night in it. How did you find me?"

"I ran into Baxter back on the *Bonaventure* this morning and he told me where you were. I returned his Cadiz chart to him, by the way, so you're off the hook there. I hope you made a copy."

"Yes, between playing the spoons for hours on end, rowing a skiff from one end of this harbor to the other and back again, and nearly being blown out of the water by our own cannon fire discharged directly in my ear, I had very little to do except—"

"Never mind. I can get a copy if we need it. Swallow this gruel I've brought you, and let's be on our way before you entirely miss the remarkable exploits of this day. Captain Bellingham saved a yawl as a memento from one of the prize ships we burned, and I borrowed it to fetch you, so let's go. Never fear," Malachi laughed, seeing William's extended blistered hand. "I borrowed the oarsmen too."

They descended the ladder and seated themselves in the yawl behind four oarsmen before William asked. "What have I already missed?"

"Vice-admiral Borough finally caught up with Drake on the *Bonaventure* this morning and attempted to dissuade him from carrying our raid into the inner harbor for fear our ships would be embayed if the wind should die."

"I imagine 'attempted' is the pivotal word in that sentence."

"Right. Drake listened but he went on preparing a small fleet of pinnaces and frigates and then led them with his launch right into the Inner Harbor while Borough was still talking. We had learned from our Portuguese informants last night that the Marquis of Santa Cruz himself—essentially the father of the Spanish navy—had anchored in that inner harbor his own magnificent 1200-ton galleon which was being prepared as the flagship for the Armada that Santa Cruz hopes to lead soon against England."

"Just the kind of bait Drake can't resist!"

"Right. His fleet of frigates and pinnaces attacked and burned it just after dawn this morning. Then they burned ten more ships loaded with supplies—tar, biscuit, wheat, and seasoned timbers for water casks along with dozens of brand new cannon—all scheduled for delivery to the Armada. Unfortunately, the steady breeze which had been our friend so far, decided to grow fitful and almost quit completely about an hour ago, so Drake brought us all back to the Outer Harbor to protect our galleons with their flapping sails."

"Why did he burn everything? Didn't he realize how happy his countrymen would be to greet such prizes sailing up the Thames?"

"True enough, but he had no choice since the tide had already gone out and several of those deep-draft ships could only leave the inner harbor during the height of the next spring tide."

"What spring tide?"

"The very high tide which occurs twice a month when the sun and moon are in conjunction and combine to produce their greatest drawing power on our oceans. We don't have such a tide scheduled for another two weeks, so we had to burn those ships or else encounter them next when the Armada visits us."

"So Borough was right about the wind, after all?"

"Oh, well, no wind lasts forever, so he had to be right eventually, but he has picked an unfortunate time to be right. Our fleet is becalmed in enemy territory, and it looks as if the Dons are organizing some attacks on us, so it would be handy if we got out of here soon."

"Attacks?"

"If you'll look over to the west a bit, you'll see the tail end of several thousand Spanish soldiers who have just marched up that spit of land into the city of Cadiz to defend it against any possible attack from us. Early this morning we saw three hundred cavalrymen ride into the city. That kind of swift military response means that our time here is limited, so whatever plans Drake may have had for the sacking of Cadiz are out the window."

"But a few of our small craft are still sailing around burning ships, so it doesn't look as if the Spanish reinforcements are scaring them off."

"One of the prisoners we picked up this morning told us that the duke of Medina Sidonia is in charge of those 300 cavalry and 3000 foot and has issued statements condemning our attack and promising the people that revenge will be taken against us. When Sidonia took over the defense of Cadiz, he said he wished 'the enemy would come out of their nests and prove if they were better at fighting than at creeping about in the dark attacking crewless ships which could not resist with more than their wooden hulls.' [8] He has heartened the populace so they are ready to seek revenge on us for the night of terror we inflicted on them last night."

"What can they do?"

"The guns at the big fort have been firing steadily since he got here, but we're still out of range, so there is little effect. At the middle of the hourglass, however, the Dons have managed to drag up a huge old bronze culverin, eighteen feet long, which can throw an 18-pound ball two miles without much accuracy. They're not firing often, but they did manage to land one random ball this morning on the *Golden Lion* from a mile away, and it cut the leg off Borough's master gunner. Because the wind was slight, Borough's crew laid an anchor forward by boat and warped the *Lion* out of range in the direction of St Mary's Port. That's in the northeast corner of the outer Bay, about four miles across from Cadiz.

"I remember seeing it on the map."

"Because the *Lion* was isolated, six galleys attacked it. But enough wind came up to swing her sideways, and she beat them off. Then she took up a position between them and St Mary's Port, shutting them out of their protective lair. Drake saw Borough's trouble and sent the *Rainbow* here with three merchantmen to help him as soon as the wind stirred again. Let's clamber aboard the *Rainbow* now and check in with Captain Bellingham, then wait with the rest of our fleet for enough wind to say good-by to Cadiz.

I suppose you're still hungry."

"Egad, yes. I'm praying for an early dinner."

CHAPTER 5:
THE GENTLE TOUCH OF A POET

On the Rainbow that afternoon:

"Malachi," Captain Bellingham greeted them, "you're just in time to help us solve a little problem—if you'll lend us your man for awhile." He smiled at William and started to greet him too, but a fierce feminine scream from his cabin interrupted his greeting.

William's eyebrows shot up. "What's going on in there?"

"That's the problem," Bellingham sighed. "We have a highly hysterical detainee and need somebody to calm her down so we can search her. She was one of only two people who were inadvertently left alone in a room for a few minutes during which time a very valuable, bejeweled broach disappeared from our booty box."

"No guard on the box?" Malachi asked, grinning.

"He was running errands. Everything is so disorganized with all this excitement, you know, but our Admiral had his eye on that broach, so we wouldn't want it missing if he asks to see it again."

"Tell whoever is in charge that I will be glad to guard the box the next time your regular guard is called upon to—"

"Never mind that now. I remember Malachi mentioned once that you had a way with women that completely puzzled him, and I'm wondering if you can possibly calm her down. I must warn you she's pretty crazy. She will not allow any man to touch her, and we have no other woman aboard."

"Is she English?"

"No. I'd say neither English nor Spanish. She refuses to communicate with us at all on personal matters."

"Sounds like a bucket of cold water over her head might do some good," William suggested.

"That's out," Bellingham growled. "We've already questioned the man who was also in the room, but he didn't hold up well to the interview and is presently being carried ashore to some out-of-the-way spot. The command feels we already have enough diplomatic complications from this raid without inviting more, and since the woman acts as if she is important, I think it best we take it easy on her."

"Is she pretty?" William asked.

"Aye, like a black widow spider without the red dots as far as we can tell."

"So you want me to see if she has the dots?"

"The dots are up to you. See if she has the broach. It's incredibly valuable. Can you do it?"

"Search an hysterical woman from top to bottom, you mean?" William scratched his head. "I can try."

"I must warn you she screams at every man who approaches her."

"I'll need some help. Women are impressed by calm self-assurance in a man, and nothing conveys that impression better than a wardrobe which reflects understated taste. Give me five minutes' access to your officer's shore-side closet and then a period of uninterrupted time with her so I may calm her down."

"The wardrobe is behind you," Bellingham directed. "Dig in."

They watched William make his selection and had only one comment.

"Nobody wears a big heavy cape like that on board," Malachi observed. "It would get caught on everything."

William whirled about and the cape swirled out. "Women like a little flash. It catches their eye."

"Good luck," Captain Bellingham said as he opened his cabin door only to be greeted by a shriek of fury.

"If one of you fish-smelling escombros ingles have come back to lay a hand on me, I'll rip los ojos right out of sus cabeza! Madre de Dios! I will not submit to your assumption of guilty-until-proven-innocent! Nunca!"

William entered the cabin and bowed extravagantly, swirling his cape about him. "A million pardons, Senorita. Those clumsy oaf seamen have insulted you, but methinks 'twas your beauty that stunned them out of their manners. My word, darling girl, your hair is the shiniest of ebony. A flock of ravens must have crowned you with a bouquet from their own wings."

The woman took a good look at him. "Who are you?" she asked suspiciously but quietly, putting a hand to her hair.

Bellingham's eyes blinked in surprise, and Malachi shrugged as if to say, "I told you so." They closed the cabin door.

"I am just a poor poet, fair lady, a mere writer of words, come to offer you a humble apology from the captain of this ship, from his officers, and from his men. They have just emerged, as you know, from the violence of war and are still enmeshed in the simple expedient of might over right. 'Twas inexcusable they should dare to touch you. Please sit, senorita, and tell me how I can serve you."

"Well, Englishman," said the young woman," it appears your Admiral Drake is adding a new chapter to his list of transgressions against the Spanish Empire. I can only imagine King Philip will have a mighty fit when he hears of this raid."

"My lady, I beg you to understand," William replied. "Your king has been intimidating our little island for two years now with rumors of his great armada coming to overwhelm us. I believe our Navy is trying its utmost to reduce the number of ships he plans to bring against us."

"He's not my king," she scoffed. "It delights me to see Spanish ships burning, but I'm sorry that Portuguese ships are part of the blaze."

"So are we, senorita!" agreed William, very pleased. "Portugal has been much mistreated by Philip. Are you, by chance, Portuguese?"

She held out her hand. "Inez O'Toole. Portuguese mother, Irish father. Neutral dealer in leather goods, caught up in the toils of a foreign war. The shipment of leather vests and pants and whips and belts I was carrying to Spain from Ireland is now going up in flames aboard my small ship in the harbor. It breaks my mercantile heart to see it, although I wouldn't mind spending a short time by that blaze since I find it so damp and chilly here in this cabin."

"Oh, I'm sorry. Please permit me." William whipped off his cape and draped it over her shoulders. "My name is William, and I'm very sorry to have to acknowledge that warfare often brings about incidental casualties that we seldom hear about. Was that shipment your livelihood?"

"The leather goods can be marked off as a bad harvest year, but I lost my ship as well, and that will put me out of business until I get another. It was just a small 20-ton craft, but it did get me here and back. I don't suppose the Spanish will be in any mood to replace it since I didn't get the delivery papers signed at the fort yesterday before your people arrived on the scene with your monstrous display of cannon fire."

"Oddly enough," William smiled, "I was also quite impressed by yesterday's exhibition because I am not a regular Navy person myself, you see, and that was my first experience at such a demonstration of deadly force. I didn't realize there were that many cannon in the whole world or that we had people who could make them function so effectively or that they would produce so much smoke and noise. My ears are still ringing."

"Yes, I notice the harbor guard galleys are being quite cautious with your warships since that initial display. I must tell you the Spanish officers at the fort yesterday were very impressed by the power and range of your cannon. They were afflicted with a bit of shock and awe at how quickly your *Bonaventure* delivered a second broadside against Acuna's galleys. There was even concern expressed as to whether Spanish galleys could stand up to English warships at all, and that's a real worry for them since half the Spanish navy consists of galleys."

"You were at the fort yesterday morning and then a detainee here on one of our flagships this afternoon? That seems a little puzzling in light of your being a simple merchant."

Inez shrugged. "Easy enough to explain. Complete chaos in Cadiz since your people started shooting. Everybody rushing about to protect their families and goods. Your people picked me up on the dock when I tried to retrieve the manifest from my ship, the *Raven*. Many Cadiz citizens were panic-stricken and rushed up the path to the fort in such a mob that the commander closed the gates in order, he claimed, to better concentrate on fighting you English. Unfortunately, the crush against the closed gate was so great that two dozen women and children were pushed off the path and into the sea where they drowned."

"Good Lord! That's terrible."

"But not everybody panicked. Many presumed the town itself would be attacked, so the Spanish organized bands of men in the squares with pikes and shields and barrels of tar to light the night. You can well imagine everybody's relief this morning when the Duke of Medina Sidonia rode in at the head of three hundred cavalry."

"Yes, we saw thousands of additional soldiers march into the city, so I suspect Cadiz is safe from assault if that's what Drake had in mind. What do you intend doing now? Will you go back to Ireland?"

"I suppose I will if I ever get clear of this ridiculous suspicion of being a jewel thief. I wish now I had thought to grab something out of their precious booty box to replace my ship, but the truth of the matter is I was so dazed by the rapidly unfolding events that I could concentrate on nothing but breathing normally so I would not faint. I hate it when women faint in the middle of any kind of excitement, don't you?"

"Oh, I do, I do—unless it's the right kind of excitement," he smiled and kept his eyes fixed on hers.

She looked him up and down and smiled back. "I see you are prepared to make your search. I don't suppose my word would settle the matter for you?"

"It would for me. In my present mood, I am prepared to believe anything you say, but, afterward, I must answer to my superiors who will make me swear that I left no stone unturned in this examination, and you certainly would not entice me into swearing falsely, would you?"

"Never," she testified, "and I suppose this will be no more embarrassing than an examination by a qualified doctor. I'll simply undress beneath the cape and you can examine my clothing first."

"Quite right. No occasion for embarrassment, only for deep appreciation for such proximity to your beauty, and even for the beauty of your underclothing whose intimacy to your person I can't help but envy," he said as he examined the clothing she passed to him from beneath the cloak. "I must say, you do dress well underneath the corduroy and leather, but I can find no jeweled broach amidst such finery and I now believe whatever precious goods these flimsy things might have encased have since withdrawn and must be sought out elsewhere."

"Oh, you are a terrible flirt, English Will," she said as she tousled his hair with a soft hand, "but I do enjoy how you smooth over such an awkward moment. Are you sure your hands are warm?"

"They have been experiencing spontaneous combustion since this assignment was mentioned," he assured her.

"Let me see. Oh, you do know how to do it, don't you? But be careful. I'm ticklish. I wonder if we might use the captain's bed to facilitate this process. After all, when you're turning over stones, you need a little room to spread out."

"Exactly," William grinned and they tumbled into the bed.

❖ ❖ ❖

Almost an hour later, there came a knock at the Captain's door and a voice inquired from outside. "How about it? Does she have the broach or not?"

"I have found her to be no thief," William replied, "but she is somewhat upset and driven to hunger by the ordeal of the examination. Could we have something to eat while she has a brief period to calm down?" He smiled at Inez, who joined him with a knowing grin.

"Pack her up quickly and we'll give her something to eat as we ship her to shore. I need my cabin!" Captain Bellingham bellowed and then turned to Malachi. "You're certain your man is honest? There's no chance she's made a confederate of him by offering to share the loot?"

"Share the jewels with him? No." Malachi shook his head. "I can personally assure you his mind does not run in that direction until after he has resolved his other overriding concerns. You'll have to look elsewhere for your broach. How trustworthy is that guard who left the booty box unguarded?"

"Aye, I'll look into that when things calm down, but in the meantime, I'll get her escorted ashore—Ah, here they are," he said as the pair emerged from the cabin with Inez fully dressed and once again covered with the cape. "My men will see you ashore, young lady, and my steward will have a covered dish for you. In addition, I've prepared a short safe-conduct note for you so you won't be bothered again. I'm sorry to have inconvenienced you, but we must all be careful in important matters."

"Perfectly understandable," Inez murmured in a mild voice. "Even somewhat romantic to be taken for a jewel thief now that it's over—although, I admit I was somewhat upset by such a ridiculous accusation at the beginning. But in the end it was certainly an adventure I'll never forget." She smiled at William.

"Off you go then," Bellingham said as he handed her down the ladder to the ship's boat, "and good luck to you. Hold on now," he added. "I believe that's my cape you still have on your shoulders."

"Captain," interposed William softly. "Perhaps you would allow Miss O'Toole to wear the cape to shore and let your men bring it back."

"Oh, no-no," protested Miss O'Toole, smiling coyly at William. She slipped the cape from her shoulders, brushed it off, and handed it up to him. "It was very handy because your cabin is a little damp, Captain. But I'm much warmer now, thank you."

The boat pulled away and William watched her smile fade into the distance.

"You did a remarkable job, young man," Bellingham complimented William. "You changed a veritable witch into a reasonable human being, even if our big question was left unanswered. Hold on now. My kerchief is missing from the inside pocket of my cloak. Did you see it?"

"Inside pocket, you say?" William gulped and then regained his composure. "That is unfortunate. It must have dropped out somewhere along the line. I'm sure you'll find it in your cabin." He turned to lean over the rail and cock an ear. "What's all that shouting about?"

"If you look around a little you'll see that the Dons are attempting to send fire-ships against our anchored galleons now that the wind has died. Without coming within range of our cannon, the galleys are towing the fire-ships to a position where the tidal surge will carry them to our ships, but our frigates are having little trouble shunting them off to burn harmlessly along the shore."

"But the shouting and laughing—what's that all about?"

"Admiral Drake has joked that tonight the Spanish are doing our work for us by burning their own ships, and the English crews are shouting the joke gleefully from ship to ship throughout our becalmed fleet."

"Yes, we are becalmed, aren't we? I thought this was the time when we were most susceptible to attack from the galleys. Why are they not attacking us from our blind side?"

Captain Bellingham chuckled. "We had one last defensive ace up our sleeve to protect us against that threat because even anchored and becalmed, a galleon has no blind side as long as she has an alert crew. The galleys don't dare get any closer than 700 yards because our crews have learned to lay out anchors at opposite right angles from our bow and stern so we can swing our broadside to the enemy by quickly letting out or hauling in on the anchor cables."

"Ingenious," murmured William. "That's really comforting. I can now relax and hunt up something to eat and even locate some place to sleep until the wind comes up. I shall sleep well because you have convinced me we have nothing to fear either from those galleys or the fire-ships or the guns from the fort. Please wake me when the wind returns, so I can say good-by to Cadiz."

The wind came up at 2 am, and the English left the harbor only to be followed outside by Acuna's squadron of galleys. Drake brought his fleet about in preparation for further gunfire, but Acuna sent over a complimentary message along with some fruits and wine in an exchange of courtesy worthy of two knights of old.

CHAPTER 6:
AT CAPE ST. VINCENT: CAPTAIN
BOROUGHS GOES TOO FAR

Captain Bellingham's cabin on the Rainbow May 19, 1587:

"I am quite aware, Mr. Baxter, that you are not Captain Borough," Captain Bellingham said patiently. "There's really no need to keep reminding me. You've been asked here to give the informal side of Captain Borough's views and opinions during this past month's unfortunate disagreement. We will shortly dispatch a convoy of our captured ships back to England with our sick and disabled aboard, and it's important that they carry details to the Privy Council about the arrest and confinement of the Vice-Admiral of the fleet during this past month. After all, it is not every day that such an officer is stripped of his command and confined to his cabin for the duration of the expedition, and the Council will want to know how and why it happened."

"Are you saying," Baxter asked, "that the *Golden Lion* will remain on station here with Vice-admiral Borough confined aboard rather than be permitted to accompany the prize ships in the return trip to England where he may explain his side of the story to the Privy Council?"

"No mention of special circumstance for the *Lion* was made in Drake's report to the Council, was it, Malachi?"

"Not a word," Malachi said. "Admiral Drake usually prefers to thrash out personnel matters when the expedition has returned to England, so it would be a surprise if he dispatched one of our most powerful ships to home waters while there might still be combat ahead."

Bellingham nodded. "It's certainly no secret that the Admiral intends to maintain our fleet for an extended period here at Cape St. Vincent, where we are the cork in the bottle of Spanish supplies which their Mediterranean ports are prepared to send around into Lisbon Harbor. The Armada preparation is standing still while we have its supply train bottled up."

"How much longer can we stay around this Cape?" William asked.

Malachi chuckled. "I think Drake answered that best in the letter to Walsingham I copied for him this morning. He said that in addition to the month we've already spent here, we'll stay *'As long as it shall please God to give us provisions to eat and drink and that our ships and wind and weather will permit us, you shall surely hear of us near this Cape of St. Vincent where we do and will expect daily what her Majesty and your honours will further command. There must be a beginning of any good matter but the continuing to the end, until it be thoroughly finished, yields the true glory......God make us all thankful again and again, that we have, although it be little, made a beginning on the coast of Spain'."* [9]

"'Continuing to the end' makes it sound like he plans to stay quite a while longer," William said.

Malachi nodded. "In addition, he asked that supplies and reinforcements be sent here as soon as possible."

Baxter coughed. "Perhaps I shouldn't say so, but Drake's statement that we have only made a little beginning on the coast of Spain doesn't sound like him at all. He usually doesn't deal in understatement when measuring his own achievements. I recently heard him boast that we had not only struck a heavy blow against the Armada preparations by capturing or destroying thirty-seven of the major Spanish ships in Cadiz Bay, but we had also succeeded in humiliating the King of Spain by singeing his beard on his native soil."

"Excuse me, Mr. Baxter," Malachi said, "but you seem to be coloring Drake's remarks with a quill you borrowed from Captain Borough. The truth of the matter is that we did destroy thirty-one Armada ships at Cadiz, and we are in the process of sending another six prizes home heavily laden with supplies the Armada will never get, so the number thirty-seven doesn't seem to me a boast as much as a bookkeeping entry. The singeing of Philip's beard, which you characterize as a boast, is simply a chilling, understated reference to a widely circulated quotation after the Muslim fleet was destroyed at the battle of Lepanto back in 1571."

"Really," said Mr. Baxter. "Do tell."

"The Sultan minimized the loss of his fleet by saying, "When the *'Venetians sunk my fleet they only singed my beard. It will grow again. But when I captured Cyprus I cut off one of their arms'*." [10] Rather than boasting about singeing Philip's beard, Drake is obviously warning England not to rest easy in light of his success at Cadiz because the King of Spain's fleet will grow again. He told Walsingham, *'I assure your honour the like preparation was never heard of nor known as the King of Spain hath and daily maketh to invade England….which if they be not impeached before they join will be very perilous…..This service, which by God's sufferance we have done will breed some alterations…[but] all possible preparations for defense are very expedient…..I dare not almost write of the great forces we hear the King of Spain hath. Prepare in England strongly and most by sea'.*" [11]

"He still sounds like a boaster to me," Baxter persisted. "But tell me, was any mention made of Vice-Admiral Borough in the report?"

"He wasn't mentioned," Malachi said, "so the *Golden Lion* will remain on station with the rest of the fleet when we send the prize ships home tomorrow. How are the *Lion's* crew handling the imprisonment of their captain, Mr. Baxter?"

"To be perfectly honest, I must tell you that among the *Lion's* officers there is growing discontent with the confinement of Vice-admiral Borough, and a mounting apprehension that Drake may decide to deal with him as he did with poor Doughty on the Around-the-World trip. All of them think that Drake is guilty of over-reaching in his treatment of an experienced senior officer who is simply trying to help out by sharing his vast knowledge with our present commander."

"That's what we must attempt to explain to the Council before this rift between our expedition's commanders becomes even more serious," Captain Bellingham said. "If our small group can prepare a somewhat non-partisan explanation of the conflict for the Council, we may head off serious consequences before they arise. It seems to me that if we explain this quarrel openly and emphasize the older officer verses the newer officer and the regular Navy opposed to the irregular Navy—so to speak—we could go a long way in defusing this situation in the minds of the Council members."

"Just so it's understood from the beginning that only Vice-admiral Borough can speak for Vice-admiral Borough," Baxter insisted.

"You have established that point not only clearly, Mr. Baxter, but often," Bellingham smiled. "As a matter of fact, I apply the same condition to myself. Only Admiral Drake may speak for Admiral Drake, but since those two principals have reached the point of refusing to speak to each other, it is left to those of us who have sailed with them for many years to attempt to shed light on the present disagreement for the report to the Privy Council. It certainly would be best if the two commanders could resolve their differences in person, but as we all know, their strong convictions do not permit them to ebb and flow in unison."

"Which is not an ideal atmosphere in which to conduct the Queen's business or to guide her fleet," Malachi added.

"Exactly," said Bellingham. "Apart from the safety and honor of England, the lives of over two thousand of our mariners are still at stake here until we fetch them safely home. I'd like you to keep that point well in mind when you report to the Council, Malachi, although frankly, I suspect they'll be more impressed by the prizes we've taken and the blow we've dealt to the Armada's preparation. I doubt if Santa Cruz can sail against England anytime this year after the success we enjoyed at Cadiz last month."

"And since then I bet we've sunk or burned at least one hundred of their fishing smacks along with all those coastal cargo boats carrying tons of hoops and staves," William added. "Why in the world were they transporting so many of those things?"

Malachi smiled. "When you start gathering wartime supplies, hoops and staves rank right up there with cannon and powder. From those raw materials, the coopers fashion the water-proof casks which protect the store of water and wine and fish and meat and biscuit—all of which make it possible for ships to undertake long journeys in the first place. Without such casks, the biggest fleet in the world would be limited to week-end sailing."

William said, "I must say those well-seasoned staves really made a nice, aromatic fire, unlike the fishing boats which generate a real stink as they burn. It must be all that fish oil."

Bellingham frowned at William. "Excuse me, Malachi, but must he be here?"

"He's learning the business," Malachi assured him, "And he backs me up in note-taking, because, God help me, I have slowed down over the years."

"And he is a very good oarsman," Baxter added, "although a bit sulky at times, but a navy can never carry too many good oarsmen, you know."

Captain Bellingham sighed deeply. "I believe we can keep today's primary concern in better focus if we develop our discussion chronologically. Let's start at the beginning. Mr. Baxter, it was clear from the first day that Captain Borough had unsettled issues with Admiral Drake's decision to enter Cadiz Bay, did he not?"

"Damn right he did. As we all know, Drake called the captains together before we ever entered the harbor and issued his orders without giving the other captains a single minute to voice their opinions at his so-called Council of War. His procedure was completely outside the customary boundaries of the conventions of the true English Navy which were established by Henry VIII specifically to permit—"

"Yes, yes, Mr. Baxter, we're quiet aware of the historic background of the naval War Council, but perhaps our time could best be served here if you simply listed the objections Captain Borough had to the strategy Admiral Drake employed on that occasion."

"Very well. Vice-admiral Borough protested Drake's decision to enter so abruptly into Cadiz Bay and characterized the Admiral's action as the height of rashness when he plunged into a strange harbor without fresh knowledge of the forts and channels situated therein. Vice-admiral Borough also objected to the fact that there was no debating of alternative strategies, no deference given to the opinions of senior officers, no formal orders issued, and no presentation of a proper challenge to the enemy before the attack took place. In short, it infuriated Vice-admiral Borough that Drake did not abide by any of the conventions of naval warfare that have governed the actions of all true naval officers ever since King Henry VIII—"

"Yes, yes," Bellingham interrupted. "So as soon as the three-day battle of Cadiz Bay was over, Captain Borough felt obliged to write Admiral Drake a scathing letter in which he recorded his disapproval, did he not?"

"Well now," Baxter said, "if we are to develop this discussion chronologically as you suggested, let's pay a little more attention to the actual passage of time, shall we? As I recall, the letter to which Drake reacted so violently—to the complete surprise of Vice-admiral Borough, I might mention—was written after we left Cadiz on April 22 (O.S.) and swung west and then north to try to capture Recalde who, we had learned, was at sea with a small Spanish fleet. On April 30 (O.S.) we broke off the chase just short of Lisbon because Drake decided Recalde had probably reached the sanctuary of that well defended harbor, and we swung south again after Drake announced in another brief War Council that he intended to capture the Sagres fort at Cape St. Vincent."

"Excuse me, gentlemen," Malachi said, "I hate to interrupt the flow here but the Council insists on being able to find these specific locations on one of Hukluyt's maps, so if you don't mind, let me make a note of distances at this point. As I recall, Cadiz is just fifty miles north of the Strait of Gibraltar and thirty miles north of Trafalgar Cape. The Sagres fort at Cape St.Vincent is two hundred miles northwest of Cadiz along the coast where Spain runs into the bottom of Portugal, right?"

Bellingham nodded, "And Lisbon is 120 miles further north of Cape St. Vincent, which incidentally is not only the southwest corner of Portugal but also the southwest corner of the European continent, so whatever naval force controls Cape St. Vincent controls all the naval traffic between the Mediterranean and Lisbon."

"I hesitate to mention it at this point," Malachi added, "but I always think historical background adds resonance to current discussions. So let me just say that Sagres Castle was the headquarters of Prince Henry the Navigator of Portugal while he mapped out the sea explorations which made Portuguese explorers the most successful navigators of the last century, and his efforts directly resulted in the discovery of the East Indies and India and helped in locating the West Indies and the New World. As such, Sagres Castle had become something of a shrine for all map-makers, mathematicians, and mariners until Drake saw the unfortunate necessity of burning it down."

"A small matter compared to his other transgressions," Baxter sniffed. "Vice-admiral Borough certainly saw the strategic importance of Cape St. Vincent, but he definitely did not agree that the Sagres fort had to be captured to exercise dominance over that key point. He insisted control could be maintained from the sea without setting foot on shore because he realized any invasion of a sovereign's native soil con-

stituted an act of war. It was upon that occasion that he informed Drake in no uncertain terms that the Admiral was overreaching his commission and exceeding his
Royal instructions since he was never authorized to seize King Philip's land and make
a camp thereon."

"And Captain Borough thought it wise," Bellingham spoke crisply, "while he was
sending a letter to question Drake's strategy and his judgment and his violation of
naval customs, to also characterize Drake's motive for taking the fort at Sagres as a
simple desire to boast; *'Thus have I done upon the King of Spain's land'*. [12] At that point,
Captain Borough seems to be suggesting that Captain Drake's motive amounted to
little more than one dog's desire to piss on another dog's tree."

"Let's just say he lessoned Drake just as senior naval officers have lessoned junior officers since time immemorial," Baxter clarified. "He then concluded his letter
handsomely by clearly explaining what his purpose had been in addressing Drake in
that fashion: *'I pray you take this in good part as I mean it: for I protest before God I do it to
no other end but in discharge of my duty towards her Majesty and the service'*." [13]

"It is unfortunate," Bellingham said, "that Captain Borough did not realize that
questioning Drake's judgment meant he was undermining Drake's authority and also
calling into question Drake's ability to command—very serious charges, which no
commander could ignore while he was busy confronting the enemy. That's why Borough was arrested, stripped of his command, and confined to his cabin for the remainder of the journey."

"This conflict need never have reached that point at all, you know," Baxter insisted,
"if Drake had only listened to Vice-admiral Borough right from the beginning as he
should have done."

"Somewhat beside the point at this stage, I'm afraid," Bellingham murmured, "but
it must be admitted that Captain Borough made sense on some of those issues. Capturing the fort at Sagres was not only dangerous but could be looked on as an act of
war even if Drake didn't choose to look at it that way."

"How else could you look at it?"

"Those of us who sailed with Drake on his raids in the New World knew what
he had in mind," said Captain Bellingham. "Since he intended to disrupt Spanish
shipping by stationing his fleet off Cape St. Vincent for a time, he obviously needed a
handy harbor in which to keep his ships healthy by careening them for maintenance
just as he had always done on his other voyages. Every six to eight weeks, he laid up
each of his ships in turn in order to scrape the hull, pump the bilges, renew the ballast,
clean and fumigate the crew's quarters, and do whatever caulking and painting was
needed. The Sagres Harbor was handy for such work, but the Spanish fort overlooking that anchorage was a direct threat, so it had to be put out of commission."

"He sure decommissioned her when he dismounted her cannon and tumbled them down the cliff to be retrieved by our boats," William added gleefully. "I'll never forget seeing Drake himself joining his men to pile bundles of faggots soaked in pitch at the base of the castle gate while the defenders were pouring musket shot down on them. No wonder his men will follow him anywhere."

"I can only hope somebody thinks to point out to King Philip," Malachi said, "that Drake never actually occupied the fort once he had reduced its threat to the Sagres anchorage. That distinction might save us from going to war over the incident."

"One can only hope," Baxter persisted, "that in the future, the Queen will choose military commanders who recognize the distinction between cannonading an enemy's harbors and setting up an encampment on his soil. Had she chosen more wisely on this expedition, she would have avoided some of the diplomatic headaches which will visit her very shortly as a result of the unauthorized and reckless actions taken here in her name."

"Be careful, Mr. Baxter," Captain Bellingham warned, "or you'll soon join your Captain under arrest. We are still in enemy waters, and we will tolerate no broadcast of doubt about Admiral Drake's ability to command."

"You asked for Vice-Admiral Borough's opinions on the matter, and mine happens to match his exactly," Baxter declared, "so it seems to me—"

A quick rap on the captain's door interrupted him, and a junior officer entered quickly. "Sorry to disturb you, sir, but the *Bonaventure* is signaling, and you asked to be notified."

"Sorry, gentlemen," Bellingham said as he leaped up. "Our business will have to wait. Why don't you visit our galley and refresh yourselves until I can get back to you. Malachi, you better come with me," he said on his way out.

"Eat your fill but remember to save some for me," Malachi said as he joined Bellingham.

"I wonder if you could summon a mess boy for us," William asked the junior officer who had remained stationed at the cabin door.

"I'm sorry, sir, but you may not be left unattended in the Captain's cabin while he's gone. Charts and things, you know. There is a ward room directly adjoining and a mess boy may be summoned from there."

William and Baxter entered the wardroom, summoned a mess boy, ordered something to eat and relaxed in the fond expectation of enjoying a well organized meal after the snatch-and-grab arrangements which had dominated their eating habits during the past month. The meal arrived just as Malachi breezed back into the room.

"No time to lose," he announced. "It's up and at 'em time. The *Bonaventure* just sent a very abrupt and surprising message. Every ship in the fleet is to leave the coast of Spain twelve hours from now at dawn tomorrow with all hands on board. All traffic with the shore is to be halted immediately and every ship is to be fully manned and prepared for an extended journey."

"Zounds," William exclaimed. "That's strange. I thought we were staying put for a while."

"So," Baxter smiled, "Drake's faulty judgment has finally awakened to the reckless endangerment he has caused by invading the land of another monarch without a declaration of war. I can only hope he remembers who attempted to point out that danger to him right from the beginning and that he is now ready to consult with those officers who may very well be better informed about such matters than he is. It seems to me it is not too late even now, if he is willing to come, hat in hand—"

"Excuse me, Mr. Baxter," Malachi interrupted him, "but I suspect you are running down the wrong road. We are all speculating, of course, but I've known Francis Drake for a long time and I've never once seen him worry about what others may regard as a mistake on his part. Neither have I ever seen him go back to clean up what others might regard as the mess he made. All of his energy is directed to going forward, so I think you can safely attribute this sudden change of tactic to a new plan of attack on somebody somewhere."

"What you say does not hide the fact that we are again confronted with another glaring illustration of Drake's rashness and lack of judgment," Baxter contended. "We still have ships in our fleet that have not finished taking on fresh water. We have ships that have not yet completed the task of shifting their sick and disabled to the returning prize ships. We have crews ashore that will have to scramble to get forges and other equipment back on board before we sail off. Doesn't our esteemed admiral know that twelve hours is simply not enough time to complete the maintenance and dispatching of a large fleet? It takes long range planning and not some big dramatic rush with bugles blowing to put an effective fleet out on the water. It certainly behooves us to take the time to do the thing right."

"Who might we be attacking next?" William asked Malachi, "and where?"

"Hard to say," Malachi conceded, "but my first guess would be that Drake has come into possession of some Portuguese pilots who have agreed to guide him through the dangerous, well-defended channels up the Taugus River and into Lisbon harbor. If we could slip our fleet past those harbor defenses, we could blow Philip's dream of building a conquering armada right out of the water. We know that Lisbon is presently full of Spanish warships just waiting to be fitted with the new cannon which we scattered across the bottom of Cadiz Bay last month. Sooner or later, Santa Cruz will scrape something together to arm his galleons, of course, but in the meantime, what a four-star festival our gunners would enjoy if we could bring them alongside those unarmed galleons for just a an hour or two!"

"If we're really leaving tomorrow," Baxter said, "I better return to the *Lion* and tie up some details. I must say, however, before I go, that despite my misgivings about Captain Drake, I hope your speculation about the Portuguese pilots is correct, Malachi, because I recognize that turning English cannon loose inside Lisbon Harbor would do more good for the Queen and the future of England than any argument about who should command our fleet ever could."

"We can only hope," Malachi grinned. "William, you get back over to the *Bonaventure* where there is copy work for you. I'll ride along with Mr. Baxter to the *Lion* and rejoin you in a day or so after I make an official copy of Captain Borough's map of Cadiz harbor to include in the report to the Council."

Chapter 7:
THE SAN FELIPE TREASURE SHIP

Walsingham's Whitehall Office one month later, 6-20-87 (O.S.)

Milles, Walsingham's secretary, ushered Malachi and William into the outer office and introduced them to his companion. "This gentleman is Stan Green, who has just brought us the heart-warming estimates from the capture of the *San Felipe*. The boss will be back in a few minutes." Milles showed them to seats.

"I understand," said Milles, "you and your apprentice have been separated since before the *San Felipe* was taken, Malachi."

"True," said Malachi, one hand on William's shoulder. "One day short of a month. This is the first time I've seen William since May 21, when Admiral Drake ordered us all to leave Cape St. Vincent within twelve hours."

"Not a good thing, losing your man," chuckled Milles. "How did you get separated?"

William spoke up. "I was eating on Captain Bellingham's *Rainbow* when Malachi went to the *Golden Lion* with Baxter. After that there was great confusion, and it was the last I saw of him until now."

Malachi smiled. "The whole fleet had escorted the prize ships, with the sick and injured aboard, until they turned north on the track to England while we continued west toward the Azores. That direction surprised all of us, but we concluded that Drake's hurry was caused by information he had gathered about Spain's gold and silver shipments from the New World arriving in the Azores. He kept our destination a closely-guarded secret, which probably contributed to the breakup of our fleet after we ran into a vicious storm just three days out from the Spanish coast, and the fleet was well scattered after forty-eight hours of buffeting."

"I got very seasick," William mentioned.

"Because of the secrecy, no rendezvous point had been established," continued Malachi, "so, just after the storm, some of the ships decided to go their own way. The London group of tall ships that had been with us from the beginning turned for home. They claimed their food was running low, and they had damage from the storm, but I suspect they had grown tired of burning barrel staves and missed the comforts of home. The crew of the *Golden Lion* decided Drake was a madman, who had dishonored their captain, so they mutinied, put Captain Borough back on the bridge, refused to rejoin the fleet, and sailed home after confining me to an officer's cabin because I was identified as a 'Drake-man'."

"But the *Golden Lion* was seen to survive the storm," said William, "and to leave the fleet thereafter, so Drake assembled a drumhead court-martial and had Borough condemned to death for treason and desertion. How is that particular drama playing out here at home? Has Borough been taken up yet?"

"The death verdict has been pretty much ignored at Court, where there is a growing impatience with Drake's tendency to kill off his second-in-command in the middle of his voyage," Milles said. "Borough has friends in London who interceded for him, so I don't think he's in any real danger unless he is fool enough to sail again under Drake. From this episode, however, there is a mounting conviction among Council members that Drake operates pretty much as a heavy-handed tyrant at sea."

"But he wins the day, ignoring bad advice!" cried William.

"Right," said Malachi. "People at Court were much more concerned with the morality of the situation before the capture of the treasure ship, *San Felipe*, drove all other considerations from their mind."

Green spoke up. "She's a prize ship worth £114,000—almost equal to half the Queen's annual allotment."

Milles laughed softly. "When they brought her into port, all other concerns were tossed to the seagulls along with the rest of the refuse. The careful distribution of such treasure leaves no room for talk of other matters."

"How much do I get?" William asked.

"You're very fortunate," said Milles. "You will be among the first to know because Mr. Green is just waiting for a chance to deliver that distribution chart to the boss, but I suspect we can talk him into letting us have a peek at it first. How about it, Stan?"

"I am supposed to turn it over to Mr. Walsingham in person," Green said, "but I suppose it wouldn't hurt if—"

"Hold on," Malachi commanded. "Before my man is swamped in new-found riches, let him give us details of the actual capture. Don't forget that I was confined to a cabin on the *Lion* while he was aboard the *Bonaventure* with Drake. Fill us in if you will, William."

"Let me first say I was still suffering from my mal-de-mar, as I mentioned, but when we raised Sao Miguel in the Azores, I was somewhat snapped out of my misery by the astonishing sight of that monster carrack, *San Felipe*, loaded with the precious treasures of Asia, sitting there waiting for us."

"How big is she?" Milles asked.

"At fifteen hundred tons, she was exactly the size of our three biggest warships put together, and she loomed like a huge oak tree over our bramble bush galleons. Let me tell you, the fact that our Admiral had led us unerringly for a thousand miles through storm and strife to confront the richest prize in all the oceans of the world, left every man in that fleet breathless for a time and in complete awe of Sir Francis Drake. There was even renewed speculation that perhaps the Spanish were correct when they claimed Drake had a magic mirror in which he could trace the movements of all ships in all oceans."

Malachi snorted. "The magic mirror story doesn't hurt anything and Drake rather enjoys seeing himself cast as a wizard, but the truth of the matter is far less magical. We have since learned that Drake was tipped off about a ship heavily laden with spices returning from the East Indies."

"But who would be in a position to give him such information?" William asked.

"Probably one of those coastal caravels which trade up and down the African coast and then beat their way homeward to Spain. We intercepted several such vessels off Cape St. Vincent, and one of them must have mentioned seeing the *San Felipe* down around Cape Verdes along the central African coast. Drake knows that Portuguese ships homeward-bound from the Spice Islands in Asia, instead of taking the trouble to beat their way up the African coast against the prevailing northeast Trade Wind, will often make one long reach across that wind from Cape Verdes to the Azores and then run home to Lisbon on the prevailing westerly winds."

"So all he had to do," smiled Milles, "was estimate her average speed and pick out the right spot to intercept her without even consulting his magic mirror."

"And he did a proper job of that," Malachi nodded, "because that's exactly what the *San Felipe* did, and that's why she was right where he calculated when you cornered her. But I'm curious about the capture. Did she fight at all, William?"

"Even after the departure of the *Lion*, we still had six galleons and numerous pinnaces left to confront her. Surprisingly, she did fire a few rounds at us from small swivel-mounted guns in her forecastle and afterdeck before surrendering gracefully. At first we were puzzled why she never opened the gunports of her big guns, but—

we found later—her gundecks were completely crammed with trade goods, and after such a long journey, many of her crew were too sick or weak to work the guns even if they had been able to clear them."

"Did you get a chance to check the cargo?" Malachi asked.

"Oh, yes, I was part of the crew recruited to do an informal manifest and my nose danced with delight when it encountered the sweet smelling fragrance below deck from the mountains of nutmeg, ginger, clove, cinnamon, and pepper which they had carried from the Orient. There were also treasures for my eyes in the piles of silk and ivory along with gold and silver in addition to a handsome array of jewels. Let me tell you, it was an intoxicating experience just to run inventory on that trove of treasure, and my sea-sickness was quickly squeezed from my head by my scramble to find figures to adequately reflect her worth."

"I'll confess, my reaction to the treasure was the opposite of yours." Green chuckled, "When I learned that the estimated value of £114,000 made the *San Felipe* the richest prize ever to sail into an English port, my mind surged with such pride that my head began to swim."

The group joined Green's appreciative chuckle, and he went on to say, "We have calculated the value of the *San Felipe* and her cargo to be a little over three times the value of all the ships and cargoes burned and taken in Cadiz Harbor. Her capture will be particularly galling to King Philip because the *San Felipe* was his personal property, and her loss will undoubtedly put him in further debt to Continental bankers who are still lending him money but are now charging him 25% interest because it is felt that Drake's raids have made him a greater risk."

"Speaking of money," William said, "you mentioned that the treasure from the *San Felipe* was ready for a split. How much did each of my shipmates and I end up with, anyway?"

"Well, you know," Green explained, "there are major distributions before it gets down to the average seaman. When the money from the prizes captured at Cadiz was added to the £114,000 from the *San Felipe*, it totaled £140,000. First off, of course, the Admiralty Office takes its ten percent, which comes to £14,000. We then have £126,000 left to split into thirds for the ship owners, the victualers and the crews."

"Egad, this is exciting!" William exclaimed. "We're talking about a veritable mountain of money here! I don't know that I ever want this kind of anticipation to end, it's so exhilarating. But I guess I do—how much do I get?"

"Of that £126,000," Green continued, "the Queen gets over £40,000 because she is both ship owner and victualer. That's enough money to buy her a brand new fleet of fifteen *Elizabeth Bonaventures* since they can be built for £2,600 each."

"And how does our brilliant Admiral make out after bringing us to the prize in the first place?"

"Pretty well," Green said. "Drake is also a ship owner and victualer in the venture, so he will get over £17,000–the equivalent of a nobleman's estate."

"So if we subtract the Queen's £40,000 and Drake's £17,000, that leaves £69,000 to divide among the 1100 or so of us who were in on the actual capture. Egad," William cried as he rubbed his hands together, "that will put a nice bulge in my purse. '*I am giddy; expectation whirls me around*'." [14]

"Try and keep your feet on the ground," Malachi advised, "and be a little more realistic in your expectations. You've left out the London merchants, who admittedly were not in on the capture but were part of the venture group, so they are entitled to their return on investment. That means you can subtract another third from your £69,000. which leaves you with £46,000. The inclusion of the London group, of course, also validates the claim of their crewmen, so you must add another 1100 claimants which thereby cuts your share of the £46,000 neatly in half."

"Ha!" William exclaimed. "That doesn't seem quite fair, but I guess business is business. You did, however, forgot to exclude the *Golden Lion* crew from your estimate. If we drop that crew of 250 mutineers from the final computation, we only have to add 850 to my group of 1100 for the final split; although, for the life of me, I don't understand how or why they are as eligible as those of us who actually stood up to the gunfire from the *San Felipe* and risked our lives in the front line of battle in order to procure this treasure."

"Didn't you say you were sick in bed with your mal-de-mar during the actual battle?" Malachi asked.

"Oh, well," William shrugged, "you know what I mean. Let's see now. We are down to 1,950 crewmen to divide up the remaining £46,000, and I think, even speaking conservatively, that will put into the purse of each of us just about….." he broke off to scribble hastily on his foolscap.

"I don't mean to whittle on your illusions," Malachi said, "but no charges have yet been filed against the crew of the *Golden Lion* nor against Vice Admiral Borough, and I doubt if any ever will be, so they are still eligible for their cut of the prize money."

"Bloody hell!" William exclaimed, "My money is disappearing faster than if I actually had it in my purse!" He heaved a deep sigh. "All right then! We add the 250 mutineers back to the group and finally end up with 2200 crewmen all set to divide the £46,000. Is that right, or are there more exclusions and exceptions?"

"About one hundred officers will each get a double share, of course, so just base the split on roughly 2,300 crewmen," Green advised, "and that will take care of them. Without running the actual figures then, I would estimate each man would have close to twenty pounds coming."

"That's before administrative costs are subtracted, of course," Milles cautioned, "but I think it would be safe to say each crewman will see close to fifteen pounds, which comes to about five years' pay for the average London worker. Not bad for a three-month holiday on the high seas."

"What a joy it will be to finally have some real money of my own in my purse!. You wouldn't believe how difficult it has been to go so long without—but stay! Where and when will I collect my share? Should I go back to the *Elizabeth Bonaventure* and stand in line for my money? Is that the way it's done?"

"I can check the amount you have coming now if you'd like," said Green, "I have copies of the fleet's muster roles right here. In addition, it may relieve your mind to learn that I have been empowered to evaluate how much of a claim each crew member has to the prize money, so we can resolve your case right here and now." Green opened the ledger he carried under his arm. "What's your last name, William?"

"Last name?" William gagged.

"Right," Green chuckled. "You can't expect the government to issue money to everybody named William, can you?"

"Yes, I see. That may be a problem, but everybody knows I was with the fleet."

"I hesitate to spoil your fun," Malachi said, "but officially, you were never really assigned to any one ship, but rather to whichever small craft could ferry us about the fleet to perform our duties as clerks."

"You were a non-registered, non-combatant who was sick in bed during the capture of the *San Felipe*?" Green asked ominously.

"Just a minute now," William insisted. "I may have been laid up for a time in the Azores' action, but I served dutifully on a boat crew during the Cadiz raid."

"Were you part of a boarding party or part of a gun crew?"

"Neither, as it occurs. As it fell out, my assignment was to recruit some of the embargoed mariners of the port who might help us identify which ships were worth pillaging."

"Good," said Green. "That's an important assignment. That should qualify you. How did you manage to recruit them?"

"I played the spoons for what seemed like endless hours."

"Spoons? I don't quite understand."

"Forget that," William decided. "I was second in command of a separate naval vessel which patrolled the entire length and breath of Cadiz Bay for many hours to complete a vital mission for the Vice-Admiral of the entire English navy."

"Would that be the man who Admiral Drake later condemned to death as a traitor and deserter?" Green asked.

"That's beside the point," William insisted. "The point is I was in complete charge of navigating that vessel, and I guided it to a successful completion of the mission."

"That's fine. What was the name of the vessel?"

"Name? It had no name. It was a very small vessel."

"A skiff, you mean, without a name and doubtless without a muster role too. I see." Green paused to fold up the ledger he had opened, and said, "I suppose there is no real rush in validating your claim right here and now when it can easily be looked into in greater detail when things straighten themselves out at a later date."

"I heard that tone," William scowled. "What does that mean? I have nothing coming? I was there. I was shot at! I had cannon balls pass directly over my head no more than five feet away!"

"From the Spanish cannon at the Cadiz fort?" Green asked.

"Well no," William conceded. "As it occurs those were from the *Bonaventure's* broadside, but that makes little difference in terms of the danger involved."

"Let me make sure I have this straight. You say you were not behind our cannon while it was shooting at the enemy, but you were, instead, out in front of the guns where our enemy was gathered?" Mr. Green asked with wonder in his voice.

"Perhaps you're right, Mr. Green," Malachi interrupted. "All of this can wait for a later examination, and in the meantime, William, you need not be too discouraged. We will certainly get you some money somewhere, and in a pinch, you could have some of mine."

"Yours? How could you be listed on a muster role if I'm not?"

"The *Golden Lion* had to list me when they assigned me to a cabin."

"You have money coming and I don't? You weren't there and I was!"

"Try to stay calm. With a little effort, we can almost certainly establish that you were, indeed, aboard one of her Majesty's ships for three month's time, and that will automatically entitle you to at least a seaman's pay of fourteen shillings a month for wages and victuals. We will, of course, have to deduct half of that for the food you ate during that period, but I'm certain you can count on coming out of this with a full twenty-one shillings free and clear."

"Shillings?" William moaned. "Traitors get pounds while I get shillings? Naked, skinny shillings for me, you say, while mutineers get pounds! Zounds! *To have seen much and to have nothing is to have rich eyes and poor hands.*" [15]

"It's not all that bad," Malachi advised. "Let me take you off to the side here and review your experience without bothering the rest of these gentlemen." They said their goodbyes and left. "Think of it this way. Even with little financial return, you were treated to memorable adventures which you will relish for the rest of your days, and you got a good start in filling that reservoir of experience which you mention so often."

"Yes, Yes, full reservoirs will be handy later on, but at the moment, it is a full purse I have in mind, but there is no hope for me. I am betrayed by an errant fate at every turn."

"We must all pay a planetary penalty for our residence on this intriguing orb," Malachi counseled, "and everybody is bound to encounter occasional misfortune along the way."

524

"But it's not occasional! Misfortune haunts me and pursues me and leads me to feel:

> *How weary, stale, flat, and unprofitable*
> *Seem to me all the uses of this world!*
> *Tis an unweeded garden*
> *That grows to seed.*
> *Things rank and gross in nature*
> *Possess it merely.* [16]

"Oh, try not to run on like that, or people will think you have hit bottom, so they will hesitate to trust you or lend you money or let you marry their daughters. Try instead to see life as a tankard already half-full. Get something to look forward to. Generate some enthusiasm as you did after you signed up for the second colony attempt in Virginia."

"Oh, by the good Saint George, that's right! Malachi you are a wonder! You always know how to lead me down the expanding path which suits my spirit so well! By Gadfrey, I will make the colony experience the greatest adventure of my life. The new world is just crying out for a poet-in-residence to broadcast to the world its wonders and riches! Oftentimes, a poet who succeeds in a foreign land is then welcomed effusively and rewarded generously at home. I can hardly wait. When do we leave?"

"Well, perhaps it was ill-advised of me to bring up that particular possibility in your present mood. However, as you may recall, there is a time constraint on Raleigh and his people to get that colony established as quickly as possible, so it is not too surprising that they moved up the departure date quite a bit."

"That's no problem. I can be ready in a very big hurry. I don't need a week to prepare. My needs are simple enough when I respond to such a golden opportunity to really turn my life around and finally get something done. And our office need not worry at all about my getting those regular reports sent back as soon as any ship makes the return trip. I know just the kinds of things our office wants to hear about in terms of what is working over there and what is not. I know they'll be sharing those reports with Raleigh, so I will pay very close attention to the things which seem to foster a realistic understanding with the native Indians, and permit the colony to set itself up on a permanent basis instead of having to limp home after a disorganized year like the last attempt did. So two or three days is plenty of time for me to be ready. What is the new departure date?"

"They left early last month."

"Oh, My God! Disappointments do not pursue me singly or even in pairs, but they come down on me in battalions and finally erode away my native courage. I think I better take a nap. But first, let me digest the bitter truth. What were the circumstances of their departure? Who went in how many ships? Was John White still in charge when they left?"

"He was," Malachi affirmed. "Raleigh appointed him governor of the joint stock company and granted him a coat of arms and also produced emblems for each of his half dozen assistants in order to set up a government of sorts to establish responsibility and keep the colony functioning."

"How many people went?"

"Fourteen complete families which came to 89 men, 17 women, and 11 children. They are all either English or Irish workers from various crafts and guilds, so they had no loafers or slackers among them. As a matter of fact, they followed Hakluyt's advice on taking people with a variety of skills for the new venture."

"Will they settle in Roanoke again?"

"Oh No! Absolutely not. It was decided that the lack of a deep water port was too great a drawback—in addition to being a real hazard—for the establishment of a permanent base, so they'll set up the new colony a hundreds miles north of Roanoke in Chesipik Bay where Lane's group did some exploring last year and found adequate depth for safe mooring and more farm land with less swamp than around Roanoke."

"What about Indians?"

"That remains to be seen, but Governor White is determined to make every effort to reach a friendly arrangement with them, and if that fails, there are countless islands in the bay which could be turned into fortified settlements against the Indians or the Spanish. The switch from Roanoke to Chesipik is an intelligent one because there are many more alternatives available once you have command of a deep water port. From there, it would be easy to mount attacks on the Spanish gold shipments which pass just fifty miles offshore on their way back to Spain."

"What kind of shipping did the new colony have?"

"Raleigh provided them with the 120 ton flagship *Lion* which made the trip in '85 and a medium sized flyboat along with a pinnace. The plan is to have the *Lion* go back and forth to England for supplies and have the flyboat and pinnace stay with the colony for exploring."

"Did John White's daughter, Eleanor, go with them?"

Malachi frowned. "You always did have a problem with the fact that she is now Ananias Dare's wife, didn't you? No matter, however, since she is already pregnant and safely out of your influence. She hopes to give birth to the first English baby born in the New World and plans to call the child 'Virginia' if it's a girl."

William shrugged. "Very nice but I can only imagine she had a rough passage if she tackled such a difficult trip while pregnant, but as I recall, she is a sturdy and spirited young woman, so I imagine she will do well."

"Aside from all those details there were no big surprises about the makeup of the expedition except that only a few of those who returned last year decided to repeat the experience."

"Perhaps that's just as well. That group seemed to start with some major misconceptions which probably prevented them from ever succeeding with the project, but it sounds like this group is much more realistic and level-headed, so I predict they will experience nothing but a resounding success in this new venture. Who did they select as captain and pilot?"

"They decided experience counted heavily in such an important post so Raleigh selected Simon Fernandez as captain of the flagship."

"Uh Oh."

PART VIII: A VISIT WITH MONTAIGNE.

Chapter 1:
THE WAR OF THE THREE HENRYS

Riding to Bordeaux, France, by coach: Oct. 22, (N.S.), 1587:

"We may be in France for some time," Malachi said, "so I better fill you in on some of the more prominent policy makers."

"Please do," William replied. "I'm especially confused by reference to the War of the Three Henrys which apparently is between several Frenchmen who happen to be named Henry. Surely that's not the reason for the war, is it?"

"No, indeed," Malachi chuckled. "Even in France things have to make more sense than that. The religious war which has plagued the French for the last thirty years is a result of the classical confusion over which bloody doctrinarian sword—Catholic or Protestant—is most pleasing to the Prince of Peace; in short, which faction has the approval of the Almighty in disposing of all dissenters."

"How many major factions are we talking about?"

"Three, and as it happens, each of the contending forces is led by a man named Henry. The French Protestant party—or Huguenots, as they are called—is led by King Henry of Navarre of the Bourbon family. The Royal party is led by a member of the Valois house who is the present King of France, Henry III. He happens to be something of a luke-warm partisan in the religious debate, but he is heavily influenced by two major string-pullers operating behind the throne to keep the royal family closely allied with the Catholic party."

"And one of those would have to be a 'Henry' to make the trilogy complete."

"Right. The third is Duke Henry de Guise—from the house of Guise-Lorraine—who is the head of the powerful French Catholic League. De Guise is usually allied in policy with the King and his mother, Catherine de Medici, who happens to be the other major influence on the King. De Guise carries a great deal of influence with the Crown because Philip of Spain subsidizes him handsomely to defend the Catholic cause in France, and fresh gold has many times its real value in a government whose resources have been squandered by decades of internal bloodletting."

"Does Spain's gold give Philip a major voice in French affairs?" William wondered.

"It might seem so," Malachi said, "but fortunately for England, Henry III and his mother do not always agree with de Guise, nor with each other, for that matter. The three of them are such volatile characters, there is no telling at any given moment which two are more closely allied against the other. Catherine, however, usually gets more credit than the other two for igniting the St. Bartholomew's Day Massacre back in 1572 at the wedding of the Huguenot King Henry of Navarre with Catherine's daughter, Margaret of Valois. The wedding was supposed to reconcile the contending religious factions, but, instead, it set them further apart."

"Major bad news for a wedding that starts with a massacre,' William shook his head.

"It is said that Catherine had to harangue her son for several hours to get him to set in motion the slaughter of Protestant wedding guests which started in Paris and then rampaged across France for six weeks and by some estimates ended up killing between twenty and thirty thousand of the Huguenots. It was said that the Pope had a commemorative medal struck to mark the event, and Philip of Spain celebrated the destruction of so many heretics for three days, while the bridegroom, Henry of Navarre, barely escaped with his life from the grand treachery."

"Protestant Henry, I take it, married a Catholic princess, and together they rule Navarre. Where is Navarre anyway?"

"It's a small and ancient kingdom lying in the mountains between France and Spain, and its king is part of the royal French bloodline. Since the last of the Valois heirs died in '84, Huguenot King Henry of Navarre is now the heir-apparent to the French throne if anything happens to Catholic Henry III. Walsingham thinks that Navarre might be the single person capable of uniting France if he inherits the French crown anytime soon. Walsingham says it is inevitable that Navarre will have to turn Catholic in order to ascend the throne simply because a French king who cannot enter Paris would be a bird without a nest."

"Paris is strongly Catholic?"

"About 95% Catholic, and the other 5% better keep very quiet about it. Navarre's conversion would inconvenience England for a time, but it would profit us in the long run. If Navarre can get a boot down in each camp, he might be able to stop the Catholics and Huguenots from killing each other by uniting them under one flag, and then France could once again assume her proper role in the structure of European society."

"Proper role?" William asked.

"To serve as a buffer zone between England and Spain," Malachi explained. "If fate happened to put Navarre on the French throne, he could unite the existing military forces of his country—who now waste their energy chasing each other—and easily take Flanders from the Spanish. He could give Spain enough to worry about so Philip might forget about us for a while. That's why Philip keeps Guise supplied with funds to keep the civil unrest churning in France while he attends to the Dutch rebels without interference. And, eventually of course, attends to us English heretics when he finishes with the Dutch."

"But meanwhile, peace in our time, eh?" William asked.

"Always a popular idea," Malachi nodded, "and just about as much as mortal man can manage amidst the shifting political currents. But, fearful of losing a powerful ally in Protestant Navarre, Elizabeth wants his conversion delayed as long as possible, even to the extent of approving more men and money to influence that purpose. That's why we're traveling coach to Bordeaux instead of riding horseback. We're taking English gold to Navarre."

"Ah well, every comfort is gratefully accepted," said William, bouncing high over the bumps of the road, "especially those bestowed by an appreciative Queen who decides to recognize and reward our special service."

"That's right," said Malachi, holding on to the side of the rocking coach. "The open purse indicates Elizabeth is strongly interested in delaying Navarre's conversion, or at least learning beforehand the exact moment the event is likely to occur. We can't influence Navarre directly, of course, but we know he consults frequently with Michel de Montaigne, the fifty-five-year-old former mayor of Bordeaux. I once did some work for Montaigne, and we have since visited each other occasionally on business. Montaigne is a Catholic who serves as Navarre's back-door link to Henry de Guise's Catholic League, so he is the very person most likely to know how much authentic pressure is being exerted on Navarre for a quick conversion."

"Authentic pressure?"

"The leaders of the French Catholic League must cry out publicly for an immediate conversion in order to justify the gold which Spain has supplied to them over the years. Privately, however, they're all aware that the day Navarre turns Catholic is the day Philip turns off the spigot of gold from Madrid, and the day the League must begin to share power with the Huguenots over large sections of France. Their purpose in life will erode along with their financing—not a pleasant prospect for any administrator."

"So, privately, many in the Catholic League will lean against an accommodation with Navarre?"

"That's what we're counting on," Malachi nodded. "For a while anyway, we expect them to set unreasonable demands in the negotiations to keep him from jumping the fence too quickly. We're going to visit Montaigne in his home in the country because there is plague again in Bordeaux. He's very open and candid and loves to talk, so we'll see what we can wheedle out of him."

"That's why you're having me read his book of essays? To help wheedle him?"

Malachi nodded. "I'm pleased that you are finding time in our travels to read his book because I expect you to keep him engaged while I finish off the delivery of English monies to Navarre's people. It would jeopardize Montaigne's status as an honest broker between contending parties if he were forced to recognize what I was up to while we were guests in his home, so we must be extra cautious. In his ingenuous way, Montaigne often gets as much information out of me as I do out of him, so I want to change the equation by encouraging him to converse with you. I'm sure the exchange will so startle him that I won't be missed for a time, and when I return, I'll be able to fish unnoticed in his troubled waters."

William brought forth his copy of *Essays*. "There really isn't much of a story line here, you know,"

"That's to be expected," Malachi assured him. "Essays are not stories so much as informal, candid examinations of the world at large from a personal perspective. Montaigne is honest and open in his writings, and he grants his audience the greatest boon in Christendom."

"What's that?"

"He doesn't moralize. He doesn't preach. He offers an examination of interesting topics in a good-humored, somewhat skeptical fashion, and when you're finished reading, you know as much about the subject as he does because he conceals nothing. I find him a very refreshing voice in a partisan world which only too readily cultivates deliberate confusion."

"I don't suppose there's an English translation available?"

Malachi frowned. "You know, if you spent half as much energy working as you do avoiding work, you would lead a much more useful existence."

"A short season for the greatest boon in Christendom, I'd say," William observed. "Oh, well. But, tell me, what do you and Montaigne find to talk about?"

"Apart from everything else," Malachi explained, "Montaigne and I share a common interest in governments which have managed to be successful over long periods of time. We have spent our lives binding up the small wounds of our separate kingdoms, only to be tumbled about periodically by the large injuries which random events sometimes inflict. We're growing old and thoughtful. We would like to see more continuity in modern governments, so we might relish our retirement and pass a treasury of hope and trust to our posterity."

"And there have been stable institutions in the past?"

"When we read the history of successful governments, our interest naturally centers strongly on the Romans who kept the civic machinery going for over a thousand years and, as a matter of fact, occupied England along with most of the known world for many of those centuries."

"I've heard of the roads and the ruins," William acknowledged.

Malachi nodded. "They were in England from fifty years before the birth of Christ to four hundred and fifty years after, and their influence is still with us. You know the Latin word 'castra' means 'camp', so the old Roman garrison camps have left their name on the present English countryside in the form of towns like Lancaster, Manchester, and Winchester."

"How did the Romans handle the pull-out? Did they appoint a king before they left?"

Malachi chuckled. "No time for niceties. They left in a real panic because all sorts of barbarians were hammering at the gates of Rome at that time, but let me get back to that another day, because right now I need to finish telling you about Montaigne before our visit. His deep interest in Rome came about in a curious fashion. He was born to a low noble family on the estate of Montaigne which he presently holds. His father was displeased with the results of public education in France, so he decided to educate his son in a unique way."

"Unique how?"

"He put him in the charge of a tutor who spoke only Latin to him from his birth to his fifth year. Even the house servants were compelled to manage enough Latin so that Montaigne never heard a word of French until he was six years old. So Latin, oddly enough, is his native tongue, and practical politics is one of his primary interest areas. He has twice served two-year terms as Mayor of Bordeaux, so there are few intricacies of city government unknown to him. During most of his lifetime, he has watched the contending Catholic and Protestant armies sweep back and forth across his estate year after year, killing each other as they go. And even though he is Catholic himself, his deepest distress is seeing Frenchmen killing other Frenchmen of whatever religion."

"So he distracts himself by cultivating an interest in the Romans?"

"Montaigne's interest in history is much like my own: to find happy times and discover how they got that way. The dream of all aging government functionaries is to assure their own pensions by leaving a little stability behind. Over the years, I have come to regard Montaigne as the wisest of my French contacts and, by good fortune, the source with the best connections."

"Connections in Bordeaux?"

"Throughout France. He is Navarre's close friend and advisor. In addition, he is a personal friend of Henry III, the king, and has dedicated his *Essays* to him. He is also acceptable to the de Guise faction as a Catholic who has been the honorable intermediary between the League and the Huguenots. No ordinary man in France is as well informed as Montaigne, and no advisor closer to Navarre than he. Just as Walsingham does, Montaigne sees Navarre as the only hope France has for unity after thirty-years of religious blood-letting."

"Even though Navarre is Protestant?"

"For the moment he is, yes, but Navarre is a practical man and he knows his conversion would help heal the split which has divided France so murderously for so long. A leg down in each camp may not be good theology, but it is good politics."

"Does Elizabeth see it that way too?"

"The Queen knows well enough that you seldom get served more than half a loaf at diplomatic dinners. Protestant or Catholic, Navarre is anti-Spanish to the bone, so the Queen knows she is lucky to retain at least that much alliance with France against Spain because it would be dangerous if those two ever allied themselves against us. I want you to study Montaigne as closely as you can and try to remember everything about him because some slip on his part, some unaccustomed gesture or phrase, if we can detect it, might give us our best tip on when Navarre's conversion might take place."

"I may not be able to remember everything all at once," William pointed out. "It would help if I had some sort of guideline. I know Montaigne wrote this book of essays, and he does talk about himself; but, in truth, I know nothing of his social characteristics."

"Not a bad idea." Malachi thought for a moment. "In conversation, I'd say Montaigne is exceedingly affable and good natured and fills his discussion with colorful comparisons and examples. In short, he speaks very much as he writes."

"He speaks like his essays read?"

"That's right," Malachi nodded. "The word 'essai' means 'test' in French, and in his writings he tests his personal observations of the world against every other person's version."

"Does he ever express your own views?"

Malachi clasped his hands together. "He is like a brain-brother at times. It's a fascinating experience to peek into another man's mind through his writings and see him put words around some of one's own hazy glimmerings."

"I'm surprised to hear you admit your 'hazy glimmerings,' Malachi." William smiled.

"I should never have admitted to it," laughed Malachi. "You will notice that Montaigne has a bit of a memory problem, so in conversation he often discusses the material he wrote five years ago when his book of essays came out."

"He has forgotten the words?"

"Not the words or ideas. He has them down pat. He has simply forgotten that he included them in his book. Don't be surprised when I ask rather simple-minded questions of our host. He likes to pursue a subject to some depth, but I sometimes grow weary of obscure Greeks cross-referenced to unknown Romans and paralleled to distant Egyptians. Nobody has that kind of education anymore. I can usually jump him from one page to another if I ask the right question."

"Is he doing well commercially with his essay writing?"

Malachi shrugged. "Depends on the deal he made with his publisher, but the book itself is doing well. Montaigne is already credited by many with creating a whole new literary form, and many Englishmen—Francis Bacon being prominent among them—are eager to give it a try. Henry III of France received the first copy, and, as I said, the volume was dedicated to him."

"I suppose stroking the higher-ups is pretty standard procedure for getting published?"

"Yes, indeed. Dedications are nearly always to patrons or monarchs. Pretty hard to get anything printed without some influential person to clear the path, and amazingly easy to work any business as long as you hold the favor of your prince."

"I intend to dedicate my first creation to the gloriously average people just so they will know that they too are worthy of respect for the role they play in making the world function as it does."

Malachi guffawed. "That would be quite proper for your copy-book scribbling, but you still must have some patron to clear the way to get anything printed legally, and, in England at least, it's easy for us to check on anything which has been printed illegally. Our office regularly inspects the few print-shops we have, and we keep a record of their type faces, so we know where to go if something seditious or libelous appears in print. Actually, there are no public print shops in England."

"You're not forgetting about the Puritans, are you?" William asked with a grin, bouncing lightly on the coach seat.

"Hardly," Malachi laughed. "Not public at all, but only too private. Their published tirades against Anglican clerics have been a real thorn in Walsingham's side for over a year now—even though he himself is a Puritan—and he lets his underlings feel his displeasure often enough. He thinks we should have been able to track them down long ago, and he's probably right about that. Every press takes large amounts of paper and ink."

"Can't we check things like that?"

"Yes, we can. The quantities required are unusual enough that they can easily be traced. That's the way we knocked off the Seminarian's paper a few years back, but this time the merchants who sell those supplies are not reporting any unusual sales. We suspect the Puritans continue to confuse us by moving the press around to different areas and purchasing supplies piece-meal at many different locations. Despite their posture of rigid rectitude and sanctimonious solicitude, it appears in the end that the Puritans are really tricky bastards like the rest of us."

"Could one wagon hold a printing press?"

"Maybe. Miniaturization has probably reached the point where one press could just about fit in one wagon," said Malachi. "Easily concealed too by covering the load to protect it from the rain. It would be heavy, of course, but so is most freight. To catch them, we would have to stumble on them or else get some informer inside. How do you look in black?"

"I could dress like a Puritan, I suppose, but black is not my best color, and I'm afraid I would not fit well into any group which looks with disfavor on pleasure. How long do we expect to stay with Montaigne? Should I unpack the bags?"

Malachi shrugged. "No telling beforehand. Overnight or a few days, depending on Montaigne. If he personally greets us at the front door, it means the flag is up for company. If his man directs us to the back door, however, it means we should bother him as little as possible. I still have my own errand to complete, but you have no assignment until next week in Paris, so it would be a real educational opportunity for you if we happen to catch him in a convivial mood."

"I'm certainly looking forward to getting off the road for a few days, or more exactly off my bums. I think perhaps a saddle is preferable to a coach."

"Now, William, pay attention. I want you to try very hard to be civil should Montaigne invite us to stay. He runs a very informal household once you are in the front door, and guests are left pretty much on their own during the day. Montaigne loves to chat with them in the evening, however, especially about his own writing, and there is much to be learned if an ambitious beginner keeps a respectful ear open. I hope I can count on you to be a good audience."

"I love the loose-host arrangement," William said as he stretched and yawned deeply. "It will give me a chance to catch up on my sleep. Has Montaigne no wife then?"

"He does, yes, and at least one child, though several have died young. I have never met Madam. How much of his book did you read?"

"I spot-read it. First essay, last essay, middle essay. I like to get the feel of the thing before I spend too much time on it."

"How did it feel?"

"It revealed to me an interesting man, very candid and of broad interest, but a trifle skeptical. He also seems to have a real problem sticking to the subject."

"Please withhold such critiques until we are well in the door, seated at the fire, sipping a glass of Madeira and ready to confront the inanities of the world."

"I'll do my best."

Chapter 2:
MONTAIGNE'S ESSAYS

At the Chateau:

They soon arrived at the Chateau de Montaigne, thirty miles east of Bordeau, and were greeted at the front door by the owner himself, a full-faced, balding gentleman of less than middle height, dressed in a silk houserobe. He extended a warm handshake to Malachi. "Bienvenue, mon ami! It has been a long time since last you visited me."

"Indeed, Michel. You have become a famous author since then," said Malachi warmly. "I hope we find you and your wife and daughter well."

"Mon'sir Montaigne," said William, stepping forward, "I'd recognize you anywhere from your book."

Montaigne stared at him for a moment, then smiled. *"Everyone recognizes me in my book, and my book in me."* [1]

"Only a great writer could say such a thing," said William politely. Malachi grinned, waiting.

Montaigne shook his head. *"In truth, the good authors humble me and dishearten me too much. I am inclined to do the trick of that painter who, after painting a miserable picture of some cocks, forbade his boys to let any real cock come into his shop."*

"Your writing is full of just that sort of reference," William exclaimed. "You must read a great deal, but how do you keep all those references straight?"

"I write at home," confided Montaigne. "[Here] *in a backward region, where no one helps me or corrects me, where I usually have no contact with any man who understands the Latin of his*

Paternoster. I would indeed correct an accidental error, and I am full of them, since I run on carelessly. But the imperfections that are ordinary and constant in me it would be treachery to remove."

"So you have nobody close at hand to help you with the tedious chore of close editing?"

Montagne laughed heartily. *"I have been told, or have told myself: 'You are too thick in figures of speech. Here is a word of Gascon vintage. Here is a dangerous phrase.' (I do not avoid any of those that are used in the streets of France: Those who would combat usage with grammar make fools of themselves.) 'This is ignorant reasoning. This is paradoxical reasoning. This one is too mad. You are often playful; people will think you are speaking in earnest when you are making believe.' 'Yes,' I say, 'but I correct the faults of inadvertence, not those of habit. Isn't this the way I speak everywhere? Don't I represent myself to the life?"*

At last Malachi interrupted. "It is very agreeable, my friend, to discuss these things here with you in the open dooorway, but you are not dressed for the chill of the outdoors as we two are. Perhaps—"

"Malachi, mon ami, you know my judgment keeps me indeed from kicking and grumbling against the discomforts that nature orders me to suffer, but not from feeling them. *I who have no other aim but to live and be merry, would run from one end of the earth to the other to seek out one good year of pleasant and cheerful tranquility. A somber, dull tranquility is easy enough to find for me, but it puts me to sleep and stupefies me; I am not content with it. If there be any persons, any good company, in country or city, in France or elsewhere, residing or traveling, who like my humors and whose humors I like, they have only to whistle in their palm and I will go furnish them with essays in flesh and bone."*

William whistled into his palm.

"Bon! Bon!" laughed Montaigne. "Oui, entre vous! Come in! I'm afraid I run on carelessly at times. Hospitality first, toujour!" He led them inside, holding Malachi's arm affectionately. "Come in by the fire, s'il vous plait. Quelle pleasure, mon ami, to see you."

The two older men exchanged pleasantries, recalling when they had last been together and the main events of the time, while William looked at the book titles on the library shelves.

"Well, old friend," said Malachi at last, draining his glass of wine, "before we settle into more friendly chit-chat, I have some small business in the neighborhood to attend to. If you'll excuse me for an hour, my youthful companion here has much to learn from us old dogs, if we can bring ourselves to confide in him."

"Certainment, ami," Montaigne assured him. "Your man here seems a very lively fellow. We will entertain each other well, n'est-ce pas?" He jumped up as Malachi bowed himself out.

"Mon'sir," said William as Montaigne returned to his place, "I find it very interesting that you should be a pioneer in the literary field with your essays."

"Oui, it seems an obvious form, does it not, for sharing thoughts and insights? I have experimented with it for many years: a letter, as it were; addressed to every man. *I have recently turned fifty-six,*" he confided puckishly, *"six years beyond the age which some nations, not without cause, had prescribed as such a just limit of life that they allowed none to exceed it."* [2]

"A bit precipitous, I would think," said William. "You seem very fit, not in any way near your "limit of life."

"Oui, *I still have flashes of recovery so clear, though inconstant and brief, that they fall little short of my youthful health and freedom from pain.*"

"I sometime have streaks like that myself," William confided. "They certainly perk up my tennis game."

"I am not speaking of vigor and sprightliness; it is not reasonable that they should follow me beyond their limits. My face immediately betrays me, and my eyes; all my changes begin there, and seem a little worse than they really are. I often move my friends to pity before I feel the reason for it. My mirror does not alarm me, for even in my youth I have more than once found myself thus wearing a muddy complexion and an ill-omened look, without any serious consequences; so that the doctors, finding inside me no cause responsible for this outward change, attributed it to the spirit and to some secret passion gnawing me within. They were wrong. My body is often depressed; whereas if my soul is not jolly, it is at least tranquil and at rest."

"Sounds like healing-by-faith to me," William said; "but faith always has its zigs and zags. You must surely have had some experience with real sickness?"

Montaigne nodded. *"Oh oui, I had a quartan fever for four or five months, which quite disfigured me; my mind still kept going not only peacefully but cheerfully. If the pain is outside of me, the weakness and the languor do not distress me much. I know several bodily infirmities that inspire horror if you merely name them, which I should fear less than a thousand passions and agitations of the spirit that I see prevalent. I have made up my mind to my inability to run anymore; it is enough that I crawl. Nor do I complain of the natural decay that has hold of me—anymore than I regret that my turn of life is not as long and sound as that of an oak. Is that you knocking, jeune Guilliam?"*

"I'm just knocking on wood that you'll be able to keep on crawling for a long time to come."

"Merci," said Montaigne. "You are most thoughtful."

"I find your reference to having a jolly, tranquil soul very refreshing," William said, "but my stop-and-go, here-and-there kind of job offers me no opportunity for the time and repose necessary to cultivate such a desirable soul-set. I have to twist my imagination cruelly out of shape to even begin to picture the happy circumstances which permit you such a comfortable outlook."

"I treat my imagination as gently as I can," Montaigne sighed, *"and would relieve it if I could, of all trouble and conflict. We must help it and flatter it, and fool it if we can. My mind*

is suited to this service; it has no lack of plausible reasons for all things. If it could persuade as well as it preaches, it would help me out very happily. Would you like an example?" [3]

"Well, actually, I'd like to stick with your treatment—or should I say mistreatment—of your imagination since it interests me very much."

Montaigne's voice took on an edge. "I hope you do not intend to make a habit of interrupting the flow of my thoughts, young man."

William shrugged apologetically but murmured, "This seems rough treatment for a guest who simply wants to inquire about how you treat your imagination."

"Mais oui," Montaigne admitted, his buoyancy returning. "I can't have a guest complain of the treatment he receives in my house, so as your conscientious host, I agree that when there is a difference over the agenda, I will naturally give way to whatever is best for my guest whether he knows it or not, and, on that principle, I will proceed with my example, if you don't mind."

"In that case, I'll be happy to hear it," said William while he poured himself another glass of wine.

"S'il vous plait, have another drop of the wine," exclaimed Montaigne softly. "I was explaining, you may recall, *how my imagination helps me out in life. It tells me that it is for my own good that I have the stone; that buildings of my age must naturally suffer some leakage. It is time for them to begin to grow loose and give way.*"

"I've heard of the 'stone'. Very painful kidney condition, they say."

Montaigne nodded, *"It's the commonest ailment of men of my time of life. On all sides I see them afflicted with the same type of disease, and their society is honorable for me, since it preferably attacks the great; it is essentially noble and dignified—That of the men who are striken by it there are few that get off more cheaply; and at that, they pay the penalty of an unpleasant diet and daily doses of loathsome medicinal drugs, whereas I am indebted solely to my good fortune.....The others have to pay a thousand vows to Aesculapius, and as many crowns to their doctor, for the easy and abundant outflow of gravel which I often get through the kindness of nature. Even the propriety of my behavior in ordinary company is not disturbed by it, and I can hold my water ten hours and as long as anyone."*

"But why should you?" asked William.

"Why should I what?"

"Have to fool your imagination. Isn't it always on your side to begin with? Doesn't it always stand ready to soften life's little bumps for you?"

"You're very lucky, young man, if that's the way yours works," Montaigne laughed somewhat bitterly. "I'm afraid that many educated people have imaginations so fettered with conscience that they may not let themselves off as slyly as you do. *If you suffer from the stone as I do, you would soon come to realize the fear and pity that people feel for this illness is a subject of vainglory for you. There is pleasure in hearing people say about you: There indeed is strength, there indeed is fortitude! They see you sweat in agony, turn pale, turn red, tremble, vomit your very blood, suffer strange contractions and convulsions, sometimes shed great tears from your eyes, discharge thick, black, and frightful urine, or have it stopped up by some sharp rough stone that cruelly picks and flays the neck of your penis—"* [4]

"You seem to have some very understanding friends," William acknowledged, "or perhaps some who are easily entertained."

Montaigne nodded. *"—meanwhile keeping up conversation with your company with a normal countenance, jesting in the intervals with your servants, holding up your end in a sustained discussion, making excuses for your pain and minimizing your suffering."*

"Oh well, as you say, as long as the propriety of the moment is not shattered by.... ahh...all that other stuff happening. It serves to remind me that Malachi has often warned me there is much more going on in each social scene than I seem to be aware of."

Montaigne laughed. "You're not alone there. Courtly parties I've attended have always seemed to me mystifications wrapped in perplexities, doused in dilemmas, and obscured by bewilderment and confusion, but I'll confess, you can't beat the service."

"I don't know anything more about social occasions at that level than I do about the man in the moon," William admitted.

Montaigne cleared his throat. *"There is a certain type of subtle humility that is born of presumption, like this one: that we acknowledge our ignorance in many things, and are so courteous as to admit that there are in the works of nature certain qualities and conditions that are imperceptible to us and whose means and causes our capacity cannot discover. By this honest and conscientious declaration we hope to gain credence also about those things that we claim to understand."* [5]

"I don't boast often of my understanding," William admitted. "I'm reluctant to do so partially because of my recent head wound, but also because my job has confronted me with many strange and miraculous happenings, both at home and abroad. I would be extremely hard-put to select the most puzzling."

Chapter 3:
THE SEED OF LIFE

Same location:

"We have no need to go picking out miracles and remote difficulties; it seems to me that amongst the things we see ordinarily there are wonders so incomprehensible that they surpass even miracles in obscurity." [6]

"You have something in mind, I perceive."

"Mais, oui," Montaigne replied. *"What a prodigy it is that the drop of seed from which we are produced bears in itself the impressions not only of the bodily form but of the thoughts and inclinations of our fathers! Where does that drop of fluid lodge this infinite number of forms? And how do they convey these resemblances with so heedless and irregular a course that the great-grandson will correspond to his great-grandfather, the nephew to the uncle?"*

"I've never given that side of love-making much thought."

Montaigne smiled. *"Speaking of the stone, 'It is probable that I owe this strong propensity to my father, for he died extraordinarily afflicted with a large stone he had in his bladder. He did not perceive his disease until his sixty-seventh year, and before that he had had no threat or symptom of it, in his loins, his sides, or elsewhere. And he had lived until then in a happy state of health, and very little subject to diseases; and he lasted seven years more with this ailment, painfully dragging out the last years of his life. I was born twenty-five years and more before his illness, at a time when he enjoyed his best health, the third of his children in order of birth."*

"But you inherited his ailment anyway."

Montaigne nodded. *"Where was the propensity to this infirmity hatching all this time? And when he was so far from the ailment, how did this slight bit of his substance, with which he made me, bear so great an impression of it for its share? And moreover, how did it remain so concealed that I began to feel it forty-five years later, the only one to this hour out of so many brothers and sisters, and all of the same mother? If anyone will enlighten me about this process, I will believe him about as many other miracles as he wants; providing he does not palm off on me some explanation much more difficult and fantastic than the thing itself."*

"What do all the others say?" William asked.

"What others?"

"Socrates and Plato and all those old-timers you quote so often in your essays. They must have given such a serious matter some thought. What do they say?"

Montaigne laughed. "They had to work without the benefit of modern medicine remember, but *Pythagoras says that our seed is the foam of our best blood. Plato, the flow from the marrow of the backbone, which he argues from the fact that this spot first feels the fatigue of the business. Alcmaeon, a part of the substance of the brain; and a sign that this is so, he says, is that the eyes grow dim in those who work immoderately at this exercise. Democritus, a substance extracted from the whole mass of the body; Epicurus, extracted from the soul and the body. Aristotle, an excrement derived from the nourishment of the blood, the last that spreads through our members. Others, blood cooked and digested by the heat of the genitals, which they judge from the fact that in extreme efforts men give out drops of pure blood."*

William winced. "Does that mean it's safe to frolic until then?"

Montaigne scowled at him, and William turned to a new topic. "I understand you know the King of Navarre personally. Is it true——"

Montaigne interrupted. "Would you like to learn what is said to be the woman's part in this process?"

"Yes, indeed." William said. "Please go on."

"Aristotle and Democritus maintain that women have no sperm, and that it is only a sweat that they discharge in the heat of the pleasure and the movement, which contributes nothing toward generation; Galen and his followers, on the contrary, that without the meeting of the seeds, generation cannot take place."

"So there's no concurrence even among our deepest thinkers?"

"C'est vrai. *Here we see the doctors, the philosophers, the jurists, and the theologians at grips with our wives, pell-mell, in the dispute over how long women carry their fruit, and myself, I back up, with my own example, those of them who maintain the possibility of an eleven months' pregnancy. The world is built of this experience; there is no little woman so simple that she may not have her say about all these contested matters; and still we cannot come to an agreement."*

"A lot of simple women say nine months," said William.

"Few women have a head for numbers," said Montaigne, dismissing the subject. He rose to pour more wine.

"I couldn't help noticing, Mon'sir," said William seeking another subject, "that your family name is the same as the name of your estate: Montaigne. You must be very proud of passing on the family name in that manner."

"...it is a base practice, and of very bad consequence in our France, to call everyone by the name of his land and lordship; nothing in the world causes more confusion and misconceptions about families. A younger son of good family cannot honorably abandon an estate that has been settled on him and by whose name he has been known and honored. Ten years after his death the estate goes to a stranger, who does the same thing with it: guess where this leaves us when it comes to knowing who these men are?" [7]

"Do you fear some future Montaigne may sully the name?"

Montaigne ignored him. *"We need seek no other examples than those of our own royal family: so many divisions, so many surnames; meanwhile the original of the stock has escaped us. There is so much liberty in these mutations that in my time I have not seen anyone elevated by fortune to any extraordinary greatness who has not promptly taken on new genealogical titles not known to his father, and been grafted into some illustrious stock. And, by good luck, the most obscure families are the best suited to falsification. How many gentlemen have we in France who are of royal blood by their account? More, I believe, than the others."*

"We have much the same thing in England," William admitted. "No sooner does a man have a good year or two in sales, than he solicits the services of what Malachi calls 'Heralds-for-hire' to produce a coat of arms for him."

Montaigne shook his head sadly. *"Coats of arms have no more security than surnames. I have azure powdered with trefoils or, with a lion's paw of the same, armed gules in fesse. What privilege has this design to remain privately in my house? A son-in-law will transport it into another family; some paltry buyer will make it his first coat of arms; there is nothing in which more change and confusion is found."*

William sighed deeply. "Believe me, I know a great deal about the confusion of names since I'm having so much trouble finding my own."

Montaigne shrugged, "We make much too much of names. After all, *how many people are there in every family with the same name and surname? And in different families, centuries and countries, how many? History has known three Socrateses, five Platos, eight Aristotles, seven Xenophons, twenty Demetriuses, twenty Theodores; and just guess how many it has not known?"* In the final analysis, *what prevents my groom from calling himself Pompey the Great?"*

"I must admit a groom so named would really stick in my memory."

Montaigne laughed softly. "An aid to memory, bon! I need it. *The more I distrust my memory, the more confused it becomes. It serves me better by chance encounter; I have to solicit it nonchalantly. For if I press it, it is stunned; and once it has begun to totter, the more I probe it, the more it gets mixed up and embarrassed. It serves me at its own time, not at mine .And if I were to live a long time, I do not doubt that I would forget my own name, as others have done."* [8]

"You don't have to tell me," William groaned.

"Alors, ami. You are not alone. *Messala Corvinus was two years without any trace of memory, and this is also said of George of Trebizond. And in my own interest I often ruminate about what sort of a life theirs was, and whether without this faculty I shall have enough left to support me with any comfort; and looking at it closely, I fear that this defect, if it is absolute, ruins all the functions of the mind. 'It is certain that the memory is the only receptacle, not only of philosophy, but of all that concerns the conduct of life, and of all the arts', as Cicero writes."*

"I can only hope my loss is neither absolute nor permanent," said William.

"It has happened more than once that I have forgotten the watch-word that I had given three hours before, or received from another, and forgotten where I had hidden my purse, in spite of what Cicero says about that."

"What does he say?"

"I forget," said Montaigne, scratching his head. *"And I am so good at forgetting that I forget even my own writings and compositions no less than the rest. People are all the time quoting me to myself without my knowing it."*

"Without attribution?" William inquired with a knowing smile. "That's certainly unscholarly if nothing worse. What is the Montaigne House policy on giving credit to others in print?"

Montaigne laughed heartily. *"Anyone who would like to know the sources of the verses and examples I have piled up here would put me to a great deal of trouble to tell them...I leaf through books, I do not study them. What I retain of them is something I no longer recognize as anyone else's. It is only the material from which my judgment has profited, and the thoughts and ideas with which it has become imbued; the author, the place, the words, and other circumstances, I immediately forget."* [9]

"Most convenient," William observed.

"And yet I have begged them only at well-known and famous doors, not content with their being rich unless they also came from rich and honorable hands; in them authority and reason concur."

"All the more reason they should receive mention," William insisted. "How would you like it if your book were permitted to slide into oblivion like that?"

"It is no great wonder if my book follows the fate of other books, and if my memory lets go of what I write as of what I read, and of what I give as of what I receive."

"Don't the French schools teach you how to footnote?"

"In my present mood, I see all of that as trivia for scholars to mull over," Montaigne chuckled. "A man's words should ring out as his own without any label."

"They might well do so if one could fit his ideas to some memorable metrical pattern in order to write something other than straight prose," said William. "That's what I have in mind, once I start."

Malachi entered the room in time to hear the exchange. "No time like the present," he said. "Let's hear some of whatever it is you have in mind."

"C'est vrai," Montaigne said, leaping up to usher Malachi to his waiting chair. "Any young man who entertains the remotest possibility of doing some memorable writing in the future, should certainly seize the present moment to exhibit a certain original-ity in his ordinary conversation, n'est-ce pas?"

"Originality, you want, eh?" William said. "Let me ask you, Mon'sir, how often you borrow from other writers for your own works?"

Montaigne laughed with delight. *"Let people see in what I borrow whether I have known how to choose what would enhance my theme. For I make others say what I cannot say so well now through the weakness of my language, now through the weakness of my understanding. I do not count my borrowings, I weigh them. And if I had wanted to have them valued by their number, I should have loaded myself with twice as many. They are all, or nearly all, from such famous and ancient names that they seem to identify themselves without me."*

"As it happens, I don't recognize any of them," William grumbled.

"Small wonder," Montaigne grinned, "English schools being what they are. Nev-ertheless; *"In the reasonings and inventions that I transplant into my soil and confound with my own, I have sometimes deliberately not indicated the author, in order to hold in check the temerity of those hasty condemnations that are tossed at all sorts of writings, notably recent writings of men still living, and in the vulgar tongue, which invites everyone to talk about them and seems to convict the conception and design of being likewise vulgar. I want them to give Plutarch a fillip on my nose and get burned insulting Seneca in me. I have to hide my weakness under these great authorities."*

"Doesn't that approach open the door to a bit of plagiarism if you indiscriminately mix together your lesser writings with their better ones and count on your reader to pick one from the other?"

"For this I am obliged to be responsible," Montaigne acknowledged, *"if I get myself tangled up, if there is vanity and faultiness in my reasonings that I do not perceive."*

"That's exactly what I have frequently told him," Malachi said, smoothing ruffled feathers. "William's judgment seems to question every effort made to guide it along sensible paths, and he ends up completely bereft of the benchmarks of sound thinking which he should have picked up long ago."

"What do I know?" William shrugged. "With my handicap, I really can't be ex-pected to be knowledgeable about everything overnight."

"Before you trot out your excuses—" Malachi began, but Montaigne halted him with a raised hand.

"Knowledge and truth can lodge in us without judgment, and judgment also without them; indeed the recognition of ignorance is one of the fairest and surest testimonials of judgment that I find" [10]

"Thank you," William said.

"I have no doubt that I often happen to speak of things that are better treated by the masters of the craft, and more truthfully....Whoever is in search of knowledge let him fish for it where it dwells; There is nothing I profess less. These—" he paused to tap his manuscript— *"are my*

fancies, by which I try to give knowledge not of things, but of myself. And if I am a man of some reading, I am a man of no retentiveness."

"You need an editor or a keeper or somebody to organize things for you when it's time to give credit," William insisted.

Montaigne sighed happily. *"I have no other marshal but fortune to arrange my bits. As my fancies present themselves, I pile them up; now they come pressing in a crowd, now dragging single file. I want people to see my natural and ordinary pace, however off the track it is. I let myself go as I am."* [11]

"But it really wouldn't be too much trouble for you to keep a file of some sort," William suggested.

"I should certainly like to have a more perfect knowledge of things," Montaigne admitted genially, *"but I do not want to buy it as dear as it costs. My intention is to pass pleasantly, and not laboriously, what life I have left. There is nothing for which I want to rack my brain, not even knowledge, however great its value."*

This admission was followed by a period of thoughtful silence, broken finally by William. "If knowledge is not your object in reading, I wonder what is."

"I seek in books only to give myself pleasure by honest amusement; or if I study, I seek only the learning that treats of the knowledge of myself and instructs me in how to die well and live well. 'This is the goal toward which my sweating horse should strain,' as Propertius writes."

"Do you ever just quit reading a book in the middle?" William asked.

"If I encounter difficulties in reading, I do not gnaw my nails over them; I leave them there, after making one or two attacks on them. If I planted myself in them, I would lose both myself and time; for I have an impulsive mind. What I do not see at the first attack, I see less by persisting. I do nothing without gaiety; continuation and too strong contention dazes, depresses, and wearies my judgment. My sight becomes confused and dispersed. I do not take much to modern books, because the ancient ones seem to me fuller and stronger; nor to those in Greek because my judgment cannot do its work with a childish and apprentice understanding."

"I know just what you mean," Malachi grinned.

"Among the books that are simply entertaining, I find, of the moderns, the Decameron *of Boccoccio, Rabelais, and* The Kisses *of Johannes Secundus, if they may be placed under this heading, worth reading for amusement."* [12]

"That's exactly what I say to my friends," William agreed.

"I will also say this——" Montaigne's twinkling eyes rested on William, *"if I may— that this heavy old soul of mine no longer lets itself be tickled, not merely by Ariosto, but even by the good Ovid; his facility and inventions, which once enchanted me, hardly entertain me at all now."*

"Is Ovid the one people say is really..ah...graphic?" William asked.

"I wouldn't be surprised," Malachi said. "He writes freely and enthusiastically of human love-making."

Chapter 4:
ENCHANT WITH ELEGANCE OR
BAFFLE WITH BOCCACCIO

Same location:

Montaigne continues, "*It has often struck my mind how in our time those who set them-selves to write comedies—like the Italians, who are rather happy at it—use three or four plots from Terence or Plautus to make one of their own. They pile up in a single comedy five or six stories from Boccaccio.*"

"That seems like a waste of raw materials if you're thinking in terms of long term literary production." William said. "Why are they so inefficient?"

"*What makes them so load themselves with material is the distrust they have of being able to sustain themselves by their own graces; they have to find a body to lean on; and not having enough of their own to entertain us, they want the story to amuse us. It is quite the contrary with my [ideal] author; the perfections and beauty of his style of expression make us lose our appetite for his subject. His distinction and elegance hold us throughout; he is everywhere so delightful— 'Clear flowing and most like a crystal stream,' writes Horace—and so fills our soul with his charms, that we forget those of his plot.*"

"If you can't enchant them with elegance, baffle them with Boccaccio, eh?" snick-ered William.

"C'est vrai," Montaigne chuckled. "That is how the minor writers work."

"But is it accepted procedure for a writer to operate in that fashion?"

Montaigne lifted his shoulders in a Gallic shrug. "It is tolerated but not ad-mired."

"But if a man threw in a little verse to cloak the borrowings, perhaps—" William mused. "There's no telling just how far—you say Boccaccio is a good source for plots?"

"The best," Montaigne nodded. "I often wish he could furnish France with a fictional plot to show her a way out of her troubles."

"Yes, hmm, if France could be the lady with three lovers—"

"At this point," Montaigne said sadly, "one of those lovers would have to be a miracle worker. After so many years of bitter killing, there is a mounting chorus of ancestral voices crying out for revenge from every graveyard in France. Peut-etre, Henry of Navarre could be that miracle-working lover, who could rescue Lady France and stop the villainous partisan killing. He would need the support of every French subject, of course, but they are tired of thirty years of internal bleeding and need only the rallying cry of a hero such as Navarre, and a clear code of values. Lady France is in the same position that Plato mentioned in the Republic: '*I wonder if we could contrive… some noble lie that would in itself carry conviction to our whole community'.*" [13]

"And I presume you have that noble lie in mind, old friend," said Malachi.

Montaigne's eyes twinkled. "Alors, Navarre recently confessed that Paris might be worth a mass after all, so I wouldn't be too surprised if we did get our noble lie, but I don't know when, mon ami, if that's what you're fishing for."

William waited as the silence lengthened between the two, then ventured. "All writers seem to follow down the same creative paths generally. How close do you think a writer should permit himself to follow his artistic patrons before he is actually copying them?"

"*Let him know that he knows, at least. He must imbibe their ways of thinking , not learn their precepts,*" Montaigne smiled. "*And let him boldly forget, if he wants, where he got them, but let him know how to make them his own. Truth and reason are common to everyone, and no more belong to the man who first spoke them than to the man who says them later. It is no more according to Plato than according to me, since he and I understand and see it in the same way. The bees plunder the flowers here and there, but afterward they make of them honey, which is all theirs; it is no longer thyme or marjoram. Even so with the pieces borrowed from others; he will transform and blend them to make a work that is all his own, to wit, his judgment. His education, work, and study aim only at forming this.*" [14]

"But at some point," William insisted, "isn't the successful borrower obliged to his fellow-artists to publicly reveal the assistance he accepted along the way?"

"*Let him hide all the help he has had, and show only what he has made of it. The pillagers, the borrowers, parade their buildings, their purchases, not what they got from others. You do not see the gratuities of a member of Parliament, you see the alliances he has gained and the honors for his children. No one makes public his receipts; everyone makes public his acquisitions.*"

"Egad," William exclaimed, "if we add hiding of receipts to your earlier instruction of boldly forgetting your sources, you have created an ambiance in which a writer could really roll up his doublet and do some significant work—if only a situation could be arranged to sustain him while he creates."

Montaigne shook his head. "Don't waste your time worrying about situations because they don't matter. They change."

"What does matter then?"

"It is the understanding, Epicharmus used to say, that sees and hears; it is the understanding that makes profit of everything, that arranges everything, that acts, dominates, and reigns; all other things are blind, deaf, and soulless. Truly we make it servile and cowardly, by leaving it no freedom to do anything by itself. Who ever asks his pupil what he thinks of rhetoric or grammar, or of such-and-such a saying of Cicero: They slap them into our memory with all the feathers on, like oracles in which the letters and syllables are the substance of the matter."

"Assuming such learning is for our own good," William ventured.

"C'est vrai," Montaigne nodded. *"To know by heart is not to know; it is to retain what we have given our memory to keep. What we know rightly we dispose, without looking at the model, without turning our eyes toward our book. Sad competence, a purely bookish competence."*

"Are you suggesting that we change our approach to education?"

"Certainment!" Montaigne exclaimed. *"Our tutors never stop bawling into our ears, as though they were pouring water into a funnel; and our task is only to repeat what has been told to us. I should like the tutor to correct this practice, and right from the start, according to the capacity of the mind he has in hand, to begin putting it through its paces, making it taste things, choose them, and discern them by itself; sometimes clearing the way for him, sometimes letting him clear his own way. I don't want him to think and talk alone, I want him to listen to his pupil speaking in his turn. Socrates, and later Arcesilaus, first had their disciples speak, and then they spoke to them. 'The authority of those who teach is often an obstacle to those who want to learn.' writes Cicero."* [15]

"You contend, then, that we learn best by doing?"

Montaigne nodded: *"I wish Paluel or Pompey, those fine dancers of my time, could teach us capers just by performing them before us and without moving us from our seats, as those people want to train our understanding without setting it in motion; or that we could be taught to handle a horse, or a pike, or a lute, or our voice without practicing at it, as those people want to teach us to judge well and to speak well, without having us practice either speaking or judging."*

"That's exactly what I am forever hinting to Malachi," William confided.

"Which part do you hint at?" Montaigne inquired politely.

"Well, during my bond period, you see, I am kept so busy that I never get consulted on any of the decision making. How can I form a judgment unless I'm permitted to sit in on policy considerations, and how can I be expected to learn anything if

I am kept scurrying about endlessly on minor errands and am offered no leisure time for serious study?"

"You are not looking at your job properly," Montaigne advised him pleasantly. *"For this apprenticeship, everything that comes to our eyes is book enough; a page's prank, a servant's blunder, a remark at table, are so many new materials."*

"Or a drunken porter or a grasping money-lender?"

"I think you are beginning to get the idea," Montaigne laughed.

"Or ungrateful children or jealous generals?"

"Essentially, that's it, yes, but let me go further. I don't think we ought to try to teach children anything they can't learn standing up."

William chuckled, "That would certainly turn the educational world on its ear, but wouldn't it play hob with things like toilet-training?"

Montaigne looked at him quizically, "You have learned well the art of playing the vulgar lout," he laughed.

"I like a bit of comedy to relieve the intensity of serious talk," William said. "So, Mon'sir Montaigne, perhaps you could suggest which writer can increase my knowledge of important matters quickest and teach me the easiest way to write well in the shortest time. When people are caught up in my particular circumstances through injury, to whom should they turn for a quick starting point? Where should they go to find intelligent instruction?"

"I'd try Plutarch first if I were you," Montaigne advised. *"He is so universal and so full that on all occasions, and however eccentric the subject you have taken up, he makes his way into your work and offers you a liberal hand, inexhaustible in riches and embellishments. Just to see him pick out a trivial action in a man's life, or a word which seems unimportant: that is a treatise in itself. It is a pity that men of understanding are so fond of brevity; doubtless their reputation gains by it, but we lose by it. Plutarch would rather we praised him for his judgment than for his knowledge; he would rather leave us wanting more of him than satiated. He knew that even of good things one may say too much.'* Why Do such matters interest you?"

"You may have forgotten, Mon'sir, but I plan to do a little writing myself as soon as I fill my reservoir of experience and settle down. And find a worthwhile subject, of course."

Montaigne winced as though attacked by a small insect. "I'm sure the world can hardly wait for all your requirements to be favorably fashioned; nevertheless, *wonderful brilliance may be gained for human judgment by getting to know men. We are all huddled and concentrated in ourselves, and our vision is reduced to the end of our nose. Socrates was asked where he was from. He replied not 'Athens', but 'The World'. He, whose imagination was fuller and more extensive, embraced the universe as his city, and distributed his knowledge, his company, and his affections to all mankind, unlike us who look only at what is underfoot. When the vines freeze in my village, my priest infers that the wrath of God is upon the human race*

...Seeing our civil wars, who does not cry out that this mechanism is being turned topsy-turvy and that the judgment day has us by the throat, without reflecting that many worse things have happened, and that ten thousand parts of the world, to our one, are meanwhile having a gay time."

"What do you think would be the effect if we could all somehow share each other's misery on a daily basis?" William mused.

"How do you mean?"

"You know, if somebody developed a carrier-pigeon postal service for the whole country as Darius did for the Persians, or somebody came up with a breed of horse that could gallop across France in a few hours, so we could all hear of the day's late news each evening before we went to bed?"

"The daily news from all over France?" Montaigne cried. "You'd go stark raving mad in a month. You'd become convinced evil ruled the world. You'd board up your house and never go out. *Pourquoi?*"

"Just curious. I'm always amazed to hear of bloody wars being won or lost in far-off places—like here in France—while I wasn't even aware they were going on, and then I wonder if I am better off not hearing of them."

"Myself, considering their licentiousness and impunity, I am amazed to see our wars so gentle and mild. When the hail comes down on a man's head, it seems to him that the whole hemisphere is in tempest and storm. And a Savoyard said that if that fool of a French king had known how to play his cards right, he would have had it in him to become chief steward to the Duke of Savoy. His imagination conceived no higher dignity than that of his master. We are all unconsciously in this error of great consequence and harm. But whoever considers as in a painting the great picture of our mother Nature in her full majesty; whoever reads such universal and constant variety in her face; whoever finds himself there and not merely himself, but a whole kingdom, as a dot made with a very fine brush; that man alone estimates things according to their true proportions."

"That's exactly what I'm going to show," exclaimed William, "when I really get into my writing mode."

"Which part?" Montaigne inquired.

"All of it."

"Bon chance."

Chapter 5:
OLD WORLD PARALLELS
WITH THE NEW WORLD

Same location:

William chuckled, "Oh, I know well enough there are limits—I'm not completely naïve'—but I believe one must set his sights well above any fetters because, after all, there have always been limits. They come as a badge of the species."

"C'est vrai," Montaigne laughed, "and some of our most-revered limits have not stood up well to the great grinder of passing time."

"Time, eh? I thought real limits were imposed by nature?"

"Perhaps they are," Montaigne said, "if only we could perceive them. The truth is we have not quite outgrown a tendency to put limits on ourselves through our false assumptions about natural things."

"For example?"

"Europe has spent over a thousand years genuflecting to the cosmic view of a Greco-Egyptian astronomer and mathematician who died about 150 AD," Montaigne explained, "and we didn't learn until a few years ago that he had neglected to include half the world in his geographical boundaries of our Earth."

"The New World!"

"Right," said Montaigne. "*Ptolemy, who was a great man, had established the limits of our world; all the ancient philosophers thought they had its measure, except for a few remote islands that might escape their knowledge....Behold in our century an infinite extent of terra firma, not an island or one particular country, but a portion nearly equal in size to the one we know, which* has just been discovered. The geographers of the present time do not fail to assure us that now all is discovered and all is seen. The question is if Ptolmy was once mistaken on the grounds of his reason, whether it would not be stupid for me now to trust to what these people say about it; and whether it is not more likely that this great body that we call the world is something quite different from what we judge." [16]

"Well, with Captain Drake and others traveling about—"

"Plato holds that it changes its aspect in all regards: that the sky, the stars, and the sun at times reverse the movement that we see in them, changing east to west. The Egyptian priests told Herodotus that since their first king, who lived eleven thousand and so many years before (and of all their kings they showed him effigies in the form of statues sculptured from life), the sun had four times changed its course; that the sea and the land change alternately into one another; that the birth of the world is undetermined. Aristotle, Cicero, say the same."

"It all sounds very thoughtful," William observed.

"In the most famous of the Greek schools, the world is held to be a god made by another, greater god, and is composed of a body and a soul that dwells in the center of it, spreading by musical numbers to its circumference; divine, very happy, very great, very wise, eternal. In it are other gods, the earth, the sea, the stars, which entertain each other with a perpetual harmonious agitation and divine dance, now meeting, now separating, hiding, appearing, changing order, now in front and now behind."

"Actually," interrupted Malachi, "many parallels exist in various cultural interpretations of the Deity's design throughout the world."

"Not only in religion," Montaigne said, "but in other areas as well. In truth, considering what has come to our knowledge about the course of this terrestrial government, I have often marveled to see, at a very great distance in time and space, the coincidences between a great number of fabulous popular opinions and savage customs and beliefs, which do not seem from any angle to be connected with our natural reason. The human mind is a great worker of miracles; but this correspondence has something or other about it that is still queerer: it is found also in names, in incidents, and in a thousand other things."

"'A very great distance' could only mean the New World, right?" asked William.

Montaigne nodded. "Nations were found there that never, so far as we know, had heard anything about us, where circumcision, for example, was in credit."

"Well, there is the matter of coincidence as you mentioned," William pointed out, "but one similarity does not a sameness make."

"And this example reminds me of another amusing difference: for whereas there were some nations who like to uncover the end of their member, and cut off the skin in the Mohammedan and Jewish fashion, there were others who had such great scruples about uncovering it that with the help of little cords they wore their skin very carefully stretched and fastened above, for fear that this end might see the air." [17]

William winced. "That's different, all right."

554

"And this difference too, that, whereas we honor kings and festivals by dressing ourselves up in the finest clothes we have, in some regions, to show complete disparity and submission to their king, the subjects presented themselves before him in their vilest clothes, and on entering the palace put some old torn robe over their good one, so that all the brilliance and ornament should be the master's"

Malachi broke in with a chuckle, "That's hardly what Elizabeth would regard as a proper Court."

"That is a difference, oui, but there are other parallels," Montaigne assured him. *"There were states and great governments where our fasts and our Lent were represented with the addition of abstinence from women. Where our crosses were in credit in various ways: here sepulchers were honored with them; there they applied them, and especially the Saint Andrew's cross, to defend themselves from nocturnal visions, and placed them on children's beds against enchantments; elsewhere they found a wooden one, of great height, worshiped as the god of rain, and that very far inland. There they found a very clear likeness of our shriving priests; the use of miters, the celibacy of the priests, the art of divining from entrails of sacrificed animals, abstinence from every kind of flesh and fish in their food; the fashion among the priests of using a special language, and not the vulgar one, when officiating. And this fancy, that the first god was ousted by a second, his younger brother; that they were created with all comforts, and that since, because of their sin, these were cut off from them, their territory was changed, and their natural condition made worse."*

"A direct replay of our Garden of Eden experience," Malachi observed, "with Cain and Able thrown into the mix along with original sin."

"Exactament," Montaigne grinned, "except theirs may have come first."

"Strange indeed," William acknowledged. "These New World societies sound very civilized. How could that be?"

Montaigne grinned. "They also believed that *'they were once submerged by an inundation of waters from heaven; that only a few families escaped, which cast themselves into high mountain caves, which caves they stopped up so that the water did not get in, having shut up many kinds of animals inside; that when they felt the rain stop, they put out some dogs, which having returned clean and wet, they judged that they water had not yet gone down much; later, having sent others out and seeing them come back muddy, they went out to repeople the world, which they found full of nothing but snakes."*

"The Noah story too, eh?" William exclaimed. "And a little of Saint Patrick thrown in. This is getting pretty spooky."

"In one place the Spanish explorers *came across the belief in the day of judgment, so that the people were strangely shocked by the Spaniards for scattering the bones of the dead while searching the tombs for riches, saying that these separated bones could not easily come together again."*

"Strange sparks are struck by competing cultures," Malachi observed. "I suppose there were parallels in everyday life too?

"Almost too numerous to mention." Montaigne said. *"Traffic by exchange, and none other; fairs and markets for that purpose; dwarfs and deformed persons to adorn the tables of princes; the practice of falconry according to the nature of their birds; tyrants' subsidies; refinement in gardening; dances, tumbling; instrumental music; coats of arms; tennis games, games of dice and of chance in which they grow so heated as to stake themselves and their liberty; no medicine other than that of charms; the system of writing in pictures."*

"In pictures?" William gasped.

Montaigne nodded and resumed. *"Belief in a single first man, father of all nations; worship of a god who once lived as a man in perfect virginity, fasting and penitence, preaching the law of nature and religious ceremonies, and who disappeared from the world without a natural death; the belief in giants; the custom of getting drunk on their beverages and of competition in drinking; religious ornaments painted with bones and death's-heads; surplices, holy water, sprinklers; women and servants competing in offering themselves to be burned or buried with the dead husband or master; a law that the eldest succeed to all the property, and no portion is reserved for the younger but obedience."*

"Like our primogeniture," Malachi observed.

William shook his head, "Well beyond the scope of coincidence, I'll warrant," he said, "and yet that series of similarities sets a man to wondering if his own religious faith is lessened or augmented by awareness of how many fundamental characteristics the Christian church shares with the other major religions of the world."

"Don't get confused," Montaigne cautioned him. "In matters of faith it is always best to think very clearly, especially when there are people with swords and stakes roaming the land."

"Easier said than done," William shrugged.

"These empty shadows of our religion that are seen in some of these examples testify to its dignity and divinity. It has insinuated itself to some extent not only into all the infidel nations on this side of the world by some sort of imitation, but also into these barbarous ones as by a common and supernatural inspiration."

"Are you suggesting God himself has inclined them to imitate us?" William asked.

"Who else could do it?" Montaigne shrugged.

"You think he directs them to follow us all the way down the line?"

"No, no. I can only imagine that would bore the Almighty, who seems to require diversity in human endeavor in order to remain interested in our species. They follow for a while and then branch off."

"Branch off?"

"For instance they share our belief in purgatory *...but in a new form; what we ascribe to fire they ascribe to cold, and imagine the souls both purged and punished by the rigor of extreme cold."*

"Well. not much difference there when you consider the possibilities," William mused. "I suppose extreme heat or cold are both quite able to torture and inconvenience us humans."

"I should mention," said Montaigne, "that I have talked to men from the New World, so much of my knowledge of these similarities and differences is first hand."

"Ah, that is a great thing, Mon'sir!" exclaimed William. "We hear much of the European reaction to the New Word people but very little of what the Indians think of us. Can you tell us more?"

"Mais oui! C'est vrai that the impressions of the Indians have been seriously understated in the midst of Europe's loud reaction to them, but we have recorded a few isolated voices. *Three of these men, ignorant of the price they will pay some day, in loss of repose and happiness, for gaining knowledge of the corruptions of this side of the ocean; ignorant also of the fact that of this intercourse will come their ruin—which I suppose is already well advanced; poor wretches, to let themselves be tricked by the desire for new things, and to have left the serenity of their own sky to come and see us!—three of these men were at Rouen, at the time the late King Charles II was there* in 1562 . Charles was eleven at the time." [18]

"It's almost as if our culture served as the Eden-apple of their culture," said Malachi.

Montaigne nodded. *"The King talked to them for a long time; they were shown our ways, our splendor, the aspect of a fine city; after that someone asked their opinion, and wanted to know what they had found most amazing. They mentioned three things, of which I have forgotten the third, and I am very sorry for it."*

"That old memory thing again," said William sympathetically, "but up to this point, Mon'sir, your memory has been functioning very well."

"Oui, I still remember two of them. They said that in the first place they thought it very strange that so many grown men, bearded, strong, and armed, who were around the king—it is likely they were talking about the Swiss of his guard—should submit to obey a child, and that one of them was not chosen to command instead. The second thing the Indian visitors found amazing is that the poor did not take the rich by the throat or set fire to their houses. *They have a way in their language of speaking of men as halves of one another; they had noticed that there were among us men full and gorged with all sorts of good things, and that their other halves were beggars at their doors, emaciated with hunger and poverty; and they thought it strange that those needy halves could endure such an injustice."*

"Did you get a chance to explain our society to them?"

"I had a very long talk with one of them; but I had an interpreter who followed my meaning so badly, and who was so hindered by his stupidity in taking in my ideas, that I could get hardly any satisfaction from the man. When I asked him [the visitor] what profit he gained from his superior position among his people—for he was a captain, and our sailors called him king—he told me it was to march foremost in war. How many men followed him? He pointed to a piece of

ground, to signify as many as such a space would hold; it might have been four or five thousand men. Did all his authority expire with the war? He said that this much remained, that when he visited the villages dependent on him, they made paths for him through the underbrush by which he might pass quite comfortably. All this is not too bad—but what's the use? They don't wear breeches."

Malachi guffawed. "—and thereby are judged uncivilized and primitive for lack of proper attire."

"I get rid of mine too when I want to be uncivilized," William offered lightly.

"You manage quite well with them on too, I've noticed," laughed Montaigne.

"I wonder if thinking of other men as halves of themselves permits them to be kinder to each other than we sometimes are in our part of the world," William mused. "It would be like stepping on your own toes to mistreat anyone if you really felt that way."

"This idea has some relation to that other very ancient one, which consists of thinking that we gratify heaven and nature by committing massacre and homicide, a belief universally embraced by all religions. Even in the time of our fathers, Amurath, at the taking of the Isthmus, immolated six hundred young Greeks to his father's soul so that this blood should serve as a propitiation to expiate the sins of the deceased. And in these new lands discovered in our time, still pure and virgin compared with ours, this practice is to some extent accepted everywhere; all their idols are drenched with human blood, often with horrible cruelty. They burn the victims alive, and take them out of the brazier half roasted to tear their hearts and entrails out. Others, even women, are flayed alive, and with their bloody skins they dress and disguise others, and there are no fewer examples of constancy and resolution. For these poor people who are to be sacrificed, old men, women, children, themselves go about, some days before, begging alms for the offering at their sacrifice, and present themselves to the slaughter singing and dancing with the spectators." [19]

"It seems to me, they are already heavy contributors without having to solicit alms for an offering."

"Gods don't like to be short-changed," Malachi observed.

"The ambassadors of the king of Mexico, to give Hernando Cortez an idea of the greatness of their master, after having told him that he had thirty vassals, each of whom could assemble a hundred thousand fighting men, and that he lived in the most beautiful and strongest city under heaven, added that he had to sacrifice to the gods fifty thousand men a year."

"Zounds! Could he find that many singing and dancing volunteers? Even the king of Mexico would have a hard time rounding up that many sacrifices."

"Indeed, they say he fostered war with certain great neighboring peoples, not only to exercise the youth of his country, but principally to have enough prisoners of war to supply his sacrifices. Elsewhere, in a certain town, as a welcome to the said Cortez, they sacrificed fifty men all at one time."

"Wheee," William whistled. "They better learn to use welcome mats or they'll soon run out of people."

"I will tell this one story more. Some of these people, having been beaten by Cortez, sent to acknowledge him and seek his friendship. The messengers offered him three sorts of presents, in this manner; 'Lord, here are five slaves; if you are a cruel god that feeds on flesh and blood, eat them, and we will bring you some more. If you are a good-natured god, here is incense and plumes; If you are a man, take these birds and fruit'."

"Which did Cortez take?"

"He took all three," Montaigne said, "and went on to capture the most beautiful and strongest city under heaven as a bonus."

"How long did the Spanish fool the Indians about being gods?"

"Not very long," Montaigne laughed. "As soon as the Indian servants realized the white man's bowels functioned exactly as their own, suspicious muttering was heard."

"It says something against familiarity, doesn't it?"

"Oh, there are no secrets from servants."

"You mentioned earlier," Malachi said, "that you had a poor translator for your conversation with the New World Indian, but it is a wonder that translators—good or bad—are available in the first place for such out-of-the-way people?"

"This one was a ship-wrecked priest who had lived with these Indians for twenty-five years. He couldn't keep his hands off the tribe's nubile maidens, however, so he was defrocked for his transgressions after the maidens had been welcomed into the true faith. The trouble in the exchange was that his French was terrible, and my Spanish is no better."

"Much can be lost in translation," Malachi nodded.

Chapter 6:
NO RESPECT IN LOVE MEANS NO GLAMOUR

Same location:

Montaigne sighed, shifted in his easy chair, and nodded, "C'est vrai, and it reminds me that faulty translation is a big problem in communication for many of us, especially between men and women."

"Why especially between men and women?"

"Because of...that law that commands them to abominate us because we adore them and to hate us because we love them." [20]

"It's always possible, however, to catch them on the upswing," William smiled, "and with a little luck a man might translate the right moment into the right motion in gaining their most fervent favors."

"C'est vrai," Montaigne chuckled. *"Oh, what a terrific advantage is opportuneness! If someone asked me the first thing in love, I would answer that it is knowing how to seize the right time; the second likewise, and the third too; it is a point that can accomplish anything."*

William nodded agreement.

"I have often lacked luck, but also sometimes enterprise: God keep from harm the man who can laugh at this. These days love calls for more temerity, which our young men excuse on the pretext of ardor; but if the women considered the matter closely, they would find that temerity comes rather from contempt. I used to be scrupulously afraid of giving offense, and I am inclined to respect what I love. Besides, in these negotiations, if you take away respect you rub out the glamor."

"You feel boldness rises from contempt, mon'sir? In my experience—"

"I like the love-making of the Spaniards and Italians, more respectful and timid, more mannered and veiled. I don't know who it was in ancient times who wanted his throat as long as a crane's neck so as to relish longer what he swallowed. That wish is more appropriate in this quick and precipitate pleasure, especially for such natures as mine, for I have the failing of being too sudden." [21]

"Well, that happens to a lot of us," said William sympathetically. "Have you tried thinking about something else?"

"Pardon?"

"To slow yourself down. Think about dusting your library or sharpening your quill or making up rhymes."

Montaigne snorted. "I spend much of my life lusting for this one experience, and you advise me that while I am in the midst of it, I should try to think about something else? Is that what your advice amounts to? Mon Dieu, your mind may be capable of such unnatural dis-association, young man, but I am happy to say, mine is not!. My passion must take its cue from the actions of the ladies. *In order to arrest its flight and prolong it in preambles, everything among them serves as a favor and a recompense: a glance, a bow, a word, a sign. If a man could dine off the steam of a roast, wouldn't that be a fine saving?... If the ladies spin out and spread out their favors in small amounts, each man, even to miserable old age, will find there some scrap of pleasure, according to his worth and merit.*

"Ahem," Malachi interrupted, "I have known ladies who would spin out the preambles indefinitely."

"He who has no enjoyment except in enjoyment, who must win all or nothing, who loves the chase only in the capture, has no business mixing with our school. The more steps and degrees there are, the more height and honor there is in the topmost seat. We should take pleasure in being led there, as is done in magnificent palaces, by divers porticoes and passages, long and pleasant galleries, and many windings."

"Zounds, I was never creative enough to think of long hallways and passages in quite that way before," William confessed. "I'm really going to enjoy my next trip to the museum, and I begin to see why certain types of men are drawn to the study of architecture."

Montaigne nodded thoughtfully. "One must have sympathy for the ladies, however, because *our mastery and entire possession is something for them to fear infinitely. Once they have surrendered to the mercy of our fidelity and constancy, they are in a very hazardous position."* [22]

"Surely, the majority of men can be counted on to be fair and constant!"

"Women are not wrong at all when they reject the rules of life that have been introduced into the world, inasmuch as it is the men who have made these without them. Furthermore, it has long been known that women generally are incomparably more capable and ardent than we in the acts of love." [23]

William was lost in thought, so Montaigne continued.

"Let them dispense with ceremony a bit, let them speak freely; we are but children compared with them in this knowledge. Hear them describe our wooings and our conversations, and you will realize full well that we bring them nothing that they have not known and digested without us." [24]

William shuddered, then snickered. "Thank God they are a little shy and circumspect in public."

"If this natural violence of their desire were not somewhat held in check by the fear and honor with which they have been provided, we would be shamed. The whole movement of the world resolves itself into and leads to this coupling."

"Ah," sighed William. "Were it only so. But you must admit that war and killing and such run a mighty close second." Malachi nodded in agreement.

"What has the sexual act, so natural, so necessary, and so just, done to mankind, for us not to dare talk about it without shame and for us to exclude it from serious and decent conversation?" asked Montaigne. *"We boldly pronounce the words 'kill,' 'rob,' 'betray'; and this one we do not dare pronounce, except between our teeth."* He got up to pour more wine for his guests. *"Everyone shuns to see a man born, everyone runs to see him die. For his destruction we seek a spacious field in broad daylight; for his construction we hide in a dark little corner. It is a duty to hide and blush in order to make him; and it is a glory and a source of many virtues to be able to unmake him."*

"Well, well," said Malachi. "The notion of a 'spacious field in broad daylight' smacks of a young man's game."

Montaigne chuckled . *"According to the privilege of my age....I counsel them abstinence, as I do to us; but if this generation is hostile to it, at least discretion and modesty."* [24]

"Indeed, discretion and modesty are much better than abstinence," nodded William. "And it would take a lusty sort of wench to agree to that open field in the daylight arrangement."

"Plato shows that in every kind of love the defenders are forbidden to yield easily and promptly. It is a trait of greediness, which they must cover up with all their art, to surrender so heedlessly, completely, and impetuously. By conducting themselves with order and measure in granting their favors, they beguile our desire much better and conceal their own. Let them always flee before us, I mean even those who intend to let themselves be caught; they conquer us better in flight, like the Scythians."

"I notice once the lasses make up their secret minds about a man, he is often subtly enticed down the path of dalliance," grinned William.

"Indeed, according to the law which nature gives them, it is not properly for them to will and desire; their role is to suffer, obey, consent. That is why nature has given them a perpetual capacity, to us a rare and uncertain one. They have their hour always, so that they may be ready for ours...And whereas Nature has willed that our appetites should show and declare themselves

prominently, she has made theirs occult and internal, and has furnished them with parts unsuitable for show and simply for the defensive." [25]

"Au contraire! I don't know about you, but one of the greatest pleasures of my life is the unveiling of their beauty. I love it when they unveil for me, because it shows me they truly lust for me."

"Perhaps yes, perhaps no," smiled his wiser companion. "Women have many motives. *We are in almost all things unjust judges of their actions as they are of ours. When Alexander was passing through Hyrcania, Thalestris, queen of the Amazons, came to find him with three hundred warriors of her own sex, well mounted and well armed, having left the remainder of a large army that was following her beyond the neighboring mountains; and said to him, right out loud and in public, that the fame of his victories and valor had brought her there to see him, to offer him her resources and power in support of his enterprises; and that finding him so handsome, young, and vigorous, she, who was perfect in all her qualities, advised him that they should lie together, so that of the most valiant woman in the world and the most valiant man who was then alive there should be born something great and rare for the future. Alexander thanked her just the same for the rest; but to allow enough time for the accomplishment of her last request, he stopped in that place thirteen days, which he celebrated as lustily as he could in honor of so courageous a princess."*

"Ah," William sighed. "That's a classical reference one can relish! And was their union blessed? Or did the Amazon queen go on to other lovers so that no one knows?"

"History doesn't make an issue of it." Montaigne conceded. "Mais, in a strange sort of way, inconstancy is perhaps somewhat more pardonable in women than in men. *The inclination to variety and novelty is common to us both, and action involves more effort than submission, and consequently they are always able to satisfy our needs, whereas it may be otherwise when it is up to us to satisfy theirs."*

"How so?" asked William, surprised.

Montaigne and Malachi looked at each other and shrugged in unison.

Chapter 7:
A WRITER OWES HIS COMPLETE
PORTRAIT TO HIS READER

Same location:

"*Nature should have contented herself with making age miserable without making it also ridiculous,*" grimaced the Frenchman. "*I hate to see it, for one inch of wretched vigor that heats it up three times a week, bustle about and swagger with the same fierceness as if it had some great and proper day's work in its belly: a real flash in the pan...He who can await, the morning after, without dying of shame, the disdain of those fair eyes that have witnessed his limpness and impertinence, has never felt the satisfaction of having conquered them and put circles around them by the vigorous exercise of a busy and active night. When I have seen one of them grow weary of me, I have not promptly blamed her fickleness; I have wondered whether I did not have reason rather to blame nature. Certainly she has treated me unfairly and unkindly and has done me most enormous damage.* You know what Priapea says about that:

> '*But if the penis be not long or stout enough...*
> *Even the matrons—all too well they know—*
> *Look dimly on a man whose member's small.*'"

Montaigne took a heavy pull on his wine glass, leaped to his feet and declared: "Nevertheless, by God! *Each one of my parts makes me myself just as much as every other one. And no one makes me more properly a man than this one. I owe a complete portrait of myself to the public. The wisdom of my lesson is wholly in truth, in freedom, in reality...*" [26]

"Are there people who do that sort of thing?" William asked.

"Do what?"

"You know, portraits of your parts, like you said. It seems to me it should be done when a person is still young and active. Do you, perhaps, remember an artist or sculptor you could recommend?"

Both of the older men laughed heartily. "Vous est droll, cheri," cried Montaigne. "But I must share with you a thing I have learned and believe to be worth remembering in spite of our memory problems, yours and mine. *Wisdom, goodness, and happiness depend on our treating ourselves, not with complacency and laxity, but with a measure of fairness and kindness. The golden rule must work both ways. Only if we accept our limitations without rancor can we recognize the privilege and dignity of being human. To do so is the highest achievement of human wisdom. To compose our character is our duty, not to compose books, and to win, not battles and provinces, but order and tranquility in our conduct. Our great and glorious masterpiece is to live appropriately.*"

"Oh, gad," groaned William. "Would you have me repent then my ambitions to write and thus risk myself outside myself?"

"You misunderstand me, cherie. Writing and seeking fame and fortune are in your very nature. Do not repent of that! Your repentance, in fact, *would outweigh the sin. I know of no quality so easy to counterfeit as piety, if conduct and life are not made to conform with it. Its essence is abstruse and occult, its semblance, easy and showy.*" [27]

"Oh, good," cried William. "I can seek fame and fortune and still live appropriately!"

Chapter 8:
THE KING OF NAVARRE CELEBRATES THE COUTRAS VICTORY

Chateau de Montaigne: October 22 (N.S.), 1587:

"I hate to break up a pleasant evening, Gentlemen," William said as he gazed out the window, "but you appear to have armed horsemen surrounding your compound, M. Montaigne."

Montaigne muttered, "Not again!" and crossed to the window. "I've had these local toughs brace me before, but as soon as they see my estate is undefended, their hackles are lowered and they revert to the clumsy louts God intended before they promoted themselves to be defenders of whichever true faith they happen to favor. Let me see if I can make out an insignia before they come knocking, so we may avoid bloodshed by greeting them properly as Catholics or Huguenots."

"Yes, let's avoid bloodshed by all means," murmured William.

"Hold on now! Those are Navarre's men! But that's impossible. All accounts indicate he just defeated the royal army under the Duke of Joyeuse two days ago at Coutras twenty miles north of here. How he attained that victory against a superior force is a real mystery to everybody, but what in the world is he doing here?"

"What's mysterious about a battle where somebody wins and somebody loses?" William inquired.

"Joyeuse had the best army either side had seen in France for many years. The King could hardly do enough to please his current favorite when that force was assembled; it contained hundreds of France's leading nobility in the midst of its 40,000 men. It's frankly unimaginable that they were not only defeated—as the reports have it—but completely destroyed by Navarre's military which, in truth, is much less distinguished either in titles or numbers, and was reported to be trapped at Coutras when the battle began."

"But Joyeuse is not really an experienced military commander, is he?" Malachi asked.

"Well, at age twenty-five," Montaigne shook his head, "he has whatever experience he gained from frittering away the first royal army the king gave him before he assumed command of this second one which he also seems to have managed to mismanage. We only have rumors so far, however, but we will soon get clarification from our visitors."

"Mid-twenties!" William exclaimed. "That's my age. What in the world is he doing in charge of an army of 40,000 soldiers? How can such things happen? Is he part of the royal family?"

Montaigne chuckled. "He is now. King Henry Valois has made him both a Duke and a brother-in-law since he has married the king's sister. Joyeuse is a lot like what we hear of your young Essex. Young, handsome, valorous beyond measure, impetuous, insistent, quarrelsome, and desperately seeking personal glory in the service of his country. A stimulating companion for a month of so, doubtless, but bound to get on the nerves of ordinary mortals after a time. Our good King Henry Valois has shown in the past that he requires a little down-time from such intensity. The king waxes and wanes in choosing his favorites as he does in so many other areas."

"Are you suggesting that your French king may have sent off Joyeuse with a new army in order to gain a little peace from an insistent favorite?"

"I'm recalling that recent court gossip has mentioned that the king has lately been paying a lot more attention to another favorite, young Duc de Epernon. Some have been led to speculate that Henry may have deliberately set-up Joyeuse against Navarre, knowing that recklessness and consumptive valour do not often hold up well against such a cool campaigner as Navarre has proven to be."

"You think Henry hopes Joyeuse might get some of the noisy insistence knocked out of him?" William ventured.

"At least that," Montaigne nodded, "but Navarre may have done him one better, because nothing has been heard from Joyeuse since—" a heavy knocking at the door interrupted him and Montaigne crossed the room to answer.

"I'm sorry, M. Montaigne," said the uniformed figure in the doorway, "if our sentries seem threatening, but my royal master will be by this evening lightly attended, so we must be certain there are no rabid Catholics within reach. Who are these men?" he gestured to Malachi and William.

"Come in please," Montaigne invited. "I remember you. You're Navarre's aide-de-camp, Captain Gaspard Villefort, are you not? These are my honored house guests and pose no danger to your master. As a matter of fact, Malachi is one of Queen Elizabeth's couriers and has been instrumental in transporting the English gold which has kept you in good wine for the past year."

"Pleased to meet you," the Captain shook Malachi's hand and said, "keep up the good work, and this other?"

Montaigne shrugged. "Malachi's apprentice. Unimportant. But this will not be just a social call? Henry certainly has more important business at hand than dining with a worn out civil servant."

Villefort grinned. "Consultation. The king has more favorable options opened to him after Coutras than he has ever had before. He confesses that he is unaccustomed to choosing between pleasant alternatives, so he wants to thrash them over with you."

"Pleasant alternatives are my glass of wine," grinned Montaigne. "Speaking of which," he beckoned William to fetch the wine tray. "Perhaps before the consultation, it might save time if you set out some of the options. But, hold on.....you were at Coutras, were you not?"

Villefort nodded. "Right in the middle," he smiled at the memory.

"We've all heard the rumors of the tremendous victory, of course, but how was it accomplished? Your master has survived for years by winning skirmishes but avoiding pitched battles against the larger royal forces. What made him change his tactics?"

"Joyeuse himself brought about the battle with his overnight quick march, and then presented us with victory with his quick cavalry charge."

"Details man," Montaigne insisted. "How did the battle go?"

Navarre's man took a long drink of his wine, shook his head and said, "I still haven't quite made the transition from the chill of certain destruction to the warmth of a resounding victory."

"Have another glass—it will help," Montaigne filled his glass. "Please go on."

"As you said, our army has always avoided pitched battles and we were doing our best to avoid this one too. Once we heard that Joyeuse was in the neighborhood with 40,000 of the most avid Catholic Leaguers in France, we decided to pull back to the hills and valleys around B'earn, because it was obvious that Joyeuse outnumbered us nearly three-to-one and would try to pen us up along the Biscay coast and cut us to pieces. Our scouts had reported the Royal army twenty miles off when we went to sleep in Coutras."

"You planned to be up and away in the morning?"

"Right. We mounted the usual outposts, but no defensive disposition was made of the cavalry or infantry. We simply didn't expect to fight there at all. We thought we'd slip right around Joyeuse and into our home country where we have numerous hilltop fortresses where we could laugh a siege to scorn."

Montaigne nodded. "That strategy has always worked in the past."

"We were in the worst possible defensive position at dawn when our sentries indicated the Valois cavalry had reached our outposts just outside town."

"Navarre's cousins were with him, I presume," Montaigne said.

Villefort nodded. "The elite of the Bourbon stock were there; Prince de Conde' and Count de Soissons along with the king, and just about every other dignitary in the Huguenot hierarchy. Guise had a chance to strike a blow not only against the Huguenots but against the whole Protestant cause, the Reformation itself. He could have strangled that cause in France and perhaps in all of Europe if he could have killed off our leaders in the field that day."

"When you say 'Guise', do you mean the royal army of Joyeuse?" William asked.

"That's right," replied Villefort. "It is Guise gold supplied by the Spaniards which maintains the Catholic League, and it is Guise himself who promotes the tactic of taking no prisoners when the battle is against the Huguenots. That's why Joyeuse has been a particular favorite of his as a commander who systematically kills our wounded in the field and slaughters garrisons which have surrendered to him under terms. Make no mistake about it. Joyeuse was in a real hurry to corner us at Coutras where he could kill every one of us, but his reckless effrontery not only saved the lives of our troopers but completely destroyed his own very impressive and very well-dressed army."

"But how? He must have surprised you with his overnight march. How did you set up defenses so quickly?"

Villefort laughed. "By a frenzied application of catch-as-catch-can military tactics. I presume you know the layout of the city of Coutras?"

Montaigne nodded. "I remember the houses are situated on a single cobblestoned street along a narrow sliver of land between the Dronne and the Isle Rivers, and the bridges to cross those rivers are very narrow and do not lend themselves to large military operations."

"Correct. You have a good eye, sir. Because we expected no fight, our forces were split into three groups. Our light horse and two regiments of foot had already crossed both rivers along with our three-cannon artillery unit. Navarre and his officer corps spent the night in the village where they had a late night meeting, and our rear guard of cavalry and arquebusiers had yet to cross either river when we heard the Joyeuse cavalry that morning pushing in our pickets about a mile away."

"My God!" Montaigne exclaimed. "What an opportune moment for the Leaguers to hit you!"

"They would have rolled us up and utterly destroyed us, but Joyeuse's eagerness to get at us had left his foot strung out for fifteen miles along the Chalais road while some of his cavalry had reached us after trudging all night in their effort to force a battle on us that morning. They got their wish but not for an additional two hours which they needed to reassemble. Our King Henry has a well deserved reputation for moving fast, and he brought that skill into full display during those hours."

"Excuse me," said Malachi, "but if I'm following you correctly, one of the options open to Navarre at that point was to join the group already across both rivers and ride off to save himself with part of his army while leaving his rear guard to cover his departure before they were cut down. I only mention that option because so many other commanders have done just that in history, and I wondered why he didn't. After all, he seemed to be facing extinction for himself and his cause by staying."

"Unthinkable!" Villefort rumbled. "The King of Navarre would never do such a thing! Just as we are loyal to him, he is loyal to us. He has always stood beside us in the front line of every battle we have ever fought.....including Coutras."

Malachi shrugged good naturedly. "No offense. Just covering the contingencies. All right, how did he use the next two hours?"

"King Henry surveyed the surrounding countryside with a quick glance and ordered a general advance to an open meadow at the north end of the village. He recalled our three cannon and set them up on a small hill to the left of the new front, not very high but elevated enough to cover most of the meadow with enfilading fire. The meadow formed a natural amphitheater sloping gradually upward away from us for several hundred yards and marked at the top by a stand of woods from which the royal army was beginning to appear."

"Aren't you always supposed to take the high ground to set up your defenses?" William asked.

"Traditionally perhaps," Villefort said patiently, "but adjustments are necessary if the enemy is already on that ground. Navarre positioned most of our infantry on the right with swampy ground behind them and pikes in front. He dressed out our heavy cavalry into four squadrons of ten horsemen wide by ten deep along the bottom of the meadow, and he lined detachments of our best arquebusiers in the gaps between those squadrons with instructions to hold their fire until the enemy were within thirty paces. Our light cavalry was stationed on our left at the rear of some marshy ground with a brook running through it. Directly behind our entire position ran the swift and deep Isle River so we knew we had little room to back up if things went wrong."

"And Joyeuse must have been ready just about then," Montaigne suggested.

"I can only imagine he emerged from those woods licking his chops like a hungry wolf at the prospect before him as he gazed down the length of that meadow at our defensive position and considered the most effective way to deploy his heavy cavalry. He could come at us in the arrowhead phalanx form which the Romans used so effectively, or he could charge us in squadrons which in effect would assault our position with simultaneous battering rams of bunched horsemen. Either of those choices might well have overwhelmed us but he decided on another." He paused for a sip of wine.

"Carry on, man," Montaigne urged. "His decision obviously made the difference between victory and defeat. What did he decide?"

Villefort smiled. "First, a little background. From the pennons and banners we collected after the battle, we know that Joyeuse had attracted the flower of the French court to follow him into battle against us. He had recruited well over four hundred gentlemen, Lords, and knights along with 40 barons, counts, dukes and marquises, many of whom were dressed in the finest gold-leaf encrusted armour. Their presence cut down the Duke's alternatives when it came to setting the formation for the cavalry charge."

"How? Why?" William asked

"Because he had four hundred and fifty valiant courtiers whose honor demanded that their pennons appear in the first line of battle when the charge was made. Joyeuse pleased all of them by deciding to attack us with one long, unbroken double line of heavy cavalry with the flower of the French court stretched across the middle of the first row. The military advantage of the double line is that it can swoop down on the enemy's compact defense and envelope them by sweeping its wings around behind them."

"Good Lord!" William exclaimed. "That means they would have you surrounded."

"That was the plan," the Captain nodded. "From the prisoners, we later learned that Joyeuse imagined he could crush the Huguenot cause with one overwhelming charge which would sweep over and around us and confine us to a bloody killing field in the middle. He promised his officers that not one heretic—including King Henry of Navarre—would leave that field alive. His promise pleased the Leaguers so much that there was a good deal of shouting and hooraying and cavorting their horses about as they pranced themselves into their double row at the head of the meadow."

"How were they armed?" Montaigne asked.

"The Duke had insisted that they attack with lances, and so just before they came at us, they took the time to festoon those lances with pennons and banners and clumps of colored ribbons in honor of the ladies of the court. After that nicety had been attended to, however, I must confess that just before they charged, they presented the most fearsome spectacle it is possible for a soldier to confront. The entire top of that dewy meadow was rimmed with thousands of stern, sober well-armed riders poised with lances raised just waiting for the trumpet call to release an avalanche of galloping horsemen pounding down that field to strike a deadly blow against the despoilers of the true faith."

"Were you frightened?" William asked.

The Captain laughed, "I've campaigned for ten years with my master and never before faced such certain death. It was a new experience for me. I don't know if I was frightened or exhilarated. I know I was more awake than I have ever been in my life, more alert. After I had feasted my eyes on the fearsome, shiny image which Joyeuse had assembled for us at the head of the meadow, I turned to consider my comrades. We were all dressed in the rather drab leather and mail that ten years of skirmishing brings you to, and our cavalry was armed only with short swords and pistols."

"Only one pistol?" William asked.

"Only one," the Captain nodded. "But most of them were the new wheel-locks that can be fired with one hand. Lucky to get one shot off, however, in the midst of a melee. Most cavalry men shoot right away and then drop the gun and quickly grab their sword for the rest of the battle."

"My thinking exactly," said Montaigne. *"I should advise the use of the shortest weapons, and those we can answer for best. It is much more sensible to rely on a sword that we hold in our hand than on a bullet that escapes out of our pistol, in which there are many parts—the powder, the flint, the lock—the least of which, by failing, will make your fortune fail. You strike with little certainty the blow which the air carries for you. But as for the pistol...I think it is a weapon of very little effect, and hope that some day we shall abandon the use of it."* [28]

"How was your king dressed for the battle?" William asked.

"Henry? He was dressed just like the rest of us. You couldn't tell him from an ordinary trooper except he sat his horse at the head of our cavalry. Believe me, if color and glitter could win military battles, we were doomed from the beginning that day."

"I've often wondered about the advisability of a military commander dressing distinctly," Montaigne reflected. *"Considering how important it is to safeguard the leader of an army, and that the enemy's aim is chiefly directed at his head, whom all the others hold to and depend on, it seems that one cannot question this course, which we see has been adopted by many great leaders of changing attire and disguising themselves on the point of battle. However..... when the captain is unrecognized by his men, the courage they derive from his example and presence fails them; and losing sight of his customary marks and insignia, they judge him either to be dead or to have fled in despair of success.....Alexander, Caesar, and Lucullus liked to be marked in battle by rich arms and accouterments of a particular shining color; Agis, Agesilaus, and the great Gylippus, on the contrary, used to go to war obscurely covered and without the trappings of command."* [29]

"I've never heard of those last three," William said.

"See!" said Montaigne.

"All very interesting and pertinent too," said the Captain patiently and politely, "but if you are still interested in the battle of Coutras, perhaps you'll permit me to get on with the story?"

"Certainly," Montaigne waved him on. "Sorry. I sometimes get carried away."

"So there we were quietly singing our battle hymn to put us in the mood as we waited for their trumpet to sound the charge."

"You have a battle hymn?" William inquired. "May we hear it?"

"Certainly," the Captain smiled, "and believe me it cuts down on the gnashing of teeth time during the critical period just before the action starts. Our hymn begins like this. After clearing his throat, he sang quietly. *'This is the day which the Lord hath made; we will rejoice and be glad in it,'* and that's our signal to start our slow trot while being careful not to outpace our arquebusiers."

"Psalm 118; 'The Lord is on my side'," Malachi observed. "Very appropriate."

"Excuse me, but I like to be well-oriented while hearing such compelling experiences," William said. "Were you mounted as Navarre was?"

"Indeed I was. In the first row behind him in a place of honor for myself and for my faithful old warhorse, Siegfried."

"He sounds like a true friend."

"I hesitate to confess that after such long acquaintance, I have formed a very strong feeling about the animal that I have groomed and curried and stroked so often, and upon whose back I risk myself riding into combat."

"Such feelings are nothing to be ashamed of," William assured him. "After all, it's perfectly natural if an emotional bond is cultivated between a man and an animal with whom he has shared so many intimate and sensual experiences. That stroking business gets to all of us. Nothing to be ashamed of at all. However, it might be best if you did not discuss such a relationship publicly. You know; don't ask. don't tell."

The Captain frowned at William. "You are grossly over-reading my meaning, and I do mean grossly. I recently read an article which more successfully summarized my feeling for old Siegfried. I forget who the author was, but he expressed my feeling very well when he said: *'Our ancestors, especially in the time of the wars with the English, in all serious engagements and pitched battles, fought most of the time on foot, so as to trust to nothing but their own strength and the vigor of their courage and their limbs for anything as dear as honor and life. No matter what Chrysanthas in Xenophon says, you stake your valor and your fortune on that of your horse; his wounds and his death bring on yours as a consequence; his fright or his impetuosity make you either rash or cowardly; if he fails to respond to bit or spur, it is your honor that must answer for it.'* For those reasons, I have decided to turn Siegfried out to pasture and switch to the infantry when things calm down a bit." [30]

"Oh," said William.

"That piece sounds very familiar to me," said Montaigne. "I must have read that exact opinion someplace. But please, Captain, it must now be time for Joyeuse to sound his trumpet."

The Captain nodded. "He was still fussing over the alignment of his cavalry when our veteran gunners got our cannon into action and tore holes in their double line with eighteen or twenty solid shot before their artillery replied. Joyeuse must have noticed he was losing valuable men while dressing his ranks, so he signaled his trumpeter to blow the charge and the double line surged forward."

"Good Lord," William exclaimed, "I imagine that many horses would make the earth itself tremble."

Villefort nodded. "Immediately the whole meadow began to vibrate when that magnificent assemblage started their slow trot in our direction. But within moments those avid Leaguers could not contain their growing excitement which they quickly transmitted to their mounts through impatient spurs. Their goading generated an accelerating rumble of hoof beats which quickly resounded like approaching thunder throughout the amphitheater as two thousand riders galloped madly over the intervening three hundred yards to be first to plunge their lances into our four hundred who were still trotting steadily into their center singing louder and louder." His voice rose as he sang:

> "The Lord is on my side; I will not fear:
> What can man do unto me?
> It is better to trust in the Lord
> Than to put confidence in man.
> It is better to trust in the Lord
> Than to put confidence in princes." [31]

"Yes, yes, very nice" Montaigne exclaimed impatiently, "but isn't three hundred yards quite a stretch to gallop tired horses downhill and still have anything left when they get there?"

"Correct," said the Captain. "I heard troopers beside me mutter, 'Too soon,' when the Leaguers put the spur to their animals. Our arquebusiers, however, remained well disciplined and when the Catholic cavalry reached thirty paces in front of them, a thunderous roar of gunfire drowned out the sound of hoof beats for a few seconds and the first row of the double line in front of the shooters dissolved into a chaotic tangle of tumbling horses, thrashing legs, and catapulting riders. Our four squadrons, meanwhile, quickened our trot to crash directly into the galloping horde of riders before us, and when they encountered our tightly packed formation, their line of gasping animals splashed apart like a wave upon a rock. The middle of the meadow instantly became a grotesque pit of writhing, thrashing, shrieking animals and moaning men who were quickly overridden in the midst of their despair by the second wave of exhausted mounts whose overnight exertion, lengthy charge, and downhill momentum left them no ability to pull up on the dewy grass, so they plunged directly in on top of their wounded and dying comrades with their lances leveled.

"Good God. Horror upon horror!" William exclaimed.

"In little more than the blinking of an eye the battle was decided by that collision in the center. Some of their riders in the wings did flank our sides only to find the river behind us, so they had to pull up in disarray and were soon dispatched by our infantry. It's hard to judge time on such occasions, but I believe the rest of the fighting lasted no more than fifteen minutes against their disheartened infantry who turned and ran when they saw their cavalry destroyed."

"Did Joyeuse get away?" William asked.

"Our troopers boxed him in as he tried to escape. He dismounted, threw down his sword, discarded his helmet, and announced grandly; 'My ransom is a hundred thousand crowns'. [32] He was, however, dealing with men who had all lost friends and relatives to his murderous temper after other battles, so there was no discussion among them. One veteran trooper stepped down, put a pistol to the head of the Duke of Joyeuse and blew away any chance of ever collecting that kingly ransom."

"Good," said Malachi. "Well deserved."

"Navarre finally commanded our troopers to kill no more of the fleeing enemy, since the bodies of three thousand common soldiers already littered the field. In addition, there were more than four hundred knights, lords, and gentlemen who died alongside enough dukes, barons, marquises, and counts to make up the greatest loss of nobility France has ever recorded in any other battle of the last century."

"How can you get such accurate figures of the nobility in the midst of such confusion and chaos?" William asked. "Isn't there a history of inflated body-counts in military affairs?"

The captain rose to cross to the window. "If you'd like," he growled at William, "I'll stick your nose in the bloody banners and pennons that make up the cargo of the cart my men have just parked in the courtyard. You can do the counting yourself."

"I was just asking," William replied as he peered at the cart through the window. "It's clear they were collected from the battle field with that blood and mud all over them, but why are you carting such grisly trophies around the countryside?"

"Navarre wishes to present them to La Belle Corisande as a tribute to her beauty and as a fond farewell."

"I'm well acquainted with several of the women in the kitchen," William confided, "and I'm sure I could get them to wash and clean and press those trophies for you before he turns them over to what's-her-name. Women prefer clean presents, I've noticed, or at least those which have the appearance of being first-hand.'

The Captain looked at him in astonishment. "You can't seriously be proposing to wash off the hard-earned blood and mud before the presentation to La Belle

Corisande? You may know something about the women in the kitchen, young man, but, believe me, you know nothing about real ladies."

"I only thought——" William was interrupted by a commotion in the courtyard as they saw new horses entering the compound.

"There is Navarre now," said the Captain. "He's early. I wonder what's up."

"Get the door," Montaigne said to William. "Malachi, would you mind taking notes if Henry will permit?"

"Glad to," Malachi smiled and brought forth a pad and quill.

William opened the door and a slight wiry man in his mid-thirties brushed past him and crossed the room with the functional flexibility of a well-oiled whip to embrace Montaigne in the study.

"Michel!" he shouted

"Henry," said Montaigne. "What in the world are you doing here? Was not La Belle Corisande at home?"

Navarre chuckled. "Probably, but confusion dictates who comes first on this occasion, as it has on so many others lately. On my way over there I was informed that my trophy cart has ended up in your courtyard instead of hers, so I had to change plans and seek out your fatherly advice even before I sought to reap the profits such a presentation will surely elicit from the sultry, sensual Mademoiselle Corisande. Captain Villefort, will you be good enough to instruct your men to deliver that cart to the proper location, and tell the young lady I'll be along directly after I squeeze some advice out of my old friend."

"Immediately, sir." Villefort saluted and left.

"I suppose, you're dying to hear the details of the Coutras affair?" Navarre smiled and rubbed his hands together as he prepared to relish the telling.

The three men in the room exchanged a troubled glance and Montaigne spoke. "We'd be delighted to, Henry, but as it occurs, we just finished dragooning the whole story out of your Captain Villefort."

"What!" Navarre barked. "That scoundrel has stolen my thunder? Oh well, I suppose we all earned the right to relate our part of such an amazing adventure. I suppose we'll be telling that story for the rest of our lives. Did he also follow orders to inform you of the alternatives now open to me which I'd like your opinion on?"

"He was just getting to that part when you arrived," Montaigne assured him.

"Good. We'll take it from there, and I can seek out the young lady all the sooner. Perhaps a listing of the possibilities which confront me would be best. Is there paper available?"

"This is Malachi," Montaigne introduced him. "The best scrivener on the Continent. "Would it suit you if he took notes?"

"Malachi, yes," Navarre shook his hand. "You had something to do with a very special delivery I received from your Queen, I remember. I would welcome your note-taking since the future of France may be decided in this room tonight if Michel will only give me some advice I can use. And this other must be your wine server who is safe enough or Villefort would not have left him in the room with us, so let's begin." And he held out a hand to William as though it held an absent wine glass.

"Now that you've disposed of Joyeuse," Montaigne inquired while William served, "which other royal army would you be tempted to confront?"

Navarre chuckled. "I'd like a little rest before I go after any of them, but I suppose Matignon would be my first choice with his small Catholic army of 4,000 just south of us. He was on his way north to rendezvous with Joyeuse, but I imagine he has already learned there is no point in pursuing that course, so he is sitting still to regroup his thinking. I could easily wheel my army about and fall on him before he decides to hole up in Bordeaux. If we neutralized him, that would be the end of royal armies south of the Loire River, so the southern half of France would be entirely in the hands of our Huguenot forces. Certainly a desirable objective but there are pluses and minuses to eliminating Matignon that I would like your opinion on."

"And the first would be who Paris would send to replace him, I would guess."

Navarre laughed aloud. "Oh, I knew I came to the right man to examine the possibilities. Absolutely correct. Matignon is Catholic, of course, but he is not a bloodthirsty Leaguer like Joyeuse. He is a moderate, reasonable man who is absolutely faithful to the King of France, so he would be completely trustworthy if I became king."

"I make that out as one minus for Catholic and one plus for faithful to the crown," William chimed in.

"Yes," said Navarre slowly, "my thinking exactly. Young man, it's perfectly all right if you keep score along with us, but please do so silently so that all of France may have your opinion in reserve if we happen to lose track."

"Glad to, sir.

"In the balance then, Michael, I would think Matignon is better left in place than risk the appearance of some young, fresh, rabid Leaguer whom Guise is bound to send to replace him. Southwest France has had more than its share of murderous interfaith killings for awhile, so my inclination is to give everybody time to relax and begin the difficult process of reconciliation. We simply don't need another handsome, young favorite of the king sent to see how many of us he can kill in order to please the royal court at Paris. What do you think?"

"Like you, Henry, I think the pluses have it. Without Joyeuse, Matignon is not strong enough nor aggressive enough to come after you, and he is reasonable enough to recognize the desirability of a temporary stalemate for both of you, so I think you can profitably disregard him for the time being. Who else do you have to worry about?"

"I don't know if worry is the right word, but sometime in the near future, I'm scheduled to join forces with the largest foreign army to enter French soil in recent times."

Montaigne nodded. "You mean the Germans and Swiss that Baron von Dohna and the Duke of Bouillon are leading through Lorraine at this moment?"

"You do stay current, don't you," Navarre smiled. "That's right. Dohna is leading 8,000 of the formidable German reiters cavalry, and another 8,000 of German mercenary infantry. In addition Bouillon has recruited 18,000 Swiss, and four or five thousand of my Huguenots have already joined them. Right now that army of some 40,000 should just about be approaching the upper Loire River if they have followed my advice to stay away from the 40,000 man army Henry Valois has stationed thirty miles southwest of Paris with the Duke of Epernon in command of the van and the king himself in command of the main body."

"Good God!" William exclaimed. "Another 40,000 man army with a 25 year old favorite leading them! What in God's name is going on around here? Where are they getting all those mobs of 40,000 people anyway?"

"Young man," Montaigne commanded. "As long as you are a guest in this house, you will learn there are times to keep your immature mouth tightly sealed until you are spoken to. If you open it out of turn again, I shall have you sent off to muck out my stables. To leave you something to think about in your sullen silence, let me mention that Henry Valois also recruits liberally from the Swiss. A significant portion of his 40,000 army are Catholic Swiss regiments traditionally recruited by the French government when they feel the need to take action. In addition to the Swiss, however, France has no trouble getting thousands of Frenchmen to join the army because my countrymen enjoy dressing up once in a while and putting on those flashy uniforms gives them a chance to discard the baggy, shapeless clothing they ordinarily wear."

"Here, here," Navarre raised his wine glass in salute. "I must remember to use you the next time I am on a recruiting drive, Michel. And to be fair, I should point out to you, young man, that you and your country have a great deal to do with turning so many armed men loose on French soil. Where do you imagine the money comes from so I can hire the services of Baron von Dohna and the Duke of Bouillon and their men?"

"You mean?"

"Correct. Your Royal Mistress is the unofficial paymaster of the Protestant cause in all of Europe just as Philip of Spain serves that office for the Catholics. But let's get on with our analysis so I do not keep the young lady waiting. I intend to finish business here and then ride like the wind to reach her place just as the cartload of love potions arrive."

"Will you then join forces with Dohna and Bouillon?" Montaigne asked.

"That's well worth considering," Navarre nodded. "The plus side is that with such numbers, we could easily besiege Paris and force Henry Valois to fight or flee, and I could end up on the throne."

"That's a major plus," Montaigne murmured, "at least for your Huguenot cause."

"But that's not the way I want it. I have already pledged that I will leave the country rather than take the field against France's legitimate king. I did not destroy a royal army at Coutras, I destroyed a Catholic army which was bent on destroying me, and I can only wish that the Duke de Guise had ridden beside Joyeuse that day. I would regard it as a major minus if I usurped the throne from the legitimate sovereign of our people. I can live patiently with Henry III because he is willing to live patiently with me."

"But, unfortunately, the Duke de Guise is not a patient man," Montaigne admitted.

Navarre nodded. "It was de Guise who upset the apple cart of domestic tranquility when he forced the king against his will to revoke the Edict of Poitiers whose moderate terms permitted French Catholics and Protestants to live in peace together. To have the heir to the throne wrest the crown away from the legitimate king by force would do nothing to resolve the present bloodletting in France, so I will have none of it."

"If you don't join forces with the Germans and the Swiss, what will you do?" Montaigne asked.

"I'm very glad we had this discussion, Michel, because you have made me realize that all I really want is to contact Henry Valois by some secret messenger, and tell him I will rest my arms and let nature take its course as to who sits on the throne as long as he agrees to stand up to de Guise and reinstitute the Edict of Poitiers."

"Your men will drift off if you don't undertake another campaign," Montaigne warned.

"Let them," Navarre decided airily. "After all, they gathered heaps of swords and shields from the Coutras battlefield to show their wives and sweethearts, so let's give them a chance to relish their glory. Fighting men need their rest and recreation."

"Don't you mean wives or sweethearts?" William inquired.

Navarre looked down his nose at the young man. "You may say 'or' in England, young man, but in France we say 'and'."

"Those rich spoils have always been a bit of a problem to me," Montaigne said.

"How do you mean?" Navarre asked.

"If one had to choose whether to keep one's soldiers richly and sumptuously armed or armed only for necessity, it could be advanced in favor of the first course—which was the course of Brutus, Caesar, and others—that it is always a spur to honor and glory for a soldier to see himself adorned, and a stimulus to greater obstinacy in combat, since he has to save his arms as his property and inheritance; the reason says Xenophon, why the Asiatics in their wars took along wives and concubines with their dearest jewels and treasures." [33]

"They probably realized how attracted women are to men in uniform," William offered.

"On the other hand," Montaigne continued, *"Lycurgus forbade his soldiers not only sumptuousness in their equipment but also to despoil their conquered enemies, wanting, he said, their poverty and frugality to shine as bright as everything else in the battle."*

"As we learned in Holland," William observed, "an amazing number of military officers—for one reason or another—are convinced that poverty and frugality best suit the men under their command."

"So Henry," said Montaigne, "you may retire from the public stage and take your rest along with your men?"

"At the moment, I am certainly inclined that way, but a final decision will wait to see what repercussions the victory at Coutras brings about. After all," he smiled," it is within the scope of human behavior that the Duke de Guise may finally see the light and turn Protestant when he contemplates how soundly we thrashed his best Catholic army."

All four men chuckled at the prospect, and William took the opportunity to observe:

> *"All the world's a stage,*
> *And all the men and women merely players;*
> *They have their exits and their entrances,*
> *And one man in his time plays many parts."* [34]

"So if de Guise turned Huguenot," he added, "and Navarre turned pacifist, it would be only in keeping with the other oddities we have encountered in this unique world of France because;

> *"This world's a city full of straying streets,*
> *And death's the market place where each one meets."* [35]

Montaigne said politely, "We have really important matters that need further discussion. Perhaps you wouldn't mind—"

"The thing is," William continued, "that I am impressed that very important matters—often bloody matters—seem to get settled quite frivolously here in France."

"Frivolously?" Navarre frowned.

"I gather, sir, that one of the big reasons you fought and won an incredible victory at Coutras was so you could dump a cartload of bloody banners on the bed of your soon-to-be-estranged paramour. Is that a fair statement of fact?"

"Not really one of the reasons," Navarre muttered. "Part of the process of things, actually."

"But you are leaving her?"

"Yes, our relationship has run its course, but she has been good to me and deserves some farewell recognition."

"And how many innocent, ordinary men have lost their lives to play out this little domestic drama?"

Navarre shrugged. "We lost a few hundred and they lost in the neighborhood of five thousand, but these things are bound to happen. It's in the nature of things."

"And I gather that the big reason Henry Valoise sent his favorite, Joyeuse, out to meet you in battle was that he had grown tired of him, and hoped you would teach him some manners on the battlefield, so the king would then be free to spend more time dallying with his new favorite, the Duke of Epernon."

"You seem strangely well informed of current French affairs," Montaigne muttered.

"And further, that Henry Valois didn't really care if you smashed up Joyeuse's army since it was a Catholic League army anyway, and as such, any success it enjoyed would reflect glory on de Guise rather than on the king himself."

Navarre nodded. "My hope is that the king will recognize that we did him a favor in smashing Joyeuse. Anything which curbs the bargaining power of de Guise is a big plus for the French people and a large step toward the reconciliation which must soon occur in this country before we run out of people."

Montaigne cleared his throat noisily and addressed William. "Something really puzzles me here about what you've just said, young man. A few days ago you were completely ignorant of French politics, and when I say ignorant—well, never mind that for the moment—but now you seem incredibly well informed if I may say so, and, yet, I don't recall discussing any of these specifics with you at any time."

"You ought to spend more time in your kitchen," William shrugged. "The girls out there talk of these matters all day. They are particularly impressed by King Henry Valois' endless fondness for rash, reckless, handsome young courtiers who seem to stir up endless trouble."

"It must go with the territory," Malachi observed, "since our Queen seems to suffer from the same tendency."

"Essex," said Montaigne and they all nodded.

PART IX: WITH RALEIGH IN IRELAND; NOVEMBER, 1587

Chapter 1: FLORENCE TEMPTS RALEIGH AT BARNSTAPLE

Black Dog Inn, Barnstaple, England: November 1587:

"I don't know how well you know Raleigh," said Angelo the agent, "but I do some business in Devonshire, so I've heard all the stories about him for years, and I've often been forced to take into consideration his point of view in order to get any business done."

"And what have you decided?" Malachi asked.

"I think Raleigh is perfectly capable of shopping around his plan to colonize the New World if he can't get the backing he wants here in England."

"You mean shop it around outside of England? Go to work for some foreign country?" William asked.

"I'm perfectly aware that everything he says is wrapped in the flag of England and the glory of the Queen, but in the end, Raleigh is a businessman, and as such, he knows if you can't make a sale in one location, you move to another market."

"I don't think Raleigh would do that." William murmured.

"Maybe not," said Angelo, "but it's pretty obvious he does have something big cooking away in that steaming kettle on his shoulders, and I'm convinced he'll get it done one way or another, even if he has to seek funding elsewhere."

"He could do that? Make discoveries and set up colonies for some other country even though he's English himself?"

"Of course," Angelo shrugged. "Whichever country pays the cost of the expedition gets to claim the results. Plenty of legal precedent on that principle. The Italian, Christopher Columbus, shopped his expedition around to several countries, even here in England, before he finally got Ferdinand and Isabella to back him with a handful of Spanish jewels ."

"So, for a trifle of trinkets, Spain thereby laid claim to the entire New World?"

"That's the way it works. But, don't forget, you English have also profited from the enterprise of Italian explorers. In 1497, a Venetian named Giovanni Caboto took your money to hire out as an explorer and discovered Newfoundland for you."

"I believe we call him John Cabot," William pointed out.

"Changing his name doesn't change his blood," Angelo smiled. "His discovery of Newfoundland—just five years after Columbus landed in the West Indies—was the first recorded sighting of land on the North American continent, you may recall, and as such was deserving of greater recognition than Giovanni ever received."

"How much did he get for such a rare accomplishment?" William asked.

"I believe your Henry VII—grandfather of your Queen—awarded him £10 for such a monumental discovery, and later, when the importance of Caboto's work sank in a bit, he added a small pension. The king did, however, along with Bristol merchants and London financiers, help him organize and finance a second voyage the next year."

"I hope he got his due recompense for the second trip."

"There's really no telling," Angelo shrugged. "He departed from Bristol in May of 1498 with five well stocked ships, one stopped in Ireland for needed repairs, and the other four, along with Giovanni Caboto, were last seen sailing west from Ireland, but they were never heard from again."

"Exploring is obviously a dangerous business," William said. "Raleigh's cousin Humphrey Gilbert was reported to be 'devoured and swallowed up of the sea' just four years ago, when his pinnace disappeared beneath the waves as his companion vessels were warning him that his craft was unsafe in such turbulent weather."

"I read about that someplace," Angelo nodded. "I thought at the time he had no business attempting his exploration of the American coast in such a small vessel as the 25-ton Sparrow. I had to admit, however, that even though he wasn't Italian, he went out with a bit of flair when it was reported that he went down singing the hymn, 'As near to God by sea as by land'."

"How big was Cabot's ship?"

"The Mathew was 50-tons, but she was a caravel which can handle the rough seas much better than a pinnace."

"The caravel is the one developed by the Portuguese, isn't it?"

"Right. And even though it was more weatherly at sea than a pinnace because it incorporated some triangular lateen sails along with square sails in its rigging—which permitted it to sail up to 5 points on the wind—it didn't always protect its occupants either. The Portuguese explorers, the Corte Real brothers, Gaspar and Miguel, were sailing caravels when they disappeared in separate incidents in 1501 and were never heard from again."

William shook his head. "It's a real shame that so many great men can just disappear like that without our gaining any knowledge from their fate. Just think of what we might learn if we could determine what really happened to so many of them."

Anglelo chuckled. "Interesting speculation, but we might learn some things we didn't want to know just as Girolamo, the brother of Giovanni da Verrazzano, did when he watched his brother vanish right before his eyes in 1528."

"Verrazzano. Another Italian? Did he sail for Italy?"

"No. The Italian city-states were still not well organized enough to support such expeditions, other than providing them with leaders. After Spain financed Columbus and your Henry VII granted a charter to Caboto, the French King, Francis I—a cousin to your Henry VIII—felt left out enough to recruit an Italian explorer of his own. He commissioned Giovanni da Verrazzano for several expeditions in the 1520's. After the first trip, Verrazzano correctly reported that the whole American coast between Newfoundland and Florida was a fresh, promising world of its own without a passageway to Cathay, but many explorers ignored his discovery and went on with the futile search for such a profitable garden path to the silks and spices of Asia. Some explorers however—Davis and Frobisher for instance—respected his finding and sought the passageway north of those boundaries. Someday, somewhere, Giovanni da Verrazzano deserves an outstanding tribute for his rare perception."

"Good luck to him on bridging the gap between having earned recognition and receiving it," William said, "but his exploration of the American coast sixty years ago meant that France could have laid claim to that whole area just as Spain did to the West Indies. Why didn't they?"

"Oh, yes. King Francis might have inserted several colonies in that territory if he had not been so preoccupied trying to recover from being held prisoner for a year after the defeat of his army in Italy. But the French always have reasons of their own for doing things or not doing them; for instance, if they had sponsored such New World colonies, they might not have had enough national energy left to fight wars with you English or to kill each other off in their bloody religious feuds."

"You mentioned Verrazzano made several trips for France. How did he make out on the others?"

"The second was a profitable trip to South America for a load of Brazilian logwood which is used in the process of dyeing cloth. The profits from that trip helped finance a third trip which proved fatal when he stopped at a West Indian island close to where Columbus first landed. Verrazzano anchored well offshore, as was his custom, and he and his brother were rowed close to shore in the ship's boat. He saw a large number of natives lining the coast so he waded ashore to greet them while his brother kept the ship's boat just outside the line of waves."

"Did he have presents to offer them?"

"More than he knew," pronounced Angelo. "Those were the fierce, bloodthirsty Carib tribe whose habits were unknown to the Europeans up until then, but Verrazzano quickly learned that he had walked with open arms into the hands of merciless cannibals. They killed him quickly, cut him into pieces and sat on the beach feasting on his body while Girolamo sat moaning softly in the boat as he watched his brother disappear piecemeal before him."

"Interesting history," Malachi said quietly, "but back to the business at hand. What would be Raleigh's prospects for foreign backing if he did decide to go international?"

"I'd imagine one of the Italian states would snap him up on such a proposal. Genoa, perhaps, which is always full of sly-headed fellows whose eyes have grown green from watching mountains of gold and silver—uncovered originally by their native son, Christopher Columbus—shipped directly into Philip's coffers in Madrid. If you ever feel the need to spend a really miserable evening, you could hardly do better than having some drunken Genovese explain to you in endless detail how much more pleasant his life would have been if only his forefathers had sense enough to back their native son as he attempted to pour all that treasure into their laps. Believe me, it rankles them daily that they messed up such a golden opportunity nearly a century ago, and I'm convinced, as a matter of fact, I'm positive, there are several Italian states which would give very serious thought to making another grab for the big payoff."

"Are we just chatting idly here," Malachi smiled, "or are you about to unfold something significant?"

Angelo smiled. "You're right. It's time to quit pretending. I am a Florentine business agent who has been commissioned by the council of my city to make just such an offer to Sir Walter Raleigh. I've been told, Malachi, that you could get me access to him since he seems to be out of favor at Court at the moment. Is he in Ireland?"

"I'm not at liberty to say," Malachi said, "but I can say that I am scheduled to see him sometime in the next two weeks, so I can offer you my messenger service if you'd like."

"I would like," Angelo said as he withdrew a small pouch heavy with coins from his doublet and began hefting them in his hand as he went on talking. "Not only would we like to have our offer presented to Raleigh, we would be very pleased to get his response with all possible speed."

"I can promise delivery of your message if so commissioned," Malachi said as he watched the pouch bounce up and down, "but a response is up to Raleigh. He may choose to think the matter over, and my duties may take me elsewhere in the interim. If you have a residence here in London, I'll leave your address with him, and he can respond when he finds time, but I must warn you that he already has so many pots boiling, you must have patience as you await his reply."

Angelo laughed, "Patience comes painfully to Florentines, but the events of the last sixty years have thrust it into our very vitals! It is somewhat disheartening to grow up in a culture which, during your entire lifetime, is coming down from an astounding economic high. We still have old men in Florence who tell stories of a city which was the center of all the trade from the east. All the jewels, jade, silks, perfumes, and ivory of the entire Ottoman empire in addition to the cloves, cinnamon, nutmeg, and pepper of the far East Indies once flowed exclusively through Florence. We were the European entry port for all the camels out of the desert and the dhows out of the Red Sea."

"A happy middle-man position," William observed.

"Happy and profitable," Angelo acknowledged. "Huge fortunes were made every day by Florentine merchants who accepted delivery from the Asians in the morning and sold the cargo manifests to the Dutch, French, English, German, and Spanish merchants after lunch. It was a wonderful way to do business; get rich without ever leaving your easy chair. Our trans-shipping service kept all our workers and mariners busy unloading and loading ships, and every merchant and inn-keeper profited thereby. Even the arts prospered to the point where some present historians are beginning to refer to the last hundred years as a Renaissance of the arts in Italy."

"Really?"

Angelo nodded. "But our exclusive arrangement dwindled after Vasco de Gama circled South Africa in 1496 and opened Portuguese trade with the Far East. Because they were actually on the scene with the Asian owners of the valuable spices, the Portuguese were permitted to bargain for exclusive rights to buy up the aromatic seasoning of the Spice Islands. They no longer had to haggle with lowly agents at the other end of the trade routes as Florence still has to do. In business, you know, the closer you can get to the man who has the power to say 'yes' or 'no', the nearer you are to cornering a franchise—which leaves the opposition out in the cold. Even your Drake on his remarkable Around the World Trip arranged an exclusive trading agreement with the Sultan of Sumatra just because he happened to be in the neighborhood."

"That was only eight years ago," William pointed out. "Perhaps you Florentines should travel more."

"Possibly so," Angelo shrugged. "It's a wonder to me that our City-states became so accustomed to a quick return on all investments and to having the money come to us while we lounged at home that we completely ignored the changing world conditions. God knows we build the best ships in the world and cultivate some of the finest seamen in existence, and then we send them off to explore for other countries while we confine our examination to the Mediterranean Sea where we already know every current and inlet."

"Why is that, do you imagine?"

"Ordinary Italian sailors won't sail far off because they don't trust their wives at home."

Malachi shook his head. "History takes some strange turns for some odd reasons."

"So Florence has gradually declined during my lifetime as our far Eastern trade has been carried in larger and larger ships around the Cape of Good Hope. We are no longer the exclusive middleman between Asia and Europe. As a result of this disconnect, our profits have declined, the arts have suffered, and our people are unemployed. Everything in Florence during my lifetime has been cutback and reduction. It's hard to grow on a job when you are always required to reduce and contract. That's why we are determined to expand or go broke trying."

"That's where Raleigh comes in."

Angelo nodded. "We want Raleigh to establish a colony for us in the New World. We would prefer the southern part—more like the Mediterranean climate—but Spain has the south pretty well fenced off, so we'll have to settle for something further north. There are only three European colonies there now so we'll use them for rough boundaries; the Spanish in Florida, Raleigh in Virginia, and you English in Newfoundland to the north. We thought someplace between Florida and Raleigh would be nice, not as cold as it would be further north."

"You plan to use it as a trading base?"

"That's right. We are tired of being cut out of profitable trade. If we could set up an Italian colony there, we could talk to the head man—somebody named Powhatton, as I understand it—and get exclusive rights to transship their goods back to Europe."

"What kind of goods do you have in mind?"

"God knows. That's what makes commerce so exciting. New fields to profit from, and then you never know if we might strike it rich in the north just as Philip has in the south. We'll send in priests first to shame the natives for their nakedness, and then we'll send in the cloth and shoe merchants with the latest Italian fashions. That way, we don't have to do any of the actual digging for the gold ourselves; the Indians will bring it to us to buy clothes to cover their shame."

"And the humanitarian assumption here is that the natives will also eventually profit from the relationship?" William asked.

"Correct. We'll give then a quick lesson in commerce, but I want you to emphasize to Raleigh that this is a long range project for us. We would not expect to reach the turn-around point in such a colony for at least seven years. We know it will be expensive, but we have the funding lined up. I believe that's Raleigh's big worry here in England. As I said, we have learned patience in Florence, so we are in it for the long haul. The city fathers are not only ready to risk municipal funds but also their personal estates to see this thing through. Tell Raleigh that. In short, with his help, we think it possible to quietly maneuver our blocked pawn down to the last rank and see Florence emerge once again as a newly crowned queen of commercial enterprise!"

"Good thinking there. Stay up-beat in the exploring business," Malachi advised. "Incredible over-head before you see any return. Discouragement comes easily, I'm afraid."

"That's why we want Raleigh. They say he has a hard head."

"There may be a touch of Dutch blood in him for sure. He is not easily discouraged."

"Do you think he would be interested?"

"Only he can answer that, of course, but frankly, I'd be surprised if he were. Even though he is out of royal favor at the moment, the Queen has shown no sign of permanently punishing him. I know Raleigh thinks he will regain Elizabeth's goodwill as soon as he can find another cloak to throw in her path."

"Cloak?"

"Anything unique or novel or profitable. The Queen has eclectic tastes, but they center around those touchstones."

"Commendable woman, I'm sure, but you will make our proposal to him nonetheless?" Angelo placed the purse on the table between them.

"Oh, yes, I will deliver your message," Malachi said and slid the purse into his cloak, "and I can just about guarantee that Raleigh will spend an evening very soon entertaining your proposal at supper. He likes new ideas and certainly the thought of an unlimited budget will get his strict attention."

"Nobody said 'unlimited'," Angelo pointed out.

Chapter 2:
SAILING TO IRELAND WITH RALEIGH'S PLANTS

Aboard the Maura Belle on the Irish Sea:

"*I am gone though I am here*," [1] William sighed as he relaxed across a coil of rope on the deck of the *Maura Belle* as she cut through the waves. "I think journey by sea is the sweetest form of travel simply because you don't have to do anything to get there unless you are part of the crew. They set the sails and we just go cruising along as smooth as silk, perfectly free to occupy our thoughts with whatever pleases us."

"Nearly correct," Malachi nodded, "unless bad weather erupts and then we become part of a frantic crew doing whatever needs doing in order to stay afloat."

"But I see no bad weather on the horizon," William ventured, "and nothing but fair winds behind."

"Let's hope it stays that way."

"Just for fun, I've been brushing up on some of the simple navigational clues Mr. Hauklyet taught me, and I notice our ship is pointed about 90 degrees to the right of where the sun stands in the sky. Since it is just now noon, that means the sun is directly south of us, so that means we are sailing west, right?"

"Almost exactly right within about one degree of latitude," Malachi nodded. "Youghal is at 52^0 North, and our departure port of Barnstaple is at 51^0 North, so we'll swing a bit to starboard when we sight the Irish coast. About eight more hours of sliding along this northeast wind will do it."

"Add that eight to the six which have elapsed since we left England, and it is essentially a 14-hour trip then from England to Ireland. That's good for the tobac plants because they may be a little tired of sea air after coming 3,000 miles from the New World."

"Don't print any schedule with those numbers," Malachi advised. "The weather is perfect for us at the moment, but this trip could still take two weeks if the sea turns sour. As it is, as soon as we leave the St. George Channel, we'll require a couple more hours to swing around the south coast of Ireland in the direction of Cork in order to reach Raleigh's place at Youghal."

"What do you mean leave the St. George Channel? We're out here in the middle of the water. Where else are we going to go?"

"The geographers are dueling this one out just as they are in settling the final designation between the Narrow Seas and the English Channel. The Irish insist that the body of water between our two countries should rightly be called the Irish Sea just as they have always called it since the days of St. Brendan the navigator. When we cross the mid-mark in our journey, we start referring to this body of water as the Irish Sea."

"What actual mileage is involved in crossing between the two countries?"

"Depends on where you start. Ulster in the north is practically within hailing distance of Scotland in several places. As a matter of fact the Irish and Scot clans summon reinforcements from each other with smoke signals when they have trouble with the English. The distance is almost the same as between Dover and Calais, about 22 miles, but they can relay the signals through small islands between them. Further south along the jagged coastline, there is almost exactly 75 miles of open sea between Holyhead in Wales and Dublin. Here in the south it is about 140 miles between Barnstaple and Youghal because the Irish coastline diverges somewhat to the west."

"If I'm not mistaken, that's the same kind of construct you explained to me in visualizing the English channel between France and England: A funnel shape starting in the North Sea with a twenty-two mile neck between Calais and Dover and flaring out to about 140 miles as it enters the Atlantic Ocean 350 miles away at the other end of the Channel."

"Very good," Malachi said. "You have a perceptive engineering mind to see that resemblance without a map handy. The funnel shape is not quite that pure, however, since the bulk of Wales bulges out prominently from our side, but then so does the Cherbourg peninsula jut out from the coast of France, so your impression is substantially valid."

William laughed. "It suits my poetic soul to see our country protected on each flank by a funnel that will strain any invading adversary."

"It will do that," Malachi acknowledged. "The compression of water caused by that funnel shape often produces complex, unpredictable tides and currants which our people have learned to live with, but which bedevil foreign merchants to the point that they often request pilot ships to escort them along our coast."

"Whoa! Why has Captain Fernandez swung our ship off course to the south so suddenly?"

Malachi considered for a moment. "Clearly, he has decided to do something else before he delivers us to Ireland; no doubt something to do with that ship I see coming over the horizon from the direction of Spain. You may not know that the west and south of Ireland have for a long time done most of their trading with Spain. That commercial exchange helps to explain why Munster—the southwest corner of Ireland—feels less allegiance to the English crown than do other portions of Ireland. As a matter of fact, that vessel may be carrying the King of Spain's daughter."

"What? That ship might contain Spanish royalty? "Princess?"

Malachi chuckled, "Try to think poetically for a moment. The Irish use timber, hides, ironwork, fish and anything else they can tear loose to buy shiploads of wine from the Dons, and that warm, red wine is regarded so affectionately by thirsty Irishmen that they refer to it as the King of Spain's daughter. It is apparent our captain has suddenly developed an overwhelming curiosity to see if there is royalty approaching on that ship."

"It looks like a simple fishing vessel to me," William said. "I don't understand why we would interrupt our journey to pursue some poor fishing boat. You may recall Raleigh commanded us rather forcefully to get his tobac planted in Ireland as soon as possible. I'm sure he'll see this needless pursuit of other ships as an unforgivable delay since it is taking us directly away from Youghal."

Malachi could not conceal his excitement. "Her lines are Spanish well enough, and Fernando has the bone in his teeth! Our Captain knows full well Raleigh's feelings will not be hurt if our trip is delayed in pursuit of a possible prize. Believe me, Raleigh encourages his captains to be extra-ambitious in prize-taking by sharing the booty liberally with them. I've heard him shout down those who object to his buccaneering tendencies by openly declaring—often late at night when drink has been taken—'It is a worthy endeavor to be vigilant along England's coast as long as we have foes afloat.'" Malachi chuckled. "Some nights I think Raleigh is more afloat than the foes."

William frowned. "I know Raleigh expects us to deliver these tobac plants while they are reasonably healthy, and it doesn't seem to me a good idea to add random acts of piracy to the shock they have already suffered from traveling from the New World. Frankly, they looked a little travel-worn when we loaded them in England."

"I'd go very easy with that piracy talk if I were you," Malachi whispered. "There are men aboard who would take it as a personal threat since that particular charge could result in a man being hung. The men prefer to think of themselves as patriots protecting their home waters from invaders and profiting only from the debt owed by Spain for past depredations on English shipping. They'd like you to join their brotherhood by thinking that way too."

"Miniature Drakes, eh?"

"That's right! Now be a good fellow and hop up on the bulwark and strike a threatening pose to see if you can't draw first-fire from that vessel we're closing on. That way, you'll earn the forgiveness of the crew for all your grumbling and grousing."

"That perch doesn't look at all safe," William said. "Frankly, I would prefer to stay right here. In fact, I insist on the full protection of my rights as a bonded apprentice."

"Try not to be so simple," Malachi growled. "With your broken brain, you don't even know your rights unless I inform you of them."

"Never-the-less, I insist upon their full protection. I can't imagine that any master has the right to risk the life and limb of his apprentice over and over again."

"What risk?" Malachi demanded. "You're just as safe atop the bulwark as you are crouched here behind it. Captain Fernandez obviously intends to seize the moral high-ground by enticing that other ship to loose off the first shot, so that if this interlude happens to get to Admiralty Court someday, we can claim—with a clear conscience—that we were attacked first. Don't worry. The other ship is already jumpy because they can plainly see that we're closing on them on this tack. You won't have much trouble setting them off if you put yourself into the part. Now's the moment!" Malachi urged. "We're close enough. Jump atop the rail there like a good lad and invite them to fire on us."

"Odd's blood! Invite how?"

"Attack their nerves. Wave your fist menacingly and shout threats and obscenities at them."

"Don't rush me! What kind of obscenities?"

"The Dons are very touchy about religion and valor, so start with something like 'Lily-livered, Cat-lickers' and then work out some grossly obscene variations along those lines. Wave your sword about as you prance menacingly along the rail, and see if you can't frighten them into letting off at least one shot."

William recoiled. "Right at me! I'm afraid such a response would be a disproportionate rebuke of my performance."

Malachi scoffed, "You worry about the oddest things. You'll be in the safest spot in the world if they aim at you because the Spaniards have no real naval gunners. Their idea of naval gunnery is to keep all guns loaded in order to discharge one mighty salvo at point-blank range just as they grapple and board. That strategy clears a lot of decks for them, but it leaves their gunners with no experience in judging the pitch and roll of the ship under sail when they aim their cannon. They have no practice at all in reloading under fire; indeed, some of their big guns must be reloaded from outboard. Can you imagine the fun English musketeers in the rigging would have with such an arrangement? Don't worry. Not only will they not hit you, there's hardly one chance in a hundred they'll hit this ship."

"That's funny," William said, "because I remember hearing somewhere that the Spaniards were very good with their cannon."

"On land, they are," Malachi agreed. "Most military people agree they are the best in the world with their field-cannon, but, paradoxically, they are the worst in the world with their sea-cannon."

"How can that be? Isn't the shooting process the same on land and sea? "load-and-fire-and-aim kind of thing?"

"You certainly have a quick grasp of military fundamentals," Malachi chortled, "but in Spain it's not the same thing at all. The leading noble families of Spain have supplied the Spanish Army with artillery officers for generations past. That branch is particularly attractive to young noblemen who enter the service, so that for the rest of their lives they may share a soothing mix of mild Madeira and military-memories with fathers, uncles, brothers, and, eventually, if they survive, with their own sons, and possibly even their grandsons."

"But the leading families have not supplied the navy?"

"That's right. There is no tradition of naval gunnery because that particular endeavor is such a new science. Young noblemen are reluctant to risk their military careers in a service where personal glory seems so ill defined and so solitary. Spain did respond to King Henry Vlll's development of the broadside, however, by installing more guns in their galleons, but they have used them mostly to terrify the Indians in the New World and to scare off buccaneers along the Spanish Main. The discharge of their naval cannon is like the trumpet call at the Rose Theater: it is meant to draw attention to the ensuing action, so there's nothing to worry about. Hop on up there now and get started."

"You're absolutely positive they can't hit me if they shoot?"

"It would be such a rare occurrence," Malachi assured him, "that every man on both ships would remember it with awe until his dying day. *It would be argument for a week, laughter for a month, and a good jest forever.*" [2]

"Well," William smiled, "That's not really what I had in mind as my legacy to humanity, but I guess being a good jest forever should be immortality enough for any man."

"Get on up with you now!" Malachi commanded. "It's time for you to perform!"

"I'm on? Where's my sword? Does it look more menacing on my right hip or my left?"

"We're closing fast! Curtains up! GO!"

William climbed up on the rail. "I can't balance up here. I'm no acrobat. I can't even stand up! How menacing can a person look in a crouched position?"

"Leap onto the rat-lines with vigor!" Malachi ordered. "Get busy before you discourage our crew altogether!. Leap!"

William leaped onto the rat-lines, swung about a bit, and turned back toward Malachi, "I have something important to say."

"Good," Malachi shouted. "We can use a little inspiration, but keep it short!"

"When I leaped to this vantage point, my attention, like that of my shipmates, was completely focused on the drama of the upcoming encounter in front of us, but as I swung about, I realized we are being overtaken by that ominous, dark cloud rushing in on us from the rear. Doesn't that mean a big storm is just about to hit us? It doesn't look good to me."

"B'God," Malachi exclaimed as he looked to the stern, "that came out of nowhere. It looks like the heavens are on the side of the Dons today, so climb down from there before somebody shoots you, and let's get some hatches battened down."

❖ ❖ ❖

After landing at Youghal on the south Irish coast:

"I'm sorry indeed to see this kind of mess," said Tiny O' Toole, Raleigh's storekeeper at Youghal, as he pawed through the plants they had brought from England. "Sir Walter must surely have sent healthy plants for transplanting, but these are dry and listless as though they had been soaked in saltwater. Ah well, we can still stick them in the ground, but methinks your long delay in fetching them has done them in entirely."

"We would have brought them in better shape," William assured him, "if Captain Fernandez had not decided to go buccaneering—thereby risking our very lives along with the health of the tobacco plants—and sailed us into a storm that nearly killed us instead of fetching us immediately to Ireland as he should have done."

"Fernandez chasing prizes, eh?" O'Toole chuckled. "Might as well try to keep the fox from the henhouse." He lifted one of the dry tobacco plants and found a potato tangled in the roots. "Why did you bring this other?" he asked. "Isn't this the Indian plant from the New World, po-ta-toe?"

"Oh," said William, "I just packed some in there to keep the tobacco plants from crushing each other."

O'Toole hefted one of the brown rollers. "Did you ever taste one of these fellers?" he asked.

William nodded, "They have little taste until you mash them up and lash them with butter. Then you can't find a better belly-filler, even if some think they are slightly poisonous because they grow below ground."

O' Toole laughed. "That might be just the thing here in Munster. The Desmond Rebellion killed everything above ground, but I don't see much future for them here if they are tasteless. I'll plant these tobac plants now, Malachi, and give them two weeks to recover. If they stay dead, you'll be wantin' to fetch more plants from London." He chuckled. "If we can't get a commercial crop of tobac to grow over here, however, Sir Walter may end up doing most of the smoke-drinking all by himself."

"I don't know about that," Malachi said. "He's creating quite a following in London with his silver pipe. He has many of his set calling for greater supplies since he has taught them to fascinate the ladies by blowing smoke rings and expelling smoke through their nostrils. Raleigh, himself, holds every audience enthralled with his smoky legerdemain, so I can only imagine he'll find some source for new supplies even if it means importing them from the New World."

"I know Mr. White still drinks smoke too," William said. "He learned it from the Indians during his stay in the New World. He says drinking smoke is good for your health."

"Only time will tell," Malachi observed.

Chapter 3:
WITH RALEIGH AT YOUGHAL

"You are young, William, in addition to your other problems," Malachi observed carefully, "but that is no excuse for you to prance along the very precipice of self-destruction so consistently—at least not twice in two days."

"I realize I still have much to learn," William responded rather stiffly, "and I accept you as my mentor as well as my master, so tell me what I've done wrong."

"That's sensible," Malachi muttered. "To begin, when Raleigh arrived last night after a tiring trip from England and quite worried over his sudden disfavor in the Queen's eyes—for some offense whose nature I have not yet learned—all he wanted was a hot meal, a puff or two from his pipe, and then his bed for a long rest. When he lit his pipe, however, you intervened. Why, in God's name?"

"The simple explanation is that I was living out my part as you have advised me to do. When you assigned me to gossip-in-the–kitchen duty while maintaining my stay-in-the-background persona here at Raleigh's place, I chose to be an old servant on his way home after a long and honorable career in a great Anglo-Irish house outside Tralee. I flatter myself I have a very clever costume which I regard as 'respectably shabby'. I used our make-up kit to show advanced age and even armed myself with a serviceable mangle of old Irish gibberish, enough to gain confusion and cause delay whenever needed. I have cultivated the ability to stagger and stumble in a convincing manner, and I can usually make myself almost completely inconspicuous. Last night, however, I may have been guilty of over-acting to some degree."

"Yes, indeed! Sneaking up behind Sir Walter at the kitchen table and pouring a pail full of wash-water over his head is a scene which not only offended my eyes but left me in a state of high apprehension for fear one of the servants should squeal on you."

"I'm thankful, for once, for the complete obscurity that loathsome glib provides. Much as I despise wearing such a ludicrous mop, I have to admit that it succeeds in covering one's face in such a way that no witness under oath could distinguish a man from his mother. Because the servants accept me as a respectable brother worn out in their honorable profession, they would never give me up without the offer of a hefty reward from the master—which, happily, shows no sign of being forthcoming. More to the point of my action, however, I was deep in the part of an older Irish retainer springing to the aid of his master when danger loomed."

"Danger loomed, eh?" Malachi sneered. "He was simply lighting his pipe. You've seen that done before. You've even done it yourself."

"Don't you see! The personal me is familiar with the lighting-up process, so the real me was not surprised when Raleigh lit his pipe, but that was not true for the old servant me who has spent his working years in an isolated community and had never seen anybody light up before. You keep telling me to play my parts more convincingly, so my servant-self saw only that Raleigh—who was, after all, my temporary master as host of the house—must have set himself on fire since a plume of unexplained smoke was coming out of his nose and mouth. I saw the need to take action, so I assessed my inner-actor self, counseled quickly with the spirit of the character I was playing, and determined that the old servant would protect the master at all costs. So I put the fire out, yes. But I did so by acting out what was expected of my character, which is the strategy you have always advised for staying out of sight. You always warn me to make no furtive moves if I wish to remain unobserved, so I was just playing my part to the hilt."

"Ah well, cease your babble. You may have had your reasons. Still, it seems like a minor miracle that you managed to escape identification in all the confusion. You disappeared quite suddenly."

"I just got rid of the glib and straightened up. I was immediately befriended by a very nice young maid who appeared—for her own odd reasons—to enjoy her master's discomfiture enough to quickly make friends with the real me."

"You were providentially lucky that Raleigh was tired enough to go off to bed without pursuing the matter when no culprit was immediately identified. That's why I was amazed to hear you again tonight put yourself in a position of being sliced to pieces by Sir Walter's sword. I fear that such random miracles in your favor will only encourage you in further adventures, but I assure you that gentlemen can be quite murderous when their honor is so grossly offended. You threw the entire company into a state of frozen horror with your impertinent question."

"I still don't know what all the excitement was about," William confessed. "Sir Walter drew his sword, it's true, but then fell down drunk. I'm not sure what he had in mind."

"Yes," grated Malachi. "This world will always be a great mystery to you, as you slither and slide your way through it, leaving nothing but havoc and despair in your wake. I have to give you credit, though; you stand right there in the middle of the chaos as though you were detached from the turmoil you have created. A casual observer might mistake you for the candy-man at the county fair selling his sweets as you distribute provocation and lunacy to anyone who will meet your eye. Do you have any idea how close you came tonight to having your guts pierced by cold steel?"

"I did notice he was stammering there at the end when I inquired about the Smerwick matter, but I attributed that to the drink he had taken."

Malachi snorted. "Inquired indeed! Your exact words, as I recall, were, 'How did it feel, Sir Walter, to lead your men onto the grounds of the Smerwick fort and spend two hours hacking and stabbing 600 unarmed prisoners to death as they cowered and begged for mercy in four different languages?'"

"Did I say four? I forgot to count the native Irish among them. That makes five."

"Once again fortune interceded in your favor. Had Raleigh taken one less tankard of ale tonight, he would have reached you with his sword."

"Chilling thought, right enough," William shrugged, "but, on the other hand, I'm always sorry to have a good meal interrupted in the middle like that. I know I bear some responsibility in the matter, but the truth is that most companies are really much too tired after a busy day to generate real drama unless they are stirred up. I am supremely interested in unique experiences, so I quiz those who have had them. Raleigh's role at Smerwick was certainly a singular one. Good God! Leading the slaughter of 600 unarmed people—all in a day's work—should prompt rare reactions in any man. That's the kind of thing I'm really interested in: unique experiences that serve to illustrate various things."

"Illustrate what various things?"

"I haven't figured that part out yet."

"Well," Malachi laughed, "tonight, once again, you came within a hair's-breadth of this life's most unique experience, and only good fortune kept you alive, so you better start imposing meaning on your short existence before your just-deserts catch up with you. You are lucky in this particular case because Raleigh will forget everything in the morning—he always does when he drinks—but still, you've got to learn to control yourself in company. Your dining-room antics sour the beer in my belly, and I can't digest my meals when my life is constantly put at risk by your reckless behavior."

"That's very touching," William said. "Does that mean you would defend me against Raleigh if actual violence broke out?"

"Think whatever gives you comfort," Malachi advised, "but the truth is that Raleigh—and any other gentleman so offended—would undoubtedly take my life along with yours since I was guilty of presenting you. You must learn the rules of gentlemanly behavior if you are to survive in company." Malachi took a book from his pocket and handed it to William. "Take this volume up to the room and spend the night memorizing major portions of it."

"What is it?"

"The Courtier by Baldassare de Castiglione. It was first published in Italy in 1528 but was translated into English about twenty years ago. Since then, it has set the style for the behavior of aristocratic gentlemen in such matters as dress, manners, bearing, ethics, conversation, intellectual interests, and the keeping of pleasant company generally."

"Brush up on Baldassare, eh?"

Malachi grimaced. "It might help not only in polishing your own behavior but in helping you understand people in our society who have taken Castiglione to heart and patterned themselves on his definition of gentlemanly behavior."

"I sense you have someone specifically in mind."

"Sir Philip Sydney you know about already, but from what I've seen so far, the 'Faerie Queene'—a poem now in the process of being created by our upcoming host, Edmund Spenser—embodies Castiglione's vision of a gentleman. The Courtier, by the way, also favors the ladies greatly in promoting their education by pointing out how desirable it is for a woman to be skilled in all the arts as well as in conversation. After reading Castiglione, thoughtful fathers who want their daughters to marry well can no longer neglect schooling them."

"I don't have much trouble with women where behavior is concerned."

"Your success with women has always puzzled me," Malachi growled. "I assume they mistake your addled brain for innocence, so they feel safe to play the strumpet for you. But fortune has two sides, and before long your accumulation of worldly experience will melt the mask of innocence you affect and reveal you as the die-hard, philandering lecher you really are. After that, you will have as much difficulty as any of us in charming the gentle creatures into a bout of fondling."

"Thank you, Malachi. As far as I can recall, that's the first time you've nearly hinted—even in a left-handed way—that I may be learning something. But, you know, I can't get what Raleigh did out of my mind. Killing 600 people in cold blood!"

"A soldier's blood is never cold when he is about his business," Malachi assured him. "Raleigh was only following Grey's orders, and don't forget, they did show mercy to the 100 officers and gentlemen they held for ransom."

"Well, yes," William sneered. "That touch of mercy must have greatly relieved the 600 as they waved goodbye. I heard from a servant that it was Raleigh himself who advised Grey to kill all 600 on the spot as soon as they surrendered."

"Mayhap he did," Malachi shrugged, "but the truth of the matter is there was a great deal of confusion about the terms of the surrender. At the time, it was also believed there were rebel Irish forces close at hand who might have rushed in and freed the foreign troops to fight again. In a strictly military sense, it was the right decision. Grey barely had enough men to guard the prisoners and still take the field against O'Neill if he decided to swoop in with his 5,000 troops. The ships that brought those unfortunate men to Ireland had been run off by our Channel Patrol, and there was no facility in all of Ireland to detain 700 prisoners. Who was to feed them? Who clothe them? Who guard them? So what were the English to do? I've heard Raleigh say— always in his cups, mind you—that it was the dirtiest duty he ever did in sixteen years of military service. He had to change swords three times because the blades were dulled from striking bone."

"Good God! Horror upon horror."

"You can afford to look at it that way, but, humanity and morality aside, it made a lot of sense as a military decision."

"I couldn't do it, even under orders," William testified.

"That remains to be seen. If such a duty ever does confront you, don't forget that a soldier only refuses such an order once and then he becomes number 601."

"Even so."

"Ah, you love to think of yourself as a special case: the man with clean hands."

"Well, I believe a person should grant himself as much luster and esteem as he possibly—"

Malachi snorted. "You have no idea how much our lives are like units of communication between monarchs exchanging messages, a period here or an exclamation mark there. *As flies to wanton boys are we to our monarchs. They kill us for their sport.*" [3]

William paused thoughtfully. 'That is an eye-opening vision. Did our queen approve such mass extermination beforehand?"

"There was no time for anything like that. Immediate action had to be taken to protect English lives. Elizabeth appoints military commanders to make on-the-spot decisions. She is then free to approve or disapprove their actions."

"Did she approve?"

"No reaction at all in public, although in private she expressed irritation that the 100 officers and officials were spared. Elizabeth is not opposed to heavy duty executions if the offense is significant. When the Catholic noblemen of Northern England staged a rebellion in 1569 with the object of installing Mary, Queen of Scots as

Queen of England, Elizabeth did not hesitate to have over 800 people hanged after the rebellion had been snuffed out."

"She hanged 800 English noblemen?"

"Well no, not exactly. That would cause too much confusion and disorganization. She had a handful of the principle nobility hung, drawn, and quartered as ringleaders, of course, to discourage such inclinations in the future, and then she simply confiscated the estates of 57 of the lesser traitors, to help the Crown defray the expense of putting down the rebellion. She also had her soldiers lay waste to the whole area by destroying the crops in the fields and storehouses and confiscating the farm animals to teach the whole area a lesson."

"Wait a minute now. Who were the other 795 people who were hanged?"

"Some of them were the people who actually followed their leaders in rebellion. Eighty were hanged in Durham where the actual revolt began and an additional 615 were selected from the neighboring towns and villages which had been surrounded after the revolt was crushed. The Earl of Sussex ordered his commanders to select the 'meanest of the people' from those communities and: 'to make very great example' of the people they picked. The hanging was done in a hurry, so that after the object lesson had been administered, Elizabeth's costly forces could be disbanded." [4]

"Yes," William said as he slowly shook his head, "it's only too clear that monarchs often have far greater financial problems than those of us who are only struggling to survive. But as I understand it, some of those who were executed were only following the orders of their noble leaders."

"Yes," Malachi nodded. "That's what they all say, and that's what makes the administration of justice so difficult at times. Elizabeth doesn't hesitate to take harsh steps when they are needed and she takes them without apology. She issued no public opinion about the executions at Smerwick since none was needed because the backstage sponsors of the ill-fated 600 kept silent for fear of revealing their participation. It solved a problem for England, and that's all the Queen cared about. Monarchs can't permit themselves to get bogged down in yesterday's problems nor in today's lawn-bowling schedule, or they'd have to stint on future matters. She sent a clear-cut message to King Philip and to Pope Gregory as well, and that's all that really counted."

"Spain and Rome armed the 700?"

"That's right. Rome gave its papal blessing in 1578 to James Fitzmaurice, fiery cousin to Gerald Fitzgerald, the Earl of Desmond—who was temporarily under English confinement at the time—and then after one false start, Rome and Madrid sent Fitzmaurice in Spanish ships with a 700-man polyglot crew of Italian mercenaries and Spanish volunteers to carry on a holy war against the heretical Elizabeth in southwest Ireland. The expedition was given no official commission when they sailed, and that's why they were executed and not treated as prisoners of war when they surrendered at the Smerwick fortress. Without a commission, they were simply a band of armed cut-throats descending on Ireland's West Coast for an exercise in pillage and rape just as the Vikings did for hundreds of years. The Smerwick thing was exactly as if we had scooped up 700 pirates in one grab, and we all know what happens to pirates."

"What would have happened if the invaders had a commission and obviously were prisoners of war?"

"Pretty much the same thing, I guess," shrugged Malachi. "There was still no place to put them."

Chapter 4:
LUNCH WITH RALEIGH THE NEXT DAY

In Youghal:

Showing no sign of the prior night's confusion, Sir Walter Raleigh inquired of Malachi the next morning, "An epic poem, you say, praising the Queen?"

"Praising her extravagantly," Malachi chuckled. "I've only transcribed bits of it myself on visits to Hap-Hazard—and I certainly make no claim to poetic sensibility on my own behalf—but I am taking the liberty of borrowing the opinion of the fine gentlemen who gather at Bryskit's cottage outside Dublin, when I say it is a major piece of work. They were unanimous in their approval when Spenser read part of it to them."

"Edmund Spenser, you say?" Raleigh mused. "Yes, I know the man well. He was Lord Grey's secretary during the Desmond Rebellion. Did a good job for us too in dealing with London."

"The same man," said Malachi. "And for that valuable service, he was granted an eight-thousand acre parcel of the confiscated Desmond estate adjoining Lord Roche's holdings, about thirty miles north of here at Kilcolman, between Cork and Limerick."

"Or astride Roche's land from the complaints I've heard in London," Raleigh chuckled. "These Anglo-Irish Lords like Roche don't yet realize they've had their fair share of years to make this land profitable for the Queen, and by every measure imaginable they have failed to do so. It's time for them to get out of the way and let our Undertakers have a go at it. But now you tell me that one of our own Undertakers in the middle of Ireland has written an epic poem to the Queen. I must confess such an oddity fascinates me. What does Spenser call his poem?

"The Fairey Queene."

Raleigh grinned. "And no doubt the fairey queen is a virgin queen?"

"As far as I could tell," Malachi replied.

"That's good. She'll like that," Raleigh mused. "She fancies that image for political reasons as well as personal. I'd like to hear the poem. See if you can't fetch me a copy when it's completed, Malachi, and tell Spenser I would consider buying the work if it makes a suitable present for the Queen. It's no secret I could use a little something to get back in her good graces."

"You're in it, you know," William put in.

"In it? In the poem itself?" Raleigh exclaimed. "Oh, I really must hear it then. When will you next see Spenser, Malachi? Can you get me an invitation?"

"You can't be serious, sir," Malachi said. "There is not a single home in all England or Ireland that wouldn't welcome a visit from the redoubtable Sir Walter Raleigh."

"I don't mean that kind of visit. Poet-to-poet is what I want. Would Spenser himself read it to me? There is always so much more illumination in the voice of the author."

William waved his wine glass in happy circles. "From what I've heard, he'll read it to every tinker and tradesman he chances across in the lane."

Raleigh stared for a moment, then shrugged and moved the wine bottle out of William's reach as Malachi said, "What he's trying to explain, your Honor, is that Master Spenser is eager to share his efforts with any appreciative audience, so there will be no trouble setting up a reading. We'll visit Spenser in a week or so just after we see the Lord Deputy in Dublin, and I'm sure he'll be overjoyed at the prospect."

"Good," Raleigh nodded. "Arrange a visit for me as soon as possible. Drop all other business but the Queen's. You know Spenser, do you?"

"Indeed I do, sir. We did business together often during the Desmond Rebellion. I carried many of Lord Grey's dispatches back and forth between Ireland and England during the late campaign. As a matter of fact, Master Spenser owes me a bit of a favor from the past, but we won't need to mention that once he hears you are interested in his work."

"Splendid! Then I'll count on you to deliver my message and return soon with the reply."

Malachi cleared his throat. "I'll certainly let you know, sir, as soon as possible. In any case, I think you can safely count on a visit about ten days from now unless I notify you otherwise."

"That's good," Raleigh nodded. "I'll need another week here to see that my tobac is well planted and then I'll be free to follow along. Tell Spenser not to go to any trouble.

Nothing formal. God knows I've had enough of the hypocrisy and hollowness of Courtly ritual for a time, and Ireland hardly seems the proper setting for pompous pretense and foolish flattery."

"I'll tell him you'd like it to be poet-to-poet."

"Just right. And assure him I'll bring some of my best stuff, so we may trade back and forth."

"He'll enjoy that, I'm sure," Malachi smiled, "as long as he gets to go first."

Raleigh chuckled. "I guess we're all the same in the end."

"How about the potatoes?" William asked.

"What?"

"Will you also plant the potatoes? Malachi and I risked our lives to carry them across to Ireland."

Raleigh frowned, and looked at William closely, "Do I know you? There's something vaguely familiar about your voice. Way back in the dark recesses of my mind, I seem to recall a quarrelsome voice very much like yours. Were you at our supper last night?"

"Excuse me, your Grace," Malachi broke in. "This worthless scoundrel is my apprentice, and he is certainly the last person in the world to be offering advice about what to plant in Ireland. As a matter of fact, he is required elsewhere at this very moment to prepare our luggage for travel. Get going, young man."

"I will, but first I would like to ask Sir Walter a question I didn't get a chance to ask last night when our meal ended so strangely."

"There's no time for that!" Malachi snapped. "Get about your duties this instant!"

"Hold on now, Malachi," Raleigh instructed. "I don't remember much about our supper last night, but if your young man has a question from that meal, I'm sure it will help me fill in some of the blanks I'm experiencing."

"I'm sorry, sir," Malachi persisted, "but as you well know, time is fleeting and we must make preparations to carry out your wishes, so I'm sure that whatever questions he may have——"

"That won't serve," Raleigh insisted. "I'm sure we're on to something here and I intend to pursue it. You will do me a personal service, Malachi, if you will attend to your preparations yourself and let me get to the bottom of something with this inquisitive young man. You are excused."

"Yes, my Lord," Malachi said and rolled his eyes skyward at William as he left.

"And now," Raleigh said as he stood up, loosened his sword in its hanger, put one booted foot up on the bench, and leaned over the table to speak directly to William. "before we discuss what happened last night, let me hear that voice one more time. What is your question?"

"I hope it's not too complex for you, your Grace, but I would really like to get the inside story of the Desmond Rebellion. I have heard enough disconnected bits and pieces of the affair lately so that I'm completely confused about what I now realize was a key event in Irish history—an event in which you played a major role, unless, of course, the significance of the event and your participation in it has been exaggerated."

"Well, this is certainly an amazing coincidence," Raleigh relaxed and resumed his seat on the bench across from William. "On my sea trip to Ireland just yesterday, I spent some time musing what I should do when my adventuring days are done and I end up with some spare time on my hands. I decided I would commit myself wholeheartedly to further serve my country and my Queen when that reflective time of life comes by writing an authoritative, History of the World."

"You mean you'll tell the whole truth about what goes on behind closed doors at Whitehall?"

Raleigh chuckled. "Even truth may be pursued too recklessly. I have already written out a cautionary prefatory pledge to remind myself to keep my pen at a workable aesthetic distance from my material. My first page will say: '*Whosoever in writing a modern history, shall follow truth too near the heels, it may haply strike out his teeth*'." [5]

"I think that's right. Every writer deserves a little wobble room."

"And I can think of no better way to cultivate realistic historical objectivity for that monumental task than by forcing my mind at this very moment to clear itself of nagging suspicions and attempt to piece together for you the story of the Great Irish Rebel Earl who helped destroy the southwest quarter of Ireland and brought more death and destruction to his people than any man before or since."

"The Earl of Desmond," ventured William.

"The very man. Gerald Fitzgerald. Let me take you back twenty-two years to 1565, when the two largest titled landowners in Ireland brought thousands of their followers to a field not far from here just outside Affane, and there they did their best to kill each other. The fourteenth Earl of Desmond, Gerald Fitzgerald, and the tenth Earl of Ormond, Thomas Butler, between them owned pretty much the entire southwest portion of the land mass of Ireland, close to one quarter of the entire country. By ancient grants and right of chieftaincy, Fitzgerald owned 800,000 acres or about 1550 square miles of this province of Munster, and Butler owned a little less of the neighboring province of Leinster."

"How many Providences are there in Ireland?"

"Only five. Ulster, Connaugt, Meath, and the two I've just mentioned."

"But the titles of Fourteenth Earl and Tenth Earl must mean such holdings were in their families for hundreds of years. Who made them earls to begin with?"

"Many of those titles and estates were granted over the years to noble Norman families after William the Conquerer invaded England back in 1066. For many years thereafter, the leading Norman families were encouraged by their monarchs to spread Norman influence, and they were granted titles and extensive land holdings in Ireland to make their dispersal comfortable. Our good King Henry VIII also made lords of many Irish chieftains during this century and turned over to them large tracts of monastic lands to insure their loyalty to him in his argument with the Pope."

"Sounds like a good deal for the chieftains. Titles and land for a little loyalty."

"Not quite that simple," Raleigh smiled. "To get the land, the chieftains also had to agree to adopt the English custom of primogeniture where the eldest son inherits everything rather than having the clan elect a new leader every time an old leader dies. Henry felt such a change would put some badly needed continuity into our control of Ireland and help reduce the culture of clan allegiance by making the noble Irish families more beholden to the English crown which had to approve the inheritance."

"Did that change work?"

"To some degree it did, but the truth of the matter is that even today the clan chiefs are the most powerful force in Ireland once you leave the protection of the English garrisons set up in the pales of Dublin, Cork, Waterford, Galway, and Limerick. So there is still work to be done in breaking up the power of the clans because of the 'Dictum of Hibernia Hibernescit'."

"I beg your pardon."

"'Ireland makes all things Irish'." Raleigh paused for a rueful chuckle. "Burghley speaks sadly of the process of assimilation being reversed in Ireland because this land grabs the invaders and turns them into raving Irishmen who are much more avid than the native Irish. Like the Vikings before them, the Norman families with few exceptions have disappeared into the Irish landscape without any trace of the English language or English law or English customs and, indeed, even without much respect for the English monarch or the tax collectors of the crown."

"They don't pay their taxes?"

"'Few pay little' is the way I've heard the situation summarized by knowledgeable people. The Irish use the rental and leasing money they collect from their holdings not to help relieve the expense which Elizabeth suffers for keeping the peace in this country, but rather to build their own private armies. They indulge themselves by fighting their own petty battles without the least concern for the best interests of England. The Fitzgeralds and the Butlers were arguing over the collection of rents in Munster when they battled it out at Affane twenty-two years ago, and Elizabeth decided then it was time to put a stop to private armies by telling them *'No sword shall be drawn in this realm but the Queen's which shall touch only the guilty'*." [6]

"And she made it stick?"

"It's still a work in progress," admitted Raleigh.

"Even after twenty-two years?"

"Twenty-two years and half a million lives."

"500,000 people! Like who? How?"

"Some of everybody you can imagine. Irish and English, Catholics and Anglicans, Gallowglass and pikemen, kerne and horseman, guilty and innocent, traitor and bystander, herder and farmer, men and women—not to mention a few hundred Spanish and Italians thrown into the mix. For many years the Irish wars have been regarded as 'The Englishman's Grave' since thousands of the Crown's soldiers have died here from scurvy and dysentery even before the axes and cross-bows take their toll. An enormous number of people die off to the side away from the major battles."

"Who do you mean?"

"In a six month period from late 1581 to early 1582 the area surrounding Cork was under siege by the rebels and lost one-third of its residents—about 30,000 people—from hunger and sickness brought about by famine and plague. In addition to the death of people, the livestock of southern Ireland have nearly all been killed off, and the property of the area hasn't fared much better after all the burning and looting that has occurred."

"And the Earl of Desmond caused all this?"

"He did his share although we kept him out of action in the Tower and under house arrest in London for seven years after he was shot in the hip in the battle of Affane. Good soldier story there, incidentally," Raleigh grinned. "As Butler's men lifted Gerald onto their shoulders to be carried off the battlefield where he had just lost 300 Geraldines—as his people are called—they mocked him by jeering, 'Where now is the mighty Earl of Desmond?' and he replied, 'Where he belongs. Riding on the backs of the Butlers.'" Raleigh chuckled and shook his head. "It's hard not to admire a man who soldiers on through it all, even if he was a traitor."

"So he was judged a traitor and his lands confiscated, but how did the war continue if he was out of action?"

"Hold on now. Final judgments are hard to come by at Whitehall. As a matter of fact, the Queen often takes months to make decisions. But then, of course, she demands results in days. The truth is that nobody knew exactly what to do with Desmond when Butler answered the Queen's summons to have the two of them appear before her in London after the Affane battle. It was easy enough to let Butler go home because he is one of the few Anglican earls in Ireland, and his family has always supported the Queen's policies in Leinster by supplying troops to put down local disturbances against the Crown. On a personal note, Butler is cousin to the Queen through the Boleyn side and was brought up in a noble house in London and was for a time a childhood companion to the then Princess Elizabeth, who called him 'Black Tom'."

William shook his head. "It is curious how personal all of this wrangling must be to the upper-crust since they all seem to be related."

"More personal than you can imagine between the Butlers and the Fitzgeralds. The Countess of Desmond, Eleanor Butler Fitzgerald, besides being a very close confidante of the Queen because she was also raised in England, is, of course, the wife of Gerald, but she also happens to be the mother of Thomas Butler."

"What? I'm really confused now. If I understand what you've just said, that means Gerald Fitzgerald and the man he set out to kill at Affane are father and son. Is that possible?"

"Step-son really," Raleigh smiled, "despite the fact that Butler is two years older than his step-father. Thomas Butler's father, the Ninth Earl of Ormond, died after Thomas was born, and the Countess of Ormond found something she liked in the Earl of Desmond and married him despite being twenty years his senior. Since that time, Eleanor has spent many days riding back and forth on horseback between one castle and another—often between hillsides teeming with throngs of opposing gallowglass and kern patiently watching her passage for hours and days—thirteen days on one occasion—to see if they were to fight or retire—as she tried to bind up the wounds between her son and her husband. But the men and their families have remained bitter enemies despite her efforts."

"I hope she didn't marry with her mind set on changing them," said William. "But you said Butler was considered safe enough to release back to Ireland?"

Raleigh nodded. "And, of course, Desmond was not. Although he was only a tepid Catholic, he was a strong home-rule man and disputed any Crown policy which interfered with his ancient rights to rule all of the Desmond territories just as he pleased. It was also believed he would not have shown up at all in London if Butler hadn't fetched him on a stretcher, because for one thing, Gerald's father—the Thirteenth Earl of Desmond—had refused an invitation from King Henry many years before to have Gerald raised as Thomas Butler was in a noble house in London, which would, of course, have permitted him to see how government really worked and would have made him much more amenable to guidance from the throne."

"So if Gerald was out of action for seven years, where did the war come from?"

"During his confinement, Whitehall gradually came to realize that Munster with its fine meadows and plentiful water could be a great larder of cattle and grain and represented a treasure trove of fees and rentals if the land could be worked properly. The Irish have never really farmed to any advantage because they still prepare the soil by tying a plow to the tail of a horse and when that tail is all pulled out, they throw up their hands and turn to cattle grazing."

"Well at least that makes them shifty instead of shiftless as I've heard some charge," William smiled.

"You could say that," Raleigh said, "but basically, they still prefer a nomadic existence where they take their cattle into the mountains for the fresh grass in the summer and down into the valleys in the autumn. A healthy, outdoor existence with little manual labor and an opportunity to travel suits them just fine—plus the opportunity to visit and sample the ale in different communities, of course. Since forty percent of the Irish landscape consists of bogs and forested mountains, you can well imagine that the seasonal movement of herds puts a premium on control of river fords, stream crossings, and clear passages and, consequently, the landscape plays a significant role in Irish history."

"But where did this new speculation on the future of Munster leave the Earl of Desmond?"

"Some of the Whitehall wise-heads reached the major conclusion that England would be better off getting rid of Desmond entirely and putting some sturdy, reliable Anglican Englishmen with military experience in charge of utilizing the land intelligently. They hoped thereby to cultivate greater political stability in the province and to enhance the flow of revenues returned to Whitehall and, not incidentally, to plant a permanent English military presence which would solidify Munster's allegiance to the Crown and dampen Spanish interest in the area."

"Does that mean they would confiscate Desmond's land?"

"Oh, yes," Raleigh nodded, "but they wanted the land transfer to be perfectly legal and above board, so they cleverly loosened Gerald's confinement from the Tower and increased his pension so he could move freely under informal house-arrest in Southwark and Bankside where he frequented the stews and did some drinking and finally ran across the daring seadog, Captain Martin Frobisher. Together the two hatched a plot to smuggle Gerald down the Thames and out of England before he was missed. Frobisher, however, was operating as a government agent the whole time and finally turned Gerald in while he was standing on the London dock in disguise, ready to travel, and armed in defiance of the Queen's command."

"Entrapment! Seems dishonorable somehow."

"Some might think so," agreed Raleigh. "But Whitehall argued he was free not to fall into the trap. Anyway, he was charged with violating his parole and plotting treason, so his execution was considered because that would have neatly attainted his title, confiscated his property, and opened the door to establishing the English Plantation in Munster. The entrapment must have caused some administrative uneasiness, however—particularly on Burghley's part, I'll wager—and Gerald was offered an alternative to total destruction. To save his life Gerald was squeezed enough to plead 'I, the Earl of Desmond on the 12th day of July, 1568, hereby acknowledge my offences, my life being in peril…and relinquish into her Majesty's hands all my lands, tenements, houses, castles, signories, all I stand possessed of, to receive back what her Majesty please allow me'." [7]

"And what did Elizabeth allow him for donating 1550 square miles of Munster to the Crown?"

"Basically, she allowed him another four years of house arrest in Southwark while one of my relatives took advantage of the open door to Munster lands."

"A Raleigh moved in?"

"Not quite. Sir Peter Carew was my cousin from Devonshire and had up until 1568 always been something of a ne'er-do-well country knight who had more ambition than land. He saw his chance to exercise his dynastic tendencies when the Privy Council decided to promote the establishment of the Munster Plantation by awarding substantial estates to any wellborn English gentleman with military experience—since he would have to evict the Irish tenants—who could prove that he had a prior claim to Desmond lands. All he had to do was present to the compliant Council half-believable documents—Carew's were accepted even though they were mostly illegible because, it was legally contended, they had at some point, unfortunately, been trampled underfoot—and also agree to turn over to London a reasonable fee and a portion of whatever profits proceeded from the land, and he would be in business as quick as he could clap on his hat."

"After he evicted the Irish."

"That was the tricky part, but Carew was determined to clear Munster for himself and other lackland English knights including his kinsman and mine, Humphrey Gilbert, as well as Sir Richard Grenville and Desmond's jailor in Southwark, Sir Warham St. Leger. Since Carew went to Ireland as a would-be landlord rather than as the commander of a royal military force, he prepared for the operation by rounding up all the English ne'er-do-wells and Irish bonaghts he could locate to rout out the small Munster landholders whose title to their land—granted by the deposed Earl of Desmond—were suddenly declared invalid and they were, consequently, trespassing on Carew's newly acquired property."

"Who are the bonaghts?"

"They are those men who have proved so lacking in social graces or moral ethics that they have been cast out by the clans, if you can imagine such a thing." Raleigh smiled. "They are masterless men who have turned into drifting, mercenary plunderers. While they are grabbing what they can, they don't mind in the least shedding a little blood as they terrorize the countryside with killings and burnings to make the area uninhabitable for the former occupants, but Carew believed they were just what he needed to cleanse the land for a new beginning, so he turned them loose. The problem with such men, of course, is that once started, there's no stopping them, and Carew's men went much too far."

"How much further can you go than burning and killing?"

"They encroached where they should not even have dreamed of going. They not only plundered Desmond lands, they intruded on the territory of the Kavanaughs and the Burkes, and finally they killed whatever chance the first Munster Plantation had of succeeding by foolishly sacking and burning the prosperous city of Kilkenny, the very seat and residence of Thomas Butler. Don't forget now, Thomas Butler is the Earl of Ormond, who, in a very real sense, opened the door to Carew's sudden acquisition of valuable land in the first place, so you can see how far out of control the situation had careened when his property was destroyed. Ironically, at the time of the attack, Butler was in London filing suit to get some of the Desmond lands for his family."

"When you say they killed the prospects of the first Munster Plantation, are you implying there was a second one?"

"You are seated in the very midst of it." Raleigh smiled and waved about the room of his rebuilt residence at Youghal. "Let me explain. Even though Sir Peter Carew was my cousin, I am very pleased the man is no longer with us. He died peacefully enough in 1575, and thereby removed from the Irish scene one of the most arrogant, irrational human beings ever to cultivate chaos in an area only too receptive to such entertainment."

"But from '68 to his death in '75, Carew managed to create chaos aplenty, I take it."

"In the winter of 1568, Carew had succeeded in running off some Irish and setting up small English farms in his newly acquired territory in Idrone and Carlow, but when he crossed the line into Butler territory and burned Kilkenny, he not only shocked and alarmed every lord who held land in Ireland, he also set in motion what we now call the first of the Desmond Wars."

"So it was Carew's attack on Butler that started the Desmond Wars?"

"Right. Until Carew struck his land, Thomas Butler had rightfully been regarded as the staunchest ally the Queen had in Ireland, but when other Irishmen saw such a loyal subject suddenly attacked and the very seat of his power pillaged and burned and his people savagely killed and his wife publicly violated by a group which had the approval and encouragement of the Privy Council, they reached a chilling conclusion. If that could happen to Butler, it could happen to any one of them. They saw no explanation other than that the attack represented the first step of a royal policy to strip the Irish Lords not only of their lands but of their honor and dignity as well, so every land owner in Ireland got busy locking his gates and sharpening his weapons."

"But the Irish had accepted some evicting and dispossessing during that winter?"

"Not exactly. Any Englishman who was planted on an estate out of the shadow of Carew's mercenaries soon found his throat cut by one of the evicted Irish who were hiding out in nearby woods feasting on shamrocks. The organized resistance to the

English plantation effort in Munster quickly arose when one of the Desmond cousins, James Fitzmaurice, in the absence of Gerald, appointed himself Captain of the Desmonds. Fitzmaurice quickly led the Desmond gallowglass of the MacSheehy and MacSweeny clans into rebellion against the English plantation plan, and he was soon joined in rebellion by the apprehensive Irish landholders throughout Munster."

"Who are the gallowglass?"

"Good people to avoid if your mind is set on a long life," Raleigh chuckled. "I don't know if you've ever heard of the Viking berserkers who entered all battles with a steely determination to kill or be killed, and who accepted no condition in between—they didn't do nuance on the battlefield. The gallowglass seem to me to be direct descendants of those notable warriors in both strategy and weaponry. They are professional, mercenary fighters for hire to anybody who can afford them. I had occasion recently to write out a letter for one of my men who had spent more time collecting battle scars than he spent learning his letters. He said the gallowglass were:'*picked and selected men of great and mighty bodies, cruel without compassion. The greatest force of the battle consisteth of them, choosing to die rather than to yield, so that when it cometh to bandy blows, they are quickly slain or win the field. They are armed with a shirt of mail, a skullcap of steel, and a skein [dagger]: The weapon they most use is a battle-axe, six-foot long, the blade whereof is somewhat like a shoemaker's knife; the stroke thereof is deadly where it lighteth*'." [8]

"I've noticed the Irish certainly have their fair share of big, burly people to handle such cumbersome weapons as six-foot axes, but I also see plenty of small, wiry, agile chaps in this country who, incidentally, do most of the talking. What do they do during battle? Hold the horses?"

"Oh no. The lighter, swifter people who are called the 'kern' represent the light Irish infantry, and it is their job to skirmish in front of the gallowglass and along their flanks with swords and short spears which they call darts. Protected only with plated leather, they move swiftly to try to disrupt our formations and cause confusion in our ranks. They often use their darts to kill or injure cavalry mounts, and with their short swords, they gang up on stragglers and on anybody who breaks formation or ends up on the ground, but they are no match for well—drilled pikemen or for determined cavalry."

"You said the gallowglass resemble the Vikings in weaponry as well as strategy. Does that mean their weapons are out of date?"

"Only a few hundred years behind the times," Raleigh snickered. "The English army has long since replaced skullcaps with morions which are safer headpieces because their curved brim peaked in front and back better deflect the enemy blows, and we long ago replaced shirts of mail with steel breastplates for better protection. The few Irish cavalry units we encounter still ride with pillions on the saddle behind the rider instead of with stirrups, and as a consequence, they can't hold their seat as well when they charge and must hold their lances above their heads when they attack. We haven't seen weaponry like that in England since the Battle of Hastings six hundred years ago."

"It all seems like another demonstration of the idea that the Irish are hard-headed as far as change is concerned, but it is puzzling why they are so slow to advance in the combat area where they spend so much of their time and energy."

"Don't let anything I've said create the impression that their old weapons are ineffectual. They can still impose terrible harm at close quarters, and that's why all of our strategies are to hold them off with pikes while we fire at them with our muskets."

"You said Fitzmaurice appointed himself as Captain of the Desmonds, and I wondered if that was the way such officers were usually designated?"

"It's a common enough office in the hierarchy of the clan, but it's usually not a self-appointed office. Fitzmaurice gained a lot of fighting muscle, however, when he upped the ante against Carew and the Crown by declaring that his forces would fight not only against the English effort to seize Irish lands but also against the Act of Religious Uniformity and the Oath of Supremacy by which the Established Church of England—the Anglican—had supplanted the Catholic Church in Ireland as well as in England. In championing the cause of Catholicism in Ireland, he not only hoped to inflame his own people with the energetic magic of religious fervor, but also to get support from Rome and Spain in his campaign to drive the heretics out of Ireland.

In the meantime, however, he proposed to curb the burning and pillaging of Carew's people, by killing everybody connected to the plantation effort, and also by carrying out a scorched earth policy of burning and pillaging everything in the path of Carew's marauders. That traditional military strategy eventually defeated Carew's forces and sent all the English survivors fleeing naked for their lives to the coastal cities of Youghal, Kinsale, Waterford, and Cork."

"With both contending forces burning and pillaging the countryside, I can only imagine that would result in a great reduction of the annual food supply."

"That was exactly the situation before Sir Henry Sidney, the Lord Deputy of Ireland set out to hunt down Fitzmaurice with regular English forces. One year later, Sidney had finally driven Fitzmaurice and his irregulars back into the mountains of Kerry and pulled the teeth of the rebellion's support by plundering and burning the lands and hanging the estate people of those Irish lords who had gone out to join Fitzmaurice. The rebel lords were forced to return home and beg the Crown's pardon so they might protect what was left of their property.

By the end of 1569, Sidney had achieved a stalemate with Fitzmaurice, but he was recalled to London because he insisted on imposing equal taxes on all the Irish Lords without making exceptions for the favorites of the Queen. As you may know, Elizabeth has little patience with administrators who strike her as being politically impractical. The responsibility for finishing the job and rounding up the Desmond Captain was assigned to Sir John Perrot."

"Did Perrot change the strategy once they had the rebels isolated in the mountains? Did he go in after them?"

"He made that mistake at first and suffered for it. He complained to Burghley in 1571: *'This work of trotting the mountains and marching the bogs is not suited to English soldiers. The Irish flee where hounds can scarce follow and much less men'*. But it's clear that Sir John Perrot is a quick learner and very soon he began to fight like the Irish. By 1572, he again wrote to Burghley, obviously delighted with his own ambush ability: *'The Irish ran from our trap and fled into the bogs, where my soldiers followed them barefooted, carrying light cavalry lances which there serve better than pikes. They returned with a trophy of fifty heads, with which I decorated the market cross of Kilmallock'.*" [9]

"Where is Kilmallock?"

Raleigh pulled a rough map from his doublet. "You'll see on this map of Ireland. Kilmallock is a significant town in central Munster because it is known as the 'Sallyport of the Geraldines' as they come east out of the Kerry mountains, and its control by Perrot indicated that Fitzmaurice was pretty well bottled up. Perrot became discouraged, however, after two years of losing men to ambush and ague from the damp and the bogs, and he was also stung by Whitehall's complaints of lack of progress, so he departed from custom and challenged Fitzmaurice to a personal duel on horseback. The Captain of the Desmonds didn't show up for the fight, so he was humiliated in all eyes, and the Irish thereafter have always held a grudging respect for Perrot even as they laugh at him for turning into an Irish warlord issuing personal challenges."

"Not showing up must have hurt Fitzmaurice's ability to recruit new fighters."

Raleigh shrugged. "Most of his men were leaving anyway to keep from starving because the ravaged hills of Kerry held little food for anyone. In the spring of 1573, Fitzmaurice was hard driven enough by the blockade to surrender to Perrot in a formal ceremony with the sword pressed to his breast. Since he came in freely, he was allowed to leave freely, and he soon fled to France to recruit new allies in his effort to chase the heretic Queen out of Ireland."

"So in short, they ran him off after four years but not before he upset the Munster Plantation idea?"

"Right," Raleigh nodded. "The plantation plan was killed for the time being because the Munster countryside had been completely laid to waste. Whitehall debated the wisdom of reestablishing Gerald again in his home territory in order to get Munster back in shape, and because Gerald was reputed to despise his cousin, it was hoped his return to power would forestall any return of Fitzmaurice. Gerald was escorted to Dublin to await the Queen's final decision on his disposition, but Dublin Castle couldn't hold him and he quickly escaped. His journey back to Kerry—which is the western most section of Munster and has always been the seat of Desmond power—became a public spectacle as he discarded his English clothing along the road and donned the dress of an Irish chieftain to the cheers of the kern and gallowglass who escorted him in triumphant return."

"Did his escape make him a hunted man again?"

"That was carefully considered, especially after he dismissed the officers Perrot had put in place for the governing of Munster and replaced them with his own people. He also returned the Catholic Church to the community, returned the community to clan rule, and started soliciting clan chiefs for the next fight. Whitehall considered putting a price on Gerald's head, but Elizabeth was bone tired of the expense and trouble of Irish Wars, so she accepted the advice of Burghley who counseled, '*You must conciliate Ireland; allow the chiefs to continue their ancient greatness, take away the fear of conquest lately grafted in the wild Irish, and wink at disorders which do not offend the crown*'. [10] In September 1574, Gerald was therefore invited to submit to Sidney at Cork in order to be officially pardoned and then fully restored as Earl of Desmond along with the revenues, privileges and the full rights of his hereditary estates."

"After they almost killed him the first time!" William exclaimed. "That's really the kind of unprincipled, expeditious policy-making that Machiavelli was talking about."

"It was felt that Gerald was far less of a threat to the Crown than his cousin since he did not invoke the kind of blind religious fervor that Fitzmaurice induced in the rebels."

"The lesser of two evils," nodded William.

"Unfortunately, that's what policy-making often amounts to. For the next few years, Gerald did avoid major troubles with Whitehall, but he clearly dallied with the demands of the Crown by offering them transparent alibis and flimsy pretenses in place of the taxes and fees they attempted to collect. He told them that without that money, he could not support adequate forces to maintain the Queen's law or guarantee the safety of her subjects, and reminded them that his forces had often served the Queen by hunting down outlaws and woodkern."

"Woodkern?"

"Robbers and thieves living in the woods because they're so bad at their craft they can't afford to live in a community. Desperate, dangerous people, to be sure, and well worth the catching, but Burghley complained he had seen very few woodkern heads and pointed out that Gerald was known to travel often with an expensive company of 500 gallowglass. Gerald replied that he needed that much protection because of all the enemies England had left when they devastated Munster in pursuit of Fitzmaurice. Burghley contended further that 500 gallowglass were far too many for the present situation, and some of the money saved by cutting ranks could be forwarded to London. Gerald next turned his Irish cheek to Burghley by denying he had any gallowglass at all, and deflected further London instructions by offering delays and deceptions to anything London ordered. He went so far in 1576 that it was felt his evasiveness was severe enough to amount to treason. He was again judged a traitor and a 500-pound prize put on his head, but cooler heads quickly prevailed and that designation was withdrawn."

"He sounds like a man who likes a lot of excitement."

"Not always. For the next couple of years, he kept pretty quiet, hunting deer with his brothers John and James while he strengthened his island castle at Askeaton against any attack which might arise after Fitzmaurice returned with whatever armed force he could drum up on the continent."

"Did England know that the Desmond captain would return? Were we keeping track of him?"

"Oh, yes. Walsingham doesn't let danger like that slip off the page. Ever since Fitzmaurice left Ireland in 1572, Walsingham's people had shadowed him as he went from France to Spain to Italy seeking allies to help him expel the heretic English from Catholic Ireland. The French refused to help because they still had the Alencon-Elizabeth wedding boiling in the possibility pot. King Philip of Spain still had his hands full and his forces occupied with the revolt in the Netherlands. Pope Gregory was always reluctant to operate openly against Elizabeth, but under the table he did offer 300 jailbirds—Italian musketeers—if somebody else would transport them."

"Would Fitzmaurice take jailbirds?"

"He would take anybody he could get for the kind of work he had in mind, the rougher the better. So the Captain of the Desmonds persevered, and by late 1578, as Walsingham quickly learned, he had enlisted a formidable army of Catholic sympathizers, avaricious plunderers, and casual adventurers to the number of 4,000 who were being assembled in Lisbon on Spanish ships and almost ready to sail."

"My word! 4,000 is a fair sized army."

Raleigh nodded. "Enough to pose a real threat if they succeeded in reaching Ireland because they were well armed and commanded by a veteran Italian officer, Hercules of Pisa, under the general command of Thomas Stukeley, a renegade English soldier of fortune who had shown himself in past adventures to be both courageous and competent—even if greedy and foolhardy. They also had a Papal nuncio for spiritual guidance in the Jesuit Nicholas Sanders, who promised papal forgiveness for any who killed the English heretics."

"They must have encountered some rough seas on the way because I remember hearing that just 700 of them landed the next year on the Dingle Peninsula only to be executed at uh,uh——I forget the name of the place."

Raleigh frowned for a moment. "It's strange that the name Smerwick sticks in your throat as it sometimes does in mine, but no matter. Whitehall continued to believe the best bet England had against Fitzmaurice succeeding would be the resistance Gerald would lead against the man he reputedly disliked so intensely."

"Did that strategy work? Did Gerald perform as expected?"

"As fortune would have it, his loyalty wasn't tested for another year. One fine morning in 1578, good King Sebastian of Portugal noticed the fine army assembling on his docks in Lisbon and decided that was a good moment to settle a little argument he had with his neighbor to the south, the King of Morocco, so he commandeered the whole outfit, ships and all, and along with the Portuguese and German mercenaries he already had lined up, sailed them all off to Africa."

"Was that a Catholic versus Moslem argument?"

"Not really. Much more a trade argument and piracy problem. The disagreement turned into a major battle at Alcazar, however, and killed nearly everybody involved including the King of Portugal, the King of Morocco along with the pretender to the throne of Morocco, and Hercules of Pisa, Thomas Stukeley, and most of the people Fitzmaurice had lined up to help him in Ireland. Quite apart from what that deadly African battle did to the Irish invasion plan eight years ago, England has yet to feel the full brunt of the aftermath from that fight. The death of the King of Portugal permitted King Philip of Spain to seize the throne of Portugal with its safe harbors on the Atlantic."

"Safe harbors?"

Raleigh nodded. "Especially the well-protected port of Lisbon which will make a splendid staging area for Philip's proposed armada. In addition to the crown, Philip also gained control of the Portuguese colonies in India, Africa, and Brazil. More important, perhaps, it gave Spain the largest navy in the world by adding a veteran merchant fleet of large, seaworthy East Indiamen in addition to twelve well-built Portuguese galleons—which we will undoubtedly get a close view of when they come against us."

"But Fitzmaurice came on anyway with his remaining force?"

"Right. He scraped together 700 of the original group and landed them at the most extreme southwest corner of Ireland on the Dingle Peninsula in June of 1579. They were not all Spanish and Italian, however. The final count showed 80 Spanish soldiers, 300 Italians recruited from the jails of Rome, some exiled Irish clerics along with Fitzmaurice's underlings, a handful of English and an assortment of Continental adventurers including Portuguese, Flemings, French, and a small group of women connected to the various groups."

"My word. That sounds like an international group."

Raleigh nodded. "It was enough to get the second Desmond War started. At this time, Gerald maintained a friendly relationship with Sir William Drury, Lord Deputy of Cork, who was preparing an English force to confront Fitzmaurice. The Desmond Captain himself left his invasion force at Dingle and went off to recruit the Geraldines who had strong Catholic feelings to help his fight for religious freedom. In his absence, the mixed group of mercenaries did what they came to Ireland to do. They burned and sacked the small Catholic community of Dingle even after it had greeted their landing with flowers and dancing in the street, and then they moved on to the Smerwick fortress nearby."

"I guess those villainous jailbirds didn't want anybody to think they came that far just to dance and sing."

Raleigh frowned, intent on his narrative. "In the meantime, Drury attempted to set up negotiations with Fitzmaurice by sending two older gentlemen who were long-time friends of the Desmonds to talk things over and get some idea of what the invasion force intended. At that time, however, Gerald's two brothers, Sir John and Sir James, decided to make a show of unity with Fitzmaurice by beheading the two old family friends and by joining the hundreds of Catholic Geraldines who were ready to take the field against the English force."

"'Tis a comedy of errors," groaned William.

"And it gets worse," agreed Raleigh. "Drury activated Nicholas Maltby, the president of the Province of Connaught, who quickly burned some of Gerald's castles and killed some of his people in order to get the Earl of Desmond to show his true colors. But Gerald not only did not come out openly to join the rebellion but instead offered some of his gallowglass to serve as scouts for Drury in pursuit of Fitzmaurice."

"Drury didn't accept such a suspicious offer, did he?"

"Oh, yes, that arrangement wasn't too unusual. As a matter of fact Maltby's English army included a large force of Irish provisionals fighting for him, but, of course, that group was well-acquainted with Maltby's deadly, iron-handed discipline, so they behaved themselves as expected in the field. Maltby continued a campaign of burning and sacking more Geraldine properties, and, of course, hanging the occupants in order to drive Fitzmaurice and Sir John out in the open to protect their people. In the meantime, Gerald not only made no overt moves against the Crown, but turned his son over to Drury as ransom for his loyalty. Maltby, however, was absolutely convinced that Gerald was plotting something big, so he pursued him relentlessly."

"Let me see now. Drury and Maltby were leading English armies against Fitzmaurice and Sir John Fitzgerald, who are leading groups of Irish rebels. But Gerald Fitzgerald, the Earl of Desmond, was just hanging out in his castle without joining anybody after lending some of his gallowglass to the English army under Drury. Was Gerald plotting something?"

"I think he was plotting with himself about how to remain the Earl of Desmond by walking a very narrow path with a precipitous drop-off on each side. After three years in the tower and four more under house arrest, he had been convinced by Whitehall that he would be deprived not only of his life but that his family would lose forever his title and his estates if he brought the Geraldines out in open rebellion against the crown. On the other hand, if he failed to act against the depredations being visited on his people and estates first by Carew and then by the English armies of Drury and Maltby, he could lose not only the respect of his tenants but also the allegiance of the clan leaders scattered across Munster. It seems clear, however, that by offering his son as ransom, he was determined at that time not to join the rebellion."

"That should have been convincing."

"It was for a time, but even while Gerald sat musing at Askeaton, Fitzmaurice set about burning and pillaging the Irish villages which had housed Maltby's forces, and laying siege to Cork and some of the other coastal cities. Maltby retaliated by burning houses and crops and hanging everybody he suspected of supporting the Desmond Rebellion. Attention was called to the fact that while Gerald never openly broke out in support of the rebels, his personal bodyguard of 1200 gallowglass reduced itself to 60 overnight while Fitzmaurice shortly gained 1140 new fighters."

"Which probably confirmed Maltby's suspicion about Gerald."

"Commanders like Maltby don't entertain suspicions. As much as anything, Maltby is the instrument of the unforgiving Puritan purpose in Ireland, so the appearance of Gerald's gallowglass in Fitzmaurice's force only reinforced Maltby's convictions, and he continued to provoke Gerald by burning his castles and killing his people whenever the opportunity arose."

"Trying to goad Gerald into open rebellion?"

"I think he was. I think Walsingham had instructed him to settle the Desmond thing once and for all, and he got a big break in that direction in August of 1579 when Fitzmaurice was finally run to ground and killed in one of those bizarre Irish episodes which arise out of nowhere at the crossing of a stream."

"August, eh? Only three months after Fitzmaurice landed his invasion force back in Ireland."

"That's right. He was traveling about the Kerry countryside he knew so well with a small staff planning further attacks on Maltby's people. They camped overnight under Barrington Bridge close to Limerick, near the northern borders of Desmond's territory. As usual, his men went out to fetch fresh horses for the next morning's ride. They took one from a simple Irish churl who was plowing his field, and the farmer followed them back to the bridge to complain to whoever was in charge. Fitzmaurice assured the man that his horse was a noble sacrifice in the cause of Irish freedom and for the Holy Mother church, and then went off to eat his supper. The churl cared nothing about such abstractions but only desired to have his field plowed, so he went immediately to report the theft to his lord, Theobald Burke, who happened to be an Anglican and an Anglophile."

"Bad news for Desmond."

"Right. Burke gathered some men and rode to confront Fitzmaurice across a small stream near the bridge. The Captain of the Desmonds was also mounted and identified himself by shouting, 'For the Pope!' and Burke replied, 'God save the Queen and devil take James Fitzmaurice!' One of Burke's musketeers then fired across the stream and the ball caught James full in the chest in what proved to be a mortal wound."

"It always seems odd to see such a powerful and influential person finished off in such a casual encounter."

"Not quite finished. It appears the Fitzgeralds die hard because James spurred his horse across the stream and drove his sword into the throat of Theobald Burke, so that he had company for his journey to eternity. Before he departed, however, he instructed his men to cut off his head and hide it so Maltby could not display it at his headquarters."

"My word! Fitzmaurice was still planning his future even as he lay on his death bed. Did his death bring Gerald out?"

"No. Instead, Gerald's brother, Sir John Fitzgerald, inherited the 3,000 fighters Fitzmaurice had gathered and went on to soundly defeat the English army at Springfield, where Drury himself was fatally wounded. Whitehall believed that the Irish gallowglass which Gerald had lent Drury for reconnaissance had led the English forces into an ambush, so all patience with the Earl of Desmond was lost once again, and Sir William Pelham was sent over to replace Drury and to confront Gerald. While the transfer of command was going on, Maltby formed his well trained troops into blockish bands to soundly thrash Sir John's gallowglass at Monaster even though the Irish outnumbered the English."

"Blockish bands?"

"A variation of the Spanish square. We form up several rows of pikemen facing outward on each side of a square and station our musketeers inside the square to fire on the charging gallowglass who are busy trying to chop their way through the wall of 18-foot pikes. It's a good formation for stopping the ferocious rush of the gallowglass who come on so strongly that their first row at times becomes impaled on the end of the pikes so that their blood runs down onto the hands of the pikeman."

"Do the gallowglass ever overrun such formations?"

"Sometimes they do succeed in hacking their way into the square and then it's unfortunate for anybody they can reach with their 6-foot axes, but often they are forced to retreat and that's when well-drilled squares stay in formation and pursue them.

That's exactly what Maltby's people did and before the day was done, they managed to dispose of 500 of Sir John's Geraldines."

"The blockish band formation sounds like a wonderful defensive maneuver. Why don't the English use it more often?"

"You can bet we use it every chance we get, but there are two conditions that must be met before it can be utilized. First, the pikemen must be well drilled in the formation beforehand because there's no opportunity for training on the job. The slightest miscalculation in aligning and maintaining the pikes would let the Irish pour into the square to slaughter our people who would at that moment have their backs turned and their weapons pointed outward. Second, the formation is only possible in open country where it's feasible to station the pikemen shoulder to shoulder. That's why the Irish like to attack in narrow passages and stream crossings and other places where it's impossible to form up into blockish bands."

"Well, I guess in a military sense, the Irish would be dumb not to stack the deck in their favor."

"Right. They do very little formation drilling in their training, so they count heavily on the surprise frontal assault and the hidden ambush. Many English leaders were afraid that the Earl of Desmond had some kind of surprise attack in mind when he did not openly lend his title and prestige to the rebellion despite Maltby's efforts to goad him into open resistance, so the newly-arrived Pelham issued an ultimatum to Gerald. Either he would come out to attend a meeting with Pelham and renew his allegiance to the Crown or he would be declared a traitor." Raleigh paused to smile. "I hate to admit it, but it's no small wonder that Gerald refused to come out since he had been placed in our custody several times in the past at just such meetings."

"Did Pelham carry out his threat?"

"He did and declared Gerald a traitor in November 1579 and thereby set off the Second Desmond War, because Gerald immediately mounted his white charger and rode off to battle against the Crown with the whole southwest of Ireland rising behind him. Gerald spent the first months of angry defiance redistributing the confiscated farms back to his hungry peasants and gathering his forces. Then he did an odd thing in attacking and pillaging of all places a town which the Desmonds themselves had built, right here in Youghal, where they constructed the port for this city and erected many of the public buildings." Raleigh waved around him.

"That must have surprised London."

"It did, indeed, and it's still hard to understand because Gerald's people tore down the town walls and burned the public buildings. The English officials were dragged out and hanged, and the women of the town were divided into lots and each lot assigned to a different clan for entertainment purposes. At the same time Sir John Fitzgerald led a force which included the Spanish and Italian troops to run off the

English garrisons at Castlemaine and Castleisland and ended up burning and sacking another Desmond center, the town of Tralee. I think Gerald wanted to strike a nerve in England, and he certainly succeeded with Elizabeth because upon hearing of the outrage, she was heard to roar, 'Which idiot declared Desmond a traitor before we had him in hand'?"

"That's getting at the heart of the matter, all right."

Raleigh nodded, "Insightful administrative thinking even if after the fact. The vindictiveness of Maltby and the clumsiness of Pelham had tipped a regional revolt into a widespread civil war which finally alarmed the Queen enough to put aside for a moment 'the French Cause' of possibly marrying the heir-apparent to the French throne and to give ear to her advisors who warned her that the Irish situation was about to spiral out of control. This was the period during which she had banned Walsingham from her presence because of his thorny advice on the marriage, so she had not been kept up to date on the unrest in Munster."

"Did she take action?"

"I'll say she did! The Queen was finally fed up with the endless wrangle Ireland represented because it was so unresponsive to intelligent administrative direction, and it refused to show any inclination to share the expense of keeping the country safe and civilized. Elizabeth always counted very heavily on solving Irish problems by a skillful application of bribery and coercion, but when that policy failed to quiet the unrest in Munster—and especially when foreign troops were brought onto the scene—she grew angry enough with the Irish that early in 1580, she was heard to shout; *'Enough! Cry havoc, and let slip the dogs of war'.*" [11]

"My word, that sounds like some kind of Rubicon had been crossed in her mind."

"Exactly. She ordered up a second army to back up Pelham's force to finally grind the rebels into the dirt of their own territory and be rid of them forever. So in early 1580, Thomas Butler, the Earl of Ormand, was called upon for the second time to command a royal army and ordered to join Pelham in putting down the rebels. Before getting the campaign started, however, he had other problems to solve. He watched his men suffer sickness from lack of food and become ineffectual from lack of arms. Fairly disgusted, he wrote bitterly to the Privy Council knowing full well Elizabeth and everybody at Court would see his letter."

"Did you see it?"

"Not at that time. I was still here in Ireland fighting it out on a daily basis, but I did see a copy later when I was on good terms with the Queen, and I was impressed at how typical his letter was of all communications from English forces in the field."

"Typical how?"

"Butler wrote; *'I require to be victualled, that I might bestow the captains and soldiers under my leading in such places as I know to be fitted for the service, and most among the rebels.*

I was answered there was none. I required the ordinance for batteries many times and could have none, nor cannot as yet, for my Lord Justice sayeth to me, it is not in the land. Money I required for the army to supply necessary wants, and could have but 200 pounds, a bare proportion to leave with an army. Now what any man can do with these wants I leave to your judgment. I hear the Queen mislikes that her service has gone no faster forward...I would to God I could feed soldiers with the air, and throw down castles with my breath, and furnish naked men with a wish, and if these things might be done the service would on as fast as her Highness would have it. This is the second time that I have been suffered to want all these things, having the like charge that now I have, but there shall not be a third time; for I protest I will sooner be committed as a prisoner by the heels than to be thus dealt with again'." [12]

"Did he get his supplies?"

"Enough to get started on what he and Pelham agreed would be a mutual sweep from east to west right through the province of Munster and turn it into 'as bare a country as ever Spaniard set his foot in'. No living thing was to be spared."

"I guess that means women and children too."

"Everybody, without exception. The Irish Chronicle complained, '*It is not wonderful that they should kill men fit for action, but they killed blind and feeble men, women, boys and girls, sick persons, idiots, and old people.*' [13] As a soldier myself, I know that hard work must at times be done in the field, but I think it is unfortunate that some military commanders like Pelham become so steeped in blood, they lose their sense of perspective and appear gleeful when they report to the Queen how they have carried out her commands, little realizing that her tender sensibilities might easily be aroused by their grisly details and her orders might thereby be hastily revised."

"Were her tender sensibilities aroused?"

"They were eventually by such reports as Pelham shared with her. For instance one read; '*We consumed with fire all inhabitants and executed the people wherever we found them. My manner of prosecuting is thus: I give the rebels no breath to relieve themselves, but by one of your garrisons or other they be continually hunted. I keep them from their harvest, and have taken great preys of cattle from them, by which it seemeth the poor people that lived only on labor, and fed by their milch cows, are so distressed as they follow their goods and offer themselves with their wives and children rather to be slain by the army than to suffer the famine that now in extremity beginneth to pinch them'.*" [14]

"Good God, doesn't anybody care about the lives of the ordinary Irish people? The ones they call the churls? It seems to me the big fight is between the Irish lords and the English governors and they both kill the 'mere' Irish to intimidate the other side and to use the dead bodies as a scoreboard to see who's ahead. Can't the brave fighters on each side confine their killing to each other instead of destroying the poor people who can't fight back?"

Raleigh reflected for a moment. "Once again you seem to lose the perspective of the big picture. Let me attempt to enlighten you anew. First of all, Whitehall had to do some cold-blooded accounting on the progress of the English plantation project in Ireland. The Privy council was forced to conclude that every evicted Irishman who was left alive added up to a dead English colonist somewhere down the line. It was quickly realized that turning evicted people loose to entertain their murderous thoughts was a serious miscalculation in planning, and would essentially doom the plantation project. Don't forget that Ireland is not exactly a civilized society where mutual agreements may be reached peacefully. After examining the evidence carefully, a recent commentator on Irish affairs, Barnaby Rich wrote; *'The Irish would rather still retain themselves in their sluttishness, in their uncleanliness, in their rudeness.... than they would take an example from the English, either of civility, humanity or any manner of decency'.*" [15]

"Speaking of humanity, isn't there something warped in justifying mass murder on a lack of cleanliness or politeness? Doesn't that reaction seem to you a bit over-done?"

"You don't seem to realize the gulf between our two countries is much wider than the width of the St. George Channel," Raleigh admonished him. "For instance, the average Irishman baths just twice a year: when he gets drunk and falls down in a stream while leading his herds to and from the mountains in the spring and fall. On the other hand, many English gentlemen take a full-body bath nearly every month, and if they attend the Court regularly, they augment that cleansing by applying personal fragrances to their body and clothing because Elizabeth has a very sensitive nose as far as unpleasant odors are concerned. I fail to see how your mind can entertain the slightest resemblance in the two situations."

"And that justifies killing the great unwashed?"

"It's clear that you non-military types don't really understand the exigencies of warfare. Sweeps of the sort we're discussing tend to be all-inclusive because if a commander takes the time to particularize who should live and who should die, it slows everything down and blunts the effectiveness of the military movement. It was far more efficient to decide that every living person they found in the province was a Geraldine—as they could well have been—and to deal with them as such."

William choked out a question. "How many did they manage to deal with?"

"Pelham didn't list numbers, but Butler estimated that Pelham had killed 10,000, while the Ormond forces recorded that they had killed 41 rebel officers, 800 notorious traitors, and between 4,000 and 5,000 other people in the nine months it took them to sweep through Munster."

"How in the world do they kill so many? Do they shoot them?"

Raleigh shook his head. "None of the armies have that much powder, and swords are so quickly blunted on bone and gristle that they ordinarily settle for the old reliable standby: they hang everybody."

"Did they get Gerald?"

"Not directly, but they got a good start on the disintegration process which ate away his support and finally brought him to bay in 1583."

"What? He lasted another three years after the clean sweep?" cried William in astonishment. "How? By my calculation, you've mentioned nine armies which have burned and plundered and slaughtered the people and property of Munster Province in the years between 1568 and 1581. First there was your cousin Carew pursued by Fitzmaurice who was pursued by Perrot, and then Sir John Fitzgerald broke out and was pursued by Drury and Maltby. And finally Gerald was chased by Pelham and Butler. Is that right? Who and what was left to support Gerald's continued resistance?"

"Try not to get so involved emotionally that you cause me to lose my objectivity in this matter," Raleigh instructed him. "If you are really that concerned with numbers, I think you should count Sir Henry Sidney's army as number ten because he took a turn in the field in pursuit of Fitzmaurice before that noteworthy rebel was replaced by Sir John Fitzgerald, Desmond's brother."

"Oh, yes. Sir John. Whatever happened to him when Gerald broke out?"

"He campaigned along with his brother for a time, but he ended up being another of those who met his end in an odd turn along the clear passages and stream crossings of Ireland. He was dispatched in January 1582 when he turned a bend in a road with a small group of his men on horseback and was suddenly confronted by a large group of English cavalry coming the other way. The English were just as startled as he was, and there was confusion for a moment as the Irish group attempted to dash their way through the English troops. Some made it, but one soldier caught Sir John with a lance thrust which slowed him enough so that another was able to shoot him off his horse."

"If you'll forgive me for saying so, it begins to sound like the English forces bring the rebels to ground more effectively in casual encounters than they do in planned operations. I suppose the final accounting of Gerald Fitzgerald was over some equally unimportant incident?"

"As a matter of fact he was finally brought down because his people stole some laundry to protect themselves against the chill of the Phantom Mountains, but they made the mistake of leaving O'Moriarity's wife naked when they grabbed her woolen dress, and Gerald finally lost his head for that thieving insult. But that's ahead of our story, so let me finish up where we left off. As I recall, you asked where Gerald got any further support after Pelham and Butler swept Munster clean, did you not?"

"I did. It seems to me there couldn't be anyone or anything left that would support a rebellion."

"You're losing sight of the big picture again. It was mostly the homebodies who were hanged because the rebels themselves were never confined to towns or farms, so they were able to avoid the sweep and, not incidentally, also avoid the plague which usually spreads within communities. In addition, it must be remembered that one of the strongest recruiting axioms for military service—especially during famines—is the realization that the men with the weapons are the last to starve."

"So, in effect, they were living healthy, carefree, outdoor lives, almost like they were on a picnic?"

"Please," Raleigh raised an admonishing hand. "Such sarcasm ill befits a scholastic review of historical happenings. Desmond's breakout had ignited the torch of rebellion all over southern Ireland, and many of the clans which had been sitting on the sidelines finally jumped into the fray. The Viscount Baltinglas, James Eustace from Kildare, declared his strong Catholic sympathies aloud and managed thereby to inflame the O'Byrnes and the O'Tooles from the Wicklow Mountains just south of the Dublin Pale and encourage them to stage a series of raids directly into that seat of the English government in Ireland."

"Did Gerald swing east to help them?"

"No. He was busy besieging and assaulting the coastal communities of Cork, Kinsale, Waterford, and Youghal with the fresh supply of fighters sent to him by the O'Keefe and MacAuliffe clans who had finally decided to join the fray."

"I see on the map that all those coastal communities are pretty close together. Why didn't they form a mutual defense association so they could help defend each other when they were attacked by the rebels?"

"That was attempted but the system broke down because every time they attempted to summon aid from each other, the starving beggars who surrounded those communities killed the messengers so they could eat their horses."

"I don't understand why the coastal cities which could get fresh food supplies by sea didn't show more Christian mercy to the people who were starving on their doorstep. At least feed them enough to reduce them as a threat, so the cities could get their messages in and out safely."

"The community of Waterford learned to their sorrow that the quality of mercy must be carefully strained during a famine because they did bring some of the starving people into their community and fed them, but their mayor was then forced to report to Burghley; 'On Good Friday the city opened its gates to 1100 starving men, who, when they had eaten, fell to plundering and housebreaking and it took three weeks to get rid of them by beating out the stronger ones and coaxing the weaker'." [16]

William mused, "Yes, that is unfortunate. That kind of incident could give a bad name to the whole business of starvation." He paused to frown at himself and then continued, "So Gerald succeeded in setting everybody at each other's throats again, eh?"

"Right. English outposts were soon aflame from Cork to the Dublin Pale, and confusion rode supreme when rumors circulated of further Spanish landings scheduled for the Dingle Peninsula. Many Englishmen began to fear that the great Irish spiral of chaos and death was poised once again to suck up and destroy all civilized life in the country. Whitehall finally became alarmed enough about the double threat from the Wicklow mountains and the foreign troops forted up at Smerwick that it pulled Pelham out of the game and dispatched Lord Grey of Winton with the largest contingent of English troops ever sent over to the Irish Wars."

"Was he experienced in Irish warfare?"

"No, but his education came very quickly. After being invested as the new Lord Deputy of Ireland in an impressive formal ceremony in Dublin, he marched his quickly-assembled but ill-trained force through the city just as Sidney and Perrot and Drury and Pelham had done before him. I can only imagine rebel leaders like James Eustace and Fiach MacHugh took careful note of him from the heights of the Wicklow Mountains where they sat with their men polishing their swords and refurbishing their cross-bows and axes in addition to cleaning up their few muskets."

"Did Grey have a specific plan?"

"Yes. He intended to eliminate the threat from the Wicklows before marching west to take care of the foreigners at Smerwick. Grey was anxious not to be seen as an indecisive or lingering kind of commander—as his father was reputed to have been—so counting heavily on the superiority of the English pikemen against whatever rabble the Irish had assembled, he immediately marched his men directly into the Wicklow mountains. He thereby validated a key observation made by one of our English soldier-writers on the scene, Barnaby Rich, who concluded, '*The inexpert captain and the unlearned physician do buy their experience at too dear a rate, for it is still purchased with the price of men's lives*'." [17]

"The Irish were waiting for him?"

"I can only imagine they could hardly conceal their glee when Grey marched directly into the four-mile-long, one-mile-deep glen of Glenmalure at the entrance to the Wicklow Mountains. As is the custom in the military, Grey invited all the outstanding officers present in Dublin to accompany his campaign to drive down the center of the glen along the sluggish River Oure and flush the Irish off the steep hillside to be taken down by his pikemen and musketeers. Some of the younger commanders did accompany him, including my young nephew, the son of Sir Peter Carew, who entered the glen in full armor. Maltby, who was on leave in Dublin for the investiture ceremony, also joined him, but it must be noted that the experienced commanders who had suffered most from trying to dislodge the Irish in broken country—Pelham, Perrot, and Butler—found better things to do that day."

"So far you have set up the coming engagement as an over-confident commander leading poorly-trained troops into a well-prepared ambush."

"That was the recipe exactly, and the results were highly predictable in the eyes of the seasoned commanders. Grey led his men into the worst defeat English forces ever suffered in Ireland up until that time. I spoke at length with Sir William Stanley after the event and he gave me a first hand account of the happening. He led the rear guard of the army, so his men entered the glen last. He said the four mile length of the glen was full of slippery rocks, stones, bogs, woods and underbrush with a swampy, sluggish river full of loose stones meandering through the bottom where Grey proposed to march."

"I can only imagine it would be difficult to remain in lockstep over such ground."

"That's right. The terrain quickly forced the English troops to break their marching formation and to spend more time choosing their footing than observing the Irish concealed on the hillside. Stanley said the Irish lay all along the woods they had to pass, behind trees, rocks, crags, logs, and in covert areas in the underbrush where they were concealed by their mantles. From their cover, they fired down on our ranks with their muskets and cross-bows and began to take a heavy toll. Stanley soon began to encounter dead and wounded English all along the river bottom."

"The English were unable to respond?"

"Halfway through the glen, Stanley realized that the forward sections must have experienced so many casualties that they had decided to abandon the river bed and climb the steep slope to get out of the glen."

"Which would take them right through the surrounding ring of Irish?"

"That was the problem, of course. It was impossible to climb the slope without using both hands and feet, and that meant they were breathing hard with their blades still encased and their pikes dragging behind them when they finally climbed high enough to confront the unforgiving and well-rested kern and gallowglass who were smiling down on them. Hundreds of dead and wounded English soldiers began tumbling back down the slope in such numbers that their bodies soon clogged up the river in some spots and turned the water red with soldier blood. To add to the horror, Stanley saw gallowglass descend to the river bed and expend their fury by cleaving and cutting those English bodies with their axes so no wounded were left alive. Stanley escaped the trap, but there were three English commanders and 500 soldiers who did not get out. He doubted if the Irish lost a single man."

"Weren't the English protected by their armor?"

"No. Actually it killed many. Young Peter Carew, for instance, became so overheated and exhausted from climbing in his suit of armor that he couldn't stand upright when he reached the enemy, so they killed him where he lay and made a coffin of his metal suit."

William moaned.

Raleigh nodded grimly. "'*There are few die well that die in battle*'. [18] Nevertheless, every battlefield holds lessons for the survivors and some men do learn those lessons. Maltby, for instance, offered several insightful suggestions to Whitehall after the battle. He pointed out that the English uniforms of bright red and blue doublets along with the white kersey hose made our men prominent targets on the green-brown hillside of Glenmalure and in Ireland generally. He seemed particularly offended that the money we waste on parade ground appearances put our men at greater risk on the battlefield. He wrote; '*Their coats stand them in no stead, neither in fashion nor in giving them any succor to their bodies. Let the coat money be given to some person of credit with which, and with that which is lavished on their colored hose, they may be clothed here in Ireland with jerkins and hose of frieze, and with the same money bring them every man an Irish mantle which shall serve him for his bedding, and thereby shall not be otherwise known to the rebels*'." [19]

"Frieze is that shaggy woolen stuff, isn't it? So Maltby was saying we ought to dress our soldiers more like the rebels, so they would not serve as such ready targets?"

"Exactly," Raleigh nodded. "It's a great idea, but Whitehall will have none of it because the English army would look like a bunch of ragamuffins during parades just when the policy-makers like them to look pretty."

"Was Grey disgraced by the Glenmalure defeat?"

"Oddly enough, he was not, because there was still plenty of work to be done and little time to do it. Grey sent the loyal Earl of Kildare to negotiate with O'Neill in the north after some rumor that the Ulster people might be encouraged to come down for the fight in light of how successful the rebels had been at Glenmalure. O'Neill commands 5,000 men so it was felt he was well worth bribing to stay clear, and that arrangement assured Grey free passage to the west with the survivors of the Glenmalure debacle to try his luck against the foreigners at Smerwick.

On the way into Munster, Grey picked up more men from Butler who decided to stay home to defend his boundaries and from Pelham's group of Cork defenders, who moved north to join him. Then Captain Winters brought him 1,000 more men by sea along with the heavy siege pieces which had just finished smashing Gerald's castles at Askeaton and Carrigafoyle, so Grey approached Smerwick with close to 4,000 men—even after subtracting the several sergeants and the score of his own soldiers Grey had executed on the road for unauthorized foraging."

"Killed his own men? Isn't that a little unusual? Isn't foraging just another word for hunting up something to eat? It isn't considered to be as serious as pillaging or plundering, is it?"

"No, it isn't, and most commanders, though they frown on it, soon forget about it. But Grey has a reputation for being a bit of a bloody man and not overly concerned about the lives of his soldiers. It must be admitted, however, that as the commander of so many different groups of soldiers, he might have felt an object lesson was called for to show who was in charge of such a polyglot force."

"Did the invaders at Smerwick know Grey's army was coming after them ?"

Raleigh nodded. "They had mounted fourteen medium-sized culverins on platforms built just inside the wall of Smerwick, and for one day they showed us they knew how to use them in a spirited exchange with our siege pieces, which we mounted on a hill overlooking the fort. They also had enough muskets, powder, and ball to furnish an army if the Irish had supplied one, and Gerald promised the Italian commander, Sabastiano di San Joseppi, that he would respond with 4,000 fighters if the fort raised a black-and-white flag to indicate they needed assistance."

"So Grey had about 4,000 against the 700 in the fort, but the defenders always have the advantage, don't they? Behind solid walls?"

"Usually that is the case," Raleigh nodded, "but Smerwick is not a fortress in any real sense. In reality, it is an open enclosure, 350 by 100 feet, surrounded by a make-shift earth and stone barrier which Fitzmaurice originally set up as a supply depot and not as a fortification able to withstand siege. After our siege guns knocked out their culverins and destroyed their gun platforms, and after Gerald failed to bring in the 4000 fighters in response to the fort's black-and-white flag signal, and after the November chill made itself felt on those Mediterranean people and they began to suffer real thirst because the nearest source of fresh water was a half-mile outside their enclosure, some of them began to curse the Pope and Philip for sending them on such a fruitless assignment, so they decided to sue for terms."

"Simply surrender, you mean?"

"Nothing simple about it. Much has to be decided. If quarter is promised to the surrendering group, the victors are honor-bound to live up to their word and keep the prisoners alive and finally ransom them off. If they surrender at discretion, they are subject to whatever mercy the victor cares to extend to them. Intense negotiations were conducted for three days by Grey's staff and de San Joseppi's people. An odd assortment of translators was needed to conduct the business in five different languages because few of the invaders spoke either English or Gaelic while Grey's people spoke little Italian and were not fluent in Spanish and spoke no Basque at all."

"Basque?"

"That's who most of the Spaniards turned out to be," said Raleigh, "and that's why it's not surprising there were some hard feelings and confusion after the executions had been carried out about what had been agreed to at the negotiations."

William swallowed hard. "Yes. The executions."

"Six hundred were put to death while the officers were held for ransom. The Irish among them were broken on the wheel and then drawn and quartered as traitors, and even the few women among them were put to the sword despite some of them pleading their bellies."

"Ah yes, carrying a child," murmured William. "You were on duty that day, were you not?"

Raleigh stiffened. "That reminds me. Did I ever get a straight answer from you on whether or not you were at our supper table last night?"

"I've lost track. Do you perchance remember what was served?"

"Yes, there was undercooked venison for one thing because the Irish eat all of their meat half-raw and, in addition, it was somewhat unappetizing because they have never gone to the trouble of learning the secret of using sauce to get that gamy taste out of their meat. When duty calls the English soldier to serve in Ireland, however, he must accept the fact that there will be drawbacks in almost every phase of daily existence, so there is no sense complaining about them, and the only sensible thing a man can do is discipline himself to seek out the bright side. I do recall the meal was somewhat saved by the appearance of a tasty pork-pie which must have been prepared by some Englishman who wandered into the kitchen. I suddenly realize I haven't eaten for a long time, and perhaps we should take a break. Are you hungry?"

"That would suit me fine, but out of consideration for your deep desire to cultivate some historical perspective, maybe it would be a good idea if you first sharpen up your ability to summarize, by condensing the rest of the Desmond War history."

"Quite right. The belly must wait when duty beckons and summarizing quickly will give me even more appetite. During the surrender negotiations then, Grey called on the intruders to produce a commission from a recognized head of state which would have authorized their invasion and made it a legitimate act of war. They could produce none, so Grey pronounced them beyond mercy, and they were summarily executed as brigands and robbers, even though some people later said he lured them out by offering mercy and then had them killed."

"Did he?"

Raleigh shrugged. "Who can say what was decided with five languages being shouted by at least that many emotional and desperate translators, many of whom had their lives hanging on what was decided. Enough to say, it's over with, so let's get on to the end of Gerald. From 1580 to November of 1583, his ability to annoy the Crown ebbed and flowed according to how many men he could summon. Sometimes he commanded only a few dozen and sometimes a few hundred, but the loyal clans still sent him new fighters every spring. Shortly after the death of his brother, Sir James, in 1582, he put together 1,000 kern and stunned both Pelham, who was protecting Cork from siege, and Grey, who had returned to Dublin to try his luck with the Wicklow Mountains again—by striking deep into the Golden Vale of Tipperary and Clonmel."

"Golden Vale?"

"The richest farm land in Ireland, which had not been subjected to quite as much burning and killing as some other areas. The Crown was both amazed and appalled by the attack because they thought they had Gerald on the run, and they thought they were forcing him to react only in a defensive fashion. They had him cornered several times during this period, but he always managed to slip away into the familiar woods, often by leaving faithful gallowglass behind to buy escape time for him even as they died in the process. The Crown grew so irritated at their inability to corner him, they even gave serious ear to St. Leger's suggestion that they completely defoliate Munster by cutting down all the trees to eliminate his hiding places. That proposal was abandoned, however, when it was realized that it would take 3,000 woodcutters several years under the close protection of 5,000 soldiers to get the job done."

"Kind of like swatting a fly with a hammer."

"Right. In truth, however, the sand was finally running through the hour-glass for Gerald. Famine had been used as a weapon of war by Pelham and Butler in 1579, and starvation had thereafter gained a firm footing in the land, so that desperate, famished people became a very common sight in nearly every community touched by the Desmond War. Even English soldiers were driven to sell their horses to Irish butchers who thereupon served them up to English officers at premium prices. The Crown had to bribe many of those officers to stay in Ireland long enough to finish the job by offering them free land from Gerald's confiscated estates. All of Munster was hurting from hunger so the burning of the Golden Vale crops tightened everybody's stomach another notch and began to strip away the native support that the Earl of Desmond had always enjoyed."

"I can well imagine it would be an unforgivable act in the minds of hungry people."

"It was especially unforgivable in the minds of the Privy Council who finally decided the only person who could run Gerald down was another Irishman, so once again they called on the Earl of Ormond, and Thomas Butler took up the chase after relieving Grey as Lord General of Munster. This time he had the backing of some Geraldines who were tired enough of the killing and hunger, that they sued for pardon from the Crown, and it was granted to them liberally by Butler, who then invited them to uncover Gerald and collect the £1,000 prize money that Whitehall placed on his head."

"Somebody once explained to me that the Irish culture makes betrayal impossible to avoid for the average Irishman. Do you think England's being here has anything to do with the cultivation of betrayal?"

"I don't know, but I think we would get very little done in this country without Irish informers. I know that the head money offered on Gerald helped to turn most of Munster into a pursuing army, so that by November 1583, his course of destruction had been run, and he was driven to hiding in a small cabin in the Phantom Mountains about six miles from Tralee."

"Phantom Mountains?"

"Just inland from the Dingle Peninsula in Kerry so that by late November each evening brings a spectral sea-mist sweeping inland from the Atlantic to chill the body and confuse the mind. A wonderful place to hide so long as you're dressed for it, but Gerald and his few followers were not, so they foraged the surrounding hills and found a few cows and some woolen clothing at the house of Maurice O'Moriarty who was absent at the time. Part of the warm clothing, however, came off the body of Mrs. O'Moriarty and when Maurice returned, he took that theft so unkindly that he gathered the O'Moriarty clan and they went hunting the Phantom Mountains for both the dress and the £1,000 head money."

"And they had the home ground advantage."

"Right. After trekking up and down the mountains for two weeks, they finally located a remote cabin, chased away some men hanging about, and found a woman, a child, and an elderly, grey-haired man who could barely stand from the pain of an old hip wound. They managed to break his arm in an effort to get him to talk, and he finally bolted upright and shouted, '*I am the Earl of Desmond. Save my life!.*' And one of the O'Moriartys replied, '*Thou hast killed thyself long ago, and now thou shalt be prisoner to the Queen's majesty and the Earl of Ormond*'." [20]

"So they took the Earl of Desmond into custody one more time?"

"Not exactly. After uttering such a formal denunciation and impressive policy, they decided to reconsider when they faced the prospect of carrying the crippled Earl the six miles to Tralee, so they lessoned their burden by cutting off his head and then bringing that trophy to Sir William Stanley at Castlemaine, where they were rewarded with the £1,000."

"And the head, I imagine, was made part of some barbaric display."

"Not immediately. It was sent to Kilkenny, where Butler could finally gaze on it with satisfaction, and then sent off to London where it is said Elizabeth spent one whole morning staring at it on a table before her. Finally it was mounted on a spike over London bridge."

"Was the hip injury the same one Gerald suffered at Affane?"

"I think it was. I imagine the mist and dew of the mountains probably aggravated the hip, but I wouldn't be surprised if that injury bothered Gerald during the whole eighteen years we chased him. The condition was unfortunate for him, of course, but it serves as a very handy bookend for me in closing my discussion of the Desmond Wars from Affane to the Phantom mountains. Any questions?"

"Only one. Why do you not wear your drop-pearl cape here in Yonghal?"

Raleigh laughed and clapped William on the shoulder. "I do enjoy a young man who has his eye out for the main chance. Let's go get something to eat. I think your master will soon be ready to take you on the road."

Chapter 5:
WITH SIR JOHN PERROT'S SCRIVENER

In Dublin:

"You'll never hear a single word from me about any private detail, no matter how miniscule, of my master's life," said Sir John Perrot's scrivener, decisively. He took another pull on his tankard. "Whether you come after me with red-hot pinchers or ice-cold daggers, it would make not one whit of difference to me. Specific private details in the life of the Lord Deputy of all Ireland are safe with me because I would never renounce my loyalty even in the face of imminent torture and death."

"I'm afraid you grossly overestimate my interest in your master," William chuckled. "I was just inquiring politely while I was trying to get the inn-keeper's attention, so please don't speak further if you feel at all uncomfortable in sharing another round, and I'll be on my way."

"On the other hand, there exists a vast reservoir of public stories about Sir John's affairs, and repetition of those anecdotes does not offend moral principle because Sir John himself delights in telling them publicly. Everybody in Ireland knows well enough that he is almost certainly the bastard half-brother to Elizabeth—and when you see him you'll know why—the spitting image of the Queen's father, good King Henry, so he is treated very deferentially by everyone, because no man knows when the Queen might decide to reclaim her own. As a matter of fact, Sir John Perrot has only one real enemy in all of Ireland today, and that's his own loose tongue which, mark me, will get him in serious trouble one of these days."

"Does he drink?"

"In Ireland?" Clark, the scrivener, smirked. "It's a rare night that Sir John in his cups doesn't utter some remark that would be traitorous in one who was less favored. He's a bluff, good-humored man much like his father, but his assumption of the big-brother role in criticizing the Queen's policies could easily be used against him by his enemies at home. He's very popular with the native Irish, however, despite having destroyed eight hundred of them in one battle."

"Surprising," said William. "I didn't know the Irish were that forgiving."

"It's difficult for them to harden their hearts against Sir John ever since he challenged the self-proclaimed Captain of the Desmond forces to a winner-take-all single combat on horseback in front of both armies in 1572 during the first of the Desmond Wars. Perrot was the Lord President of Munster at the time, and he had grown weary of chasing James FitzMaurice and his Catholic cohorts through the Irish bogs. The Desmond bunch were busy laying waste to Elizabeth's master plan of establishing a Munster Plantation of hundreds of trustworthy Anglican Undertakers after the eviction of hundreds of Catholic Irishmen from their ancestral lands."

"Didn't the Irish resist being forced to leave?"

"Oh, yes. The evicted Irish were so successful in resisting that many would-be Undertakers decided they could get much better value for their money elsewhere than having their throats cut on some lonely Irish plantation, and the Queen's master plan slowed to the point where Sir John finally issued his challenge."

"That's what I call confrontational diplomacy! But was Perrot up to that kind of thing? I mean you seldom think of diplomats riding out on their horses for a do-or-die discussion."

"He would have been ready twenty years earlier when he was a champion participant in the English courtly jousts, and he probably still envisioned himself atop some huge English charger galloping full tilt at his opponent while his 280 pounds provided a resolute backstop for the sturdy English lance with which he intended to unseat the fiery FitzMaurice. The Captain of Desmond, however, had a different vision. As the challenged party, he had the right to name the terms of the combat, and he chose to discard the English lance, sword, and shield in favor of the short spear—which the Irish call a dart—and the broad-bladed sword, both of which I imagine Sir John could handle. But then FitzMaurice showed that streak of Irish cunning which so often surfaces at key moments, by declaring the battle would be fought on the backs of Irish hobs."

"Irish hobs? Aren't they those frisky little horses the Irish ride without stirrups so that their feet drag the ground?"

"That's right, but they don't frisk much underneath 280 pounds."

"Could Sir John refuse such conditions with dignity?"

"Few could blame him, I think, but on the designated day, he chose instead to ride out into the clearing in the Kilmore Wood between the two armies and sit there all day in the misting rain on that sagging Irish pony waiting to clash broad-bladed Irish swords with the Captain of Desmond. FitzMaurice never rode out, but he finally sent a messenger with a note which said: *'If I do kill the great John Perrot, the Queen of England will but send another President into this province, but if he do kill me, there is none in Ireland to succeed me, or to command as I do now'.*" [21]

"Very wise, but perhaps not too brave after stacking the deck in his own favor."

"Exactly what many of the Irish felt, so they can't help admiring Sir John. They are always intrigued by a headstrong, flamboyant character, especially a witty one, and that's exactly what Sir John Perrot is."

"Stay witty in Ireland. A good rule to remember."

"Sir John despises the straight-laced, chin-up, book-smart gentlemen the Queen usually sends to aid him in his work. Perrot would much rather have men who have some feel for Irish customs and traditions even though he tried to smother those very elements early in his career because he felt they contributed to the general lawlessness of the Irish. He prohibited the wearing of Irish mantles and the growing of thick Irish forelocks which concealed identity and ordered the Irish under pain of punishment or imprisonment to dress like Englishmen. He even outlawed bards, rhymers and messengers, and insisted that Irish women close up their open smocks and cloth themselves in decent attire."

"Did such alterations calm things down?"

"When he noticed those changes only increased the crime and violence in Irish life, he backed off and decided that this country could not be forced to change overnight no matter how badly it needed it."

"He may be right about that from what I've seen so far."

"He also sees a lot of things wrong with direct rule of Ireland from England even though he's part of it. The present arrangement presumes that the Privy Council in London can make wiser decisions about Irish affairs than can the Council in Dublin which works directly with the native chieftains who have controlled their people for hundreds of years. We can't turn this country into the peaceful and profitable paradise it could easily become, without the help of the Irish people. It can't be done by decree from London alone, and well Sir John knows it."

"What does his present policy hope to achieve?"

Clark shrugged, "Gradual change based on fair treatment is what he hopes for. All that England has ever wanted out of Ireland for the trouble of governing them is to bank a little profit. Since all past experience indicates profit is somehow out of the picture, he thinks we should turn our attention to policies where we somehow break even, because we don't know how long the English people will support such a losing proposition."

"There's no question about who owns the land?"

"None whatever! It's clear as a bell under English Law. If the Irish clan chiefs—or the red Indians of the New World, for that matter—think they can weasel out of their land deals by dying off so conveniently, they have another think coming. Under their laws, of course, their chiefs do not have the authority to sell the lands for longer than their own lifetimes since the property in their culture belongs to the group rather than to any individual. Despite their law, however, a legal contract was joined—they sold and we bought—so our present ownership of the land simply shows what happens when a primitive legal system encounters a civilized legal system head-to-head just as the Almighty intended for the furtherance of his glory."

"God is a land-grabber?"

"I'd be a little more careful about what I said if I were you," Clark advised. "I think you have already had too much to drink, and you better find some place to sleep it off before a bailiff is summoned to witness your blasphemy."

"One more round and then I'm off," William smiled. "But thanks for the warning. Do the Irish deserve the extra concern Perrot is exerting in their behalf? Will they act out the part of good soldiers in following his leadership?"

"Oh, yes," said Spenser's scrivener. "If he is well led, your average Irishman will give a good account of himself in battle; so long as he is allowed to go forward, or so long as his fellows are watching him. Off by himself, however, he will lurk and peer along any pathway that might promise advantage for his personal safety. He really has no compunction whatever in choosing underhanded stealth to attain his ends. Ambush comes easy to him because betrayal is built into his social structure."

"Built in? Hard to believe. Are you sure?"

"No question," the scrivener replied. "The system offers the Irishman no choice but betrayal since he is born into a tangled web of competing allegiances which ebb and flow and wax and wane by night and day. By remaining loyal to some interests, he betrays others which are, periodically, in competition with the first."

"Are we talking religious differences here?"

"Hardly!" Clark scoffed. "Everything in Ireland doesn't get decided on Sunday, you know. There is precious little room around Irish council-fires for ecclesiastical elbows when clan business is at hand. Every Irishman owes his first allegiance to his clan and to its chief. Within that clan, however, there are always competing splinter groups intent on feathering their nests by lining up with the next logical heir. After his clan allegiance, every Irishman owes his loyalty to neighboring allied clans with whom his chieftain has agreements. However, there are often night-time border skirmishes and cattle-raids going on with those neighbors, so that particular loyalty sometimes goes to bed with the sun. Next, he owes allegiance to the Anglo-Irish lord who now owns the ancestral lands from which his clan operates as tenants and guardians. That lord may, periodically, rent the entire clan out as fighting men to earn some money or to settle some dispute, so it is not unusual for clans to encounter former allies, even neighboring clans, hired out to the other side, in the middle of a battlefield, and inter-clan loyalty, of course, is the first victim in such a confrontation."

"Where does loyalty to their religion fit into the picture?" William asked.

"Most Irishmen set aside a single hour every Sunday to render sincere deference to their faith, but at all other hours, their involvement hangs in the air out of reach, much like the wonderful incense they burn at their mass."

"Are the mercenary clan armies the only way of settling things here in Ireland?"

"Only the temporary solution," said Clark. "Most of the unrest in this land comes from angry property disputes which end up sending hired fighting men into bloody and ironic combat."

"Ironic?"

"Totally ironic in the sense that it is pointless," said Clark. "The bloodcurdling war whoops amidst the clatter and clang of the battlefield stand in stark contrast to the muted, dusty files in Whitehall where four-hundred-year-old records of Irish land holdings are kept, and where property disputes are really decided no matter how many dead men are strewn across the field of battle. While the clan is in the field, the lord meanwhile has full-time lawyers in Dublin and London working to see how much more of the clan's ancestral property he can take over by paying up taxes-due or by somehow producing musty deeds where none existed before. The recent group of English Undertakers have learned that game so well that it is not unusual for them to double their Irish holdings in a few years since they have such sympathetic listeners in London."

"When does the Queen's direct representative enter into the loyalty picture?"

"Right now. The Irishman next owes his allegiance to the Lord Deputy, the highest ranking English officer in Ireland. That officer's policies, however, may change overnight, depending on the Queen's moods and on the particular convictions which each Lord Deputy brings to the job. The recent appointment of my master, Sir John Perrot, to replace Lord Grey—who was finally deemed too bloody by Whitehall—was a stunning change in terms of settling Irish land disputes, because Sir John has much more sympathy for the claims of Irish landholders than his predecessor had, and he's very suspicious of the paperwork produced so conveniently by some of the English Undertakers."

"We are to dine with your master this evening," William confided, "so I am happy to hear he is one who provokes drama by unseating the status quo. We've attended some dinners where the dessert was the dramatic highlight of the evening."

"Oh, I think you can count on Sir John taking your mind off the food," the scrivener smiled, "but it won't be tonight. The Lord Deputy has been called away to settle some malfunction at the Crown's Redemption Center just beyond the Pale. Some-body didn't show up for work, so the dinner has been postponed for a time."

Malachi entered at that point with a well-dressed chap. "We're switching signals for a short time to help the Lord Deputy," he said to William. "The dinner has been delayed for two days, so I want you to accompany Donald Campbell here on a bit of government business during that period. You'll be temporarily stationed at the Re-demption Center south of Dublin, and Mr. Campbell will explain your duties to you. Go off with him now, and I'll send for you in time for the supper with Sir John."

"Just a minute now," William said. "What is a Pale and what are we redeeming at the Center?"

"Quickly then," Malachi conceded, "while Master Campbell fetches the horses. The Pale is an area populated by enough English and Anglo-Irish that they are fairly secure from major attacks by the Irish rebels. Dublin is a good-sized Pale, and Cork and Wexford and Limerick are smaller ones, but such areas are not absolutely safe as indicated by the recent hit-and-run nighttime raids on the cattle herds of Dublin by the Irish lurking nearby in the Wicklow Mountains. We just have to do our best to discourage them, and that's where the redeeming station is important, but I'll let Campbell explain all of that to you on the trip to your station. Try not to irritate him, and don't introduce any discussion of Edmund Spenser. He seems unduly upset since some of Spenser's old friends in Dublin have proposed that the Queen extend a £ 20. pension to that poet to subsidize his creative efforts. Here is Campbell now with your horse, so I'll be on my way. Remember to behave yourself down there until I send for you."

Chapter 6:
ON THE RIDE TO THE REDEMPTION CENTER

En route:

"Did I understand Malachi correctly that there might be a government subsidy in the future for the poet Spenser?" William inquired.

"That proposal has been advanced," Campbell admitted, somewhat sourly. "I rather think the £ 20 figure is double what would be fair if Spenser were merely a poet, but I suspect the generous proposal is recognition of the fact that with his recent award of the castle at Kilcolman and the adjoining plowlands, he has become one of our body of loyal Undertakers here in Ireland."

"'Merely a poet', did I hear you say?" William asked quietly.

Campbell nodded. "Of course I am pleased to see one of our number gain due recognition, but sad experience has taught me that no one in the kingdom has an ear to hear how enormous are the expenses the Undertaker must bear; and I'll be man enough to admit that we brought some of the problem down on our own collective estates."

"Really?"

"When our Munster Plantation Corporation agreed that no Undertaker could employ or encourage any of the native Irish, the cheap labor supply vanished overnight. You can't imagine how expensive everything is when you have to beat the bushes for workers—I mean who else is there in this God-forsaken land except native Irish? Ah, well, the point here is that if you are forced to bargain with the people you hire, you often end up paying them a reasonable wage, and you might be surprised to see just how deeply such gestures cut into your profit margin.

The ironic part is, of course, that in the end, after we have hired the very thin layer of non-Irish, we have no choice but to sign on the very people we had just voted to cut off entirely, and, to add indignity to our plight, we must offer them good wages and conditions in the bargain."

"Pretty disquieting, I imagine."

"Well, we have no choice, and I soon learned that in bargaining, the native Irish have a strong streak of cunning when they sense they have the upper hand. I have concluded that a mysterious, fanciful humor is imposed on the people of this hapless land when the Atlantic Ocean blows mettlesome clouds from the New World across Ireland like a publican blowing foam from a pint, and that spirit rains down on every Irish lake and river from which the people draw their drink, and it inflicts on them a curious, whimsical vision which encourages them to make light of both logic and reason. That's the only explanation for why careful planning in London and thoughtful administration in Dublin so often produce the exact opposite of the goals desired by the crown."

"But you think a poet should get only half—"

"Exactly!" Donnie Campbell cut the air decisively with the flat of his hand. "Poets can live on bread crumbs, and they can get a mountain of such nourishment for £ 10 per annum, with a fine medium grade Madeira from a respectable year thrown into the bargain."

William spoke slowly and distinctly, "Is there some value in your judgment which is not apparent to the naked eye? I have it on the best possible authority that if anything, poets need more, not less, so they do not feel trapped in the economic morass which hinders their creative fancy like a coating of tar engulfing a swan. Not only more but much more! A £ 20 annual pension is certainly not to be sneezed at since it assures a man a certain level of courteous treatment for the rest of his days, but it should not be the end for which a true poet strives."

Campbell frowned. "Did you say 'much more'?"

"I happen to know the Queen gives the Earl of Oxford £1,000 per annum."

"He's a nobleman. They're different. Noblemen are born in debt and are usually greeted at birth by hundreds of dependents who will stand around for many years encouraging the newborn to climb out of his crib and start whipping things into shape."

"That different? A fifty-to-one ratio of difference? Are you trying to tell me that an art piece of any sort would be fifty times greater or finer if created by one who is judged noble because of his ancestral background than that of someone—who may very well be noble for all he knows—but who has fallen onto hard times which do not, however, detract from the integrity of his effort, nor from his proposed future achievements?"

"I have no idea what you are babbling about," Campbell said, "but give me a moment to explain to you why this Redemption Center assignment is an important one for me. In accepting this duty, I have volunteered to do a personal favor for the Lord Deputy in hopes that he will look with compassionate understanding on my most recent land acquisition application to enlarge my holdings in Ireland."

"Why shouldn't he approve it?"

"Unfortunately, the ancient deed which supports my claim was chewed on by goats before it was splattered with cow flops, so there is some difficulty in reading it correctly. Its authenticity, therefore, requires a sympathetic interpretation if I am to go forward with my plans, and I've heard Sir John does not always look with favor on such damaged documents. I'm hoping, however, that one favor deserves another in this case. That's why it's important we pull together to get this job done right."

"This might be a good time then to explain to me what I am supposed to do at the Redemption Center."

"Yes, indeed. Since you will be distributing funds from the royal treasury, it is extremely important that your duties and responsibilities are crystal clear to you right from the beginning. I want you first to give careful study to this list that has been prepared for you." He handed a list of names to William.

"Distributing funds, eh?" William smiled. "Very interesting. Are these the people who get the money?"

"Some are and some are not, but first let me set up our chain of command. I will establish residence at the last comfortable inn south of Dublin where you can always reach me if you need further direction. You will proceed toward the Wicklow Mountains from which most of the trouble comes. The Redemption Station is directly in the foothills, so be vigilant because there are wicked people traveling those roads." Campbell chuckled. "But then, if there weren't, we wouldn't have this assignment, would we?"

"Wicked people. eh? I'm afraid I'm still not quite clear on the details of my duty."

"You'll notice that the list in your hands includes a dozen or so Irish clan names. Read them off, because those are the people with whom you will be dealing."

"Let me see here. 'O'Conner, MacCarthy, Daly, O'Brien, McSweeny, O'Toole, Burke, O'Byrne, MacSheehy, Kavanaugh, and O'Neill.'"

"Good. Now you see that each family in the listing has an 'R' or an 'L' after its name? The 'R' indicates a clan that is now in rebellion to the Crown and those are the people we're after. The 'L', on the other hand, is a clan that is loyal to the Queen at the moment and is helping us round up the rebels that infest the Wicklow Mountains and descend periodically for fiery raids on Dublin Town."

"I notice that some R's are crossed out and replaced with L's and some L's crossed out and replaced with R's. Do the families change allegiance or does this indicate an administrative error?"

"It indicates the administration does its utmost to keep the listing current, but at times there is a lot of back and forth movement. The big thing is not to pay rebel families for loyal heads, because that sends the wrong message to all the clans. You can, however, pay them for other rebel heads, and, as a matter of fact, pay them double if they can prove the head is from a rebel greater than themselves. I'm in a bit of a hurry. Are you sure you have all of that straight?"

"What is all this about heads?" William asked in astonishment.

"That's what a Redemption Center is," Campbell explained slowly. "They bring in the rebel heads and we pay them in coin of the realm for contributing to the safety of the community."

"They cut off people's heads?"

"That's right. There's no other way of keeping the accounting straight. Some suggested early on that we pay on receipt of ears or fingers, but fortunately wiser heads prevailed. There can be no wily Irish tricks possible when the head is presented."

"But how does one know a McSweeny head from a MacSheehy head?"

"I'll leave a man with you behind the screen in your office who knows the families, man and boy. He will advise you with one cough for loyal and two for rebel. However, he must not be seen by anyone because half your customers will consider him a traitor."

"Which half?"

"That changes with your visitors, but that's not your problem. Don't make the job more complicated by taking on incidental worry. If he happens to disappear, however, let me know and we'll get you another one. You just pass out the silver in judicious fashion and everything will be fine."

"I guess I can handle that as long as your man directs me intelligently."

"He'll do that all right, but of course, it's up to you to notch the ears."

"Notch the ears?"

"That's right. We certainly don't want to have to pay for the same head twice through some cunning Irish trick, so we can't leave that duty up to your Irish helper. The Englishman who has the responsibility of passing out the Queen's silver also has the duty of notching one ear on each of the heads he pays for."

"Let me make sure I have this straight now. You expect me to cut off the ear of people who have already had their heads cut off?"

"No, no. Not the whole ear. Just cut off that little tab on the bottom, so if you encounter that head again, you will recognize it."

"But that means I have to handle the bloody heads."

"You must anyway. It's what we call an official head-count. They must be removed from the baskets one by one. These Irish are not above false-bottom baskets you know. You could easily pay for a basket of five heads only to find later that the contents were only four heads and a glib covering a false bottom."

"Let the buyer beware, I guess," said William with a sigh.

"Nobody ever said civil administration was an easy job. What really bothers me, however, when I'm doing the redeeming personally, is when the carrier of the basket bears a striking resemblance to the contents of the basket. Makes me wonder how many family squabbles get settled under the guise of serving the Queen."

"Do I pay if I get suspicious?"

"Oh, you must pay as long as they give sworn testimony that the heads are rebel heads."

"Just a moment now. Do you seriously expect me to accept sworn testimony from a man who comes in the door with a basket full of human heads under his arm?"

"That's the procedure. London certainly does not want to waste its money on fakes, so testimony must be taken for the record."

"How long has this cruel business of trafficking in heads been going on?"

"It might seem cruel to you at the beginning, but you will soon learn that the Irish people are very hard to impress, and the taking of heads has been part of their warfare pattern for hundreds of years. English administrators must deal with them in terms they understand or risk losing their respect."

"The respect of the people who cut off the heads of other people?"

"I'm afraid you'll have to refer yourself to Machiavelli on the distinction between 'fear' and 'respect', but I know that when Whitehall was seeking a firm commander to control the unruly Irish, Sir Walter Raleigh recommended his own half-brother, Humphrey Gilbert by saying, *'I never heard nor read of any man more feared than he is among the Irish nation'.*" [22]

"I hesitate to ask what would impress the man who personally wore out three swords in leading the execution of 600 unarmed prisoners to say such a thing?"

"Like many adventurous Englishmen, Gilbert spent part of the early seventies in Ireland helping to establish Elizabeth's Munster Plantation and dealing with the resistance from the Desmonds. For a time he was in charge of the area around Kilmallock in Kerry. I remember the policy statement he sent in a letter to Sir Henry Sidney; *'My manner of dealing was to show them all that they had more need of her Majesty than she of their service; neither yet that we were afraid of any number of them, our quarrel being so good. I slew all those from time to time that did belong to, feed, accompany, or maintain any outlaw or traitors; and after my first summoning of any castle or fort, if they would not presently yield it, I would not afterward take it as their gift, but perforce, how many lives so ever it cost, putting man, woman, and child of them to the sword'.*" [23]

"He sounds very pleased with himself."

"And well he should be. His policy not only earned him the obvious respect of his half-brother and the fear of the Irish people but his commander, Sir Henry Sidney, also knighted him on the spot after one of his outstanding victories."

"Gilbert must have accumulated hundreds of heads with such policies, and am I to understand he did something really unusual with them?"

"Right. Just to make it clear to the rebels that they were not dealing with any soft-hearted, namby-pamby administrator, he impaled the heads along the pathway to the front door of his headquarters to impress the dignitaries who came to call."

"Oh, my. Impale to impress, eh? I guess that's enough orientation to get me ready to perform my duty. Did you say I give them thirty pieces of silver per head?"

"Traditionally, yes. That's the price."

Chapter 7:
AT DINNER WITH SIR JOHN PERROT

Evening:

"I'm sorry your experience at the Redemption Center caused you to lose your appetite for a time, but this assembly of prominent Irish officials whom we have just joined," Malachi explained as they seated themselves at the table, "is called together periodically because that's the way Sir John Perrot likes to run his government. This group includes several of her Majesty's most experienced officials, some military, some civil, with some merchants thrown in. Perrot will usually ask each in turn to present his most important recommendation for better government in Ireland. If you can control your manners, you may be permitted to remain at table during the discussion and possibly learn something worthwhile."

"You may count on my best behavior so long as the vittles are toothsome."

"My compliments to your kitchen staff, Patrick," Sir John Perrot later said to his steward after the dinner, "for a splendid repast." He turned to his assembled guests. "Let me take this opportunity, as we digest our meal, to mention the policy I intend to pursue in the many land disputes we have before us, so that local policy may be an extension of national policy. Take Lord Roach here. He's an excellent example of what I'm talking about. His land has been in his family for hundreds of years. He treats his tenants well and has always supported the Queen, even if one of his sons did backslide for a few weeks and ride into rebellion with Desmond some years ago. Young people will do things like that no matter what their fathers say, but the son's foolishness is now being used as an excuse to annex some of Lord Roche's lands and turn them over to these plantation people. That's ridiculous! Surely Elizabeth knows she's feeding rebellion if she permits Raleigh and those other land-hungry Undertakers to steal the land that rightfully belongs to the Anglo-Irish. God's teeth, she has most of Munster—eight hundred thousand acres, 1,550 square miles, nearly a fifth of Ireland—to distribute among her favorites now that she has confiscating Desmond's lands, so she has no business permitting her people to chisel further by falsely claiming that Lord Roche aided Desmond. London has recently granted eight-thousand acres to Grey's secretary, Edmund Spenser, including pasturage that the Roche family has held for generations past. Unthinkable!" Perrot smacked a huge fist on the table hard enough to bounce all the glasses, and William remembered tales of Henry VIII's strength.

"You seem to suggest that the Undertakers are an organized group of land-grabbers," Lord Norris suggested.

"Exactly," Perrot growled. "What disappoints me most, I think, is that nobody seems to notice that the Undertakers are all Grey's men, civil or military. Seven years ago the Queen sent them to Ireland to make this nation peaceful and profitable for the Queen, and they end up grabbing everything in sight. Lord Greys' group was rewarded with tracts of land from Desmond's estates for putting down the rebellion and eliminating the ringleader. Elizabeth gave each of them either eight-thousand or sixteen-thousand acres of Desmond's holdings to begin with, and some of them have doubled their estates in three years' time by lawsuits and accusations like this one. You can't sensibly take a man's land from him because his son—or his stable-boy, for that matter—ran off and joined the rebels for a few weeks. The son didn't take Lord Roche's people out with him. That's not rebellion—that's youthful exuberance!" He slammed the table again.

"In any case," continued Perrot, "it's not a good reason to confiscate a father's lands unless you want to drive that father, and many more like him, into open rebellion. I know that's not what Elizabeth wants. I know she wants a peaceful Ireland—although I think she has pretty well given up on seeing profit from this land anytime soon. She destroyed Desmond because no one could deal with him. He was a madman, but Desmond is the first Irish noble house she's ever struck down. She knows as well as any ruler that there has to be a hierarchy in a society or else you have chaos. The Irish lords are the necessary intermediary between Dublin and the mass of Irish people. Elizabeth doesn't want to destroy those lords; she just wants their concurrence in her policies. But to gain that end she must deal sensibly with them. Elizabeth is aware of that, so it's surprising when blatant injustices like this robbery of Roche's lands occur, and they falsely appear to have her approval. You even had audience with the Queen, Lord Roche, did you not?"

"I did," Roche replied. "She granted me a full hour in her audience chamber. She confessed herself to be completely tired of hearing about Irish land disputes, but because my family had served her so well, she would make an exception in my case. I explained to her about this Spenser person and the meadow stolen from me. She was sympathetic enough to dictate a letter to the council in my favor, and I thought the matter was settled. You assume once you get the Queen on your side—"

"What happened?" Lord Norris asked.

"The letter went to the council, and I was advised to file suit, which I did. And nothing further came of it."

"Why not?"

"You can't effectively be heard in the courts if your request for judgment keeps getting returned to you for reapplication because you didn't dot an 'i' or cross a 't'. It's clear the legal people have both the power and the inclination to churn your case forever if you object to their Undertaker project, and reapplying means starting over."

"With the Queen?"

"That's right. My experience made it vividly clear to me that English Undertakers have good friends in English courts, so I'm simply going to have to make life as miserable for this Edmund Spenser fellow as I can."

"I can't much blame you," Perrot nodded. "Without bloodshed, however."

"I won't start it," Roche promised. "I'll just offer whatever inconvenience or threat or horror I would offer to any trespasser on my land."

"Just act sensibly and we'll have no trouble between us," Perrot's voice hardened a bit, but then assumed a social smoothness when he addressed the group. "How much land did she end up giving Raleigh anyway? Was it really the forty-seven thousand acres I've heard rumors of? What in the world would a man do with that much land?"

"Grow potatoes." William suggested.

"Grow what?" The group buzzed with confusion.

"Very easy to grow," William explained. "Just stick them in a small mound. Takes very little effort or attention. Raleigh said that would suit the Irish just fine."

"Are they fruits or vegetables or what?" Roche asked.

"Vegetables, I'd say, of the nightshade family," Malachi offered, "but very wholesome, I'm told. They do need some doctoring, however, to bring out the best flavor, and nothing in the world suits that purpose better than a thick layer of roast beef gravy which makes them absolutely mouth-watering and a sure cure for a rumbling belly. Raleigh wants to plant tobac here as well."

"Will that stuff grow here?" Perrot wondered. "Somebody asked me the other day if you could make bread from tobac?"

Malachi chuckled. "You probably could, but you might have trouble getting anyone to eat it. I've heard some say you can tuck a chunk of tobac in your cheek and draw juices from it which pleases the chewer for a time until he spits it out, so who knows what will come of it? Raleigh is certainly promoting it heavily. He's already created the market for it in London by drinking smoke from his silver pipe for any who will watch."

"While I was in London," Roche said, "I heard he even got the Queen to try it."

"Yes," Malachi said, "but it made her cough. She said she noticed that people who drink a lot of smoke end up with blackened teeth, so she'll not take up the habit. Raleigh is clever enough, however, to keep her interested. He recently bet her that he could actually weigh the smoke that the tobacco produced, and Elizabeth jumped right in since she enjoys a wager now and then. Raleigh produced a scale and weighed a plug of tobacco before stuffing it in his pipe and smoking it. He then weighed the remaining ashes and declared the difference between the two was the weight of the smoke. The Queen was amused enough to pay up and comment, *'I've seen many in my Court turn money into ashes, but you are the first I've seen turn ashes into money'*." The group enjoyed a quiet chuckle at the Queen's reaction.

"Yes," Perrot growled, "he's clever enough to set her up for those punchy endings along with his pretty face, but Jesus Christ Almighty, forty-seven thousand acres' worth of clever and pretty?" Perrot shook his head. "I think that's overdoing it a bit, however," he heaved a deep sigh and continued, "little as I care for Raleigh, I hope he succeeds with his tobac crop. If he makes a profit from growing the stuff, others will follow, and Ireland may finally have a cash crop that stands up to warfare. That's where the famine comes from in Ireland, you know. The field crops burn so easily that the Irish food supply is the first casualty every time there's a flare up. Do the tobac plants burn easily?"

"I don't think they are very flammable until they are dried," Malachi said, "but I don't really know. Obviously the intention is to burn them somewhere along the line in order to drink the smoke. They're not good food, however, so I don't think they are the answer to surviving in warfare."

"It doesn't sound like a solution to that particular problem anyway," Perrot mused. "The rich seldom starve, of course, but the ordinary people need something to sustain them even as wars rage around them and all the fields burn, but I guess tobac isn't it."

"If it turns out to be a cash crop," Lord Roche said, "I'll plant some in the disputed field if I am allowed to retain my own property."

"You will be," Sir John Perrot assured him. "I know the Queen values loyal subjects very highly over troublemakers and will come to realize it is a big mistake to let her administration rob decent people of their land. Nothing will drive them into rebellion faster. Ireland has to change, and it is changing slowly, but if we are to end with a peaceful, profitable land, the Irish people must be convinced that the Queen's administrators are dealing fairly with them, and that means this Edmund Spenser person must not be allowed to rob you of your ancestral lands."

"Speaking of troublemakers," Lord Carpenter asked, "How much of a threat does the O'Neill represent to commercial interests in Ireland at the moment?"

"Mark me well," Sir John Perrot advised his audience. "The day will soon come when O'Neill succeeds in arming his people with wheel-lock muskets, and then he'll pose an imminent threat to all of us. Frankly, I'm amazed King Philip has so far made no formal effort to run arms up to Ulster. It wouldn't surprise me one bit if the Dons decided to supply O'Neill with plenty of firepower in order to create a flanking diversion for England and draw off our troops just as Spain comes after us frontally with the invasion fleet they're building. But after the bloody nose Spain got in the Smerwick business, there's no recent evidence that they're taking a hand in Ireland as a matter of national policy."

"What kind of evidence would you recognize, Sir John?" Lord Norris asked.

"I would think the appearance of some Spanish galleons accompanying an arms shipment to Ulster would indicate that King Philip and the Prince of Tyrone were doing more than talking. As a matter of fact, we do know that Spanish navy people have recently taken soundings of the harbors in Ulster, so they obviously have something big in mind, and if they take action together, we really have a problem on our hands because O'Neill has plenty of men and Philip has plenty of guns."

"How many men?" someone asked.

"O'Neill has every lord in the North," Perrot explained, "and, of course, he always has the O'Donnells, so I'd estimate he could put fifteen thousand men on the road to Dublin in a week."

"Why doesn't he?" asked another.

John Perrot laughed. "In simple terms, he knows better. The recent military lessons played out here in Ireland are not lost on O'Neill any more than they are on us. Anytime we can see his Gallowglass coming, and we can meet them in the open, we can destroy them with our pikemen and musketeers assembled in blocked bands. When they catch us in the passes or at the fords, they inflict heavy casualties before we can organize our defense, but as long as the pikes keep them out, the wheel-locks can tear them to pieces. The musketeers have been well trained in reloading and by firing at a range of only twenty-five-feet between the rows of pikemen directly into the Gallowglass mass, each gun can kill one of the axemen every two minutes, and I must tell you there are few experiences in life as gratifying as watching one of those fearsome savages who is so intent on dismembering you, perish right before your eyes. A heart-warming spectacle, believe me. I have never come out of such an encounter without saying a special blessing for the man who invented the wheel-lock. It lets us kill them before they get close enough to swing their axes among us. An ideal military arrangement. But, of course, the balance of power could shift very suddenly if Tyrone should arm his people with muskets."

"Could he train large numbers in the use of such radically new weapons overnight?" someone asked.

Lord Norris answered. "Obviously not. Don't forget these are the mere Irish we're talking about. We've all seen in the past how slowly they learn any new employment. I don't know that we have quite as much to worry about as you are suggesting, Sir John—at least not in the immediate future, if you'll forgive me for saying so."

"Oh, I'll forgive you well enough," Perrot laughed, "and so will O'Neill when he hears how lightly you hold his threat, and he'll feel free, thereby, to cut out your tongue someday and serve it for his dinner. But to return to the pertinent inquiry about the training of O'Neill's army. He already has some Spanish military advisors up there with him now—just visiting, it is said—and he still has a special order from the Queen left over from the old days permitting him to arm and train one small band of men for his personal protection. In typical Irish fashion, O'Neill chooses to interpret that permit to mean he may train only one small band at a time, so he trains one group, then sends them home to train their garrison, and replaces them with another bunch. In that fashion, he has probably already instructed a third of those fifteen thousand men in handling weapons and in basic battle strategy."

"Sounds like a tricky bastard," one of the merchants observed.

"That's a good beginning in describing O'Neill," Perrot agreed. "He is one of only two men I can think of who have consistently outmaneuvered Elizabeth and somehow convinced her to forgive them over and over. The other is, of course, Cormac MacCarthy, the Lord of Blarney Castle whose gift of gab is so convincing," Perrot paused to chuckle, "that our exasperated Queen has taken to denouncing him—along with any who use a silver tongue to overwhelm her good sense—as being 'full of Blarney.'"

"May I ask if O'Neill is training his men to use wheel-locks at the moment?" Lord Norris asked.

"Good question," Perrot replied. "I'd expect such instruction to be a dead giveaway of plans already laid, but no, he's not training all of them in musket fire yet. Nothing disproportionate. If he should start such a program, it would mean that he has reached an agreement with Philip and is expecting an arms delivery from Spain to Ulster. Our naval people could do wonders with such a notification, I'm sure, so all of you must keep your ears open in your travels and keep those helpful tongues wagging, even if it means standing an extra round of somebody's refreshment. I'll recompense any expense which results in obtaining good information."

"Sir John," spoke up another merchant. "I hope I'm not opening a cask of worms here, but you have invited us to express ourselves candidly at these gatherings, have you not?"

"I have indeed," Perrot affirmed. "No other way to dig out the truth. Get on with it."

"Like many merchant adventurers, my firm lost heavily when our holdings were burned up in the Desmond Rebellion, and I have recently heard that particular conflict could have been avoided if Elizabeth had been paying more attention and was not such a stickler for courtly flattery. Do you find any truth in such charges?"

"Oh, I don't think Elizabeth requires any more flattery than any other prince," said Sir John Perrot, "and a lot less than some, but still if you are going to do business with the Queen, you must play the game. Even some of her closest advisers are banished from the Court periodically for bad manners, and sometimes the country suffers from not having those people on the job."

"Suffers?" someone asked.

Perrot shrugged. "We could have quenched the Desmond Rebellion without destroying the whole southwest corner of Ireland if Walsingham had been left to mind the store."

"Where was he?"

"In September, 1579, I talked to him in London at Leicester House after he had been banished from the Court for his comments about the Queen's proposed marriage to the Duke of Alencon, the heir-apparent to the French throne. Leicester House had become the headquarters for the Puritan-bred opposition to her marriage to the man they called 'The Frog'. She was forty-six then, already on the chancy side of child-bearing. Burghley, who was in favor of the marriage because it might provide a legitimate heir to the English throne, constantly praised Elizabeth's body and posture which he professed was still ripe for children. The Fox stayed in her favor by that approach and left the opposite view to Walsingham who was opposed to the union, because—among other things—Alencon was not only a Catholic but a French Catholic as well. In Spain they call Walsingham 'The Spider' with good reason, but every once in a while he gets tangled in his own web."

"I'll wager this was one of his more outspoken moments."

"Right. He was against the marriage, so he felt obliged to tell the queen quite frankly that her royal body sagged a bit and appeared to him to have passed the safe child-bearing years. She dismissed him from the court in September, and he did not resume his standing until the next year. That's how the Desmond rebellion got so far before we brought it down. There was nobody minding the London end of the intelligence gathering, because we sent plenty of notice that Desmond was working himself up to break out. Walsingham, however, stayed busy at Leicester House for the remainder of that year, plotting to thwart the marriage."

"I remember it was said he wrote the long letter Sir Philip Sidney delivered to Elizabeth denouncing the marriage," Malachi said.

"Right. Even though Sidney signed the forty-five hundred word discourse denouncing the proposed union, Walsingham's hand is apparent in the listing of compelling reasons against the event. But Walsingham had to operate outside the Court all the rest of that year and was not once given audience with Elizabeth when he might have spread some alarm over the growing threat from Desmond. He suffered personally, yes, but the real damage was done in the performance of his duties. Desmond had already lit the fuse in Ireland, and we could all see that nothing was being done to discourage him because Elizabeth was nursing hurt feelings from the marriage argument and would not take the time to listen to the warnings of her advisors."

"Was she in love with the Frenchman?" William inquired diffidently.

"Who can say? During the four years of the on-again off-again discussion of a marriage, she appeared at times to be toying with him so she could play the heir to the French throne against the Spanish, but at other times she seemed genuinely fond of him. She did realize that having an heir by any prince would quiet a lot of criticism— or advice, if you will—in her Council. But she was certainly distracted by the experience, and little was decided on other issues during that time. Ordinarily, the Queen loves to hold Court no matter what the problem, but she came later and later to business each day while that marriage dispute raged and finally dismissed Walsingham and his thorny council altogether from her Court. That turned Desmond loose to destroy the whole southwest of Ireland. Ah, well, we'll take every precaution to hold rebellion down, but meantime—" Sir John stood and saluted the group with his glass before finishing its contents— "It is said that '*Every man hath business and desire*', [24] and I think we have finished business for the evening. Let us commence with the other."

PART X: WITH SPENSER IN IRELAND; DECEMBER 1587

Chapter 1:
VISIT WITH SPENSER AT HAP-HAZARD

Early December, 1587:

"You're in for an interesting evening if you keep your ears pricked," said Malachi, as they rode their cart to Spenser's place at Kilcolman. "Edmund Spenser likes to hear from everybody who is ready to approve his work, so you are under direct orders to applaud vigorously whatever he chooses to grace us with."

"If we're graced with good food, the applause will follow."

Malachi nodded. "It never hurts for a sensible audience to bolster the artists' self-esteem in order to pave the path for the appearance of his Muse, so be very careful tonight. Above all else, do not point out any little oddities in his verse form which you imagine you detect, or I'll have you sent immediately from the company."

"Not even helpful suggestions?"

"Those particularly," Malachi growled. "Also remember that Edmund Spenser is a renowned and respected poet, read and admired even by the Queen. He has influential friends at every level of both English and Irish politics, but since such seed-beds of good fellowship often produce withered vines along with the blossoms, it is not surprising that he also has an enemy or two at each of those levels."

"You mentioned that he calls his estate 'Hap-Hazard', and I wonder how much thought he put into using such a mundane name."

Malachi frowned. "As such an accomplished versifier, Edmund Spenser has earned the right to call his estate anything he damn well pleases, and there could hardly be more than a single soul throughout the realm who could muster the barefaced arrogance to second-guess him. And yet, defying all odds, here you are. Remarkable."

"'Hap-Hazard' is not a very impressive name for the estate of a man with the kind of poetic sensibility people suggest Spenser has," William insisted. "Of course the repetition of the 'ha' sound is pleasing to the ear but—"

"Poetic sensibility, bah! He calls the estate Hap-Hazard because Spenser is acutely aware of what has happened time after time to small English landholders in Ireland and what might happen to them again at any moment. Not only are estates destroyed, but owners are placed in mortal danger. The lucky ones will arrive at the gates of Cork running for their lives, stripped naked of all possessions including their clothing, which they will have traded for safe passage along the road. Indeed, they will be fortunate if someone has not cut off their noses or ears when they run out of better things to barter."

"How often does that happen?" gasped William.

Malachi shrugged. "It's sporadic. It doesn't happen every year, of course, but it's hard to get through a decade without a significant flare-up of some kind. In 1569 and then again in 1579, outbreaks during the Desmond Wars sent hundreds of English settlers fleeing for their lives to the English garrisons in the coastal communities. And, of course, some estate owners simply disappeared."

"Do these outbreaks occur just because the Irish are anti-English?"

"That's part of it," Malachi nodded, "but the bigger truth may be that the Irish love to squabble over land and cattle. Every estate pensions a gang of thugs to patrol its boundaries—the Kern and Gallowglass have that duty on their home estate when they are not off to battle. When boundary disputes arise, fighting men from each side go at each other a time or two, and eventually the estate owners meet to settle the matter sensibly; however, those owners, in their own turn, often fall to further argument, and each hurries his claim off to Dublin for legal settlement. While they wait for a judgment from Dublin—which must wait, in its own good turn, for a judgment from London—they each find it practical to augment their force of head-knockers by recruiting loose bands of fighting men from every corner of the land."

"And that's when the battle begins?"

"Sometimes," said Malachi, "but often the build-up is an attempt to intimidate the opposition, so the fighting is delayed. The clans often number five or six thousand fighters so when they gather, the armed men are billeted at every home for miles around, just waiting for the fun to begin. On those occasions, there is great dislocation of sleeping quarters, and legitimate apprehension arises on the part of property owners, husbands, and fathers in the surrounding area. If the Irish can't take you at a disadvantage, they may delay the battle, which results in their forces forever sneaking around to out-flank each other, or setting up ambushes by burning, pillaging, and taking advantage of the women as they move in order to draw the enemy to the disturbance. The trick is often ignored by the opposing force, however, because they are preoccupied with setting up their own ambush. Many professional soldiers prefer such forays and sallies to the actual battle."

"Less risk and less stressful, I should imagine."

"It makes a quality difference if no one is shooting back," agreed Malachi. "Anyway, the opposing forces usually circle each other warily for a time before any battle, and during that period, everybody in the surrounding countryside is at risk both for his estate and for his life—in short, Edmund Spenser's mortal existence is at hazard here in Ireland." [1]

"Do these opposing forces sneaking back and forth mean the same women could be taken advantage of by rival groups on the same day?"

Malachi nodded. "Happens often, no question. The falling-back troops don't do as much socializing as the coming-on troops obviously, but they get in as much burning and pillaging as they can. Funny thing is that many of the old soldiers I have talked to—men who have seen action in France and the Low Countries as well as in Ireland—feel that the Irish women are taken advantage of more easily than most."

"I wonder what that means?"

"Some say their erotic feelings are somehow closer to the surface."

"Their eyes do sparkle with some wonderment," William observed.

"Don't be misled by that sparkle which is but a simple refraction of the abiding mist and is easily discounted by intelligent men," Malachi pointed out, "but there is no denying they do beam a saucy twinkle at times. I may have to get some horse-blinders for you if I expect to get any work out of you."

"I'll try to look away when such danger lurks," William smiled. "Did I understand you to mean a local dispute could flare up and engulf Spenser without any involvement on his part?"

"Local or national makes little difference when the Irish trail their pikes up to your front door. The local conflicts flare faster is all. As a matter of fact, just as we heard from Lord Perrot, Spenser is in the middle of just such a dispute right now with his neighbor, Lord Roche. They both claim title to a pasture of some two hundred acres. Spenser claims it was in the land grant he got from the Crown, and Roche claims it has been part of his family's estate for hundreds of years. Roche's thugs have already trounced Spenser's handy-men a time or two at the disputed field, and they each have been to Dublin to argue their case and send petitions to London."

"Time now for a gathering of the Gallowglass?"

"Roche already has some living on his estate, but Spenser would have to hire some if he intended to out-muscle Roche for the pasture."

"Will he do that?"

Malachi laughed. "I doubt it. He knows Ireland too well to risk inviting such people onto his property even for a short time. If they refuse to leave when their work is done, his only recourse would be to hire a larger group of thugs to pitch them out, and then the new cluster must decide to leave or stay. Only then he would be dickering with a bigger, stronger assembly whose expenses he is still picking up. They will be too cunning to defy him openly about leaving since they are always concerned about next year's employment. Instead, they simply delay their departure by offering compelling reasons every week to explain why they may not relinquish the land at that particular moment: 'May we have one more week, please, your Honor, while the Grandmother is buried or the baby is born or the lost child found or the herds gathered.' In typical Irish fashion, the week's delay runs into a month's malingering, a year's loitering, and a decade's dalliance."

"Compelling reasons by the week, eh? They must be very creative chaps, for all their slovenly appearance. I'll have to see if I can milk some plot lines out of them when we get a chance to visit."

"You'll see plot lines enough if trouble should explode while we're visiting Hap-Hazard because once the action starts, both armies head directly for the English houses in search of the best loot."

"That doesn't seem quite fair if the English are not involved in the original argument."

Malachi hooted. "The English are involved in every dispute, according to Irish thinking. Believe me, when the countryside is ravished, English properties burn first."

"So what can Spenser do if he doesn't hire thugs of his own?"

"Very little after all his handymen are laid up, except stay clear of the pasture without renouncing ownership entirely, keep a token presence near the field, circulate letters and petitions in London, and hope for the best."

"With his civil and military background, Spenser should have better connections in London than Roche, shouldn't he?"

"Ordinarily, I'd say that was true because all those men who, like Spenser, served under Lord Grey in Ireland have well-placed London friends who awarded them the land grants in the first place and are still eager to see their program of English Undertakers succeed. Those friends usually determine Irish land disputes heavily in favor of the London-appointed Undertakers, but Lord Roche is a special case. As Perrot mentioned, Roche even had a personal conference with the Queen about the pasture. Pretty hard to be better connected than that unless you happen to have a handful of London lawyers in your pocket."

"Is Spenser retired now or is he still in government service?"

"Essentially, he is in the process of retiring after serving her majesty's government in Ireland for many years in major civic and military administrative posts. In addition to being considered a talented English poet, Spenser is also one of the greatest Irish scholars of all time, having read everything in existence on Irish history. During his service to Lord Arthur Grey of Wilton during the Desmond Rebellion, Spenser dealt with the top people in all areas of this country for many years. He is on speaking terms with the leaders of the three major power-groups in Ireland."

"Three major power-groups?"

"The native Irish chieftains, the Anglo-Irish families, and the Lord Deputy's government in Dublin. Those three are the power brokers. Their individual interactions with London keep the political pot boiling, and Edmund Spenser knows the whole system inside and out."

"Let us hope he is not reluctant to share his knowledge with her Majesty's couriers."

Malachi sputtered with laughter. "Reluctant hell! You can't shut him up! Spenser and I did some business together a few years back and saved ourselves a serious reprimand from London by covering each other on a delayed letter. When I'm on hold in this part of the country, I usually stay with Master Spenser and earn my keep by taking notes and doing fair copy for him. We've spent many pleasant evenings over dinner trying to pump information from each other. He knows of my gift of memory, so he tries to trip me into indiscreet recall by praising me effusively. It's a childish device on his part, of course, so I feel pretty silly when I fall for it each time. Fortunately, after two jars, he usually ascends to a trance-like state—kept aloft by the updraft of his own voice—and in that state, he discourses at length on his view of the present state of Ireland. With suggestions, of course."

"Suggestions?"

"Oh, yes, he's full of them and some of them are fascinating. All in all, Spenser is a splendid dinner companion. He knows all the clan affiliations and every by-way in Ireland. He knows which passes to block and which towns to garrison in order to rule with the guiding hand of the benevolent big brother he assumes England represents in Ireland. He has the perfect administrator's mind, cranking away, blissfully unaware that his entire effort is based on a flawed premise."

"Ah, a flawed premise."

Malachi nodded. "His presumption is that Irishmen are simply uncivilized and untrained Englishmen, and that they only need strong guidance in order to repair the deficit and begin to catch up."

"So that whatever worked in England will work here?"

"That seems to be the assumption," said Malachi, "but, of course, it won't. I'm afraid it's a little more complicated than Spenser's excellent administrative mind will ever grasp. He likes relationships and responsibilities nailed down and cemented up, but the Irish bog is the wrong place to count on firm footing."

"Step carefully in Ireland," grinned William. "I can remember that. Does he use his poetry to present his political views?"

"Not so you would notice. Although his poetry is a bit overdrawn at times for my taste, it is a classical exercise in poetic references, intricate analogies, and abstract arguments, all tied together in a bouquet of vaporous clouds."

"Did he ever speak aloud on why he wrote 'The Faerie Queene'?" You know; the motivation. I'm always interested in what gets a writer started, because you never know when such knowledge might come in handy."

"As a matter of fact he did. He made his purpose crystal clear—in his terms—in a recent letter he said; *'In the Faerie Queene I mean glory in my generall intention, but in my particular I conceive the most excellent and glorious person of our soveraine the Queene, and her kingdome in Faery land. And yet in some places els, I doe otherwise shadow her. For considering she beareth two persons, the one of a most royall Queene or Empresse, the other of a most virtuous and beautifull Lady, this latter part in some places I doe expresse in Belphoebe, fashioning her name according to your owne excellent conceipt of Cynthia, (Phoebe and Cynthia being both names of Diana)'."* [2]

"Good Lord, he has divided the Queen into enough people for a dinner party! I suppose all writers presume clarity from a personal point of view."

Malachi chuckled. "I wouldn't be surprised. It pretty well requires a university education to appreciate Spenser, so I'm sure you wouldn't care for his poetry."

"Try me. You said you took notes on some of his work. Let's hear it."

"You're on!" Malachi grinned. "Let me see if I can remember a bit that has some chance of appealing to your taste. Ah, yes…

> *'Under the porch a comely dame did rest,*
> *Clad in fair weedes, but fowle disordered,*
> *And garments loose, that seemed unmeet for womanhed.'"* [3]

"Garments loose. That's promising," murmured William.

> *"'In her left hand a cup of gold she held,*
> *And with her right the riper fruit did reach,*
> *Whose sappy liquor, that with fulnesse sweld,*
> *Into her cup she scruzd with daintie breach*
> *Of her fine fingers, without fowle empeach,*
> *That so faire wine-presse made the wine more sweet;*
> *Thereof she usd to give to drinke to each*
> *Whom passing by she happened to meet:*
> *It was her guise, all straungers goodly so to greet.'"*

"That's not bad at all," William said, "but who was the guy?"

"What guy?"

"Oh, come on now, play fair. Are you trying to tell me that her dainty breech squeezed some sappy liquor out of a fullness swelled and there was no guy around?"

Malachi reflected for a moment. "You know, with your shameless, licentious imaginings, you might enjoy Spenser more than most people would. Let me give you a little more where there is actually a gentleman around. I should warn you, however, Spenser has finished three books so far, and in each one there is a hero who is tempted by a nearly irresistible enticement which he is finally able to resist because of his virtue and purity."

"Oh, well. Even sad endings can be entertaining. Let's hear it."

> "'As Guyon hapned by the same to wend,
> Two naked damzelles he herein espyde,
> Which therein bathing seeme'd to contend
> And wrestle wantonly, ne car'd to hyde
> Their dainty parts from vew of any which them eyed.
>
> Sometimes the one would lift the other quight
> Above the waters, and then downe againe
> Her plong, as over maistrere'd by might,
> Where both awhile would covere'd remain,
> And each the other from to rise restraine;
> The while their snowy limbes, as through a vele,
> So through the christall waves appeare'd plaine;
> Then suddenly both woud themselves unhele,
> And th' amorous sweet spoiles to greedy eyes revele.
> Whom such when Guyon saw, he drew him neare,
> And somewhat gan relent his earnest pace,
> His stubborne brest gan secret pleasaunce to embrace.
>
> The wonton maidens him espying, stood
> Gazing a while at his unwonted guise;
> Then th' one her selfe low ducke'd in the flood,
> Absht, that her a stranger did avise;
> But th' other rather higher did arise,
> And her two lilly paps aloft displayd,
> And all that might his melting hart entise
> To her delights, she unto him betrayed:
> The rest hid underneath, him more desirous made.'"

"That's right," William exclaimed. "If you can get them to compete for which is most shameless, you are in for a very exciting evening!"

> *Withall she laughe'd, and she blusht withal,*
> *That blushing to her laughter gave more grace,*
> *And laughter to her blushing, as did fall;*
> *Now when they spide the knight to slacke his pace,*
> *Them to behold, and in his sparkling face*
> *The secret signes of kindled lust appeare,*
> *Their wanton merriments they did encreace,*
> *And to him beckned to approach more neare,*
> *And shewd him many sights, that courage cold could reare'.*" [4]

"This is very exciting! Keep going."

"No, that's a good spot to stop for two reasons. First, because you might be quite disappointed when you learn that Guyon is a champion at repressing his animal impulses and ends up being easily drawn away from the encounter by a helpful friend, and secondly, because here we are at Hap-Hazard and there is our host at the gate."

Malachi kept his distance while he exchanged pleasantries with Edmund Spenser. "Well, to tell you the truth, Master Spenser, the manure cart is a magic carpet through the trouble spots in any land. Every country has its contentious crossroads where bands of patriots or partisans or insurgents or ruffians or God knows what-all—gather to blockade your passage and threaten you with harm for reasons known only to themselves. This cart gives incredible access to public roads which are blocked to many travelers. Everybody steers clear because of the nauseating stench, and people assume you are local because such loads are usually hauled only as long as one can hold his breath, usually from one field to another. You are waved through every check-point, so there is no stay or delay in your progress clear across the land. Yes, I'd have to say the manure cart is the flying carpet for travel in every country."

"Get your man to run it down the road to leeward if you don't mind while we discuss its obvious inconvenience in addition to Raleigh's inquiry." Edmund Spenser requested as he sniffed daintily.

Malachi laughed and signaled William to move the wagon before addressing Spenser. "A quick scrub will undo the after-effects, sir, and a clean set of clothes. As I said, Raleigh says he can make it up by next Sunday if you approve. Will that be all right?"

"I'll be delighted to have him, and Sunday is just right. Mr. Eudox and I should be finished our chat by then, and I would be honored to host the redoubtable Sir Walter Raleigh. How is he taking the Queen's displeasure?"

"Oh, he's very concerned. More than once I've heard him mutter, 'Out of favor, out of fortune', but Raleigh is a creative business man. He'll recapture the Queen's favor with some grand stroke, never fear. You've heard about the gesture with the cape?"

Spenser laughed. "Everybody has. A bit of theatrical nonsense but effective none-the-less. At times I think the Queen has a fondness for foolish gestures."

"When they exaggerate a subject's devotion to her, she loves them, but woe betide the man whose foolishness costs the Queen a single shred of dignity or an ounce of treasury. That man will encounter a very different audience for his foolishness."

"Yes," said Spenser, "I handled Lord Grey's requests for funds to pursue his campaign against Desmond, so I know how it goes when Elizabeth is displeased by something."

Malachi chuckled, "Ah, the good old days. If the Raleigh invitation is all set, then, I must run a few more errands in the neighborhood and then tomorrow ride back down to Yougal."

"You're welcome anytime," Spenser assured him. "I couldn't ask for better company than the best informed town-crier in the kingdom, but I'm sorry to hear your duties carry you off so quickly. I could certainly use your excellent amanuensis service for a few days to record my discussions with Mr. Eudox, but you must respond to Sir Walter's request, of course. I suppose Mr. Eudox can take notes as we go, but that will slow us down terribly in preparing a blueprint for Ireland's future."

"No need to despair, sir. I have readily at hand my apprentice, here, who is an outstanding amanuensis. He strikes a fairer copy than any man I know including— although it pains me to admit it—my own self, and I don't need him on my business tonight, so he may serve you for a day or two if it please you. He has already mastered the art of the short-scribble recently developed—"

"Short-hand," corrected William softly.

"Really? Well, we'll try and make do with him, but it won't be the same." Spenser looked William over. "You can transcribe at conversational speed, I presume?"

"Most assuredly," William said.

"Excellent. Your service will permit us to ramble freely without distraction. As a matter of fact, if you were completely out of sight, it would lend freedom to the flow of our thoughts, so I'll place a screen around your desk in the corner, and I'll set a glass of wine behind the screen, so you may refresh yourself during our thoughtful pauses."

"Thank you," said William.

"Arrange your pen and paper accordingly. Mr. Eudox will join me in about two hours. Try to be out of sight when I return. Malachi, I'd like a private word with you before I go. Perhaps your man could wash up and find duty elsewhere for a short time?"

"Oh, certainly," William responded, "Which way to the kitchen?"

Spenser pointed the way, then leaned forward to Malachi. "Tonight's discussion is quite important, Malachi. Much more so than would appear on the surface."

"Oh?"

"Yes. It will appear to be nothing more than an idle exchange between myself as a retiring civil servant and a young man newly appointed by London as an administrator to this land, as I was so many years ago..." Spenser paused and appeared lost in thought.

"In reality, however..." Malachi prompted.

"Yes. I'll actually be representing a collection of very experienced administrators attempting to change England's present policies by passing along recommendations on how to govern this unruly land intelligently. Mr. Eudox represents the new group which has recently assumed its duties in Ireland. He is a personal friend, and while he is only a minor official, his family has money, so he knows everybody worth knowing in London. He is the trusted pipeline between my old group and the new group which is just arriving to assume their duties. My faction of experienced officials are convinced that the failure of English policy in Ireland is due to two main causes."

"That is impressive pin-pointing."

"First, we are convinced that Irish policy is made by people in London who know very little about how Irish society actually functions, or, if you prefer, how it dysfunctions."

Malachi smiled. "I've seen this land in both moods, your Honor."

"And secondly, we feel that past English policy was always based on political expediency. It was fashioned only to solve the problem in the short term and not designed to root out the real causes of unrest and discontent in Ireland. So these notes are meant to clear up those two faults and prepare the way for an intelligent and profitable governance of this country."

"Obviously then, this is not simply an annual report."

"More of a warning, really, pointing out the hidden pitfalls of trying to apply logic and reason to the business of governing the Irish."

"And solutions?"

"We'll offer solutions as we go along. It will be easier to follow our thinking that way. Finally, I hope to put all of these suggestions into a book which I intend to call, A View of the Present State of Ireland."

"So the notes may end up being published?"

"Right. That's why I want your assurance that your man is up to the job."

"He's the best transcriber in the world right now, sir, and you must know how much it hurts me to confess that," Malachi chuckled, "but there is no sense denying it."

"Good. I'll want three copies. One for Mr. Eudox to circulate among the civil servants; one for Walsingham to get Burghley to read to the Privy Council and hopefully bring to the attention of the Queen; and one for my file on the future book."

"No problem," Malachi assured him.

"Is your man fast? May we speak at conversational speed?"

"Like lightning, sir. He even records laughs and sighs."

"You make him sound like a wonder, indeed. Of course, he'd leave the laughs and sighs out of the final copy."

"He'll do it anyway you like it, sir. As a matter of fact, that's his motto, and he means it as long as you are patient with him."

"Patient with Mr. Lightning?" Spenser inquired good naturedly.

"He recently suffered a head injury which causes him at times to forget his manners. He just needs to be reminded occasionally."

"Oh well," Spenser laughed. "We'll sort that out for him in a hurry. We maintain a strict level of servant compliance in this household and we speak sharply to those who deviate. I'll talk to him myself before Mr. Eudox comes down."

"Patience is all it takes, sir, and you will get good work from him."

"Laughs and sighs too. How extraordinary."

Malachi nodded, "He'll doodle if you pause for breath. Fastest transcriber in the world and the most accurate. Never makes a mistake. Never blots a line."

"Remarkable."

Malachi nodded. "Marvelously gifted he is in some areas and completely remiss in others, such as the important matter of punctuation. The words seem to come to him easily enough, but he has to think through the punctuation."

"Little matter," said Spenser. "I'll straighten that out in the copies. See that your man is well placed, and I'll see if Mr. Eudox is ready, but before that, one last thing, Malachi."

"Yes, sir, what is that?"

"I want your professional assurance that Mr. Eudox and I will be presented with clear transcripts of our full conversation by noon tomorrow."

"Barring rebellion or fire, sir, rest assured you will have the fair copies by then, for so I shall instruct my man forthwith, and I will also emphasize the importance of the subject matter, although, I imagine, that will be apparent even to my somewhat inexperienced servant as soon as you start your discussion."

"Positively," Spenser nodded. "No escaping it. These notes really will be a concerted effort to communicate to the Queen some of the realities of the Irish situation which she must acknowledge if she is to avoid falling down the same old Irish rat-holes which have swallowed English policy in the past. As it is now, Elizabeth divides all her time between raging at her officials to do more to solve our problems in Ireland and then turning around and blaming them for mistreating 'her loving subjects'. All the while she is wooing the worst of the rebels for a lasting peace. Under those conditions, policy-making is impossible because the rulings from London chase their own tails like a bitch in heat."

"And as I understand it, sir, the suggestions you'll offer are more than just your personal thoughts on the matter."

"Right. They will represent the thinking of the group that has met at Briskett's Dublin cottage for many years. It was not unusual to have most of the civil and military administration of Ireland at those gatherings, and tonight I will attempt to convey to Mr. Eudox that group's best thinking on many aspects of governing this disorderly nation. In a very strong sense, then, whatever notes proceed from our discussion will represent the mature thinking of an assemblage of concerned and experienced civil servants who are on their way out, so they have no further political axes to grind. In a somewhat subdued sense, these notes will represent a blueprint for the policy which the Queen must pursue if she wants to turn the Irish situation around."

Malachi whistled through his teeth. "I can well see why you are concerned with quality of the transcript for such valuable material. No room for error in such important matters."

"Since I've already pointed out the strategic significance of these notes, I know you'll realize how important it is that they not fall into certain hands—O'Neill's, for instance. The Prince of Tyrone seems to have an ear in every house in Ireland. There is no official document—no matter how securely it is handled, if it goes through a single pair of Irish hands—but O'Neill will have a copy as soon as the legitimate recipient does. And sometimes sooner."

"No question about that," agreed Malachi. "I've even heard Walsingham himself whistle in open admiration at the intelligence O'Neill has at hand not only here in Ireland but in England as well, and, as we both know, that good old Puritan doesn't whistle for many."

"Which leads me to an over-riding question, my old friend. Can your man be trusted? Are you sure he's on our side?"

"It is true," Malachi acknowledged, "that O'Neill has a long arm in this country, but even Ulster's bloody hand can't touch the mind of a man who has already barricaded his brain against any outside influence. His mind exists in a hazy, far-off land of his own making and does not welcome strangers. He is dead-center loyal on that basis alone."

"Never-the-less, I intend to exercise the closest possible supervision—with your permission, of course—until those fair-copies are in my hands."

"Close supervision, sir?"

Spenser nodded. "I shall take the precaution of limiting him to only enough materials to produce three fair-copies. He shall be confined to his quarters until I have the copies—and his notes as well—in my hand at noon of the next day. Food will be brought to him periodically. Delay invites mischief in cases like this. I want you to explain all of this very clearly to him even before we begin, so there will be no misunderstanding later on."

"Absolutely," Malachi said. "Best policy. Did you say you want his notes too, sir?"

"His notes, indeed. I want no fourth copy of these proceedings leaving my control. Our inability to keep important documents away from enemy hands is, to my mind, a national disgrace and shows a serious lack of attention to security on the part of every English official in Ireland. I know most administrators let scriveners walk off with their personal notes after fair-copies have been produced because they don't realize that such notes constitute an additional copy. Undoubtedly, such is the source of much of O'Neill's information."

"William's notes are pretty complex," Malachi cautioned.

"I don't need to read them," Spenser smiled. "As soon as I check the fair copy, I shall destroy the notes. My purpose is served as long as the notes don't fall into enemy hands—or remain in the hands of your man, for that matter, because, if you'll forgive me for saying so, he does sound quite disconnected from rational thought at times. Laughs and sighs indeed!"

Malachi shrugged. "He has good moments and bad moments socially because of the head injury which happened to throw us together. Interesting story there if a man could get it on paper."

"Really?" said Edmund Spenser. "You must tell me all about it sometime, but at the moment, I hope we are crystal clear on the particulars here."

"Yes, sir. Crystal clear. Close supervision, no additional writing materials, this time tomorrow, and three copies plus his notes."

"Good! Make sure your man is ready in two hours. Incidentally, in addition to his thorough scrubbing, make sure he is perfumed before we begin."

"I'll see to it, sir," Malachi assured him and turned to the kitchen to find William and deliver his instructions.

"So I'm on duty this evening," grinned William.

Malachi smiled, "You will, no doubt, profit from my departure. I've spent many a happy night recording Spenser's thoughts on poetry and, as you know, even recorded some of the very lines of his 'Faerie Queene'. Excellent stuff though a bit over my head. I appreciate a meat and bread kind of poetry with a strong story line, and Spenser's flights of fancy exceed my grasp at times. You claim an interest in such areas, so I thought you would welcome an opportunity to peer into the workings of a true poetic mind."

"Yes, indeed, such a discussion will be most welcome after the petty details most of our work entails. I will enjoy wafting off to the heaven of poesy."

"Don't forget the agenda for the evening's discussion is strictly up to the host, but I think you can count on his getting to poetry sooner or later. Now do a double-wash on that manure stink, dig some clean cloths out of our bag, daub on some perfume water, get comfortable in your station, and record whatever is said. In addition, of course, I expect you to curb your habitual impudence, lad."

"Oh, come, Malachi. You must have noticed lately how much I've matured, but if you keep correcting me, '*You do draw my sprits from me/ With new lamenting ancient oversights*'." [5]

"We'll see. I will check with Spenser when I get back, and I am prepared to welcome any degree of maturity you have exhibited."

Chapter 2:
SPENSER SAYS SWORD WILL SOLVE IRISH PROBLEM

Later the same evening:

Two hours later, Edmund Spenser escorted his guest into the room and seated him before the fire. The transcriber sat well out of sight in the corner.

"We are well aware," said Mr. Eudox, "of your lengthy civil service here in Ireland, Edmund, and we hope to profit directly from the enormous repository of valuable information about this poor wretched country which you have accumulated."

"In all modesty," Spenser said, "mine can be but one of many views of this land, but it is true that my experience has taught me many painful lessons, which I will be happy to pass along if it will aid her Majesty's government. I'll attempt to respond to whatever inquires you care to make. You will join me in a glass of Madeira?"

"Wine is food for thought," Eudox nodded.

Spenser crossed to the wine cabinet and smiled at Master William safely ensconced behind the screen with quill poised. "Begin," he whispered and returned to his seat.

"I will deeply appreciate it," Eudox said, "if you can cast any intelligent light at all on the mystery of Ireland. All I know at present is that for nearly four hundred years England has spent millions of pounds and thousands of lives trying to civilize this bog-ridden country without a single detectable sign of improvement. Would you regard that as an accurate impression?"

"That seems to me a very perceptive and honest view of our past policies in Ireland, even if a trifle overdrawn," Spenser chuckled, "but a conscientious administrator can't give up the ship, you know."

"Edmund, if you would," Eudox said, "help me out here. We spend a lot of time in London establishing sensible policies for Ireland, but our efforts disappear into the mist as soon as they cross the Irish Sea. What's going on?"

"The harsh truth is that affairs in Ireland just seem to spin out of control periodically for no apparent reason. They call it the *'Deadly Irish Spiral'* in Dublin..*There have been diverse good plots devised and wise counsels cast already about reformation of this realm, but they say it is the fatal destiny of this land, that no purpose whatsoever meant for her good will prosper or take good effect; which whether it proceed from the very genius of the soil, or influence of the stars, or that almighty God hath not yet appointed the time of her reformation, or that he reserveth her in this unquiet state still, for some secret scourge which shall by her come unto England, it is hard to be known but much to be feared'."* [6]

Eudox laughed. "It begins to sound as if you need a long rest, Edmund, worn weary in the heroic performance of day-by-day duty. Surely there are no problems in Ireland which a crisp, efficient administration can't handle. We need only determine the targets of our attention to foster alleviation. Now, basically, what would you say is wrong with Ireland?"

"Surely, Eudoxus, the evils which you desire to be recounted are very many and some of them are of very great antiquity and long continuance; others more late and of less endurance; others daily growing and increasing continually as the evil occasions are every day offered."

"Let me just jot those down," said Eudox. "Might come in handy if we wander off the track, some are of 'great antiquity...more late...and daily growing'...was that it?"

Spenser hesitated for a moment and then said, "I have this all outlined someplace so you need not list the evils."

Eudox quit scribbling and said, "Tell them then in the same order that you have rehearsed them. For there can be no better method than this which the very matter itself offers, and when you have reckoned all the evils, let us hear your opinion for redressing of them, after which there will perhaps of itself appear some reasonable way to settle a sound and perfect rule of government by shunning the former evils and following the offered good; the which method we may learn of the wise physicians which first require that the malady be known thoroughly and discovered, afterwards do teach how to cure and redress it, and lastly do prescribe a diet with strait rules and orders to be daily observed, for fear of relapse unto the former disease or falling into some other more dangerous than it."

An inquiring voice arose from the amanuensis' station. "Does anyone out there care if I compress this a little bit? You know...ah...catch the gist of it, so to speak, until we get to the pertinent parts? For instance, I've written that Eudox just said, 'Go to it.' Does that express the spirit of the thing adequately, or is further modification necessary?"

Eudox started at the sound and twisted around in his chair. "Who in God's name is that?"

"Alas," said Edmund Spenser, "it is my secret amanuensis. Let me see what's bothering him. What seems to be the trouble, young man?"

"I'm not one to complain, you understand," said William, 'but I need a little relief from such a rambling sentence as that last. I can handle quite a bit of complexity in sentence structure, you understand, but I simply ran out of breath trying to find a spot to fix a period in that one."

"My...my sentence, you say?" Eudox sputtered.

"I don't mean to strike a sour note, of course. There's much can be said in favor of your sentence structure."

"Oh?"

"My, yes. The dangling parenthetical thoughts you leave twisting and squirming through your sentence like so many lecherous goats and monkeys, certainly compel the close attention of your listeners."

"So what's the problem then?" Eudox gritted.

"The punctuation for such disjointed entities befuddles my mind. Don't forget that punctuation is always a judgment call for the transcriber. The truth is that such a long, chopped-up sentence wears me out in a hurry as I scramble to mark coherence in your mutterings. For the sake of future harmony between us, let's just see if we can't compact our thoughts a bit. How about it?"

Spenser and Eudox turned to stare at each other.

"Effrontery personified! Impudent upstart!" Eudox waved his fist at the screen in the corner by the liqueur cabinet. His hand rested on the hilt of his sword.

"There, there," said Spenser, "It's not time yet for such strong measures. It's only a servant who has not yet learned his place. Not unusual these days, I'm afraid, and I've already been warned about this one. I'll just step back and straighten him out quickly, if you'll excuse me for a moment."

"I'll stand ready," Eudox promised.

Spenser rose and walked to the screened-in corner until he could peer down onto the smiling face of William.

"Let me take a moment here to review your position in this household, young man," Spenser said. "Your master is a guest under my roof. You are his servant. Therefore, you are a servant of the house which is hosting your master. You don't change social positions just because you change households, you know."

"Oh, I realize that well enough, sir, since it has been drilled into me one way or another ever since I can remember, and that's one of the big reasons why I really appreciate the splendid hospitality which has been extended to me at your lodging. Even with your poetic sensibility, you could scarcely imagine some of the dreadful conditions under which I am asked to work. However, the meal which I enjoyed in your kitchen today was so good that I confess I could not resist a third helping."

"Yes, I've already received alarming reports from my kitchen, but that can wait. The point at the moment is that as a guest's servant, you are subject to the commands of the Master of the house you visit."

"Yes, I understand all that. That's the way the system works. Fair or unfair, there is ultimately little concern for individual differences, and yet it is those very differences which—"

"AND I commanded you to sit quietly behind the screen and transcribe our discussion, did I not?" Spenser demanded.

"I wouldn't really say 'commanded.' It seemed to me you were pretty polite about it,"

"My up-bringing, I presume," conceded Spenser, "which sometimes operates against me in situations like this."

"Like what?"

"Never mind!" snapped Spenser. "Young man, I command you to close your mouth this instant, open your ears, take pen in hand, and transcribe word-for-word the discussion which is about to ensue. Is that quite clear?"

William nodded. "Could you say something about poetry? That's my major concern here tonight."

Spenser drew back in astonishment. "Poetry?" he gasped. "What in the world are you talking about? This is a government discussion, and you're certainly not in charge of it, so what does poetry have to do with anything?"

"It soothes my mind," William grinned at him. "I can transcribe like a fury after I contemplate even for a moment the poetic process in all its myriad guises. I don't even have to hear poetry. Even a short discussion of the process will set my quill spinning with delight for the rest of the night."

"A desirable prospect," Spenser mused. "Let me see now..."

"Is there something I may help you with back there, Edmund?" Eudox called.

"Please don't trouble yourself," Spenser said. "It's all settled, so sit back and relax. I'll be with you in a moment."

He moved behind the screen and whispered to William. "All right then, a deal. I'll lead us into a short discussion of poetry, and then you'll do your duty quietly on the other subjects. Agreed?"

William smiled, nodded, and picked up his pen. "Ready," he said.

Spenser returned to his chair and grinned tightly at Eudox. "I'm afraid everybody has servant trouble these days. Now where were we?"

"Hold on now," said Eudox, "I don't much like this business of a hidden scribe taking down my every word. Are you up to something, Edmund?"

"Oh, no," Spenser said and waved his hand as though to clear the air between them, "Nothing like that."

"Have some of your old friends in Dublin asked you to run a file on the thoughts of the new man in town?"

"Nothing in the world like that, Eudoxius, old friend, and please accept my apologies for a clumsy servant. I thought only that our discussions in the past have proved so fruitful that we might enjoy having a transcript of the full discussion rather than rely on your scribbled notes. I fully intended for you to have a copy too—as a surprise gift, I thought." Spenser grimaced. "I've already made all the arrangements for your copy. You may check if you wish."

"No, no," said Eudox, "the word of a gentleman is quite enough for me. Still I'd prefer to be told beforehand."

"Perfectly understandable," Spenser nodded. "Sensible too. We'll see to it. In the meantime, I hope you won't let this little misadventure cast a pall over our discussion because I value you highly as a spirited interlocutor. You bring out the best in me, and I would like to put you at your ease before we continue."

"Bosh, Edmund. You're making too much of this. I was simply startled by the suddenness of the circumstance. Let's return to our discussion. You were saying, I believe, that your experience has taught you that there are many evils in Ireland. Would you care to be a little more specific? It aids understanding, you know."

"It does indeed, old friend," Spenser smiled. "I will then according to your advisement begin to declare the evils which seem to be most hurtful to the common weale of this land, and first those which I said were most ancient and long grown; and they are also of three kinds; the first in the laws, the second in customs, and last in religion."

"Ah, I love sub-heads in discussions," Eudox declared. "There's something almost poetic about such attention to detail, such assured organization. A very soothing balm for anxious minds. Perhaps that's what I miss most here in Ireland: no sub-heads."

"Yes, poetic." Spenser mumbled and scratched his head.

"Speaking of poetry, Edmund," Eudox said, "It might surprise you to learn that I sometimes let my fancy run free and wonder what it would be like if I grew up as a young man amidst the chaos of Ireland and was swept into the whirlpool of conflicting Kern and Gallowglass clans, whose bloody vortex swallows up most of Ireland's skimpy resources. I must confess, I doubt if, under those circumstances, I would have emerged as quite the same English gentleman I am today."

"Little question about the result of such upbringing," Spenser shook his head sadly. *"Those be the most loathly and barbarous conditions of any people I think under heaven for from the time that they enter into that course they do use all the beastly behavior that may be to oppress all men. They spoil as well the subject as the enemy, they steal, they are cruel and bloody, full of revenge, and delight in deadly execution, licentious swearers and blasphemers, common ravishers of women, and murderers of children."* [7]

Eudox seemed to recoil. "These be most villainous conditions. I marvel then that ever they be used or employed, or almost suffered to live. What good can there be then in them?"

"Oh, it's never a good idea to underrate them," Spenser cautioned. "Yet sure they are very valiant and hardy, for the most part great endurers of the cold, labour, hunger, and all hardness, very active, and strong of hand, very swift of foot, very vigilant and circumspect in their enterprises, very present in perils, very great scorners of death."

"Impressive," Eudox acknowledged. "Surely by this that ye say it seems the Irishman is a very brave soldier?"

Spenser nodded. *"Yea, truly, even in that rude kind of service he beareth himself very courageously, but when he cometh to experience of service abroad, and is put to a piece or a pike, he maketh as worthy a soldier as any nation he meeteth with."*

"Yes," said Eudox, "I have often heard our military people decry the waste of so many Irish fighting men in tribal warfare, when they could just as easily be dying for us on the Continent to some worthwhile purpose. But let us, I pray you, turn again to our discourse of evil customs amongst the Irish."

"Quite right," Spenser said with a sudden smile and a glance at the corner. *"First let me get at one of the least noticed yet most insidious influences in the land. There is amongst the Irish a certain kind of people called the bards, which are to them instead of poets, whose profession is to set forth the praises and dispraises of men, in their poems or rhymes, the which are had in so high regard and estimation amongst them that none dare displease them for fear to run into reproach through their offence and to be made infamous in the mouths of all men; for their verses are taken up with a general applause, and usually sung at all feasts and meetings by certain other persons whose proper function that is, which also receive for the same great rewards, and reputation besides."*

Eudox said, *"Do you blame this in them, which I otherwise have thought to have been worthy of good account, and rather to have been maintained and augmented amongst them, than to have been disliked? For I have read that in all ages, poets have been had in special reputation, and that meseems not without great cause, for besides their sweet inventions and most witty lays, they are always used to set forth the praises of the good and virtuous, and to beat down and disgrace the bad and vicious, so that many brave young minds have oftentimes, through the hearing the praises and famous eulogies of worthy men sung and reported to them, been stirred up to affect like commendations, and so to strive unto the like deserts."*

Spenser smiled. *"It is most true that such poets as in their writing do labor to better the manners, and through the sweet bait of their numbers to steal into the young spirits a desire of honour and virtue, are worthy to be had in great respect, but these Irish bards are for the most part of another mind."*

"Oh?"

"They seldom choose unto themselves the doing of good men for the ornamentation of their poems, but whomsoever they find to be most licentious of life, most bold and lawless in his doings, most dangerous and desperate in all parts of disobedience and rebellious disposition, him they set up and glorify in their rhymes, him they praise to the people, and to young men make an example to follow."

Eudox shook his head sadly. *"I marvel what kind of speeches they can find or what face they can put on to praise such lewd persons as live so lawlessly and licentiously upon stealths and spoils as most of them do or how can they think that any good mind will applaud the same?"*

Spenser nodded. *"There is none so bad, Eudoxus, but that shall find some to favor his doings, but such licentious parts as these, tending to the most part to the hurt of the English, or maintenance of their own lewd liberty, they themselves being most desirous thereof, do most allow, besides these evil things being decked and suborned with the gay attire of goodly words, may easily decline and carry away the affection of a young mind that is not well staged, but desirous by some bold adventure to make proof of himself."*

"Is it simply the school system's failure to teach respect for the rights of others?"

"Not entirely," Spenser said. *"For being—as they all be—brought up idly without awe of parents, without precepts of masters, without fear of offence, not being directed or employed in any course of life which may carry them to virtue, will easily be drawn to follow such as any shall set before them, for a young mind cannot rest if he be not still busied in some goodness. He will find himself such business as shall soon busy all about him, in which, if he shall find any to praise him and to give him encouragement, as those bards and rhymers do for little reward or a share of a stolen cow, then waxeth he most insolent and half-mad, with the love of himself and his own lewd deeds."*

"Monstrous," said Eudox; "I don't understand where they can find the language to reward such villainies."

"As for the words to set forth such lewdness it is not hard for them to give a goodly gloss and painted show thereunto, borrowed even from the praises which are proper unto virtue itself, as of a most notorious thief and wicked outlaw, which had lived all his lifetime of spoils and robberies, one of their bards in his praise said that he was none of these idle milksops that was brought up by the fireside, but that most of his days he spent in arms and valiant enterprises, that he did never eat his meat before he had won it with his sword, that he lay not slugging all night in a cabin under his mantle, but used commonly to keep others waking, to defend their lives, and did light his candle at the flame of their houses to lead him in darkness, that the day was his night and the night his day; that he loved not to lie long wooing of wenches to yield to him, but where he came he took by force the spoil of other men's love, and left but lamentations to their lovers..."

"Egad, that hardly seems like poetic fare to me."

"Exactly," said Spenser. *"And further that his muses was not the harp nor the lays of love, but the cries of people and clashing of armour, and that finally he died, not bewailed of many, but made many wail when he died, that dearly bought his death. Do you not think, Eudoxus, that many of these praises might be applied to men of best desert?"*

"Indeed!"

"Yet are they all yielded to a most notable traitor. And amongst some of the Irish not smally acccompted of, for the song when it was first made, and sung unto a person of high degree, there was bought as their manner is for forty crowns."

"Forty crowns! Holy Mother of God!" came a shout from the screened-in alcove. "That's almost as much money as Marlowe got for *Tamburlaine*! It's clear that the Irish know how to do some things right."

"Silence yourself!" Spenser commanded the corner. "Let's ignore him," he said to Eudox, "and get on with the business of undoing the present Irish government so we may recast it in such a form as to offer a final solution to the Irish problem."

"Are you seriously suggesting, Edmund, that in order to solve the Irish troubles once and for all, we must completely eliminate the present government of Ireland and start over again from the very beginning?" Eudox asked in some wonder.

"I do so, Eudoxius," Spenser said. *"The longer this government thus continueth, in the worse case will this realm be.....for the Irish do strongly hate and abhor all reformation and subjection to the English, by reason that having been once subdued by them, they were thrust out of all their possessions, so as now they fear that if they were again brought under they should likewise be expelled out of all."* [8]

"I can't imagine why they'd feel that way. Surely they know that under English law, even sore losers get their day in court—sooner or later." Eudox laughed. "If they think they have troubles now, wait till we bring in another batch of Undertakers to take charge over here—all with proper papers, of course. The Irish better enjoy the good times while they have only a light halter to constrict them!"

"Yes, more English would help a lot," said Spenser. *"Every day we perceive the troubles growing more upon us, and one evil growing upon another, insomuch as there is no part sound nor ascertained, but all have their ears upright, waiting when the watchword will come that they should all rise generally in rebellion and cast away the English subjection to which there now little wanteth, for I think the word be already given and there wanteth nothing but opportunity... It is vain to prescribe laws where no man careth for keeping them, nor feareth the danger from breaking them, but all the realm is first to be reformed and laws are afterward to be made, for keeping and continuing it in that reformed estate."*

Eudox sipped his wine and chuckled, "Pre-emptive reformation, eh? Militant nation-building? We may have left you too long in the bogs, Edmund, old boy. You're beginning to see an Irishman lurking behind every bush."

Spenser stiffened, then smiled. "Our group of veterans-in-the-field is only too happy to offer our recommendations to you newly arrived younger-sort, and we wish we might also transfer our actual experience to you, but I suppose nature dictates that we must all learn life's important lessons the hard way to insure that we don't forget them in a hurry."

"Always eager to learn," a subdued Eudox responded. "But to resume, Edmund, I'm afraid I was genuinely puzzled by your suggestion to ignore the law altogether in changing Ireland's government. How then do you think is the reformation thereof to be begun, if not by laws and ordinances?"

Spenser struck the table with a clenched fist. *"Even by the sword, for all these evils must first be cut away with a strong hand before any good can be planted, like as the corrupt branches and the unwholesome boughs are first to be pruned, and the foul mass cleansed or scrapped away, before the tree can bring forth any good fruit."*

"Ah, I really enjoy your use of gardening metaphors," Eudox said. "It's such a pleasant way to speak of otherwise unpleasant subjects. I pray you then, declare your mind at large how you would wish that sword which you mean to be used in the reformation of those evils."

Spenser cleared his throat. *"The first thing, must be to send over into this realm such a strong power of men as that shall perforce bring in all that rebellious rout of loose people which either do now stand out in open arms or in wandering companies do keep the woods spoiling and infesting the good subject."*

"Stay a moment, Edmund," Eudox said. "Surely the Madeira is going to your head. *You speak now of an infinite charge to her majesty to send over such an army as should tread down all that standeth before them on foot and lay on the ground all the stiff-necked people* of this land, for there is now but one outlaw of any great reckoning, to wit, the Earl of Tyrone, abroad in arms, against whom you see what huge charges she hath been at this last year in sending of men, providing of victuals and making head against him, yet there is little or nothing at all done; therefore it were hard counsel to draw such an exceeding charge upon her, whose event shall be so uncertain."

"Ah ha!" Spenser cried. "True, indeed, if the event should be uncertain, but the certainty of the effect hereof shall be so infallible as that no reason can gainsay it, neither shall the charge of all this army which I demand be much greater than so much as in this last two years' wars hath vainly been expended, for I dare undertake that it hath cost the Queen above £200,000 already; and for the present charge that amounteth to very near £12,000 a month, whereof cast ye the count; yet nothing done. The which sum, had it been employed as it should be, would have effected all this that I now go about."

"You seem to be suggesting something here, Edmund, which is not quite clear to me. What would you do with the money? How mean you to have it employed, but to be spent in the pay of soldiers and provision of victual?"

Spenser beamed. "Right so, but it is now not disbursed at once as it might be, but drawn out into a long length, by sending over now £20,000, and next half year £10,000, so as the soldier in the meantime is for want of due provision of victual and good payment of his pay, starved and consumed, that of 1,000 which came over lusty, able men in half a year, there are not left 500 and yet is the Queen's charge nevertheless, but what is not paid in present money is accounted in debt, which will not be long unpaid, for the captain, half of whose soldiers are dead, and the other quarter never mustered nor seen, comes shortly to demand payment here of his whole account, where by good means of some great ones and privy sharing with the officers and servants of other some, he receiveth his debt, much less perhaps than was due, yet much more indeed than he justly deserved."

Eudox shook his head, "I sometimes think that compensating errors are the very heart of good government. But back to logistics. How many men would you require to the finishing of this which ye take in hand, and how long space would you have them entertained?"

"Verily," said Spenser, "Not above 10,000 footmen and 1,000 horse, and all those not above the space of one year and a half."

Eudox seemed surprised. "Surely, it seemeth not much that ye require, nor no long time, but how would you have them used? Would you lead forth your army against the enemy and seek him where he is to fight?"

Spenser shook his head, "No, Eudoxius, that would not be, for it is well known that he is a flying enemy, hiding himself in woods and bogs, from whence he will not draw forth but into some straight passage or perilous ford where he knows the army must needs pass....I would divide my men in garrison upon his country, in such places as I should think would most annoy him."

"But how can that be with so few men?" Eudox asked. "For the enemy as ye now see is not all in one country, but some in Ulster, some in Connaught, and others in Leinster."

"Easy enough, if the troops be well laid out across the land. I would wish the chief power of the army to be garrisoned in one country, that is strongest, and the other upon the rest that are weakest, for example, the Earl of Tyrone is now counted the strongest. Upon him would I lay 8,000 men in garrison, 1,000 upon Feagh MacHugh and the Cavanaghs, and 1,000 on some parts of Connaught to be at the direction of the Governor. These 8,000 of Ulster I would divide likewise into four parts, so as there should be 2,000 footman in every garrison...The four garrisons thus being placed I would have to be victualled beforehand for half a year, which ye will say to be hard, considering the corruption and usual waste of victuals. But why should they not as well be victualled for so long time as the ships are, usually for a year, and sometimes two, seeing it is easier to keep them on land than on water?"

Eudox shrugged, "No reason I can think of."

"Hereunto would I also have them have a store of hose and shoes with such other necessaries as may be needful of soldiers, so as they should have no occasion to look for relief from abroad, or occasion such trouble for their continual supply......for the enemy, knowing the ordinary ways by which their relief must be brought them, useth commonly to draw himself into the straight passages thitherward, and oftentimes doth dangerously distress them."

"Yes, crafty enemies always strike at the supply lines, but we can handle that problem later. How would you use the garrisons?"

"These four garrisons, issuing forth at such convenient times as they shall have intelligence or espial upon the enemy, will so drive him from one stead to another, and tennis him amongst them, that he shall find nowhere safe to keep his creet nor hide himself, but flying from the fire shall fall into the water, and out of one danger into another, that in a short time his creet, which is his most sustenance, shall be wasted with preying, or killed with driving, or starved for want of pasture in the woods, and he himself brought so low that he shall have no heart nor ability to endure his wretchedness; the which will surely come to pass in very short space, for one winter's well-following of him will so pluck him on his knees that he will never be able to stand up again."

A voice from the alcove suggested, "It might work to our advantage, Gentlemen, not to use Irish words alien to your transcriber in the discussion because that slows down the whole recording process. From the context, I presume the word 'creet' refers to the herd of cattle or goats with which the insurgents sustain themselves, but would that word be spelled with one 'e' or two?"

Before Eudox could complain, Spenser stood up and declared, "Since we started so late and were unfortunately interrupted on several occasions, let's get a good night's sleep and start early tomorrow afternoon. In the meantime, young man, I expect to see your fair copy of the present discussion by noon at the latest, so I may judge if my patience in this matter is worth the trouble. I will also pass additional observations to your master regarding upstart behavior, and I'm sure he will have something to say to you before he leaves us. In the meantime, I expect you to stay clear of the kitchen until your work is finished. Is all of that quite clear?"

William nodded and Eudox murmured, "Well done, Edmund!"

Chapter 3:
"I WILL NOT HESITATE TO USE A HORSE-WHIP ON HIM!"

Noon the next day:

"I've only known him a short time myself, sir," Malachi explained, "but I can assure you positively that he means well, so it's just a matter of instructing him in a few simple rules which have been neglected in his upbringing, and I'm sure there will be no repetition of such untoward behavior at future discussions."

"That's somewhat reassuring," said Edmund Spenser, "because his fair copy does show outstanding transcription abilities, just as you said. As a matter of fact his finished report of yesterday's discussion practically writes my book for me, and I would hate to lose him because of a few irregularities in behavior. I would like to see the result of the note-taking technique which permits him to record every sentiment so accurately. Somehow those notes must be crystal clear to him."

"Oh, they are that all right," Malachi assured him. "But you won't be able to read them unless you can decipher chicken scratches."

"Are you trying to tell me something?"

"Biggest mess you've ever laid eyes on! Couldn't decipher it in a million years!"

"What kind of package have you sold me here, Malachi?"

"And yet! Time after time, he will produce from that gibberish, crisp, clear transcripts that please everyone concerned. For those of us who have watched him work, it is an absolute wonder—not quite water into wine, perhaps, but very close. It's the one thing he does supremely well while he botches everything else, as you witnessed last night. What is it the French call that kind of mind-set? Idiot savant, I think."

"I'm glad to hear of the 'savant' reference," Spenser said, "because I had figured out the rest of it myself, but since he does the job that well, I'm sure we can work our way around his odd behavior. You said he works with that new fangled shorthand system we've been hearing about?"

"He does work with that, yes, but he adds a few refinements of his own which make his notes secret even from those of us who know shorthand. Just for fun I left a set of his notes with Philippes to see if he could make sense of them—you know him, don't you?"

"Of course," Spenser said. "I know him well: thin, blondish, pock-faced man with squirrelly little eyes. Walsingham's man-in-the-backroom, always ready to do some deciphering or forge a little something for the boss."

"That's him," Malachi nodded. "Best in the world at the deciphering game, and he couldn't make tails nor heads of those notes. So I'm afraid you will have to treat my man with some patience until the job is done since he is the only one in the world who can read his notes."

"Is there some way to tie his tongue? He asks the oddest questions."

"Slip him a small glass of port now and then—but only half-a-glass, mind you—that usually quiets him, and, as a good Christian, you might think in terms of helping to educate a genial inanity. The urgency of the time beckons outstanding individuals to step forward and volunteer their guidance in areas like public education in order to stem the tide of growing social unrest. We can't sensibly count on the Queen to do it all, can we?"

"Certainly not," Spenser nodded. "I suppose in this case the payoff is worth the trouble. At least Mr. Eudox will not be inconvenienced by taking notes himself, and—just between the two of us—he often loses the thread of the conversation if he gets caught up in his own transcription. Perfectly natural, I know, but bothersome, none-the-less, when the discussion should proceed apace. You must assure me now, Malachi, that you will have a few strong words with your man before you depart. Don't leave all the attitude adjustment to me."

"Absolutely. And please let me add that I've already detected faint glimmerings of improvement in him after having been under your roof for only one day."

"Many social boors are lacking only forceful instruction," Spenser nodded. "Let's see if we can't immerse him in civilized behavior for a few days and then pass him along quickly to others who are presently living lives much too calm for their own good."

"Excellent strategy, sir, if I may say so."

"And keep a close eye on him, Malachi. I still don't trust that fellow somehow."

"Well, sir," Malachi said with a smile, "You'll have to start trusting him soon."

"Oh? Why is that?"

"He'll sense it quickly enough if you don't put your complete faith in him. I've seen it before, and he'll remember it as a slight if you should ever need a favor from him."

"Favor? From your apprentice? Have you turned toss-pot entirely, Malachi? I hope to live a long and happy life without ever once requiring a favor from your underling."

"I wouldn't use belittling terms either. He's very sensitive in some areas."

"What in God's name are you rambling about, sir? The man is a servant! I don't care what he senses and what he doesn't. Let him keep the hell out of the way and do his job. It unnerves me to have servants who call attention to themselves—it's unseemly and highly embarrassing in front of company. The servant's job is to serve the master in an efficient manner, unseen and unheard. That's what I expect, and I'll settle for nothing less in this house!"

"I don't blame you for that, sir, if you can manage it."

"Manage it? I want you to tell him for me that while I was very patient with him last night, I will not hesitate to use a horse-whip on him should his behavior not improve. With your permission, of course."

"Oh, go to it, by all means," Malachi said, "if you think it will do a bit of good, but I'll tell you something frankly. Ironically enough, despite his position in our society and despite his behavior problems, he still expects to be treated with dignity, respect, and patience. Yes, a great deal of patience. He does erratic things when he is not so treated, and I'm afraid that horse-whip remark would not please him at all."

Spenser sighed deeply. "You obviously have some reason in mind, Malachi, why I should be concerned with what this servant thinks and feels. Please come to the point."

Malachi shrugged, "Only if you meant what you said about security."

"Of course I meant it. If every official in Ireland kept a conscientious check on his documents, we would soon cut off O'Neill's ears and have some chance of mounting an effective campaign against him. Don't forget, these little skirmishes we're presently having with the Ulster forces are simply preparations for all-out war when O'Neill decides he has enough men trained and armed. He'll strike in earnest soon, believe me, unless we stop him. That's why he must never see the military suggestions embodied in our current discussion, or else he will burn the countryside for miles around the strategic garrison towns I've mentioned and leave our troops stranded in the middle of a scorched earth."

"That's exactly what I'm thinking of, sir, the security. That's why it would be just as well to treat my apprentice civilly. He doesn't object to that."

"Out with it, Malachi. I'm losing patience."

"From a security standpoint, you must trust him completely at the very moment you ask him to hand over his notes because he may not give you the right ones if he feels slighted, don't you see?"

"He might give me others?"

"He has pockets and bags of notes. Always scribbling, wherever we go. No one else can read them, so I don't worry. He has left a trail of indecipherable litter clear across England. The odd twist is that he has hindered the efforts of our foreign enemies—who sometimes follow us—by having them waste endless hours trying to make sense out of the notes which they have already squandered time and money collecting."

"But why would he give me the wrong notes?"

"That is what I'm explaining, sir," Malachi said patiently. "He wouldn't think to trick you if he is treated civilly, but if he is driven to petulance—and that's not much of a trip for him—there's really no telling what kind of fast shuffle he might subject you to just for the hell of it, and then, erratically enough, he might just decide to offer clear copies of your plans to the ballad-singers in Dublin."

"The ballad-singers! Oh my God, and he already has the names of the garrison towns. Dignity and respect, you say?"

"And I mentioned patience too, didn't I? Not likely to forget the wear and tear on that particular virtue."

"Still in all," Spenser reflected, "total security would always depend on his good graces since he's the only one who can read the notes. If a conscientious administrator really wanted iron-tight security, he might hire one of the ruffians in which Ireland so much abounds and have him lay in wait some dark night—"

"I would take that personally, sir—very personally, indeed," Malachi said quietly. "I know it doesn't show on the surface, but he is a very valuable man, and I would miss him."

Spenser cranked up half a grin, "Don't worry. Just permitting my mind to free-float there for a moment as any conscientious administrator must do periodically. No harm done. If you say he is valuable, you must be aware of something that is not apparent either to the naked eye or to the probing mind. I'll rest somewhat comfortably in your judgment if you assure me he is safe enough as long as he is well treated?"

"Absolutely," Malachi nodded, "Idiot-Savants are often misunderstood people."

"With really bad manners," Spenser insisted. "But I think I can work around our quandary, Malachi, by simply taking the trouble to initial his notes each evening." He rubbed his hands together. "That will permit me to keep track nicely even if I can't read the notes themselves."

"Splendid idea, sir."

Chapter 4:
TRUTH REARS ITS HURTFUL HEAD

Later that evening:

"Let us resume our discussion," Spenser suggested genially, as he poured out two and a half glasses of wine and walked the latter over to the corner without comment.

"Splendid idea," Eudox agreed. "As I was about to ask you, Edmund, what is the explanation for this unbelievable business of many of our countrymen switching names when they come to Ireland? It is simply unthinkable that any English gentlemen would exchange his proud name for an Irish one in order to join the ranks of the Anglo-Irish. Good God, man, some of those Irish names can't even be pronounced by a proper Englishman."

Spenser managed a bitter laugh. "Oh, the Anglo-Irish fixed that problem soon enough and presented Dublin with a new problem in administrative supervision. *They not only changed names, they also switched languages from English to Irish, and thereby, I might add, brought to bear against her Majesty's legal forces a new array of delay-and-distortion devices to further entangle legal and civic matters, particularly at tax-collection time. I have to find fault with the abuse of language, that is, for the speaking of Irish among the English, which, as it is unnatural that any people should love another's language more than their own, so is it very inconvenient and the cause of many other evils.*" [9]

Eudox shook his head. "I can see where it could become an administrative nightmare communicating with speakers in such a barbaric tongue if proper steps are not taken forthwith. I suppose when I get over my shock at the name-changes, I'll have to face the language situation as an administrative problem and, if we are going to communicate at all with such difficult people, we'll have to live elbow-to-elbow with Irish-speakers right there inside our Dublin headquarters." He leaned over to whisper confidentially to Spenser. "Although, off the record, Edmund, I think if we are going to civilize the native Irish, the first thing we ought to do is ram our language right down their throats if only to let them know who is boss."

Spenser nodded. "It hath been ever the use of the conquerer to despise the language of the conquered, and to force him by all means to learn his. So did the Romans always use, insomuch that there is almost no nation in the world but is sprinkled with their language...I think it were strange that the English being so many and the Irish so few, as they then were left, the few should draw the more unto their use."

"There must be some kind of explanation for such an odd turn of events," Eudox mused. "*Is it possible that an Englishman brought up naturally in such sweet civility as England affords could find such liking in that barbarous rudeness that he should forget his own nature and forgo his own nation?* [10] A true Englishman should never change his ways just because he finds himself abroad amongst strangers."

"I suppose that the chief cause of bringing in the Irish language amongst them was specially their fostering and marrying with the Irish, which are two most dangerous infections, for first the child that sucketh the milk of the nurse must of necessity learn his first speech of her, the which being the first that is enured to his tongue is ever after most pleasing unto him, insomuch as though he afterwards be taught English, yet the smack of the first will always abide with him, and not only of the speech, but of the manners and conditions."

"Yes, I suppose if you permit English children to be brought up in the homes of Irish wet-nurses, those children will not only be forced to share the poor living conditions, but they will also be subjected to a lifetime of maudlin Irish lullabies rattling through their head."

"Right, and don't forget, the young children be like apes, which will affect and imitate what they see done before them, specially by their nurses whom they love so well. They moreover draw into themselves together with their suck, even the nature and disposition of their nurses, for the mind followeth much the temperature of the body; and also the words are the image of the mind, so as they proceeding from the mind, the mind must be needs effected with the words; so that the speech being Irish, the heart must needs be Irish, for out of the abundance of the heart the tongue speaketh."

"By good St George," Eudox stood up and struck a pose. "I hereby resolve that as soon as we get things humming in Dublin, we will do something Draconian to stop this flight of decent Englishmen into the ranks of the eternally unwashed, unlettered, illiterate, barbaric denizens of this blasted island."

"That is certainly an admirable objective, Eudoxius," Spenser said, "but take care not to overset such grandiose plans by your misstatement of history."

"What do you mean misstatement? The proof is there for all to see."

"*But you have not looked closely enough. For where ye say that the Irish have always been without letters, ye are therein much deceived, for it is certain that Ireland hath had the use of letters very anciently, and long before England.*" [11]

"What! What are you saying?" Eudox dropped back in his chair.

"I am a great respecter of truth wherever it rears its hurtful head," Spenser said. "During the period from 500 AD to 1100 AD—the period which historians are now calling the Dark Ages—Irish scholars had a nearly exclusive possession of the written language of all the countries in Europe, including our own. It may seem ironic now, but there is no question that Irish scholars and monks helped spread learning and literacy to all of Europe for many centuries. Even such outstanding historical figures as the illiterate Charlemagne, the King of the Franks who was appointed the first Holy Roman Emperor in 800 AD, in recognition of his outstanding administrative ability. But he could barley have functioned at all without the literate Irish scholars who did the paper work for him in stabilizing the Christian Church by converting the Saxons, legislating justice and security for ordinary citizens, and igniting a virtual Renaissance of learning throughout much of Europe."

Eudox took several deep breaths as he stared at Spenser in astonishment. "Is it possible? How comes it then that they are so barbarous still and so unlearned being so old scholars?"

Spenser shrugged, "Educational fads come and go but that they had letters anciently it is nothing doubtful, for the Saxons of England are said to have their letters and learning and learned men, from the Irish, and that also appeareth by the likeness of the character, for the Saxon's character is the same with the Irish. Exactly the same letters."

"Are you seriously contending that the Irish taught the English their letters?" Eudox asked in some alarm.

"There is no question about it," Spenser nodded. "No question at all."

"How many people know about this?" Eudox whispered.

"Scholars and historians mostly. Few of the common sort."

"Good God! That bit of knowledge sticks in a man's craw. Let's try to keep a lid on it because there's no sense making matters over here worse by distributing such inflammatory information."

"I don't think you have to worry. Few care except the scholars. The vulgar sort turn their minds quickly to other things."

"Why don't the Anglo-Irish mothers nurse their own babies?" came a query from the alcove.

Spenser smiled, so happy to have his observation validated that he seemed unaware of the question's source. "Some say it's bad for a woman's figure, but I never found that to be true. As a matter of fact—strictly off the record, you understand—" He took a deep pull from his wine glass. "During the few moments of opportunity I have had over the years to inspect various aspects of the female body close-up, so to speak—" He paused for a knowing leer at Eudox.

"Excuse me, Edmund," Eudox interrupted, jerking his thumb at the amanuensis' corner and making a scribble-motion with the other hand, "but perhaps you'd prefer to save personal reminiscing for your memoirs?"

Spenser caught his breath as though stopped in mid-stride, glanced quickly at William's corner, and nodded to Eudox. "Perhaps you're right, old friend. Perhaps it's best not to mix the two subjects."

"If you don't mind, Edmund, I would like to revisit your puzzling suggestion about the calendar for best campaigning against the Irish. Do you truly think the winter-time fittest for the services of Ireland? How falls it then that our most employments be in summer, and the armies then led commonly forth?"

"*It is a grievous error,*" said Spenser. "*It is surely misconceived for it is not with Ireland as with other countries, where the wars flare most in summer, and the helmets glisten brightest in the fair sunshine, but in Ireland the winter yieldeth best services, for then the trees are bare and naked, which use both to clothe and house the kern, the ground is cold and wet which useth to be his bedding, the air is sharp and bitter which useth to blow through his naked sides and legs, the kine are barren and without milk, which useth to be his only food, neither if he kill them, then will they yield him flesh, nor if he keep them will they give him food, besides being all in calve, for the most part they will through much chasing and driving, cast all their calves and lose all their milk which should relieve him the summer after.*" [12]

An angry voice rose from behind the amanuensis' screen. "How would you like someone to do that to your mother?"

"I beg your pardon," Spenser cried in dismay.

"Cows are mothers and calves are their children, you know, so it wouldn't take too much poetic sensibility to imagine your own mother being chased wildly through the countryside while she was trying to give birth to people like you, now would it?"

"This is preposterous!" Eudox growled. "My sword is at your service, Edmund, if you would like to teach this rude upstart a mortal lesson right here and now!"

"Tut, tut, Eudoxius," said Edmund Spenser. "Times are changing, and we must change with them. Servants today take no responsibility for their actions and seek no forgiveness when they amaze the company with their vile manners. I'm afraid we must all face up to this startling realization and begin to work from there. We must attempt to set up a relationship beyond the chilling displeasure of what we have to put up with."

Eudox looked somewhat perplexed. "A relationship based on what?"

"I think a little patience is in order. A little respect. A touch of dignity perhaps."

"This is your house, Mr. Spenser, so you may do whatever you want in it, but I must tell you frankly, I think you are letting yourself in for big trouble by not having that presumptuous wretch horsewhipped immediately and thrown off your property forthwith."

"Plenty of time for that later if necessary," Spenser assured him. "Let me just step back there and see what's bothering him."

He rose and crossed quickly to the screened-in alcove. It smelled strongly of sweet wine.

"How is the note-taking coming?" he asked gently.

"Cows are people too, you know, jushh like you and me."

"Yes, indeed," said Spenser. "Cows are important. But the notes? How are they coming?"

William pulled a wad of notes from his doublet and slammed them on the desk. "Notes all over the plashh...never run out."

The slurred speech brought Eudox to the alcove for inspection. "Égad!" he cried. "The sot is drunk out of his head!"

Spenser glanced at the open wine cabinet. "Jesus, Mary, and Joseph! He's knocked off two full bottles of my best Madeira."

William pulled more notes from his doublet and crumpled them into the pile on the desk. "they's plenty for ever'one," he declared.

"Excuse me, young man," Spenser said patiently, "but I have not yet initialed to-day's notes. Would you mind pointing them out to me, so we can get right to work tomorrow?"

William stared at him for a moment and then said: "*To-morrow, and, to-morrow, and to-morrow / Creeps in this petty pace from day to day...*" [13]

"I'm sure you're right about that," Spenser said, "but would you mind indicating which are the notes of this evening's discussion, and then we'll see that you get right off to bed. I know a scrivener's job can be quite exhausting. I was a secretary myself in the past, you know."

"O, *call back yesterday, bid time return.*" [14].

"That's fine," said Spenser, "but save it for later. Let's just take care of the notes now."

William scooped up the notes, crumpled them further, and shoved the mass beneath his doublet. "There you are, sir," he smiled, "all shafe and shound."

Eudox spoke to Spenser's ear. "I hate to tell you this, Edmund, but I got a good look at one of those scraps he's waving about, and they are not notes at all. They are mostly scattered dots and jots."

"He has his own system," Spenser explained, "so I'm sure it will be all right in the morning when he's had a little sleep. And Master William?"

"Sir?"

"Do me a little favor and number the pages you take of our discussion, if you would."

"Number?"

"Yes. Number." Spenser explained patiently. "Mark the first page 'one' and the second page 'two' and the third—"

"Got t'idea," William broke in. "Be happy to oblige. Have m'own mark for numbers too, y' know."

"My," said Spenser through clenched teeth, "that is interesting, but let's get you off to sleep now so you may get up early and get to work on those fair copies from your... ah...notes. You may recall I was to have them in hand by noon tomorrow."

"Noon, hell!" William boomed. "Fair copies m'business. I d'cide the time, b' God! I'll hand you copies b'dawn tomorrow or m'name isn't—oh, well." He lurched to the door and was escorted to his bed.

"Astounding," said Eudox.

"I'll have a word with his master in the morning," Spenser promised grimly.

Chapter 5:
WILLIAM AUDITIONS AS A GALLOWGLASS

The next morning:

"No matter how long I live," Malachi said to William, "I will always be impressed at how often life resembles a rock sticking out of a mud puddle."

"A rock?"

"I saw the nice, clean, shiny upside of that rock this morning halfway to Yougal when I intercepted one of our messengers going south and saved myself the rest of the trip by sending him on to confirm the invitation to Raleigh. However, the muddy, dirty, unappetizing side of the stone was upturned before my eyes when I returned to Hap-Hazard an hour ago and Spenser entertained me with a discussion of your behavior yesterday."

"Before you start on me, let me remind you that despite feeling very tired for some reason—I may be coming down with something—I did get the fair copies done and have already handed them over in good shape."

"Yes, Spenser mentioned how much he appreciated the results and how perplexed he is by the whole situation. He and Eudox have talked it over extensively and they have concluded that your somewhat giddy behavior is probably a result of pent up energy because your active young body has been deprived of outdoor exercise by the pressure of your recording and copying duties."

"Exercise?"

"They feel they are partially responsible for having overscheduled and overworked you and for not giving you enough time to pursue more leisurely activities. After all, it is good for a man to stop and smell the roses occasionally, so they suggest it would be a good idea if you got a little exercise while I take notes this evening just to get rid of your tendency to fidget while you are working, and then you can make your splendid copies from my notes tonight."

"Fidget?"

"They'd like you to participate in a little outdoor drama they are arranging for the neighbors."

"A part? Outdoors? Like an interlude?"

"Exactly. They wonder if you would like to take a leisurely stroll around the boundaries of Hap-Hazard after lunch just to survey the estate and gain some knowledge of the local wonders. Your evening would be free."

"I could handle that, certainly. It might even improve my appetite. But what role will I be playing?"

"That becomes apparent when you realize Spenser must make some response to the increasingly aggressive displays Roche's men are making around the disputed pasture—without bringing real Gallowglass onto his land."

"Aggressive displays?"

"You know the sort of thing: cursing and spitting and waving their battle axes at any who come into sight."

"Dreadful. Spenser should complain to the authorities."

"Oh, he does that, regularly, but it does little good." Malachi said. "Mostly, he hopes to pretend he's hiring his own fighters, and at least give Roche something to think about for awhile. A temporary measure until something legal gets done."

"How can he do that?"

"Just dress up a few men as Gallowglass and parade them around a bit."

"He'll have to find people who are pretty husky. All those men have massive chests."

Malachi nodded. "Axe-work is good for the chest. We'll put a double doublet on you, and nobody will know the difference under the mantle."

"On me!" cried William, backing away in horror.

"It's a part! Costume and all! You're always saying you'd love to be on stage, so here's your chance! Incidentally, don't try to exchange curses with the men at the boundary because they are MacSheehys and speak only Gallic, and you would confuse and enrage them with a foreign tongue."

"Enrage them?"

"Don't get thrown out of focus here, because this part is fashioned in heaven for you specifically, and you would regret to your dying day that you turned down this chance to play a role that suits you so well."

"'Til my dying day! Egad! Suits me so well, you say?"

"Your usual style will augment this part nicely. The roll simply calls for some belligerent and bellicose growling and vigorous axe waving, so it would be impossible for even you to overact the part."

William thought for a moment. "You say both men thought this would be a good part for me?"

"Yes, indeed. They thought it over very carefully and concluded this would be the ideal means of protecting your health."

"Just as you say, it is a part," he sighed, "and their request opens wide the door for me to ask a favor of them before we leave. But in the meantime, any chance we could dummy up a prop axe? Those real ones are both heavy and sharp."

Chapter 6:
THE 'IRISH SPIRAL' TAKES HOLD

Next afternoon:

"If you don't mind, Edmund," Eudox said, "now that we are relaxed and comfortable," he paused for a satisfied glance at the quiet alcove where Malachi had assumed the duties of the amanuensis, "let's take a closer look at your campaign calendar, in light of the crime statistics which the bureau collects from the Continent. *I have heard it said of some that were outlaws, that in summer they kept themselves quiet, but in winter they would play their parts, and when the nights were longest, then burn and spoil most, so that they might safely return before day.*" [15]

"*That's probably true in countries where law-breakers are considered outcasts who must sneak and skulk from both the civil authorities and their neighbors,*" Spenser said: "*But it is far otherwise with a strong peopled enemy, that possess a whole country, for the others being but a few are indeed privily lodged and kept in out villages and corners nigh the woods and mountains by some their privy friends to whom they bring their spoils and stealths, and of whom they continually receive secret relief.*"

"Not much we can do about the home-field advantage, of course," Eudox mused, "But your advice seems to be that we use the military during the winter to throw Ireland's economy into chaos—that is what I call a very interesting idea from an administrator's viewpoint, quite apart from any humanitarian considerations, of course. War is, after all, war. You can't hide it. What immediate results might we expect if we undertook such a campaign?"

"*The open enemy having all of his country wasted, what by himself and what by the soldiers, findeth then succour in no place. Towns there are none of which he may get spoil, they are all burnt, country houses and farmers there are none, they be all fled, bread he hath none, he ploughed not in summer, flesh he hath, but if he kill it in winter he shall want milk in summer. Therefore if they be well followed but one winter ye shall have little work with them in the next summer.*"

"Sounds promising, but, of course, there are always administrative problems, as you well know. What would you do with those people who want to surrender as soon as your campaign is announced? Even among the Irish there must be some sensible miscreants. Would you have them received?"

Spenser shook his head. "No, but '*at the beginning of these wars, and when the garrisons are well planted and fortified, I would wish a proclamation were made generally to come to their knowledge that what persons soever would within twenty days absolutely submit themselves—excepting only the very principal and ringleaders—should find grace. I well know that the rebels themselves—as I saw by proof in the Desmond wars—will turn away all their rascal people whom they think unserviceable, as old men, women, children and hinds, which they call churls, which only waste their victuals and yield them no aid but their cattle, they will surely keep away. These therefore, though policy would turn them back again that they might rather consume and afflict the other rebels, yet in a pitiful commiseration I would wish them to be received.*'"

"Very considerate of you, indeed," Eudox observed.

"Well, you know," Spenser said, "*This base sort of people doth not for the most part rebel of himself, having no heart thereunto, but is of force drawn by the grand rebels into their action, and carried away with the violence of the stream.*"

"I know just what you mean, and certainly a twenty-day grace period would get such a campaign off to an admirable Christian start by making provision for people hoodwinked into rebellion by their own treacherous leaders. Even London could hardly complain of such generosity."

"But afterwards—" Spencer's voice hardened. "—*I would have none received, but left to their fortune and miserable end. My reason is, for that these which will afterwards remain without are stout and obstinate rebels, such as will never be made dutiful and obedient, nor brought to labour or civil conversation, having once tasted that licentious life, and being acquainted with spoil and outrages will ever after be ready for the like occasions, so as there is no hope for their amendment or recovery, and therefore needful to be cut off.*"

"I can well imagine that the pillage and rape experience could get to be a pretty heady life-style for certain kinds of men," Eudox mused. "But what then shall be the conclusion of this war, for you have prefixed a short time of his continuence?"

"*The end I assure me will be very short and much sooner than can be in so great a trouble—as it seemeth—hoped for. Although there should none of them fall by the sword, nor be slain be soldier, yet thus being kept from manurance, and their cattle from running abroad by this hard restraint, they should quickly consume themselves and devour one another.*"

"Excuse me for saying so, Edmund, but that seems very hard to picture when I see cows and crops in every field."

"*The proof whereof I saw sufficiently ensampled in those late wars in Munster, for not withstanding that the same was a most rich and plentiful country, full of corn and cattle, that you would have thought that they would be able to stand long, yet ere one year and a half they were brought to such wretchedness, as that any strong heart would have rued the same.*"

"You say you actually saw the proof of this condition?"

Spenser nodded solemnly. "*Out of every corner of the woods and glens they came creeping forth upon their hands, for their legs could not bear them. They looked anatomies of death, they spake like ghosts crying out of their graves, they did eat of the dead carrions, happy where they could find them, yea and one another soon after in so much as the very carcasses they spared not to scrape out of their graves, and if they found a plot of water cress or shamrocks, there they flocked as to a feast for a time, yet not able long to continue therewithal, that in short space there were none almost left and a most populous and plentiful country suddenly left void of man or beast. Yet sure in all that war there perished not many by the sword, but all by the extremity of famine, which they themselves had wrought.*" [16]

"Yes, it's always best when they bring it on themselves like that. But tell me frankly, Edmund, are such results possible in so short a time? I mean it's one thing to paint a rosy picture with words and quite another to get something done in the field. Will this plan work?"

"*Let me assure you of something important,*" Spenser said. "*The strength of all this nation is the kern, gallowglass, horseman, and horseboy, the which having been never used to have anything of their own, and now living upon spoil of others; make no spare of anything, but havoc and confusion of all they meet with, whether it be their own friends' goods or their foes', and if they happen to get never so great spoils at any time the same they waste and consume in a trice, as naturally delighting in spoil, though it do themselves no good.*"

"But they can still flee from our soldiers," Eudox pointed out. "And that's been the problem all along. How will your plan slow them down?"

"*Whatsoever they leave unspent, the soldier, when he cometh there, he havocketh and spoileth likewise, so that between them both nothing is very shortly left.*"

"Which leaves the soldiers short of food too."

"Can't be helped. That's why *supply is always half the battle. And yet this is very necessary to be done, for the soon finishing of the war. And not only this in this wise, but also all those subjects which border upon those parts are either to be removed and drawn away or likewise to be spoiled, that the enemy may find no succour thereby, for what the soldier spares the rebel will surely spoil."*

"Burn out the neighbors too, eh? Yes, that seems well thought out."

"No choice in the matter if you really intend to give your policy a chance to blossom and bear fruit."

Eudox finished his wine, slapped his belly noisily a time or two and said to Spenser, "You know, Edmund, it's very comforting to sit here and paint rosy pictures of quick military victories in this country, but we both know that your plan, if undertaken, to completely exterminate the rebels—who must constitute at least half the country from the trouble they cause—will be soundly denounced by bleeding hearts at every level of government, not the least of whom may be the Queen herself as well as her chief councilor, Lord Burghley. Because a military campaign based on your urgings probably would come to an abrupt halt before completion, the Irish government in Dublin should have a cover operation going at the same time, so we could switch horses in mid-stream if Royal outcry arose against this idealistic but bloody formula which you advise."

"Cover story, eh?"

"Yes. What practical means could we use to lessen the strength of the Irish without putting them all to the sword?"

"You remember I told you that the Irish tribes and septs require from their members an allegiance which English Law can seldom usurp?"

Eudox nodded, "You said they even went without a surname in order to share such common tribal names as *Hannigan, Flannigan, Milligan, Gilligan, Duffy, McCuffy, Malaughy, Mahone*—my, they do roll off your tongue once you start!"

"Be careful now, Eudoxius," Spenser warned as he glanced at Eudox's empty wine glass. "It's surprisingly easy to get caught up in a tempo which is alien to every civilized—"

Eudox slapped the arm of his chair in rhythm and resumed chanting: *"Mattigan, Pattigan, Lanagan, Flanigan, Fagin, O'Hagan, O' Hoolihan, Flynn—"*

"It's the Irish Spiral!" Spenser exclaimed in mild alarm. "It's got right hold of you. Quickly now, jump up, wave your arms about and take a series of deep breaths to expel the evil air."

Eudox jumped up and stamped his feet as he continued chanting: *"Donnegan, Monnigan, Fogarty, Hogarty, Kelly, McAuliffe, McGinnis, McGinn—"* [17]

Spenser brought him to a halt by dashing a glass of water in his face.

Eudox subsided and shook his head. "Very strange. Something took me over against my wishes."

"Yes," said Spenser, "Not unusual, I'm afraid, and *that is exactly why methinks it should do very well to renew that old statute that was made in the reign of Edward the Fourth of England, by which it was commanded that whereas all men then used to be called by the name of their septs.....and had no surnames at all, that from thenceforth each one should take unto himself of a several surnames, either of his trade or facility or of some quality of his body or mind, or of the place where he dwelt, so as every one should be distinguished from other or from the most part; whereby they shall not only not depend upon the head of their sept as now they do, but also shall in short time learn to forget his Irish nation.*" [18]

William strode into the room, still in his gallowglass costume, just in time to overhear Spenser. "How could you tell?" he asked.

"Tell what?" Spenser inquired.

"If a man's surname were 'Dainty' or 'Thrashy', for example, how could you tell if that quality applied to his body or to his mind?"

"Do you know anybody named 'Dainty' or 'Thrashy'?" Spenser snarled.

"Not at the moment," William shrugged, "but you never know when you'll come across one."

"I shall leave such considerations to those who regard such minutia as significant," said Spenser.

"Very good, Master Spenser," Malachi said as he left the alcove and joined the informal group with notebook in hand. "You quoted good King Edward almost word for word. But as I recall, Edward's statute read: '*That every Irishman that dwells betwixt or amongst Englishmen in the county of Dublin, Myeth, Vreill, and Kildare...shall take to him an English surname of one town, as Sutton, Chester, Trim, Skryne, Corke, Kinsale; or colorer, as white, blacke, browne ; or art or science, as smith or carpenter; or office, as cooke, butler, and that he and his issue shall use this name.*' No explicit mention of 'quality,' however."

Spenser laughed aloud. "You're like the elephant, old friend: you never forget. That's good. It keeps the discussion honest to have such a referee. The truth is I thought the addition of 'qualities' to Edward's list was a good idea generally; society could certainly use a few more Honest Cecil's in our market place or Thoughtful Percival's in the Commons."

"What would you do with the Mac's and O's?" Eudox asked. "I hear they're a special problem."

"They are, indeed," Spenser confirmed, "and that is why I also wish all the 'Oes' and the 'Macs' which the heads of septs have taken to their names to be utterly forbidden and extinguished, for the same being as old manner—as some sayeth—first made by O'Brien for the strengthening of the Irish, the abrogating thereof will as much enfeeble them."

"That's the way things are tending," Malachi offered. "I know that people with the 'Mac' or 'O' preface to their name are already forbidden to enter the town of Galway because they are regarded as trouble-makers."

"Controlling people by labeling them is an interesting idea," William mused.

"Essex county back in England did much the same thing years ago," Malachi said. "They matched people's names with their craft, and now Essex is overrun with Chandlers, Coopers, Sawers, Saddlers, Thatchers, Tinkers, Masons, Glovers, Drapers, Cutlers, Millers, Turners, Watermans, Wheelwrights, and Curriers."

"I know a women named 'Twitchbottom,'" William offered.

"And I know a young man who should be named 'Insolent Bumpkin,'" Spenser said.

William laughed, "At least people would remember his name. I'll have to find something clever like that."

"Good luck," said Spenser. "Now, in summary, Mr. Eudox, don't forget timing is of the utmost importance if you were to undertake this campaign."

"In winter, I remember," Eudox assured him.

"Not just the timing in Ireland, but the timing in England. The campaign must be pressed so vigorously that the Queen will not have a chance to change policy just as success is near in the surge for extermination of the undesireables."

"I do well understand you," Eudox assured him. "But now when all things are brought to this pass, and all filled with these rueful spectacles of so many wretched carcasses starving, goodly countries wasted, so huge a desolation and confusion, as even I that do but hear it from you and do picture it in my mind, do greatly pity and commiserate it, if it shall happen that the state of this miserly and lamentable image of things shall be told and feelingly presented to Her sacred Majesty, being by nature full of mercy and clemency, who is most inclinable to such pitiful complaints, and will not endure to hear such tragedies made of her people and poor subjects, as some about her may insinuate, then she perhaps for very compassion of such calamities will not only stop the stream of such violence and return to her wanted mildness, but also con them little thanks which have been the authors and councilors of such bloody platforms." [19]

"That's exactly what happened after the Desmond Rebellion," Spenser said, "if you recall."

Eudox nodded. "So I remember that in the late government of that good Lord Grey, when after long travail and many perilous assays, he had brought things almost to this pass that ye speak of, that it was even made ready for reformation.....like complaint was made against him, that he was a bloody man, and he regarded not the lives of her subjects, no more than dogs, but had wasted and consumed all, so as now she had almost nothing left but to reign in their ashes.'

"Was the Queen impressed?" William asked.

"Oh, yes," Eudox nodded. "Ear was soon lent thereunto, all suddenly turned top-sy-turvy, the noble Lord eftsoons was blamed, the wretched people pitied, and new counsels plotted, in which it was concluded that a general pardon should be sent over to all that would accept of it; upon which all former purposes were blanked, the governor at a bay, and not only all that great and long charge which she had before been at quite lost and cancelled, but also all that hope of good which was even at the door put back and clean frustrate; all which whether it be true or no yourself can well tell."

"Too true, Eudoxius. The more the pity," said Spenser. "That is why I so strongly advise you to get the money up front if you launch this campaign, so you may solve this damnable Irish problem once and for all."

"Hear, hear!" Eudox saluted and raised his glass.

With the recording session over, Malachi sent William off to prepare fair copies and summed up the visit with Spenser. "We'll be on our way first thing in the morning," Malachi said. "Before we go however, I did want to ask how you are doing with *The Faerie Queene*. Are you almost finished?"

Spenser smiled. "Thank you for your interest, Malachi. Yes, I'm close enough to the end that I have just completed my dedication. As you know the overriding thrust of the work is to affirm my admiration and loyalty to the Queen. I thought the dedication would be a good place to make my allegiance clear without, however, subscribing to the fawning, obsequious testimony of so many recent writers, and in all modesty I think I have succeeded admirably in producing a subdued yet sincere tribute which Elizabeth might enjoy. Would you like to hear it?"

"I would feel privileged, sir, particularly because, like yourself, I too am somewhat offended by the smarmy, oily, groveling, unctuous dedications which have grown so popular lately, and I would welcome a dignified, restrained note of tribute to some inspirational figure."

"Exactly the tone I have aimed at," Spenser said with enthusiasm. Listen to this dedication: *To the Most High, Mightie, and Magnificent Empresse, Renowned for Pietie, Vertue, and All Gracious Government, Elizaberth, By the Grace of God, Queene of England, France, and Ireland, and of Virginia, Defender of the Faith, etc., Her most humble Servaunt Edmund Spenser, Doth, in all Humilitie, Dedicate, Present, and Consecrate these His Labours, to live with the Eternitie of Her Fame.* [20] Well what do you think?"

Malachi coughed discreetly into his closed fist. "Very well done, Sir. It is a trifle awkward to have to keep including France as part of her purveyance since England was run out of there in 1558, but I know that's the way her official title still reads, so what's a person to do? I thought it charming that you made up for the inclusion of such outdated material by also incorporating her New World acquisition of Virginia into your tribute. That should please her mightily."

"Yes indeed, I thought that a nice touch myself."

"I certainly want to thank you for your hospitality and for your thoughtful guidance of a young man who could easily go bad if we did not all combine our efforts to keep him on the straight and narrow. You certainly showed an admirable patience with him, Sir."

"Now that it's over, Malachi," Spenser said, "I'll admit to you that this week has been the most trying I've experienced since the combat days of the Desmond Rebellion. Every day I've had to balance how much I wanted the extraordinary fair copies he kept handing me—you were right about that: he does have the finest fist in the land—and I therefore had to balance those copies against the dramatic display of insolence and bad manners he exhibited daily."

"As if he were on stage, you mean?" Malachi asked with a knowing grin.

"That's it!" Spenser shouted. "That's it exactly! As if he were on stage...and he didn't even notice there was no one in the audience."

"Characteristic," Malachi nodded.

"But I'm glad it's over, Malachi, because I don't know how much more my patience could take. I'm sorry to see you go, of course, since we had so little time to chat, but I'll admit I'm not sorry to see the last of you-know-who, even if he does the best transcription I've ever seen."

"Well said, sir, and on the mark as well, but perhaps a trifle previous."

"How so you mean?"

"I'm afraid I must ask you to stretch your forbearance one last evening, Sir, because you-know-who has made a request of the House."

"Indeed?"

"He tells me he would feel very rejected if he has to leave without reading his half-finished sonnets to you and your company."

"Half-finished sonnets!" Spenser sputtered and shook his head. "Inconceivable," he concluded. "I suppose I have no choice?"

Malachi shrugged. "Not if you expect him to deal honestly with you about the notes when we leave. Actually, this proposal, as ridiculous as it sounds, is a big step for him in the social graces. He has asked me to act as his intermediary to get you to request this sonnet-reading in your drawing room this evening."

"I must request such inanity?" Spenser cried. "Do I have to be there?"

Malachi smiled. "It would be even more pointless without you, sir, but please believe me, you are making a worthy contribution to the education of this young man. In the recent past, he would have barred the door at dinner and produced sonnet bits from his doublet unannounced."

Spenser shook his head. "I can't imagine what our world is coming to, Malachi—astonishing behavior on the part of our young people. This reading won't take long, will it?"

"If you critique quickly it will be over in a flash. After all, how long does it take to read a dozen or so half-finished sonnets?"

"A dozen or so, you say? Perhaps I better make sure my liquor cabinet has been replenished. It's a sad host who can't offer alternatives to his beleaguered guests, because you say he insists on Master Eudox being there too?"

"Yes, that was his request, Sir."

Spenser shook his head sadly. "The world we knew for so long," he muttered, "has turned topsy-turvy overnight, and we are now governed by unruly apprentices."

PART XI YEAR OF THE ARMADA: JANUARY TO JULY, 1588

Chapter 1:
THE REGIOMONTANUS PREDICTION

The Blue Boar Inn in London, January 1, 1588

"Who was this Regiomontanus fellow anyway," William groused, "and what business did he have leaving us so many dire predictions? Gadzooks, the taverns are full of people who should be enjoying the birth of a new year instead of shaking in their boots over woes and worries that we never knew existed. If it's not the Armada coming after us, it's all the earthquakes and bloody rain and floods and pestilence and darkness at noon and snow in the summer that the Dutch almanacs are forecasting for this year." William shook his head. "It begins to look as if 1588 may go down in history as the year of universal worry whether anything happens or not,"

"And well it should," Malachi said. "People have worried about this fatal year for over a century now, ever since Johannes Muller von Konigsberg—called Regiomontanus for short—predicted that in 1588, mankind would experience enormous changes because the stars in the heavens were aligning themselves in a certain fashion in order to pinpoint this exact year. Before you ask, let me mention that Regiomontanus was unquestionably the greatest European astronomer and mathematician of the last century. Apart from his astronomical forecasts, he constructed an astrolabe which navigators like Christopher Columbus have since used, and he devised trigonometry tables from which Copernicus and Galileo and Kepler and others have since profited."

"But basically he was a fortune-teller?"

"Not exactly," Malachi smiled. "Even today, many highly educated men believe that our fortunes are foretold by the movement of the stars and their placement at the time of our birth."

"What utter nonsense'" William decided. *"Men at some time are masters of their fates: The fault....is not in our stars but in ourselves."* [1]

Never-the-less, conscientious astronomers like Regiomontanus feel the need not only to chart those movements, but to point out their influence on the lives of individuals and on the well-being of countries and continents, as is the case with his most famous prophecy."

"Perhaps he made the whole thing up as I do myself when I cast horoscopes or read palms for the ladies."

"I suspect his interest was more scientifically inclined than your lechery-laden approach to the ladies, so instead of plucking beguiling details from thin air, he went to the trouble of doing some hard work beforehand."

"I've only heard bits and pieces about empires crumbling and the earth and sea changing places. What did he say exactly?"

"Actually, the 1588 prophecy appeared before Regiomontanus took an interest. Some say that old magician, Merlin of King Arthur's time, originated the prediction and wrote it on a marble slab which has recently been unearthed by an earthquake just in time to renew interest in every corner of Europe where Empires might be scheduled for decline."

"Was Merlin a real person?"

"Hard to say. Nevertheless, just about one hundred years ago, Regiomontanus became interested in the prophecy and, using his skills as an astronomer and a mathematician, he set out to forecast a picture of the heavens during 1588. He found that during a total eclipse of the moon which is due in March of this year, there would be an unusual alignment of Saturn, Jupiter, and Mars in the moon's own house, and he saw in that powerful conjunction the probability of giant upheavals of land and sea which would bring about catastrophic changes in the world as we know it, changes so powerful, they would cause empires to dwindle and decline."

"That sounds like his own opinion, even assuming he got his charts right."

"Not entirely," Malachi shook his head. "His prophecy was soon supported by a group known as the scriptural numerologists, who believe that all human history since the time of Christ is divided into a series of cycles whose boundaries are revealed by computing various multiples of the numbers ten and seven to establish beginnings and endings and then paralleling those boundaries to events in the Bible. The individual cycles are believed to terminate in some highly significant event, and they believe further that the series of cycles ends in 1588, so this should be the year of some really gaudy finale."

"The Apocalypse?" William gasped.

"We have yet to discover what this year will bring us," Malachi grinned, "but the numerologists feel the cycle before this one ended when Martin Luther pinned his 95 theses on the Wittenberg Church door, and then openly defied the Pope by refusing to travel to Rome to defend his position because he knew he might never be allowed to return to Germany. Since that time, every soul in Europe has been influenced by Luther's rejection of Papal authority, so it's clear the last cycle did end in a monumental event."

"What year did he turn down the invitation?"

"1518. Just seven times ten brings us to 1588."

"Spooky."

"Maybe so," Malachi said, "but well substantiated in the minds of scriptural numerologists by the fact that the Jews were held captive by the Babylonians for just seventy years."

"But you say this is the last cycle of the series, so we should expect something really exceptional?"

"Oh yes, I'm sure the numerologists will be disappointed if we don't get the final Day of Judgment or at least the second coming of Christ or Armageddon or something of that dimension, but let me give you Regiomontanus' own words so you may ponder them yourself:

> *A thousand years after the virgin birth*
> *and after five hundred more allowed the globe,*
> *the wonderful eighty-eight year begins and*
> *brings with it woe enough. If, this year*
> *total catastrophe does not befall, if land*
> *and sea do not collapse in total ruin, yet*
> *will the whole world suffer upheavals,*
> *empires will dwindle and from everywhere will*
> *be great lamentation.*
> Regiomantanus of Konigsberg (c.1460)[2]

"But he doesn't say which empires or how many or even who will be doing the lamenting?"

"Oh no, prophets are very careful not to spoil the fun by including too many suffocating specifics."

William grinned. "That part of the prediction about the land and the sea collapsing in total ruin must be a very disconcerting thought for Parma who appears to have a big amphibious assault on England planned for sometime this year. The Spanish empire itself may well be nervous since King Philip rules more land at the moment than any man in history, and the Catholic Church is certainly an empire of sorts. I don't imagine England would qualify."

"Not unless you count the Roanoke colony. We don't know if that's still functional since Richard Grenville's five-ship fleet was recently stopped by the stay-order on all shipping just as he was about to sail to Roanoke with fresh supplies and he was, instead, ordered to join Drake's fleet in preparation for meeting the Spanish. Poor Governor White was very disappointed at being kept at home by the stay-order because his daughter and granddaughter, Virginia Dare, haven't been heard from in some time."

"If England doesn't qualify, how about France?"

"I'd say France qualifies at least twice since it is so divided. The Catholic League represents one empire of a sort, which may be subject to dwindling if Philip cuts off their gold subsidy, and the Huguenots represent another empire which could decline if anything happens to King Henry of Navarre."

"How about the government in Paris?"

"Oddly enough that's probably the only place those other two empires agree with each other. I imagine Henry de Guise and Henry of Navarre would both agree that France would be better off without the feckless Henry III on the throne with his precious minions and lap dogs in attendance, so I think you'd be safe in saying there are three French empires in the dwindling competition this year."

"Seen this way, the Regiomontanus prediction could indeed make many European rulers nervous."

Malachi nodded. "Emperor Rudolph II of the reduced Holy Roman Empire is himself an avid astrologer who is highly aware of the prophecy, so I can only imagine he has deep forebodings that his ancient Empire will continue to dwindle—unless he is completely preoccupied with casting the horoscope of the latest stallion added to his stable. His brother Maximilian is not much better off because his empire is also up for grabs since he is falling behind a Swedish nominee in a bitter contest for the throne of Poland."

"It sounds like the prophesy is of most concern to the rulers and kings of the world, which I guess is not too surprising."

"Oh no. Apart from the prospect of empires crumbling, there is also throughout the continent a wonderful anticipation that the day of Final Judgment may at last be at hand, so the Catholics look forward to the spectacle of the Protestants being tortured and burned for their heretical impiety and the Protestants are salivating for the same view in reverse of the Anti-Christ Romans."

"Are the Spaniards at all nervous since their empire is so large?"

"Not in Seville or Madrid because Philip has made it quite clear that he regards such forecasts of future events as idle at best and impious at worst, so every government official, for his own safety, is committed to quietly viewing the prophecy as the end of the Protestant empire in all its forms."

"The King can undoubtedly intimidate his own office holders, but how about the ordinary soldiers and sailors? How are they responding to the possibility of catastrophic change?"

"You're right. On the docks of Lisbon, the situation is quite different. The almanac printers in Amsterdam sold a lot of their books last year by featuring the dire consequences and frightening portents that are about to descend on some empire somewhere, and many of the soldiers and seamen gathered for the Armada have responded to that warning bell by jumping ship. Our reports from last month indicate that Spain is having a hard time holding her crews together, and must impose harsher and harsher penalties on those who desert or those who circulate any kind of discouraging predictions."

"Whee," William exhaled. "It begins to sound like the whole of Europe is a giant stage wherein we will view a very compelling drama as this year unfolds. Do we have any vacation time coming up?"

Malachi chuckled. "You'll get a vacation at the same time Walsingham does, which will be never. Our first assignment this year is to help establish a dependable system of messengers to carry communications throughout the realm. We'll need to set up horses and riders and stations and special passes, so we could be busy for months because London insists on knowing as quickly as possible anything suspicious that occurs on the coasts of England or Ireland or Scotland. We will also be inspecting the beacon warning system which has received some bad marks recently."

"You mean the fires-on-the-hill arrangement?"

Malachi sighed deeply. "It seems to me your succinct abbreviation of such an important precaution doesn't quite catch the inherent drama of citizen participation in our national defense. I prefer the summary I heard recently from one of our Venetian visitors: *'Against all invasion'* he observed, *'they have this, to me, admirable arrangement. The whole countryside is diversified by charming hills, and from the summits of those which are nearer to the sea they sweep the whole horizon. On these summits are poles with braziers filled with inflammable material which is fired by the sentinel if armed ships of the enemy are sighted, and so in a moment the news spreads from hill to hill throughout the kingdom.'* [3]

"Poles? More than one? Is that in case they have a false alarm or two?"

Malachi shook his head. "For once, we're better organized than that. On the Isle of Wight, for instance we have an east beacon station and a west station, and if either of them sees a dozen or so ships in convoy off the main shipping routes, they have instructions to raise a flag they call an 'ear' to alert the other station for confirmation of the sightings before they light the beacons."

"Suppose the other station is looking the other way and doesn't see the ear?"

"Oh, they'll see it all right because as soon as the ear is hoisted, one of the watchers goes to the nearest church and wildly clangs every bell in the belfry. Those church bells have essentially been silenced for a year now in preparation for this warning system, although local churches have been allowed to use one bell at weddings and funerals and at Christmas time. When other churches hear the incredible clanging from all the bells ringing together, they'll add their own inventory of cacophony to the dissonance, and for miles around, care-free calmness will go out the window along with sound sleep, and the trained bands will scurry to their duly appointed assembly points."

"So when they get confirmation of a sighting, the watchers will then light up their braziers?"

"Yes, but only after carefully counting the number of suspicious sails involved. They'll light one brazier if they see twenty to thirty sail and two fires for thirty to fifty sail and all three if they see fifty or more of what could be enemy vessels."

"And you say these beacons are manned by ordinary citizens and not the military?"

"That's right. Every Tom, Dick and Marmaduke takes his turn."

"It's very impressive to see that when our country is in peril, ordinary English citizens can be counted on to forget their every-day passions and pleasures and stand forth at rigid attention until the foe is vanquished. Very impressive and very comforting at the same time."

"Yes," Malachi chuckled, "They can be counted on as long as some responsible party is periodically checking up on them."

"Checking up?"

"In every district the Justice of the Peace is responsible for seeing that the beacon hilltops are effectively manned; to insure constant vigilance, they have ordered all benches and resting places removed from the hilltops. Despite such precations, however, JP's have been forced to hand out dozens of citations for absenteeism, inattentiveness, drunkenness, gambling, and sleeping on duty."

"Oh, so it's not much different from the military, after all," William mused.

Chapter 2:
THE REPORT FROM SPAIN

March 1588. Deptford Dock:

"That's Benjamin White coming down the gangplank now," Malachi informed his apprentice. "In a minute we'll know if he managed to visit the Lisbon docks during his trip to Portugal. If he did, we should get some account of how the death of Admiral Santa Cruz last month has affected the construction of the Armada fleet. At least we'll learn who King Philip has selected to replace Santa Cruz."

"Why is an Englishman doing business with the Spaniards while they are building a fleet to attack us?"

"The Spanish have licensed him to help them modernize their accounting system which has never quite caught up with the influx of gold and silver from the New World. They complain their old system keeps them always in debt to the money-lenders, so they're hoping he can pull them over to the other side of the ledger. His business is not war-related, so the Spanish permit him to stay as long as he behaves sensibly and does good work for them. Walsingham, of course, loves the idea since it gives us another English eye to see what the Dons are up to."

"You mean he's a spy?"

Malachi sighed deeply. "In the eyes of sensible people, Ben White is simply a casual observer who has just returned from an interesting trip abroad and may have a story or two to relate about his travels. You may sensibly refer to him as a business agent if you wish, but forget all about that spy business. Now, let us see if we can draw a few anecdotes from him without exerting too much pressure and without affixing too many labels to him, shall we?"

Malachi greeted White and introduced him to William. He winced as his apprentice burst forth, "So what did the king of Spain decide? Who did he pick?"

The elderly merchant held up his hand, smiling coolly. "Hold on there, young man! You seem completely bereft of dramatic sensibility. Don't you realize that a man with a good story in hand does a disservice to his audience if he is driven past the point of dramatic intensity by being badgered into disgorging act five in place of act one? King Philip did decide, and his selection is a very curious one, but only if you are aware of what the death of Santa Cruz means to the Spanish navy and to the Armada undertaking generally."

"I have not been to Spain recently," William confessed, "but I understand that Santa Cruz had assumed almost deity status in the minds of the Spanish people. It seemed to me he was held in the same kind of warm regard and deep respect that Hawkins and Drake enjoy from the English people."

"Exactly right," White agreed. "Santa Cruz was the unquestioned father of the Spanish navy for the last twenty years, and he directed Spain's ships in their two most notable victories during that period: the Battle of Lepanto in 1572 and the battle of Terciera in 1583 when several Continental claimants attempted to occupy the offshore Portuguese colonies which were left without a monarch after King Sebastian was killed in Africa."

"That would be the Azores," said Malachi.

White nodded. "And he has, of course, been a driving force for building the Armada from the first day it was considererd. As a matter of fact, for several years before it was undertaken, Santa Cruz had offered Philip a series of detailed plans for the building of a flotilla powerful enough to strike fear into the hearts of the heretical English pirates. And into their 'underhanded Queen' as well."

"His 1586 plan to invade England called for 556 ships," Malachi added, "so he certainly didn't underrate the opposition. Our recent reports indicate, however, that as Spain recovers from the death of Santa Cruz, the Armada preparations will be delayed somewhat, and even when completed, it seems unlikely they will be able to muster even one third of his original plan, perhaps one-hundred-and-fifty ships. I'd be interested, Ben, in your estimate of their progress when you went through Lisbon. Did you get a chance to look at their dock works?"

"As you know, Malachi, Spain makes very little effort to cordon off the Lisbon dockside because that splendid harbor is such an international trade center in addition to being the assembly point for the Armada. The city is always full of foreign merchants and seamen, and many of the native Portuguese—who do the actual work on the docks—still see the Spanish as intruders and invaders of their native city, so they resent any attempt by Madrid to control their movements. That makes it easy for others to walk there as long as they have sense enough to look busy. Spanish officials did check my commercial license a time or two just to make sure I had legitimate business interests in the area, but their security was pretty perfunctory by our standards. I saw enough to say that the death of Santa Cruz has left them at something of a stand-still in preparing their Armada.'"

"How could you tell?" William asked.

"There are huge piles of shipbuilding timbers and spars and cable sitting beside half-finished galleons, but most of the shipyard people seem to be standing around waiting for somebody to tell them to get busy. I didn't see the kind of frantic construction energy that Santa Cruz was able to generate while he was in good health. I'm afraid Philip's daily demands to get a fleet out on the water and let God take care of the details, eventually forced that conscientious, sixty-three-year-old warrior to take to his bunk, turn his face to the wall, and forget his earthly deadlines."

"So it will be up to whomever Philip picked to put the pieces back together," Malachi observed. "How well equipped is the new man to get that done?"

"You are a tricky one, Malachi," White smiled, "but I'm not quite ready for the final revelation. Let me first proceed through the candidates available for this important assignment. After all, the success or failure of this Grand Enterprise will rest squarely on the shoulders of the man Philip has chosen, and that choice will also reveal to us a great deal about the thinking of King Philip."

"At least let us know if it was a navy man," Malachi requested. "Did he pick Recalde?"

"You do know your Spanish commanders, Malachi. Juan Martinez de Recalde would have been my choice too. At sixty-two, Recalde is somewhat older than the other navel commanders, so he has much more seafaring experience. He is a skilled navigator and a daring and resourceful seaman who has successfully commanded Spanish fleets for sixteen years. In 1579 he landed 700 Spanish volunteers in Ireland during the Desmond Rebellion, and in 1583, he served as Santa Cruz's second-in-command in their victory for control of the Azores. As much as any other Spanish commander, he knows the ability of England's naval forces, so he is not likely to underestimate us as an opponent. Being held in high regard by the other Spanish officers and having recently conducted a charting reconnaissance of both the English and the Irish coasts, Recalde would certainly seem to be the logical choice to lead the Armada."

"But he was not picked," William prodded.

"I haven't said so yet," White smiled, "because the fiery Don Miguel de Oquendo is little more than a half step behind Recalde in experience and comes close to being a Spanish version of our Francis Drake. He carries the reputation of being a very adventuresome and daring commander who handles his ship 'like a light horseman', according to the sailor's tales. He saved Santa Cruz's bacon during the Terceira battle of 1583 by sailing his ship between two enemy craft that were hammering the old Admiral, and Oquendo boarded and captured the French flagship. That kind of flamboyance and rashness is typical of the Spanish military generally and may be exactly what the Armada needs from their leader to get the job done, so I would have regarded him also as a very logical candidate for the job, or at least second-in-command to Recalde."

"Past tense," William observed quietly.

"And then we have Don Pedro de Valdez, an experienced commander who was wounded in a skirmish with English ships while he was in charge of Spain's Indian fleet, so he is also unlikely to take England's naval powers lightly should they meet in battle. Don Pedro may be more strategically inclined than the others—something like our John Hawkins—since it was he who persuaded Philip that the Spanish ships should be armed with heavier artillery, being convinced that the English intend to fight any future navy battle with cannon at long range rather than by grappling and boarding."

"And a good job of persuading he did," Malachi nodded. "We just got a copy of Philip's warning to his captains of our plan to use firepower to overcome the Spanish advantage in manpower, in which he wrote, '*It must be borne in mind that the enemy's object will be to fight at long distance, in consequence of his advantage in artillery...the aim of our men, on the contrary, must be to bring him to close quarters and grapple with him*'." [4]

White nodded. "I know the Spanish have recently doubled their orders for big cannon from all the Continental suppliers. Unfortunately—it is rumored—such suppliers include some English firms who have found it very profitable to trans-ship their product to Spain through Italy or the Netherlands. Anyway, Valdez could have been Philip's choice if a premium were put upon strategic thinking."

"Was it?" William asked.

"Don't rush me," White said. "Just three logical candidates left and only two of them are naval commanders. The first of those two would be Don Hugo de Moncada, but he is not a serious choice because he has spent most of his career in charge of the oared galleys of the Mediterranean fleet and has not had as much experience as the others with pure sailing vessels. He does, however, at this moment, command a squadron of the newly developed Spanish ships which attempt to combine the advantages of the galley and the galleon in what they call the 'galleass'. The galleass is a sailing ship which can also be propelled by oars."

"That sounds just like the galley," William offered.

White shook his head. "Much bigger than a galley. It's a major war-ship. It carries 300 soldiers compared to the galley's 90 and 300 rowers compared to the galley's

220. The new dimension allows the construction of a gun deck above the heads of the rowers' station, and that new deck enables the galleass to mount a formidable array of fifty cannon compared to the skimpy five on the regular galley. The new vessel would be particularly effective in a battle during which the wind died and the sailing vessels were left practically immobile. Because of its size, however, the galleass is not quite as maneuverable as the galley which can whirl about in its own length and can reach a short-term, ramming speed of 12 knots in a dead calm. The new vessel can move right along if the drummer gives the rowers a frisky beat, though it's not particularly quick under sail."

"That sounds like a great idea," William responded. "If there were no wind, a galleass could row among the sailing ships and shoot at them from angles which didn't expose it to broadside fire. Does England have any vessels like that, or have our shipbuilders entirely missed the boat, so to speak?"

"Hold on there, young Master Mariner," Malachi chuckled. "As Ben knows, the galleass has yet to be tested in combat against a well-armed galleon, and it is a real novice in dealing with the turbulent seas of the Atlantic Ocean. It is also rumored to be a somewhat cumbersome craft since that extra high gun-deck, along with its fore and aft castles, makes it top-heavy enough to be cranky in choppy seas and reluctant to answer the helm even in fair weather. In the end, it may turn out to be nothing more than a sentimental Spanish gesture to hold onto the galley configuration which has served them so well in the Mediterranean for hundreds of years, but I advise we not rush into production until we see how well they hold up to battle in the tumultuous ocean."

"And," White added, "the truth is that for Moncada to be chosen as commander of the Armada, he would have to overcome a reputation for having a pride so thinskinned that he bristles easily even in exchanges with his superiors, something like our Martin Frobisher. It has also been rumored, however, that a fleet of his galleasses would lead the Armada, so who can say if one of those odd vessels might not be the flagship of the fleet."

"Not me, certainly," William said.

"So if Moncada is an improbable choice, what other navy man is left as a contender?" Malachi asked.

"Another naval commander with vast experience—but one who is an unlikely candidate because he is despised and hated by all the other Spanish commanders—is Don Diego Flores de Valdez."

"Despised and hated, why?" William asked.

"Apart from being regarded as a touchy and quarrelsome man who is fiercely jealous of other captains, including his cousin, Don Pedro de Valdez—Don Flores is remembered by the entire Spanish navy as being the commander who abandoned a brave and popular fellow officer named Sarmiento in the Straits of Magellan. They had been sent to that location by Philip to establish defenses against the possibility that the English might repeat Drake's successful circumnavigation of the globe. The obstacles to their success in that bleak area were considerable, however, and Don Flores soon soured on the project.

"So what did he do?"

"He sailed home without Sarmiento, which marked him not only as a failure but as a treacherous escort in the eyes of his fellow commanders. He did command trans-Atlantic fleets for twenty years, however, so he is thought to be a competent seaman."

"It's hard to imagine he would be appointed if he is so universally disliked," Malachi observed, "and that leaves only the non-naval officer for consideration before we hear the unraveling of this puzzle."

"Right," said White. "Not navy perhaps, but he is military to the core, born and bred for battle. Most of his experience, however, has been with Spain's cavalry on land, so he has very little experience at sea although for a short time he did command a squadron of the Neapolitan galleys."

"Why in the world would King Philip pick him then?"

"I didn't say he did, but you can bet the thought crossed his mind because Don Aonso de Leyva is a bright, dashing young officer who is very popular with Spanish society generally, and he is a special favorite of the King who often treats de Leyva as though he were a favored prince in the Royal household. It is not too much to say that Leyva is the Spanish equivalent of our late Sir Philip Sidney, admired by every noble family in Spain, and those families would set up a distinct clamor to enlist their sons in his service if he were appointed commander."

"But he was not?"

"No, he was not," White laughed, "and I finally have to admit neither were any of the other logical contenders."

"Ah ha!" exclaimed Malachi. "The King of Spain had exactly the same problem our Queen had in choosing a commander of our fleet who would not ignite jealousy and anger on the part of our other sea-captains."

"So that's why Elizabeth selected Lord Howard of Effingham over Drake or Hawkins," said William.

"Exactly right," Malachi nodded. "Among other prevailing antagonisms in our fleet, both Martin Frobisher and his second-in-command, Edward Fenton, are openly hostile to Drake, and Captain William Borough has little good to say about his former commander since he was condemned to death by Drake for disagreeing with him during the action at Cadiz. Since Borough is a favorite of the Queen, his death sentence has been pretty well ignored and Borough is still on the job although assigned to the command of England's only galley in the Thames, away from Drake. And Hawkins stepped on a lot of well-entrenched toes when he reorganized the Navy Department and modernized the Queen's warships, so he has his own detractors among his Navy board colleagues."

"So if either of them were selected, there might be mutiny?"

"Open mutiny is unlikely, but still there might come a time for England in combat when a personal animosity prevented our forces from acting in unison, and that failure could prove disastrous for both our navy and our country. By appointing a noble like Charles Howard as Lord High Admiral, Elizabeth has presented our seamen with a familiar hierarchy, and effectively squelched whatever jealousy might arise from asking our mariners to obey the orders of a mere commoner even if he be knighted. I'll wager King Philip made much the same choice."

"Quite right," White smiled, "but Philip went even further a-field in his choice than did Elizabeth because she at least picked a man who is steeped in naval tradition and experience. The office of Lord Admiral has been in the Howard family for many years since his father, two of his uncles, and his great grandfather held the post before him. It doesn't hurt, of course, that Howard is a first cousin to Anne Boleyn, the Queen's mother."

"But Philip picked a rank outsider?" Malachi suggested.

White laughed and said, "Before I reveal that choice to you let me ask you to do a little playacting. I'd like each of you to pretend you are the King of Spain for a moment, and let's see what your reaction would be to the situation I shall now relate."

"I like this part," William said. "I've always imagined that if I were ever type-cast in a role—"

Malachi interrupted, "We are enthroned with scepter in hand, Ben, so please relate away."

"I would enjoy your royal reaction to the response the king received from one of his greatest grandees after he appointed that man to replace Santa Cruz as the commander of the Armada. The response is lengthy, so I will only present you with the salient excerpts from it. He wrote to Philip; *"I humbly thank his Majesty for having thought of me for so great a task, and I wish I possessed the talents and strength necessary for it. But, Sir, I have not health for the sea, for I know by the small experience that I have had afloat that I soon become seasick, besides I have bad rheumatism..The force is so great, and the undertaking so important, that it would not be right for a person like myself, possessing no experience of seafaring or of war, to take charge of it..I possess neither aptitude, ability, health or fortune for the expedition...The lack of any of these qualities would be sufficient to excuse me, and much more the lack of them all, as is the case with me at present..For me to take charge of the Armada a-fresh, without the slightest knowledge of it, of the persons who are taking part in it, of the objects in view, of the intelligence from England..would be simply groping in the dark, even if I had experience, seeing that I should have suddenly and without preparation to enter a new career. So, Sir, you will see that my reasons for declining are so strong and convincing in his Majesty's own interests, that I cannot attempt a task of which I have no doubt I should give a bad account.. for I do not understand it, know nothing about it, have no health for the sea, and no money to spend upon it."* [5]

"That sounds like a man who is not looking for work," Malachi smiled.

"But what would you say to him if you were king?" White asked. "Or might you have him hanged out of hand?"

"I know what I'd say," William offered. "I would put such a craven response into its proper perspective by telling him; *'The devil damn thee black, thou cream-faced loon!'* [6]

"My word!," White exclaimed, "That's monarchial enough to have come from Elizabeth herself, but even sovereigns must curb their self-indulgence if they are to end up with the man they want for the job."

"You're saying King Philip was not put off by such a response?"

"Not in the least. Whatever King Philip's faults might be, he is certainly not lacking in patience. He wrote immediately to his cousin, Don Alonso Perez de Gusman el Bueno, twelfth Senor and fifth Marques de Sanlucar de Barramada, ninth Conde de Niebla and seventh Duque de Medina Sidonia, and discounted his beg-off letter with a single sentence: *'Duke and Cousin..All of what you say I attribute to your excess of modesty. But it is I who must judge of your capabilities and parts, and I am fully satisfied with these. As for the good health which you say often deserts you at sea, we must believe that God will grant it to you in that great day dedicated to His service..You yourself should proceed to Lisbon with the haste made necessary by the concentration there of a mighty armada, uncaptained and awaiting your orders. I charge you to do this, and also to acquaint yourself fully with the object of this enterprise; how it is to be conducted; and the manner in which your plans may be coordinated with those of the Duke of Parma, my nephew."* [7]

"The Duke of Medina Sidonia again," Malachi mused. "We saw him last year in charge of the defense of Cadiz during Drake's attack. On the second day, Sidonia marched into the city with three thousand infantry and three hundred cavalry to combat our naval forces, and probably prevented a sack of the city if that's what Drake had in mind. Sidonia might have been better off, however, fetching some long-range culverins, because even though the city's shore batteries made some noise during the two days our people spent in the harbor burning and seizing Spanish ships, no English vessel was hurt by their cannon fire, and no English seaman lost. I can only hope Sidonia is equally successful in his new position."

"I find it hard to believe King Philip would chose him after his all-too-candid response to the appointment, but I suppose the king knows something we don't know," William said.

"That is indeed the case," White said. "The Duke of Medina Sidonia has been tested by Philip before, and the king was obviously pleased with the result because he goes on to say; *'The experience I have had of your efforts to secure the good management of my property leads me to hope for your careful management of all relating to this Armada. You should try to keep intact as best you can, the wealth it represents, knowing what it has cost to assemble, and the financial difficulties it has caused.'*"

"Pick the people who already have money of their own to handle yours, eh?"

"Essentially correct," White nodded, "but probably not for the shady reason you are intimating. A monarch must always be aware of the ratio of wealth within his country. If he finds a nobleman whose personal fortune has grown to outstrip all others in the kingdom, the king must give that man additional duties to match his profits, or else the crown may shortly encounter a rival who can hire more soldiers than can the king. After all, kings are really only overgrown barons, so they are quite aware of how easily a threat might arise from that direction."

"You mention the ratio of wealth," William said. "How much could one man accumulate without drawing unwelcome attention from the throne?"

"As soon as a subject's annual income reaches about ten percent of the King's income, the monarch must make sure that subject is not profiting from the nation's economy without putting something back. That's one of the big reasons why Sidonia was chosen to lead the Armada even if he is not a navy-type; he is the wealthiest grandee in all of Spain, so it is time for him to shoulder some of the cost of governing the kingdom. Philip does know, for instance, that despite Sidonia's poverty plea, he has already contributed nine million maravedi to the cause and could be induced to scrape up a good deal more if it were needed for the success of the Enterprise."

"How much is a maravedi worth in real money?" William asked.

"Money comparisons are always a complicated matter as the people at the currency exchange often explain with ill-concealed glee," White pointed out, "but nine million of anything is obviously a healthy pile of money. I know a day laborer in Spain gets six maravedi a day and it takes 374 maravedi to make a gold Spanish ducat whereas it takes 240 pennies to make a gold English pound. Assuming those gold coins are roughly equal in value, it would appear a maravedi is worth two-thirds of a penny. If we then stretch our rounding out of figures to the limit, we might assume nine million maravedi could amount to as much as £25,000 of English money."

"Just one tenth of our Queen's annual income," Malachi mused, "So that's the amount which might excite the Queen if one of her subjects succeeded in reaching £25,000 on an annual basis."

White nodded. "That person could count on further duties at that point. It seems odd that in England more and more of the men called for that kind of public service in recent years have come from the merchant class and fewer and fewer from the old nobility, but in Spain that group is still exclusively drawn from the nobility."

"Which partially explains Senor Sidonia's qualifications for being chosen to lead the Enterprise," Malachi smiled. "His testimony to Philip about being ignorant of the preparation of the proposed fleet, however, is a trifle misleading since he has already sold them fruit from his orange groves in San Lucar and shipped them large supplies of dried fish from his commercial fishing operation. As a matter of fact we have reason to believe he is the single largest supplier of such foodstuffs, so he is already notable in our eyes as being one of the most efficient of the Spanish victualers in terms of delivering the goods on time. I imagine that in addition to being aware of Sidonia's wealth, Philip also had in mind his cousin's proven ability as an administrator when he set him the task of getting the fleet ready to sail."

"He certainly wasn't chosen for his war-like tendencies," White agreed. "As a noble, Medina Sidonia was schooled in the arts of war, but he has never shown any ambition in that area. He has, however, been notably successful in organizing his territory of Andalusia both as the primary source of Armada food supplies and the mustering center for volunteer manpower for the fleet. He has organized Cadiz harbor as a marshalling yard for reconditioning ships to be dispatched to Lisbon when they are in finished form. Unlike most Castilians, he does not wear his pride upon his sleeve, so he does not mind working quietly behind the scenes. In all truth, Medina Sidonia seems rather a quiet, friendly, religious chap who would be just as happy to stay home in San Lucar and tend his orange groves."

"But he would respond to Philip's summons, of course," Malachi observed.

White nodded. "Like all loyal Spaniards, he leaped into the saddle upon the King's direct insistence and has made his way to Lisbon, where I can only imagine he is presently busy making sure the big guns aren't installed on the small ships, and insisting also that all the cannon balls not be stored in the slow, unarmed supply ships. Philip obviously feels that the unfinished work left behind by Santa Cruz's sickness and death can best be addressed by a trusted administrator rather than by a naval expert. The truth is that despite his protestations, Medina Sidonia knows more about the preparations for the Armada than any other single soul, so it is not surprising that the King has waved off his objections to the assignment."

"That sounds like Philip may have picked the right man to straighten out his supply lines," Malachi concluded, "but what about military tactics and strategy? Did the king pick a second-in-command who understands how to use the navy after it leaves the docks?"

"I'll leave that judgment up to you. He did pick Sidonia's Naval Advisor from the list of military leaders I've already mentioned. Guess which one?"

"Well," Malachi considered, "it wasn't Recalde or you wouldn't ask the question, so I'll nominate the younger Oquendo as an intelligent choice."

"Considering how far off the mark all of our foregoing assumptions have been," William said, "I'll enter into the spirit of the thing and select the army man to lead the Spanish navy. De Leyva, was it? The dashing one?"

"Not Oquendo," White said to Malachi, "but the mention of Don Alonso de Leyva is very close because Philip did pick him to command the soldiers on board the Armada, and since their number will probably hit close to twenty-thousand as opposed to eight-thousand mariners, you can readily see it is an important appointment, and probably a good one for Spain. That still leaves the Navy without a second-in-command, so let me draw his identity from you in another fashion. Which of the men mentioned so far would you think least likely to be chosen as Sidonia's chief-of-staff of the whole Grand Enterprise?"

"The person whose only experience was in command of galleys in the Mediterranean?" William ventured.

"Moncada," White said. "No, not him."

"The direction your questions have taken, and the perverse enjoyment you get from these drawn out revelations can mean only one thing," Malachi said. "He appointed Don Diego Flores Valdez."

White slapped his thigh in satisfaction at what he obviously regarded as a huge joke. "That's exactly what he did! From a field of competent, adventuresome commanders, the king picked the two men he could absolutely count on to follow his instructions to the letter; dependable, predictable men who would not risk his fleet by indulging in any flights of personal initiative which deviated from the highly detailed instructions he will undoubtedly give them for successfully carrying out the enterprise."

"Let me see if I have a clear picture of what you're saying," William said slowly. "When and if the Armada does arrive with nearly 30,000 fighting men, it will be led by a reluctant, rich, landlubber who is really a fruit-and-fish-salesman without experience at sea, and he will be advised in naval matters by a chief-of-staff who is universally despised by the entire Spanish navy?"

Malachi shook his head. "It's hard for me to believe that Philip appointed Don Flores. He certainly knows the absolute disdain in which the other naval commanders hold the man. Philip's monarchial mind may have over-reached itself with a choice he will soon come to regret. I know that a king's royal commands should overwhelm whatever trivial animosities exist within the ranks of his well disciplined military, but we are, after all, speaking of mortals here, and sometimes their feelings of hatred and envy sink a shaft so deep into their vitals that it is well beyond the recall of a mere king."

"The other Spanish maritime officers agree with you," said White. "They would all prefer to have a respected naval commander in charge of the whole operation. As a matter of fact, Racalde nominated himself to lead the Armada and then added that Oquendo was also well qualified to handle the responsibility. Exactly the choices you and I would have made if we were on the side of the Spanish. As it occurs, of course, we are on the side that may well profit from the doubtful choices the King of Spain has made. Only time will tell."

"Yes," William chuckled, "Let's hope *the whirligig of time brings in his revenge* [8] But in the meantime can't we get after them by attacking Spanish ports again as Drake did last year? What's holding up that fruitful enterprise?"

Malachi replied. "Elizabeth is fearful we will be invaded if she permits Howard to take the fleet south and thereby leaves England's shores unprotected. She keeps them from sailing off by refusing to victual her navy ships for longer than a month at a time, which means that with a little bad weather, they could just about reach Spain before they had to turn around and come home if they wanted to keep eating."

"I don't imagine that suits Drake," White said.

Malachi nodded. "I think Drake has almost convinced Howard that England's coast would still be safe if he sailed south on favorable winds from the north or northeast, directly into the face of the Spaniards if they attempted to attack us by sailing north from Lisbon. Howard is a good naval man. He can see the sense in the thing, and, in the end, I think he will convince the Queen to turn Drake loose under the condition that the fleet return at once if the winds shift to favor the Armada's advance on England. A steady northeast wind could put Drake off Spain's shore in five days, but a nice strong wind out of the southwest could put Sidonia on top of us in a week."

"Why the difference?"

"Because the Spanish warships must restrict their speed to match the pace of their big, round, slow urcas which will be carrying—among other things—much more than a month's supply of victuals, you can bet. As a matter of fact they will carry several things which may surprise those of us at home."

"You mean the whips and things I hear the ballad singers shouting about?" William asked.

"Really?" said White. "I hadn't heard that. I guess I've been gone too long to catch up with homeland security. How does it go?"

"I don't remember all of it, but I do remember a few lines sung to the tune of 'The Valiant Soldier'." William threw back his head and sang out:

> All you that list to look and see
> What profit comes from Spain,
> And what the Pope and Spaniards both
> Prepared for our gain.
> Then turn your eyes and bend your ears,

And you shall hear and see
What courteous minds, what gentle hearts,
They bear to thee and me!
They say "they seek for England's good,
And wish the people well!"
They say "they are such holy men,
all others they excel!"
These holy men, these sacred saints,
And those that think no ill:
See how they sought, against all right,
To murder, spoil, and kill!
Although they meant, with murdering hands,
Our guiltless blood to spill;
Before our deaths, they did devise
To whip us, first, their fill.
And for that purpose had prepared
Of whips such wondrous store,
So strangely made, that, sure, the like
Was never seen before.
One sort of whips, they had for men,
So smarting, fierce, and fell,
As like could never be devised
By any devil in hell.
The strings whereof with wiry knots,
Like rowels they did frame,
That every stroke might tear the flesh,
They laid on with the same.
And pluck the spreading sinews from
The hardened bloody bone,
To prick and pierce each tender vein,
Within the body known;
And not to leave one crooked rib
On any side unseen
Nor yet to leave a lump of flesh,
The head and foot between.
And for our silly women eke,
their hearts with grief to clog;
They made such whips, wherewith no man
Would seem to strike a dog.

Although their bodies sweet and fair
Their spoil they meant to make,
And on them first their filthy lust
And pleasure for to take.
O Ladies fair, what spite were this!
Your gentle hearts to kill!
To see these devilish tyrants thus
Your children's blood to spill.
What grief unto the husband dear!
His loving wife to see
Tormented so before his face
with extreme villainy.
Even as in India once they did
Against those people there
With cruel curs, in shameful sort,
the men both rent and tear;
And set the ladies great with child
upright against a tree,
And shot them through with piercing darts;
Such would their practice be! [9]

Malachi chuckled at the overdrawn drama and asked White, "Did you perchance see any bales of such wicked instruments on the Lisbon dock?"

"Those particular threats may have been inserted by the Dutch Almanac printers to liven up their sales," White grinned, "but the real threats are not so obvious. I heard many English exiles voice loud complaints against our Queen and her advisors, and they offered equally loud assurances to the Dons of the feeble fight that can be expected from the English against the overwhelming power of the Spanish forces, especially after those forces are joined by the tens of thousands of secret English Catholics they expect to link up with the invading Dons."

"Tens of thousands, eh?"

"Most on the Continent feel at least one-third of our countrymen are still secret Catholics. Some others say one-half and a few think two-thirds, but I think those high percentages are mostly from the exiles themselves who spend a great deal of time convincing each other that huge hoards of Papists will turn out to greet the Dons with bunches of flowers and dancing in the street."

"They might be a little disappointed on that score," Malachi said, "because we have plans to intern about a hundred of the Catholic fire-brands if things do heat up. If some few others come out for the invaders, it will be without their leaders."

White grinned. "I doubt if the Dons count seriously on such help, but the Spanish gentlemen who do lend ear to such nonsense seemed all of the opinion that they have only to set foot on our shore and our lands and women will be theirs for the taking. The officers and gentlemen who are getting ready for this voyage are spending quite a bit of money on dressing themselves richly, assuring themselves of good success and presuming that it will be easy to cover their expenses by the booty they will take in England. Many of the Spanish nobility are arranging to take a portion of their wealth with them in case they have to dicker with each other for our choice estates. They are prepared to carry that wealth around their neck in the form of gold chains, some of which are eight feet long and weigh as much as five pounds."

"Five pounds, eh?" Malachi chuckled. "I hope such an adornment does not hinder their swimming stroke because I know England's fleet is prepared to salute those stoop-shouldered voyagers with every bit of welcome we can possibly stuff into an 18-pound round shot."

Chapter 3:
HOWARD JOINS DRAKE AT PLYMOUTH

Plymouth, May 23, 1588:

"Whyn't they listen to the man what knows?" Sammons the sailor cried out to Malachi in exasperation. "If Drake 'ad 'is way, you can bet we would 'it Cadiz again just like we did last year. Certain I could use another payday like that. Everybody's talking about the nice fat plums sprinkled along the Spanish coast, from Cadiz to Corunna. The ports're crowded with Armada preparations. All kinds o' craft jammed together bein' built or under repair, most 'thout sail, some 'thout guns mounted. What a day our gunners would 'ave! I'd give a goodly piece to relive them three days we 'ad at Cadiz! Even seamen's thirds brought a nice fat purse for each o' the lads, and you can bet that if a little dribbled down to us, the shareholders was well pleased."

"Yes," Malachi chuckled, "and it didn't hurt either that you did such an outstanding service for your country while getting rich in the bargain. But Howard is still Lord High Admiral of England's fleet, and Howard is much more conservative than Drake, much more like the Queen. Not only does he represent nobility as opposed to a rash commoner like Drake but responsible nobility who must think past the exhilaration of a free-wheeling raid on Spain's coast and must regard the possible consequences of such a satisfying action."

"Is't possible Drake 'as pulled back since they made 'im a knight?"

"That may be partially true, but he did, nevertheless, score a substantial policy victory in February when he convinced the Council to let him set up a western squadron of thirty-eight sail here at Plymouth, so that our whole fleet wouldn't be bunched up around the mouth of the Thames where it has traditionally been stationed. Here at Plymouth, we're in a much better position to protect the western mouth of the English Channel."

"Aye, we be 'ere in Plymouth with only 'alf a crew on each ship, and even those be on a scant ration of four-to-six so Drake can build 'is secret 'orde of food that London don't know about. Them big brains at Whitehall keeps us low on vittles so as we can't raid Spain on the sly."

"Four-to-six what?" William asked.

"Six men is fed the rations of four," Sammons explained, "but plumping the galley larder involves the seamen roundin' up part o' their vittles from the townfolk. They promises to pay when we get paid, but that puts the patience of the townfolk on trial, you c'n bet."

"True enough," Malachi nodded. "Essentially, Burghley and the Queen fear an attack by our fleet into Spanish waters would leave our own coast substantially unprotected even though Seymour has our other fleet with thirty-one sail patrolling between Dover and Calais at the eastern end of the English Channel."

"They could just haul Seymour's group o'er to the west end of the Channel and 'ave it all covered."

"That would suit Philip just fine because that would leave the way open for Parma to transport his tercios across from Dunkirk to Dover without waiting for the Armada ships that are planned for his escort—just what Philip would love to see happen."

"Fat chance they'd get far afore thousands of 'em ended up shot to pieces along wi' them flat-bottomed, river-barges they plan to row across. Don't forget them Dutchies have patrolled that coast agin' the likelihood of Parma's crossing for quite some time. Them Zeeland shoals keeps our deep-draft galleons from venturin' too close t' shore, but them Dutchie flyboats drafts only eight feet so they can sail right over them shoals just as easy as Parma's flat-bottomed scows. Their cannon would do wondrous damage to barges packed wi' Spanish troops and 'orses. Some of them big, flat-bottomed boxes be big enough to 'aul thirty 'orses, I 'ear tell, so it follows they be remarkable clumsy lessen they 'ave an absolute calm sea for crossin'. As for that, they might 'ave a long wait for calm in the Narrow Seas. Little danger them gettin' past Maurice of Nassau's Dutch navy in the first place."

"You are assuming, Sammons, that the Dutch are determined to protect the English coast at all costs," said Malachi, "and that they see some wisdom in preventing sixteen or seventeen thousand of Parma's regulars from leaving their country because that would spoil all the fun of fighting it out with them on Dutch soil."

"What are you saying?" cried William. "Do you think the Dutch might deliberately let Parma transport his tercios over to England?"

"Not quite. I have no doubt the Dutch will strike Parma's forces every chance they get unless the price is too high, or unless some Dutch commander simply decides Holland is better off without so many armed Spanish soldiers on its soil and takes his flyboats fishing while the Spanish are crossing."

"Betray us!" Sammons shouted. "After we 'ave spent money an' blood to protect 'em from Phillip's taxes and the bloody Inquisition?"

"Just examining possibilities," Malachi shrugged. "Don't forget the Queen has publicly labeled the Dutch rebels 'an ungrateful rabble', and she is still negotiating secretly for a truce with Parma with or without the consent of Maurice of Nassau. She seems to feel that if she pulls the English troops out of the Netherlands, Philip may give up the idea of invading England, and she will be saved a great deal of expense. It doesn't help the situation, of course, that many of the Dutch have come to see the English garrisons stationed in their key cities as more of an occupying force than a liberating one. The days of greeting us with flowers and dancing in the streets are long past, and Leicester, of course, has returned to England in virtual disgrace after frittering away two complete, well-financed English armies without disturbing the Spanish in the least. All in all, I don't think England should be too surprised if we are soon confronted with a self-serving decision from the Low Countries which cuts England out of the decision-making all together."

Sammons shook his head. "Them's shocking ideas. Hard to imagine any country being so bloody ungrateful. Where the 'ell is their loyalty?"

"Loyalty is a mixed ingredient in this muddle," Malachi cautioned him. "It hasn't been so long ago that the Dutch watched a number of their frontier cities handed over to Parma without a fight because the foreign commanders felt more loyalty to their Catholic beliefs or to the sanctity of their personal purse. When Leicester left Holland last year, he amazed the Dutch by placing two of his friends, who were well known Catholics, in command of two of Holland's most strategic cities. When objections were raised, he shouted them down by proclaiming that he trusted both men with his life."

"And he's still alive," observed William.

"That's right, but the cities are gone. One of those friends, Englishman William Stanley, the Catholic governor of the strategic city of Deventer—which is the capital of Overijssel province—turned the keys over to Parma and then fled to the Spanish side with the special force of 1500 Irish Kern he commanded and announced he was now serving God instead of the devil. On the same day, another of those personal friends, Rowland Yorke, who was left in charge of the fort which commands Zutphen, simply opened the gates and let the Spanish take over. The French Catholic commander of the fort at Wouw accepted sixteen thousand guineas from Spain for turning the place over to Spanish regulars. With those notable betrayals in mind, the Dutch Council of State is presently making angry, unpleasant noises about the strategy of having important Dutch defenses commanded by foreigners."

"If that be the case," Sammons said, shaking his head, "You're likely right. Seymour 'ad best stay where he be in case some Dutch navies decide to fill their purses 'n look t'other way when Parma makes 'is move. Where does that leave our attack on Spanish shipping? Drake knows we need to 'it Spain before she 'its us, or be he still shoutin' in the dark?"

"It's not so dark anymore," Malachi assured him. "Many voices have joined him. I think Drake has softened up the Queen with a series of notes he has written this spring, arguing his strategy that England's first line of defense should be on the coast of the enemy. Shortly after he was allowed to set up the Eastern Squadron at Plymouth he wrote to say that since Philip intends to invade England *then doubtless his force is and will be great in Spain.* And the queen should not fear any invasion of her own country but should instead *seek God's enemies and her Majesty's wherever they may be found.. for that, with 50 sail of shipping, we shall do more good upon their own coast than a great many more will do here at home.'* [10]

"In April he wrote her again: *'Most renowned Prince, I beseech you to pardon my boldness in the discharge of my conscience, being burdened to signify unto your highness the imminent dangers that in my simple opinion do hang over us..The promise of peace from the Prince of Parma and those mighty preparations in Spain agree not well together..these preparations may be speedily prevented by sending your forces to encounter them somewhat far off and more near to their own coasts, which will be cheaper for your Majesty and her people and much dearer for the enemy. The advantage of time and place in all martial actions is half the victory, which being lost is irrecoverable. Wherefore, if your Majesty will command me away with those ships which are here already, and the rest to follow with all possible expedition, I hold it in my poor opinion the surest and best course.'"* [11]

"Oh aye, that there was a good stroke tellin' our sweet Sovereign how much cheaper t'would be to fight it out in Spain," Sammons laughed. "There's the way to get to her, all right. How about Burghley? E's the man who writes the warrants for supplies. Did Drake write 'im?"

"He did indirectly when he sent the same arguments to the Privy Council: *'My very good lords, next under God's mighty protection, the advantage again of time and place will be the only and chief means for our good; wherein I most humbly beseech your good Lordships to persevere as you have begun; for that with fifty sail of shipping we shall do more good upon their own coast than a great deal more will do here at home.'"* [12]

"But he has been urging that strategy since the attack on Cadiz without much of an audience, hasn't he?" asked William.

"For several months, a key group of English planners have been debating Drake's approach, and I think they're now just about convinced of the wisdom of his way. The group included Lord Burghley, Admiral Howard, Sir Walter Raleigh, and the captains Drake, Hawkins, Fenner, Sir William Winter and Howard's cousin, Lord Seymour. After much debate they had Lord Admiral Howard recently pen a letter to Walsingham which said, *'The opinion of Sir Francis Drake, Mr. Hawkyns, Mr. Frobisher, and others that be men of greatest judgment and experience, as also my own concurring with them in the same, is that the surest way to meet with the Spanish fleet is upon their own coast, or in any harbour of their own, and there to defeat them.'* [13]

"Now that there sounds more like!" Sammons exulted as he rubbed his hands together. "I'll make sure me sea-bag be packed and bed down close to dockside, waitin' for me recall t' prosperity. The good word from gunner Starkey this morning be that Howard's due into Plymouth Sound today wi' sixty-seven more ships to join Drake's thirty-eight. That there's the makin's of a pretty good fleet if they sail agin the Spanish coast, an' speak o' the devil, here is Starkey hisself."

Gunner Starkey shook hands all around and joined the table. "Fleet can't leave 'til they decide who's boss," he told them. "As't stands now we'll shortly 'ave two Admirals of the English Navy in the 'arbor. Glance out that there window to the left, you'll see Howard's group on its way into the Sound this minute. Look close at 'is flagship, the *Ark Royal,* an' see e's flying both 'is Lord Admiral's flag and 'is Vice-Admiral's flag."

"Aye," said Sammons. "That be the *Ark Royal* now, what used to be the *Ark Raleigh* when Sir Walter 'ad it built last year. 'Tis said he turned it over to the Queen's navy to pay off some of 'is debt to 'er, but what's it mean, Howard flying both flags?"

"'Tis a sign 'e wants peace 'twixt him and Drake, two admirals in the same 'arbor, as 'twere. Now lookee to the right! There's Drake in his *Revenge,* leading 'is ships out to greet the newcomers, but still flying 'is admiral's flag. Drake be a man o' passion, an' if 'e objects to bein' ousted by Howard, we may see a exchange of cannon fire right 'ere in Plymouth Sound before we even get to the Spaniards."

Malachi chuckled. "Your profession has made you so blood-thirsty, Starkey, that you are seriously underrating Drake's desire to get at the Spaniards. The last thing in the world that man will do at this moment is cause trouble at home which may get him called off the fight. There is only one decider of such appointments in this kingdom and—unless she has recently changed her mind in the matter—she has already chosen Howard. If the loser doesn't dip his flag in respect to the Queen's choice when the two meet, I'll buy the next round. If he does dip his flag, it would seem to me only fair if each of you would be sporting enough–"

"Oh aye, our queen be a canny lass," Sammons interrupted, "but she may well 'ave made a mistake appointin' Howard over Drake. Us swabs follows Drake into battle because there is always profit at the end."

"What's that you say!" snarled Starkey. "She could never appoint an upstart like Drake! That base-born scoundrel be little more than a pirate for all 'e's the ablest sea-cap'n we got."

"Aye, exactly who we need if they come at us wi' cannon and pikes," Sammons insisted. "A fighting sea-cap'n! Howard c'n handle the London end of it like the courtly mariner 'e be, and Drake c'n do the fightin' like the cunning, hard-bitten scraper 'e 'as always been."

"Drake may be the best cap'n of a single ship or even a squadron, but 'e'd never do to control a entire fleet. 'E would clap his junior officers in irons for darin' to share in 'is decision-making, which is what he done on every trip 'e's made. Cut off Doughty's head, ye recall, and tried to do the same to Borough after the Cadiz raid."

"Oh, aye," said Sammons, full of sarcasm, "And Howard will confer with everybody this side o' the Pope afore he weighs anchor. Think ye Sidonia will give 'im that kind o' time?"

"When the Spanish come, the English fleet will 'ave to act sensible, not reckless," Starkey insisted. "'Tis true they will no doubt confer often times on how to handle them one-hundred-and-fifty enemy ships, but that's only good sense. The other English cap'ns trust Howard, and some of 'em don't trust Drake, seeing 'im as greedy and arrogant. "sides, 'e ain't regular navy, so lots 'o officers might 'ave a hard time following 'im."

"Ah well, gentlemen," broke in Malachi, "all of our sea captains have a bit of an ego. It comes from being in full command of a small slice of England at sea. If a man had no big head before that experience, he'd have one after it."

"Sort of like playing God," said William, grinning.

Starkey ignored both comments. "Elizabeth ain't impressed by a loose-cannon like Drake. She would never ignore tradition nor bypass her own cousins, the Howards. A round for the table for our new Lord Admiral!"

"And I'll buy a round for Drake," cried Sammons. "Zounds, Drake ain't goin' to accept a reduction in rank an' a loss of pay just to please one of them Whitehall fellows. Drake's earned the 'onor on the 'igh seas, and it's 'im the Spanish fear. I say there'll be trouble."

"I find it interesting," said William, "that two regular seamen should differ so much over nobleman versus commoner as Lord Admiral."

"For one thing," Starkey explained, "nobles 'ave the 'abit of command. They are used to giving orders and 'aving those orders obeyed."

"Howard 'as nothin' over Drake there," grumbled Sammons. "Just ask Doughty and Borough."

"That's the point. Nobles can exact obedience 'thout cuttin' off a man's head or threatenin' a body with execution. Men 'ave the habit of obeying 'em even if they grumble a bit behind their backs. Also, Howard c'n get more supplies for the navy from Whitehall than Drake could, and 'e could mayhap speed up the sailor's pay. Might be e'd even open up his own purse if worse come to worse. And as the Queen well knows, a noble 'as much more to lose than a commoner if things go wrong."

"An excellent point," said Malachi. "Our sovereign lady keeps a keen eye out for any handy fall-guy when things don't go her way. It might surprise many of our countrymen to find that while they were extremely pleased with Drake's heroic attack on Cadiz last year, Elizabeth was quite annoyed with him because she felt his action interfered with her peace negotiations and that his attack finally helped convince Philip to sail against us in response to Drake's desecration of Spanish territory when he invaded their mainland at Sagres during that raid. The Queen is very reluctant to turn the control of England's future over to military leaders who see no distinction between cannonading a country's harbors and setting up camp on the mainland of their territory. Her irritation with Drake may partially explain why she chose Howard for her Lord Admiral, and why she's unlikely to change that appointment now."

"Look!" cried William. "Drake is dipping his Admiral's flag to Howard!"

"You called it, Malachi," exclaimed Starkey. "The issue has been decided!"

"Bloody 'ell," cursed Sammons. "There'll be no glory in't now for us boys."

"The Lord Admiral is pulling down his Vice-Admiral's flag to ship over to Drake's ship," pointed out Starkey. "Now we'll 'ave all of our nautical ducks in a proper row."

"Ready to face something no navy has ever faced before," Malachi reflected over his tankard.

All three listeners turned their attention to him. "The Spanish Armada, you mean," asked William.

Malachi nodded. "Hundreds of sail-driven ships are about to confront each other with massed broadside cannon fire in a battle royal for the very survival of our country. The outcome of this titanic struggle is still very much in doubt, no matter how many assurances we are offered by good John Hawkins and his fellow ship builders."

"And from the stout hearts of oak who man those ships!" shouted Starkey, and the men all joined him in an early toast to victory.

"Yes, that's the spirit, all right," smiled Malachi, "at least until we get our feet wet. Are you gentlemen aware that a mere seventeen years ago, the largest naval battle yet known took place in the Sea of Corinth just off Lepanto in Greece, where the combined Christian forces of Spain, Venice, and the Papal States met the Muslim military fleet in an attempt to arbitrate who would get the lion's share of earnings from the profitable Asian spice trade?"

"That was back when they still fought in galleys, wasn't it?" William asked.

"It was," Malichi nodded. "Together, the two fleets fielded, if you'll allow me a poetic stretch, close to five hundred galleys, all oar-driven. Essentially, the battle strategy for those vessels involved punching holes in enemy hulls by ramming, while shooting their bow-mounted cannon as often as they could reload. They then boarded each other across a plank in the bow and came to hand-to-hand fighting with pistols, pikes, knives, swords, and grenades."

"Grenades?" prompted William.

"Ceramic jars full of oil to be smashed on the enemy's deck and ignited. Even with those primitive methods, at Lepanto they managed to destroy close to 250 of those vessels and to make fish-food of thirty-five-thousand participants, mostly Muslims, during that historic encounter."

"No sailing ships involved?"

"The few sailing vessels that were in the neighborhood were warned to sail off and stay out of harm's way. Now, when we look at the incredible changes that have occurred in those intervening seventeen years, it is easy to see—"

"You left out who won," William observed.

"Yes, I did, didn't I," Malachi said with mock patience. "Are you Christian or Muslim?"

"I like to think I am a solid Christian, but I guess only God knows for sure."

"Then ask him for the score sheet from Lepanto, but in the meantime, let me call your attention to the greatest single change you are likely to witness in your lifetime. We are watching the eclipse of an epic era, Gentlemen," Malachi pronounced solumly. "As a matter of fact, we are standing inside the cover of a history book only now being written."

"How do you mean?" William inquired.

"For thousands of years, the oar-driven galley has dominated nautical battle-fields, but at this very moment you are watching them being abandoned for the fighting ships you see passing before you. With sail-driven ships used for the first time by both sides, you can bet that this upcoming battle will reveal strategies and results never before witnessed by human kind. Such monumental technological change occurring practically overnight is enough to make a man stop in his tracks and wonder whether the world is speeding up like a child's carousel to pitch us all off into the vast abyss of eternity, past comprehension of the apparatus which doomed us."

"It may doom some," Starkey said, "but I be just as 'appy to make my fight from behin' my eighteen pounders instead of crossin' some slippery plank to get at the buggers."

"That's right, Sammons added, "they can have yesterday, but I'll take today. Sailing may be hard work, but it's easier than rowing. Hey, Drake is raising his vice-admiral's flag so I guess that settles that." Sammons and Starkey drifted to the window to witness the transfer of command of the Plymouth fleet.

"Good Lord, Malachi," William exclaimed, "the way you describe the up-coming event makes it sound like the curtain is about to go up on one of the greatest historical events of all time, and it's happening right at our front door. I wouldn't miss it for the world, not for a woman or a drink or a nice soft bed!"

"Before you get too far out on a limb," Malachi said, "let me remind you that your attendance here is no longer in your control. You'll have to be with me."

"What does that mean? Where will you be?"

"I'll be in Holland very shortly and so will you."

"I don't understand. Won't we be here for the fight?"

"Hard to say. How soon would you guess the two fleets will collide?"

"From what everybody was saying, I would have guessed about a week after they left Lisbon. Now I have to consider that, as you've pointed out, none of the daily trade ships from Spain have shown up for the last two weeks. You said that must mean Philip has stopped all shipping out of Spanish ports, and he would only do that to conceal the fact that his Armada has sailed. How sure are you about such long-range guessing?"

"I'm sure enough to be very puzzled about why they haven't yet appeared off our coast."

"Could you be wrong?"

"That is among the possibilities," Malachi conceded, "but it is more likely still that they got scattered by some of the regular bad weather in the Bay of Biscay and Sidonia decided to hole up in one of the Biscay ports to reassemble his fleet and do some minor repairs. I imagine they'll be here in another week just as you and I are on duty in the Netherlands."

"I find it very hard to believe that they can ask us to miss the biggest battle—"

"They didn't ask. There's work for us there."

"So we'll miss the whole thing."

"That's very likely," Malachi nodded, "but you can read all the reports later, so you won't really miss anything. Get packed. We leave for the Ostend Peace Conference with Parma's people in an hour. We have money to deliver to our soldiers there and messages to convey to our commissioners. Once delivery is made, we may be asked to take some minutes of the meetings if, indeed, they have finally decided on the seating arrangement and the size of the conference room and the shape of the table and the other wonderful minutia which has occupied their serious consideration for the past six weeks."

"Doesn't all that pointless delay make it clear that what everybody is saying is true? That Parma is just leading us on with this peace proposal to keep us off guard while they get ready to attack us?"

"That is very probable," Malachi conceded, "and there is absolutely nothing we can do about it since we are not policy makers. Ours is not to reason why; ours is but to do or suffer the consequences. Drink up and we'll go pack."

William paused beside Sammons and Starkey as he was leaving. "I suppose you boys will be in the thick of it," he murmured unhappily.

"We c'n only hope!" was the cheerful reply.

Chapter 4:
WITH CERVANTES AT THE WINDMILL

Outside Ostend, July 14, 1588

William lifted a loaf of bread, a round of cheese, and two bottles of wine from his pack and set them out on the small table.

"You're a good provider, lad," said Malachi, rubbing his hands. "I hope you didn't have to stoop to stealing."

"Well, let's just say I didn't have to pay for all of it with coin of the realm. A maid at the inn—"

"Yes, yes, spare me the sordid details, but try to appreciate the benefits you obviously enjoy from the ordinary people when we have you dressed up as a gentleman. Just remember we are in a very delicate spot here between the English and Spanish lines, so make every effort not to reveal our location to anybody. What we don't need now is a patrol from either side sniffing around to see what we're up to."

"What are we up to?"

"I'm expecting company, so grab that broom and straighten this place up a bit. It looks like the miller sometimes lives here and sometimes doesn't, and this is the time he doesn't. I'm always amazed that our Office is able to find such uncomfortable rendezvous spots for our meetings. It is the one area in which they are truly gifted."

"This is certainly close and cozy living, but it seems quite livable if you could get used to the noise and the machinery running right down through the middle of the kitchen. Does this moaning and groaning go on all the time?" William put his palm against the hollow, tree-like shaft which plunged from ceiling to floor in the middle of the small kitchen. "I can feel the cogs in there turning."

"Most of the moaning and groaning comes from the gearing system above us when the wind rotates the sail and spins the horizontal shaft behind it. The gears transfer that turning motion onto the vertical shaft you feel inside that post. When you mix those giant stone and wooden gears up there, you are likely to get some noise. Beneath our feet is a lesser gear turning a smaller horizontal shaft which runs out the side of the mill and rotates the outside water wheel to scoop water out of the lake beside us. That water is then transferred by sluice or trench or pipe to a canal beside the lake and run out to one of the nearby rivers for deliverance to the sea, thus creating more farm land for the Dutch."

"Are all the windmills we passed on the way over here pumping water?"

"No. Some are engaged in that centuries-old process of grinding wheat and corn to make flour for bread just as was done in Biblical times, although now—in our advanced industrial age—the grinding is done by a machine instead of by the women of the village. Some mills are grinding other odds and ends or sawing timbers. But water pumping accounts for most of the activity and for most of the mills because draining water is a survival necessity in a land which is lower than the sea. If you are in this country very long, you'll notice that the water-pumping mills are often set up in a series quite close to each other because of the limitation on the lifting power of the water wheels."

"What limitation? It seems to me these windmills could go on forever, day and night."

"If the cups on the wheel are too hefty, or if the diameter of the wheel is too great, the weight of the water they attempt to raise will offset the lifting power of the mill and stop the mechanism—especially in lighter winds—so generally they limit the lifting power of each mill to five feet. That means if the Dutch are draining a fifteen-foot lake, they must use three mills next to each other but with a five-foot difference in the elevation of the water wheels so the lowest one can lift the water five-feet to feed the middle mill to be passed on to the higher one and transported from there to the sea. Wind and water have been the story of the Dutch since they started draining this land back about 1400."

"That kind of challenge must require clever engineers and very persistent people."

"It does that and more. It serves to make them ingenious. When you're here awhile you'll notice that many of the windmill sails that are not moving have been left braked in different positions, and you'll soon learn that those positions send messages to the whole community just as sailors at sea sometimes use flags to send messages to other ships."

"Messages how?"

"Windmills are always placed in cleared, prominent positions to catch the uninterrupted wind; therefore, they are usually in the sight of everybody in the community. By tradition the four arms turn counter-clockwise because the sail cloth is mounted to the right of the wooden arm so that the miller may hold onto the arm with his left hand while he climbs the frame to maintain the sailcloth with his good right hand. During storms the sail must be tied down so the wind doesn't overpower the braking system and permit the mechanism to run wild."

"So everybody in the community knows which way the sail turns?"

"Right, so when they see a windmill with the up-most sail braked just short of the vertical position, about one-o-clock on the face of a clock, they know a festivity is in order because that is the 'coming' position and indicates that a wedding or birthday or holiday is about to be celebrated."

"And if the upper sail stops just past the vertical, it's a downer of some kind?"

"Very good. You show some poetic insight at times. If the sail is stopped at about the eleven-o-clock or the 'going' position, it means mourning or sadness of some kind. If the sail is stopped with one arm in the vertical or 'cross' position, it means the mill has finished the work at hand and needs more wheat or corn to be ground. If it stops with the upper sails of equal height in the X position, it usually means a skilled craftsman like a carpenter is needed for repairs. The variations are too numerous to mention, but that's enough to give you some idea of how clever the Dutch are."

"Yes. Very clever and very hospitable, which leads one to wonder why they didn't offer us a less noisy assignation point."

"This spot really was assigned to us by Whitehall, which must feel that the continual racket will prevent us from being overheard when we conduct—"

Malachi was interrupted by a pounding at the door accompanied by a shout: "Saludo amigos! It is I, Miguel Cervantes."

"Good Lord," William cried, "A sneaky Spaniard!" He grabbed the broom, flung open the door and fell upon the enemy with such vigor that he drove him backward and down, still desperately clutching the bag he carried with his one good arm.

"Stop! Stop! You fool," cried Malachi as he rushed to pull the broom from the flailing arms of his apprentice.

"He's an underhanded Spaniard, Malachi! Use your sword! Get him before he gets us!"

"No, no, lad! Hold your fire! This is my good friend, Senor Cervantes. Get out of the way and let me help him up." Malachi suited action to words and pulled the Spaniard to his feet and dusted him off while he apologized. "I'm sorry, Miguel. I'm afraid young people today tend to be precipitous because they watch too many stage plays. I'll keep a halter on him from now on."

Cervantes had trouble catching his breath, but he finally muttered, "You keep some very odd company, Malachi, in the midst of such a delicate operation."

He put down the bag he was carrying and, holding himself as erect and stiff as a weary traveler could manage, he turned to address William. "And you, whoever you turn out to be, need to know just who it is you have subjected to such an insult, so take a good look. *The man you see here with the aquiline countenance, the chestnut hair, the smooth, untroubled brow, the bright eyes, the hooked yet well proportioned nose, the silvery beard that less than a score of years ago was golden, the big mustache, the small mouth, the teeth that are scarcely worth mentioning, the body of medium height, neither tall nor short, the high complexion that is fair rather than dark, the slightly stooping shoulders, and the somewhat heavy build, this I may tell you is the author..commonly called Miguel de Cervantes Saavedra. He was a soldier for many years and a captive for five and a half, an experience that taught him patience in adversity. In the navel battle of Lepanto he lost his left hand as a result of a harquebus shot, a wound which, however unsightly it may appear, he looks upon as beautiful, for the reason that it was received on the most memorable and sublime occasion that past ages have known or those to come may hope to know'."* Cervantes paused and then snarled, "I trust you can now understand how deeply I resent your belittling reference to me as 'an underhanded Spaniard'!" [13]

"Sorry about that," William said as he brushed off Cervantes' doublet. "Who held you captive for all those years?"

"The Barbary pirates," Cervantes snapped, opening the bag he had carried in. "But none of that matters now. What's important at this moment, Malachi, is that your favorite Madeira seems to have survived the onslaught, so let's toast our reunion and—" he paused to glare at William— "worry about other things later."

"Excellent idea, amigo," Malachi agreed while he busied himself opening a bottle and filling glasses for himself and Cervantes while explaining, "Please forgive my apprentice, Miguel, for his belligerent behavior. I think your Spanish greeting startled him. I guess I should have prepared him better for your appearance."

The two friendly foes toasted each other for having survived another year as successful civil servants and then exchanged small purses, which they clinked merrily.

"May I ask," inquired William, nodding at the purses, "how long you gentlemen have maintained this rather unique but obviously lucrative relationship while in the uniforms of nations which are warring with each other?"

"Such arrangements benefit our countries and help to feed and cloth their agents," Malachi pointed out. "I sometimes think that only agents themselves know how slippery this world can be for people who are on this job. Please don't forget that we live at a time when a country may be Catholic one day and Protestant the next, where subsidies may be granted one day and revoked the next, and where orders, once given—"

"And where honest men may be thrown into the dungeon by the Inquisition at any hour of any day," Cervantes added.

"A man needs to be loyal to something," Malachi said, still addressing William, "and as long as that loyalty is returned, a man would be a fool not to share it. Among older agents, there is an understanding that we will exchange enough information so our masters will feel good about paying for it. We don't trade secrets, you understand—there's nothing traitorous going on here—just information which will become public knowledge a week or two later without our efforts."

"Why should anybody pay for it then?" asked William, sulking slightly.

"First sight of any policy change is valuable information for office-holders who want to be on top of things with their response when public announcements are made, so they are willing to pay for early notification. In effect, Whitehall pays Miguel and Madrid pays me, so this exchange really has the under-the-table approval of both our governments, and sometimes it's the only real money we see in a year's time, so here's to payday!" Malachi raised his glass in one hand and his purse in the other to lead a salute to mutually beneficial arrangements. Cervantes raised his glass with his one good arm and joined him enthusiastically.

"I noticed the purse you got from Senor Cervantes was somewhat bigger than the one he got from you," William said to Malachi, "Are the coins so different in size?"

Cervantes answered, "Dios! You are new to the business. Philip always pays more than Elizabeth. Every monarch on the continent pays more than your Queen. As a matter of fact, among people in the business she is called a 'parsimonious bitch' for good reason."

William bolted to his feet and dropped his hand to his dagger, "How dare you say that about our Queen!"

Malachi rose quickly to place a restraining hand on William's shoulder. "Whoa," he commanded. "Steady up there, young man. You've already caused enough trouble today. This is shop talk for professionals. Save your anger for the people who are trying to kill us. Miguel is simply reporting what the Continent says of Elizabeth, so cool off or take a walk."

"No, no, amigo," Cervantes protested. "It pleases me to witness a little chivalry in this world even if it be misdirected. The young man is quite right although he does seem a bit overcharged. Our talk grows too rough at times, and probably our minds along with it. I'm glad to be reminded that I should make a habit of thinking more often in chivalric terms."

"It might not hurt either of us," Malachi conceded.

Cervantes' voice struck a note of exquisite politeness. "Is your apprentice aware that the King of Spain and the Queen of England know each other personally and therefore have few illusions about the financial tendencies of the other?"

"You will soon discover, Miguel," Malachi chuckled, "that William's lack of knowledge is formidable despite my Herculean efforts to augment it for him."

"Know each other how?" William asked.

"Philip became your Queen's brother-in-law when he married Elizabeth's half-sister, Queen Mary, back in 1553. I believe you English call her 'Bloody Mary' in view of her attempts to educate your Protestant heretics. During his stay in England, Philip met several times with Princess Elizabeth, and you can bet those two took each other's measure very closely. When Mary died and Elizabeth was crowned in 1558, there was talk of Philip and Elizabeth marrying, and our King asked only that your Queen turn Catholic, so the union would be blessed in the eyes of God. Your Queen played her usual yes-no game with the proposal for some time, but finally the Spanish ambassador had to report to Philip: *'She says she cannot marry Your Majesty because she is a heretic'.*" [15]

"Was there any discussion of your King changing over to our true religion?" William ventured.

Cervantes glared at him. "In a sense, the Armada effort is really a kind of delayed lover's spat. Philip and Elizabeth have succeeded in dancing around each other militarily for many years now. Either country could have gone to war at anytime for the offences committed by the other: the seizure of merchant ships, the confiscation of precious cargoes, the letters of reprisal, the burning of Cadiz, and the English raids in the West Indies. But such incidents have always been handled diplomatically between England and Spain because diplomats are cheaper to maintain than armies and navies."

"And just as expendable when the time comes," Malachi added.

"Oh, si. Running the foreign diplomat out of the country has come to equal the opening broadside in establishing hostilities."

"As Mendoza learned when he was sent packing from England for his part in the Throckmorton plot five years ago."

Cervantes tilted back his stool in a burst of laughter. "And Mendoza awaits his revenge in Paris at this very moment. He thirsts for it! When you insult a Spaniard, you have an enemy for life." He fixed a hard eye on William and said, "It will help you to stay healthy if you remember that. An enemy for life!"

"But if Philip was rejected by Elizabeth thirty years ago," William said, ignoring the comments of the Spaniard, "why did it take him so long to react? Can't he take a hint? Is his brain slow?"

"Hey, you!" Cervantes protested with a touch of tired anger.

"Me?"

"Si! You need to appreciate what has worked in favor for your country. We used to call our king 'Philip the Profound,' because he operated so prudently, but this quarrel with your queen has stung him so deeply that he has cast off all caution. It was always obvious to his advisors that he had a soft spot in his heart for Elizabeth because he permitted her liberties that he would not accept from any other European monarch or from Drake and all the rest. He always accepted her transgressions with a grim smile, but all of that changed the evening she decided to attend the play with the Venetian ambassador."

"What play?"

"An obscure political play in which Philip was characterized as a ridiculous figure at whom Elizabeth was seen to laugh. The play didn't matter, countries sport each other on a regular basis. The fact that the Queen laughed at him didn't matter that much: those two had shared such laughs many years before. The fact, however, that the Venetian ambassador saw her enjoying a play which ridiculed the King of Spain did matter. Those Venetians are avid communicators, you know, and before a month was out, every royal court in Europe had the story, including Madrid. Something very deep inside Philip hardened at that time."

"He became Elizabeth's enemy?"

Cervantes nodded. "Si. He could no longer privately assume that he was the back-stage protector of your fascinating but unpredictable queen. He had to acknowledge the truth of what his military advisors had been telling him for many years: Elizabeth had completely lost respect for him. He is still grim when Elizabeth is mentioned, but now the smile is gone. He threw caution to the wind and put this Grand Enterprise in motion with an energy and zeal which you might not have expected even in a much younger man. For three years now, Spain has marched to the drumbeat of preparing the fleet. Every community in the land has responded with supplies for the Armada and with a substantial, if not whole-hearted, enthusiasm for the sacrifices they must absorb to teach you heretics a lesson."

"I think it remains to be seen who teaches who a lesson," William huffed.

"The only point here is that Philip is an accomplished and admirable monarch for whom I feel the greatest loyalty. He is not to be belittled in my presence if we are to spend a civilized evening together. In short, you don't punch my Philip and I won't pinch your Elizabeth. There is still much of interest to be exchanged about policy-makers without making it personal."

"I only said—"

Cervantes stiffened in a tense arch with his head held high and his good hand on his dagger. "The rules are now clear, and honor demands action be taken if they are not observed, so be very careful, comprende?"

"I still don't understand," William persisted, "why it took King Philip so long—"

Malachi interrupted as Cervantes rose swiftly to his feet. "William, take your broom outside and stand guard while Miguel and I talk over some very secret matters. Alert us immediately if there are any intruders in the neighborhood." William shouldered his broom and marched outside.

"Now tell me, Miguel, about this latest excommunication. Did the Church have you thrown in jail for the same reason as before?"

"Pretty much so," Cervantes nodded, "and although I was quickly freed this time, it leaves me uneasy when I consider that my release came either through divine intervention or through some fortunate clerical error. Getting out of bed each morning, a man can only wonder which way his life will turn when those Inquisition idiots open their record books to determine which among us are not most pleasing to God. The truth of the matter is that those asses wouldn't recognize the true God if he pissed in their ear! They are cruel rather than merciful, arrogant rather than humble, unforgiving rather than charitable, and oppressors rather than defenders—I could go on, but you get the idea. They are, in short, the exact opposite of everything I admire in Christianity."

"Hold on now," Malachi grinned. "Don't you mean that you admire in Catholicism?"

"No, no. Mine is the classical philosophical view," Cervantes insisted. "I include you heretic English bastards as Christians too if it helps make my argument."

"And our Puritans," Malachi grinned, "do you also regard them as Christians?"

"Too much so," Cervantes laughed. "They are as willing as the Inquisition to burn or tear apart any who do not toe their mark. They may be few in number at the moment, but their constant growth is a sure sign of trouble down the road for your government. You may yet hear much more from your Wentworth fellow before he's done."

"Yes," Malachi said. "We recently did hear more and had to pop the man into the tower for a time, so you see Spain is not the only country that locks up its troublemakers. But it seems to me you've made a regular habit of being thrown out of the church and into the jail, Miguel."

"Only twice so far, gracias a Dios. It's a disquieting feeling, let me assure you. Spiritually, you are left very much on your own. The only good thing about my futile soul-searching to justify my excommunication is that the effort does drive me to drink." Cervantes paused for a healthy swig from his glass.

"I'd say you are still very Catholic if you are working so hard to find reasons to excuse your Church's actions," Malachi observed.

"I'm not really doing that," Cervantes said. "I'm only trying to find a clear passage for my thinking, and that's why I welcomed this trip north to contact you. As soon as the Church excommunicates a person, they set the Inquisition on his trail, and you know how those ecclesiastical agencies are. If one doesn't get you, the other will. I've been 'under observation' as they like to call it, since they threw me out. You know as well as I do, amigo, that any man under constant surveillance is likely to end up in jail for one reason or another. Christ himself was driven to his crucifixion gesture out of realizing that we are all sinners. Being followed makes me so self-conscious that I end up doing foolish things. I spend time peering out of windows and around corners when I should be adjusting my trousers before going out in public."

"I assume you didn't lead your observers here," Malachi said.

"My years as a slave of the Barbary pirates did wonders for my ability to employ deceptive actions to mislead any company which I find oppressive. I arrived here un-accompanied and relaxed for this meeting—until your associate greeted me in such a rude manner."

"Being wounded at the front will give you something to boast about when you get back home," Malachi chuckled.

"Si, I know all about returning home from the front as a wounded hero. I was born, to judge by my inclination to arms, under the influence of the planet Mars. Mars befriended me; I acquired the name of a good soldier. The emperor distinguished me, I made friends, and above all, I learned liberality and good breeding, one learns this in the school of a Christian soldier. I returned home with riches and honours, intending to remain some days there in order to enjoy the society of my parents who were both living and of the friends who expected me. But that which men call fortune, for my part I know not what she is, envious of my tranquility, turning the wheel she is said to hold, threw me down from the summit on which I had been placed into the depths of misery wherein you see me now." [16]

"What would you say went wrong?"

"It's this business of fitting into the everyday work scene and earning my twelve reales a day that I have difficulty with. The King's Purveyor General's personal Dep-uty himself put the rod of authority into my hand to gather fodder for the fleet. I have the authority to break locks, search homes, confiscate goods, and do almost anything to get an accurate picture of the supplies available. Naturally, we don't use rough stuff unless we have to. We nearly always manage to strike a commercial bargain for the goods, but the problem begins when we have to pay with a royal promissory note because Philip is using what little ready-money there is to get the ships ready to sail."

"Where in the world does all that gold and silver from the New World go?" Mala-chi exclaimed.

"A lot of it goes to the money-lenders, of course, because we never seem to get caught up, and the military takes most of what's left. We have armies and navies all over Europe, don't forget, and in the New World too."

"Yes, indeed," Malachi grinned, "but Drake found you spread a little thin over there, didn't he?"

Cervantes shrugged, "Outposts get battered. That's what they're for. Early warn-ing systems. Your Captain Drake has cut a pretty picture for a time, I'll admit, but he'll run out of luck one of these days just as all pirates do. His day is coming, quien sabe?"

"To Captain Drake's big day then," Malachi proposed and they clinked glasses to their separate views. "Tell me, Miguel, did you have any training before they sent you out as a purveyor?"

"They warned me at the training sessions in Seville that I should attempt to cultivate national and civic pride in each community before I strike a commercial bargain for the grain, fodder and oil. I was told not to use the heavy hand of confiscation except under extreme circumstances. The idea was to get people in a good enough mood to accept the King's promise of future payment for this year's supplies. I remember my first day on the job, I made a very impassioned and pretty plea to the city fathers of Sorrento to respond to the King's call for a crusade against you wicked heretics, and I was shocked to find the city fathers visibly unmoved by a performance which I rated, modestly enough, as not quite brilliant, but certainly bright enough to move the average audience."

"They had heard it all before?"

"Worse. They had not yet been paid for last year's crops."

"Nobody mentioned that at the training sessions?"

"Not that I recall," Cervantes muttered. "Anyway, everyone is reluctant to pile one bad deal atop another, and I don't just mean the town fathers either. The Church owns most of the granaries in Spain and regularly receives surplus crops as offerings, so they control a great deal of the supplies the fleet needs."

"But if the King says the fleet needs supplies, doesn't the Church have to turn them over to him? What's the problem? Isn't Philip their nominal head?"

"Tut tut," Cervantes chided him. "Even a monarch as absolute as Philip may not move power from his left hand to his right without going through the bookkeeper's bee-hive, which justifies its existence by producing endless scribble which only they can interpret—after they collect a fat fee. Another classic case of the fox taking up residence in the hen house."

"Couldn't Philip just commandeer everything in sight?"

"He could but he might thereby lose the sympathy of the Spanish Catholic Church which could very well turn to Rome for the redressing of their grievances. The Pope would be happy to take them under his wing, and he would certainly support them in any effort to get their property back. Rome and Madrid are in a constant struggle to establish leadership of the Catholic Church. The Church leaders tend to align themselves with whichever ruler permits them to prosper."

"And you don't mean just spiritually, I take it?"

"Si. The claim is always made that spiritual and commercial are the same thing in the Church, but it's very complicated." Cervantes paused for a sip of wine. "The real problem is that the King issues commands at the national level without much regard for the realities of the local level where the bargains must be struck—the wheels within wheels business, the overlapping jurisdictions, the whole complicated mess, which ends up with a man being excommunicated for doing his duty."

"But how could something like that happen?"

"The church authorities of Sorrento absolutely refused to release their grain to me until they collected for the crop they turned over to us last year. Still, I had to meet the quota which Seville had imposed on me for that region, and there was no way of doing it without the grain the Church controlled, so I did what I had to do in order to keep faith with my office: I confiscated the Church grain."

"So you took from Peter to pay Philip, and they bounced you."

"Again! They have some ancient Canonical law which I am charged with breaking whenever I take possession of Church property, so out I go after the local Dominicans characterize my proceedings as being contrary to Divine Law."

"Can't Seville straighten it out?"

Cervantes shrugged. "They've got the same problem all over the country. I suppose they're working on it, who knows? It's hard to get anything done in Seville. They kept me waiting in the outer office for four months to get my purveyor post. I still haven't been paid after a year on the job."

"Egad, man, how do you live?"

"I pay for everything with notes on the government."

"You could get in trouble that way."

"Si!" Cervantes laughed. "But I'll do the job assigned me, come what may, and hope they can straighten it out later."

"You're a good soldier, Miguel," Malachi saluted him. "We're having trouble gearing up too," he admitted. "Big talk in the taverns about how much each community can contribute, but when collection day arrives, we are likely to hear a chorus of far-fetched excuses to mask poor performances. How is your supply thing going generally?"

Cervantes raised his hand. "An exchange! I'll show you mine if you'll show me yours. Spain for England."

They clinked glasses. "A deal. You first."

"Si, compadre. I suppose if I were Purveyor General of Spain instead of a regional magistrate, I would have a clearer view of the whole operation and might be able to shrug off the numerous incidents of spoilage, wastage, and shameless profiteering going on all over my region. The national operation must have a tremendous capacity for absorbing the spoilage which occurs when the carts don't arrive for transport or when the mills don't grind their quota or when the grain rots in the field for lack of granary space. Dios, I've seen enough of that, but I've also seen a steady stream of loaded carts plodding clear across Spain carrying supplies to the fleet, and it is an impressive sight despite the waste."

"They must figure the percentages are in their favor if they can deliver one cart out of each pair."

Cervantes nodded. "So if I were the Purveyor General, I would be very optimistic about supplies piling up on the Lisbon docks. I would even hope your rascally Drake might be tempted to take a shot at them as he did at Cadiz last year. We'd love to see him try to get up the Taugus River into Lisbon harbor. We'd catch him under our shore guns in those long, straight stretches and shoot holes through his fleet and through his damnable reputation and right through his smart arse! Madre de Dios, we'd blow him so high——"

"Calm down, Miguel," Malachi advised. "Have a drink and talk supplies, not Drake."

"Si, we'll get him yet. But you're right, that can wait. At the local level then, it's a little depressing. I spend so much time keeping endless records of every transaction—especially where confiscation is involved—that I don't have time to defend myself against the city fathers and the Church authorities who plot continuously to denounce and excommunicate me in order to save their grain. I don't know how such black-marks will look on my record in years to come, but I can't imagine they will help me earn a government pension anytime soon. As you know, all governments clean house periodically for one reason or another, and the first to go are always those who have been flagged by the prevailing faction. Ten years from now there will be no chance to explain. Those insidious black-marks on my record will be given greater weight than any explanation I am permitted to offer. It really makes a man feel small, while all the time he would simply like to leave a favorable record of his passing."

"Our supply people are always complaining about the burden of book-keeping," Malachi said, "and now you tell me it's a problem in Spain too."

"Si, si. You simply wouldn't believe it," Cervantes shook his head. "*I must pick out the best mills in an area, arrange for grain storage to prevent spoilage, take random test samples of the crop, divide the grain into workable lots, ship it off to the mills at the right time, and keep detailed notes on every movement. Then I must make sure both the Church and City are duly represented to supervise the cleaning and winnowing. We are all required to be present on the threshing room floor during the whole process. We have to weigh not only the wheat and chaff, but the very dust itself. We have to notarize all of these records and send them off to Seville, where copies are made for Madrid.*" [17]

"That must entail some very long workdays."

"It's not the time so much as the aggravation which wears a man down. Ordinarily, as a purveyor, I spend my working hours with men who have not only been arguing with me for days and weeks about quotas and deadlines, but have also fixed critical eyes and ears on my speech and actions to detect any blasphemous or heretical inclinations which I might display. It is not a good fellowship thus assembled, by any gauge, so that even the solitary paperwork is a welcome diversion although it be a wearisome task. Nothing reduces a man's sense of self like being forced to squabble over petty details. So," Cervantes paused again for a sip of wine, "how goes the purveyance game in merry old England?"

Malachi shrugged. "About the same. All communities complain that the quotas which were dictated by the Privy Council are unfair and do not take due account of the ease with which the neighboring communities could provide a bigger share of the grain or guns or men or ships or taxes. Our people are reluctant to respond to what are introduced as temporary impositions for fear that they will be made permanent if the communities do not put up enough of a howl. Unfortunately for the English fleet, the competent and honest, long-time Surveyor of Victuals for the Navy, Edward Baeshe, retired last year and was replaced by James Quarles, who has impressed people early on as being either a knave or a fool for his inability to keep the fleet supplied with fresh food."

"Some profiteering afoot, you think?"

"The jury is still out on that," Malachi nodded. "The truth is that the counties around Plymouth, Devon, and Cornwall are not much given to agriculture, so the pickings are pretty slim for grain and meat in that area. That means that most of the victuals must be shipped around from London, and the weather does not always cooperate in that endeavor. We are lucky, though, that one of Quarles' agents, young Marmaduke Darrell, has been active and alert in gathering supplies and has even spent some of his own money to stockpile things he knows we'll need. Sir John Laughton described the efforts of Darrell by saying he *was scouring the country round, buying up what he could, more like a mess-steward with a market basket than the agent-victualler of a great fleet'.*[18]

Both men enjoyed a chuckle at the image of such a spectacle. "Darell even delivered some supplies to the ships before he received official authorization to do so, but he was reprimanded when his impudence was discovered. Even he, however, has not been able to prevent the one occurrence which turns English mariners surly and sulky."

"Slow pay?"

"Sour beer. The problem of gathering the supplies is so immense that they never end up with enough hops in the right place for proper brewing, so we get great stores of beer that turn sour as soon as the ships clear harbor."

"Si," said Cervantes. "We have the same thing. Some of our wines travel better at sea than others, so Philip issues strict orders on which should be used up first."

"Philip gets involved right down to that level of detail, does he?"

Cervantes laughed. "The King never runs out of suggestions to aid his commanders in carrying out his wishes. No detail is too small for his attention. It is certainly touching that he takes such close care with his kingdom, but it makes slow work of decision making, I'm afraid. I mentioned the four-months wait for my appointment earlier?"

"Dreadful," Malachi agreed. "But now to business. Your message said you had something for me?"

"Si," said Cervantes digging into his back pack and pulling clear a thin roll of manuscript. "You're not going to believe this, but I am about to hand you a complete listing of all the supplies already gathered for the Armada, and a listing of the ships and officers Philip intends to send against you."

"An authoritative listing?"

"From Madrid with Philip's signature."

"None better," Malachi nodded, "unless it's a trick. Tell me, Miguel, have you suddenly come to your senses and switched sides? Does Madrid know you have this listing?"

"Oh, si. You wouldn't get it otherwise," Cervantes smiled. "When Madrid sends official information to every outpost in the Old and New World, they know copies will appear shortly in royal courts throughout Europe. That's the price Philip is willing to pay to make sure his voice is heard throughout his empire, so there can be no misunderstanding about what the boss wants done. We have a lot of security on official documents just as you have, but Dios knows there are always mistakes made, documents lost or misdirected, and men on both sides who broker such information to different governments for a fat fee."

"I've heard," Malachi nodded.

"So they knew this listing would be public knowledge before long—especially since Parma's people have already 'misplaced' a copy—Seville decided to get something out of the early exposure before the list was widely circulated, so they had me bring you this copy to build my credibility with you. Now, of course, you must give me something I can use to show them what a valuable contact you are for us."

Malachi shook his head. "They're all the same. English and Spanish administrators are interchangeable."

Cervantes laughed. "If they only knew how much alike they are, they wouldn't bother distrusting each other so much."

Malachi busied himself with opening the manuscript and noticing the title: *'The most puissant and most happy Fleet of the King of Spain, against the realm of England'.* [19] "Good Lord," he breathed as he read, "these are astounding numbers. *One-hundred-and-fifty ships including sixty-four galleons and eight thousand sailors and twenty thousand soldiers and four thousand noblemen and gentlemen with servants.* How many is that? About thirty-two thousand Spaniards in all even before we count Parma's seventeen thousand regulars coming over from the Low Countries? Awesome!"

Cervantes nodded. "Philip wants you to know that he's not holding back. Every noble house in Spain is sending its best people against you."

"And in addition to the names of the ships, here is a listing of their ordinance, armor, *gunpowder, and the victuals they carry including mountains of bacon, cheese, beans, rice, fish, oil, vinegar and other provisions like sails, hemp, candles, lanterns, spades, shovels, wheels, carts, and baskets. I would have to guess those earth moving tools are the supplies your engineers will need in case they have to build bridges or besiege forts on their march to London. And finally this listing of thousands of names of governors, captains, noblemen, and even of gentlemen volunteers.* Quite incredible."

"It was thought that an official list of those who were deserving would come in handy when the booty of England is distributed," nodded Cervantes.

"That is keen down-stream thinking all right—even if a trifle presumptuous—but I can only imagine the primary purpose of such a listing is to strike fear into the very vitals of any possible opponent to Spain's ambition. Sensible men everywhere will have to confront the image this advertisement brings to mind of a fleet of Spanish warships bobbing about in Lisbon harbor being stocked to the gunnels with munitions enough to attempt whatever Grand Enterprise Philip has in mind. My God, if this proposed fleet is ever fully assembled, it will undoubtedly constitute the greatest naval force the world has ever known!"

"Si," said Cervantes, "and your shock and awe seem to me a very sensible reaction to the plan."

"It is impressively ambitious," Malachi concluded. "And I'll be very surprised if some of England's slow-movers don't get into action when they see the extent of the force that is to come against us. So we're very happy to get this wake-up call, Miguel, and in return, I have for you a copy of the supplies we have already assembled at Dartmoor— which your people can use as a cross-check because we know that our Croft has already turned a copy of this list over to your Mendoza."

"Good. Madrid will like that. They love to cross-check. It makes them feel they have a handle on things."

"Whitehall is the same way," Malachi nodded. "Permit me to ask about your arm. How are things going there?"

"Sore and painful at times but no matter. I still have one healthy sword arm, and I've always felt pleased the Turks didn't shoot off my writing hand at Lepanto or I'd be in a sad fix."

"You've got more writing plans?"

"Si! As you know, I've already done a few minor stage plays. My first novel, *La Galatea*, printed three years ago, was a pastoral piece which I now realize did not best display my humor or my realism, but I do have a major work in mind which still needs some thinking through."

"Ah well, then," Malachi joshed him, "you're in the same position as my apprentice, thinking through what you will write sometime in the future."

Cervantes responded, "I hope you don't mind my being perfectly frank with you, compadre, but your apprentice seems to me like a very odd sort."

"I think you can safely say he is a *medley of good sense and madness,*" [20] Malachi admitted, "although the truth is there's no dealing with him on any level when he has on his antic disposition."

"Good sense and madness, eh?" Cervantes mused. "A medley of such a mix. If a writer happened to have a creative bend, he could strike some dramatic fire with such a character."

"Are you still so inclined?" Malachi asked with a sly smile.

"More than most," Cervantes responded. "I like the madness idea because it gives the writer a great deal of leeway in building suspense to entertain his reader, who doesn't know what the character will do or say next. Of course, it would have to be some kind of systematic madness—really crazy people tell us nothing except that madness exists. A semi-madman, on the other hand, could turn to and fro, back and forth, and react oddly to ordinary circumstances to the amazement of all around him."

"Not crazy all the time, then, only in patches?"

"But I would need to think of something that sets him off."

"Like greed, you mean?"

"Too sordid and common," Cervantes pronounced. "Hard to get reader sympathy if your character is deserving only of contempt."

"Occasional greed, then?"

"No such thing."

"Ruthless ambition?"

"Machiavelli pretty well covered that."

"A religious man, perhaps, caught in an unsavory world," Malachi suggested.

"That has the makings, but we've already heard the monastic point of view from Rabelias and Erasmus and Boccaccio."

"And from Luther and Calvin," Malachi added.

"Amen," Cervantes said as he crossed himself.

"An innocent of some kind, perhaps?" Malachi suggested. "Have him knocked in the head, like my man. Plenty of excuse for explaining things that way."

Cervantes shook his head. "A cheap, shabby device that any author worth his salt should be ashamed to offer to his readers, but I might be driven to such expediency unless I can devise something better. Any more suggestions?"

"That's all the help I can offer you at the moment," Malachi said as he rose from his seat and wandered over to look out the window. "And I now begin to wonder if our abstract discussion of the writing art does you any good since, in the end, you must apply specific words to your foolscap, so it seems to me that these discussions amount to little more than what I observe my young friend doing out there in the yard."

"What?" Cervantes asked and joined Malachi in looking out.

"The young fool is using his broom to joust with the arms of our windmill," Malachi chuckled. "If he's not careful, this machine will catch his broom and knock him on his backside."

"Tilting at windmills!" Cervantes shouted. "Madre de Dios! What a world of imagination he has just opened for me!"

"You must be careful of such revealing comments, amigo," Malachi warned.

"Careful of what? Disclosing the creative process at work?"

"No. The reference to the mother of God in your exclamation. It will always reveal you as a Catholic to careful observers. We Anglicans choose not to make an icon of Mary."

William reentered the kitchen with his broom in two pieces and Malachi greeted him jovially, "Here is our knight-errant now whose latest contribution to the literature of the world is a broken broomstick!"

"And his cap set askew to match his doublet, rumpled by the giant opponent who has bested him." Cervantes egged on the wellspring of humor and the two older men fell into a chorus of laughter.

"It is strange," William said haughtily, "*how hurtful are the tongues of decent men when they are well soaked in alcohol. O God, that men should put an enemy in their mouths to steal away their brains! That we should with joy, pleasance, revel and applause transform ourselves into beasts!* [21] Is this single bottle all that's left? The two of you drank it all up?"

Malachi and Cervantes looked at each other and shrugged. "You would not begrudge us," Malachi explained carefully, "if your experience had permitted you to share our recent discourse. When friends attain such ethereal heights in converse—" he winked at the grinning Spaniard— "the material goods which transported them to that celestial plane are of no concern. If you had been partner to our discussion, you would be wiser for one thing and less thirsty for another. As it stands now, you may have the first draw from the last bottle."

"Thanks very much, indeed," William muttered before inhaling a hefty swig. "I don't suppose there is anything left to eat either?"

Cervantes burst into laughter. "You know," he said to Malachi, "I enjoy this squire of yours despite himself, and I begin to appreciate that his simplistic mind offsets your own free-floating sensibility and brings you back to earth occasionally for some practical considerations. There is a great deal to be said in favor of simple-minded peasant types as companions on the road."

"Just a moment now—" William huffed.

"Did you ask about food?" Cervantes asked slyly.

"Food? Yes, indeed!" William exclaimed. "Is it possible—"

Cervantes held his sides to keep from bursting with laughter. "Did you hear that?" he roared to Malachi, who joined him in guffaws. "Decoyed right out of his sulk by the simple mention of food. He is almost of another species altogether as far as comprehension is concerned, and I can see a lot of benefit in having him remain so. If I were you, I wouldn't be in any hurry to lose his entertainment value by returning him to normal intelligence—if, indeed, he was ever there in the first place."

Malachi wiped the tears from his eyes and pulled himself together. "I also got you that copy of the arrest warrant you asked for." He handed Cervantes a folded paper, which the Spaniard examined quickly.

"Irony of ironies," Cervantes chuckled. "In this particular case, Malachi, you have better connections on my native soil than I do. I couldn't sneak a copy of my arrest warrant out of Madrid without re-arousing some very unwelcome official interest in my guilt or innocence about something I don't remember which happened nearly twenty years ago. You, however, just snap your fingers across the seas and the deed is done. I'm very glad you were able to get this for my family record without fuss because I don't really need any more inquiry from either the government or the Church. It occurs to me that I have not profited in the past when they have chosen to make their interest in me personal enough to come and visit me."

"Would you say it is your memory that has let you down," William asked, "or is this a more serious lapse?"

Cervantes frowned. "I beg your pardon?"

"When you said that you could not remember stabbing Antonio de Segura to death in a fight brought about by a duel challenge in Madrid in 1569, as charged by this official document—which, indeed, I have read—did you mean your memory had failed you in the intervening years, or did you mean that the incident seemed so unimportant and common, that you choose not to make a special memory of it?"

"Kill a man and not remember?" Cervantes frowned. "You have yet to see battle, young man. I simply meant that I didn't know the next morning what had transpired on that fatal occasion, and I didn't know anymore about it the next week when they charged me with the murder. I did remember there was no duel involved. The authorities just made that up to explain the unexplainable."

"What unexplainable?"

Cervantes shrugged. "All I remember of that evening is that it started with drinks and laughter amongst recent acquaintances, and ended with shouts and curses in a dark byway where swords were drawn and blood spilled in a general melee. Nobody knows who did what to whom in that inky tumult. I was myself stabbed brutally through one shoulder and lost considerable blood in the adventure, but I didn't notice anybody being charged with assault on my person, did you?"

"No, we just have this one arrest-warrant against you, but I couldn't help but chuckle a bit at the funny quirk of fate the warrant embodied."

"Quirk of fate?" Cervantes inquired.

"Yes, it struck me how hard it is for people to avoid their destiny, almost like that Greek story of Oedipus. In addition to calling for your arrest, this warrant ordered your right hand be chopped off. By running off to avoid arrest in 1569, you managed to evade that fate which, however, finally caught up with you, although in a left-handed way, of course—two years later at the Battle of Lepanto."

Cervantes looked closely at William. "Si, funny quirk indeed," he muttered. "I didn't much like your expression that I 'ran off' to avoid arrest, young man. What I did do was reach an intellectual decision about policy makers generally and, acting on that estimate, I removed myself from their jurisdiction."

"Oh, that's different. What decision?"

"It has always surprised me that ruling powers feel so free to nominate culprits on flimsy evidence under the pretext of keeping their society well-ordered, as they like to say, but actually to conceal the pact they all eventually hold with the dark powers."

"Really? Satanic, you mean?"

"No other explanation," Cervantes shrugged. "How could the civil authorities possibly know who stabbed who on that murky night when even the participants were rendered sightless by the impenetrable darkness unless those authorities consulted with the occult?"

"Did you mention your satanic theory to the authorities when they came to pick you up?"

"I didn't wait around for them. I skipped off to Italy for several years. Had I been picked up, I doubt if I would have opened that particular line of speculation with them, because they are humorless to a man and would regard such a suggestion as dangerous lunacy at best and heretical utterance at worst. Prison or the stake would be their predictable response to such a line of thinking. Government people are so busy maintaining civil order by pin-pointing malefactors and evil-doers, they have little time for self appraisal and none at all for confronting the complexities of justice."

"Nominate a culprit and the problem is solved."

"That's the policy," Cervantes nodded. "A point of view only too prominent with the authorities in your London as well as in Madrid and Rome."

"What was the big attraction in Italy?"

"Everything! I liked all of it. *I'll never forget the beauties of Naples, the feasts of Palermo, the abundance of Milan, the banquets dear to the Lombards, and the succulent meals served in all the inns of the peninsula. Oh, those wonderful chickens, pigeons, ham and sausages!* [22] They certainly compare favorably with the cold slab of cod we are lucky to get at any Spanish inn."

William licked his lips. "I very much admire your highly-selective memory. Did you get over to Rome at all?"

Cervantes nodded. "*I was very deeply moved by my visit to the Eternal City. Just as from the claws of the lion, we can intuit his bulk and his ferocity, so does Rome manifest herself in her fragmented marbles, in her mutilated statues, in her crumbling arches, in her ruined baths, in her magnificent amphitheatres and in the infinite relics of the bodies of martyrs who have been interred in this city.*" [23]

"Sounds like some first-class civic neglect to me," William observed. "The baths are gone too, you say? Too bad. I had looked forward to a real Roman bath at least once in my life, but as is so often the case when I set my mind on something—"

"They were destroyed hundreds of years ago."

"Small consolation for a bitter disappointment," William said. "I had planned to make a real occasion of taking that bath, of getting all dressed up in my finest clothing to show that an Englishman's respect for the ancient cultures has not gone to sleep."

"Finest clothing, indeed!" Cervantes chuckled. "Gathered, no doubt, from the ends of the Earth. Instead of cultivating a distinctive national dress of your own, you English are so lacking in style that you are forced to steal the oddments of your attire from every country in Europe with a touch or two from the Turks thrown in. Your own Thomas Dekker in his *Seven Deadly Sins of London*, tells us, '*The Englishman's dress is like a traitor's body that hath been hanged, drawn, and quartered, and is set up in various places; his cod-piece is in Denmark, the collar of his doublet and the belly in France; the wing and narrow sleeve in Italy; the short waist hangs over a Dutch butcher's stall in Utrecht; his huge slops speak Spanishly. And thus we that mock every nation for keeping of one fashion, yet steal patches from every one of them to piece out our pride*'."

"The worst job of borrowing we ever did was when we lifted that damnable ruff from your people," Malachi growled.

"The ruff from Spain?" William said. "I didn't know that."

"They are a nuisance in bed," Cervantes laughed.

"Obviously, you remain a gentleman until quite late in the evening," Malachi chuckled. "I was thinking, though, that it's very difficult to play your cards close to the chest while peering over that one-foot rampart. A single night of card playing in company always leaves me with a neck-crimp next morning. It occurs to me such inconvenience is altogether too high a price to pay to remain fashionable, especially when the pain comes on top of my customary losses—but I seem powerless to change anything."

"Oh, no, you're not going to lure me into another game of cards with that 'customary losses' enticement," Cervantes declared. "I'm always impressed by how ready you acquisitive English are to strip a poor working man of his meager rewards, but I refuse to fall for your traps and snares this time and fully intend to return home with my payment intact."

Malachi drew back in mock shock. "It's particularly impressive to be labeled 'acquisitive' by the subject of a King who has spent the last forty years systematically looting the gold and silver from half the world. Yes, that accusation from that particular source really cuts deep."

"It is God's way of financing His good works," Cervantes explained.

"You're sure then that God Himself is a Catholic?" William asked.

"God a Catholic? What are you talking about? It's the same thing!" Cervantes drew a deep breath and then addressed Malachi directly. "No matter how well a society works otherwise, they all seem to produce a surplus of these simple-minded young men who feel their arrogant questions can unseat the spiritual tranquility already solidified in the minds of thoughtful men."

"And when they're not busy casually casting doubts on the beliefs of perfect strangers, those striplings spend half their time wenching," Malachi added, "half their time gambling, half their time attending plays, and then over-indulge themselves in that wonderful theater of erotic frolic which they call sleep. I sometimes wonder what good they are at all."

"Very insightful," agreed Cervantes. "Your arithmetic may be a trifle wobbly, but your characterization is precise. It's obvious your apprentice is not fooling you one bit. He's so simple that he reminds me very much of a servant I have back home. *Sometimes of so acute a simplicity that it is no small enjoyment to guess whether he is simple or cunning. He has roguish tricks which condemn him as a knave, and blundering ways which confirm him a fool. He doubts everything and yet believes everything; when I imagine he is crashing head-foremost into folly, he bobs up with some shrewd or witty thing which sends him shouting up to the skies.*" [24]

"That answers my big question," Malachi smiled. "The young are here so that the more mature among us may enjoy poking fun at them while they ignore us completely. But now that it's dark, Miguel, I must break off and dispatch this information to the English camp down the road. I can only imagine Madrid would want their intimidating list to reach Whitehall as soon as possible. I'll only be gone a short time. Why don't you rest a little, and we'll swap stories when I get back. You too, William. Take a nap. Or must I take you with me to insure peace and harmony?"

William grunted as he curled up on the bench. "Egad, Malachi, do you think me an argumentive bumpkin?"

But when Malachi returned an hour later, he was greeted by Cervantes pacing outside the mill. "You better get as much work out of that upstart apprentice as you can tonight, because when morning comes, I'm going to teach him some manners with my sword."

Malachi shook his head as William appeared in the doorway. "You two better taper off before you lose your reason entirely. We are not so secure in this location that you can permit personal quarrels to put us at further risk, so forget about the argument, whatever it is."

"I've heard all about the Spanish temper, and now I get to see it," William testified.

"Dios, I'll kill him yet!" Cervantes shouted. "You better spend your few remaining hours in sincere apology to your Maker, young man, and make some attempt to shorten the term of your eternal damnation." He turned to Malachi. "Do you happen to have a whetstone handy, Malachi? The point of my sword could use a little attention."

"I'm really surprised it has gone this far," said Malachi. "My apprentice usually gets along famously with all company."

"Does he call them names?" Cervantes growled through clenched teeth. "Does he openly insult them and their family, or does he reserve that special treatment for Spanish citizens?"

"I suspect whatever problem you're having is mostly in translation, Miguel. After all, your English isn't really that good, and William doesn't always make sense in his native tongue either. If you'll just give me a minute to catch my breath, I'll be happy to mediate whatever dispute you assume has arisen."

"It's too late for that. The insult has been offered, and as soon as I locate my gauntlet, I intend to fling it full in his face."

Malachi turned to his apprentice. "How did you manage this one? What did you say?".

"Nothing. It came out of the blue. I still don't know why he's so upset. I can only say that you have some very odd friends."

"I was simply trying to explain to him," Cervantes said, "the plight of the literary artist in Spain, why it is so hard for a writer to make any money unless his name is Lope de Vega—who relies mostly on quantity for his income—in his mid-twenties, that man has already written dozens of plays. But the sincere writer who is pursuing quality rather than quantity has a tough job living off his writing. When I explained that to him, I didn't expect sympathy, you understand, perhaps a little understanding from a brother in poverty, but what I got was the scoffing of a base-born scoundrel whom I can only characterize as an *Ill-mannered, vulgar, ignorant, ill-spoken, foul-tounged, insolent…… audacious back-biter!*" [25]

"He gets that way sometimes," Malachi confessed.

"Ill-spoken?" William shouted. "I don't know that I'd call attention to any deficiency in language skills if I were you, Senor Cervantes. I realize you are speaking in a foreign tongue, but still—"

Malachi held up a mollifying hand. "At ease, if you please, gentlemen. You are already so far into dispute that my ears are beginning to rattle. It serves no worthwhile purpose to add fuel to the fire. Let us seek a resolution instead."

"At dawn he shall find his final resolution," Cervantes promised.

"Be sensible, Miguel. I know there are hidalgoes and cabalaroes and even Grandees who like to join their kitchen staff in the wringing of chicken necks and butchering of ducks, but surely you are not among that blood-thirsty group?"

"He insults everything I stand for," Cervantes insisted, "and there is no solution other than he die in disgrace at dawn."

Malachi nodded. "Very intelligent to set a tough and inflexible bargaining position to start things off, but don't forget, my old friend, there are other considerations here in addition to Spanish honor."

"Considerations?"

"Practical considerations. I will have nobody to cart my luggage home if you dispatch my helper. Not a major issue, I'll admit, but still, in terms of sheer practicality and outright inconvenience—"

"I can see your point, Malachi, and I have no desire to trouble you personally, but some satisfaction is still required for the grievous insult which that vulgar person—"

Malachi interrupted in a soothing fashion. "I'm sure we can work something out once we learn the exact nature of the insult."

"I was explaining the ins and outs of the Spanish literary scene to him, and I had just finished enumerating the four basic reasons why it is so difficult for a proper writer to prosper in my country—"

"Sounds innocent enough."

"Until he offered a fifth reason," Cervantes fairly hissed.

"It was one you had overlooked," William explained, "and since you were examining the reasons so closely, I thought in all fairness, you should include the possibility that you have no talent."

"Talent!" Cervantes shouted as he lurched to his feet. "Talent, you say! Why I have more talent in this little finger—" he held up his bandaged stump. "Ah, well, this other little finger then—more talent than any misbegotten son of an English harpy possesses in his whole body!"

"Now, now, Miguel," Malachi said gently, "we have maintained a friendly and profitable relationship for many years because we have had the good sense to stay clear of serious ethnic slurs, and up until now we have always been sensible enough to leave our mothers out of it. Much may be said in jest, I know, but—"

"Sorry, Malachi. You're right, of course, but if there is anything in this world that curdles my spleen, it is a young, arrogant, know-nothing, who professes literary ambitions and presumes to pass a caustic and unfeeling judgment on those of us who have already experienced public acclaim for our writings, and who compares word-for-word his so-called writings with my published works. I'm a little hazy on what constitutes literary merit in England, but I personally do not regard half-finished sonnets as an accomplishment worth flaunting."

"Oh, he read those, did he?"

"The height of inanity," Cervantes shook his head. "I've never had an experience like that before, bewildering and repulsive at the same time, but once was enough for me. If he tries that stuff again, Malachi, no power on this earth will stop me from—"

"Now, now, Miguel, we are seeking a solution here. Let's attempt to bend our energies in that direction, shall we? It seems to me the crux of the problem is literary merit, so let's work from there." He pulled his pack toward him. "And see what I brought back from the English camp. Not as fine as your Madeira, but quite adequate. And more bread and cheese for you, William. If you mind your manners. And apologize."

"Food? Yes, I apologize," said William as he reached for the pack while Malachi opened one of the bottles of wine and poured.

"What solution do you suggest?" grumbled Cervantes, taking a glass.

"You two can duel with words instead of with swords. You each claim some literary ability along with some knowledge of rhetorical devices, so let's put your skills to the test."

"Against him?" Cervantes snorted. "Professional against amateur? He would be better served on the end of my sword."

"Don't be too sure," Malachi said. "I've seen him work. Nothing organized, you understand, but his off-the-cuff stuff is sometimes pretty good."

"We'll see," Cervantes smirked. "What do you have in mind?"

"I'll call out some literary device and you each supply me with an original example as quickly as you can."

"A timed thing?" William asked.

"No pressure," Malachi said. "Take a full ten minutes if you need it in preparation. Your entry will be judged strictly on originality, sincerity, and aptness of thought."

"I'm ready," said Cervantes.

"Personification," Malachi announced.

"What's that?' William inquired.

"When you give to an abstract idea or an inanimate object the properties of a person," Malachi explained.

"I'm not sure."

"Watch me," Cervantes said and struck a pose. *"O fatal poverty, why do you insist on persecuting gentlemen and well-born souls more than other people? Why do you oblige them to smoke their shoes for lack of wax, and wear the same threadbare garment, odd buttons of silk hair, and even glass? Why must their ruffs be, for the most part, pleated and not starched? Wretched is the poor gentleman who, to ginger up his honour starves his body, and fasts unseen with his door locked; then putting on a brave face, sallies forth into the street picking his teeth, though that is an honorable hypocrisy, seeing that he has eaten nothing and thus has naught to pick! Wretched is he whose honour is extremely shy, and who thinks that at a league's distance people can see the patch on his shoe, the sweat stains on his hat, the threadbareness of his clothes, and even the cravings of his famished belly."* [26] Cervantes bowed to his small audience.

"It seems to me you strayed from the personification of poverty—although, I admit, the picture is touching," said Malachi thoughtfully. "Would you care to say more about poverty itself?"

"Come now," Cervantes objected. "We were just starting a new thing, and I volunteered to go first for the sake of illustration. Let's see what our youthful contender has to offer before you are allowed to tax my effort."

"Quite right. Good principle," Malachi nodded. "No taxation without representation."

"I think I've got it," William said. "How's this? *Tomorrow and tomorrow, and tomorrow, creeps in this petty pace from day to day, to the last syllable of recorded time; And all our yesterdays have lighted fools the way to dusty death. Out, out brief candle! Life's but a walking shadow, a poor player that struts and frets his hour upon the stage, and then is heard no more."* [27]

"Pretty cute," Cervantes observed, "slipping that metered verse in there. Malachi, you will recall when judgment is passed that your instructions did not call for metered personification."

"I'll disregard it entirely," Malachi assured him.

"And I hope you noticed that his whole piece was little more than an extended mixed metaphor."

"Oh, be fair now, Miguel. He clearly had the candle as life. I'm ready to lean his way a little on the first contest since he stuck more closely to the subject although I must admit you both adjusted nicely to the structure of the competition. I must warn you, however, that each of you needs to work much more within the directions I spell out hereafter." Malachi paused to sample his wine. "Ready?"

Both men leaned forward and nodded their readiness.

"Argumentation," Malachi announced.

"Excellent choice," Cervantes said. "It permits me to return to the discussion I was having with your baggage-man when he ended all civil discourse by casting such—"

"Perhaps," Malachi interrupted, "in the common interest of reconciliation, it were best not to characterize past statements in an inflammatory fashion. Let us just steer around them." Malachi wiggled his hand like a fish to illustrate.

Miguel Cervantes suddenly shouted "*Away with those who say that letters win more fame than arms!*" [28]

"That isn't exactly what I said," William corrected him.

"*Since, then, arms as well as letters requires mind, consider which of the two minds is exerted most, the scholar's or the warrior's.*"

"There's no way of measuring such abstractions." William murmured.

Malachi shushed him speedily and waved Cervantes to continue.

"*I speak of human letters, whose end is to regulate distributive justice, and give to every man his due; to apply good laws and cause them to be strictly observed, an end most certainly generous and exalted, and worthy of high praise, but not so glorious as the aim of arms, which is peace, the greatest blessing man can enjoy in this life. This peace is the true end of war, and by war and arms I mean the same thing.*"

"Wait a minute now, you're mixing me up. Did I just hear you say that war was peace?"

"If you interrupt again, my boy, you will be in danger of disqualification and forfeiture," warned Malachi.

Cervantes smiled. "*If we admit this truth, that the end of war is peace, and in this it excels the end of letters, let us consider the physical toils of the scholar and the warrior and see which are greater.....The hardships of the student are, first of all poverty, not that all are poor, but I wish to put the case as strongly as possible, and when I have said that he endures poverty; no more need be said of his wretchedness, for he who is poor lacks every comfort in life.*"

"Amen!" William added, softly.

"*But when their education is finished, we have seen them rule and govern the world from an arm-chair, their hunger converted into feasting, their cold into refreshment, their nakedness into rich raiment, and their sleep on a mat to repose on fine linen and damask, the just reward for their virtuous efforts.*"

"The prospect of feasting and of rich raiment does carry a lot of appeal for a certain kind of people," William pointed out.

"*On the other hand, when we consider the soldier we find that there is no one poorer in poverty itself, for he depends on his wretched pay, which comes late or never, or on that he grabs with his own hands, at the imminent risk of his life and his conscience.*"

"How about that pillage factor?"

"Worthy of note perhaps but not really as attractive as it appears when you consider that those who profit most from pillage are those closest to the heat of battle and they are the very ones who don't always make it out alive or in one piece. In the final analysis the soldier is obviously worthy of more admiration than the scholar For at every step he is in danger of losing his life."

"Isn't that a trifle melodramatic?"

"What fear or poverty can threaten the student compared to that which faces a soldier who, finding himself besieged and stationed as sentry in the ravelin or cavalier of some beleagured fortress, perceives that the enemy is mining towards the place where he stands, yet must not stir from there on any pretext nor shun the danger which so nearly threatens him?"

William stirred uneasily on his bench but said nothing.

"All he can do is give notice to his captain of what is happening, hoping that he may remedy it by some counter-mine, but he must stand quietly his ground in fear and momentary expectation of suddenly flying up to the clouds without wings and dashing down to the abyss against his will."

"That would be tragic, certainly, but how often could something like that be expected to happen in one individual soldier's lifetime?"

"You want percentages, eh? All right, if this be thought a small danger, let us see if it is equaled or surpassed by the clash between two galleys prow to prow in mid ocean."

"Oh, good, good," Malachi approved. "You're going to hearten the breed by mixing a little comparison in with your argumentation. As I recall, Miguel, 'galleys prow to prow' describes exactly your situation at the battle of Lepanto when you were fighting off the deck of the *La Marquesa* against the Turks in 1571."

Cervantes nodded, "You have an excellent memory, Malachi."

"And that's where you lost your hand and got your medal for gallantry," Malachi added.

"It's not really fair for the referee to intrude partisan information while the contest is being waged," William pointed out.

"He's right, you know," Cervantes acknowledged. "But let me get back to describing a more imminent danger than guard duty presents when we see two galleys meeting head-on at sea. *Both of them locked and grappled together leave the soldier no more space than two feet of plank at the beak-head to stand upon; but though he sees in front of him so many ministers of death threatening him as there are pieces of artillery pointing at him from the opposite ship, no farther than a lance's length from his body, and though he sees that the first slip of his foot will land him in Neptune's bottomless gulf; nevertheless, with undaunted heart, inspired by glory which spurs him on, he allows himself to be a mark for all their fire, and endeavors to force his way by that narrow path into the enemy's vessel. And what is most to be admired is that scarcely has one fallen, never to rise again until the end of the world, when another takes his place; and if he too drops into the sea, which lies in wait like an enemy ready to devour him, another and yet another succeeds without any time elapsing between their deaths."*

"Now that is perilous, indeed," William acknowledged, "when even your own protective armor would drag you inexorably down to a watery grave at the instant of your first misstep on a slippery plank."

Cervantes nodded. *"In all the perils of war there is no greater courage and boldness than this. Blessed were those ages which were without the dreadful fury of those diabolical engines of artillery, whose inventor, I truly believe, is now receiving in hell the reward for his devilish invention, by means of which a base and cowardly hand may deprive the most valiant knight of life. While such a knight fights with all the bravery and ardor which fire gallant hearts, without his knowing how or where there comes a random ball, discharged by one who perhaps ran away in terror at the flash of his own accursed machine, and cuts short and ends in an instant the life of one who deserved to live for centuries to come."*

"You seem to have a bit of a knightly fixation, I'd say," William snickered. "But basically that's why I try to avoid the battlefield."

"Fear of muerte?" Cervantes asked.

"Simply to avoid sinking too soon into that ocean of obscurity and foregoing my destiny of making sure my name is remembered for centuries to come."

"Remembered for what?"

"I'm still examining the possibilities there."

"It's your turn, you know,' Malachi said. "If Miguel is finished, that is."

"Yes, I'm finished. I sort of trailed off there at the end, I know, but let it stand, and let's see what this young hot-shot has to offer."

"Argumentation, you say? Give me a moment." William's brow furrowed. Finally, he lifted his head.

> *"To be or not to be: that is the question:*
> *Whether 'tis nobler in the mind to suffer*
> *The slings and arrows of outrageous fortune,*
> *Or to take arms against a sea of troubles,*
> *And by opposing end them. To die, to sleep,*
> *No more, and by a sleep to say we end*
> *The heartache, and the thousand natural shocks*
> *That flesh is heir to! 'Tis a consummation*
> *Devoutly to be wished. To die, to sleep,*
> *To sleep, perchance to dream: ay, there's the rub,*
> *For in that sleep of death what dreams may come*
> *When we have shuffled off this mortal coil,*
> *Must give us pause. There's the respect*

> *That makes calamity of so long life:*
> *For who would bear the whips and scorns of time,*
> *Th' oppressor's wrong, the proud man's contumely,*
> *The pangs of despised love, the law's delay,*
> *The insolence of office, and the spurns*
> *That patient merit of the unworthy takes,*
> *When he himself might his quietus make*
> *With a bare bodkin?"*

"Very thoughtful," Cervantes conceded, "but it is only an argument with one-self. It seems to me that should be labeled a sub-category of classic argumentation, Malachi."

"Excuse me, Miguel, but I don't think he's quite finished."

> *"Who would fardels bear, I say,*
> *To grunt and sweat under a weary life,*
> *But that the dread of something after death,*
> *The undiscovered country, from whose bourn*
> *No traveler returns, puzzles the will,*
> *And makes us rather bear those ills we have,*
> *Than fly to others that we know not of?"* [29]

"Come on now," Cervantes argued, "you can't tell me that's original! And he's do-ing that meter thing again, Malachi. I think disqualification is in order on the basis of the evidence at hand, and he didn't dress it up with any hint of comparison either."

"He's right, you know," Malachi nodded. "Miguel made a big jump with his instant mix of comparison. Can you whirl about adroitly enough to show us something other than that slings and arrows stuff? Get away entirely from the woe-is-me approach and brighten it up?"

"Brighten it up, you say!" William shouted. "All right, how about some contrast then? I've just given you the darker side of life.....the whips and scorns that beset us, but now permit me to show you how we should exhault at being alive and we should remain open to the lessons which nature holds out to us."

> *For so work the honeybees,*
> *Creatures that by a rule in nature teach*
> *The act of order to a peopled kingdom.*
> *They have a king and officers of sorts,*
> *Where some, like magistrates, correct at home,*

> *Others, like merchants, venture trade abroad,*
> *Others, like soldiers, armed in their stings,*
> *Make boot upon the summer's velvet buds,*
> *Which pillage they with merry march bring home*
> *To the tent royal of their Emperor.*
> *Who, busied in his majesty, surveys*
> *The singing masons building roofs of gold,*
> *The civil citizens kneading up the honey,*
> *The poor mechanic porters crowding in*
> *Their heavy burdens at his narrow gate,*
> *The sad-eyed justice with his surly hum,*
> *Delivering o'er to executioners pale*
> *The lazy yawning drone.* [30]

"Ha!" Cervantes shouted. "Your writing is just about on a par with your knowledge of husbandry. We raise honeybees at home. They have no Kings or emperors! Everything in their society centers around the Queen, so your entire presentation is one of ignorance which makes even more valid the decision to disqualify you on the evidence at hand. How about it , Malachi?"

"Hold on now, Miguel. You are right to complain on the honeybees, but his mislabeling the leader does not change the effectiveness of the contrast. As far as originality is concerned, I must admit I've seen him do this stuff before. I can't for the life of me trace it to any source. I've concluded his head is full of disconnected dialogue floating off in space without reference. Against my own personal feelings in the matter, but responding to my conscience as arbiter, I'm afraid I'll have to award him another laurel leaf on that one, Miguel. His entry was much better organized and more compact than yours."

"I'm sorry you see it that way, but I remain convinced you are letting his shameless manipulation of meter sway your judgment."

"On my honor, I am not," Malachi swore.

"Speaking of honor," Cervantes said as he took a hearty nip from his wine glass, "let's make it three out of five."

"You're on," said William.

"Sorry gentlemen, but this contest will have to wait because we have business in Ostend we must attend, so shake hands and part peacefully"

Chapter 5:
THE OSTEND PEACE CONFERENCE

Inn at Ostend, Flanders, July 16, 1588:

"It took some arranging, but in a few minutes," Malachi said, "we will meet Otto Doerter, who does a lot of business in the Netherlands, so eat up and tell me about the conflict you had with the Italian waiter yesterday."

"The obstreperous Italian waiter, you mean," William insisted.

"How did you know he was Italian?"

"Oh, I recognize all those 'i' and 'o' endings all right. He cursed me in Italian, which lead me to conclude the Dutch should really do something about their immigration policies. They are simply inviting trouble if they permit impolite foreigners to run loose in their country."

"Such a mix of people is not unusual at a conference which is being conducted in four languages: English, Dutch, Spanish, and Italian. Perhaps he was a translator."

"No, he was a waiter all right because he was making notes on the menu pad when I directed him to reheat my pork pie, and he cursed at me and went on with his note-taking."

"But you don't speak Italian. How did you know he was cursing at you instead of explaining that he was simply off duty?"

"Speak it or not, when I hear a string of words ending in vowels muttered at me with threatening gestures, I know what's going on. These Mediterranean types who get so involved in mundane tasks like checking the daily menu, amaze me when there is so much of importance going on around them if they would only open their eyes and be receptive to their surroundings. This Doerter fellow doesn't sound Italian."

"Hardly," Malachi laughed. "Otto is now a citizen of Flanders although he was born in Germany, and he presently makes his living as a broker for Baltic wheat and corn which he sells mostly to the Spanish."

"Is he on our side?"

"More or less," Malachi said, "but we still need to be careful what we tell him because he is often in the presence of the Dons and might let something slip. He takes business flyers here and there on the market and often goes along with his cargoes as factor. As a matter of fact, he was in Cadiz last year during Drake's raid and he had to stand by to watch one of his major investments go up in flames when a cargo of his wheat and corn burned aboard one of the ships in the harbor."

"Does he hold that against us?"

"Not noticeably. Herr Doerter pretty well accepts the ups and downs of his complicated trade. He is fluent in Flemish, Spanish, and English and makes commercial deals with all three countries. When wheat is not being harvested, he often trades English cloth for Flemish butter, cheese, and salt fish which he trades to the Spanish for the gold he uses to buy more English cloth."

"But how can we trust him if he trades with the Spanish?"

"We have little choice. Many of the Dutch trade with the Spanish in order to finance their war against them. The seven northern Provinces, particularly the coastal ones of Holland, Zeeland and Flanders—which are mostly Protestant—can't permit a simple war to interfere with the commerce they carry on with their best customer, or they would have very little income. They count on the profit from that exchange to defend themselves against the intrusion of the Inquisition."

William shook his head. "This world is very complicated."

Malachi chuckled. "It is that. Get your notebook out because here comes Herr Doerter."

They greeted their visitor and supplied him with a mug of beer.

"Well, Otto," Malachi said, "if the peace people are all sitting down, I must presume they have finally agreed on the size and shape of the conference table."

"Ach, ya," agreed Herr Doerter. "Elizabetha haf sent her Englisch commissioners to Flanders in February to negotiate peace mit Parma's peoples. These English and Spanish haf spent four months on the giffing of presents and compliments before they are deciding on the kinds of tables and chairs they would find most comfortable."

"What kind of people do they usually send on such missions, Herr Doerter?" William asked. "It seems to me it would be something of a holiday if a man were housed and fed and had only to decide which furniture suited him best. Is there any chance we could sign up for such duty?"

"You hardly fit the bill," Malachi grinned. "England's commissioners include two aristocrats—the Earl of Derby, and Lord Cobham—and three older and well-educated men—Sir James Croft, Dr. Dale and Dr. Rogers."

"From mein observation," said Herr Doerter, "Croft iss looked on by many peoples as senile because he holds strong Spanish sympathies, unt the two doctors they spend much time presenting speeches in Latin mit many classical allusions nobody else can understand. Derby and Cobham, however, haf been giffen compliments for the fine job they haf done, setting up and hosting der community diningroom for gatherings of commissioners. After dat tangle of furniture-deciding, they haf voted on meeting here at Ostend, which ve Hollundisch unt Englisch haf so recently captured from der Spanish."

"Even though Parma might counterattack here at any moment?"

"Nein, attack iss not likely now," said Herr Doerter. "Der Spanish haf taken few aggressive actions for these several months. But das ist wahr. Parma was quite irritated by the selection of Ostend for the meeting. He looks at Ostend still as Spanish territory, so he haf sent representatives, not come hisself. I tink the Spanish are content to wait for results of peace negotiations before turning der tercios loose again."

"It's all a stall, you know," Malachi said, "to keep us from mobilizing our defenses against the coming attack of their Armada."

"Yah, that's what many peoples say," Herr Doerter conceded, "but agreement on that issue is not by all. Pope Sixtus hafs large distrust of Spanish intentions because of continual battle mit Philip for control of Catholic Church. Not too surprising that Pope, for one, tinks Philip has no intention to invade England."

"How does he explain the creation of the Armada?" William asked.

"Two reasons. To run 'brag' to frighten Elizabetha into peace settlement unt to create traditional 'diversion abroad' that all monarchs haf arranged now unt then to get troublesome noblemen out of their presence for a time unt to focus the people's attention on things other than shortcomings of government. Pope is so sure Philip will not invade England that he haf pledged that on der first day a Spanish soldier sets foot on Englisch soil, he vill not lend but gif King Philip one million gold ducats for der cause. Very impressive offer because, as ve all know, Pope Sixtus does not spend his treasure so easy."

"So he's daring Philip to invade us?" William said.

"That's what it amounts to," Malachi said, "although he doesn't think it will happen, or he wouldn't have risked that much money. How about the peace terms, Otto? Any hint on those?"

Herr Doerter shrugged. "Nein, notting official. Rumor ist that Philip must get return for investment he haf made."

"What kind of return?" asked William, wide-eyed.

"Der back-door diplomacy haf hinted that Philip asks Elizabetha to withdraw from Netherlands, to curb Drake's attacks on Spanish colonies in New World, and to foster toleration for Catholic worship in England. Then he might call off conquest of England." [31]

"Not bloody likely!" exclaimed William. "What about toleration for Protestant worship in Holland?"

"Big sticking point, yah," admitted Herr Doerter. "King Philip hafs intention of clearing world of Protestant heresy—no matter how many of the peoples he hafs to burn. Accommodation mit Protestants in Holland would amount to compact mit Devil in his mind. Not likely to occur."

"Elizabeth has hinted that she would withdraw from the Netherlands if the Spanish would also withdraw," Malachi mentioned. "That would neatly skirt around the issue of Philip having to tolerate Protestants because such twin withdrawals would leave no outside authority in the country to enforce religious membership. The Dutch would be free to sit in whichever pew they choose. Of course, the Queen is also thinking strategically because a Spanish withdrawal would eliminate a large, threatening military presence from sitting on England's left flank, just one tide away."

"It's insane that King Philip would insist on toleration of Catholic worship in England while refusing to tolerate Protestant worship in the Netherlands," mumbled William.

Doerter laughed, "You know little about nature of zealots, yung mann."

"The longer a man is king, the less he feels the need to justify anything," Malachi observed, "but all of this has me wondering if Philip and Sixtus might just be faking an argument between themselves to throw sand in our faces about the threat of the Armada. After all, we know that the Armada left Lisbon weeks ago, although God alone knows what happened to it after that."

"Ahem!" Herr Doerter coughed. "Make that Gott and close associates."

"You know?"

Herr Doerter nodded. "They haf contrary winds for der two weeks after they left Lisbon, then a great gale damaged some ships and scattered others. They haf took shelter in port of Corunna in northern Spain to repair ships and get in new supplies. Soon, I tink, they will be ready to resume journey north, but ist still uncertain whether they come against England or simply take reinforcements to Parma. Certain they hope to scare Elizabetha out of Holland and to curb Drake and others in New World."

"If the King of Spain thinks to frighten Elizabeth, he is in for a rude awakening," Malachi growled. "He will quickly learn what everybody in our country has already discovered time and time again. While it is very easy to upset Queen Elizabeth, it is impossible to frighten her. She still has hopes that these peace negotiations will succeed because she regards Parma as an honorable man. She will support the peace effort until the last minute, but there are no illusions in England about where the Armada will strike if it should put to sea again."

"Ach, how you are so sure when all of Continent is mystified?"

Malachi hesitated, then said, "We are in possession of Philip's rather cynical assurances that the peace conference is a put-up job just to delay our defense preparations. In a recent message to Parma, the King said: *'But to you only, I declare that my intention is that these negotiations shall never lead to any result, whatever conditions the English may offer. On the contrary, the only object is to deceive them, and to cool them in their preparations for defence, by making them believe such preparations will not be necessary. You are well aware that the reverse of this is the truth, and that on our part there is to be no slackness but the greatest diligence in our efforts for the invasion of England, for which we have already made abundant provision in men, ships and money. Although we enter thus into negotiations, without any intention of concluding them, you can always get out of them with great honour by taking umbrage about some point of religion, or the other outrageous proposals they are likely to make.... Thus you will proceed, now yielding on one point, and now insisting on another, but directing all to the same object to gain time while preparations for the invasion are completed'."* [32]

"God's teeth!" William exclaimed, "Philip has been reading his Machiavelli again."

"Ya, das ist wahr," agreed Doerter. "That is voice of master, ya. I haf much amazement at Walsingham's ability to gather up der documents, but please—don't tell me how it vas got. Such secrets, ya, means much moneys spent and maybe some blood spilt. I tink I better to stay out of it, ya. Peace conference is doomed to go nowhere then. Elizabetha she knows, of course, about Philip's instructions?"

"Yes, indeed," Malachi assured him. "Walsingham wouldn't dare hide such revealing material from Her Majesty, but the Queen must still feel it's worth pursuing the possibility of luring Parma away from his allegiance to Spain because that would cut the risk to England neatly in half. We could probably defeat the Armada alone or Parma alone, but if the Spaniards really succeed in mounting a coordinated land and sea assault on England, we could be in serious trouble."

"Danka, Malachi, for sharing mit me such information. I won't forget. Unt now I must go. A conscientious merchant, he must not hesitate too long, else money-grubbing fellows will buy up all der food stuffs, ya, which will be in short supply when commerce ist interrupted by upcoming conflict. Please, enjoy der beer. Ist by me."

Swigging down his stein of beer, William paused to comment. "I hope there is a very special place in heaven for appreciative people who are also generous."

"Generous and informative," Malachi concluded. "I don't know if there is another living Englishman who is in possession of the information that Doerter just gave us. By God. Contrary winds for two weeks and then a gale in the Bay of Biscay is reason enough to delay the Armada, They've had time enough since, however, to refit and spruce up at Corunna, and undoubtedly they will attack England any day now. Headquarters must learn of this immediately. After so long a wait some of our countrymen may have relaxed their vigil, and that can't be allowed to happen. We're off for England this very minute, my boy, to let Walsingham and Drake know the threat has been renewed."

"They want you at headquarters right away, Malachi," said a middle-aged man, who joined them at table without preamble. "Travel papers have been issued for you.""

"Any idea what's up, Eddie?" asked Malachi as he stood up.

Eddie shrugged. "None, but they sent me on the *Briget C.* to fetch you. She's small and she's spare but she'll cross the Channel faster than any other ship afloat, so it means they want you in a hurry You'll be in Dover in three hours on the prevailing north-east breeze."

"That's good. We'll drop a messenger at Dover to ride up and notify Walsingham and then we'll sail that breeze right down to Plymouth and Drake. Let's go," Malachi motioned William and started off.

"My beer!" protested William.

"Leave it. There'll be drink wherever we go. Eddie, you'll cross with us and make the trip to London. I want somebody I can count on to make sure Walsingham is alerted."

"Good enough," Eddie said. "One thing more. Headquarters has asked that we all keep our eyes peeled for the Duke of Parma, who, we've learned, spent the entire day yesterday right here in Ostend taking notes on our defenses in preparation for a possible counterattack. If we could have nabbed that man, we might have turned aside the proposed attack on England."

"Didn't anybody recognize him?" William asked in astonishment. "I would think a real live Duke would be hard to miss if people would only open their eyes and be receptive to their surroundings."

"Nobody on our side noticed him," Eddie shrugged. "He spent the whole day disguised as an Italian waiter inspecting menus."

"An Italian inspecting menus?" William groaned and smacked his fist into the palm of his other hand. "I knew I should have checked up on that man because he seemed so out of place, so surly, so foreign and sinister-like. Good Lord, I might have saved England if I had taken the time to act on my suspicions! Imagine that. A hero to the whole country! The truth is, however, that I was afraid that any further inquiry would bring forth more of his fiery retorts, and I doubted if my pot pie could hold its little heat during further exchanges, so I just left him there while I went off to finish my meal. If I had only known! I now realize that 'our doubts are traitors, and make us *lose the good we oft might win, by fearing to attempt.'* [33] My word but I'd love to have one more crack at that guy!"

Malachi smiled. "Don't despair. It is said that Parma bears a charmed life, so it is no surprise that he got away from you. With any luck at all, however, we should fetch Plymouth by tomorrow night even after dropping Eddie in Dover, and my instincts tell me we'll get there just about the same time the Spaniards do, so you'll get your chance to work your vengeance against the whole Spanish fleet."

Malachi grinned and led his mortified apprentice down to the dock for the trip to Plymouth and the coming confrontation with the mighty Spanish Armada. "Our adventures are not over yet, William."

❖ ❖ ❖

INVITATION TO READERS

Stay alert for Volume II—the further adventures of William and Malachi as they continue their secret missions, participate in the strategies, and sabotage during the English engagements with the mighty Spanish Armada, and finally encounter Queen Elizabeth herself.

REFERENCES

PART I LEARNING THE ROPES

[1] Shakespeare, *Macbeth*, V:v

[2] Giovanni Boccoccio, *Decameron, 9*[th] *Day, 10*[th] *Story*

[3] Shakespere, *Measure for Measure*, I:ii

[4] Papal Bull of 1570

[5] Thomas Dekker as found in Norman

[6] Thomas Heywood as found in Norman

[7] Thomas Nashe as found in Bridenbaugh

[8] Carl B. Bridenbaugh

[9] Nashe as found in Wells

[10] Nashe in Wells

[11] Nashe in Wells

[12] Nashe in Wells

[13] Nashe in Wells

[14] Nashe in Wells

[15] Nashe in Wells

[16] Nashe in Wells

[17] Nashe in Wells

[18] Shakespeare, *Troilus and Cressida*, I:iii

[19] Gamini Salgado, *The Elizabethan Underworld*

[20] Bridenbaugh

[21] Gabrial Harvey as found in McMichaels

[22] Shakespeare, *Henry V*. III:i

[23] Lord Oxford as found in Evans

[24] Shakespeare, Hamlet, I:ii

[25] Shakespeare, *Hamlet*, II:ii

[26] Michel Montaigne, *Complete Works*, xiv

[27] Shakespeare, *Othello*, lll:iii

[28] A. L. Rowse, *The England of Elizabeth*

[29] R. Howell, *Sir Philip Sidney*

[30] Lord Burghley as found in Rowse, *The England of Elizabeth*

PART II TUG OF WAR: CATHOLICS VS PROTESTANTS

[1] Shakespeare, *Troilus and Cressida*, IV:v

[2] Ovid, Publius, *Book I, Alegia* V.

[3] Christopher Marlowe, *Tamburlaine the Great*, Pt.2, III:ii

[4] Bishop Bancroft as found in Ivor Brown

[5] Burghley as found in A. L. Rowse, *England of Elizabeth*

[6] Rowse, *England of Elizabeth*

[7] Carolly Erickson

[8] Fuller as found in Erickson

[9] Peter Wentworth as found in Erickson

[10] Erickson

[11] Shakespeare, Troilus and Cressida, III: iii

[12] John Stubbs as found in Erickson

[13] Erickson

[14] Shakespeare, *Henry V, Prologue.*

[15] Shakespeare, *Hamlet*, III:iv.

[16] Francis Bacon, Essays, "Of Ambition"

[17] Stephen Greenblatt, Sir Walter Raleigh

[18] Niccolo Machiavelli, *The Prince, VI: "On New Principalities Acquired by One's Own Arms and Skill."*

[19] Machiavelli, *The Prince, XIX: "On Avoiding Being Despised and Hated."*

[20] Machiavelli, The Prince, XIX: "On Avoiding Being Despised and Hated."

[21] Machiavelli, The Prince, VIII: "On Those Who Have Become Princes through Wickedness."

[22] Machiavelli, *The Prince, V: "How Principalities Should Be Governed that Lived by Their Own Laws Before They Were Occupied."*

[23] Machiavelli, *The Prince, XXV: "On Fortune's Role in Human Affairs and How She Can Be Dealt With."*

[24] Machiavelli, *The Prince, XXV: "On Fortune's Role...."*

[25] Machiavelli, *The Prince, XXV: "On Fortune's Role...."*

[26] Count Carlo Sforza, *The Living Thoughts of Machiavelli*

[27] Machiavelli, *The Prince, XVIII:* "How a Prince Should Keep His Word."

[28] Machiavelli, *The Prince, XVII:* "On Cruelty and Mercy, and Whether It Is Better to Be Loved Than To Be Feared or the Contrary."

[29] Durant, Will & Ariel, *The Reformation Vol. VI*

[30] Machiavelli, *The Prince, XXVI:* "An Exhortation to Liberate Italy from the Barbarians."

[31] Elizabeth's quote on O'Neill found in Henry Warren

[32] Henry Sidney's letter as found in Warren

[33] Shakespeare, *Hamlet*, I:iii

[34] Shakespeare, *Hamlet*, I:iii

[35] Lady Sidney's letter as found in Warren

[36] Philip Sydney, "*A Discourse of Irish Affairs*" as found in Warren

[37] Letter of Languet as found in Warren

[38] Warren

[39] Letter of Lord Burghley as found in Warren

[40] Philip Sydney's letter to brother David as found in Warren

[41] Philip Sydney's letter to Molyneux as found in Warren

[42] Molyneux's letter to Philip Sydney as found in Warren

[43] Letter of Philip Sydney as found in Warren

PART III THE ENGLISH NAVY

[1] J. Stowe, in J. Hampden, *Francis Drake Privateer*

[2] William Camden as found in Hampden

[3] Stowe in Hampden

[4] Hampden

[5] Shakespeare, *All's Well that Ends Well*, V:ii

[6] Drake's "Gentlemen and Mariners" speech as found in James Williamson, Age of Drake

[7] Elizabeth I as found in Hampden

[8] Drake as found in Hampden

[9] Shakeseare, *Henry IV, Part 2*, III:ii

[10] Williamson, *Hawkins of Plymouth*

[11] Williamson, *The Age of Drake*

[12] Hampden

[13] Warren

PART IV THE ADVENTURERS AND SCHOLARS

[1] Elizabeth's charter as found in Williams

[2] Fuller letter as found in Williams

[3] Seneca as found in Stephen Greenblatt

[4] Elizabeth as found in Greenblatt

[5] On Raleigh as found in Robert Lacey

[6] Elizabeth's rebuke of Bishop of Ely, found in Greenblatt

[7] Raleigh letter as found in Greenblatt

[8] Eleanor G. Clark

[9] Clark

[10] Durant, Will & Ariel, *The Reformation Vol. VI*

[11] Richard Hakluyt as found in Clark

[12] Clark

[13] Exchange between Elizabeth & Raleigh as found in Lacey

[14] Raleigh's poem as found in Lacey

[15] Francis Bacon, *Essays, "Of Plantations"*

[16] Hakluyt as found in D.B.Quinn, Raleigh and the British Empire

[17] Lane's letter to Walsingham as found in Lacey

[18] Bacon, *Essays, "Of Plantation"*

[19] Bacon, *"Of Envy,"*

[20] Bacon, "Of Studies,"

[21] Bacon, *"Letter to Lord Burghley,"*

[22] Bacon, *"Of Regimen of Health,"*

[23] Shakespeare, *Hamlet,* V:i

[24] Bacon, *"Of Discourse"*

[25] Bacon, *"Of Cunning"*

[26] Bacon, *"Of Discourse"*

[27] Bacon, *"Of Discourse"*

[28] Bacon, *"Of Cunning"*

[29] Bacon, *"Of Regimen of Health"*

[30] Catherine Bowen

[31] Bacon, *Letter to Lord Burghley*

[32] Bacon, *"Of Great Place"*

[33] Bacon, *"Of Great Place"*

[34] Bacon, *"Of Nobility"*

[35] Bacon. *"Of Nobility"*

[36] Bacon, *"Of Expense"*

[37] Bacon, *"Of True Greatness of Kingdoms, Estates"*

[38] Bacon, *"Of Dispatch"*

[39] Bacon, *"Of Simulation and Dissimulation"*

[40] Shakespeare, *Hamlet,* II:i

[41] Bowen

[42] Shakespeare, *Troilus and Cressida,* III:iii

[43] Bacon, *"Of Discourse"*

[44] Bacon, "*Of Simulation and Dissimulation*"

[45] Bacon, "*Of Studies*"

[46] Bacon, "Of Studies"

[47] Bacon, "*Of Marriage and Single Life*"

[48] Bacon, "*Of Marriage and Single Life*"

[49] Bacon, "*Of Love*"

[50] Bacon, "*Of Love*"

[51] Bacon, "*Of Marriage and Single Life*"

[52] Bacon, "Of Love"

[53] Bacon, "*Of Cunning*"

[54] Shakespeare, Sonnet *xviii*

PART V THE PLOT TO KILL THE QUEEN

[1] Nostrodamus as found in Fraser

[2] J. E. Neale, *Queen Elizabeth* I

[3] Shakespeare, *King Lear*, I:iv

[4] Shakespeare, *Henry IV*, IV:v

[5] Neale

[6] C.Read, *Mr. Secretary Walsingham*

[7] Read

[8] Francis Malachi McAuliffe, *Of All the Bloody Cheek*, Title

[9] Will and Ariel Durant, *The Story of Civilization, Part VII*

[10] Durant

[11] A.L.. Rowse, *England of Elizabeth*

[12] Jenkins, *Elizabeth the Great*

[13] Rowse, *England of Elizabeth*

[14] Rowse, *England of Elizabeth*

[15] Rowse, *England of Elizabeth*

[16] R. Howell, *Sir Philip Sidney*

[17] Howell

[18] Howell

[19] Howell

[20] Howell

[21] Gamini Salgado, *The Elizabethan Underworld*

[22] Salgado

[23] Thomas Kyd, *The Spanish Tragedy*, II;ii

[24] Kyd, IV:i

[25] Shakespeare, *Hamlet,* III:ii

[26] *Hamlet*, III:ii

[27] *Hamlet*, III:ii

[28] *Hamlet*, III:ii

[29] Read

[30] Shakespeare, *Macbeth*, I:v

[31] Read

PART VI ROANOKE COLONY RETURNS: TRAITORS DIE

[1] Robert Lacey, *Sir Walter Raleigh*

[2] Samuel Eliot Morison, *The European Discovery of America*

[3] Morison

[4] Lacey

[5] A.D.Wraight and V.F.Stern

[6] Morison

[7] Morison

[8] Francis Bacon, *"Of Plantations," Essays*

[9] Morison

[10] C. Read, *Mr. Secretary Walsingham*

[11] Seneca

[12] William Camden, *History of Princess Elizabeth*

[13] Read

[14] Read

[15] Carolly Erickson, *The First Elizabeth*

[16] Read

[17] Henry Warren, *Sir Philip Sidney*

[18] A.L..Rowse, *The Expansion of Elizabethan England*

[19] Durant, Part VII

[20] Rowse

[21] Shakespeare, *Midsummer Night's Dream*, IV:i

[22] Garrett Mattingly, *The Defeat of the Spanish Armada*

[23] Mattingly

[24] Elizabeth Jenkins, *Elizabeth the Great*

[25] Jenkins

[26] Ed. Note: Every English sovereign since Elizabeth is descended from Mary Stuart.

PART VII DRAKE'S CADIZ RAID: APRIL 1587

[1] Garrett Mattingly, *The Defeat of the Spanish Armada*

[2] Mattingly

[3] William Shakespeare, *Troilus and Cressida*, III:iii

[4] Mattingly

[5] Neville Williams, *The Sea Dogs*

[6] Shakespeare, *Measure for Measure*, IV:i

[7] Shakespeare, *Hamlet*, I:iii

[8] A.M. Hadfield, Time to Finish the Game

[9] Mattingly

[10] Mattingly

[11] Mattingly

[12] Williams

[13] Williams

[14] Shakespeare, *Troilus and Cressida*, III:ii

[15] Shakespeare, *As You Like It*, IV:I

[16} Shakespeare, Hamlet, I:ii

PART VIII "VISIT WITH MONTAIGNE

[1] "*On Some Verses of Virgil,*" Montaigne's *Complete Works*

[2] Ibid.

[3] "*Of Experience*" Montaigne's *Complete Works*

[4] Ibid.

[5] Ibid.

[6] "*Children and Fathers*" Montaigne's *Complete Works*

[7] "*Apology for Raymond Sebond,*" Montaigne's *Complete Works*

[8] "*Of Names,*" Montaigne's *Complete Works*

[9] "*Of Presumption,*" Montaigne's Complete Works

[10] "*Of Books,*" Montaigne's *Complete Works*

[11] Ibid.

[12] Ibid.

[13] Montaigne's *Complete Works*

[14] "*Education of Children,*" Montaigne's *Complete Works*

[15] Ibid.

[16] "*Apology for Raymond Sebond,*" Montaigne's *Complete Works*

[17] Ibid.

[18] "*Of Cannibals*" Montaigne's *Complete Works*

[19] "*Of Moderation*" Montaigne's *Complete Works*

[20] "On Some Verses of Virgil" Montaigne's *Complete Works*

[21] Ibid.

[22] Ibid.

[23] Ibid.

[24] Ibid.

[25] Ibid.

[26] Ibid.

[27] ibid.

[28] Montaigne's. *Complete Works*

[29] Montaigne's. *Complete Works*

[30] Montaigne's. *Complete Works*

[31] Bible. *Pslam 118.*

[32] Mattingly

[33]] Montaigne's. *Complete Works*

[34] Shakespeare. A*s You Like It.* II:vii

[35] Shakespeare. *The Two Noble Kinsmen.* I:v

PART IX WITH RALEIGH IN IRELAND: NOVEMBER 1587

[1] *Much "Ado About Nothing.* IV:i

[2] *Henry IV . Prt. 1.* II:ii

[3] *King Lear.* IV:i

[4] Carolly Ericson, *The First Elizabeth*

[5] Sir Walter Raleigh, *The History of the World. Preface.*

[6] Berleth

[7] Berleth

[8] Berleth

[9] Berleth

[10] Berleth

[11] *Julius Caesar.* III:I

[12] Berleth

[13] Berleth

[14] Berleth

[15] Berleth

[16] Berleth

[17] Berleth

[18] *Henry V* IV:i

[19] Berleth

[20] Berleth

[21] Berleth

[22] Berleth

[23] Berleth

[24] *Hamlet.* I:v.

PART X WITH SPENSER IN IRELAND: DECEMBER, 1587

[1] [Editor's note] In 1598, Edmund Spenser and wife had to flee to Cork after Kilcolmin was burned and a child (possibly his) was killed.

[2] Stephen Greenblatt, *Sir Walter Raleigh*

[3] Spenser, "*The Faerie Queene*"

[4] Spenser, "*The Faerie Queene*"

[5] Shakespeare, *Henry IV, Prt. 2*, II:iii

[6] Edmund Spenser, A *View of the Present State of Ireland*

[7] Spenser

[8] Spenser

[9] Spenser

[10] Spenser

[11] Spenser

[12] Spenser

[13] Shakespeare, *Macbeth*, V:v

[14] Shakespeare, *Richard II*, III:ii

[15] Spenser

[16] Spenser

[17] Steve Graham, "*Dear Old Donegal*," lyrics.

[18] Spenser

[19] Spenser

[20] Spenser, *Dedication*

PART XI: YEAR OF THE ARMADA: JANUARY-JULY. 1588

[1] Shakespeare, *Julius Casear*. I:ii

[2] Mattingly

[3] Armento

[4] Lewis

[5] Lewis

[6] *Macbeth,V*:iii

[7] Littleton and Rae

[8] *Twelfth Night*, V:i

[9] Littleton and Rae

[10] Lewis

[11] Littleton and Rae

[12] Graham

[13] Littleton and Rae

[14] Bergin

[15] Howarth

[16] Bergin

[17] Armento

[18] Lewis

[19] Hakluyt, *Principal Navigations*

[20] *Don Quixote,* xiv: 2

[21] *Othello*, II:iii

[22] Bergin

[23] Bergin

[24] *Don Quixote,* xxiv:1

[25] *Don Quixote,* xxiv:1

[26] *Don Quixote,* x: 2

[27] *Macbeth,* V:v

[28] *Don Quixote,* xxii:1

[29] *Hamlet,* III:i

[30] *Henry V,* I:ii

[31] Armento

[32] Howarth

[33] *Measure for Measure*, I:iv

❖ ❖ ❖

BIBLIOGRAPHY

(Includes this Volume I and forthcoming Volume II)

A

Aesop	*Aesop's Fables*
Akrigg, G.P.V.	*Shakespeare and the Earl of Southampton*
Andrews, K.R.	*Drake's Voyages*
Armesto, F.	*The Spanish Armada*
Armitage, Angus.	*The World of Copernicus*
Asley, M.	*Great Britain to 1688*

B.

Bacon, Francis.	*Essays and New Atlantis*
Bainton, Roland H.	*Erasmus of Christendom*
Bald, R. C.	*John Dunne – A Life*
Bartel, Roland.	*London in Plague and Fire*
Beckingsale, B.W.	*Burghley –Tudor Statesman*
Berleth, Richard.	*The Twilight Lords*
Black, J. B.	*The Reign of Elizabeth: 1558-1603*
Boccaccio, Giovanni.	*Decameron*
Bowen, Catherine.	*Francis Bacon & The Lion and the Throne*
Bradbrook, Muriel.	*The School of Night.*
Brewer, Derek.	*Chaucer in his Time*
Bridenbaugh, Carl B.	*Vexed and Troubled Englishmen 1590-1642*
Brown, Ivor.	*Shakespeare In His Time*
Brownlee, Walter.	*The First Ships Around the World*

Bryant, J.A.   *The Compassionate Satirist*
Budiansky, Stephen   Her Majesty's Spymaster
Burton, E.   *The Pageant of Elizabethan England*
C
Cahill, Thomas.   *How the Irish Saved Civilization*
Camden, William   *History of Princess Elizabeth*
Castiglione, Baldesar.   *The Book of the Courtier*
Cervantes, Miguel.   *Don Quixote*
Clark, Eleanor G.   *Raleigh and Marlowe*
Collinson, Patrick   *The Elizabethan Puritan Movement*
Corbett, Julian.   *Drake and the Tudor Navy*
Cranfill, Thomas M.   *Rich's Farewell to Military Profession*
D.
Dorson, Richard.   *America Begins*
Downs, Robert B.   *Books that Changed the World*
Du Maurier, Daphne   *Golden Lads*
Durant, Will & Ariel.   *The Story of Civilization, Vol. VI. The Reformation*
Durant, Will & Ariel   *The Story of Civilization, Vol. VII.*
Dyer, T. F.   *Folk-Lore of Shakespeare*
E.
Enck, John   *Jonson and the Comic Truth*
Ericson, Carolly   *The First Elizabeth*
Evans, A.J.   *Shakespeare's Magic Circle*
F.
Fallon, N.   *The Armada in Ireland*
Feiling, K.   *A History of England*
Frame, Donald.   *The Complete Works of Montaigne*
G.
Gallagher, Ligeia.   *More's Utopia and its Critics*
Gardiner, J.H.   *The Bible as English Literature*
Graham, W.   *The Spanish Armada*
Greenblatt, Stephen.   *Sir Walter Raleigh*
Grenfell, Morton   *Elizabethan Ireland*
H.
Hadfield, A.M.   *Time to Finish the Game*
Halliday, F. E.   *Shakespeare in his Age*
Hampden, John.   *Francis Drake Privateer*
Hardy, Evelyn   *Survivors of the Armada*
Harrison, G. B.   *Shakespeare*

Harrison, G. B.   *An Elizabethan Journal*
Hauben, P.   *The Spanish Inquisition*
Held, Robert.   *Inquisition*
Hilton, D.   *Who Was Kit Marlowe?*
Holmes, Martin.   *Shakespeare's Public*
Holt, Victoria.   *My Enemy, the Queen*
Horizon Book   *Shakespeare's England*
Horizon Book   *The Horizon Book of the Elizabethan World*
Hotson, J.L.   *Mr. W. H.*
Howell, R.   *Sir Philip Sidney*
Hunt, Mary Leland.   *Thomas Dekker*
I.
Irwin, M.   *That Great Lucifer*
J.
Jenkins, Elizabeth   *Elizabeth the Great*
Johnston, Arthur.   *Francis Bacon*
K.
Kautsky, Karl.   *Thomas More and his Utopia*
Kenny, R.   *Elizabeth's Admiral*
Kingsley, Charles.   *Westward Ho!*
Knight, W. Nicholas.   *Shakespeare's Hidden Life*
Koning, Hans.   *Columbus: His Enterprise*
L.
Lacey, Robert.   *Sir Walter Raleigh*
Landstrom, Bjorn.   *Sailing Ships*
Lee, Sir Sidney.   A *Life of William Shakespeare*
Lewis, Michael   *The Spanish Armada*
Littleton, Taylor D. & Rea, Robert R.   *The Spanish Armada*
M.
Michiavelli, Niccolo   *The Prince*
Mattingly, Garrett   *The Defeat of the Spanish Armada*
McAuliffe, Frank Malachi.   *Of All the Bloody Cheek*
McCollum, John, I.   *The Age of Elizabeth*
McMichael,G. & Glenn,E.M.   *Shakespeare and His Rivals*
Miner, M. & Rawson, H.   A *Dictionary of Quotations from Shakespeare*
Morgan, Kenneth O.   *The Oxford Illustrated History of Britain*
Morison, Samuel Eliot.   *The European Discovery of America*

N.

Neale, J. E.   *Queen Elizabeth*

Norman, Charles.   *Christopher Marlowe The Muse's Darling*

O.

P.

Peck, Dwight.   *Leicester's Commonwealth*

Pendry, E.D. Editor.   *Thomas Dekker Selected Prose Writings*

Pinciss, Gerald   *Christopher Marlowe*

Plaidy, Jean   *The Spanish Bridegroom*

Q

Quinn, David B.   *North American Discovery Circa 1000-1612*

Quinn, David B.   *North America from Earliest Discovery to 1st Settlement*

Quinn, David B.   *England and the Discovery of America*

R.

Read, C.   *Mr. Secretary Walsingham*

Rowse, A.L.   *The English Spirit*

Rowse, A.L.   *The Expansion of Elizabethan England*

Rowse, A.L.   *The England of Elizabeth*

Rowse, A.L.   *The Poems of Shakespeare's Dark Lady*

Rowse, A.L.   *Shakespeare's Self Portrait*

Rowse, A.L.   *The Elizabethans and America*

S.

Salgado, Gamini.   *The Elizabethan Underworld*

Schoenbaum, S.   *William Shakespeare, A Compact Documented Life*

Seltzer, Daniel. Editor   *Robert Greene Friar Bacon and Friar Bungay*

Count Carlo Siorza.   *The Living Thoughts of Machiavelli*

Sitwell, Edith.   *The Queen and the Hive*

Smith, L. B.   *Elizabeth Tudor*

Spenser, Edmund   A *View of the Present State of Ireland*

Strachey, Lytton   *Elizabeth and Essex*

Summers, C. J.   *Ben Jonson*

T.

Thomas, William Holland   *Book of Raleigh's Letters*

Thomson, George Malcolm   *Sir Francis Drake*

Thornbury, G.W.   *Shakespeare's England*

Tillyard, E.M.W.   *The Elizabethan World Picture*

Trevelyan, G. M.   *History of England*

U.

V.

W.

Warren, Henry.   *Sir Philip Sidney*

Wells, Stanley. Ed.   *Thomas Nash*

Wernham, R. B.   *After the Armada*

Williams, Kathleen. Ed.   *20th Century Interpretation of 'The Praise of Folly'*

Williams, Neville   *The Sea Dogs*

Williamson, James, A.   *The Age of Drake*

Williamson, James, A.   *Hawkins of Plymouth.*

Wraight, A.D. & Stern, V.F.   *In Search of Christopher Marlowe*

X.

Y.

Youings, J.   *Raleigh in Exeter*

Z.

❖ ❖ ❖

5369832R0

Made in the USA
Charleston, SC
04 June 2010